EFFECTS OF WAR

on a

GODLESS DOG LOVER

KB FUGITT

January 28-2014

Heather & Bill,

Life can present us with many challenges, but if we remain hopeful and believe anything is possible it can be an amazing, incredible and beautiful journey. Enjoy the read.

K—

This is a work of fiction. Names, characters, places and incidents are either the product of the author's imagination or are used fictitiously. Any resemblance to actual events, locales or persons living or dead is entirely coincidental.

©Copyright 2013 by KB Fugitt

All rights reserved. No part of this publication may be reproduced, stored in a retrieval system or transmitted in any form or by any means—electronic, mechanical, photocopying, recording or otherwise—without the prior written permission of the author, except for brief passages quoted by a reviewer in a newspaper or magazine. To perform any of the above is an infringement of copyright law.

Layout and cover design: Esther Hart, www.heartsolutions.com

Cover image: Freyja Zazu, zattazoo.blogspot.ca

Published by Heart Solutions

ISBN –   978-0-9683364-8-9

Acknowledgements

No book can be started or finished without inspiration and that can come from the here and now, or the beyond. With that in mind, a big thank you goes out to Maureen O'Connell, the late Irene Wolt and The Irene Wolt Lifetime Foundation for inspiring me to pursue this project. You have been and always will be so very special, encouraging me to *write* for over forty years. I hope I haven't let you down. If we keep paying it forward, so many others will benefit. To Nicola Furlong another big thank you. When the seed was planted you shared your writer's knowledge and it helped the seed grow. To Roy Crichton for sharing a document dear to his heart. To my *family* at *The Aria* who were always inquiring, "How is the book coming along?" In ways you don't know, you gave me strength to press forward. To the wonderful staff at the Victoria Public Library. Your assistance in research did not go unnoticed. Rebecca Kennel, if as they say, timing is everything, then your fresh pair of eyes could not have come along at a more perfect time. Freyja Zazu, how did you manage to read my mind and create the exact image for the cover that I was thinking? I'm guessing extreme talent. Finally, to my amazing editor Esther Hart of Heart Solutions. Esther, the second time we met I expressed to you it was fate that brought us together, and it will keep you as my editor and friend for life. Simply put, I couldn't have done it without you.

For my darling wife, Vicky

Every step I take is toward you,
never away.
You give me ten million reasons for living,
each and every day.
Into my troubled life you brought a bright blue sky
and soothing sunshine.
I will be forever yours,
if you would like to be forever mine.

Table of Contents

Acknowledgements i
Every Day is a Gift 1
A DOG NAMED BUDDY   5
   Where It All Began 6
   Three Months Later - Early Fall 31
   1964 - Life at the Lake 42
   Late August – 1965 54
   Easter – 1967 66
A DOG NAMED TIMEX   83
   Early Fall - 1967 84
   The Card Game 108
   Three Months In 118
   Letter from Tommy 124
   A Dog's Life 129
   What Made Me Do It? 142
   Full Alert 158
   Rehabilitation 179
   California Calls 191
TIMEX IN LOS ANGELES – 1970   213
   Road Trip 214
   New Highs 216
   Why Doesn't He Call? 242
   Nightmares 259
   Home for a Visit 268
   Drugs Take Their Toll 287
   Permanent Change 305
   Home Again 317

A DOG NAMED BEN — 328
- More Healing 329
- New Life in Alaska 360
- Love in the Wilderness 368
- Loss 383

A DOG NAMED DAISY — 410
- Goodbyes and Gratitude 411
- A Special Place 422
- Carolyn Meets Amy 432

Every Day is a Gift

CAROLYN LOOKED AT the clock on the kitchen wall as she dried her hands on a tea towel. She had been standing over the sink doing the morning breakfast dishes, looking out the window and thinking to herself what another glorious day it was going to be. When you live in the North Country and summer is saying good-bye, you need to take advantage of these days you know will be leaving soon. The summers in Alaska don't last forever. You have to enjoy every second of every day no matter what the weather is outside. She intended to do just that. As her late husband Tommy used to say, "Every day is a gift."

"Every day is a beautiful day. Make the best of it," was the creed Tommy Franklin had lived by. Life was meant to be enjoyed. He would proclaim it every morning after he got his socks on that yes, it's true, every day is a gift. He would joke that if he could get his socks on in the morning it was going to be a good day. Tommy had a lot of good days in his life and he managed to get his socks on all by himself right up until the very end. For those he left behind every day was still exactly that, a precious gift.

Carolyn missed hearing those words from her soul mate, but she had promised him she would echo them in his memory on a daily basis. If sometimes she forgot, which she rarely did, one of her two daughters would remind her.

"Every day is a gift, Mom."

And every day she started off the morning routine by telling her dog, Daisy, what Tommy believed about the privilege of living. That we are lucky to have this opportunity to enjoy life on a daily basis.

"Every day is a gift, Daisy."

When Tommy was alive and announced that proclamation, someone would always be within hearing distance. Especially at the end, Daisy was always there listening.

Upon hearing those words the family dog would know it was time to go outside and get the morning paper. Ah, the gift of life! Ah, the magical pronouncement. Ah, the excitement of going out to get the morning paper. But more than that, *Ah! All I really want to do is go outside and pee!*

Living in the bush in Alaska, just opening the front door and letting a dog out in the morning to do their thing is not an option. There is the threat of grizzlies and wolves, which prey on family pets, to worry about. No, it's best the humans and family dog go out in tandem and Daisy was ready for the routine even before Carolyn woke up in the morning.

The very first thing Carolyn did when she got out of bed was make sure Daisy got her breakfast and fresh water. After a shower, a quick cup of coffee and some cereal, Carolyn would do the morning dishes. If her daughters, Sarah and Jessica, were up, good mornings would be tossed around, then Carolyn would brush her teeth and finally say those familiar words.

"Yes, every day is a gift, Miss Daisy girl! Are you ready to go out? Well, let's go then. Come on."

Yeah, let's go! I reeeeeeeeally have to pee.

Daisy missed Tommy as much as everyone else did. Her heart broke when she saw her family grieving after his death. Dogs can sense when there is a change, good or not so good. All a dog wants out of life is a routine and Daisy's late dad knew that, as if he had been a dog in some past life. Daisy also knew that after Tommy passed away he would have wanted it to be "business as usual." Walks and more walks and in between some sleeping, playing and eating. Tommy had told the family dog that Carolyn was someone Daisy could count on to keep that routine going after he left this world and that's how the days began rain, snow or shine. No matter how miserable it was outdoors, Daisy would get her morning walks just like Tommy had promised her. Plus her afternoon walks and her evening walks. Carolyn had made that promise to Tommy on his death bed shortly before he passed on.

"Don't worry about Miss Daisy. I'll make sure everything stays the same," she assured her husband moments before his last breath. It was a promise and when it came to promises between Tommy and Carolyn, at least in the later years of their relationship, none were broken. This morning wasn't going to be any different.

Just like every day was a gift, every day was also a little different from the one before. Yesterday it was misty and cool, today it was bright sunshine and warm. As Carolyn opened the clothes-closet door to get her light jacket and said those magical words, Daisy would jump up, wag her tail and head for the front door. Even without Dad around, Daisy knew that the routine would never alter because Carolyn, like Tommy had told Daisy on more than one occasion, was someone very, very special.

What Carolyn experienced when she walked out onto the veranda confirmed what she had suspected while she was doing the dishes and observing the early birds at her feeder. Indeed, it was going to be a beautiful day.

"Which way should we go this morning, Miss Daisy? Take the trail down to the road or just head on down the driveway?"

Daisy had no preference. Being out in the fresh air and having the freedom to exercise her legs and pee was the only thing of any importance right now. Finding the right spot to relieve herself was high on her list of things to do. When she really had to go it wouldn't take long to find that special place. Other times, if her bladder was holding up, there would be the universal dog ritual of sniffing and smelling before she found the most perfect and desirable place to relieve herself.

"OK Daisy, let's head down the driveway and you can do your business," Carolyn said walking down the steps from the veranda to the ground. That was Daisy's cue. Off she shot like a bullet and headed down the long dirt driveway.

You can't see the road from the house and vice versa. It was designed that way intentionally when Tommy built it. He didn't want anyone to see the house from the road so he could have his privacy. The driveway has a long straight stretch before it curves to the left, goes behind the evergreen trees and then does another straight stretch before it hits Crescent Rd. which is also dirt and the road you take to the town of Eagles Junction, Alaska—population thirty-five hundred. Eagles Junction is one of those small picture-postcard municipalities that is situated in the Gaston Valley surrounded by the imposing peaks of the Atwell Range. When Tommy first came to Eagles Junction to start up his business building log homes over twenty-five years ago, he knew he had come to a little corner of heaven. When Carolyn followed four years later, she felt the same. As it turned out, it was the place where they laid down their roots and raised a family. It was still heaven for her, but minus the man in her life.

As Carolyn ventured down the driveway with Daisy constantly crisscrossing and taking in the fresh new smells, she saw, as she did frequently, the two eagles that usually soared overhead at this time of day. The eagles live in the area and seem to make it a point to fly over every day and say good morning to her and Daisy. She stopped and watched, never getting tired of this privileged sight. The gathering of eagles in this region, because of the good feeding grounds, is the reason the nearest town is called Eagles Junction. She always felt honored to see the mated pair and would watch them glide overhead until they disappeared. Tommy had convinced her a long time ago that seeing an eagle was a sign of good luck. She believed it and felt blessed to live in such a lovely and breathtaking part of the planet. When she reached the mailbox and took out the morning newspaper, Carolyn checked the headlines and was amused at how sometimes a world so beautiful could go so wrong. Such a wonderful planet that took a wrong turn at some point.

At times she just couldn't understand the reasons for all the turmoil, especially when we should all be getting along. Sometimes she wondered why she even bothered to read the paper. But it was "part of the routine" and reading the newspaper, despite all the bad news, was something she still enjoyed. This paper that came from over fifty miles away and found its way into her mailbox—the only mailbox and the only house for miles around—and no matter what the weather, would always be there. And no matter what the weather, she and Daisy were always there to get it.

After Carolyn examined the headlines and turned to head back up the driveway, she saw a woman of African descent standing a couple of hundred feet away on the side of the road looking into the bush. The woman turned her head, noticed Carolyn and waved. Carolyn waved back and wondered what this woman was doing out here at the end of the road. She didn't give it much thought except she noticed it looked like the stranger was driving a pickup truck similar to one Tommy used to drive.

"OK, Daisy. Let's go back to the house and I'll read you the news, sports, weather and your favorite comics."

This was the start of the day, the start of the routine. Never changing. And weather permitting, Carolyn read Daisy the newspaper as they sat on the veranda. If it was too cool, they went inside and got cozy by the fireplace. Then, after she had read the paper, Carolyn would do some household chores while Daisy watched her every move anticipating their next excursion. It was always the same. At lunch time there would be another walk. Then another one after dinner and a short one just before bedtime. Tommy had promised Daisy that she would be looked after by a dog lover named Carolyn, and Tommy never lied. He would kid with you a lot, joke around, play tricks on you, chase you, throw the stick for you, talk to you, sing to you, do everything with you, but he would never lie.

A DOG NAMED BUDDY

Where It All Began

Brenton, Michigan – 1958

TOMMY WAS TEN years old the first time he met Carolyn. Of course it was a dog that brought them together. Over the years to come, there would always be dogs intertwined in Carolyn and Tommy's lives. Dogs that became family pets, dogs that were rescued and dogs that would rescue them. Throughout America's history, for many families the most natural thing was to have a dog—along with kids and goldfish and cats and frogs and whatever else it took to make a family feel complete. But dogs ... dogs seemed to be the common denominator that brought people together and put smiles on their faces. Dogs are a special kind of animal that, as they say, will love you unconditionally, make you laugh and make you cry, bring you happiness and bring you sorrow, but always bring you joy.

It was actually two dogs that were responsible for Carolyn and Tommy's introduction to each other. Molly, Carolyn's family dog, gave birth to the litter that gave Tommy his very first puppy that he named Buddy. Yes, Buddy. Wasn't every male dog in the fifties named Buddy? Molly was one of those Heinz 57 varieties with a lot of Labrador in her. No one knew exactly who Buddy's father was. Molly got around a lot and all the potential fathers were big. That's what Buddy ended up being. Buddy the puppy. Buddy the future wonder dog. Buddy the future hero. Thanks to Molly and Buddy, two lifelong friends met for the first time. In the beginning, if Buddy could have spoken, he would have said, "Tommy this is Carolyn, Carolyn this is Tommy. Enjoy your life together. Woof, woof!"

IT WAS MORNING on the Franklin farm in northwestern Michigan when a father and his only son were getting ready to meet a special girl for the first time. Yet the anxiety and anticipation the young boy was feeling was about getting his first puppy.

"Are you about done?" Mr. Franklin, Tommy's father, asked as he walked into the kitchen.

Tommy was finishing up his morning oatmeal and could hardly contain himself.

"Yeah, Dad. I'm done."

Where It All Began

"I told the Russells we would be there by nine and it's about a twenty-minute drive. I don't want to be late. Are you excited?" Mr. Franklin asked Tommy, who was taking his bowl over to the kitchen sink to rinse it.

"I can't wait Dad! Are you sure you don't want to come, Mom?" Tommy asked as he turned to his mother.

"I'd love to come along, Tommy, but your sister and I have made plans to go out shopping. I can't wait to see this little guy when you bring him home, though. This is so exciting!"

"Where is Kathy?" Tommy asked.

He realized he hadn't seen his sister that morning. Kathy was Tommy's favorite person and not just because she was his only sibling. They got along, plain and simple. Two years older than Tommy, she was his close friend and confidant. The age difference didn't matter. She respected him as her equal. That's how they were raised. She knew Tommy could hold his own, but if a time ever called for her to be the protective big sister, she would step up to the plate. As far as brothers and sisters went, they were the best of buddies and made it a point to look after each other.

"She's gone out for a walk with her friend, Darlene," Mrs. Franklin informed her son. "She'll be back in a little while. Are you going to share this puppy with her, Tommy?"

"Oh course, Mom. He's going to be a family dog. The only thing I want to do is name him."

Tommy began to put his shoes on as his mother sat down at the kitchen table.

" ... and have you come up with any names yet?"

Tommy thought for a few seconds. "Well, I've been going down the alphabet. I've been thinking of Arrow, Buddy, Cody, Duncan. I don't know. It'll be a good name I promise."

Mrs. Franklin mused over the names Tommy had come up with.

"I like those names. They're all good. Keep going down the alphabet and maybe one will jump out at you. I kind of like Buddy."

"Yeah, I like Buddy too, son," Mr. Franklin said agreeing with his wife of seventeen years. "But it's your call. Whatever name you choose will be perfect for our new family member."

"Thanks, Dad. I'm ready when you are." Tommy finished tying his shoes and grabbed his cap.

"Well, let's get going then!" Mr. Franklin said, kissing his wife on the cheek. "Wish us luck, honey."

Mrs. Franklin stood up from the seat at the table and wiped her hands on her apron.

"I'll walk out with you two."

As the three exited through the side kitchen door they saw Kathy and Darlene returning from their walk. Tommy waved as he and his parents made their way toward the family car. Kathy waved back and picked up the pace so she could see Tommy off.

"Hey, Tommy! Are you and Dad going now?" big sister asked.

"Yeah, we're just leaving," Tommy informed her. "We'll be back in a little while. What do you think of the name Buddy?"

Kathy walked up and took hold of her younger brother's shoulders.

"I love it! I can't wait for you to get back."

"We shouldn't be too long," Kathy's dad assured her. "It's only a twenty-minute drive over to Clear Lake. It's the Russell family. Do you know them?"

Kathy pondered for a moment.

"No, I don't think so, Dad."

"They have a daughter Tommy's age. It's her dog, Molly, that gave birth to the litter," Mr. Franklin said, opening the front driver's door and leaning on it.

"Well, in that case, Tommy," Kathy smiled and teased, "don't bring home a girlfriend instead of a puppy. We want a puppy! Got that?"

Tommy gave his sister a funny look and a light-hearted push.

"Don't worry about that. Girls are a pain in the you know what. Right, Darlene?" Tommy scowled at Darlene in a joking manner.

"Yeah right, Tommy. Just like little brothers are a pain in the you know what. I'm sure glad I don't have one," Darlene fired back.

"Let's go, Dad."

Tommy hopped into the front of his parents' car.

"Love you, little brother," Kathy kept up the innocent ribbing.

"Yeah, love you big sister. See ya when we get back."

John Franklin gave his wife Nadine another peck on the cheek, got into the car and rolled down the window. "You two behave while we're out. We'll be back with Buddy or whatever the little guy's going to be called."

"Name him Buddy," Darlene chipped in her two cents worth. "We all like Buddy, Tommy. Name him Buddy!"

Tommy leaned over in the front seat toward the driver side of the car and looked out the window at Darlene. "I don't know what I'm going to name him, we'll see."

Mr. Franklin looked at the three females standing outside the car and smiled. "Adios senoritas. We don't want to be late."

Where It All Began

Mr. Franklin put the gearshift into drive and he and his son headed out to claim their new puppy.

THE DRIVE FROM Brenton to Clear Lake was about twenty minutes depending on your choice of two ways to go. Either the direct route or the scenic route will get you there.

Describing locations in Michigan requires some clarification. When someone says, "I'm from the northwest part of the Lower Peninsula in Michigan," a lot of times the response is, "Huh?" The locals will know, but if you're not from the region you might not understand what people are talking about. Michigan is divided into the Upper Peninsula and Lower Peninsula. You could live in the north-eastern part of the Upper Peninsula or the south-western part of the Lower Peninsula or a number of variations thereof. Clear Lake and Brenton are in the upper north-western part of the Lower Peninsula. It is a part of the state that is beautiful in its own regard with the Lake Michigan sand dunes and the rolling forested hills. Cherry tree country, farm country and especially recreational fun country. A place where people who can afford it have their summer cabins on Lake Michigan or any one of the multitude of smaller lakes in the region.

The small town populations swell with summer visitors in July and August and, like someone hit a switch, everything quiets down after Labor Day. Those that are lucky enough to live there all year round feel blessed. No big cities, not in this part of the world. Not even something you would call a big town. Just small towns, with small town flavor, that breed innocence in their children. In many cases, people are born and live their whole lives there. This is where Tommy Franklin grew up and this is where he met the first dog he would ever own.

On this particular day, Mr. Franklin thought it would be a good idea to take the direct route to Clear Lake. No sense in taking the scenic route. This was business, serious business. A boy getting his first puppy was something you remembered your whole life. Mr. Franklin could remember getting his when he was about his son's age and how exciting it had been. Now it was time for his son to experience that euphoric feeling. For a young boy, getting his first puppy ranks right behind Christmas or a birthday. Mr. Franklin was feeling and living it all over again through Tommy. He watched his son as they made the trip over to the Russell farm. He could see that Tommy was excited and antsy. They said little as Tommy daydreamed about the upcoming event. The father could tell by the way his son was looking out the window and watching the scenery pass by that he was deep in thought. He was probably thinking about what tricks to teach his new friend or how to make him obey. It was going to be a big responsibility for a ten year old to take on. Mr. Franklin had explained to Tommy in a serious discussion they had a few days before that this wasn't going to be a novelty thing, it was a big undertaking. Feeding the puppy and making sure it got exercise was just part of it.

"A lot of dogs live to be between twelve and fifteen years old and even older," he had told his son. "This dog will be your friend until you're in your twenties."

Tommy understood all this and was up for the challenge. He and his dog would be best friends for a very long time and he couldn't wait to get to the Russell farm to begin that friendship. Little did he know that this upcoming encounter would strike up another friendship that would last his lifetime, longer than any dog he would ever be with. A relationship with a love that, like a dog's, would be unconditional.

"OK, TOMMY. WE'RE looking for 8373. That should be on your side of the road," Mr. Franklin said, slowing the vehicle down.

The dirt road was dry and dusty and not only did he want to keep the dust down, but he also wanted to make sure they didn't pass the driveway or hit one of the deep pot holes making the road a bit of an obstacle course. Being farm country, the driveways were far apart and if you missed the one you were looking for it meant going up the road a ways to find a place where you could turn around. Despite wanting to get to their destination as quickly as possible, driving slowly was the practical thing to do. Both father and son checked out the mailboxes as they drove down Lynden Rd.

"Did you catch that one, Tommy?"

"8255."

"OK, we're getting close. Couple more driveways, Tommy, and that should be it." Mr. Franklin glanced at his son and sensed Tommy's uneasiness. The young Franklin boy might be trying to stay cool on the outside, but was ready to jump out of the car and run the rest of the way if need be. There was a puppy waiting for him and the car wasn't going fast enough. He fidgeted a bit as he realized it had to be the next driveway.

"8373. This is it!" Tommy's dad proclaimed and pulled onto the long dirt driveway, treed on one side with an open field on the other. "Long driveway, hey Tommy?"

"Yeah, hopefully there's a house at the end of it," Tommy said looking straight ahead.

"I'm sure there is," Mr. Franklin said knowing there would be. "This driveway could be longer than ours! There's the house!"

The Russell farm house came into view as did a huge barn just beyond it. Both structures sat in a clearing with a big, old Maple tree shading the home. Mr. Franklin pulled up to the front of the house and, before he and his son could get out of the car, a young girl, the same age as Tommy, ran out the front door and up to the car's passenger side, grabbed the door handle and opened the door for the boy inside.

"Hello. I'm Carolyn! You must be Tommy Franklin."

"Hi. Yeah, I'm Tommy Franklin. Nice to meet you," Tommy said, bashfully exhibiting some typical youthful boy shyness.

"Nice to meet you too. I'm excited you're here!" Carolyn responded with genuine enthusiasm.

The young Franklin boy tried to maintain his composure as this boisterous girl greeted them. She was thrilled to the bone to meet the male Franklins.

"Hi. I'm Mr. Franklin, Tommy's dad," Mr. Franklin said, walking around the car and offering a hand to shake.

Carolyn smiled and shook his hand.

"Nice to meet you, Mr. Franklin. Here come my parents."

Mr. Franklin turned around and saw Mr. and Mrs. Russell walking down off the front porch to greet them.

"Hello, there," Mr. Franklin said as he walked in the direction of Carolyn's parents and once again extended his hand. "I'm Mr. Franklin and this is my son, Tommy."

"So nice to meet you both and welcome," Mr. Russell said, taking Mr. Franklin's hand.

"Hi, I'm Carolyn's mother, Jenny," Mrs. Russell introduced herself and turned to Tommy offering him a handshake. "Hello, Tommy. So you're after a puppy are you?"

"Yes, mam."

"Well, you've come to the right place," Mrs. Russell continued. "They're over in the barn. Let's go check them out."

The group of five headed for the barn and Tommy, instead of thinking of a puppy, was engrossed with the size of the barn. It was the biggest barn he had ever seen. His father was thinking the same.

"That's one big barn, Mr. Russell," Mr. Franklin said, stating the obvious.

"Call me Don," Carolyn's father told the elder Franklin. "My parents built it back in the twenties and it still looks the same as it did when I was a kid. It's very useful and a great place for a dog to have her litter."

Carolyn and Tommy followed behind deciding to let their parents do the grown-up talk. Carolyn had been outgoing her whole young life and was comfortable conversing with people of all ages. Tommy wasn't quite sure what to make of this girl. As Tommy and Carolyn walked side by side and she talked away, he half listened and half admired the barn that was getting bigger as they approached it.

"How do you like going to Douglas?" Carolyn asked Tommy, referring to the elementary school that Tommy attended in Brenton.

"It's fine. All my friends are there and I like my teachers. You go to Bender, right?" Tommy asked about the school in Clear Lake he assumed Carolyn must be attending.

"Yes, I do. I really like it," Carolyn replied.

"That's good. Maybe we'll both go to Filburtson when we're old enough," said Tommy, talking about the only Junior High that served the communities of both Clear Lake and Brenton.

"I would say more than likely. That would be so neat."

Tommy was trying to be polite, but his mind was now focused on getting to the barn and seeing the puppies. He barely heard Carolyn's comment.

She asked him about what sports he liked.

"Actually, baseball is my favorite sport. I play in Little League," Tommy informed her.

"I like baseball. I like watching it," said Carolyn.

"You can always come out and watch one of my games. Our home field is in Brenton at Creel Park."

Tommy thought it was kind of neat for such a young girl to be so outgoing and found her appealing for someone of the opposite sex. The Russell girl was good at making others her age feel comfortable.

The two young people continued their casual conversation as they walked and Tommy could talk baseball as long as Carolyn wanted to. But that subject came to an end as soon as they entered the barn.

Inside the barn, Tommy stopped dead in his tracks and the thought of a puppy once again momentarily left his mind. He had to stop and take it all in.

"The puppies are over here, Tommy," Carolyn said, now a few feet in front, and waved him on.

"Wow, this is such a big barn. It looks even bigger inside!" Tommy commented, speaking to no one in particular as he continued to where the others had stopped at a stall where a horse or cow would usually be kept.

"Holy moly! Look here, Tommy." Mr. Franklin stood just outside the stall while Carolyn opened the swinging gate.

"Get the boy ones out for Tommy, Carolyn," Mr. Russell instructed his daughter. "It was a male you wanted right, Tommy?"

"Yes, sir ."

"Well, there are five of them to choose from," Mrs. Russell informed the Franklin boy. "You can have your pick. We haven't promised any of them away, so you get first choice. Have you chosen a name yet, Tommy?"

"Yes, mam. I think I might call him Buddy," Tommy said, watching as Carolyn lifted the five male puppies out of their makeshift wooden box and let them run around in the hay that covered the stall floor. Molly, the proud mother who had been on her side with her children and was glad to see the humans, stood up and began wagging her tail.

Mrs. Russell beamed as she gave Molly the attention she wanted. "Hello, Molly girl. How are you today? Buddy ... that's a nice name."

"Thank you," Tommy said, engrossed in all the action going on in the stall.

Puppies everywhere. He watched them closely and suddenly realized this was going to be a tough decision. He wondered for a moment what his dad would say if he asked him about taking them all home. Probably not. Soon one caught his attention. It was the one that seemed to be the most full of beans. Jumping beans. Carolyn noticed Tommy paying more attention to the little rascal and picked the puppy up.

"Here, hold him."

"Oh, wow!" was Tommy's response. He couldn't recall ever holding a puppy before. He laughed along with Carolyn as the puppy licked his face. They both seemed to think this scene was pretty funny as the puppy squirmed and continued to lick Tommy's face. Everyone was amused at the sight.

"That one seems to have a lot of octane," Mr. Russell said.

"Yeah, Tommy. He's always up to no good. He's fun to watch," Carolyn offered her opinion as she petted the puppy being held by an admiring young boy.

Tommy put the puppy back down and in an instant the trouble maker playfully attacked his siblings who were trying to mind their own business. What was it with this little guy? Something was making him a lot more energetic than his brothers and he obviously loved an audience. The Franklins and Russells watched as the center of attention attacked his siblings in what seemed like a calculated maneuver. All in fun of course, because the only thing puppies know how to do at that age is to have fun. But was this some kind of show the little monster was putting on? Was it being done on purpose to get people to notice him? Was this the way he was going to be when he was older?

Watch me! Watch me! I'm never going to change. I'm so full of mischief! Don't you think I'm such a cute puppy?

The audience continued to watch in amusement, anticipating his next goofball antic. He didn't disappoint. His brain was going faster than his legs could take him and he was constantly tripping over his own feet ... paws. But nothing discouraged him from doing something that fit right in with this feel-good moment. It was all laughs as the humans watched the little guy go. And go. And go.

It wasn't a difficult decision after all, although the other puppy brothers were doing their best to attract everyone's attention as well in their cute passive way. It was just that this little Tasmanian devil took puppy energy to a whole new level. This was going to be the one that Tommy chose because they had so much in common—energy and the love of life— and his name was definitely going to be Buddy.

"So what do you think, Tommy?" Mr. Franklin asked his enthralled son. "Have you made up your mind?"

"Yeah, I think so," Tommy responded with eyes fixated on his future best friend.

He pointed to the one puppy wreaking havoc. "I really like that guy with all the energy."

Carolyn picked up the puppy that Tommy had pointed to, the one that had been demanding all the attention, and held him up.

"How did I know you were going to pick this one?" she marveled.

Tommy grinned and gave his new pet a pat on the head.

"I don't know, how did you?"

"I just knew. I just knew," Carolyn boasted.

"Good choice, son. I'm like you. I'd like to take them all home, but I have a feeling this one is going to be a handfull."

"Well, if he is and you change your mind you can always bring him back," Mrs. Russell said knowing that would never happen, but making the offer anyway. This was a match made in heaven. She could see it and feel it. This young boy and his new puppy would bond like boys and puppies do. The bond would be everlasting. She felt good for the Franklin father and his son and was pleased that the little rascal they had chosen was going to a good home.

"You wanna put the other ones back in the stall with their mom, Carolyn?" Mr. Russell asked his daughter.

"Sure, Dad. Good choice, Tommy," Carolyn said, "good choice." She was thrilled and feeling the same excitement as Tommy. "You two are going to have a great life together."

"Thanks, Carolyn. I'm sure we will. Thank you so much."

The Russell girl finished putting the others back in the stall with their mom and everyone headed for the barn exit. The sunshine streaked through the old planking in the doors and walls and seemed to have come out in more ways than one today. For Tommy it came every time he looked into the face of this puppy that he carried in his arms and it also came in another way he hadn't yet discovered. It came in meeting this girl named Carolyn that was so radiant and brought sunshine to all whenever they were around her.

"Thank you so much once again, Mr. and Mrs. Russell. And you too, Carolyn." Mr. Franklin offered another handshake to Mr. Russell.

"Oh, gosh. You're so welcome. I think we all feel good about this, right Carolyn?"

"For sure, Dad. Can I hold him one more time, Tommy?" Carolyn asked, holding out her hands.

"Oh, yeah," Tommy said and handed Buddy over to Carolyn for one last cuddle.

"I'm going to miss you, little guy, er, Buddy. I'll come and visit, OK? You be good and behave," Carolyn said and handed Buddy back to Tommy.

"Yeah, you'll have to come by, Carolyn. We're not that far away," Mr. Franklin extended an invitation.

Tommy put Buddy down and everyone once again watched him scramble, this time around the Franklin car. As Buddy came back around he was hot on the heels of a butterfly hoping to make it his new best friend. Or maybe it was going to be the grasshopper that caught his attention when the butterfly didn't want to cooperate. Unfortunately for Buddy, not all bugs or insects are interested in being attacked by a puppy.

Tommy scooped Buddy up. "Come on Buddy, into the car. You'll have lots of room to run around where we're going."

He put the squirming puppy into the front seat.

"Do we have your phone number, Tommy?" Carolyn asked.

"Yes, you have it," Mr. Franklin interjected. "I gave it to your dad the other night."

"Yes, we have it, Carolyn," her father assured her. "We'll give you a call sometime, Mr. Franklin, and I'll bring Carolyn over for a visit with Buddy. It will be nice to watch him grow and see how he develops."

"Anytime, Mr. Russell. Anytime." Mr. Franklin opened the driver's door and out bounded Buddy. "Hey, ya little squirt." Reacting quickly he scooped up the scoundrel before he could escape. "Tommy, I think we have a live one here."

Everyone was laughing as Mr. Franklin climbed into his car holding Buddy close to his chest.

"Don't let him get away, Dad!" Tommy showed his concern as he got into the passenger seat.

His father started up the car, handed Buddy to his son and rolled down the driver's window. "OK, people. So nice to meet you and we'll be in touch. Do drive over to Brenton sometime and see us."

"We will, Mr. Franklin. We will," Mr. Russell said, standing with his wife as they smiled in delight.

Tommy's dad put the car in reverse and turned around. Carolyn walked alongside waving and caught Tommy's eye. Their eyes locked on each other in a fixation that neither at this young age could explain.

It wouldn't be the last time she caught his eye or he caught hers. Nobody could predict what their fate was going to be. In their tender youth, these two innocent children could not have known that this moment of eye contact was a sign of their life to come. Nobody could have possibly known it was the start of a lifelong relationship that would last for more than fifty years. And nobody knew about the forthcoming pain and sorrow, joy and delight, tears and the laughter that would encompass these two as their love story unfolded.

That day, just by doing the simple task of exchanging a new puppy, Carolyn and Tommy's lives became intertwined forever. As Mr. Franklin drove his son and Buddy slowly away down the Russell driveway, Carolyn ran alongside waving. Tommy held his puppy and looked back at this intriguing girl, thinking of this encounter with Carolyn as nothing more than a brief one. She was just some girl whose dog happened to have puppies at a time when his parents thought it would be a good idea to get one. So on this day, it didn't cross his mind that this outgoing girl by the name of Carolyn was going to be someone special in his life. But all relationships have a beginning and this was theirs. Tommy took one of Buddy's paws and used it to wave good-bye to Carolyn as she stopped running and continued waving. Hello. Good-bye. The beginning.

"WELL, HE DID pretty well for his first car ride, don't ya think?" Tommy's dad asked as he and his son pulled into their driveway.

"I guess he didn't do too bad considering I held him all the way. Are you sure you like the name Buddy, Dad?" Tommy asked, needing more assurance.

"Yeah, absolutely. It's a great name. I love it!"

As the Franklin vehicle pulled up in front of the house, Tommy couldn't

Where It All Began

wait to show his mom and sister.

"Do you think Kathy and Mom will like him?"

"Of course they will, Tommy."

"Do you think they'll like the name Buddy?" Questions, questions, questions that Tommy hoped to get all positive answers to.

"Absolutely! What's not to like about the name Buddy? It's the most popular name going right now for male dogs," Mr. Franklin said. "They're going to love it, I guarantee."

As Tommy opened his door, Buddy couldn't wait to make an exit and leapt down onto the ground.

"Gees, Buddy. You don't have to be so impatient!" Tommy said, getting out of the car in a hurry just like his new friend did. "You have to be patient, Buddy."

If you had to pee like I do, you would understand. At least I didn't pee in your lap!

Buddy found a spot on the front lawn, squatted and took a record breaking pee.

"Look at that! He waited until he got out of the car." Mr. Franklin was quite impressed. "He may be hyperactive, but you know what son ... I think he's really smart."

"I think he is too, Dad. I'll keep a close eye on him when he's in the house and if he makes a mess I'll clean it up. He sure took a long pee."

"That he did, son. That he did."

All of a sudden the front screen door flew open catching Tommy and his dad's attention. It was Kathy running out followed closely by her mom.

"Oh, my gosh! Is that him? He's so cute," Kathy screamed.

Buddy, wondering who these potentially new friends were, ran toward Kathy and was quickly lifted up into her arms.

"Hello you. What's your name?"

"Buddy," Tommy informed her.

Kathy beamed.

"I was hoping you would choose that one."

"Tommy, he's such a sweetie!" Mrs. Franklin exclaimed. Mother and daughter showered the new family member with uninterrupted attention.

"It's only a puppy," Tommy thought ... oh so proudly. Kathy and Mrs. Franklin couldn't get enough of Buddy and acted a tad silly. Mr. Franklin watched. His amusement showed on his face. The puppy had his own thoughts.

Why are these humans carrying on so much? Are they trying to make me feel good? Well, they're doing an excellent job.

Yes, the love and affection coming from the humans was genuine. In the Franklin family, everything was sincere and Buddy sucked it up giving licks and kisses to all that would have them.

This is going to be a great family to live with! I'm going to rule this family. They're going to love me. I'm a puppy! I'm so cute! How could anyone resist me? My name is Buddy! I love that name! It suits me well. Put me down, Kathy. I want to run. I want to play. I want to do what puppies do. Play, eat and sleep. Play some more. Throw me a stick to chase ... or a ball. I don't care. I just want to run or go for a swim or play with other dogs. It's going to be an incredible life and you're going to love me and I'm going to love you. Now put me down, Kathy. I want to romp around and have someone chase me.

Buddy squirmed in Kathy's arms as she and her mother continued to adore him. Finally, enough squirming. Kathy put Buddy down and off he went.

"I'm guessing you picked the most energetic one, Tommy," Mrs. Franklin said, smiling to her son.

"Well, I think maybe. They were all so cute, but this guy ... there was just something about him," Tommy said as he watched Buddy run in circles.

"Yeah, Tommy," his sister said, jumping into the conversation. "You did a good job. He's just adorable. With your energy and his, I can't imagine either one of you ever getting any sleep. Good luck with that."

Tommy laughed as he watched Buddy chase everything in sight. Mrs. Franklin wondered what Buddy must have been like in his mother's womb. "Gosh," she thought, "his mother was probably glad to give birth just to get rid of him." Buddy ran toward the Franklin barn as the father, mother, sister and brother all watched. Stopping in his tracks, he realized no one was chasing him.

How come? I'll just run back to them and surely one of them will take the bait and start out after me.

As he did, Tommy fell for it and started to give chase. Off they went. Laughter was easy to come by in this family and there was a lot of it going on at the moment. Tommy dived to grab Buddy by the hind legs, but was unsuccessful. Buddy ramped it up. Kathy joined in. What great fun. Now mom joined in. Now dad. Finally Buddy was corralled by his new owners who were laughing so hard they could barely stand it. Everyone was out of breath ... except him, the puppy with endless energy. He saw he was surrounded.

What should I do? Which way can I go? There has to be an escape route.

He thought his best chance was between the brother and sister and he bolted in that direction. Tommy and Kathy both tumbled to the ground getting their hands on him, but neither one could quite make the grab. The brother and sister laughed hysterically and grabbed their sides. It was a pain that felt good. Mr. and Mrs. Franklin enjoyed the moment for all it was worth ... a memory that would be forever etched in their minds. They wondered to themselves why they hadn't gotten a puppy before now. This was too much fun. The kids were cracking the parents up with their joyous actions. These were moments every parent lived for. *Thank you, Buddy.*

Buddy? Where did he go now? Around to the other side of the house of course with Kathy and Tommy in hot pursuit. As they disappeared, all you could hear were two kids screaming about how this little canine character was going to be in big trouble when they caught him. Mrs. Franklin took a couple of steps toward her husband to stand by his side. She put her arm through his and waited with him for what they knew was going to happen next. Of course they were right. Here came Buddy around the corner of the house with their two children right on his tail. He ran toward the parents, but couldn't stop in time. He crashed into Mrs. Franklin's shins. Mr. Franklin grabbed him by the scruff of the neck and held him to his chest as Kathy and Tommy ran up. Buddy had become the center of the Franklin universe. He was now officially part of the family. Not one of the four people standing together could keep their hands off him. He was oh, so loveable, and a welcome addition to such an oh so loving environment. He would live his life here. Destiny? Fate? Whatever you want to call it, it was as Mrs. Russell knew it was going to be, a match made in heaven. Buddy had found a home. Forever and ever.

It was going to be a good life. When he finally put his head down that night for a sleep, he would come to realize that he missed his brothers and sisters and his mother, but he felt, for the moment, perfectly comfortable in his new environment.

This Franklin family is so nice. I'm a lucky puppy.

"Tommy," Mr. Franklin said as Buddy seemed to be slowing down and not squirming like when he was last held. "This guy has to be thirsty. Let's get him a drink."

Mr. Franklin put Buddy down onto the ground. Buddy was thinking the same thing.

Where's the water?

"Tommy," Mrs. Franklin said, "your sister and I bought a food dish and a water bowl for him. It's in the kitchen. Let's take him inside."

They all headed for the front door and Buddy, as if he could understand English, was right on their heels until they all got to the front steps where he decided to have a sit down. The humans made it look so easy walking up the steps, but this poor tired puppy couldn't seem to gather up the energy. They looked so high. Kathy walked back down and picked him up.

"What's the matter, Buddy? Too tired to climb the stairs? That'll teach ya. You're going to have to stop and catch your breath every now and then, little fella. Come on. We'll play some more chase later. You need some food and water."

Mrs. Franklin had already filled the food dish and water bowl as Kathy and Buddy walked in. Kathy handed him to Tommy.

"Here, he's all yours."

Tommy put Buddy down by his food bowl and in a nanosecond it became a feeding frenzy. The poor guy must have worked up an appetite. Was he actually chewing or just swallowing the kibbles? Now for some water. Must have worked up a thirst too! Yes, the poor guy. The poor, poor Buddy. Life was tough. Especially for puppies. Eat, sleep, play. Or is it play, eat, sleep? Doesn't matter. Let's just have some fun.

"So, Tommy," Mrs. Franklin said as she began prepping some food for lunch. "Where is our little terror going to sleep tonight? We haven't discussed that."

Tommy grabbed a chair at the kitchen table, not able to take his eyes off his new friend and his new responsibility.

"He can sleep in my room on my bed with me. He'll be fine"

"But if he keeps you awake at night that won't be a good thing, will it?"

Mr. Franklin and Kathy, seated at the kitchen table as well, watched Buddy chow down.

"He's not house broken yet, Tommy. You're going to have to put some papers down and train him," Mr. Franklin advised. "When he's older," Tommy's dad continued, "he'll be fine. But for now he's going to need a lot of attention and patience. He can sleep in the back door foyer if you like."

"I'd kind of like him to sleep with me if that's OK. He'll be fine. Honest. I'll look after him and keep an eye on him," Tommy pleaded with his parents.

"OK. If that's what you want, son. What do you think, Mom?" Mr. Franklin asked.

"For sure, Tommy. We trust you'll do a good job and be a good dog owner. He's all yours for the next ten to fifteen years. It's a big undertaking, but you can do it," Mrs. Franklin said, having total confidence in her son.

"Thanks, Mom. Thanks, Dad. If he misbehaves, I'll just put him in Kathy's room."

Tommy looked at his sister to see what her reaction was going to be.

"That's fine little brother, but you'll never get him back. He'll be mine, all

Where It All Began

mine. Would you like some help with lunch, Mom?"

"That would be great, honey. You can start by getting me a skillet."

Buddy finished his kibbles and slurped down a long drink as half the water went into his mouth and the other half on the floor around his bowl. He looked around at the people in the room then started off to sniff everything in sight. The chair legs, the bottom cupboards, the table legs. It was all new to him. Before today all he knew was the smell of a barn and hay that he assumed was the smell of the world. This was different and different in a pleasant way. It didn't smell like hay. It was fresh and clean. He liked it. The Franklin family watched him as he made his way from the kitchen and into the dining room.

Boy, this sure is a big house! What are these things? I saw them outside.

Buddy recalled the humans calling them stairs. He put his front paws up on the bottom one and looked up.

I wonder where they go?

Tommy and his father had followed Buddy every step of the way and watched him do his thing. Tommy looked up at his dad and smiled. "This is great entertainment," the young boy thought to himself. Buddy would like to know where the stairs went, but he didn't have the energy to attempt the climb. Besides, he wasn't too sure how to get his hind legs up onto the first step. He decided to keep all four paws on the floor and continue his journey.

Where next? What's this room over here?

It was the living room, only he had to go down two stairs to get to it. Buddy stood at the top of the steps and looked down.

Why are there all these steps? Well, it's not that far down and worth a try if I want to explore another room.

Unfortunately it was not quite as easy as Buddy thought and he did a face plant on the first step, rolled over onto the second step and then fell onto the living room floor. Father and son couldn't help but laugh.

"Ouch!" Mr. Franklin said in a low voice.

Unfazed, Buddy kept exploring, sniffing, looking and searching. Then, like it happens to every puppy who doesn't know his limits, all of a sudden Buddy plopped down next to the foot stool in front of the couch. That's it. Done. Through. Finished.

I think I need a break ... for now. I can explore more later. Right now, I'm a pretty tired guy.

Buddy lay on his side and closed his eyes. Tommy walked up to him, got on his knees and petted Buddy as Mr. Franklin looked on. Buddy gave out one of those puppy groans that only puppies can give.

"Hey, guy," Tommy said, stroking his friend, "it's too early. You can't go to sleep now. You'll be up all night if you do." Tommy picked Buddy up and slung him over his shoulder. "Let's go back into the kitchen and see what's cooking."

Tommy walked past his dad as the proud father smiled and watched his son. It had been most rewarding watching his son and Buddy interact. He thought to himself that he and his wife had made a good decision to get a puppy. Buddy was going to get lots of love from everyone here at the Franklin home. Every puppy just wants to be loved and give love and this wonderful family Buddy had come to live with had a lot of that to pass around.

AFTER DINNER THAT night Tommy was sitting on the living room couch with Buddy in his lap. The TV was on, but Tommy wasn't interested. He was content petting Buddy. Mr. Franklin sat in his favorite chair and Mrs. Franklin and Kathy shared the couch with Tommy.

"That was a good episode. I liked that one," Kathy said as the sitcom they were watching came to an end.

"Yeah, that was pretty funny. Those two guys crack me up," Mr. Franklin said, stretching his arms.

Mrs. Franklin looked over at her son and noticed his eyes getting heavy.

"Tommy, why don't you take your pal there and head off up to bed. You're looking pretty tired."

"Yeah, OK," Tommy responded groggily. "What do you think, Buddy. Do you want to sleep with me tonight?" Tommy stood up with Buddy cradled in his arms. The young boy didn't dispute going to bed. He was tired and knew it. It had been a long day. No use fighting the fatigue. He began to head for the stairs that would take him to his room.

"Good night, Mom. Good night, Dad. Good night, Kathy."

"Good night, Tommy," Mr. Franklin said.

"Good night, little brother."

"We'll come up and see you in a minute. Get yourself ready," Mrs. Franklin said, wondering if Tommy was going to have the energy to get up the stairs.

"OK. Can you bring up his food dish and water bowl?" Tommy asked anyone and everyone.

"I'll bring it up," Kathy said.

She also wanted to get one last look at this new family member before they all went to sleep. She watched her brother carry Buddy up the stairs thinking to herself that they seem attached … physically attached. She knew her brother well enough to know that from now on it was going to be the Tommy and Buddy show and that Tommy would never let go of his new best friend. She expected, as her parents did, that wherever Tommy was, from now on, was where you'd find Buddy and vice versa. There would be no separating the two. Not now. Not ever.

KATHY AND HER parents were in the kitchen tidying up.

"Anyone up for a game of Scrabble?" Mr. Franklin asked.

"Count me in," Mrs. Franklin replied.

"I promised Tommy I would bring Buddy's food dish and water bowl up," Kathy said, wanting to keep her promise.

"Do you mind if I do that, Kathy?" Mrs. Franklin asked her daughter, "and then I'll come back and play a game with you two."

"We'll set the game up, Mom. Give that Buddy a pat on the head from me." Kathy said, not objecting to her mother's suggestion.

"I'll do that," Mrs. Franklin said as she poured a little more kibble into the food dish, grabbed the water bowl and headed upstairs.

It was quiet as she made her way down the hallway to Tommy's room. His door was cracked open and it was dark inside. She used her elbow to push the door open. In the ambient light she noticed a young boy and his new puppy asleep on the bed. She put the bowl and dish near the papers Tommy had put down in case Buddy had to pee in the middle of the night. Hopefully, Buddy would figure that out if he needed to go.

Mrs. Franklin turned on the bedside lamp and looked down at the pair sound asleep. It was a scene that would bring a sense of joy to any mother and she was no different. She loved her children so much. Mrs. Franklin loved everything about her life and these were the moments that were so precious and frozen in time. She would never forget this scene and knew it. The image was in her memory bank to stay.

She mumbled under her breath, "Thank you for this blessing, Lord."

Tommy and Buddy lay perfectly still, dead to the world. Off somewhere in dreamland. They couldn't be lying any closer to each other. On top of the covers they were as one and they were going to be as one for years to come. Tommy obviously hadn't mustered up the energy to get out of his clothes and into his pajamas. His mother didn't dare wake him up now. Let them sleep. Her son would probably wake up later and get into his pajamas and under the covers by himself. No, she wouldn't disturb the boy angel and the puppy angel. This was the end of a perfect day. She bent over, softly kissed her son's cheek and quietly whispered, "I love you, Tommy." As she made her exit she stopped at the bedroom door, turned around and had another look before gently closing the door to Tommy's room.

Back downstairs in the kitchen Kathy and her father had set up the Scrabble board, popped some popcorn and poured drinks. They sat chatting when Mrs. Franklin walked back in.

"How's the Team of Double Trouble doing, dear?" Mr. Franklin asked his wife.

"Sleeping like the pair of angels that they are. Tommy couldn't even get out of his clothes or under the covers. It looked like they both just plopped down on the bed and that was it. It's so sweet. Did you get me a drink?" Mrs. Franklin asked noticing a couple of drinks on the table.

"We didn't know what you wanted," Kathy said. "Tell me what you want and I'll get it for you, Mom."

"That's OK, Kathy. I think I'll just stick with water for now."

Mrs. Franklin grabbed a glass out of the cupboard and an ice tray from the freezer and ran the water from the kitchen tap. She stared out the window above the sink into the darkness picturing the scene she had just witnessed upstairs. The reflection in the glass showed a smile on her face. She walked over to the kitchen table and took her usual seat.

"Have we drawn yet to see who goes first?" she asked the competition.

"Nope. We were waiting for you, Mom," Mr. Franklin informed his wife.

Sometimes, in front of Tommy and Kathy, Mrs. Franklin would call her husband "Dad" and Mr. Franklin would call his wife "Mom." It was quite common in a lot of families and was an expression of acknowledgement that they both enjoyed.

"OK, Dad. Pass the letter bag around and let's see who starts," Mrs. Franklin said.

Mr. Franklin picked out a wooden Scrabble letter, put it down on the table and handed the small bag of letters to his wife. He laid down the letter C and said, "Beat that!"

Mrs. Franklin reached into the bag and pulled out a letter. She held it down below table top level, looked at it and smiled. She put it on the table face up. It was the letter B.

"I think I just did," she boasted.

"Darn it, Mrs. Franklin," Mr. Franklin bemoaned light-heartedly. "You always go first. I think you looked at the letter before you pulled it out."

"That's quite an accusation there, honey. Kathy, you draw. Maybe you'll go first."

Where It All Began

Kathy pulled a letter out of the bag and looked at it.

"Looks like it's you, Mom," she said, laying down a W on the table.

"Boy oh boy. I never get to go first," Kathy's dad whined again jokingly.

It was all in good fun of course, but being competitive was in Mr. Franklin's blood and he took these games with his family very seriously. Somewhat ... kind of. Not really. Everyone picked their letters and studied them as they waited for Mrs. Franklin to play the first word. She began laughing to herself.

"Oh dear."

"Just play a word, Mom. We're waiting. You're almost out of time," her husband warned her.

"Dad, be patient. What's so funny, Mom?" Kathy asked.

Mrs. Franklin was snickering as she started to lay down a word on the Scrabble board. B-U-D-D-Y. "There Buddy. Double word. How many points is that? Let me see."

She started counting the points, but was interrupted by her husband.

"You can't play that. It's a proper name!" Mr. Franklin protested.

Mother and daughter look at each other and started laughing.

"OK you two, settle down. You're going to wake your brother, Kathy," Mr. Franklin said, pretending to be mildly upset.

Kathy couldn't help herself. What were the odds of her mother picking up those letters?

"Oh gosh, Mom. That's too funny ... and it's not a proper name, Dad" Kathy said with a smile, taking her mom's side as always.

Mrs. Franklin started picking up the letters.

"So you won't let me play that word, dear?"

Her husband tried hard to contain his own laughter, but couldn't. This was why they enjoyed playing these games together. There was always the laughing and the kidding. Playing board games or card games had become a regular occurrence since both of their kids became old enough to join in. It was more fun than when it was just the two parents playing. Stupid things were said and done that would crack the other players up. It felt good to this family of four. They would play any kind of game that brought them together. They enjoyed each other's company immensely. The easiest thing in the world was for this family to sit down and play a game. It was always the same. Dad would make his world-famous popcorn. Kathy or Tommy would poor the drinks: soda pop for the kids and usually iced tea or water for the parents if it were summer time. In the winter time it would be hot chocolate with marshmallows all around. Mom got the board game and the cards and pencils and paper to keep score on. Everybody had their job. If there happened to be a sporting event on the radio, usually baseball, that could be heard in the background as they played. It was good quality time together. This was a tight family. A loving family.

The point of it all was to have fun. Dad always played the part of the sore loser. That was his role and no one ever got tired of it. That's why he did it. It kept his captive audience laughing. If acting like a sore loser made the others laugh ... so be it. He would gladly play the part. It was the simple things in life that counted most and that's all these evening games were, something simple that they all enjoyed doing together.

"No, you can't play that, Mrs. Franklin. Buddy is a proper name. Try again," Mr. Franklin was playfully flexing his muscles.

"OK, if that's the way you're going to be, I'll see what else I can come up with, although it may take some time. I thought I had the perfect word there. Kathy is right. Buddy is not a proper name. You know ... like Mr. Franklin you're such a good buddy to me," Mrs. Franklin said, trying to stare down her husband.

With her left arm, she reached underneath the table and tapped her daughter's thigh. Kathy gave her mom a look and knew exactly what her mother was about to do. Mrs. Franklin was going to take her own sweet time coming up with another word because she knew how much it would bug her husband. She did it all the time when they played these games just to get under his skin. This was how true love worked. This was the kind of relationship the mother and father had and Kathy hoped when she got married, she could be like them, so much in love.

Mr. Franklin knew what his wife was up to and began to tap his fingers on the table and hum. Her plan was working and she knew it.

In just a second he'd say what he always said, "OK, OK. Time's a wastin'. We don't have all night."

"I'm thinking, dear. I'm thinking. Just give me a moment," Mother would reply and continue to take her time.

So it went until the game was finished and either Kathy or Mom would win. Mr. Franklin would go into his "woe is me act" and say that he wouldn't ever play the stupid game again, accusing the competition of cheating and on and on and on. Joking of course in a serious, but very transparent manner. It worked. Wife and daughter laughed.

Playing these games meant Dad had an audience and for Mr. Franklin it was all about being the entertainer and sharing a few laughs with the ones he loved. Did winning or losing matter? Not a bit. Did the fact his wife won tonight's game bother him. Not at all. Yes, he was competitive, but only for the laughs. The laughs were all that mattered.

"OK, I'm going up to bed," Kathy said as she put the Scrabble game back in its proper place in the bottom drawer of the dining room buffet and walked back into the kitchen. "Night, Mom. Night, Dad." She walked over to her parents, gave each a hug and said, "I love you."

"We love you too, dear. Good night and try to be quiet when you go upstairs," Mom said, making a simple request.

"Will do. I doubt a locomotive would wake those two up. They were looking pretty tired when they went upstairs."

Kathy grabbed a book she had been reading off the kitchen counter and headed for the stairway.

"Good night, honey," Mr. Franklin said as he watched as his daughter walk away. "Remember, tomorrow night I get to win."

"Sure, Dad. Whatever. See you guys in the morning."

Mr. Franklin went to the kitchen sink and finished cleaning the dishes and glasses they had dirtied while playing Scrabble.

"I'm going out on the porch to see if there are any stars out," Mrs. Franklin informed her husband.

"Sure, I'll join you in a second. I'm just going to go to the bathroom real quick."

"OK, dear."

Nadine opened the wooden screen door and went out onto the veranda that wrapped around three quarters of the Franklin house. It didn't take long for her to realize once she was outside that it was a perfect Michigan evening. Not too cool, not too warm and hardly any humidity. She wouldn't have expected anything less considering what a perfect day it had been. Not just with the weather, but with everything else that went on. She gazed up and wondered if she could recall ever seeing so many stars out. No sooner had that thought crossed her mind when a shooting star caught her attention. Nadine leaned against the porch post at the top of three stairs and continued to stare out at the night sky. She took a deep breath and momentarily closed her eyes. It was so quiet. When she opened her eyes again she saw the odd firefly illuminate across the openness of the yard. Even though her husband, John, was a carpenter and had his own successful construction company, they had decided long before that they would not have any barriers between the house and their twenty acres of farm, so there were no fences around the Franklin home, except for the garden. They had some manicured lawn in both the front and back, but the rest of the property was kept wild. A farm in name only, they had no livestock or big crops, just a "fair size" family garden between the house and the barn. A typical family garden with corn, beans, tomatoes, onions, carrots and lettuce. All the popular vegetables that tasted so good when picked and served the same day and were so much better than the vegetables you bought in the grocery store. Although Mrs. Franklin and Kathy got together in late summer to do some canning and every member of the Franklin family did some weeding and whatever else work needed to be done in the garden, it wasn't all consuming. It was just enough to feel good about reaping the rewards when it came time to eat what they had planted.

Then there were the fruit trees: the pear, apple and peach trees that were very popular with the kids when the fruit ripened. Nadine could see them now just a few yards from where she stood, silhouetted against a dark, moonless sky. Her apple and peach pies were always a big hit and they never lasted very long whenever she sold them at the church bazaar or a school fundraiser.

It had been a good place to live for the last seventeen years since she and John had bought the property and moved here from down state. The house itself was a classic old farmhouse built in 1908. It was in need of repair when they first moved in, but they had seen the potential and all the basics were in place including a solid foundation. With John's talents as a carpenter and her cosmetic instincts when it came to paint colors and decorating, the old house didn't look at all like it had when they first took possession of it. If you didn't know better you would have thought it was a "brand new" old-style looking farmhouse. But it was not. It simply had had a lot of tender love and care and both John and Nadine were proud of their accomplishments. They had updated the wiring and plumbing, spruced up all the woodwork and either restained or repainted all of it inside and out. It was a labor of love as they say. What was a fixer-upper seventeen years before was now a work of art and tastefully done. It was also big on the inside with a full basement, main level and an upstairs with a total of five bedrooms, four up and one down, along with three bathrooms, one up and two down. Plenty of space for everyone to play, hide, or just find some solitude. It had a modern kitchen with everything that was new and innovative in the 1950s and was bright with lots of light. It was a home now and had been since the kids were born. All the work had been completed. It was just a matter of keeping it up, something they did as a family. Everybody pitched in with their own chores to do and it was done with loving care.

Mrs. Franklin heard the screen door open and turned around.

"Hi, honey. Care to join me?" she said to her husband of almost twenty years. She knew the answer in advance.

Where It All Began

"Why I'd love to," John said predictably. He walked over and stood behind his wife putting his arms around her. He planted a kiss on her ear. "Sure is a beauty tonight, wouldn't ya say Nadine Franklin?"

"That it is," she responded.

"That Buddy is too cute don't ya think?" John stated the obvious.

Mrs. Franklin turned around and looked at her husband. "He'll be good for Tommy, and for all of us actually. We've talked about this for such a long time and it makes me wonder why we didn't get a dog before now. Every family has a dog it seems."

"Yeah, I know. You're right, dear.

"Mr. Franklin repositioned his arms around his wife's waist. "Busy lives, maybe. When I was a kid we didn't get a dog until I was about Tommy's age. I've always loved dogs. You're right. This is going to be good for all of us. Buddy is going to be a joy to have around and looking after him will teach Tommy some responsibility. I think we're all looking forward to it."

Nadine turned around once again to gaze at the stars in the sky. "You know, honey, I don't know if I've ever seen this many stars out here." She had, of course, but it never ceased to amaze her on such clear nights how many stars actually existed. Nadine took her husband's hand and held it close to her chest. "Just keep watching. I've seen a couple of shooting stars already."

The lovers stood together in silence and cast their eyes toward a mysterious universe that did not disappoint.

"Whoa! Did you see that one?" John acted like he had never seen a shooting star before. "Wow! It sure had a long tail. There must be some sort of meteor shower going on."

Nadine walked down the steps, stood on the front lawn and looked up just as another shooting star headed toward its destination.

"There goes another one. "I could sleep out here tonight if it weren't for the mosquitoes," she said slapping one she couldn't see but felt land on her arm.

"Yeah, I think the mosquitoes have found us. I'm going back inside and heading for bed. Don't stay out too late," John kidded.

"I'm coming in too, dear. Wait for me." Nadine turned and walked back up the steps, putting her arm through her husband's. "It's been a perfect day hasn't it John Franklin?"

"Yes it has, honey. It has indeed. Perfect in every way except for me losing at Scrabble."

John stopped and held the screen door open for his wife.

"There will always be tomorrow, dear. There's always tomorrow," Nadine smiled at her husband and walked back into the house.

John followed her in and as always since the day they first met, he melted when she smiled at him. "Yes," he thought to himself, "there's always tomorrow. More of the same." It was all he could wish for. More of the same. It was all he could hope for. It was all he needed out of this perfect life. More of the same.

Three Months Later - Early Fall

KATHY RAN FROM upstairs into the Franklin kitchen to answer the phone. She thought, at first, that someone else at home would pick it up, but no, apparently not. It had rung a number of times and she was surprised, when she got to the phone, that there was still a voice on the other end.

"Hello?" Kathy said, taking the phone off the base that hung on the kitchen wall by the back door. She was out of breath from the quick dash and barely got the "Hello" out.

"Oh hi. Is this the Franklin home?" a young girl's voice asked.

"Yes, it is," Kathy replied.

"May I speak with Tommy?"

Kathy had to think for a second before responding. *A girl calling for Tommy? What's with that?*

"I think he might be here somewhere, but I'll have to go look for him. You can hang on or I can have him call you back if you like."

The girl on the other end of the line considered her options. Kathy waited patiently.

"I can hang on for a minute if that's OK?" the girl said.

"Sure. I'll go see if I can find him. Can I tell him who's calling?"

"Yes, this is Carolyn Russell. Tommy and his dad came by our farm about three months ago and picked up one of our puppies. I'm calling to see how the puppy is doing."

"Oh hi, Carolyn. This is Tommy's sister, Kathy. We thought we would have heard from you before now. Buddy is doing fine. Are you going to come over and see him?"

"Yes. My dad and I were thinking of coming over in a couple of hours if someone was going to be home."

"Oh sure, Carolyn. I don't think we're doing much today. Come on over and bring your mom if she wants to come."

"I can ask her. Is Tommy going to be there?"

"I'll tie him to a tree to make sure he's here, Carolyn. He and Buddy, I'm sure, are not too far away. They're probably outside playing somewhere.

That's what those two do. You should see how much Buddy has grown. You're not going to believe it. He's getting so big."

Kathy looked out the back door window in both directions to see if she could see anyone. She noticed the family car outside so everyone had to be somewhere not too far away.

"Yeah, I can't wait to see him," Carolyn said, feeling relieved now that she knew the Franklin's were going to be around.

She had been bugging her parents for a couple of months to go pay Buddy a visit, but the summer was busy and it hadn't happened. Now it sounded like today was the day and she was bursting with excitement that could hardly be contained.

"I can't wait to meet you, Carolyn. Are you more excited to see Tommy or Buddy?" Kathy teased.

She knew who Carolyn meant, but thought she would attempt being funny. It ran in the family.

"Well, both of them actually. It would be nice to see Tommy again as well. He was really friendly when he came to pick Buddy up."

"Yeah, he's pretty nice even if he is my brother," Kathy said, trying to keep the conversation light. "But he hasn't grown quite as much as Buddy. Now, do you want me to go see if I can go find those two or do you want to just come over? I promise, we'll all be here," Kathy assured Carolyn.

"Well, if you're sure it's OK we'll just come over. My dad said right after lunch."

"That would be great, Carolyn and like I say, bring your mom. My mom is going to be home and it would be nice for you to meet her."

"OK."

"Give me your phone number, Carolyn, in case we have to call you back for some reason."

Carolyn gave Kathy her phone number and the conversation ended. Kathy walked out the front door onto the veranda and saw her mom and dad working in the garden. She didn't know why she hadn't seen them when she looked out the window while she was on the phone. Maybe they had been in the barn. She hadn't been outside this morning and it surprised her what a lovely fall day it was. Kathy headed over toward where her parents were. There wasn't much left to do in the garden this time of year except picking a few potatoes and beans and getting the soil ready for next spring. All the other vegetables were just about done, but what was left was still as tasty as ever.

Kathy stood just outside the perimeter of the garden watching her parents work together. They hadn't noticed her walk up. As she watched them she

Three Months Later – Early Fall

reflected on how lucky she was to have such a wonderful mom and dad. Kind, loving, caring. It was all any child could ask for and she felt like she had the two best parents in the world. They were easy going and hard working: Mom, as a stay at home mother and Dad with his busy construction business.

Mr. Franklin was mostly a new home builder, but he would also contract renovations and additions or just about anything to keep him busy. In fact, he would take on any job big or small if there was a buck in it. He had built up an excellent reputation in the county they lived in and he worked all over. He was a master carpenter by trade, something he had learned from his father, and he could do it all: rough carpentry or finish carpentry. He loved his work, took great pride in it and it always showed in the end product. He was a tradesman in demand and kept busy except for a couple of months a year during the winter when the weather hampered progress. Mr. Franklin had already taught his young son some carpentry skills that he hoped Tommy would use later on in life. He even visualized being business partners with Tommy one day if Tommy was interested. But that was a long way off and John would never force anything on his kids. Naturally, John and Nadine hoped that Kathy and Tommy would attend university. They always emphasized that by saying "when you go to university" not "if."

"Get yourself an education."

That was what the Franklin parents wanted most for their kids. A university degree would go a long way in life later on. But it was up to the kids to decide for themselves when that time came. What Kathy and Tommy did when they were older would be entirely up to them and they wouldn't be loved any less than they were now. This was why Kathy and her brother loved their parents so much, because the love was given back tenfold.

Mrs. Franklin, on her knees digging with a little hand spade, stood up and turned around when she noticed her daughter standing at the edge of the garden.

"Oh, hi dear," she said to Kathy.

Mr. Franklin, standing and hoeing just a few feet from his wife, took notice. "Hi, Kathy. What 'cha up to?"

"Carolyn Russell just called. You know the girl that you got Buddy from? She's coming over after lunch to visit Buddy and I told her that would be fine. Is that OK?"

"Oh sure," Kathy's mother said, putting her hands on her hips and flexing her shoulders. Gardening was hard on the back and Nadine stood up straight to relieve her aching muscles. "Did she say roughly what time?"

"Between one and one-thirty. Mrs. Russell might come too."

"And Mr. Russell?" Kathy's dad asked.

"Yeah, I'm pretty sure the three of them," Kathy replied. "They all want to see Buddy."

"Well, that's wonderful," Mrs. Franklin said, thinking what an excellent idea. She had always enjoyed meeting new people and felt that you could never have enough friends. Hopefully the Russells would become just that. "I'll go back inside then, straighten up the house and maybe get some snacks prepared."

"I'll help you, Mom, but where's Tommy?" Kathy asked "I should let him know."

"He and Buddy should be over in the back field," Mr. Franklin told Kathy. "He had a ball and I think they were headed over that way to play fetch."

The "back field" was at the rear of the barn on the northeast corner of the Franklin property. It was a wild growth of grass that was bordered by tall skinny pines growing on their neighbors' property. It was a fair-sized field of a couple of acres where a boy and his dog could run for what seemed like forever and the perfect place for Tommy and Buddy to play and where they spent a lot of their time.

"OK. I'll go see if I can find them and tell Tommy what's going on," Kathy volunteered.

"Then you two come on back to the house and we'll all have some lunch, right, Dad?" Nadine asked her husband.

"Sure thing. I could use a break," Mr. Franklin said.

"OK. I'll be back with Tommy in tow. See ya in a few minutes," Kathy said as she departed around the corner of the barn and disappeared.

In a quick minute she was walking up a sloped terrain that would take her to the back field. It was a gentle climb and a perfect hill for sledding and tobogganing in the winter. It got used all year round by Tommy and Kathy's friends for this fun activity or that one. Halfway up she could hear Buddy bark. Kathy didn't have to see them to know what they were doing. Tommy would have either a ball or a stick and would be holding it up high trying to keep it away from Buddy and Buddy would be jumping up repeatedly trying to snatch whatever Tommy had in his hand. It was the game they played until Buddy finally knocked Tommy down or Tommy fell to the ground and then it became a wrestling match with Tommy trying not to give up whatever he had in his possession that Buddy so badly wanted. That's what young boys and puppies do until one of them tires out. In the case of these two, sometimes it seemed like they never did. Sure enough, just as they came into view, Kathy saw Buddy knock Tommy down and then try to wrestle a stick away from his good

Three Months Later – Early Fall

friend. Kathy stopped and watched like she had when observing her parents a few minutes before. She was fortunate to have such a brother and blessed to be part of such a wonderful family. She didn't feel like yelling out at Tommy and Buddy so she continued walking toward them. Tommy regained his feet and as he did, seeing his sister within throwing distance, threw the stick in her direction.

"Here, Kathy. Don't let Buddy get it!" Tommy shouted, tossing the stick as hard as he could and falling back down to the ground.

"Auuugh!" Kathy screamed as the stick fell short of where she was standing and Buddy, like he had been shot out of a cannon, made a bee line toward her. She ran the few yards to get the stick and managed to pick it up a split second before Buddy got there. Kathy held it high above her head as Buddy jumped up and down trying to nab it. She started laughing and couldn't get her thoughts together enough to throw it back to Tommy. She was surprised by how high Buddy could jump and his barking hurt her ears. Tommy was yelling at her to throw it back.

"Buddy, stay down. Buddy, you're crazy," Kathy cried in near hysterics as the young puppy focused on getting his prize back into his jaws. It was his stick and no one else's and if these guys wanted to play rough, he could too.

"OK, Buddy, down. Down Buddy. Sit. Buddy sit," Kathy commanded through her joyful shrieking. Buddy, doing as he had been taught these last three months, sat down, but very reluctantly. His eyes were fixated on the stick Kathy held high above her head. "Buddy, calm down. Good boy. Staaaaaaay. That's a good boy."

Tongue hanging out, tail going ninety miles an hour, front paws tapping the ground, Buddy was ready.

Hurry up! Hurry up, Kathy. Throw the stick.

"Staaaaaay. You stay, Buddy."

Tommy watched, set to make a mad dash toward his sister.

"OK!" Kathy reared her arm back then brought it down swiftly and threw.

It was not a bad throw, but certainly not her best. It fell about halfway between her and her brother with Buddy and Tommy both in hot pursuit of it. Advantage Buddy. The stick was slightly closer to the puppy and he was much faster than Tommy. Buddy got to the stick just before a diving Tommy. He picked it up in his mouth and made off with it at the speed of light.

"Ouch!" Tommy said as he hit the ground.

The ground was hard with its collection of pebbles and stones mixed in with the tall grass. He lay on his stomach watching his proud and determined youthful dog have his moment in the sunshine once more. Buddy found his spot a safe distance away, lay down in the grass chewing his prize and tried to make it into toothpicks. Tommy smiled and thought, "It's a wonder dogs don't get splinters in their mouths when ripping up sticks ." Kathy walked up and sat in the grass next to Tommy.

"Hey, little brother."

"Hey, big sister," Tommy said, rolling onto his side and using his hand, arm and elbow to prop his head up.

"That dog is crazy, you know!" Kathy said.

"Can you believe how fast he is?" Tommy said, bouncing up onto his knees.

"Yeah, he's pretty fast," Kathy agreed, "and he sure loves to chase things."

Brother and sister watched as Buddy made short work of the stick and then sniffed around for another one. In all the excitement, Kathy had almost forgotten what she had come to talk to Tommy about.

"Oh yeah, Tommy, Mom said it's time for some lunch and the Russell family are coming over about one o'clock to visit Buddy. They called just a little while ago."

"The Russells? Oh, really," Tommy mused. "Carolyn and her parents are coming over?"

Kathy got back up on her feet.

"Yeah. They're coming for a little visit so Mom wanted us to have an early lunch. We should head back."

"Sure. Come on, Buddy," Tommy shouted in the direction of his dog. "Let's go, guy."

Buddy, ever so obedient and thinking it might be time for more play, did as he was told, ran to the Franklin siblings and jumped up on Tommy. "Buddy, stay down. Come on boy, we're going home."

Kathy began a slow trot. "Come on, Buddy. Come on."

Oh boy! More play.

He flew past Kathy at full speed in the direction of the house. He had heard the word "lunch." He'd race Kathy and Tommy and beat them both back. The two siblings started their own race against each other.

"Last one back is a rotten egg," Kathy yelled.

She thought she was going to be smart because she already had a head start on her brother. But Tommy seemed a little quicker than the last time they had raced and he closed in fast. Heading back down the slope that she had just climbed, their feet looked like they were going faster than the rest of their bodies. Kathy had won races in the past mainly because of their age difference, but now the tide had turned as Tommy was ahead by ten yards when they hit

Three Months Later – Early Fall

the flat ground just before the barn. As her brother turned the corner of the old wooden structure and disappeared, Kathy stopped. She was out of breath and conceded that maybe her little brother was in fact now faster than she was. She leaned on the back side of the barn to catch her breath and looked up at the bright blue autumn sky. Kathy was sweating. Hands on hips, she slowly walked around the barn and saw Tommy and Buddy going at it once again on the front lawn. "Those two don't ever stop," she thought to herself. It was a delightful sight and one she enjoyed witnessing. The boy and the dog were still going at it when she finally got to the house and walked up the front stairs of the veranda.

"Don't you guys ever quit?" she asked.

"Nope," Tommy replied as he lay on top of Buddy holding the dog in a headlock.

"You're going to hurt him," Kathy warned.

"I don't think so," Tommy said, knowing how rough he could be without hurting his best friend. He let go and threw another stick for Buddy to chase.

"Come on, Tommy. It's time for lunch," Kathy called to her brother.

"OK, OK."

Tommy walked up onto the veranda and as he and Kathy entered the house his sister put an arm over his shoulder.

"You sure can run fast, Tommy. You beat me good."

"Yeah, I imagine I'll beat you every time now, sis. Sorry about that."

Kathy opened the front screen door and lovingly pushed her brother through the entrance.

"Yeah, yeah. We'll see, we'll see."

CAROLYN'S FAMILY DID come by on that autumn day in 1958 and saw Buddy and Tommy and all of the Franklin family. The Russells couldn't believe how much Buddy had grown. Like all puppies, he grew fast. When you haven't seen a puppy for three months and he is growing his quickest, it is something to behold. They had seen a couple of the other puppies from Molly's litter and none of them were quite as big as Buddy. Not yet anyway. And Buddy's disposition hadn't changed either since they gave him to the Franklin family. He was still high energy and full of mischief. They all had a good laugh that day as the Franklin family shared some of their stories about Buddy's adventures or at times his misadventures, but he was still lovable Buddy. Always loveable.

Carolyn and Tommy got to know each other a little better that day as well.

While their parents had snacks and tea and sat in the kitchen chatting, Buddy started getting restless and wanted to go out again. Tommy invited Carolyn to go up to the back field to play with Buddy. She accepted the invitation and had a lot of fun throwing a ball she had brought with her. Tommy and Carolyn tried to play keep away by throwing it back and forth, but they had better not drop it because Buddy was so darn quick he would snap it up and off he would go once again. Tommy had been trying to teach his dog to "retrieve" and "drop it" ever since he got him because Buddy had a problem with giving back whatever he had between his jaws. The young boy, however, wasn't having much luck with his training methods. When Buddy got the ball, as far as he was concerned it was his to keep. So Tommy always had to resort to tricks to get the ball back. He would find a stick and as soon as Buddy saw that he would drop the ball he had in his mouth. Then Tommy would pick up the ball when Buddy darted for the stick his owner had just thrown for him. Sometimes Tommy would keep a spare ball in his pocket and rotate them. Throw one and Buddy would go get it. Then Tommy would take the extra ball out of his pocket and hold it up for Buddy to see. Buddy would come running back, drop the ball that was in his mouth and go chase the other one. That routine would go on and on and Buddy never got tired of it. The only thing that would stop the "go fetch the ball or stick game" was Tommy's arm getting sore. That's exactly what Carolyn asked Tommy that day when they played keep away from Buddy.

"Doesn't your arm ever get sore?"

"Oh yeah, sometimes."

"Mine is killing me!"

Tommy and Carolyn had quite a time conversing that day. They talked quite a bit when they were walking up to the back field and talked some more when they sat in the grass after they got tired of the keep away game with Buddy. They discussed their schools, their towns, their hobbies and of course dogs. Although Tommy was quite content just watching Buddy play while Carolyn talked, he had to admit to himself he actually enjoyed the conversation they were having. He thought that this girl he was getting to know was very nice, but dogs and sports were his thing, certainly not girls.

Not at this age anyway. That would change like it did for most boys as he got older.

After that day Carolyn and either her dad or mom came by for more visits. Tommy and Carolyn's relationship evolved into a tight friendship in Junior High and they eventually became best friends in High School. It was a friendship that endured for years through pain and sorrow, ups and downs,

Three Months Later – Early Fall

troubled times and periods of separation from each other. There were trials and tribulations and the peaks and valleys. Trips to hell and back. Then back again. Of course they were too young to know all this now on this Michigan fall day in 1958, but it was a friendship without any conditions right from the start.

TOMMY AND CAROLYN went to different schools through elementary, but when they were old enough for Junior High and High School they were in the same school district and attended both of those schools together. They had stayed in touch over the early years, mostly to Carolyn's credit, as her family would come by and visit Buddy every now and then and even more often as their parents became good friends. The Russells and Franklins would socialize at each other's houses and play cards or board games. Carolyn and Tommy would always be present and the two of them would watch TV and once in a while join in on the games. They would play with Buddy because Buddy would always be there tagging along and making a nuisance of himself. First things first. As the visits became more and more frequent, Buddy got to know Carolyn and her parents and he couldn't contain his excitement whenever the Russells came by. He loved visitors whether he recognized them or not. But the Russell's were special for reasons he couldn't explain. They just were. It was those visits that kept Tommy and Carolyn in touch and also seeing each other at sporting events when they were attending Filburtson Junior High. Carolyn was a cheerleader and Tommy played basketball. When tenth grade and high school came along they attended Lincoln High which was built in the late forties halfway between their respective communities. It was in high school where they got to know each other even better and became best friends. A fate that couldn't be avoided. Some of Carolyn's pals knew some of Tommy's friends and vice versa and they all became good companions that hung out together during those teenage years.

It was a nice circle of friends that all the parents approved of. They were typical teenagers growing up in typical small towns that you could find anywhere in America. Towns that had history and old brick buildings. Towns that were built on the American Dream. Brenton was a mirror image of Clear Lake, the town Carolyn grew up in. Both small communities had around twelve thousand people, plus or minus, and had all the amenities you would find in bigger towns, just on a lesser scale. When you grew up in these small places, this was your whole world.

There was a Main Street with just about every little business you could imagine. The hardware store, the drug store, the general store, the five and dime, a department store, a sporting goods store and a couple of women's fashion stores, everyone's favorite drive-in diner and ice cream shop and last but not least, the local bar. All thriving because they were local businesses run by local people and everybody knew just about everyone else in the surrounding area. People that lived in these relatively small towns were loyal to the locals. They would never have considered doing their shopping elsewhere. If it wasn't on Main Street, it didn't exist. On the perimeter of town would be the gas station, auto mechanic and a car dealer or two. Then on the outskirts would be the schools and churches, parks and playing fields. What more could you ask for? Perhaps a little more cultural diversity, but you could always get that by going downtown to the local Chinese restaurant. Every town had one. That and a pizza joint. Visiting one or the other would introduce you to food from other cultures. It was of course a small town version of being worldly.

Brenton was only about four miles from Clear Lake, the actual lake, not the town, which was another fifteen minutes down County Road Ninety-Five. Go figure. It could get kind of confusing if all you said was, "I'm going to Clear Lake." Which one? The town or the lake? You would have to be specific in this part of the region. "I'm going downtown to Clear Lake," or "I'm going to the beach over at Clear Lake." There was always some debate going on amongst the local elected officials about changing the name of the lake or even the town to make matters less confusing, but it never amounted to much and it never got very far in the town council meetings. In the end everyone concluded it was no big deal. The town was the town and the lake was the lake and if you lived here, it usually was nothing more than "I'm going to town," or "I'm going to the lake." When the tourists came in the summer and asked directions how to get to Clear Lake the response would be, "Which one? The lake or the town?" And so it went.

The body of water called Clear Lake was just inland from the shores of Lake Michigan on what had to be one of the world's shortest rivers, the Kama, that connected the two. You could put your boat in at the Clear Lake marina and in no time be out into the larger body of water. Clear Lake was a big time recreational lake with summer cabins and only a few permanent homes on it. The population around the lake multiplied tenfold as soon as the schools let out in late June. Most of the summer visitors were from the Chicago area. People would drive up the eastern shore of Lake Michigan and head for their summer cabins making the four-hour drive to reside in a place they called their little piece of heaven. Some out-of-towners would stay for a few days and some would stay longer. With some families, the dad would drop the family off for

Three Months Later – Early Fall

the whole summer and then come up on the weekends when he didn't have to work.

Spending the summer here was the perfect scenario whether you were a visitor or a local. The public beach at Clear Lake was big, sandy and ideal for swimming. You could barely find a place to put your blanket in the summer if you didn't get there early enough. The Clear Lake State Park was perfect for family affairs as well as the local and visiting youth. You would park your car in the gravel parking lot and unload everything you brought for a day at the beach. It was where summer romance sometimes began with the young people, and maybe lasted until September and then usually ended with a simple, "Nice to have met you." Maybe, if you were one of the lucky youth, it would carry over to the following summer. The local teenage boys would hit on the out-of-town teenage girls and the local teenage girls loved to meet and flirt with the out-of-town teenage boys, all innocent of course because it was the days of innocence. It was summer after all, when youth felt free and adventurous. The local boys liked to make the local girls jealous and that worked both ways. When school started up again in the fall, things reverted back to normal and the boyfriends and girlfriends that had been a couple in June, but flirted with others in the summer, got back together in September.

Life at "the lake" in the summertime was a perfect world for everyone. Have some fun and then have some more fun. The warm and sometimes hot and humid summers, that's when the lake was happening. It was energized by the youth, local and not so local and for that matter, energized by the out-of-towners of all ages as well. If you were lucky enough to spend time at the lake in the summer, well then, you were just plain lucky. It was all about the exuberance for life.

1964 - Life at the Lake

"Hey Richard, how old were you when you learned how to swim?" Tommy asked as he threw the football to his good friend.

It was another perfect summer day and "the gang" had decided to spend it at the beach. They knew to get there early because they were the locals and the locals knew how quickly the beach got overcrowded on a day such as this. It was mid-July, there had been record heat for the past two days and today was not going to be any different. These local teens had their favorite spot, that they always took, not twenty feet from the water. They were all here, the group that made up this close circle of friends. All twelve of them. Sometimes the group was bigger, sometimes it was smaller, but this core group of good friends usually numbered around a dozen. They had brought their blankets, transistor radios, coolers and refreshments. This was the summer of new-found independence as it was the first summer some of them had their driver's license. Tommy was one of the fortunate ones and had saved up enough money to buy a 1954 Ford sedan for fifty dollars. A steal of a deal that his mother heard about through a friend at church and passed on to her son. It was too good to pass up.

Richard had the other vehicle and between them, with five passengers in each car, they could take most of their friends anywhere. Today it was the beach. Tonight it would probably be the drive-in restaurant in downtown Brenton or Tippy's, the drive-in restaurant out in the boonies halfway between Brenton and the town of Clear Lake. Both places were magnets for the young people who had cars, or in some cases, hot rods.

Tippy's was the favorite of the two because of its location between the neighboring communities of Clear Lake and Brenton. It was easier to drive someone home if you happened to live in Brenton and your friend or friends happened to live in Clear Lake. Or vice versa. Tippy's was the place that stayed open late and you could hang out there all evening if you wished. The A&W in Brenton closed at ten o'clock and it was too early for the kids who loved being free and staying out late. Most of the parents gave their kids curfews of eleven o'clock or midnight and the young people would always take it right down to the last minute before heading home. In the summer, Tippy's stayed open until midnight every night. It was a destination for the teenagers and somewhere they could meet with their buddies and no one would ever hassle them. The owners of Tippy's knew all the kids by name and their customers always behaved. Their money was as good as anyone else's and the youth in the summertime were Tippy's biggest money maker. They came to sit in their cars, hang out and talk, but they always brought their money and that was good for business. But Tippy's would be later on tonight. For now, a dip in the lake, some football and, as always, what was a part of every trip to the beach, a keep away game with Buddy.

This was what Buddy was doing now. Chasing the football back and forth between Richard and Tommy and making a nuisance of himself. It was mid-morning and there was still a little room on the beach to do this sort of thing. The beach wasn't quite packed yet, but by lunch time anyone who wanted to toss anything would have to take it up to the grass field between the beach and parking lot where the picnic tables were.

Richard caught the football that had come his way with Buddy in hot pursuit. He held it above his head.

"Buddy, why don't you give up?" Richard antagonized Buddy by bringing the football down, holding it out in front of the dog just far enough so that Buddy couldn't snatch it and began dancing in circles. "Here ya go. Get the ball, Buddy." Richard straightened up and threw it back to Tommy and there went Buddy once again.

Richard answered Tommy's question about how old he was when he learned how to swim.

"I think I was about five or six. My parents would always bring me down here and it was a matter of survival. My dad tried to drown me a couple of times so my Mom thought it would be a good idea for me to learn to stay afloat."

Carolyn and her friend Karen, sitting on the blankets just a few feet away from Richard, overheard his remark about his dad trying to drown him. Carolyn and Richard had been dating as were Karen and Tommy.

"Your dad tried to drown you?" Carolyn asked with a quizzical look.

"Actually, it was my mom that tried to drown me," Richard fired back.

"Oh stop it Richard, before Karen and I drag you into the lake and drown you ourselves," Carolyn made a threat that challenged Richard.

"Yeah, Richard. Smarten up!" Karen added, backing up her good friend.

Richard caught the football thrown back to him just as Buddy got there. He smiled at the girls and had a thought.

"Here, catch!" he said, tossing the football over in the direction of his two female antagonists.

The ball landed on the blanket knocking over a couple of cans of soda pop as well as a bowl of chips. Buddy thought this was all part of the game and made matters worse by running onto the blanket and causing more chaos. The girls jumped up, having gotten wet from some of the sticky soda pop, and were screaming.

"Ah, Richard! Buddy! Richard, you'll never learn will you?" Carolyn yelled. "Come on, Karen. Let's go get him!"

It was time for revenge as the girls took off after Richard who was making a bee line toward the lake. Buddy had taken the football up to the picnic area, laid down in the grass and was watching from afar. He was content with having the football, although if it were any bigger he wouldn't be able to get it into his mouth. It was a funny sight to behold. Buddy thought it might be fun to go chase the people running into the lake, but he didn't want to drop his prize. He might be six years old, forty-two in human years, but he still had the energy of a puppy and, in many ways, still acted like one.

Richard ran into the water as deep as he could before diving in. The two girls were right on his tail and dove in behind him. It didn't look good for Richard, but being a good swimmer he started to get some distance between him and his pursuers. As the water got to be over everyone's head, Carolyn and Karen stopped the chase and began to tread water.

"Come on, Richard. We won't hurt you," Carolyn called over to her friend twenty feet away.

Richard stopped and began to float on his back.

"I'm really sorry!" he teased. "It was an accident. Honest!"

He was not a very good liar. He had done it on purpose and he thought it was funny. His plan worked. He had gotten the girls' attention and they had chased him into the water. Richard was like all teenage males who enjoy getting chased by girls, especially in the summer.

"Richard," Karen said in a calm tone. "You can trust us. We're not going to drown you. Come on back into the shallow water."

"I don't think so," Richard said, now swimming parallel to the shore.

He felt he was a little too close to Carolyn and Karen and he liked the thrill of the chase. It worked again. The girls started swimming and gave it their all to see if they could close the gap between them and their target. Who was going to run out of energy first?

Buddy lay on his stomach with the football between his front paws. He found it hard to breath when he put this big leather thing in his mouth. He took note of all the humans that surrounded him.

They sure knew how to have a good time.

He heard his name.

"Buddy!" Tommy shouted out. "Over here, boy."

Buddy saw his friend over by the blankets where the girls had been relaxing before Richard caused the big upset. He picked the football back up in his mouth and headed for Tommy. Enough of a breather. It must be time to play again. He reached Tommy, but maintained a safe distance so Tommy couldn't grab the football back from him. Buddy's master, however, wasn't really interested in the football any longer.

"Come on, Buddy," Tommy said, picking up the potato chips that were scattered and putting them back in the bowl. "Let's go take a dive off the dock."

At the south end of the beach, outside the parameters of the roped-off swimming area, was a wooden dock that people would dive off of. It was just far away enough down the beach that most people thought it was private. The locals knew better. It had been there since the beginning of time and no one knew how it got there or why it was even put there. It didn't matter. More than one generation had used it for sunning and diving. It wasn't being used now, however, and Tommy thought he would take advantage of that, swim the thirty feet out to it and dive into the lake. Something he had done countless times over the years.

"You wanna swim out there with me, Buddy?"

Sure.

Buddy loved the water. The air was starting to get hot and sticky and he felt overheated from all the running around he had done. Tommy didn't have to ask Buddy twice. They'd done this many times before in past summers. Buddy jumped in and with paws paddling he headed for the dock. Tommy followed.

The dock, about fifteen feet by fifteen feet square, had no ladder. So when Tommy got to it he had to brace himself up with his arms and elbows, lift himself onto his chest and then swing his legs over and roll onto the decking. Over the years as he had grown bigger and stronger, this procedure had gotten easier and easier. Now it was all done in one swift fluid motion. No problem. When he was on the dock he got down on one knee, saw his friend paddling around, grabbed him by the scruff of his neck and hoisted him up. No easy task considering how big Buddy was. Once Buddy was up on the deck and shook himself off, he knew they would both jump back into the lake like they'd done a hundred times before and swim around until they decided to go back up onto the dock or head for shore.

"Good boy, Buddy!" Tommy said, congratulating his friend on a mission accomplished.

Tommy stretched and pondered for a moment what dive he would like to do. What's it going to be this time? The cannonball? A basic head first? Naw, too simple. A twister? Maybe a back flip. He actually had never tried one of those. It might be worth a shot.

OK, let's go for it!

Tommy walked to the front of the dock where the water was deepest. He turned his back to the water and extended his arms.

"OK, Buddy," Tommy said, deciding to broadcast his dive to the world. "Here we go, for a Gold Medal at the Olympic Games. Tommy Franklin needs to get a perfect score on all the judges' score cards in order to win it all. The crowd is deathly silent."

Tommy bent his legs and sprang upward and backward as Buddy watched. When he flipped back and started to come down, his head hit the edge of the dock, knocking him out cold. He floated face down in the water as Buddy stood on the dock looking down, sensing something was not right.

I don't think this is a game or play time. Something is wrong with my master.

A red tinge surrounded Tommy's head. Buddy recalled that smell. He couldn't remember where or when in his life, but that smell meant trouble. He began to whine and panic, then jumped into the water and paddled to an unconscious Tommy whose arms were both afloat. With his adrenalin flowing, Buddy grabbed the left forearm in his mouth and struggled to swim toward shore. It was not that far, but it was physically awkward trying to tow the human toward land. Instinct told Buddy that he had to get Tommy as close to shore as possible. They finally hit shallow water which was about a foot deep. Buddy could drag Tommy no further. A small wave pushed Tommy over on his side. Buddy knew something was not right with Tommy. He stared at the youth lying in the water for a couple of seconds and then became a dog in despair.

Buddy ran toward the people just down the beach a short way away and started barking. People looked in his direction, but he was ignored. Richard scrambled out of the water still hounded by Carolyn and Karen. Out of breath, Carolyn walked out of the lake and headed back toward the blankets. She recognized Buddy's bark and looked in his direction.

"What's he barking at?" Carolyn asked her friend as Karen came up alongside her.

"He's excited about something," Karen replied.

Carolyn looked beyond Buddy and saw a body lying near the shore.

"Is that Tommy? Oh my gosh, Karen. Something's happened to Tommy!"

Life at the Lake

Both girls started running as fast as they could toward him. Carolyn called out for Richard and their other friends that they came to the beach with. Buddy had run back to Tommy, stood at his head and continued to bark. Carolyn and Karen quickly ran up with Richard and pulled Tommy onto the sand.

"Oh, my gosh. His head is bleeding!" Carolyn shouted frantically. "What happened? He's unconscious! Oh, Tommy!"

Karen yelled at one of the youth who had run up to go get a towel to wrap around Tommy's head. Richard told someone else to go find a phone and call an ambulance. A couple of adults came up and knelt down beside the teenagers.

"Turn him on his side," a man said. "We have to try and get the water out of his lungs." Carolyn, Karen and Richard turned their friend on his side. "Just hold him like that and I'll press on his back."

With Tommy half on his side, but not quite on his stomach, the man put pressure on Tommy's back, pressing hard, then releasing. "Come on, son. Let go of that water you swallowed."

Carolyn and Karen were crying, disturbed by what they were witnessing.

"Tommy, Tommy, wake up!" Carolyn pleaded through her tears. "Please Tommy, please."

The man pushed harder and faster on Tommy's back. Suddenly Tommy gurgled and coughed up water.

"That's it, Tommy. You can do it," the stranger said. "Coughing is good."

The man talked softly and remained calm.

Tommy's friends, however, were all having a tough time with the scene happening before their eyes. Buddy stuck his head in between the bodies of the youths. An upset Richard pulled him back.

"Stay out of the way, Buddy. It's OK."

Buddy's dog sense told him that his owner was not doing well. It made him feel anxious. The other adult male standing over Tommy suggested that everyone take a couple of steps back to give their injured friend some fresh air. Tommy began coughing beyond control. His eyes opened, but just barely. He moaned and tried to lift an arm. More coughing.

"He sure swallowed a lot of water," the man who had been pounding on Tommy's back said.

Tommy's eyes finally managed to stay open and he attempted to roll over onto his back. He moaned and groaned and uttered some mumble jumble.

"Tommy, it's Carolyn. You're going to be OK. Just lie still."

Their friend Ron, who had been sent to the payphone to call an ambulance, came running back up.

"An ambulance is on its way," he said excitedly.

Tommy looked at the people hovering over him. Dazed, he managed to speak.

"What happened?"

"We don't know," Karen said, cradling Tommy's head.

Buddy, hearing Tommy's voice, made his way once again to Tommy's side.

"Hey, Buddy," Tommy patted his dog on the head.

There was a great deal of relief amongst his friends as he recovered consciousness. A couple of more minutes passed before an ambulance siren could be heard off in the distance.

"Tommy, do you remember anything?" Carolyn asked.

Tommy lifted an arm and felt the towel wrapped around his head.

"I think I was doing a back flip off the dock. That's the last thing I remember. Man, my head hurts!" Tommy grimaced.

Buddy licked his face.

"Buddy, leave Tommy alone," Karen said, gently pushing Buddy away.

"It's OK, Karen. I'll be fine,"

For the next few minutes Tommy lay still as his pals consoled him and prevented him from moving. The ambulance pulled into the parking lot and two attendants got out and followed one of Tommy's friends who had run up to greet them.

"I don't need an ambulance. I'll be fine. Just drive me home," Tommy said, trying to be tough and most certainly being stubborn.

The man who had been presiding over Tommy thought otherwise.

"Tommy, you have a pretty good gouge in your head. Just lie still like your friends here say and let the ambulance attendants decide what to do."

As the two attendants walked up, the people made room for them so they could examine the injured youth. Both knelt down beside him, one at his head and one at his feet.

"Hello, what's your name, partner?" the one closest to his head asked.

"Tommy Franklin."

"Do you live around here?"

"Just outside of Brenton."

The attendant began to unwrap the towel around Tommy's head.

"Let's have a look ... whoa! Good job! You're going to need stitches, Mr. Franklin and we'll have to take you to the hospital over in Clear Lake. Have any of your friends here notified your parents yet?" the attendant wondered, looking up at the group.

Life at the Lake

"Not yet," Carolyn said. "I'll get someone to do it right now. Doug, do you know Tommy's parents' phone number?"

Doug got the phone number from Carolyn and headed off to the pay phone in the parking lot to make that call.

"Aw, gees. We don't need to worry my parents. I'm OK. I'm fine." Tommy was lying, but just the same, he didn't want a fuss made over him.

"We're going to take you to the hospital, Tommy, and have the doctors look at you," the attendant at Tommy's feet said. "We'll need your parents there for insurance purposes and Tommy, they are your parents. They're going to want to know what's happened and be by your side. You'll be OK, but you might have suffered a concussion. At any rate, we have to get you patched up."

Tommy lay back on the ground and stared up at the friends and strangers peering down at him. "What did happen?" he asked himself.

I was standing on the dock and I was going to do a back flip. I must have hit my head on the decking. How did I get to shore? Buddy must have dragged me here. He must have.

Tommy looked at Buddy, who had persisted in getting close to his master and now sat at Tommy's side. Everything was fuzzy for the injured teen. He turned his head to Carolyn.

"How did I get to shore?"

"We assume Buddy dragged you to shallow water," Carolyn answered. "Then he came running and barking and got everyone's attention on the beach," she added tearfully. "You probably would have drowned if not for Buddy here." She patted Buddy to thank him.

"Did you save me, Buddy? Hey, guy. Did you save me? You're a good boy, Buddy. A good boy," Buddy's best friend Tommy said, proud of his dog.

Buddy didn't understand why he was suddenly getting all the attention, but he sure was glad to hear his master's voice.

"Joe, would you like to go get the stretcher for our friend here?" the attendant at Tommy's head asked his partner.

"I'll be right back. Just lie still here, Mr. Franklin. You're in good hands," Joe said as he got up to retrieve a stretcher from the ambulance.

Carolyn and Karen continued to wipe away their tears and console their friend. A very lucky friend.

"It's a good idea they're taking you to the hospital, Tommy. Better to be safe than sorry," Karen said.

"... and no more back flips off the dock," Carolyn added, attempting a smile that didn't come easily.

"Yeah. I don't think I won a Gold Medal with that dive. Did anyone by chance see what the judges' scores were?" Tommy moaned rubbing his head. At least he hadn't lost his sense of humor as his mind began to clear.

"I think your score was pretty low," Richard quipped, pleased to see his good friend starting to rebound.

A police car pulled into the parking lot and an officer got out and chatted with the ambulance attendant getting out the stretcher. Both of them walked back in the direction of Tommy and his friends.

"The police are here, Tommy," Carolyn informed him.

"Am I going to jail or the hospital?" Tommy wondered in jest.

"To the hospital first, then jail," Carolyn joked back at him.

Tommy's friend Doug came back and reported that he had called Tommy's parents and they'd be at the hospital as quickly as they could get there.

"Did you tell them I was OK, Doug?" Tommy wanted to know.

"Yeah, I told them you were conscious and the hospital trip was just a precautionary thing. I tried to make it sound like you were OK."

"Thanks, Doug. I am OK."

The ambulance attendant and policeman arrived at the scene and the police officer knelt down beside Tommy.

"Hello there. Banged your head?" the officer asked.

"Yes, sir. I think I was just being stupid. I'm OK thanks to my dog here," Tommy said, acknowledging Buddy.

The policeman patted Buddy on the head. "You're lucky to have such a good canine friend. I would hate to think of your state if he hadn't been around. You're going to have to make sure he gets a nice steak for his reward," the officer suggested.

"Yes, sir. I'll make sure of that."

"These kind gentlemen are going to take you to the hospital and have the doctors look at you and clean that head up a little bit. I understand your parents are on the way. I'll head there right now and let them know I spoke with you and that you're going to be fine."

The policeman's voice was kind and comforting.

"Thanks so much, officer. I really appreciate that. I don't want them to worry," Tommy said and wondered what his parents must be thinking.

"I'll make sure they know exactly what's going on," the policeman assured Tommy.

The officer stood up as the group of teens made room for Tommy to be put on the stretcher. Buddy remained anxious and didn't understand why Tommy was being carried away.

"What about my car and Buddy?" Tommy realized half of the teens had come in his car and Buddy needed to get back home.

"I'll take your car and I'll take Buddy back to your parents place, Tommy. Don't worry about it," Richard said, letting Tommy know it would all be taken care of. "We'll manage it all somehow."

Carolyn walked alongside the stretcher as the two attendants carried her friend to the ambulance.

"Can I ride in the back with him?" Carolyn asked the attendants.

"I suppose," the one in front said. "I'll ride in the back with you two. Our job will be to keep him calm."

"I will. For sure," Carolyn said gratefully. "Thanks so much."

"Are you OK with that, Tommy?" Carolyn realized she should have asked her friend first.

Tommy had closed his eyes, but still found one of Carolyn's hands with one of his.

"Absolutely, Carolyn. That will be fine."

"Karen, do you mind?" Carolyn asked of Karen who also walked beside the stretcher.

"Not at all. Richard and I will meet you guys at the hospital and look after Buddy."

Even though it was Tommy and Karen that were a couple, Carolyn had become that "family friend" that trumps any boyfriend-girlfriend relationship and Karen understood that. She and Carolyn were best friends and there would be no petty jealously here.

Just before they put Tommy in the back of the ambulance, Karen leaned over and gave her boyfriend a kiss on the cheek.

"We'll see you at the hospital. Have a nice ride and don't give Carolyn a hard time," Karen said as she tried to keep the moment lighthearted.

"Thanks, Karen. We'll see you in a little while," Tommy replied as his grogginess seemed to come and go.

"Anything else we can do for you, bud?" Richard asked as Tommy was put into the back of the ambulance.

"Yeah, fill my car up with gas," Tommy joked as Carolyn climbed in and the back doors of the ambulance were shut. Richard chuckled, holding a whining Buddy.

Where are they taking my best friend?

"Don't worry, Buddy," Richard said, petting the dog "You'll see him later."

The ambulance drove off slowly before turning on their sirens and the group of teens headed back to their blankets and began to gather things up.

They talked amongst themselves and wondered how such a beautiful summer day at the lake could go so sour in an instant. This day, this lovely day of youthful innocence, had almost turned tragic. If it were not for the heroic actions of a dog, that always went wherever his master went, it could have been much worse. Karen folded a blanket and saw Buddy a few feet away staring in the direction in which the ambulance had driven off.

"Buddy!" she called to him. "He's going to be all right, Buddy. You were such a hero. You saved his life, boy."

Buddy ran the few steps over to Karen, needing a hug. Karen obliged. He was not sure what all had just transpired, but the hug felt good. He knew he couldn't wait to see his best friend again.

What's a hero? What's a hospital? What's a steak?

BUDDY GOT HIS steak well done and Tommy recovered from his head injury and swore he would never do a back flip off the dock ever again. Fall came and all the friends in Tommy's group headed back to school for their senior year. Twelfth grade was always special, always busy and always hard, yet everyone was looking forward to it. The last year of high school was a big one and a lot of pressure was put on young people to decide about their future. "What are you going to do when you graduate?" was the big question that would be asked many times between September and June.

"Are you going to college or university?"

"Are you going to join the military?"

"Are you going to get a full time job?"

These were tough decisions to make. With an unpopular war going on in Vietnam, it worried many parents. It had only been twenty years since the end of World War II and less than that for the Korean War. The parents of these kids had seen enough of war and many were not pleased with the possibility of their son or daughter getting involved in a dispute in a country that many had never even heard of. The young men became eligible for the draft as soon as they were eighteen and, if they hadn't received a student deferment, in all likelihood they would be called upon to do their two years in the Army. Also, in all likelihood, they would end up on a battlefield in Southeast Asia.

Most of Tommy's friends put a lot of thought into what they wanted to do after high school and a lot of them decided to attend university or junior college. A few decided to volunteer for military service with most of them choosing the Navy, Air Force or Marines. A few talked about signing up with the Peace Corps. Tommy was undecided and thought he might work in his

Dad's construction business after he graduated. That pleased Mr. Franklin as he had always dreamed of having his son work beside him on a fulltime basis. Tommy had spent his teenage summers working with his father and learning the carpentry trade and he had a natural talent for it. But he and his father both knew there would be the lingering worry of getting drafted and being shipped overseas if Tommy didn't eventually enroll in college.

The Sixties. War, assassinations, cultural change, protests. There had never been a decade that was so domestically volatile. The youth of the day were witness to it all and participated in much of what was going on. It was their country, their world. It was the young people that energized a decade like a decade had never been energized before. "The Times They Are A-Changin," as the Bob Dylan song said, and that was an understatement. Not only was the world changing, but it was changing fast. Many people of the older generation couldn't grasp it. Didn't understand it. Trying to send a man to the moon? Impossible! Color television? No way. The Cold War? Race riots! The threat of nuclear annihilation! "What's a hippie?" Not since the civil war had the authority in the United States government been questioned or rebelled against like it was in the sixties. A good time to be alive and yet a tormented decade to experience.

Despite all the worry and pressure of being in Grade Twelve, Tommy and his friends, like most teenagers, lived for the moment. It was going to be a special year this senior year. The football team went undefeated. The basketball team got into the state tournament and won a couple of games. Some couples were taking that next step from innocent petting and necking to having sex. The guys were always working on their cars and making them faster and louder. The girls thought the boys were immature. Life was all about being with your friends at somebody's house or at one of the drive-in restaurants. It was a grand time and they all somehow made it through that last year of high school. Everyone in Tommy's group of friends graduated and were high on living, partying, laughing and enjoying each other's company for one last summer before they headed off in their own direction. They accepted the challenge of going to university or joining the military or whatever suited their fancy … and one last summer with Buddy, the group mascot.

Oh, how they were going to miss Buddy, the super dog, the super hero from the summer before. He was as much a part of the inner circle as any one of them and even though he didn't know his friends would be breaking up and going their separate ways in September, he did know that what was happening right here, right now, was all good.

Late August – 1965

TOMMY'S '54 FORD pulled off to the side of the dirt road into a little gravel parking space just big enough for his car and Richard's, which pulled in next to his. It wasn't an "officially designated" place to park, but the locals knew about it and that was what made it special. It was the place where you caught a trail down to the ol' swimming hole on the Pauly River. About a seven mile drive east of Brenton, it was where the local teenagers had been coming for generations. In less than ten minutes of walking they would be on a sandy beach on the slow moving Pauly. They made a few trips here every summer.

Tommy and five of his friends, along with Buddy, jumped out of his car and started getting their things together for a day picnic on the river. The people in Richard's vehicle did the same. Everyone was upbeat and ready for a cool dip. Buddy pranced around wondering if anyone needed his help. Tommy opened the trunk of his car and out came a couple of coolers and picnic baskets.

"Tommy, give me your keys and I'll keep them safe for you," Karen said, holding out her hand and giving him "the look."

The last time the group had been here back in early July, Tommy had lost his car keys. They were eventually found in the sand, but it took a good part of an hour and Karen didn't want to go through that again. It wasn't the first time Tommy had lost or misplaced his keys.

"OK, OK. You can hold onto my keys. Good idea."

Tommy took the keys out of the trunk lock and gave them to Karen.

"Thank you, sir," Karen smiled as she took the keys and put them in her handbag.

"You're very welcome."

Everyone was set and had something to carry. It was exceptionally humid. The sun was out, but there were thunder clouds off in the distance that explained why the humidity was almost unbearable. A swim in the river would cool everyone down and there were a couple of large maple shade trees on the perimeter of the sandy beach that the kids always sat under. The trees were there for that sole purpose it seemed and had been shading kids, parents and grandparents for a long time.

Late August - 1965

Tommy carried a cooler and was leading the pack along with Buddy. A couple of the girls were singing a Beatles tune, simply because it was stuck in their head, blurting out the song between chuckles.

"Are those thunder clouds coming this way?" Tommy asked no one in particular.

"Could be," Richard said, walking just behind his friend. "They're pretty far north of here. I don't think we have to worry about them."

"OK, Richard. If you say so," Tommy replied as he continued on.

The trail the group had been walking on for a couple of minutes began to narrow and those who had been walking side by side now had to walk single file. The soil in this part of the world was sandy and was a treat to walk on. The trail had been packed down from all the years of visitors trekking on it and therefore not overgrown. Once it narrowed you knew, if you were a local, that you only had about five minutes more to get to one of the world's best river beaches ... or so the people who lived in these parts thought. In fact, if you lived anywhere around these parts you felt it had the world's best everything. Best beaches, most beautiful lakes and rivers. Most awe-inspiring fall colors. Best ski hills and trails for cross country skiing. Best fruit and soil for the big farms that grew everything. Nicest summers, except for the bugs. Most incredible thunder storms and in winter, on occasion, the northern lights. It had everything, except tall mountains. The people that lived here rarely ventured far beyond this little world of theirs. Why? Because it was all here.

Just before you got to the beach on the Pauly River you headed down a steep hill with low underbrush and into the trees that surrounded the banks of the river. This was where the kids were now, coming down the hill. They could see the beach and, as usual, they had the place all to themselves. They could drink their alcohol and make all sorts of noise and no one would bother them. It was National Forest land and the public was welcome. It was the ideal spot for a group of local youth that meant no harm to anyone and just wanted to have a good time. It was a rite of passage. Their parents had done this and now so were their children. Buddy knew where everyone was headed and decided to be the first one down to the beach. The others were close behind. The dog started to bark excitedly when his human friends arrived a few seconds after him.

"Buddy, calm down," Tommy said to his friend that couldn't seem to help himself.

If Buddy had a last name it would be, "Calm Down." He was always being told to "calm down." Buddy Calm Down ... it had a nice ring to it.

Buddy found a stick and started running in circles hoping someone would chase him. They didn't. The kids were thinking it was time for Buddy to grow up.

"You're not a puppy anymore."

That's OK. I'll just persist and sooner or later I'll get one of the humans to grab something and throw it in the river for me to fetch. It's just a matter of time.

The young people had to get organized first. Tommy put the cooler down on one of the blankets that the girls had laid out and took the lid off.

"Who wants a cold one?" he called and pulled out a beer.

The guys all accepted, of course, because it was a guy thing to drink beer down at the river on a hot summer day. The girls, being more rational and civil, choose the lemonade and other juices they had brought. It took less than a minute until beers were opened, outer garments were shed and the boys were in the river, having jumped off the four-foot embankment at one end of the beach. At the other end of the approximately eighty-foot beach was a low bank where you could walk in or out of the river. Or, as so many did, climb the maple tree that had a branch hanging over the river. They could either stand up on it and jump off into the water or hang from it and drop off.

The river at this point was only fifty feet wide and slow moving, a perfect swimming hole. World's best. You could ask any of the boys in the water right now and they would tell you there was no place like it and well worth the hike. Buddy had jumped in with the group that was playing and swam around while his master stayed up on land. The dog was going to try and find that one person who would play with him. Richard, still up on the beach, picked up the stick Buddy had forgotten about.

"Buddy ... Buddy! Look what I've got!" Richard said, waving the stick.

Buddy heard his name being called and, paddling hard, turned and looked in Richards's direction.

Richard has my stick! I didn't think anyone wanted to throw it for me. Now Richard has it and I have to get it back.

Buddy couldn't paddle fast enough to the low bank and onto the shore. Richard stood a few yards away and the dog ran toward him. Richard tossed the stick into the river and, without hesitation, Buddy jumped off the high bank and back into the water doing his best belly flop. After the big splash, Buddy got his bearings and began the search for his precious prize. There it was going downstream. He swam until he caught up to it and grabbed it with his mouth. Now life was complete. As he swam back into the group of boys he teased them by swimming just out of reach so they couldn't grab the stick. Now they were all after him. His plan was working. He had known they would all want to play with him eventually. But there was a problem; he was surrounded by humans that wanted his prize.

Now what? This doesn't look good. They're going to get my stick from me. There's an opening! If I swim fast enough I can make my escape.

He tried to swim between two boys, Carl and Steve. Carl managed to grab Buddy by the tail momentarily, but couldn't hang on. He slowed Buddy down just enough for Steve to catch up and lunge for the stick. Buddy turned away as if he had eyes in the back of his head. The low bank shore was getting closer and within reach. All of them, participants and the female observers, were enjoying the chase. One more lunge by Steve, but no luck. Buddy's feet felt the river bottom and it was game over. He made his way swiftly onto the shore where Richard and Tommy continued the pursuit. It was pointless. Once on land Buddy hit full stride and no one, but no one, was going to catch him. Yes, it was just a stick, but it was a stick that everyone wanted. Buddy knew this, so it must be worth a lot. He ran higher up onto the slope behind the beach and into the trees. He lay down and frantically chewed on the wood. The adrenalin was flowing.

Tommy called to his dog, "Come on, Buddy. We won't take your stick. It's OK, boy."

Buddy had heard it all before.

You can fool me once or twice, but eventually, even though I'm just a dog, I catch on. I know what you're up to and you're not getting my stick.

Tommy knew that no matter how slowly he approached Buddy, no matter how softly he spoke to him and tried to coax him to give it up, Buddy was too quick and bolted off as soon as Tommy or anyone else got too close for comfort.

"OK, Buddy. That's fine. If you don't want us to throw it for you, we'll all just ignore you," Tommy said, amused and laughing at his best friend.

He turned around and walked back to the blankets where he took off his shirt and shoes.

"I'm going for a dip, Buddy. The heck with you."

He took one more swig of his beer, ran and dove off the high bank, screaming out a big, "Yahoo!" He joined in with his friends tossing a foam football around. The girls decided it was a good time to start putting together some sandwiches with the food they had brought. Buddy was keeping his distance wondering why no one was paying any attention to him. He got a whiff of something in the air, stood up and took a couple of steps away from his stick. Was it the bologna and ham that the girls had brought out from the cooler? No, it was coming from another direction. It was coming from upstream. He put his nose higher in the air to get a better smell and decided to investigate. He started running toward the source of something he was familiar with.

"Buddy!" Tommy screamed from the water. "Buddy!" he yelled again. "Buddy," louder this time as some of his friends echoed his calls.

It was no use. Tommy had seen Buddy do this before. He couldn't do anyone any harm, they were in the boonies. He'd check out whatever it was and come back like he always did. He'd only go so far and then remember his stick. Someone might get it if he wasn't careful.

"Who wants a sandwich?" Carolyn yelled to the boys in the water.

The orders came in. Mustard. No mustard. Ketchup. No Ketchup. Mayonnaise. No Mayonnaise. Bologna only. No bologna. Ham only. No ham.

"This isn't a restaurant! You'll get what you get!" Karen shouted back to the boys as she stood at the edge of the high bank.

The girls preparing the food had thought at first it would be polite to ask their male counterparts what they would like on their sandwiches. But when the guys started yelling back and everyone's order was different, well, the guys blew it. The girls weren't going to make six hundred different kinds of sandwiches to keep the boys happy. It didn't work that way. There was some whining and complaining from the males in the water, and a few guilt trips thrown in the direction of the girls, but it didn't work. Karen was right, it was not a restaurant and if the guys were hungry they would eat what the girls made.

This was the scene. A scene of innocence. The way things were played out in 1965. A hot summer day. A beach. A river. Teenage boys dunking each other in the water and throwing the football. Teenage girls enjoying their own camaraderie and laughing at the boys and with the boys. Joy filled the air. It was going to be their last summer together. They had all resigned themselves to the fact that everyone was going their different ways. This was the last fling for this group of tightly-knit friends that had hung out together for so long. Through the good times and bad. Mostly good. This was the scene ... and this was the moment. A moment when youth came to realize how life can change in a split-second and how emotions can quickly go from exuberance, fun-loving laughter and not having a care in the world ... to panic and confusion.

There was a sound in the distance. The activity in the river ceased. The boys looked upstream in the direction Buddy had run off. The girls preparing the sandwiches on the beach did the same.

"What was that?" Carolyn asked loud enough for all to hear.

Late August - 1965

No one said anything, waiting to hear if there would be a follow up to what they had all just heard. It was obvious to some, but no one wanted to rush to judgment. Everything was quiet.

Richard broke the silence. "It sounded like a rifle shot!"

That was all that had to be said.

"Shit!" Tommy screamed. "Buddy!"

The girls sitting on the beach stood up and started yelling for Buddy. The boys in the water swam for shore and got there in just a few seconds. Tommy ran up to the blankets, found his tennis shoes and put them back on in a mad rush. His male friends were doing the same. Tommy quickly laced up his shoes, all the while shouting out his dog's name. He made a mad dash to the far end of the beach and headed into the thick underbrush where the noise that sounded like a rifle shot had come from. His friends, the girls and the boys, were not far behind. There was no trail through this part of the vegetation and they had to fight the undergrowth. It was no easy task. Tommy ran a short distance and stopped.

"Buddy," he yelled again and again as loud as he possibly could.

Richard caught up to a panicked Tommy.

"Come on, Tommy. We have to keep heading upstream."

There was no hesitation. Both boys started off with the rest of their friends only a few yards behind, all calling out Buddy's name. Tommy and Richard rushed through the bush like it wasn't even there, their bare legs getting scratched and cut. They ran for another minute and stopped to call out Buddy's name one more time. In the far distance, they thought they heard someone shouting back.

"What was that?" Tommy asked, looking inland and away from the river.

"It sounded like someone yelling from over in that direction," Richard replied, pointing east.

The trees here were sparse, but still enough to call it a forest. The main obstacle traveling on foot was the thick, low-lying bush that created a green curtain one could barely see through, let alone run through. The rest of the group arrived and continued to call out for Buddy.

Tommy raised his hand.

"Wait, quiet!"

There it was again. It was someone in the distance calling back to them.

"It's coming from over there!" Richard said confidently.

Ignoring the green curtain as if it didn't exist, the group headed away from the river in the direction of the voice. Tommy led the way. A couple of minutes further into the bush, it finally began to thin out and became more accessible.

Tommy and friends came into a small clearing that was a few square yards of sand dune and tall grass. He once again called out to his dog. This time the human voice that came was much closer and within communicating distance.

"Over here. Over here," the stranger called back.

Now the group knew right where to go because they were close enough to where they heard the voice. They headed in a straight line to their eventual destination. The anxiety was overwhelming not knowing what they might find. Collectively, in the back of their minds, they all knew that Buddy usually came back when he was called and that they hadn't heard a dog barking. They didn't know what to expect.

"Over here! Over here!" the man's voice now guided them as they quickly approached.

Tommy had never run this fast before and the scratches and scrapes on his legs left blood running down them. He ran into another small, grassy clearing where he saw two hunters standing over a lifeless Buddy, mistaken for a deer and shot once. Tommy stopped dead in his tracks when he first realized what had happened. His other friends ran past him screaming and crying, not believing their eyes. A few knelt down beside Buddy and sobbed.

Carolyn was one.

"Oh God, Buddy. Oh, my God no!"

The two hunters were obviously very upset and apologetic.

"We're so, so sorry. We had a deer in our sights and he just came from out of nowhere. We're so sorry," one of the hunters said remorsefully.

No one in the group really heard the men apologizing.

"Whose dog is this?" the other hunter asked, obviously shaken by the turn of events.

Tommy made his way through the group and knelt down next to Buddy.

"He's mine," he said tearfully.

How could this happen? Buddy had so many years of life left in him. We were going to be friends until the end of time.

Grief overcame Tommy as the reality of what had happened began to sink in. He put his heavy head on Buddy's side and began balling. The emotions were contagious as no one could accept this tragic end to what had been a beautiful, carefree day. Carolyn put her head on Tommy's back and wrapped her arms around him. The two hunters, who had hunted deer for years and were probably from the region and a nearby town, were torn. The one who did the shooting handed his rifle to his friend and made his way to Tommy. He got down on his knees and stroked Buddy, who lay peacefully.

"I am so, so sorry," he said, obviously shaken and sensitive to Tommy's

Late August - 1965

loss. "It was an accident. It was an accident. We're just so sorry."

Tommy didn't really hear him or acknowledge him. He was too busy crying. It was too hard for him to comprehend what had happened. All they were doing was having a good time on the beach at the river. None of them had a worry in the world. Tossing the football. Making sandwiches. And then a dog happens to get a whiff of something that refreshes his memory that maybe there was something he should go investigate. It might be a friend that wanted to play. Maybe a game of chase. Chasing something. That's what Buddy was thinking of when he ran off. Play and play some more. After all ... it was a beautiful day.

It would be fun if I find something to chase: a rabbit, a deer or a squirrel. They're waiting for me. I don't want to let them down.

Those were his pals out there waiting for him to chase after them. He didn't want them to be disappointed. He wouldn't hurt any of them. It was all about the game of chase. But on this day, Buddy never got to see exactly what he was chasing. A rifle bullet through the heart put all that to an end, forever.

Tommy couldn't stop sobbing as he kept his head buried in Buddy's side. Richard came up and put his head on Carolyn's back as she continued to cling to Tommy.

"Come on, Tommy. Let's take Buddy home. It's time to take him home, Tommy." Richard tried to be strong while sharing the tears with the rest of his friends. "Come on, Tommy. We can do this. Let's take Buddy home and bury him."

Richard felt movement from the two people below him and stood up. Carolyn did the same as Tommy made a move. He stared at Buddy, stroked him and looked at the blood on his hand. This didn't happen, couldn't be happening. He slipped his arms under Buddy and lifted him up. He stood for a moment and looked at his friends who had all been sharing his pain.

"Let's go home, Buddy. Let's go home."

TWO HUNTERS GOT up one morning to go out and do something they had been doing for years. They were just getting ready to call it a day. The best hunting was in the early morning, but it was mid-morning and it was starting to get hot. Not a good time to hunt deer. The ground was starting to crackle. The deer would hear them coming. There was no way they were going to sneak up on an unsuspecting deer. The conditions weren't right. They were heading back to their truck, not being particularly quiet, but still keeping an eye out. The deer would be lying in the shade somewhere and not moving. They would have had their morning meal and be resting, staying out of the heat. But then it happened. Just when they least expected it, there was a big six-point, white-tailed buck grazing in a grassy clearing. It surprised them. They knelt down in the bush about fifty yards away. They were upwind. That was good, but the deer still sensed something. It raised its head and slowly made its way into the thick underbrush. Its ears perked up. Did it hear something? Smell something? See something? The two hunters could still see it, but just barely. They went parallel to the clearing attempting to get a closer look for a possible shot. It was a big buck for sure, perhaps a hundred and seventy pounds or more. The deer didn't move. The hunters got within forty yards, then thirty, then twenty. The deer's ears were attentive as it nibbled on a low branch. One of the hunters knelt on the ground and looked through his rifle sight. Perfect. The deer seemed to be oblivious to them. The hunter put his finger easy on the trigger. He and his partner couldn't believe their luck. It wasn't a clear shot, but it was good enough. It was only a few feet into the bush from the perimeter of the grassy clearing. No time to wait. Time to pull the trigger. In that very brief moment when the hunter thought to himself that now was the time to fire, the deer jumped out of his sight and the dog jumped in. It happened quickly. The chase was over before it began. The deer never even saw or heard Buddy coming. Was Buddy stalking the deer? Unlikely. It didn't matter. No one would ever know. The deer was in its own little world and Buddy was looking for something to chase. It happened and that's the way of life ... and death. No need to try and explain or ask, "Why?" It was over. It happened. Wrong time. Wrong place.

"Let's go home, Buddy. Let's go home."

THE SUMMER OF 1965 ended on that sad note. This group of young people that had been friends for so long were taking their lives in different directions knowing the one friend that made them laugh the most and gave them so much energy would not be there when they came home for visits. It wouldn't be right to say, "He was only a dog." Not to this group. He was part of the "in" crowd just like his master. If Tommy was at the drive-in, so was Buddy. If Tommy was at the park or the beach, so was Buddy. The picnics, the pick-up baseball games, the winter bonfires and tobogganing parties, all those get-togethers with the gang, Buddy was there. Always there. When wasn't Buddy there? Never. But that was all over now. Wrong time. Wrong place. Buddy wouldn't be hanging out with his friends anymore.

Everyone knew in the back of their minds that this could be their last summer together. They were going to move from their youth to their early adulthood. Another transitional period. All best friends, but making their own plans for the future and soon to be going their own way. It meant going to different universities, different jobs and different branches of the military. Some were excited, some were apprehensive. They all had things in common, but the one thing they had most in common was that they were all growing up and that could sometimes be difficult. Some youth are forced by circumstances to grow up in their early teens. Others live one day at a time in the age of innocence. For this group, it had been the latter. So many years of carefree living and not a worry. They always had each other. They had school and sports and summer jobs. They had cars and great parties out in some farmer's field. They had boyfriends and girlfriends and drive-in movies and necking and petting and making out. They had break-ups and make-ups and laughter and tears. They had life and up until one fateful day, they had Buddy. "Just a dog?" No, not Buddy. He was one of them.

Life can bring joy. Life can bring pain. Life can bring change and change was in the air.

SUMMER ENDED AND suitcases were packed. Good-byes were said. Promises were made. A page was turned. Time marched on. The gang was breaking up and its members would go join a "new gang" at a college or in the military service or in the Peace Corps or a factory. Everyone went through it. That crowd you grew up with in your teen years and that you thought would be together forever, suddenly wasn't. Some would remain friends for a lifetime while others simply disappeared. The summer days at the beach or those winter night ice-skating parties on some isolated pond out in the boonies with best friends on a cold and frigid night under a bright moon were over. There would be new things to share now with new friends because time changes things. Not necessarily for the bad and usually for the good. For the kids that grew up in Brenton and Clear Lake, it had been a gifted life. Buddy would forever be in their hearts and they would talk about Buddy and tell their Buddy stories for years to come. Stories about how this wonder dog once saved his master's life and was always so much fun to be around. Whenever they talked about their youth and this crazy dog they came to know, they would pause and reflect on those days. It would bring a smile to their faces. It was a special time.

When September came around shortly after Buddy's demise, you would have thought that all the youth had left town. So it seemed to some. It felt strange. The gang had all gone their own way except for Tommy and a couple of his buddies. It was lonely and quiet around Brenton for the youth that lingered on that fall. It felt different. Weird. Everything had happened quickly: Buddy's death, Tommy's break up with Karen and her going off to university. It wasn't the most cheerful period in Tommy's young life. He and Karen had agreed not to try a long distance relationship. Tommy brought up the subject of breaking up and got no argument from Karen. Tommy had sensed that she didn't want strings attached when she went off to college and although it hurt him deeply at first, he understood why she would want her freedom.

Tommy stayed in close touch with Carolyn who had gone down state to attend a university about a two-hour drive away. They wrote each other and occasionally talked on the telephone. It was a good, healthy relationship that had been developing over the years from the time he had first met her. A strong friendship and one that they both enjoyed and felt comfortable with. Whenever Carolyn came home for the holidays, she and Tommy got together and went on their "unofficial dates" as they called them, to a movie or out to the diner. It was platonic and non-threatening, cozy and convenient. Both had gone through the boyfriend, girlfriend thing and still enjoyed being with someone of the opposite sex, but neither one wanted a romantic commitment at the time.

When Carolyn was home the two of them, on Carolyn's pleading, would go visit the Humane Society and look at dogs up for adoption. On these visits she would try and persuade Tommy to get another dog, but he was reluctant. He couldn't be specific why he didn't want another dog and was somewhat evasive whenever the subject of getting one came up. As far as he was concerned, he just wasn't ready. His heart still ached from missing Buddy. The heartbreak over what happened to Buddy would take a long time to get past. Carolyn kept trying to get him to change his mind but, for now, all the coaxing in the world couldn't do that.

He loved the times when he and Carolyn went to the dog pound together to look at dogs and take them for walks to get their exercise, but that was enough. Enough for now. Tommy was busy working in the construction business with his dad and that was the excuse he frequently used, "I'm too busy to look after a dog." That was not exactly truthful because he knew his dad would be understanding and wouldn't mind Tommy bringing a dog to work. He had brought Buddy to work in the summer when he helped his dad, so that excuse didn't fly. But in her heart, Carolyn knew the lingering pain of losing Buddy, that betrayal of life, was still haunting her good friend. It was going to take time to heal. He would get another dog one day. There was no doubt about that. The where and when no one knew or could predict. The day would come though, because Tommy was a dog person just like Carolyn, forever and true.

For the next seventeen months Carolyn and Tommy looked forward to spending their time together whenever she came home. Tommy had dates with other local girls that were quite nice, but he wasn't interested in getting too serious about anything, especially relationships. Carolyn had dates at the university she attended, but she was strictly focused on her education and didn't have a lot of time for the opposite sex, especially those that demanded her full attention. Tommy worked, Carolyn studied and they often thought of each other and how the other one was doing. The world was changing fast in the sixties and so did the lives of the young American males that had turned eighteen and weren't attending a college or university. There was always that concern about getting drafted into the Army and being shipped off to war. It worried a lot of kids and their parents. Tommy was constantly thinking about what to do with his life. He enjoyed working with his father, but there were times when he thought about joining one of the military service branches like some on his friends had done. The draft loomed large over these young adult males who happened to be in limbo, at a crossroads in their life. Tommy wasn't in the mood to go to college or in the mood for much of anything except work with his Dad and save money ... but something had to give ... and something did.

Easter – 1967

CAROLYN AND HER mom were in the kitchen of the Russell home idly chatting. Carolyn sat at the table leafing through a magazine and Mrs. Russell prepped for Easter dinner.

"Do you want some help, Mom?" Carolyn asked.

"No that's fine, dear. Read your magazine."

Mrs. Russell chopped an onion and was wiping away a tear caused by this action when she looked out the window and saw Tommy's truck coming up the drive.

"Hey, it looks like you have a visitor!" she informed her daughter.

Carolyn got up and gazed out the window to see that it was in fact her friend Tommy.

"I wasn't expecting him! This is a surprise. He said he had something he wanted to talk to me about, but we spoke on the phone earlier and I thought we agreed tomorrow would be better."

Carolyn headed out the side door and walked out onto the veranda and around to the front of the house to greet Tommy as he got out of his truck.

"Hey you. I didn't think you were coming by until tomorrow! Good to see you," Carolyn said as she walked up to Tommy and gave him a hug.

"Well ... I wasn't. But I changed my mind. I'm sorry. I'm glad you're home. I probably should have called you back."

"That's OK" Carolyn assured him. "Come on in."

Tommy stopped when they got to the veranda.

"Do you mind if we sit out here?"

"Not at all." Carolyn replied sitting on the porch swing. Tommy sat next to her.

"Not a bad day for April. Have you been getting spring fever?" he asked Carolyn starting with the small talk first that would hopefully help ease into the very important news he wanted to tell her in person. He had made the decision after their phone conversation earlier that the news he wanted to tell her couldn't wait until tomorrow.

"Yeah, it's actually quite nice," Carolyn said, closing her eyes and taking a whiff of the fresh air. "How come you decided to come over now?"

Tommy looked off into the distance and his body language caused Carolyn to become concerned. He seemed antsy. He wasn't sure how to begin and momentarily lost his train of thought. Tommy started to think that perhaps he should have waited until tomorrow and suddenly began to feel the timing might be a big whoops. Carolyn took his hand. The brief silence didn't bother her, but it was time for someone to speak.

"Tommy. Is everything OK?"

"Oh yeah. Everything is fine. Sorry. I have some news I need to share with you."

Tommy stood up feeling nervous. He hadn't felt that way on the drive over. He had been excited, but now he was feeling slightly uncomfortable.

How is she going to react?

Carolyn continued to sit, tuned in to Tommy's uneasiness. At first she had been thrilled that her friend was bringing news he wanted her to hear, but suddenly she wasn't so sure.

"Carolyn, guess what?"

If he was going to make a game of it she would play along. She stood up, smiled and peered into his face.

"What, Mr. Franklin?"

"I joined the Army!"

He blurted out the words and as soon as he did she wished she hadn't heard them. Her heart sank and her body went limp from the words her friend had just uttered. She was stunned and a grimace appeared on her face.

"What!"

Tommy repeated himself.

Carolyn turned away, walked down the steps to the front lawn and stared out into space, not believing what her ears had taken in. Tommy realized he might have made a big mistake by coming over on Easter Sunday and felt bad ... foolish. Why couldn't he have waited until tomorrow to tell her? He felt guilty at the thought he may have spoiled her day and Easter dinner with her family. She said nothing. Silence. He walked down and stood beside her.

"Carolyn ... I'm sorry if I have upset you. I'm really sorry. I was going to wait until tomorrow and I don't know why I ... ."

Carolyn turned around and faced him.

"Tommy, what have you done? There's a war going on!"

She tried to hold back tears that wanted to flow. He wasn't expecting this much of an upset and was hoping that Mr. or Mrs. Russell didn't come out of the house and see their daughter like this.

"I'm so sorry, Carolyn. Perhaps I should go."

Carolyn shook her head.

"No, don't do that. I'll be OK. I wasn't expecting this. You really caught me off guard, Tommy."

She sat down on the steps with her hands in her lap. More silence that Tommy wished would go away. He walked over and sat down beside her. It was not like they were lovers and breaking up. Yes, they were good friends, very good friends. Best friends. Maybe that's why she was so upset. Maybe her feelings for him were deeper than he realized. Or maybe it was the other way around and that's why he felt like he had to tell her today.

"Carolyn, I'm kind of excited about this. I gave it a lot of thought. They were going to draft me anyway. This is a better way to go. It's important to stop the spread of Communism in Asia."

Carolyn stared down at the ground then lifted her head up, looked at Tommy and once again took his hand.

"What do your parents think about all this?"

Tommy nodded his head several times as he thought about what to say next.

"They took it pretty hard, Mom more than Dad. I think they were mostly upset I didn't discuss it with them first. This is something I decided to do on my own. I've been thinking about it a lot. It's done. It's over and I'm excited."

Tommy was right about his parents being upset. He had told them earlier in the week when they were sitting at the kitchen table after dinner. His mother broke down in tears and his father got up from his chair, paced back and forth and started asking questions. One of them was how come he didn't talk to them about it beforehand. Carolyn wondered the same thing. The two of them talked about everything. Why did he choose not to talk to her about this? Or his parents? Tommy didn't have an answer for that. He didn't have one for his parents and he didn't have one now for Carolyn. He thought he was old enough to make his own decisions and didn't have to consult with anyone about his future plans. It didn't matter now. This decision was his and his alone. It wasn't easy telling his mother and father and they had stayed upset with him for a couple of days. It was painful for all of them. Kathy had the same reaction when he told her. More pain. But after they were given time to digest it they became supportive of what their son had done ... or at least they acted that way. No parent, right or wrong, really wanted to see their child go off to war. The Franklin family was extremely patriotic, but this war in Southeast Asia was different. Confusing.

There was too much war in the world, past and present. Now their country, this great United States of America, was involved in another armed conflict that was becoming increasingly unpopular with the American people. This was a war that, from a civilian standpoint, was hard to understand. Usually civilians trusted their politicians when they said it was a war that must be fought. This Vietnam war, for some reason, had been a tough sell from the very beginning. But soldiers were soldiers and trusted that when their leaders told them it was time to go fight, they would go fight. It was still a war, you fought for your country and you were just as brave and courageous as any soldier before you. This was what a patriotic Tommy was thinking. It was a war that had to be fought and won and he wanted to be part of it. He was sorry he had hurt his parents and his best friend, Carolyn, but this was what he felt he had to do. Get drafted or enlist. "You enlist, you get more choices," he was told. Enlisting was what patriotic men did. So he joined the Army, wanting to be part of the infantry and fight for his country. He wanted to be a soldier. A fighting soldier. And when it was all said and done, Carolyn and his parents and everyone in the community would be proud of him. In the United States especially, they were always proud and supportive of their soldiers. Carolyn stood up and looked down at the new American soldier.

"Tommy ... ," she spoke hoping that she had regained her composure. "Tommy ... ."

The American soldier looked up at her just as she began to fall apart. So much for composure. He stood up as she started crying again. Tommy held Carolyn as she clung to him tightly so that she didn't fall. What was happening? She didn't know. He didn't know. They'd find that out later on in life. For her, at this moment, it was the thought of losing a good friend and trying not to think of the worst case scenario. For him, this was the first time he realized that this girl, this best friend of his ... was more than just a friend.

MR. AND MRS. Franklin, Kathy and Carolyn sat on the bench outside the bus depot in downtown Brenton waiting for Tommy's bus. Carolyn got up and looked both ways down Main Street. Was the bus late or were they just being impatient? No, it was late. Tommy had been at boot camp for two months, but it might as well have been an eternity. It took time, but Carolyn and Tommy's families had resigned themselves to the fact that this was what Tommy wanted. He wanted to serve his country. That's all there was to it and now he had their full support. Everyone knew he would be a good soldier.

Mr. Franklin watched Carolyn look up and down the street pacing back and forth. She was anxious. They all were.

"You know, Carolyn. It's kind of like watching water boil," Mr. Franklin said to her. "The bus isn't going to get here any faster with you looking up and down the street."

Carolyn stopped in her tracks, looked over at Mr. Franklin and smiled. She knew he was right, but what else could she do? The bus was late. Why couldn't it be early? It was not winter, it was summer. The road conditions were perfect. There were other people waiting to get on the bus when it came and they were all wondering the same thing.

"I know, Mr. Franklin. If we had been late getting here the bus would have been early. Murphy's Law."

"It'll be here any minute, Carolyn," Kathy said, being the eternal optimist.

Carolyn folded her arms and stood at the curb looking, waiting. She was expecting it to come from the south end of town, but she checked the north end just in case. She turned her head to the south ... then to the north ... back to the south. Suddenly ...

"Here it comes!" she screamed.

From the south, just as it was supposed to. Of course, it would never have come from the north end of town. Mr. and Mrs. Franklin sprang up from the bench and quickly walked to the curb where Carolyn had put her hands over her mouth.

"Well, there ya go, Carolyn. Not right on schedule, but close enough," Mrs. Franklin said, trying to remain calm. "Let's hope he's on it."

That had never crossed Carolyn's mind. What if he wasn't on it? What if he had missed a connection somewhere? He was coming all the way from Kansas. A lot could go wrong between here and there.

"Of course he'll be on it, Mom," Kathy assured everyone. Optimistic and confident, that's how Tommy's sister was feeling. "He would have found a pay phone and called us if he had missed a connection somewhere," she added rationally.

Kathy was right of course. She knew her brother would be on the bus. There wasn't a doubt in her mind.

"I'm so excited," Carolyn said, walking up the sidewalk toward the bus and then whispered to herself, "It's going to be so nice to see him."

"Come on. We better get to the back of the bus depot," Mr. Franklin reminded the others who had been waiting.

Carolyn turned and looked back at the bus turning off Main Street. It would be less than a minute before it pulled off onto the side street and into the parking lot where passengers loaded and unloaded. The four of them walked through the front door and out the back just as the bus was pulling up. They were feeling the emotion of the moment. For the parents, it was about the overwhelming pride they had in their son. For the sister, it was the same, proud to be an American soldier's sibling. For Carolyn, it was a feeling she had for a friend she cared deeply about ... more than she knew and had yet to discover. The bus parked and people began to file off. Tommy was not the first one off or the second. Why? He was not the third or the fourth. Why? A dozen people got off the bus as Carolyn and Tommy's family wondered how come they couldn't see him through the windows. Twenty people were now off the bus and reunited with their friends and family. The anxiety turned into concern. The bus had to be getting close to being empty of passengers ... then there he was, in uniform. Smiling, he walked down the bus steps with his duffle bag and saw his parents, sister and Carolyn.

Mrs. Franklin couldn't help herself—she was the mother after all—and ran up and hugged Tommy.

"Oh, Tommy ... ."

"Hi, Mom."

Tommy held his mother tight. Mrs. Franklin took a step back.

"The bus was late. Gosh, look at you. You're in uniform!" a beaming mother said to her only son.

"Yes, Mom. I'm in uniform and it's good to be home."

Tommy grabbed his mother and gave her another hug. Looking over her shoulder he saw his father, Kathy and Carolyn.

"Hey, Dad."

Tommy planted a kiss on his mother's forehead then went and hugged his father.

"Hello, son. Welcome back to Brenton," Mr. Franklin said.

"It's good to be home, Dad."

Mr. Franklin grabbed his son by the biceps and looked into his eyes.

"It's good to have you home, son. We've all missed you."

"I have a lot of stories to tell about boot camp," Tommy said, looking at Carolyn and Kathy who were waiting patiently for their hugs. "I can't wait to start sharing them with you."

"I've got your duffle bag," Mr. Franklin said. "Go give your sister and Carolyn a hug."

"Finally," Kathy and Carolyn thought to themselves. They were only standing a few feet away, but wanted to stay in the background until Tommy finished greeting his parents. Tommy gave his dad a pat on the arm and looked at the two females patiently waiting. He walked over to them and nothing had to be said. Spreading out his arms the three of them had a group hug. Tommy gave each a peck on the forehead.

"Sure is nice to see the two of you," Private Franklin said. "Thank you so much for being here."

That brought a chuckle from his sister and she slapped him across the chest.

"Did you think for a second that we wouldn't, little brother?"

Tommy hugged his sister again.

"No, I knew you would be here."

He turned his attention to Carolyn.

"You look good, Carolyn. Nice to see you."

Carolyn tilted her head and smirked back at Tommy.

"Isn't it supposed to be, 'Nice to see you, mam?'"

As always, Tommy appreciated her sense of humor and was delighted to be around it once again. He had missed it.

"You're right. Nice to see you again, mam."

Carolyn followed Kathy's action and lightly tapped Tommy on the chest with her fist.

"And it's nice to see you again Private Franklin, sir. You look good in a uniform." Carolyn couldn't help herself and gave Tommy another hug. "Gosh, it's good to see you."

"We have so much to talk about. I've missed you all," Tommy said with eyes scanning the four that had come to welcome him home. "Thank you so much for your letters. They were much appreciated. I missed Brenton. It's good to be home. Are you coming over to the house?" he asked, looking at Carolyn.

"Of course I am. If I'm invited," Carolyn said, taking Tommy's hand and squeezing it.

Tommy smiled at her as he let his facial expression be the answer. Suddenly he felt like he couldn't shut up. All he wanted to do was talk. He realized how excited he was to be back home. The five of them began walking toward their vehicles parked in the parking lot a few steps away.

"… and you're going to stay for dinner," Tommy squeezed Carolyn's hand in return insisting she stay to enjoy one of Mrs. Franklin's home-cooked meals.

"You ride with your parents and I'll follow you back home," Carolyn insisted

"I can ride with you. That won't be a problem." Tommy wouldn't have it any other way. "OK with you. Mom? Dad?"

"I don't think you need our permission, soldier. We'll see you back at the house," Mr. Franklin said at they reached their cars.

Carolyn was flattered and wanted very much for Tommy to ride with her. She knew how much Mr. and Mrs. Franklin had missed their son and there would be lots of time for her and Tommy to talk and be together. For now though, it was proper for him to ride home with his parents and sister, and she wouldn't take no for an answer. Tommy put up a mild argument, which he lost, and then hopped into the backseat of his parents' car with Kathy. It was only a fifteen-minute drive and as much as she wanted to be with him, Carolyn felt she could survive the short drive back to the Franklin home by herself. Suddenly, Tommy got back out of the car to give Carolyn another hug and a kiss, this time on the lips.

"I can't wait to hear all your stories," Carolyn said, enthralled with the man in uniform.

She was feeling good because she saw that her best friend was feeling good. She was sure of that. He had done something that shocked everyone at first, but now, with the passage of time and a little understanding, it was easy to see that he was on cloud nine and proud to be wearing the uniform of the United States Army. She was pleased for him.

"Don't worry. You'll hear all my stories at least once if not a dozen times. And I want to hear everything that's going on in your life as well."

"You first," Carolyn shouted back as Tommy climbed back into his parents' car.

"OK, then. See ya at the house."

As Carolyn got into her car, she was giddy about seeing Tommy and her body tingled with the anticipation of spending time with him before he had to head off again in a couple of weeks to go wherever the Army wanted him to go. But as she waved and watched the Franklin car drive off, her mood suddenly became sullen and worrisome. The euphoria of seeing Tommy vanished as her emotions turned to overwhelming concern.

What if Tommy is sent to Vietnam? Would he volunteer to serve over there? Does he already know he's going off to war and just not telling us?

He hadn't said anything about his plans after he went back to his base. The thought of him going off to war suddenly troubled her like it had off and on since he told her he had joined the service. She couldn't wait to hear his stories, but what if he knew what his future held and wasn't telling anyone? How would they all react if he told them he was going to Southeast Asia? How would they handle that? She sat behind the steering wheel thinking about all this.

Why does there have to be war? Why do we have to kill each other? Why can't we all get along?

She worried about how she would react if Tommy in fact did go off to war and she told herself she would have to get over that. That everything was going to be OK. Everything would be fine. Tommy was doing what he wanted to do and all he wanted from her and his family was their support. He didn't want anyone to worry about him. Tommy was feeling really good about himself right now.

Just let it be. He's a great person, a great friend and he's going to be a great soldier. Two weeks is not a long time to be home. Let's be positive. Let's enjoy the time together. Life is a long journey. We'll all get through this. Tommy's parents will. His sister will. I will. This is only one chapter of a beautiful story. When Tommy gets out of the service, there will be another chapter. For now let's just get through this one and then move on.

Carolyn's thoughts were racing as she began her drive through town and into its outskirts. It was an emotional roller coaster as she went from the excitement of having him home to the worry and concern of what next? "Just let it be," she kept telling herself over and over. This homecoming had to be all about Tommy and showing him that they all loved and cared for him. A soldier needed that. All soldiers. They took up the challenge of keeping America free and safe for her citizens. It was the least his friends and family could do while he was home. Make him laugh. Let him know that he'd done the right thing. The country needed men like Tommy Franklin. Brave. Dedicated. If it weren't for men and women like him, there wouldn't be any freedom. A strong military was what made the country great.

Carolyn wiped a tear away as she pulled into the Franklin driveway, but stopped before she got up to the house. She looked straight ahead and realized she had to keep her emotions in check. It was not going to be easy and she didn't want to be a downer. "Keep it upbeat," she told herself. "Keep it light." She was glad to see him and had to be careful not to let her feelings get the best of her. She pushed on the gas to move the car forward to the Franklin home.

Be strong. I can do this. I can do this for Tommy. This next two weeks will be the best two weeks we've ever spent together. I hope he wants to spend as much time with me as I do with him. I wish that we could make the next two weeks last forever and that forever would never end.

With that thought Carolyn chuckled to herself as she pulled up in front of the house behind the Franklin car. *Forever can never end. Forever is forever.* Tommy came out of his parent's front door and rushed to greet her. She got out of her car and stood by the side of it admiring this proud person in uniform whose arms were outstretched. The excitement of seeing him came back again as she closed the car door just in time to receive another hug from her longtime pal. She rested her head on his chest.

Everything is OK now. Everything is fine. Life is good.

Easter - 1967

MOST OF THEM had thought it would never happen again, but it was happening now. Here it was the first Saturday night of Tommy being home and the majority of the ol' gang were hanging out at Tippy's. It was a made-to-order August evening for old friends who were together once again. Richard, Karen, Carl, Don, Linda, Joe, Peter, Claudia, Doug, Carolyn and Tommy, now in street clothes. It was a reunion with much energy and laughter, like it had been so many times before on a Saturday night. Everyone was talking at once. So many stories to tell because everybody had one.

"Remember when ... ?"

"Did you hear ... ?"

"Are you going to ... ?"

"Where's so and so now?"

This was the Tippy's of old. On this wonderful evening it seemed like everything had remained the same. Except the boyfriends and girlfriends that had been couples in high school weren't anymore. That didn't matter. They had matured and gotten past all that. Tonight was all about the good company they shared with each other. Their interests, goals and dreams had taken them in different directions and they seemed to have less in common than when they were in high school, but the camaraderie was still there and it was something they were all enjoying immensely. It was a magical feeling. A magical night. What a treat it was to be together again.

Saturday night at Tippy's had not changed through many generations. Some talked about their cars and motorcycles, some about their university life and others about life in the military. They reminisced about their high school days and speculated on what lay ahead. It seemed like such a long time since this last happened. These moments were now special and must be cherished. This could be their last celebration of friendship at Tippy's. Another year would go by and then another one and then three and four and they would see less and less of each other. As time passed, bumping into old friends at Tippy's would become a rare occasion and it would never be the same again after tonight. But that was the farthest thing from everyone's mind right now. Tonight, they laughed and joked. Everyone was milling about going from vehicle to vehicle trying to catch up with what was going on in everyone else's life. Drinking milk shakes and sipping on soft drinks, eating fries and sharing bites out of hamburgers. This was the way they had done it in high school and this was the way they were doing it now. So grown up, so mature, yet ... not quite.

Tommy, Richard and a couple of other guys were peering under the hood of Richard's 1965 Chevy Malibu with its 396 cubic inch motor. They were all impressed with Richard's new toy. He had gotten a draft exemption because of a kidney ailment he had had since he was a young boy. Medication was keeping it under control and he appeared to be no worse for wear, but it was just enough of an issue that it kept him out of the military. He and Tommy had discussed joining up as buddies, but as soon as the Army recruiter was informed of Richard's condition, that put an end to their dream of being in the service together. So Richard decided to work full time in the local saw mill and buy himself a fancy car. It had bucket seats, a console and a four speed. It was a two-door hard top and he was currently very popular with the local girls.

"How many speeding tickets have you gotten so far, Richard?" Tommy chided his good buddy.

Richard laughed.

"The old man told me if I get just one he'll be taking away the key. He had to co-sign so I better listen to him," Richard said. "I'm going to take it down to the strip in a couple of weeks to see what it'll do. Dad said he'll go with me. We'll crank her up and let her go."

The "strip" was the Millstone Drag Strip about fifty miles down state. It was the closest one and most of the young males went down there on an occasional Saturday or Sunday to watch the races. It was a rite of passage for "the guys" to do that. In most cases it was just so they could say they'd been there.

"Well, you got yourself a pretty hot deal here, Richard. Good for you," Tommy complemented his friend.

Richard put the hood down and Tommy looked over at Carolyn standing and talking to some of her girlfriends a couple of vehicles down. They had spent a lot of time together since Tommy arrived back home four days before and tonight they had driven out to Tippy's together in Tommy's truck. They had hardly talked to each other since they got here and that was on Tommy's mind. Richard noticed Tommy looking over at Carolyn.

"You and Miss Russell over there becoming an item, Private Franklin?" Richard asked.

Like everyone else, Richard was quite aware how much time Tommy and Carolyn had spent together since he returned from boot camp. You wouldn't see one without seeing the other.

"I don't think so, Richard. She's my female buddy. It would be a little too strange for us to be an item, as you say. Naw, she's good company, that's all."

Richard wasn't sure he believed his friend and sensed something more underneath it all.

"Yeah, she's a good kid. And smart! Everyone needs a smart friend to hang out with, Private. That's why you hang out with me, right?" Richard said as he and Tommy leaned against the front of his car.

"Yeah, that would be it, Cromley. You're the smartest guy I know," Tommy put his arm around Richard's shoulders and gave him a look. "The smartest guy I know."

Carolyn continued to chat and laugh with her girlfriends, looked over in Tommy's direction and saw him looking back at her. Everyone was having a great time. She took a sip of her soda through a straw as Tommy began walking toward her. They probably hadn't chatted in an hour and that just didn't feel right.

"Hey, soldier boy," Karen said as Tommy walked up. "We were just talking about you. Carolyn said she didn't know if you're going to Vietnam or not and we find that hard to believe."

Carolyn did in fact know. Tommy had told her a couple of nights before he was going to war. It upset her terribly and Tommy had asked her to keep it quiet and if anyone asked he would tell them in person.

"So yes or no? Are you going to Vietnam or not?" Karen persisted in a friendly manner.

Karen wasn't trying to be rude, but it was something Tommy didn't really want to discuss again in front of Carolyn. Yet everyone was going to find out sooner or later and now he was thinking he might as well get it over with. Carolyn sensed this and turned away from her friends making Tommy feel uncomfortable.

"Well, yeah, Karen," Tommy informed her and the other girls gathered around. "I'm off to Vietnam next month when I get back to base. I'll be gone a year. No big deal. It'll go by fast."

Tommy watched as Carolyn walked up to another group of friends and began talking to them.

"... and we'll be here at Tippy's when you get back. Don't worry. We'll save your spot," Karen assured him.

Tommy laughed. Karen had always been special to him, but in a different way from Carolyn. He and Karen had been boyfriend and girlfriend in high school and had experimented with sex for the first time. The physical thing was a mutual curiosity and although they were a couple at the time, there wasn't a lot of emotion involved. They were simply exploring each other's bodies and it was special in that way. But that was then and they remained good friends.

"Yeah, we'll save your spot, Tommy," Carla, another friend in the group chipped in. "And we want to hear some juicy war stories when you get back."

"OK, sure thing, Carla. You guys save my spot here and I'll buy you a burger when I get home," Tommy promised the girls while keeping one eye on Carolyn.

"All of us?" Cindy, yet another one of the females wondered.

"Yep. All of you, Cindy."

Carolyn had walked away from her other friends and over to a bench just outside Tippy's side door and sat down by herself. Tommy decided to follow her.

"Mind if I join you?" Tommy asked as he stood in front of her and offered her one of his fries in a bag he had been carrying around with him.

"No thanks. Sure, have a seat. My legs are tired. I just thought I would sit down for a minute."

Carolyn lifted her legs up and stretched them out in front of her.

"I never thought I would see the ol' gang together like this again, hey Carolyn?" Tommy said, feeling a little melancholy.

"It's great!" Carolyn agreed. "Everybody has been so busy these last few months. It's like we never have a chance to get together for anything. I didn't even go to the lake once all summer."

"Really?" Tommy was amazed at Carolyn's confession. "You didn't get there once?"

"No, not once. I've just been working all summer. Work, work, work. That's all I do. Work and work some more."

It was a half-hearted complaint as Carolyn actually really enjoyed her summer job as an activities director at a kid's camp in Pennell, not too far away from her parents' home. It was a perfect job except for the fact she had to stay there overnight Monday through Friday and did some fast talking in order to get time off when Tommy was going to be home. It all worked out and she was going to savor this time with him, especially this Saturday night. Tommy and Carolyn sat on the bench admiring their friends and relishing the moment. This was a "feel good" night.

"You feel like going out to Lake Michigan for a stroll on the beach?" Tommy asked her.

Carolyn looked at Tommy. She was quite content with what was going on here at Tippy's, but it sounded like a good offer and she didn't want to pass on it. It didn't take her long to respond.

"Yeah. That would be nice. You sure you want to leave this?" Carolyn asked, making sure she was not dragging him away if he was having a good time with their old friends.

"Yeah. I've got one more Saturday night before I leave again. Maybe we can do it all over one last time next week," Tommy said, thinking how nice that would be, but knowing it was probably wishful thinking.

"Then let's go," Carolyn said.

Tommy grabbed Carolyn by the hand and pulled her up.

"OK, partner. Let's start saying our good-byes."

It took a good twenty minutes before the two of them could break away from their friends and it was a lot harder than they thought it was going to be. They finally managed to get into Tommy's truck and start driving out to what was known by the locals as "The Point" out on Lake Michigan, about a twenty-minute drive away. Carolyn had decided to sit in the middle of the seat instead of by the passenger window. Tommy thought it peculiar at first. She had never done that before, but it was fine with him.

He had admitted to himself that ever since he got home from boot camp he was having "different" feelings toward Carolyn. Something that was beyond just being good friends. He wondered if perhaps she was feeling the same way. They had been friends for so long and he had always been content with the platonic relationship they had. He hadn't been lying whenever he claimed she was his "gal pal." They were each other's confidant and for a long time he had been her "guy pal." It worked. But now, driving out to Lake Michigan, he asked himself what they were going to do when they got there? They would sit on the beach and talk of course. Or would they? Why had Carolyn decided to sit next to him in the truck? He had always found her attractive and she knew him as well as anybody, which was part of the attraction, but as he continued to drive it hit him; he had a crush on her. However, if the feeling wasn't mutual and he made a pass at her, he would feel like a fool and never forgive himself. Tommy didn't want this to be a test; he somehow had to figure out a way to see if she felt the same way. He had too much respect for Carolyn to take a chance on blowing a wonderful friendship. His mind was racing. Would their mutual respect for each other get in the way of taking their friendship to another level? Here they were, headed out to "the point" together with not much being said as he drove.

What is she thinking?

What is he thinking?

Carolyn picked up on the lack of conversation and decided to say something. As usual. Typical her. She thought she'd just say anything to break the silence. She leaned against him and he put his arm around her. Both actions seemed normal enough. She tilted her head onto his shoulder.

"Are you going to come back to Brenton when you get out of the service?" she asked.

Tommy didn't know the answer to that, but he knew what he had to say.

"Yeah. Of course. This is home. How about you when you get out of university?"

"I don't know," Carolyn said, being more honest with her answer than Tommy was with his. "There's a lot of world out there. One of the reasons I'm taking Marine Biology is that it should give me options to work just about anywhere where there is water. So I don't know. Hard to say. I love Michigan. Good question, Mr. Franklin."

"I thought it was," Tommy said, pulling his truck into the parking lot on the shore of the lake.

"You wanna go sit out on the beach?" he asked hoping the answer was going to be "Yes."

"Yeah, let's sit on the beach. It's beautiful out," Carolyn replied already halfway out of the passenger door.

Tommy got out of his truck and before he closed the door he pulled the back part of the front seat forward and took out a blanket.

"Good plan," Carolyn was impressed he was so prepared.

"Thanks. It might beat sitting on the sand. Which direction do you want to head?"

Carolyn and Tommy walked to the edge of the parking lot where it met the beach and Carolyn sized up the situation.

"Let's go this way," she pointed to the north.

It happened to be more secluded. There weren't any houses on the beach in that direction. It was a long stretch of beach with nothing but darkness and solitude.

"Are you going be able to see OK? I've got a flashlight in the truck. I can go back and get it," Tommy offered.

"Don't be silly. I can see just fine," Carolyn said as she took off her shoes so she could walk barefoot in the sand. Tommy did the same.

"OK, then. I'm with you. Just don't get me lost," Tommy kidded.

There was a feeling of anticipation between them. A sense that this was going to be more than two friends sitting on the beach having a chat. It had begun when they left Tippy's and Carolyn decided to sit in the middle of the seat close to Tommy and it continued when she put her head on his shoulder and he put his arm around her. Both were feeling that maybe it was time to take their relationship to a point where it hadn't been before. The question for each was how this would happen without showing disrespect or having it become extremely awkward? They walked and talked making jokes and trying to keep things light. They were each hoping to get the other one comfortable and then let nature take its course.

"How about here?" Carolyn suggested a spot between two small dunes.

"Looks good to me," Tommy agreed and spread out the blanket.

They were only about forty feet away from the gently breaking waves and the sound of them helped with the mood. Carolyn sat down with her knees up and her arms around them. Tommy sat down beside her with his legs outstretched.

"Sure is the perfect evening," he said and leaned back on his hands.

"The water is relatively calm tonight," Carolyn added.

"Tommy ... ," Carolyn wanted to talk some more before anything happened. She had some questions and needed some answers. There was no rush to get into what both now hoped was going to happen next.

"Yeah?" Tommy responded looking up at the stars.

"When you go to Vietnam, can you promise me just one thing?" Carolyn asked burying her head in her arms.

"Absolutely. What is it?"

"Will you write to me as often as possible?" she lifted her head up and looked at him.

"Carolyn ... of course I will. The more I write to you the more you'll write back to me ... right?"

Tommy sat up straight and put his arm around her. She appreciated the gesture and grabbed the hand that was draped around her shoulder.

"That's right ... and I plan on writing you a lot of letters and sending you things you might need or want. You think you'll be able to handle that?" Carolyn asked wryly.

Tommy squeezed her hand.

"That would be cool. A year will go by fast and I'll be home before you know it."

Carolyn leaned on Tommy. She disagreed with his comment that a year would go by fast. It would seem like eternity and eternity was a very long time.

"I'm going to miss you, Private Franklin."

Carolyn lay on her back and looked up at the stars. There were so many. Tommy lay next to her and propped his head up with his hand and elbow.

"Can you do me another favor when you're over there?" Carolyn asked as she counted the stars. There were thousands of stars out on this night.

"What would this one be, Carolyn Russell?"

Carolyn looked at Tommy. Things were going to start moving fast any second now. She felt it. He felt it.

"When you're overseas and you see the stars out on a clear night, will you think of me?"

Tommy smiled down at her.

"When I see the stars out at night, I'll find the brightest one and think of you. I promise"

He lowered his head and pressed a soft and short kiss on her lips then raised back up to look into her eyes. She stared back at him. Was this going to be that awkward moment when they both would start laughing and wonder what in the world they were thinking? Maybe ... if it were a year or even six months ago, but not now. This feeling had been brewing for a long time, but neither one had recognized it. Now they were acknowledging their feelings for each other and there would be no turning back. It was what they wanted. It was honest, pure and genuine and now, finally, they experienced love of a different kind. Not teenage love, but love between a man and a woman. It was comforting, sincere, joyful and assuring. Youthful.

"That felt good," Carolyn said of the kiss.

"Really?" Tommy smiled at her.

He truly did admire this young lady he'd known for so long. He wondered if her body was tingling as much as his.

"Yeah, really," Carolyn answered returning his smile.

Tommy kissed her again, softly, slightly longer than the first time. He looked at her again and her eyes told him all he needed to know. He put his free hand around her waist and pulled her close to him as she put her hand behind his head and kissed him, long and deep. There wouldn't be any awkward moments tonight. There would be no hesitation, no second thoughts. What happened now would be passionate and intimate, physical and truthful between two best of friends. They had come a long way together and this was that moment that destiny had known was going to happen one day, under the stars, on the sand, with the sound of waves gently breaking on the shore.

A DOG NAMED TIMEX

Early Fall - 1967

FROM THIRTY THOUSAND feet the country of Vietnam looked quiet and peaceful. Even the beaches seemed inviting from that altitude. It had been a long grueling journey for the soldiers about to embark on the adventure of their lives. This was the place everyone had been talking about. They talked about it at boot camp and everywhere else the soldiers gathered.

"Doesn't look like much of a war going on down there," Tommy said, peering out the window of the transport plane that was on the last leg of its six-hour flight from Hawaii.

His statement was being directed to a black soldier named Will Dempsey, another private who was the same young age as Tommy. Private Dempsey was escaping the street wars back home in Detroit, where he grew up. Will leaned over and looked over Tommy's shoulder.

"Yeah well, Franklin. This isn't some company picnic they're sending us to be security guards at. You're right though, it looks peaceful down there. If this were Detroit back in July, you'd be seeing a big city on fire. You said you were from Michigan right, Franklin? Did you catch the riots back in the summer?"

"No, sorry Dempsey. I missed that party. Maybe next time," Tommy replied still looking down at the terrain below.

"Hopefully there won't be a next time," Will said calmly and dead serious. "God damn idiots just about burnt my whole neighborhood down when I was home from boot camp and they weren't no Viet Cong either. I don't know who they were, but they weren't brothers."

Will sat back in his seat and reflected on the riots that had hit Detroit that past summer and destroyed much of the city. It was a war being held on home turf similar to the one he was going off to fight in some far-off land he didn't know much about. He knew it was going to be the same thing only different. People killing each other.

Will had grown up in a rough neighborhood in the inner city of Detroit and was thankful to have two loving parents who worked hard and lived for the betterment of their children. He had managed to stay out of trouble in his teens and graduated from high school. It wasn't like all black kids had only one parent and got into trouble with the police. A lot of black youth growing up in the inner city did have two parents living at home and Will was one of the blessed ones. He had seen all too closely the challenges and temptations of living in the rough neighborhoods. The drugs, the alcohol, the murders, the prostitutes. But from his early days as a child he had been taught right from wrong by his parents. His father had a steady job at the Ford automotive plant and had worked there for years. His mother was a secretary at the high school that Will graduated from. They attended church together every Sunday as a family, he along with his two younger brothers and two younger sisters. Will had always tried to set a good example for his younger siblings. He got his diploma and after he was finished with his two years in the Army he planned on going to college on the G.I. Bill. He had set his goals high because that was what had been impressed upon him as a child. It had worked for him and it was working for all the Dempsey children. They were all good students, good athletes, good citizens and their good clean living wasn't any different from any white family living out in the suburbs. The Dempsey family lived a good life, but they lived the all American dream in a very rough neighborhood. Will's parents were involved in everything their children did, from participating in sports to all the school and church activities. The family of seven was always on the go. The challenges of raising kids in the inner city were many and Will's parents were always searching for ways to assure that their children had the best possible opportunities.

Like Tommy's parents, the elder Dempseys weren't thrilled that their oldest son had enlisted in the Army while there was a war going on. But also, just like Tommy's parents, they had come to be supportive of his decision and they would worry about their child until he got back home safe from Vietnam. It was because of their upbringing that Tommy and Will hit it off when they first met and chose to sit together on the flight over.

Racism was still very much a reality in the sixties and some white soldiers and some black soldiers chose to associate with their kind only. But not Tommy Franklin and not Will Dempsey. To them, people were people no matter what the color of their skin. The Army frowned on any hint of self-imposed segregation, but it was still there in the form of mistrust and ignorance. But that's not how these two young soldiers were raised. Their parents were colorblind and that made them colorblind. They were lucky in that regard. Racism would have been considered a sin in both families.

When Private Franklin and Private Dempsey were growing up there weren't any people of another color that lived close enough to them to make friends. If Tommy and Will had grown up as kids in the same neighborhood, it's very possible that they would have been very good friends. And now, on this flight that was about to end, these two had started a bond that would become a close and lasting friendship. They made each other laugh and were able to kid with each other. That was a good foundation from which to build a relationship, especially going into battle. They would enjoy each other's company as they served their time in the war zone. Who cared what anyone else thought. They were warriors and would look after each other's back, whether it was black or white. Red or purple. Green or blue. Orange or gray.

"What did your parents think of all that stuff that went down during the riots?" Tommy was curious as to what it must have been like to live in such a violent and chaotic time in an American city.

"They were worried about their kids, man. Shit was happening a little too close to home. Scared the hell out of all of us. Even scared me and I had just come home from boot camp. It was sad man, seeing everything getting burnt down to the ground. It was just like this place we're going to now, Franklin. Why can't we all just get along?"

Will paused while Tommy thought about what his new friend had just said. He had asked a good question. "Why can't we all just get along?"

It was the same thing Carolyn had asked when Tommy had told her he was going off to fight.

Everyone got along in Brenton. Why couldn't they get along in places like Detroit and Vietnam? He didn't want to appear naïve, so he held back from saying anything. He had enlisted in the Army to serve his country that he was so proud of. He convinced himself this was a war that had to be fought. You couldn't have the Communists taking over the world. Somebody had to stop them. Sure, his country had its own problems, but it was still the greatest country in the world. He had to fight to protect its freedom and its way of life. Someone had to do it, so Tommy joined the best-trained and strongest military on the planet. They were going to free the Vietnamese people from their oppressors and they would all be heroes. Americans were always the good guys and they had to protect the rest of the world from the evil ways of Communism. Vietnam would be just another example to show that the United States military would stand by any country that was threatened by this enemy. There was no apprehension with Tommy Franklin. He couldn't wait to land and start fighting this "red menace" as his superiors called it. But still ... it was a good question his new friend had asked.

"Why can't we all just get along?"

The plane began to make its descent and as it did, things grew quiet. The reality of the moment started to sink in.

We are going to war and some of us are not going to come back alive. Who was it going to be? The black soldier sitting next to me? The white soldier sitting next to me?

Tommy stared out the window. He had received some excellent training in the last couple of months. They all had. He felt prepared. Ready. He didn't worry about himself. If he didn't make it back alive he knew he would have died for a good cause. He worried about this soldier sitting next to him. The one with four younger siblings that looked up to their older brother. The one who had great parents like he did, but struggled to raise their children in a hostile environment in, of all places, the United States of America. He was worried about this new friend. This street-smart dude who acted tough, but loved his family as much as Tommy loved his. He thought for a moment about what would happen if this guy by the name of Will Dempsey didn't make it home. How it would affect his family? His parents? His younger siblings? It was a possibility for everyone on the plane that they might not make it back alive. They all knew it. They all had their own stories and backgrounds and somewhere they all probably had people who cared for them. They were going into battle now as a group, as a family, as a unit. They'd been told war was hell and now they were about to find out why. These soldiers from small towns and big cities. From broken families and families that were strong and united. Enlistees and draftees. Some were looking forward to the experience while others were not so enthused. For some this was their dream. Others were thinking about the dreams beyond when it was all over. Some would make it. Others would not. That's war. As time passed, some families would grieve over their lost loved one while other families would shed tears of joy when their child came home alive. It had always been this way when soldiers went off to war. Some lived. Some died.

"Why can't we all just get along?"

Will didn't feel comfortable with the quiet. Everyone seemed to be in some sort of trance. Deep thought. Even his new buddy, Tommy.

"Hey, Franklin. Whatta you gonna do when you get back stateside and get out of the service?"

Tommy continued looking out the window at this strange place that was going to be his home for the next year.

"I don't know, Dempsey. Probably go back working with my dad in the construction business. What about you?"

Will sat back and looked straight ahead. He gave it some thought.

"I'm going to go to college. Maybe take up psychology. I'd like to know what makes the human mind tick. I could be a teacher. That would be a good job. I don't want to work in no factory. I've seen what it's done to my dad. He's done well, all things considered. But it's a hard way to make a living. I wanna do something I enjoy doing. Something told me the only way to do that is to get an education. If I survive this, then that's the plan, Stan. Get an education. Raise my kids in a nice neighborhood." Will paused and daydreamed for a moment. "Where did you say you were from, Franklin?"

Tommy looked at Will. "Brenton. Up state."

"Yeah, right," Will said as he recalled Tommy telling him that earlier. "Maybe I'll raise my kids in a nice neighborhood in Brenton, Michigan. Somewhere away from the big city. Where is Brenton, Franklin?"

"It's in the upper western part of the lower peninsula on Lake Michigan," Tommy said proudly.

Will had to think about that definition for a moment.

"Hey, all I know is Detroit, man. If it's in the upper, western, lower, part of whatever, that's your problem. That doesn't tell me much. All the white people live north of us, I do know that. I can tell you where Merle's corner store is or where it was before it got burnt down in the riots. Along with Brown's Bakery and Welton's Ice Cream Parlor and Jones' Appliance Store. It's a shame, man. All burnt down to the ground."

Will reflected back to the riots that were still fresh in his mind.

"Must have been something to see the Army come in and have tanks rolling down your own street?" Tommy pondered that image for a moment.

"Yeah, it was something all right," Will said with disgust.

Will didn't want to talk about the riots. Tommy thought it must have been quite an uprising. Imagine having to call in the U.S. Army to take action against its own citizens! Especially in the United States. He couldn't possibly imagine growing up in a neighborhood like the one Will described and grew up in. It was amazing Will had survived. He was lucky to have the parents he did. Otherwise, Tommy doubted if Will would have made it.

You could have the best parents in the world, but sometimes peer pressure had an even stronger influence on young people and could send them down the wrong path. Tommy felt lucky to have lived in a small community like Brenton and to have had the loving parents he admired so much. He had to give this soldier sitting next to him a lot of credit for being such a nice person and knowing right from wrong, good from bad. Tommy was confident he would enjoy his friendship with Will. Maybe, when the timing was right, he could learn more from Will about growing up in the inner city. It sounded like the complete opposite of the environment he grew up in.

For now though, he was going to learn what hell was really like. The hell of being in a war. The sounds, the smells, the blood, the sights, the killing. It wasn't going to be anything like Brenton. It was going to be something that

Early Fall - 1967

Tommy had never experienced before. Not even close. In fact, most of those making this journey into hell were going to have their eyes opened like never before. Tommy continued to look out the window as the plane lowered its landing gear.

"Looks like we're here, Franklin," Will said, breaking the silence once again.

Tommy was suddenly feeling mixed emotions. Tommy Franklin, the true patriot, was warring the other Tommy Franklin who had stuck in the back of his mind the words Will had spoken a few minutes before, *"Why can't we all just get along?"*

"Yeah, Dempsey. It looks like we're here. Bring it on Vietnam!"

"Yeah, let's go jump into the fire, man," Will said cynically and held out a hand for Tommy to shake.

Both had joined the infantry, but they wouldn't know what their assignment was going to be until they arrived in this war-torn country.

"OK, Franklin. Whatever happens I hope we get to see more of each other. I guess we'll find out pretty quick where we're all going."

Tommy shook Will's hand.

"Yeah, Dempsey. It's been nice talking to you. I'd like to hear more about Detroit sometime. And if we end up on the same battlefield, I've got your back, Dempsey."

"Well, I appreciate that, Franklin. I got your back too, man. You're kind of cool for a white dude. Are you sure you don't have any black ancestry?"

Tommy laughed as the landing gear hit the ground. They had arrived.

"I'll have to check with my parents on that one, Dempsey. Ya, never know. You might even have some white blood in you. Hey! If you're lucky."

Will chuckled at that comment and looked past Tommy out the window.

"So, this is Da Nang! First thing I gotta figure out is how to pronounce the names of some of these places. Don't sound much like English to me. Da Nang, Poo Tang. This is going to be interesting, Franklin. This is going to be interesting."

It most certainly was going to be that, and more.

THE SOLDIERS UNLOADED from the plane that had brought them to war. To Vietnam. To the heat and humidity. To the jungle. It was not Detroit and it was not Brenton. It was not Des Moines, or Brookings. It was not New York City or Knoxville. It was not like any small town or hamlet or big city in America. It was somewhere that these brave and young soldiers had never been before. They were ready and anxious. Brave and scared. As their feet hit the ground exiting the plane, reality set in. They would fight side by side. Some would save their friends, some would lose their friends. Some of their friends would die in action.

As their feet hit the landing strip they felt ready. They were well trained, looking for a fight ... and a long, long way from home.

It was 3:00 p.m. local time and the soldiers got their first orientation right on the tarmac of the airstrip. It was quick and frank. No sense in wasting time. There was a war to be fought. In a matter of minutes they were sent to their temporary barracks to wait until they received their assignments and found out exactly where they would be stationed in this foreign land.

"Did you get what the Major said back there, Franklin?" Will quizzed Tommy as they walked toward a large group of buildings, mostly Quonset huts, a short distance away. They carried their duffel bags and looked forward to seeing their new digs.

"Kind of. Sort of. I'm just going to follow the crowd, man. I'm hungry and tired. I need a bed and some food." Tommy walked fast forcing Will to keep up. Keeping pace, another black soldier joined them.

"Doesn't look like the Hilton to me," he said, addressing Will.

Will looked at him and remembered seeing him on the plane.

"Nope, it ain't the Hilton or the Ritz. But it's going to be home sweet home for now. I'm Will Dempsey from Detroit. I saw you on the plane."

"Yeah, I was on it all right. I'm Brian Dodd from Cincinnati."

"Nice to meet you Brian. This is my white friend Private Franklin from somewhere in northern Michigan."

Tommy acknowledged the introduction.

"Nice to meet you Private Dodd. I'm from Brenton in the upper western part of the lower peninsula."

Will looked at Brian and had to contain a laugh. Brian raised his eyebrows sarcastically as if he was really impressed with what Tommy had just said.

"Franklin, don't confuse us. You're going to have to find a map somewhere and show us where this Brenton place is," Will insisted as he looked at Brian. "Shit, man. Don't mind him Dodd, he's white folk."

All three chuckled and continued walking together.

"Hey dudes, look. If I brought my boys from Brenton over here this war would be over in a week. Man, you don't mess with us."

Tommy's bravado forced him to bite his lower lip so he didn't crack himself up. He wanted the two guys walking with him to think he was serious. They didn't.

Early Fall - 1967

"Your boys from Brenton wouldn't last twenty-four hours in my neighborhood, Franklin," Will informed him.

"Less than that in Cincinnati, Private," Dodd said, also having grown up in the inner city.

Tommy looked straight ahead and smiled. He knew Brenton wasn't Detroit or Cincinnati. He thought he would try a friendly attempt at getting Will and Brian riled up. It was harder than he realized. These two guys from the big city were street smart and didn't rattle easily. They'd seen just about everything growing up on the streets of America.

"What was the war like in Detroit last July, Dempsey. Did you see any action?" Brian asked Will.

"I just got home from boot camp when the shit broke out, man. It got pretty nasty. I don't think it was as bad as the riots in Brenton last year though. I hear it got pretty ugly up there, Franklin," Will said, not letting go of the cynical comparison between where he grew up and where Tommy was from.

"Give it a rest, Dempsey. The boys from my neck of the woods are lean, mean fightin' machines. If we get through all this, you and Dodd here will have to come up for a visit and meet my boys. You'll find out what I'm talking about."

Tommy played the conversation like he'd done this before. It impressed Brian and Will. They thought they might like this white boy from somewhere up north in the state of Michigan. He seemed relatively harmless, but could talk the talk. It might work if they all got the same assignments and had the opportunity to spend time together.

"Your boys ever met a brother?" Will asked, throwing Tommy a curveball.

"Naw, I don't think so. We've just seen pictures of them. It wasn't until I joined the Army that I actually met one and saw that they were real. Brothers are kind of cool. I like brothers," Tommy continued to talk the talk.

That sealed the deal with Brian and Will. They liked this guy. A little bit crazy. A little weird and a whole lot likeable.

"You know, Franklin, you hang out with us, man," Will kidded back. "We'll teach ya how to be a soul brother even though you're the wrong color. Yeah, you hang out with us, man. Won't take long and we'll turn your skin a darker tone. You just gotta know how to strut your stuff and talk ghetto English, man. You'll fit right in."

"Ghetto English might be easier to learn than Vietnamese, Dempsey. I'll take you up on that," Tommy replied.

As the three of them walked up to the barracks that would be their home until they were given further orders in the next couple of days, they were ordered to "fall in." They'd done it many times before and knew the routine. One of the first things they had learned in boot camp was how to "fall in." As they stood at attention at the side of the barracks they were given another brief orientation on the layout of the camp and where to go to get their assignments. The first order of business was to find their beds inside the barracks and put down their belongings. Once inside the barracks, Tommy, Will and Brian chose bunks close together. After disposing of their duffel bags, they headed off as a threesome to the building not far away across the dirt and through the dust to find out where they would be assigned.

"Here comes the moment of truth, brothers," Will said to Tommy and Brian as they entered the building and got in line.

It was a big open room that was used for these occasions. There were six officers sitting at tables giving out orders to those that had just arrived and the line moved quickly.

"God, I just hope I don't get assigned to Brenton, man," Brian said, taunting Tommy and trying to get him going again. "I don't think I could do that!"

He waited for a response and Tommy bit.

"Hey, man. I'd rather be stationed there than Cincinnati. Shit, man. What the hell does Cincinnati have to offer, Dodd?"

"A lot more than some place called Brenton," Brian fired back with a laugh.

Will was the first to walk up to one of his superiors sitting at a table. Then Brian, then Tommy in rapid succession. Will got his assignment papers, walked over to the exit door and waited for Brian and Tommy. Brian walked up first.

"Well, Dempsey. They're sending me to some place called Pleiku. How about you?"

The words were barely out of Brian's mouth before Will put an arm around Brian's shoulder and held up his papers in front of Brian's face for him to read. Brian nodded his head in approval. He and Will had been assigned to the same place.

"Way to go, brother," Brian said, elated they were going to be seeing more of each other. "I don't know where the hell it is but I'm sure we'll find out soon enough. Here comes, Franklin. He's looking a little down in the mouth."

Brian and Will watched Tommy as he approached with a long face.

"You don't look too happy, Franklin," Will said, stating the obvious.

"I got assigned to Cincinnati of all places," he said with a straight face.

Brian gave him a friendly shove with both hands.

"Shit, Franklin. Give it up, man," Brian continued with the physical stuff

Early Fall - 1967

and smacked Tommy in the chest. "Where the heck are they sending you, man? Hopefully in the opposite direction of where we're going."

"Someplace called Pleiku."

Will and Brian let out a simultaneous cheer.

"You're going with us, white boy. You're going with us."

Will and Brian shared their elation with Tommy.

"Did anybody tell you guys where this place is?" Tommy asked not meaning to put a damper on the moment.

"The officer told me somewhere up in the central highlands near the Cambodian border," Will explained. "Who cares," he continued. "This Oreo cookie member is going to kick some Viet Cong ass."

Brian looked at Will as they walked through the doors to the outside.

"What the hell is that supposed to mean, Dempsey?"

Will didn't miss a beat. "Hey, some white guy fighting with a black dude on either side of him, that's an Oreo cookie, man."

"Where the hell do you come up with this shit, Dempsey? You're fuckin' crazy," Tommy said, taking the lead.

"I come up with this shit all the time, Franklin," Will boasted. "You'll get used to it."

"Pleiku here we come," Tommy replied, thinking how glad his feet were now that they were on the ground after all the flying. "Come on, assholes. Let's go find some food and water. I'm dying of thirst."

Will and Brian walked side by side just behind Tommy.

"Did you hear that, Dodd? He called us assholes!" Will said, thinking it was pretty funny. "This white kid is going to be all right. He's got nerve and that's what you need on the battlefield."

"He's still a honky!" Brian replied.

The three continued to walk toward a building they were told was the mess hall. Tommy stopped and turned around to face his new buddies. Brian, Will and Tommy all stood together.

"Hey look, Dempsey. Look, Dodd. I want you to know I'm glad, real glad, we lucked out and we're going to be together. I got your back. You won't ever have to worry about that."

Will and Brian looked at each other, started walking again and didn't bother looking back at their comrade.

"Franklin, don't get so god damn serious on us, now. We got your white ass. Everybody's got everybody's back. I smell food. Let's go," Will said, picking up the pace.

Brian followed Will and Tommy, watching as his two new buddies made their way to the kitchen. It was a good feeling for the white boy from Brenton and a soldier wouldn't get too many of those in the days ahead. Being in a war never brings too many good feelings and you hold on to them when you can. It was what kept you going.

"Hey, wait for me," Tommy called out. "I heard white boys go first in this country."

Will and Brian ignored the voice behind them and Will held up his hand flipping Tommy the bird. For the moment everything was fine and all three were enjoying themselves. Tommy caught up to Brian and Will and sandwiched himself between them.

"So this is an Oreo cookie marching off to war?" Tommy said, first looking at Will and then at Brian as both gave him a funny look. "Hey, I'm cool with that. I'm totally cool with that. I can't wait to write my friends back home about Dempsey and Dodd. They're not going to believe it. I've met two dudes of color!"

"Franklin, you're one cool dude yourself. A little strange, but I think we can live with that. Right, Dodd?" Will said, tossing the conversation back over to Brian.

"Yeah well, we'll see. We'll see. But as far as I'm concerned, he's the one with color."

BRIAN WALKED OVER and shook a sleeping Will.

"Jesus Christ! What time was it, man?" a droggy Will asked.

"Time to get up, man," Brian said. "Time to get rolling."

Will didn't bounce up like the rest of his unit in the barracks and instead slowly sat up in his bed.

"Shit, man. Can't the war wait?" he asked rubbing his forehead.

"Sorry," Private Dodd responded as he took Will's feet and put them on the floor.

It was only the Oreo cookie's third day in Vietnam, but today was the day all three would be flying into Pleiku. The honeymoon was over. Pleiku was a hotspot and needed good fighting soldiers like Will, Brian and Tommy. Not that they had ever fought in a war before, but they were ready and psyched up for the job at hand. Will was still sleepy and tried to get himself oriented. They had spent the last couple of days hanging out together and getting briefed by their superiors about what to expect from the war in general. The leaders went into great detail about what was going on in and around what was going to be their new home in Pleiku. The intensity and stress would be ratcheted up after

Early Fall - 1967

today. No matter how well they were informed about what to expect, and no matter how well trained they were, every soldier who had ever been in a battle on the ground would tell you it was never quite like what you possibly could have imagined. You could picture it in your mind, yet it was nothing like experiencing the real thing. This was where the Oreo cookie was headed, into the thick of the battle. The central highlands of Vietnam. The jungle. The hills and mountains. The heat. The monsoons. The rice paddies. It was going to be a test for the body and the mind and the consensus among them was to focus on getting home alive. The battle must be fought and you had to kill the enemy before he killed you. It was repeated over and over. Simple. It was a simple thing to do; pull the trigger. Kill the enemy.

Tommy walked up to Will who sat on the edge of his bed.

"Come on, Dempsey. This ain't Detroit where you can sleep all day and do nothing. Get dressed. Breakfast is waiting."

"Oh fuck off, Franklin. I'm coming."

Will stood up, looked around and realized he better pick up the pace. The activity in the barracks was hectic. He rubbed the back of his neck and wondered what all the excitement was about. He repeated the question to himself that he had asked a couple of minutes before, "Can't the war wait?"

"OK," he told himself begrudgingly, "let's get moving." Brian and Tommy were ready to go and sat on their beds looking at Will, waiting for him to get his act together. They were not going to breakfast without him. He was part of the team. The Oreo team.

"Come on, Dempsey. Let's go," Tommy gave his own orders.

"All right, all right. I'm ready," Will said, still trying to get his bearings and not quite as enthusiastic as his buddies. "Today's the day, eh?" he asked whoever might be listening.

"Yeah, today's the day, Dempsey. Try to contain your excitement," Brian said with a slight hint of sarcasm. "Pleiku is waiting."

PSYCHED UP AND ready for battle, Tommy still didn't quite understand it all, but he had been programmed. Programmed to do the right thing. As far as he knew he was doing it for a good cause. Yet the enemy must think the same thing or they wouldn't be fighting each other. From the plane, the jungle looked tranquil and lush. It didn't look like much was going on down there. All the soldiers had this same thought when they first flew into this country. From a distance all the landscapes looked serene. The mountains, the jungle, the deserts and oceans. It wasn't until they got on the ground that they came to realize this wasn't such a tranquil place after all.

Tommy, Will and Brian didn't do much talking to each other on the flight to their final destination. Nobody did. They spent most of the time in deep thought about friends and family back home. Sisters, brothers, parents, girlfriends. It was a time to reflect as the current reality continued to beg the question, "Who's going to survive and who isn't?" Not surviving was something no one was willing to discuss.

We'll all go home alive. One year of this and we'll all be back in our home towns and cities laughing and doing things with our families and friends. Going on picnics and to the state fairs. Going to the lake. Family reunions. High school reunions. Sitting on the front porch telling war stories and passing the time away. We'll all go home alive.

Brian couldn't stand the quietness on the plane. He was tired of listening to the hum of the engines. Sitting in the seat in front of Tommy and Will he turned around to address them.

"Hey Franklin, Dempsey, why is it so quiet? It's freaking me out? Somebody say something."

Tommy looked at Will and they in turn looked at Brian and smiled.

"What's there to say, man?" Tommy asked.

"Anything," Brian replied. "Somebody start up a conversation. Too much thinking isn't good for you. It's not healthy."

"Well, you pick a subject and I'll discuss it with you, Dodd. Any subject. If you want to talk, I'll talk," Tommy said frankly and seriously.

The silence of the soldiers on the plane didn't bother Tommy. It was just a mood they were all in and no big deal. But it bothered Brian.

"Do you believe in God, Franklin?" Brian asked Tommy.

"Aw Jesus, man. Pick another subject," Tommy joked. "When I said pick a subject, I didn't mean that subject."

"Hey, Dodd. How about we talk sports?" Will interrupted. He didn't want to talk about the subject Brian had chosen either.

"Hey, Franklin said, 'Choose a subject,' and I did," Brian said, indifferent to what his two comrades thought. "So tell me, Franklin, do you believe in God?"

Tommy sensed Brian might have a case of the nerves and needed to talk.

"I don't know, Dodd. Why should I?"

The plane suddenly hit turbulence as if on cue.

"See, Franklin, that's why. You should have said yes. Now you've upset Him."

"Relax, Dodd. What makes you think God is a he anyway?" Will said, figuring he might as well get involved in the conversation if Brian was going to persist.

"OK then, whatever," Brian continued. "You've made her mad then. Ya gotta believe, man. I believe. I believe in God. He'll look ... or she'll look after us when we're taking on the enemy."

"You really think God takes sides, Dodd?" Tommy asked as the plane hit another bump.

"Yeah, man," Brian responded, proud now that he had struck up a friendly debate. "God will always take America's side. You can believe that. We trust in God and God puts his trust in us and the American way."

"Shit, Dodd, are you fuckin' crazy? What part of Cincinnati did you grow up in?" Will wanted to know. "I grew up on the mean streets of Detroit, man. Went to church every Sunday with my parents. Listened to the gospel, sang the gospel, prayed before dinner every night. Thanked the Lord for this, thanked the Lord for that and guess what?" Will waited for a couple of seconds before continuing the debate and looked at Brian then at Tommy. They looked back at him waiting for an answer. "The fuckin' church I went to as a kid got burnt down last July in the riots. Was that God's work, Private Dodd?"

Will waited to see if he got a response from either one of his two buddies.

"Well, if it was, then God's got a funny way of conducting business," Will carried on. "I'm no 'Onward Christian Soldier' here, pal. I'm not going to rely on some God to save my black ass in this fuckin' war. I can take care of my own shit."

Will had his say and although he stated his feelings truthfully, down deep inside he hoped he hadn't offended his comrades, Tommy and especially Brian.

If people wanted to believe in a God, that was their business and Will respected that. But he had a different view of the world now as a young adult and had his own reasons for believing what he did. He didn't give his spirituality much thought and gave reality a lot of thought. What was going on in his life right now was the reality of being in a war in a faraway land and the thought of a God protecting him or favoring him didn't enter into the equation. He knew in the upcoming days and weeks as a member of the infantry how he was going to react to the unavoidable truth about facing the enemy. He'd been told it enough times already, kill or be killed. This was war and if God didn't want wars then he or she wouldn't allow for them to happen. In fact, as far as Will was concerned, if there were a God, he or she wouldn't allow a lot of the things going on in the world to happen.

No, he wasn't going to rely on prayer and a hope that a God liked him enough to get him through this war. He was not going to think for a second that a God would favor him over one of his buddies. He would rely on his training and instincts and on the comrades he trusted more than anyone or anything. His Christian upbringing had left him with more questions than answers. Will's parents still went to church and so did his siblings. That was all fine and dandy, religion no longer filled his soul spiritually. It didn't work for him. He was content in his own skin and not afraid of the consequences of being a non-believer. It wasn't going to be some God who decided if he went back home dead or alive. It was going to be fate.

He didn't join up to fight a war and preserve the American way, he joined up because he wanted to take advantage of the G.I. Bill that would help pay for his college education when he got out of the service. Being from a working class family there never was much money available to further his education when he graduated from high school. He had thought long and hard about it and he wanted to study communications and perhaps become a sportscaster, a psychologist or a teacher, especially a teacher. That was going to be in his future and part of the grand plan. But for now, the goal was all about survival and making sure he and his buddies all got out of this war alive, intact and breathing. God or no God.

The plane ride smoothed out as they started to descend on their approach to Pleiku.

"Sorry about your church getting burnt down, Dempsey," Tommy offered apologetically. "Why would anyone want to burn down a church?"

"It just got in the way of the rest of the fires that were burning down the city," Will said solemnly. "I don't think anyone did it on purpose, Franklin. Shit happens. I don't know. Ask God."

Everyone in the plane looked relieved that they had made it through the turbulence. If nerves were a little on edge before, the rough ride certainly didn't help matters. After hearing Will make his statement about what he believed and didn't believe, Brian was somewhat sorry he had broached the subject about a belief in God, but wouldn't let it go.

"Well for me, Brian Dodd, I know God acts in funny ways, but I do believe in him. Always have. Always will. To each their own, Dempsey. I respect that. You're cool, man. You're cool. I won't hold it against you and neither will God. We got your back."

Will gave his friend sitting in front of him a slap on the back.

"Hey, I appreciate that, Dodd. And if you and your God get me back home alive I'll take a trip down to Cincinnati and go to church with you. Right, Franklin? We'll both come down and go to church with you. You and your

Early Fall - 1967

God just get us back home alive, OK, Dodd? So the pressure is on, man. You and your God there, just get us home alive."

"Yeah, Dodd," Tommy chipped in. "Don't forget to say your prayers every night. We'll need 'em where we're going."

Tommy had more in common with Will's lack of belief in a God than he did with Brian's opposing view. Like Will, as a child Tommy had grown up going to church every Sunday with his family. But also like Will, the need to believe wasn't there anymore. There was no particular event or life-altering realization that had changed his way of thinking, it was simply growing up and not feeling a need for it anymore. He didn't think much about it one way or the other. Like Will's parents, his parents still went to church and worshipped, but it was no longer his cup of tea. Tommy was thankful for the way his parents had brought him up. He couldn't have asked for nicer ones. He had a great relationship with his mom and dad. They were loving and caring. They knew he had grown away from the church and religion, but they didn't love him any less. He was an adult now and if that's the path he had chosen, then so be it. He was their son and nothing could come between them, especially a belief or non-belief in a God. Tommy was who he was. He would always be their son no matter what happened in his life.

All three of these soldier's parents had kids because they wanted kids and the kids that they had were the joy of their lives. It was why they got up in the morning and went to work. It was why they joined in with all the school activities and sports events. It was why they went on picnics and to the beach. It was why they taught them how to ride bikes and drive cars. It was why they went fishing with them and made their lunches for school. Everything they did was for their kids. Kids made their life worth living. It didn't matter whether they grew up in a small town like Brenton or the ghettos of Detroit and Cincinnati, these three soldiers had loving parents and that would never change. But now their kids had gone off to war in a faraway land. What would happen to them? Would the sights and sounds of war change them? Would they come home alive? Would their prayers be answered?

Silence, just like when they were landing in Da Nang, had come back to the plane as the landing gear hit the Pleiku runway. Tommy looked around and wondered what everybody else was thinking. He had changed since joining up. Boot camp had forced him to reevaluate his feelings regarding life and death. As he studied the faces of the soldiers around him, he wished he could read their minds. Were some of them afraid of the future? Why did they join the Army? How come they joined the infantry? Did they volunteer or were they told that this was what they were going to do? Did any of it matter? They were here now. As a unit. Soldiers. Brothers. Warriors. Sons. Fathers. Uncles. All here for a common cause they'd been told. To fight and get home alive. To stop communism and spread democracy. To preserve the American way of life. To carry on the proud history of the American fighting soldier. The moment of truth had come and as Tommy continued to look around the plane, the hard reality of it all grabbed his attention ... again. Some of them would go home alive and some of them would not.

It was early afternoon and it was the humidity that first caught everyone's attention when they got off the plane. Pleiku was at a higher elevation than Da Nang, but it was not any cooler. The Oreo cookie got off and stood on the steel grid tarmac while taking in the view. They had noticed from the air on their approach there wasn't much of a jungle here. It was flat, sparsely treed with tall grass. Nowhere to hide. Everything was out in the open. The base itself was typical enough, but the landscape surprised them. They had been under the impression all of Vietnam was a thick jungle. Not here. In the surrounding areas, yes, but here at their new home it was flat and grassy except for a lone plateau off in the distance that was referred to as Kite Mountain. This was Camp Brotherhood and not many of the new arrivals had even heard of it before this morning.

Will wiped some sweat off of his brow with his forearm.

"I hope they have a big swimming pool filled with cold water," he said as he and his two buddies began to follow the others off the tarmac.

"I just hope they have cold beer," Tommy added looking around, "this place is bigger than I thought."

"Home sweet home," Brian added after assessing the new base.

"Where are we headed?" Tommy wanted to know.

"Somebody said we're headed over to the Social Club for orientation," Will replied.

"Social Club?" Brian wondered. "It better be air conditioned is all I can say."

"Yeah well, Brian," Tommy said, "if God loves us, it'll be air conditioned. God does love us, right Brian?" Tommy had to get in one last ribbing.

"Let it go, Franklin. Let it go. We'll find out who God likes and doesn't like in due time," Will responded as he focused on the buildings straight ahead.

The troops, replacements as they were called, were being led through the base by a resident officer. Sure enough, they came to a building a little bigger than an average-sized community center with a sign over the front door that said, of all things, "Social Club."

"Well, I'll be damned!" Will exclaimed. "What we have here is a Social

Club! Doesn't that beat all?"

Walking up the half dozen steps to a porch with an overhang, the soldiers began to file in.

"Where are the girls? Where's the beer. Tell 'em Private Franklin's here!" Tommy chimed as he walked through the front door.

There was more chatter now between the soldiers and generally they were feeling more relaxed, now that they were back on the ground. Once inside, the building appeared to be bigger than it had from the outside. It was a lot cooler inside too, not air conditioned, but it would do.

"This might work, hey boys?" Will asked his two buddies.

"Yep. If you can't find me, check the Social Club. That's where I'll be," Brian said, feeling better about his introduction to Camp Brotherhood.

The soldiers were ordered to fall in. A Captain Palmer stood in front with a couple of other commanding officers. It was time for the replacements' orientation. Captain Palmer, tall and slender, in his mid-forties and a lifer, began his speech. Tommy, Will, Brian and the others took it all in. They were told some things they were already aware of and some things they were not. One thing that stuck in their minds was that this was a "hot zone" and they'd see plenty of action.

"The enemy comes and goes mostly at night, but the fact of the matter is you'll never know when they're coming. This is a different war. Not a conventional one. It's hard to tell who the enemy is. They don't wear uniforms and they can be male or female of any age. They're sneaky and will use any means to kill. If you engage them in battle, that's a good thing, at least you will know who you're fighting. And they have bodies, lots of bodies. They never run out of reinforcements."

They were also told by Captain Palmer that the Americans were winning the war and it would be won all in due time. The enemy was persistent, but it was up against the best trained military in the world and the United States had never lost a war. Tommy, Will, Brian and the others listened intently. Some agreed with what the Captain was saying and others had their doubts. But agree or disagree, they were here now and when the time came they'd be ready. The superior officer continued to talk about the layout of the camp and the dos and don'ts.

"You'll settle in and it won't take long. This is a great camp. We're family here and well looked after."

He went on to say how some of them would head out tomorrow and possibly see the action they had enlisted for and hopefully were looking forward to. He wanted them fired up. It was time to engage the enemy.

CAROLYN STOOD BEHIND the family car, parked in front of her parents' house, and helped her dad load her suitcases and other belongings into the trunk. She was preparing to return for her sophomore year at university. Last year Tommy had been here to see her off. Now, one year later, things had changed dramatically and her good friend was thousands of miles away fighting a war.

"It's a good thing we have a big trunk, hey Carolyn," her father said.

Carolyn had been going through the motions of getting herself ready to leave for university and was daydreaming when her father spoke to her.

"Yeah, it sure is, Dad."

Her father had noticed her mood.

"You OK? You've been kind of quiet. Are you nervous? You shouldn't be."

Mr. Russell realized he had to arrange things differently in the trunk in order to get the last suitcase in.

"No, I'm fine. I'm as excited about university as I was this time last year. But I've been thinking about Tommy. If I have my dates right, he's either getting to Vietnam today or maybe he's been there a couple of days. I don't know. I'll have to recheck my calendar. I'm worried about him, that's all."

Mr. Russell managed to get the last suitcase in.

"There. That should do it."

He turned to his daughter and put his hands on her shoulders. He was concerned for her friend Tommy as well and selfishly was happy he had a daughter going off to university and not a son going off to war.

"Look, dear. You have a right to worry. Tommy and all the soldiers over there are doing a very courageous thing," Mr. Russell spoke softly. "We'll pray that he gets home safe and sound. But please, please, don't let him being over there distract you from your own mission here at home. Tommy wouldn't want that. It's a natural thing for all of us to worry about him, but your life here has to go on and in a year he'll be back. You concentrate on your studies. That's what Tommy would want."

The words Carolyn heard coming from her father were true, but she couldn't help herself. It had been hard ever since Tommy joined the Army. Before he left, when they were spending lots of time together, she always put on a happy face to please him. She hadn't wanted him to know what she was really thinking and how she worried about him. She wished he had gone to university, gotten a student deferment and avoided the war. Was that being selfish? Sometimes it got confusing and after the original shock of what he had done wore off, she always let on that she supported his decision. It was important to her that he feel what he was doing was the right thing and it was also important to him that she feel the same way. Her dad was right, she was looking forward to her second year of university, but it was difficult to get Tommy off her mind.

"You're right, Dad. I promise. I'll concentrate on my studies and Tommy will be fine. Should I go in and tell Mom we're ready to go?"

"Yep, I think we're all set," Mr. Russell said, closing the trunk. "I don't need anything else, so I'll wait for you two here. Just let me know if it's going to be a few minutes."

"Sure thing, Dad."

Carolyn turned and headed back into the house as her father watched. He and his wife had only the one child and they wanted the best for her. Especially an education. It meant so much to them as parents. They had always stressed the importance of an education and now the time had come once again to drive her back to school. Their baby was going back for her sophomore year. It was only a two-hour trip, but it might as well be a two-day trip. Her parents missed her that much. Carolyn could come home on the weekends if she desired or it was easy enough for her parents to go there for a visit. Both Mr. and Mrs. Russell were pleased that their daughter had chosen somewhere relatively close to attend school. Having her go somewhere far away would have been mildly upsetting. No, this was good for everyone. Carolyn was interested in Marine Biology and the school she attended had an excellent program in that field. If you lived in Michigan, you were never too far from a body of water, lake or river, big or small and as a young person Carolyn had developed a keen interest in what lay beneath the surface of the water and how life existed in such an environment. She was also interested in what lay beneath the surface of people so she had decided to take a minor in human psychology. Mr. Russell was leaning against his car thinking about his daughter's future when the two women of his life walked out the front door. He was a lucky man and knew it.

"OK, OK, we're coming, we're coming. Hold your horses!" Mrs. Russell said with all the excitement a mother could have on the day she was taking her daughter back for her second year of university life.

Mrs. Russell got to the car and opened the back door for Carolyn as her father walked around and got in the driver's door.

"In ya go."

Her mom was acting like it was kindergarten all over again. This was exactly how she had behaved last year. That was OK. It was the same emotions, only now she was older. They were all a little older. Mrs. Russell's actions tickled Carolyn and she smiled at the fact her mom was feeling a little giddy. Mrs. Russell got in the front seat and looked over at her husband.

"OK, what's the hold up? We're going to be late!"

Mr. Russell looked at his wife and said nothing. He put the gear shift into reverse and with his arm on the back of the seat, turned his head to look behind him. As he did he winked at Carolyn. He backed up, put the car in drive and headed down the driveway.

"I hope we haven't forgotten anything," Mrs. Russell said to the other two occupants of the vehicle.

"I hope so too, dear. We're not going to turn around now," her husband answered back, just kidding, as he looked in his rear view mirror and saw Carolyn staring out the window.

"Carolyn ... ? he said.

"Yes, Dad."

"When we get there, if you find out you've forgotten something, please don't worry. We'll bring it down next weekend. Just don't worry about it."

"Thanks, Dad. I appreciate that," Carolyn replied. "I think I have everything. Mom, you can always bring me down some of your baking like you did last year."

Mrs. Russell was flattered by the remark.

"I'll bring you down some of my world-famous chocolate chip cookies. How's that sound?"

"Sounds good, Mom. Bring down as many as you want. They'll get eaten I'm sure. I hope my new roommate for this year likes chocolate. We'll get along just fine if she does."

"Oh, how can anyone not like chocolate, Carolyn? If she doesn't, you'll have to ask for another roommate," Mrs. Russell joked.

Carolyn laughed.

"I can hardly wait to meet her ... and I'm sure she'll like chocolate."

Who doesn't? No one could possibly resist my mom's chocolate chip cookies!

Mr. Russell reached the end of the driveway and turned left onto the dirt road that would take them onto the two-lane paved secondary road that would then take them to the highway that put them on their way to their daughter's home for the fall, winter and spring. Carolyn looked out at the scenery. One farm after the other. One orchard after the other. Most of the foliage was still green, but there was a hint in some of the colors passing by that autumn was on its way. Her thoughts were melancholy. She knew very well she was only going to be a two-hour drive away from her parents, but it might as well be the other side of the planet. She was leaving where she grew up and it didn't matter how far away she was, she always missed Clear Lake.

No one spoke as her father pulled onto the road that would take them through town. When they reached the town of Clear Lake, memories came back to Carolyn in a flood as they always did. She remembered being young, very young, perhaps six or seven and going to the drug store with her dad for a milk shake. Going to the hardware store with him and being introduced to things she didn't even know existed. On Saturdays, she would go grocery shopping and to the fresh fruit and vegetable stand just outside of town with her mom. She recalled going to the F.W. Woolworth's store for material and fabric so her mom could make her a new dress or a costume for the school play. She remembered going to the pizza place for Friday night pizza when she became a teenager. There were many wonderful memories that put a big smile on her face. It was a great place to grow up and now it was good-bye until the next time she came home.

As they drove out of town she saw the church they attended every Sunday. Then she caught a glimpse of the elementary school she had gone to that was about a block off the highway. "It'll all be here when I get back," she told herself. "It's not going anywhere. It'll always be here." The whole town would be here. She would be back for a visit in a couple of months, but at this moment, as last year, it felt like she was leaving forever.

I'm growing up and my life is changing so fast! My second year of university already! Where did the time go?

Now they were driving by Tippy's. Carolyn knew it was coming. How many hours had she spent there the last few years? How many trips had she made there to be with her friends and hang out? Her smile got broader. Those were good times. The best of times. She could see all their faces now. It wasn't that long ago on one hand, but seemed like forever since the gang used to hang out there. It was where she and Tommy would make a bee line to whenever they had a chance. As they drove by she turned her head to look out the rear window at Tippy's one more time. As she turned back around, it was the thought of Tommy she couldn't get out of her mind ... again.

What was he doing at this very moment? How long was it going to take for him to send her his address so she could write back? How was he being treated? How would the food be? Who were his new buddies? Where were they from? Had he seen any action yet? All these thoughts suddenly consumed her. She wondered if he was thinking of her. Would he even have time? In a few minutes they would be driving through Brenton and Carolyn knew she would experience the same emotions again and more treasured memories would come back to her.

"You're awfully quiet back there," Mr. Russell voiced an observation he had been making for the last mile or so.

"Sorry, Dad. I was enjoying the scenery and thinking what a great place this is to have grown up in. I've been so lucky!"

Mr. Russell kept peeking in his rear view mirror at his daughter.

"Yeah, I think we've all been lucky to live here and I'm thinking I just might stay."

That got a chuckle out of the two females in the car.

"Oh, you think you just might stay, huh? Well, lucky for us!" Mrs. Russell kidded her husband.

"Yeah, I think I will. That is if you don't mind, Mrs. Russell," Mr. Russell said reaching over to pat his wife's thigh.

Carolyn's mom turned around in the front seat to face her daughter.

"What do you think, honey? Should we let him stick around?"

Carolyn smiled at her mom and didn't hesitate to join in on the fun.

"I think we should negotiate, Mom. What's in it for us?"

"Don't forget who's driving here," Mr. Russell warned. "I'll make ya walk if you don't say the right thing."

"OK, Dad. You can stay. Don't pout."

Carolyn always thought it was great fun picking on her dad. They had a special relationship. She didn't recall him ever yelling or cursing or arguing with anybody. He was always loving, caring and respectful, and they still liked to joke around with each other. Mr. Russell knew he was outnumbered in his household, but he loved every second of it when he was getting "picked on." Carolyn remembered the atmosphere when she was growing up as always being upbeat and positive. Her parents both had a great sense of humor and the one-liners, to this day, were always flying. There was constant laughter in their house when she was a child just like in the Franklin home. Just as she felt blessed to have grown up in such a wonderful part of the world, she also felt incredibly lucky to have the parents she did. They were her parents and not only were they very special, but just as importantly, they were her good friends.

"I'm not pouting," Mr. Russell responded to Carolyn. "All I'm saying is we have a two-hour drive ahead of us and you two better be nice."

"You're pouting, dear," Mrs. Russell joyfully insisted. "Please don't pout. If you're going to pout, then it might be a good idea if Carolyn and I walk. I can't do two hours of your pouting."

"OK, I won't pout. But only because this is a very special day. I'll save all my pouting for when we get back home and I realize our daughter isn't around because she's back at university. That's when the real pouting will start."

"That's OK, dear. I'll pout with you. It's never the same when Carolyn isn't around," Carolyn's mom said and again turned and smiled at her daughter.

"OK, you two. That's enough. Knock it off. I know you love being empty nesters and enjoy all the peace and quiet. Isn't it nice to have the freedom to do anything you want?" Carolyn inquired like a protective daughter. "I'm never away for too long and I'll be back in a couple of months for Thanksgiving."

"And we'll come down the odd weekend like we usually do, right?" Mr. Russell asked, already knowing the answer.

"Yes," Carolyn said, "You can always come down for a visit. Of course you can. I'll be happy to see you."

The kidding and conversation continued between the three for the whole trip. Rarely were any of them at a loss for words. It was a family that felt comfortable together. But whenever there was a break in the conversation, Carolyn looked out the car window, watched the world go by and thought about the life she had lived and also about a friend who had gone off to fight a war on the other side of the planet. She was here and he was there and their lives for now were going their separate ways.

The Card Game

TOMMY, WILL, BRIAN and another soldier, Paul Duncan, played cards in the shade of the local foliage. It was their second day at Camp Brotherhood and not much was happening except for more info sessions that lasted for most of the day. The four soldiers relaxed and enjoyed their break from all the lecturing they had heard that morning. They had found an old wood crate that was perfect for a card table and some five gallon buckets from behind the kitchen that, when turned upside down, made great seats. In the first twenty-four hours since they had arrived, the lessons they had learned and would continue to learn, came quickly and were intense. One thing they found out was that, when allowed, wear as little of your uniform as possible. The heat and humidity were a bit much and nothing like any of them had ever experienced before. All four sat around their makeshift card table bare-chested with bandanas wrapped around their heads to soak up the sweat. All except for Paul who, for whatever reason, wore a helmet. Will shuffled the deck of cards and prepared to deal.

"Shit, man. I can barely hold onto these things," Will said as the perspiration on his hands made the cards slippery to deal. "Any of you guys heard when winter arrives here and things start to cool off?" Will asked his card-playing friends, looking at all three and waiting for a response.

"They don't get much of a winter here, Dempsey," Paul said dryly. Corporal Duncan had been at Camp Brotherhood for six months. "This is pretty much it, man."

"That's a shame," Will said, still dealing the cards. "Having grown up in Detroit, I never thought I'd be wishing for some cooler weather, but it would be great if the temperature here dropped below a hundred. Shit! I thought I knew what hot was, but I guess not."

Will finished his deal and the soldiers picked up their cards and had a look.

"What's it like out there on the battlefield, Duncan? You've been here for a while. Does it get messy?" Brian asked Paul.

Paul didn't say anything as he studied his cards and acted like he didn't hear Brian's question. He started the hand off by laying down a card and then spoke.

"Yeah, it can get messy. You guys are going to find out soon enough. I'll give you a word of advice; don't always rely on your training. If you wanna

The Card Game

stay alive out there, sometimes you have to go with your instincts. There won't be much time to think about what you've been taught when you're in the thick of it. Ya gotta react, man. Just keep pulling the trigger." Paul's card playing audience sat and thought about what the corporal had said. "Your play, Dempsey," Paul said to Will.

"I'm thinking man, I'm thinking," Will said as he studied his cards, then laid one down.

Paul took out a cigarette from a pack lying on the top of the crate.

"Anyone else here smoke?" he asked, offering the cigarette pack around.

None of the other three participants smoked and declined his offer. Paul lit up and looked at Tommy who was eying the cards in his hand. Tommy looked back at Paul, not sure if he liked this new guy he had just met this morning.

"You ever been scared in the thick of the battle, Duncan?" Tommy asked.

"Fuck yeah, man," the Corporal responded as if it were a stupid question. "If you ain't scared you ain't human. That's what I'm saying, man. You'll find out when the bullets start flying. You'll react out of fear. Training helps, but it's going to be your will to stay alive that makes ya do what ya gotta do. You know what they say in war, 'It's either you or them.'"

Tommy played his card and his playing partner, Will, wasn't impressed.

"That ain't going to help me," Will said to his partner. "Think about it before you play, hey Franklin."

Tommy had realized as soon as he played his card it was a bad move and it was going to help Paul and Brian, who had teamed up.

"God damn it! Sorry about that, Dempsey. That was a fuckin' bozo move," a frustrated Tommy scowled.

Paul took note of Tommy's foolish play and couldn't resist making the analogy of how a simple card game could be like being in a war zone.

"Hey, Private Franklin. You gotta be a little sharper than that, man. You're in Vietnam now and it doesn't matter if it's a card game, being attacked by the enemy or whatever. A bozo move like that can get you or someone else killed. Whatever you're doing in this country, until you get back home, don't fuck up!"

"Yeah, yeah," Tommy was short in his reply.

He felt stupid, but he wasn't in the mood for a talking to. He knew he'd be on his toes when it came time to engage the enemy. This was just a card game and not the same as being in battle. Yet Paul made a good point and Tommy felt confident that he would be a good warrior when duty called.

"I know, I know," Tommy continued. "Don't fuck up. Dempsey, I owe ya one."

"It's alright, Franklin. Don't worry about it. Game's not over yet," Will said trying to be somewhat consoling.

Corporal Paul Duncan didn't have a lot of people skills before he came to fight this war in Vietnam and being here had only hardened him and made him even more cynical. He had a tendency to rub people the wrong way, but managed to get a little respect from the soldiers in his presence because he had been in the heat of battle and he knew what could happen. His personality was, unfortunately, not a very likeable one. He was a badass loner before he came to this place and that hadn't changed despite the fact he had obliged when asked by the Oreo cookie if he would like to play cards. He had resigned himself to the notion that he was not well liked. He made casual friendships whenever he felt like he could take advantage of them and it would always be on his terms. Close friends, he didn't really need. He wasn't very popular with his comrades but, up to this point, he had somehow managed to survive. For the card game, the Oreo cookie needed a fourth player and this guy just happened to be available. They could tell as they played that Paul wasn't thrilled with being in Vietnam. But you don't judge soldiers by their card-playing disposition or ability. You judge them on how courageously they fight in the trenches. Paul Duncan wasn't all that friendly, but quite possibly he could be a good fighter and someone you wanted at your side when the enemy struck. He just might be the one to save your life, you never knew in a war who was going to pull through in the crunch. It could be the idiot you're playing cards with or some soft-spoken shy kid from the Deep South.

The conversation turned to the brutality of war and the effect it had on those who thought they were prepared for it and then suddenly had to face the heat.

"You ever kill anyone, Duncan?" Tommy's curious mind wanted to know.

"What the fuck do you think, man?" Paul fired back.

Tommy stared at Paul waiting for more of an answer as the corporal eyed his cards. Tommy wondered if this guy, who thought he was so tough, was putting on an act, or was really a jerk who had been made contentious by the war.

"It's OK man. Relax," Tommy said. "You do what you got to do to stay alive, right?"

Paul looked Tommy in the eye.

"That's right, Franklin, and right now I'm playing cards to stay alive. It helps take my mind off things."

Will looked at Brian and raised his eyebrows wondering where the conversation would go next.

"That's OK, Duncan. You do what you gotta do to keep it together. I'm

The Card Game

sure after we've been here six months like you've been, we'll all be a little ornery," Tommy retorted, not knowing if Paul would react once more. He really didn't care.

"Your play, Duncan," Will said in a diplomatic tone, trying to keep the game going and hopefully lighten things up.

"Yeah, I know it's my play. I'm thinking," Paul studied his cards. Finally he laid one down. "There, you guys happy now?"

"Yeah, we're happy," Will said and laid down a card immediately following Paul's play.

"Man, you're fast, Dempsey. You must have been waiting to play that one, hey?" Brian said, impressed.

The Oreo cookie kept an eye on Paul. He had seemed nice enough when they asked him to play cards, but now their opinions had changed. He was a bit awkward to deal with, but he was also still one of them, a fighting soldier, and Tommy seemed to push the wrong buttons.

"Doesn't matter if you've ever killed anyone, Duncan. We're all infantry here and I'm sure we'll be doing whatever it is we have to do to stay alive," Tommy spoke like a veteran of the battlefield.

Paul looked up from the card table to Tommy and stared at him coldly.

"Yeah, you'll do what ya have to do to stay alive, Franklin. You're going to find that out."

Will looked at Tommy, then Paul and decided it might be time for a change of topic.

"How's your girl back home, Franklin?" Will asked.

The soldiers continued to play their cards.

"She's good," Tommy said proudly. "She's in her second year of university and that reminds me, I gotta write her a letter today. I promised her I would write when I found out what was going on. She'll be pissed off if I don't? How about you, Dempsey? How's your woman?"

"Excellent. Same one I've had since we were in ninth grade. She has a good job in a drug store and man, I miss her. I can't wait to see her again," Will said, laying down a card.

"You think she'll be there waiting for you?" Paul sarcastically asked Will.

Will wasn't sure how to take the question and now joined the others in thinking Paul just might be a smart ass. Will decided not to bite and didn't get visibly upset. They were having fun playing cards, leave it at that. Paul was difficult to like and Will, like Tommy and Brian, wasn't really enjoying Paul's company.

"Yeah, she'll be waiting, Duncan. That won't be a problem. And you,

Duncan? You got a girl back home?" Will asked, thinking Paul might relax if he talked about himself.

"I've never tied myself down to one girl, man. I've got a few waiting for me when I get back home," Paul boasted "Life's short. Why would anyone want only one gal in their life? Shit man."

Now it was unanimous. The Oreo cookie wouldn't be inviting this guy to play cards with them again. They had given him the benefit of the doubt until now but, no doubt, he was a jerk. Did war make him this way? Maybe. Or maybe this was who he was. Maybe he felt like he had to impress people. Unfortunately, he was not very good at it because nobody was impressed.

"Man, only a fool would want more than one woman in his life, Duncan," Brian figured he might as well get in on the discussion and contribute his two cents worth. "I'm a one-woman man 'cause that's all I can handle. She keeps me hopping, man. One's enough, thank you. Especially if you have a good one."

Paul really didn't care what anyone else thought. He'd had a differing opinion on just about everything that had been discussed and was not afraid to offer it up.

"To each their own, Dodd," Paul said and went back to not making eye contact. "Lots of fish in the sea. That's the way I look at it and I'll be enjoying them all when I get back stateside. You betcha!"

Tommy was thinking this guy must practice being an idiot.

These are the guys I have to fight with? He sounds like he's so full of bull shit. Talk is cheap.

Tommy wondered what it would be like in a firefight with this stranger sitting next to him. He had thought more highly of Paul a few minutes before, but now he didn't want anything to do with him. Yet, as he had thought a few minutes before, maybe he was a good fighter and would be the guy you wanted next to you when all hell broke loose. But then again … .

"You know, Duncan, I think you're full of shit," Tommy decided to take him on, but still hoped to keep "the guy talk" civilized. "I bet you got a woman back home you care about more than the other fish in the sea. Come on! Don't fuckin' bull shit us, man. What's her name, Duncan?"

The four finished the hand they were playing and Paul picked up the cards and started shuffling.

"Her name's 'fuck you.' I'm not like you fools. I play the field, man, and the women love it."

Paul started to deal as Will, Tommy and Brian found some pathetic humor in Paul's talk and actions. This guy was messed up, that's all. He had short circuited his brain at some point in his life. When did that happen? When Paul was a child? After he joined the service? Or did it happen after he went into battle and started killing? Surely he hadn't always been this way. Who knew? He might be likeable if he tried, but then again maybe not, and apparently he didn't feel like trying. He was pitiful, yet intriguing. Will had seen his kind before, and Paul was only fooling himself if he thought he was impressing someone who had grown up on the mean streets of Detroit.

"Where'd you say you were from, Duncan?" Will asked.

"I didn't," Paul replied.

"You are from planet Earth, right?" Will asked cynically.

Paul ignored Will and the four begin playing another hand.

"He's got to be from planet Earth in order to be in the United States Army, Will," Tommy spoke as if Paul were invisible. "I don't think we have any aliens in the military do we?"

Paul wasn't invisible and stood his ground.

"If they let guys like you in then it looks like they'll let anybody in, including aliens. I sure thought the Army had higher standards, but looking at you guys, I guess not."

Paul Duncan got a chuckle from the other players. His three card mates were taking him with a grain of salt now and anything he said couldn't possibly be taken seriously. He was a soldier with issues and someone who obviously had a history. But he remained with them as the game continued, as did the discussion when Brian weighed in with a smile and a question for Paul.

"Are you putting us on, Duncan, or are you really messed up?"

Paul lit another cigarette and examined his cards. He thought about Brian's comment for a while before answering.

"I'm fuckin' messed up, man. I was normal when I got here, but now I'm just fucking messed up."

"You haven't been smoking that funny tobacco I've heard about have you, Duncan?" Will asked.

"No, man. I stay away from that shit," Paul claimed. "... and you guys best stay away from it to if ya want to keep your sanity. I just smoke the good old nicotine, it's better for you."

Will had heard about the potent marijuana some servicemen in Vietnam indulged in, but he had no interest. He had seen what drugs had done to the souls in the neighborhoods back in Detroit. He had decided long ago he would stay away from that scene. Drugs had destroyed more than one friendship of his and he had seen it take down some of the best of his neighbors. He had watched them deteriorate as human beings and end up in jail or dead. The peer pressure was tough at times, but the one thing he didn't ever want to do was hurt his parents and he knew if he got involved in drugs and they found out, it would devastate them. He didn't know or even care why Paul didn't take drugs.

And then there was Tommy.

"What's funny tobacco?" Tommy asked.

Will and Brian looked at each other and couldn't believe what they had just heard. *Brenton, Michigan couldn't be that isolated from the rest of the world, could it? Tommy didn't really ask that question, did he?* Brian and Will checked out Paul to see his reaction, but Paul had no expression and acted like he didn't even hear Tommy's words.

"Did you just ask, 'What is funny tobacco?'" Brian asked, giving Tommy a look of bewilderment.

Tommy looked at Brian, then Will and wondered why they're looking at him a little dumbfounded.

"That's what I asked. I don't smoke, man. What is it?"

"It's fucking weed, man. Dope. Marijuana. Fuck man! Are you kidding me?" Paul snarled and shared Will and Brian's mild shock.

Tommy laughed at himself. It hadn't clicked when he heard "funny tobacco."

"Oh, fuck me! Yeah, yeah, yeah. I know what marijuana is. Shit! I can't believe I didn't clue in to that."

"You had us worried there for a minute, Franklin. I was beginning to wonder about you," Brian said reaching over and giving Tommy a friendly shove. "What the hell do they do up there in Brenton for fun, Franklin?"

Tommy was a little embarrassed. He wasn't that naïve about drugs even though it certainly wasn't prevalent in the part of the world where he grew up. He never had smoked marijuana and he didn't know if any of his friends ever had. It wasn't around as far as he knew and neither he nor any in the group he hung out with ever pursued it. It never crossed his mind and if it were available here in Vietnam, he'd be damned if he would try it. Like Will, he had no interest in it.

"Well, we drink beer, Dodd. Lots of beer," Tommy boasted answering Brian's question.

"Beer's bad for ya too. Drugs and alcohol, bad stuff, man," Paul said wryly.

"And I suppose those things you're smoking there are good for ya, Duncan?" Will said.

"Yeah, they're bad for ya. Gotta have at least one vice, though," Paul proclaimed. "What would life be without at least one vice?"

The Card Game

"Do your parents smoke?" Tommy asked.

"Yeah, they smoke," Paul replied, "and so do my sister and my two brothers. It runs in the family. Got a problem with that, Franklin?" Paul asked Tommy, sounding like the smart ass jerk that he was.

"No, I've got no problem with it, Duncan. It's nice that your whole family smokes. It's something you can pass down to your kids and your nieces and nephews. It's good for the economy."

Will and Brian snickered over Tommy's comment. Will looked at his watch and noticed it would be time for another briefing soon.

"Let's wrap this one up, guys. It's almost time to get back to the Social Club for some more pep talk."

Will dealt the cards for one last hand. Brian picked his up, looked at them and then looked at Paul.

"Hey, Duncan. You believe in God?"

Tommy and Will looked at each other. Gees, here we go again with the God talk. Brian hadn't let it go since they got off the plane in Da Nang. God this, God that. Brian obviously was relying on his God to get him through his time in this foreign land where there happened to be a raging war going on.

"Shit, Dodd. You've been yappin' about God since we got here," Tommy mildly complained. "What the fuck, man. God ain't gonna get us through this. Forget it, man. Give it up!" Tommy had made the point before, but decided to make it again.

"I'm just asking the man, Franklin. I like to know these things."

It was true. Brian was the religious one in this group and he was doing his own unofficial survey.

Will had to have his say about the matter before Paul could respond.

"So Dodd, who ya gonna save first out there when duty calls? You gonna ask someone who's been hit if they believe in God or not and if they don't, you move on to the next guy till you find someone who does? What the hell is that all about?"

The soldiers played their cards once and then twice around in silence before Brian spoke up again.

"No, man. That ain't how it works. We're all God's children. If ya don't believe, ya don't believe. But you are my brothers and I've got your back no matter what. That you can take to the bank."

Paul had been listening and figured it was his turn to check in on the subject.

"Hey, Dodd. I haven't been to church once in my life and I don't plan on ever going. Good for you if you believe in a God, but what about a God believing in you? If there were a God that believed in us, then he should show his fucking face. If I were you I'd be God damn tired of waiting for him to prove himself. It's a crock of shit, man. If God would just show his fucking face once then maybe I would get it. But until then, fuck it, man! Where is he?"

The heat and humidity had taken its toll. None of them had brought any water to drink and they were getting edgy.

"OK, forget it guys. I won't bring God up again. But he's watching us, man. He's watching us," Brian said, hoping to get in the last words on the subject that he felt so strongly about.

This didn't happen as Paul was also a man who felt like he had to have the final word. In fact, if someone wanted to talk about God, life and war, he was always more than happy to oblige.

"Dodd, let me give you some advice," Paul said beginning another mini-lecture. "You're going to find something out the first time you pull the trigger to kill another human being and you're going to find it out the first time another human being tries to kill you. Trust me, God ain't got anything to do with living or dying. He ain't got anything to do with life and death, man. You know why, Dodd?"

Paul had put the ball in Brian's court as Will and Tommy looked on and wondered where this was all going. Tommy and Will figured if Brian wanted to believe, then let it be, but Paul was calling him out.

"I give up, Duncan," Brian was defiant and stood his ground on a subject. "Why? Why doesn't God have anything to do with it, Duncan? Go ahead, you tell me."

The card game was over in more ways than one. Tommy and Will stood up. It was time to go. Brian and Paul stayed seated and stared at each other. Paul lit up yet another cigarette. If Brian wanted an answer, he'd give him one.

"Because, Dodd, God doesn't exist. You think he exists? Go ahead and think it. But when the time comes, man, and you get to witness what war is all about, let me tell ya something, no God that I know would allow this fuckin' bull shit to go on. You think about it." Paul stood up and started to leave, but had one more thing to say to Brian. "Say your prayers, Dodd. Say your prayers."

And that was that. This rude fellow that the Oreo cookie felt was an idiot, walked off. Brian picked up the cards, put them back into their little cardboard box and didn't say anything as Paul made his exit. Will watched Paul Duncan walk away and neither he nor Tommy said anything that might encourage him to think they should get together for another card game. For that matter, getting together again for any reason ever again just might be a mistake.

The Card Game

"Man, that's one ornery prick. Remind me, how'd we hook up with that guy?" Will asked himself and his two friends.

Brian stood up and put the cards in his trousers pocket. He thought about what had just gone down.

"I don't know, man. We needed a fourth player and he happened to be the chosen one, I guess. He's a bit too grumpy for my liking," Brian said understating the obvious fact. "Maybe next time we'll find someone else."

"Oh, come on, Brian. We don't want to hurt his feelings. He's probably not such a bad guy once you get to know him," Tommy said sarcastically.

"Yeah well, then count me out," Brian retorted.

"OK, guys. I guess we better go make ourselves look decent and head back over to the Social Club. It's getting time."

"I'm thirsty, man. I need a drink," Tommy said, taking off his bandana and wiping his forehead. "Let's get some water first."

The Oreo cookie headed off toward the barracks in search of something to quench their thirst and to freshen up before their next orientation. Each of them looked around at their surroundings as they walked, saying nothing. All three were thinking similar thoughts. They were in Vietnam now. A long, long way from home. Soon they would be doing what they were instructed to. The card game had ended, but now the war within and the war without ... had begun.

It had been said many times that this Vietnam War wasn't a conventional war. Tommy, Will and Brian had been told that repeatedly in their orientations and briefings. They had heard it on the news when they were stateside, before they even came to this place. In previous wars the United States had fought, the enemy wore a uniform and American soldiers knew who the enemy was. But this time the battles were being fought against an invisible enemy. They were male and female, adults and kids. It was hard to distinguish who was who. The Viet Cong would attack and then retreat. Then blend in with the civilians in the rural villages or the small towns. They fought hard. It wouldn't take long for the Oreo cookie to experience the bitter taste of the philosophy of kill or be killed, as Paul had said. It would change them. All three of them. War was a shitty deal. Killing others was what they had signed up for and they thought they had gone into this phase of their life with eyes wide open. They would find out, just like the ones before them, that the eyes can't believe and the mind can't comprehend what is happening when you're involved in this human invention called war.

Three Months In

"SO FRANKLIN, TELL me more about this girl of yours back home," Will encouraged Tommy as their platoon marched down a two-path trail that looked like a make-shift road through a rice field.

The Oreo cookie was three months into its tour of duty and was now battle tested. The soldiers of war marched, talked and sang together. Lived and died together. Slept under the same roof and same sky together. Ate together. Laughed together. These were the ground soldiers of war. Marching, marching, marching through a rice field in Southeast Asia and each brave and proud soldier had their own thoughts, their own feelings about this conflict. They were becoming, each at a different pace, hardened by the war and learning the value of human life. Some were more compassionate toward the locals than their comrades and those that were, learned that compassion worked to their advantage. A few were here because it was their patriotic duty to protect the American homeland, its freedom and way of life. As they marched they thought about their girlfriends and families and their pets, past and present. Some wondered why it wasn't their leaders, the politicians back home, that were here leading the charge. There were those who couldn't understand why politicians, some who hadn't even been in a war, were so eager to send other people's children into battle.

Some wars had to be fought, as strange as it seemed. These soldiers knew that. There is evil in the world. What would the planet be like if the Axis had won the First or Second World Wars? What if the enemies had conquered their country in World War II? Some wars had to be fought and Vietnam was where the United States had decided to take a stand against Communist aggression. These thoughts helped the soldiers believe in what they were doing and focus on the war they were fighting at this moment. They thought about what the day was going to bring and how many days before they'd be back home with their loved ones. Tommy's platoon marched on as family and friends back home worried about their loved ones in a faraway land. The platoon marched and hummed and sang and talked and thought.

Will's thoughts at the moment were a little different from those of the others he was walking with. As he waited for Tommy's reply, he thought about what he had seen when the riots hit his hometown. People were killing each other just for the sake of killing. Or maybe it was over a gold bracelet or a looted TV or something else of material value. It was disturbing. Will wondered to himself if the humans species knew how not to kill? Sad, this human race.

What is our problem?

"Same ol, same ol. I can't tell you much more than I already have, Dempsey. She's hitting the books at university and seems to be enjoying the college life. How's your gal doing?" Tommy responded to Will's question with one of his own.

Tommy was a few feet ahead of Will and Brian on the opposite path. He turned and looked at his two friends who had become his best buddies over the last three months. Will, Brian and Tommy were closer than ever now and never too far apart when they were out in the field.

Their platoon had left the base in helicopters early that morning to do a sweep of some nearby villages. It was a routine they were used to and they had to be on their best behavior to continue to reassure anyone they came across that the Americans were the good guys. It was an ongoing battle. It was about public relations. Today's plan was to bivouac overnight and walk back to their base tomorrow evening. Spending the night out under the stars was something nobody really enjoyed, but was happening more frequently. Sometimes they would march to where they were going and sometimes they would ride in vehicles or, like today, take helicopters and then march from their drop off points back to base. Sometimes things went well and sometimes all hell broke loose. The war never stopped.

"My gal is doing OK thank you very much, but I wish she would write more," Will said, looking out over an open flat land of rice paddies and sparse vegetation that told him if things happened to heat up here there would be no place to hide and the only thing they could do was hit the ground.

"Well, have you told her that?" Tommy suggested.

"Naw," Will replied. "In all fairness, man, she writes pretty regularly. You know what it's like getting mail. You're bummed out if you don't get something every day."

Will was right. For most soldiers, except for the Paul types who didn't care, mail was one of the things that kept them going, giving them some connection to back home and keeping them updated on family and friends. And pictures, especially pictures. Tommy had a picture of Carolyn, Buddy and him hanging on the wall above his bed back at the barracks and every time he looked at it, it made him smile. Each of the Oreo cookie members had pictures hanging up. Will had one of his girlfriend, Shirley, and him. Another one of his parents and him at high school graduation. Brian had one of his parents and him standing on the steps of their church in Cincinnati taken when he was home from boot camp. A proud soldier in uniform with a parent on either side.

"How often does your girl write, Franklin?" Will was curious.

Tommy thought for a moment, then answered Will's question.

"Every couple of weeks. She's busy studying. That's fine with me. My Mom writes as least once a week and keeps me informed about things in Brenton and my sister Kathy writes regularly. It's unusual if I don't get something every couple of days or so," Tommy said and understood that he was quite lucky in that regard.

The heat and humidity had caught everyone's attention this day. It was worse than usual and they all wondered how that could be. Just when you thought the humidity couldn't get any worse, it did. Of all the things they'd learned since they arrived in this country, it was to stay hydrated. Tommy grabbed his canteen off his belt and took a swig. He put his canteen back on his belt. The soldiers were alerted by their platoon leader, Lieutenant Peterson, about a group of villagers walking in their direction. They looked harmless, but were they "friend or foe?" There were children in the group so they were probably innocents.

"Yeah, that's about the same for me," Will said, carrying on the conversation. "My Mom writes and my brothers and sister write and they let me know what's going on in school and other stuff. Shit, man. Only nine months to go and this will all be over. Just get me back to Detroit, man."

Brian, who had moved out in front of Tommy and Will, was observing the world around him and hadn't said much until now.

The chatter continued between Tommy and Will with Brian finally joining in to say how he got mail all the time from his family, his pastor and members of his church. "That is one of the nice things about belonging to a church," Brian insisted. The congregation was a family that cared for each other. The pastor of Brian's church had requested that everyone drop a line to Private Dodd. And so the flock wrote and it made Brian feel good whenever he got their letters.

"I can ask my pastor to ask the people in my church to write you guys, if you wish," Brian proposed to Tommy and Will. "You'll get a lot more mail."

"No thanks, Dodd. I'm OK," Tommy said. "I'm sure they're nice people, but I'm good."

"Yeah, me too, Dodd. Thanks for the offer," Will said, agreeing with Tommy.

The group of locals continued to approach the infantrymen. When they

Three Months In

were about twenty yards away, Lieutenant Peterson ordered his platoon to get on one side of the trail so the villagers could pass. The soldiers were close enough now to see it all looked innocent enough. Families carrying baskets and some work implements and possibly coming back from a day's excursion in a rice field or from some other nearby village. Tommy's platoon consisted of sixteen soldiers and neither the soldiers nor the villagers seemed uncomfortable with each other as they passed. Nobody stopped and the soldiers in front said a casual "Hello" with their body language as they attempted to assure the passersby that there was nothing to fear.

Tommy, at the back of the line, watched them pass and noticed one of the adult males pulling along a reluctant and terrified big dog tied to a rope. Tommy stopped as the last of the villagers passed him by. Whether it was the heat and humidity or the far reaching effects of war or a combination of everything that had been going on these last few months, something inside of Tommy snapped. He couldn't bear witnessing a dog being treated the way this one was. It looked frightened to death. He crossed over the ten feet of short grass to the man who was dragging the dog along and grabbed him by the arm.

"Hey, you fuckin' idiot! How about if I tie you up and drag you along like that!" Tommy shouted.

The Vietnamese man took issue with Tommy's aggression and immediately resisted the soldier's interference. He yelled back at Tommy and struggled to get away from Tommy's grasp. Brian, who had heard Tommy yell, turned around to see what the commotion was all about. When he saw what was going on he quickly made his way to the two who were scuffling. The disagreement between Tommy and the man in possession of the dog had become heated, loud and caught the attention of the other soldiers and the locals.

Brian ran up and interceded. "Let 'em go, Franklin. Let 'em go!" he yelled taking hold of Tommy's arm.

"Back off, Dodd," Tommy fired back as some of the Vietnamese civilians joined the action and shouted their disapproval.

Brian tried to get between Tommy and the other man as the dog, weak and downtrodden, didn't react much to all the tussle. Lieutenant Peterson rushed up.

"That's enough, soldier. Let him go," the lieutenant screamed out.

Tommy looked at his lieutenant and then back at the shouting Vietnamese man and grudgingly decided to let the man go. In less than a minute Tommy had managed to upset the civilians, his lieutenant, his comrades, his friends. Tommy continued to curse at the man with the dog.

Brian pulled Tommy away. "Calm down, man. Calm down. That's their dinner, man. It's just a dog. It's only a dog."

Tommy seethed as he watched the man drag the dog away. Some of the children were crying and the women were panicked. The "Good American Soldier" suddenly became the "Ugly American Soldier" and all it took was a matter of a few seconds.

"Save your energy for the real enemy, Private Franklin. Not some poor guy trying to feed his family. You're way out of line here," Lieutenant Peterson said, exerting his authority firmly enough so that Tommy knew he meant it.

Tommy remained silent as Brian let go of his arm.

"It's OK, man. It's OK," Brian said, trying to calm his friend down.

Will came up as the soldiers watched the civilians continue their journey, now in fear of these foreigners.

"Hey, Franklin, keep your head, man," Will pleaded in a calm voice. "If we all get back stateside alive, I'll personally bring a dog to your house in Brenton. You got that? Let's stay focused. These people eat their dogs. This is a different world over here, man. You should know that by now. You've been here long enough. Let's go."

Will finished his little speech and put a hand on Tommy's shoulder. The soldiers turned and headed back in the direction they had been going.

"Private Dempsey's right, Franklin. It's over. Now move it." Lieutenant Peterson was visibly pissed off by what had happened and hurriedly made his way back to the front of the platoon.

As things settled down, Will and Brian flanked Tommy as the three walked.

"I can't handle seeing a dog treated like that," Tommy said defiantly. "I don't give a fuck where we are."

"Look Franklin. Let's not start another war besides the one we're fighting. Let's finish this one before we start killing each other over a dog," Will said, picking up his pace and leaving Tommy's side.

"Are you going to be OK?" Brian asked his troubled friend.

"Yeah, I'll be OK, Dodd. Thanks. I'll be OK."

Tommy stopped and looked back at the civilians getting further and further away. It pained him to think about what was going to happen to the dog. He thought of Buddy. It was taking a long time for Tommy to get over his first dog. Maybe the time would be right when he returned to Brenton to find another canine friend. That would make him feel good. Tommy stopped walking, stared down at the ground and suddenly realized what he had done. He rubbed his eyes.

Three Months In

"Come on, Franklin," Brian yelled back at his friend.

Tommy took one last look at the civilians.

Where did the dog go?

He couldn't make out the image of the dog now that the civilians were far away. He followed his comrades and remained the last in line. As he walked he asked himself what had gotten into him. He told himself he was going to have to try harder to keep it together. He was just over three months into his tour and had nine months to go. He wanted to be a good soldier and an action like he had just committed could have endangered everyone in his platoon. That's how people got killed. Tommy was embarrassed.

What are Will and Brian thinking about me now?

He had to be more careful, but his thoughts kept going back to the dog. A poor, unfortunate dog that was doomed. But Will was right. This war wasn't about saving dogs. It was way bigger than that.

As the day wore on, to Tommy's relief, all seemed to have been forgotten. Almost, but not quite. By late afternoon Will, Brian and Tommy were back into idle chit-chat as they continued their march. They picked the conversation up where it had left off a couple of hours before. They talked about their girlfriends and sports. The difference between big cities and small towns. High school and going to college on the G.I. Bill. They talked about everything except what had happened earlier in the day. It was over. Almost ... but not quite.

Will and Brian couldn't have come from backgrounds more different than Tommy's, but they had a way of making him feel comfortable. They were good for him and genuinely cared about their white friend and the feeling was mutual. Tommy was appreciative of that and the incident with the civilians hopefully was history now. His heart was pained when he thought about the dog and its fate. But there were bigger issues at hand in fighting this war. First and foremost was staying alive. Another day would come to save dogs.

Letter from Tommy

CAROLYN WAS SITTING at her desk in her dorm room when her roommate Benita walked in.

"I brought your mail up. Is that OK, Carolyn?"

Benita spoke with a heavy Spanish accent even though she had been living in Chicago for ten years, since she was eight. Born in Veracruz, Mexico, Benita's parents, along with her and her three younger brothers immigrated to the United States and ended up in Chicago where they had relatives that were instrumental in their resettling. The United States had been everything the Fernandez family anticipated. They found their new country was as advertised, the land of opportunity. Benita was a prime example of that. By taking advantage of every opportunity it offered, she became the first person in her family to graduate from high school and to attend university. Her father worked two jobs and her mother worked part-time. They rented a nice house in a culturally mixed neighborhood and one day they hoped to purchase their own home.

Carolyn had liked Benita from the first day they met and she couldn't have asked for a more perfect roommate in this her second year of university. And yes, she did like chocolate. Benita was very focused on her studies and that pleased Carolyn who was of the same mindset. They didn't lead very exciting social lives and they certainly didn't party much. They had become good friends and enjoyed each other's company immensely. Carolyn was intrigued with Benita's stories about her young life growing up in Mexico and how different it was from her own life growing up in Clear Lake. It made Carolyn feel lucky about her upbringing compared to what Benita had been through. Benita's family had struggled for as long as Benita could remember, but you couldn't tell that by her enthusiasm for life. The young Mexican girl knew she was lucky to be where she was now. She was a determined and proud student. She loved to hear her roommate's stories about growing up in the United States and especially the little town of Clear Lake. In this particular dorm room there was much laughter and little stress. The two girls' backgrounds couldn't be more different, but they had a common denominator that had taught them tolerance and understanding. They both had loving, hardworking, caring parents. It was the parents that they wanted to please and it was fate that had

Letter from Tommy

brought them together. It was a perfect match for college roommates who were driven by a common goal, getting a university degree.

"Thank you so much, Benita. That's fine." Carolyn was gracious and took the mail that her roommate had brought up from the dorm lobby mailboxes. She looked through the letters and saw that she had received another one from Tommy.

"Ah! Another letter from Tommy. Yippee!" Carolyn said gleefully as she jumped up from her desk chair.

Benita sat on her bed and began to open her own mail.

"That's exciting, Carolyn," she said, thrilled for her new friend.

She had seen how Carolyn got all giddy whenever she got a letter from this guy named Tommy who was a fighting soldier in Vietnam. Carolyn sat on the edge of her bed across from Benita and started reading the letter. The Mexican/American girl began to read a letter she had received and gave Carolyn some time before she asked about Tommy.

"So, how is your friend in Vietnam doing, senorita?" Benita on occasion jokingly threw in some Spanish lingo and her American roommate thought it was cute.

Carolyn held up a hand to signal "just a moment" and didn't say anything until she finished the paragraph she was reading.

"Sorry, Benita. He seems to be doing fine. The heat and humidity are still the same and he talks about his buddies, Will and Brian. I guess as far as a war goes, it sounds like the three of them are doing OK. He wants to come home and I don't blame him."

What Carolyn didn't reveal was how the tone of Tommy's letters had changed since he started writing from the war zone. She knew Tommy as well as anyone and now, with each letter, more and more he didn't sound like the Tommy she had known for most of her life. The language was quite colorful and he told in descriptive detail the images of war that she didn't really care to hear about. She was always glad to get his letters, but as if she wasn't worried enough about him being over there, now she was even more worried about the changes that might be taking place in his personality. The letters of late didn't sound like the Tommy she had befriended for so many years. She didn't want to be judgmental, but it was hard not to be.

War must be hell. Carolyn couldn't even imagine how being involved in one could change your view of the world. Especially as a soldier, it had to effect you. It had to change you. She wondered if the tone in his letters was because he was in such a hostile environment and ... had he really changed? *What is going on?* It was a question that weighed heavy on her mind. *Will this "new Tommy" be the one who comes home from war or will it be the "old Tommy" that everyone loved so?* She hadn't said anything about her concern in her letters when she wrote him back, but she wondered if she should.

No, I can't do that. He has enough to think about just fighting the war and I want him to know I support him in what he is doing. I just want him home and to be the same ol' Tommy.

"Gosh, why do we have to grow up so fast?" Carolyn muttered to herself.

"What did you say, Carolyn?" her roommate asked, looking up from the letter she was engrossed in.

"Oh nothing, Benita. I was just asking myself, 'Why do we have to grow up so fast?' Reading Tommy's letter, sometimes he doesn't sound like himself. I've known him since we were kids and sometimes I wish we could go back to the good old days." Carolyn paused for a brief moment as she thought about how things used to be with Tommy and their friends. "But, I guess we can't. Oh, well."

Carolyn shrugged her shoulders, held the letter in her lap and stared at Benita. Benita got up from her bed and sat down beside Carolyn.

"Don't worry about your friend, Tommy," Benita said, consoling her roommate. "He's going to be fine. When he gets back home he will be the same ol' amigo that you knew when you were in high school."

Carolyn laughed at Benita's use of the word amigo. She looked at Benita and smiled.

"Yes, Benita. When he gets home I'm sure he will be the same ol' amigo he has always been. Thank you so much for reassuring me. You are so kind."

"No problem, Carolyn."

Benita got up from the bed and sat on the chair at Carolyn's desk.

"Tommy will be just fine and I can't wait to meet him when he gets back to the great United States of America. You must introduce me to him."

Carolyn stood and walked over to the one window in their room and looked outside. It was slightly cracked opened and she could feel the fall chill air blowing in. Most of the leaves had fallen from the maple trees that grew on the front lawn of the dormitory. The ones left were still in brilliant color. Soon the snow would fly and all would be white. Winter was not far off. Thanksgiving break would be coming up next week and she couldn't wait to see her parents. She worried about her loved one overseas and the other soldiers. What would they be doing on Thanksgiving? Did they celebrate the holiday over there? Would they even know when Thanksgiving came or would the preoccupation with the war prevent such a thing? Carolyn was deep in thought.

War doesn't take holidays. War stops for nothing. Those of us that are

Letter from Tommy

stateside can sit around our dining room tables and be thankful for everything we have because of the brave soldiers who fight our wars. We pray for them. But will it change anything? Has it ever? Do we humans have any idea how to make peace?

"I can't wait for you to meet him, Benita," Carolyn said, turning away from the window and sitting back down on the end of her bed. "He's very nice and I know you will like him. He's funny and will make you laugh."

"I like to laugh," Benita said. "He is a good man if he can make you laugh, Carolyn."

Carolyn turned her head and looked back out the window from where she sat.

"Did you ever see snow before you came to the United States, Benita?"

Now it was Benita's turn to stand and gaze out the window.

"No, of course not, Carolyn. It didn't snow in Mexico. I only saw it on TV a few times. It is beautiful though. I like to build snowmen and throw snowballs. I feel so lucky to live now where it snows."

"It'll be here soon, Benita and then you and I can make a snow man together and some snow angels. How does that sound?"

Carolyn would much rather talk about the snow and the weather or anything else rather than think about how she was feeling about Tommy's letters, their content and the whole thing about this war in Vietnam.

"That sounds like so much fun, Carolyn Russell. And when your friend comes home from Vietnam we will all have a snowball fight. We will laugh and have so much fun."

The image of that in her head made Carolyn smile. It would be fun. She couldn't wait. When Tommy got home there would be so many fun things to do. So much of life to catch up on. She walked over and looked at the calendar hanging on the wall above her desk. She knew it was November, but needed to be reminded. Tommy wouldn't be home until the following August. It seemed like such a long time away. But when he finally did get home, the fun would begin again.

"Well, Benita. I will have to take you up to the lake next summer and you can see where I grew up. You will like Clear Lake and you can meet my parents and my dog, Molly who is getting very old. I miss her so much."

As she spoke, Benita gestured excitedly, jumped up and sat on the window sill.

"And then Carolyn, you can come down to Chicago and meet my family and experience the big city life. There is so much to do in the city. I love Chicago. I will take you to all the museums and art galleries."

"I've never been to a big city," Carolyn said, embarrassed by the fact.

When she was growing up her parents hadn't ventured far away from Clear Lake. Even on vacations they would head north to go camping and as a family never did visit a big city. None of her relatives lived in a city and it simply never happened. It sounded exciting to her.

"Can we go to a live theater?" Carolyn asked.

"Of course we can. We can go see a play or a concert. That will be wonderful. I can't wait!" Benita's genuine excitement was contagious.

Carolyn was thrilled with the idea of visiting a big city and doing all the things that big cities have to offer. She contemplated that for a few seconds before her thoughts turned back to Tommy and how much he might enjoy doing fun things in a big city as well. She had a picture in her mind of the two of them, along with Benita and her family, in a museum looking at all the antiquities, laughing and enjoying the experience. She could see her and Tommy holding hands and walking through an art gallery with Benita as their tour guide. Suddenly, the euphoric daydream of the three of them in Chicago having the time of their lives evaporated and was replaced by a soldier, a troubled soldier, fighting a war.

Carolyn looked at Benita and smiled. She felt lucky to have such a wonderful roommate and new friend. These thoughts become muddled with thoughts of the war, the future, a friend far away and her studies. For appearances, she maintained a happy face. It was what the moment called for. It was what her roommate wanted to see.

"I can't wait either, Benita. I can't wait!"

A Dog's Life

IT HAD BEEN a long day, a long march, and Tommy's platoon had finally found refuge and cover in thick jungle just before nightfall. The area where they decided to bivouac was different from the rice fields and sparse foliage in which they had spent the day. The terrain had changed quickly and Lieutenant Peterson informed them that most of the next day, on their way back to base, would also be spent in the jungle. This wasn't the first time the Oreo cookie spent the night bivouacked in the thick foliage. They had done it enough times to know that it wasn't their favorite thing to do. But it was usually only for one night and that they could tolerate.

Tommy lay on his bedding with his arms behind his head looking up at the stars, through a clearing in the leafy canopy. Will sat cross-legged and tried to play Solitaire in the dark with a deck of cards he always carried with him. Brian leaned up against a rock and read a small pocket-sized Bible with an equally small flashlight. Will struggled to see the cards he laid out on the ground and looked over at Brian.

"What'cha reading, Dodd?"

"The Bible," Brian replied.

"Oh yeah, right. I should have known," Will said turning back to his cards.

"You're not going to preach to us tonight are ya, Dodd?" Tommy asked as he continued to stare up at the stars.

"Naw. I'm going to give you guys the night off. I'm going to leave the ball in your court. Anything you want to know about God or Jesus, you just come to me when you need it. I'm tired of preaching to you guys. It ain't sinking in. So no more preachin'. I'm done."

"Is that a promise, Dodd?" Tommy kidded, not wanting Brian to take offence.

"Yeah, it's a promise, Franklin," Brian said, peering at his book. "No more preaching. You come to me if you want to know the truth. I'll leave it with ya."

"OK, Dodd. I'll track you down if I ever feel the urge to find out the truth."

Right now Tommy had more important things on his mind. The events of the day consumed him.

"I'm here for ya, Franklin. I'm here for you," Brian made it clear once more.

"That's comforting, Dodd."

Will gave up his attempt to play Solitaire and put the cards back in their box. He uncrossed his legs and stretched toward the sky. He too took notice how clear the night was and how many stars were out. You don't see many stars when you grow up in the big city and it amazed him whenever they spent the night away from base. For a moment, he forgot about the war and where he was and took in the soothing night sky.

"For everything that's wrong with this planet, it sure can be beautiful sometimes," Will said.

"Lots of stars out tonight, that's for sure," Tommy said, acknowledging Will's comment.

Tommy had seen it all before in Brenton.

"God's creation," Brian said, turning off his flashlight and joining the other two looking upwards.

"Somebody's creation, maybe. Who knows," Tommy said philosophically.

"Is your gal up there somewhere, Franklin?" Will asked Tommy, hoping to keep the conversation light and not let it drift into what was the meaning of life and who created the universe.

Tommy took a hand from behind his head and pointed.

"Can you see that bright one right there, straight up?"

Will and Brian looked where Tommy was pointing.

"You're talking about that bright one there?" Brian said, thinking he was pointing at the same star Tommy was.

Tommy turned his head and looked over at Brian.

"Yeah, that one. The brightest one. That's her. That's my gal."

"Looks like she's got lots of friends up there, Franklin," Will said, as he prepared his bedding so he could call it a night.

"Yeah, she's got lots of friends. That would be her. Lots of friends." Tommy rolled over onto his side and closed his eyes. "I'm gonna catch some shut eye, gentlemen. I'll see you in the morning."

Will closed his eyes, as tired as his friends.

"Are you going to behave yourself tomorrow, Franklin?" Will asked.

Tommy knew Will was referring to the dog incident earlier in the day and didn't want to address it again. It was a mistake. He knew that. Everybody made mistakes and it was done with as far as Tommy was concerned. The only thing he didn't know was who that person was that lost control of all rational thought earlier in the afternoon. It scared him to think he could be like that.

That wasn't me. It wasn't me. It couldn't have been me.

If it had been anybody else but Will asking that question, even in jest,

A Dog's Life

Tommy would have ignored it completely. But seeing it was Will making the comment, no offence was taken.

"Yeah, Dempsey. I'll be good. You know I feel like a shithead doing something like that. I'm sorry to everyone. I don't know what the fuck happened to me. It's over. You don't have to worry about it happening again. I think the lieutenant was right pissed off. I was wrong and everybody else was right. OK?"

In the dark of the night Will smiled to himself. He knew his buddy felt bad and trusted that his friend would be true to his word.

"Yeah, I wouldn't piss Peterson off again if I were you. Anyway, good-night. Tomorrow will be another beautiful day in paradise. Good-night, Dodd."

Brian, in the darkness, was putting his Bible under his pack that substituted for a pillow.

"Yeah, good-night and God bless." Brian ruffled his bedding to make it more comfortable. "The bugs aren't as bad tonight as they've been in the past, hey guys? Pretty quiet out there too. You dudes get a good night's sleep."

"Yeah, you too, Dodd," Will said, thinking the same thing as Brian, that the bugs were hardly noticeable and it was, in fact, unusually quiet.

That was just fine. They had bivouacked in the past when the bugs were intolerable and the noise from all the jungle creatures made it impossible to sleep. Tonight would be a good night for sleeping and they were thankful for that.

"Yeah, good night, Dodd. Sleep tight," Tommy said and, rolling over onto his back again, looked at the stars one more time.

His mind was racing and it wasn't easy to fall asleep. Try as he might, he couldn't stop thinking about the dog he had encountered. Then his thoughts turned to Carolyn and how much he missed her. He wondered what she was doing at this very moment. Was she thinking of him? His thoughts went back and forth between the dog and Carolyn. He closed his eyes and thought about what Will had said a few moments before, that tomorrow would be another day in paradise. His last thoughts, just before he fell asleep, were that when he got back home, it would be time to get another dog. Another companion. Another friend. It would be time to love Carolyn and be with her again. The three of them could go to Clear Lake beach and swim and he and Carolyn could play keep away with this new dog. They'd be with their friends just like old times. Will and Brian would come and visit and they would swap war stories and have beers and he'd introduce them to life in northern Michigan. He, Carolyn and the new dog would go visit Will and Brian in their home towns and meet their families. Everything would be fine in the land of the free. He and Carolyn would settle down somewhere, probably in Brenton or Clear Lake, and have kids and always have a dog as part of the family. Tommy's thoughts continued to race with all the possibilities of the future. It was not going to be easy getting to sleep. Despite what had taken place on this day, his thoughts were good thoughts and he was enjoying watching the movie in his head.

"RISE AND SHINE, gentlemen," Lieutenant Peterson said in a soft tone rousting the Oreo cookie along with the rest of his platoon. "It's time to get moving."

"Shit, man!" Will, who was still not a morning person, mumbled. He turned over, barely able to open his eyes. He squinted and saw that there was just a faint morning light.

The residents of the jungle were awakening and beginning to make noises. The birds and their friends were preparing for another day and letting the world know they were still alive. Will sat up and noticed Tommy and Brian hadn't moved.

"Hey, Franklin. Hey, Dodd. Did you hear the lieutenant? Time to get rolling."

Will slowly made his way to his feet, walked over to Tommy and gave him a kick.

"OK, OK. I'm up. I'm up." Tommy groaned and realized he had better get moving. He had to be on his best behavior today and wanted to show it right from the get go. He got up and gathered his gear together.

Will went over to Brian and gave him a kick as well.

"Hey, Dodd. God's waiting for us back at the base. We don't want to let him down. Let's go."

Brian was sound asleep and hadn't even heard Lieutenant Peterson come by. He sat up and rubbed his eyes. "Did Peterson come through here or did I dream it?"

"Yeah, he came through and he'll be back. Get it together, Dodd," Will said, encouraging his friend.

"OK, yeah. OK," Brian said, reacting slowly. "I'm ready, I'm ready."

Right on schedule, Lieutenant Peterson came walking by again to inform the Oreo cookie it was time to get some food in them and that they'd be heading out in fifteen minutes.

"Private Franklin. I don't want a repeat of yesterday. Do you understand?"

A Dog's Life

the lieutenant said, addressing Tommy in a serious tone.

"Yes, sir . Absolutely, sir."

"That's what I want to hear, Private. Let's make this day uneventful. We have a couple of little hamlets to check out on the way back to our pick up point and then we're done by nightfall. So, Franklin, be good."

"Be ready to go in fifteen minutes. I'm as anxious to get back to the base as you guys," Lieutenant Peterson said, giving a stern command.

The Oreo cookie responded in unison, "Yes, sir," as their lieutenant carried on.

Will, Tommy and Brian got out c-rations and began eating their breakfast.

"How'd you guys sleep last night?" Will asked, trying to get a conversation going that might help them wake him up.

"Sleep? What's that?" Tommy said, not the picture perfect morning person either, but at least trying to be cheerful. He had had trouble falling asleep and what sleep he did get wasn't exactly what you would call quality sleep. "Can't say I slept much at all, Mr. Dempsey. Just get me back to the base where I can crash on my bed. That'll be good. Just get me back to the base."

"I slept like a baby," Brian said in all honesty while chowing down his canned meal. His honesty, however innocent, was annoying.

Will looked at Brian and gave him a look of friendly disgust.

"Well that's good, Dodd. We're pleased you got some sleep. You'll be cheery all day today then, right?"

"Of course I'll be cheery. I'm always cheery," Brian bragged.

The three friends finished their c-rations and got organized for another days' march. At least at this time of day it was not too hot or humid. The morning light slowly got brighter and it wouldn't take long for the day to heat up. It was best to get going early and make time. True to form, Lieutenant Peterson told the platoon to get moving in exactly fifteen minutes. He had informed his men that the mission would be to keep working on public relations with the locals. He also told them to keep an eye out for any visual tidbits of information that could come in useful against the enemy.

"The Viet Cong have infiltrated everywhere. We don't know who's who. But when we encounter those that appear to be civilians, we treat them with respect. You know the routine," Lieutenant Peterson ordered.

He wanted his men to be on their best behavior. There was more to winning this war than simply seeing how many of the enemy they could kill. They needed to win over the locals and get them on their side. Not always an easy thing to do. The indigenous people could provide invaluable knowledge about a lot of things, but unfortunately, most of the rural Vietnamese were somewhat leery of American soldiers. The public relations battle was ongoing and delicate.

The Americans saw themselves as freedom fighters, not invaders or occupiers. This war was all about bringing democracy to this land, at least that's what the soldiers were told. Lieutenant Peterson wanted this to be an uneventful day, free of any distractions. He truly liked and respected all the soldiers in his platoon. He felt they were exceptional soldiers. He was proud of them and felt lucky to have them under his command. So he felt confident that the march back to base would be orderly. He also knew how unpredictable things could be in the jungle. A march could be going just fine and then things could suddenly go sideways. Lieutenant Peterson hoped today that wouldn't be the case. The first village they would visit was about two hours away if everything went well. The second village they would get to in early afternoon and they could be back at base by seven or eight o'clock that night, just before nightfall.

Less than a couple of minutes into their hike, Lieutenant Peterson walked up to Tommy and reiterated that he didn't want what happened yesterday to happen again. He reminded Tommy how out of line he had been antagonizing the civilians the day before.

"Yes, sir!" Tommy responded. "Understood, sir."

"That's good, Private. Let's just let this be a low key day. OK?"

"Yes, sir, Lieutenant. It won't happen again, sir."

Lieutenant Peterson walked off toward the front of the line to lead the way, comfortable with Private Franklin's response. Tommy didn't need to be reminded that what he had done the day before was foolish and endangered his comrades. He wanted to put it behind him and forget about it.

It was stupid! Just plain stupid!

As they marched, Tommy thought about what kind of dog he would get when he returned home. It would be a big dog, shorthair, floppy ears and he would look for it at the Humane Society where there were always dogs that needed rescuing. These thoughts made him feel good. They took him far away from the war. When he got out of the Army and became a civilian again, having a dog would be just what the doctor ordered. He got excited thinking about it. Then his thoughts, as they often did, turned to Buddy and what a wonderful dog he had been. Of course Buddy would be a tough act to follow. But all dogs were good and special in their own way. Tommy knew his next dog would be exactly that. It would be his best friend just like Buddy had been. But first things first. Get through this day and through this war and then life would be good again. Oh, so very good.

A Dog's Life

The platoon stopped by a creek to eat lunch. It had turned into another blistering hot and humid day so everyone found a spot in the shade. The sweep through the first hamlet that morning had gone well; the villagers were friendly and indicated the American soldiers were more than welcome. There wasn't anything out of the ordinary as the soldiers put on their happy faces and did some constructive public relations. Lieutenant Peterson was pleased with how things had gone and if the rest of the day went that well there wouldn't be any complaints coming from him. Will, Brian and Tommy sat together and attempted to enjoy their food.

"This stuff isn't exactly gourmet, is it?" Brian said to his mates.

It was something they'd all said many times since they'd been in Vietnam. When you spent time out on patrol, the food wasn't the greatest.

"One thing they didn't promise us was gourmet food, hey Dodd?" Will said, doing his best to get the food down.

Tommy lay back on the ground and closed his eyes. "Wake me when it's time to go, guys."

"Tired, Franklin?" Brian asked watching Tommy try to get comfortable.

"A bit," Tommy responded with a big yawn.

Five minutes later, it was time to go. Tommy may have gotten thirty winks in, he wasn't sure. He did know that he was really tired and a much longer nap would have been nice.

Brian gave him a boot. "Time to head out, Franklin. One more village to go and then we'll be homeward bound."

Everyone strapped their gear back on and then followed Lieutenant Peterson's lead. Hopefully the afternoon would go as well as the morning had.

"Shit, man. I was just falling asleep," Tommy complained.

As tired as he felt, Tommy knew he was no different from the rest in his platoon and was neither more tired nor less anxious to get back to the base than everyone else. It wouldn't be the last time he felt this exhausted and certainly wasn't the first.

"You can sleep when we get back to base, Franklin. We're all going to sleep when we get back to base. Just put one foot in front of the other and you'll be OK." Will, trying to be funny, showed Tommy how it was done in slow motion. "See how I'm doing it, Franklin? It's not that hard."

A little comedic relief in a war zone never hurt and Will's actions made Tommy, and the rest of those taking notice, chuckle. For a moment Tommy forgot how tired he was and enjoyed Will's antics.

"That's good, Dempsey. That's good. Let's see now. One foot in front of the other. I'm not sure if I can get it right." Tommy imitated Will's humorous antics and drew even more attention. Lieutenant Peterson looked back to see what all the laughing and commotion were about and laughed as well. This was what he liked to see. Camaraderie. Everyone getting along and putting the stress of war behind them, if only for a brief moment. It was good for the troops.

Thank you, Will, for bringing some laughter into the day.

The platoon continued their journey through the jungle in the heat and humidity and, like aliens from another planet, a couple of hours later stumbled into the second little hamlet to do their "sweep" and their public relations bit with the residents. They put on their happy faces, attempting to convince them that they were not the enemy but in fact were the liberators.

Most of these hamlets looked the same and it was hard to tell one from the other. It was like stepping back in time. The people living in these little villages of just a few huts had been living this way for hundreds of years. Nothing much had changed. They worked hard to get by with the bare necessities of life and seemed to be quite content with that. What more did a person need? Why would the foreign aggressors want to change anything? These American intruders, who pretended to be friendly, talked about "freedom," but the indigenous people here had always been free. They knew nothing "but" freedom. No one had ever bothered them up until now. What was freedom? The right to vote? What was voting and why would they want to do that anyway? They only wanted to be left alone. The so-called enemy of the Americans were not the people in these little villages.

It was complicated. Especially the public relations part that the soldiers had been trained in. How do you convince these people you were here to help them have an opportunity for a better life when in fact they were quite satisfied with the way they'd been living for many generations? It was a tough sell. For the most part, the American soldiers were ignored and tolerated. But today, something was noticeably different when Tommy's platoon walked out of the jungle and into this second hamlet of twenty or so huts. The residents seemed a little more standoffish than usual and weren't very receptive to the platoon's presence. No big deal. The Americans had seen it all before. Some villages were more welcoming than others and that was a fact of life. But still, the vibes here were different. It was a funny feeling and all the soldiers picked up on it. Because of their training, they naturally become more alert. Maybe there was a history of being mistreated by foreigners or even by their own kind. Maybe they had had a bad experience with American soldiers before.

Lieutenant Peterson had decided it was going to be a quick "sweep." In, out and done. Then back to the base. The soldiers smiled and tried to make

A Dog's Life

lighthearted gestures that would help assure these people that everything was OK. It wasn't going to take very long to do a walk through. It was a small hamlet and nothing looked out of the ordinary. As instructed, and as they had learned in their training, they spread out. Tommy, Will and Brian brought up the rear. Tommy kept thinking of how fatigued he felt and the heat wasn't helping. Not much was being said between the Oreo cookie members as they casually walked through the center of the hamlet. Tommy lagged behind his two comrades. He happened to look over to his right and saw the dog he had encountered the day before. It was tied up by a short rope to a post stuck in the ground outside one of the huts. He stopped and stared. He couldn't believe his eyes.

As Will and Brian carried on without noticing what Tommy was doing, he walked over in the direction of the dog. When he got to the dog he knelt down and petted him. The dog, too weak and timid to be scared or mean, accepted Tommy's gesture. Tommy looked around and saw that no one was watching. No villagers or anyone in his platoon were observing his actions. He continued to pet the dog and spoke to him in soft tones.

"You'll be OK, pal. I'm going to get you out of here. You're going to be just fine."

Tommy took out a knife strapped to his belt and cut the rope.

"Come on, my friend. You're going with me."

As Tommy started to walk away with the dog, the man who had been dragging the dog the day before came out of his hut yelling. He charged at Tommy, grabbed the rope and, like the day before, they struggled. This time Tommy was more forceful and determined to change the outcome. He managed to push the man to the ground. He pulled out his sidearm and pointed it at him.

Tommy screamed, "Fuck off, man. He's going with me!"

The Vietnamese on the ground didn't understand English and Tommy had no idea what the man screamed back at him. As the villager stood up, he continued shouting at Tommy then stormed off back into his hut. Almost immediately he came back out with a revolver of his own. The standoff only lasted for a split second. Tommy shot the man in the chest and killed him instantly.

The shot drew attention. Other villagers started to appear. Ly-Tien, the embedded interpreter with Tommy's platoon, ran up and saw the dead man lying on the ground as a woman knelt over him, crying and shouting. Ly-Tien was waving his arms and trying to get the other inhabitants of the hamlet who had gathered around, to calm down. He stopped and looked at Tommy holding the rope that was attached to the dog.

"What are you doing? What are you doing?" Ly-Tien said with disdain.

Tommy didn't know what he was doing. He knew he was standing somewhere in a foreign land holding a rope with a dog at the end of it and that he had killed a man without giving it much thought. A man that had a gun in his hand and could have killed him. It was self defense. Or was it?

What have I done?

Ly-Tien, frightened and panicked, continued to shout at Tommy in English. Words that Tommy now understood. The private stood his ground and was ready to fire again if anyone attempted to take the dog away from him. Ly-Tien turned back and began to talk desperately to the upset natives. They yelled and pointed at Tommy. They had all come: the children, the adults, the elderly. Tommy lowered his revolver and began to back away slowly, still holding the rope. Ly-Tien pleaded with the villagers to calm down. It was hopeless. Tommy didn't understand their language, but it was obvious they wanted the dog back.

A couple of men picked the body up and took the dead man into a hut. Tommy continued his retreat. He was still not thinking rationally and, holding tighter onto the rope, pulled the dog along with him. He yelled back at the residents of the hamlet.

Ly-Tien pleaded with Tommy some more to let the dog go.

"I'm taking the dog with me. He's not going to be somebody's next meal. Tell them if anyone tries to stop me I'll kill everybody and burn the village down."

Ly-Tien looked at Tommy in disbelief. He was stunned. He turned back to the upset villagers and tried once again to diffuse the crisis. Turning back to Tommy he explained intensely that time was running out and more people were going to get hurt or killed. Tommy was losing patience.

Some soldiers in Tommy's platoon had run up, including Lieutenant Peterson. He saw that there was trouble. Big trouble. He looked at Tommy holding the dog tied to the rope.

"What the hell is going on here, Franklin," Peterson shouted.

"One of the villagers came at me with a gun. I shot and killed him, sir."

Lieutenant Peterson couldn't believe what he had just heard. Will and Brian ran up and tried to help Ly-Tien settle things down, without much luck.

"Shit, Franklin. What the fuck are you thinking?" the lieutenant yelled loud enough to be heard above all the action around him. Peterson looked down at the dog and suddenly it dawned on him that what was happening must be related to the dog that Tommy clung to.

"What the hell are you doing with the dog, Franklin?" the commanding officer screamed.

Tommy yelled back matter of factly, "I'm taking him back to the base with me, sir."

The soldiers in Tommy's platoon now stood between the private, Lieutenant Peterson and the villagers. As a unit they were trying to help Ly-Tien settle matters. Peterson couldn't believe what he was hearing from his private.

"Are you out of your fucking mind, Franklin?" The lieutenant had gotten into Tommy's face to make this last statement. He stopped yelling at Tommy and let the fire in his eyes do the talking.

"The dog is going with me, sir," Tommy shouted back defiantly, knowing he was out of line, but not caring. He liked Lieutenant Peterson and had tremendous respect for him, but this was about saving a dog's life.

Lieutenant Peterson turned and looked at the commotion behind him. He had hoped so much that this day would go by without incident. Now this. He studied the scene for a moment and knew that he needed to get it sorted out quickly. He called Ly-Tien over.

"Ly-Tien, we're in total damage control here. What are the locals saying?"

Ly-Tien explained that the man Tommy had killed had a wife and two children. He told the lieutenant how the villagers felt about the American soldiers and it could only be described as hatred.

"They hate the American soldiers and just want you to go away. They want the dog back and the watch on Private Franklin's wrist."

Lieutenant Peterson had heard a lot of strange things in his life, but he couldn't believe what Ly-Tien just said about the watch Tommy was wearing. What did that have to do with anything? He had to think fast before things got more out of control.

"What the hell do they want the watch for?" a bewildered lieutenant asked Ly-Tien.

A husband and father has just been killed by one of my troops and somebody in the group wants Franklin's watch! So exactly what is a human life worth?

Ly-Tien now spoke with a very animated male who seemed to be drawing all the attention. It was a heated discussion. Lieutenant Peterson wished it would all come to an end, soon. He began to get nervous knowing they'd spent too much time here and the sweep of the village should have been over by now. His nervousness, however, didn't match his anger toward Private Franklin. Ly-Tien and the male villager had argued long enough and Peterson decided to take the initiative. It no longer mattered why the man wanted

Tommy's watch. He looked at the private.

"Franklin, give the man your watch. That's an order," the lieutenant said sternly.

Tommy looked at his lieutenant and then past him at Ly-Tien. Ly-Tien gazed at Tommy waiting for a response.

"Tell the man he's not getting the dog or the watch," Tommy said defying his lieutenant's order.

The soldiers in Tommy's platoon, still dealing with the rest of the villagers, couldn't believe what they are hearing. Will decided to intercede and began to walk toward his troubled friend just as the lieutenant screamed, "Give the man your fucking watch, Franklin and you're leaving the dog here. Do you hear me? That's an order!"

Tommy shouted right back and remained steadfast.

"Sir, the dog is going with me and the watch was a gift from my parents. It stays on my wrist!"

Ly-Tien came back up and stood between the lieutenant and private.

"The villagers have changed their minds. They say take the dog and give them your watch."

Ly-Tien stared Tommy down as the private seemed to be gazing into oblivion.

"They're not getting the watch or the dog," Tommy said.

Will had been standing next to his lieutenant and his good friend observing the heated exchanges, but had said nothing. He saw something in Tommy's eyes he hadn't seen before. It was a faraway look. The eyes didn't even look like Tommy's. There was no expression in them. No life. Where had his friend Tommy Franklin gone?

Exasperated, Ly-Tien stormed off to negotiate with the villagers one more time. Will felt he must speak up and take action. He took a couple of steps over to Tommy and, without saying anything, took the revolver out of Tommy's hand. His friend didn't resist.

"Franklin, either give them the dog or the watch or both. Make up your mind what you're going to do, Franklin and let's get the hell out of here." Will's voice was calm and it got Tommy's attention. "The lieutenant has given you an order. Let's get this over with and move on."

Tommy looked at Will. The insanity of all that was happening had taken Tommy to a place he had never been before. Will put a hand on his friend's shoulder.

"It's OK, Tommy. It's going to be OK. Make a move before someone else gets hurt." Will's voice stayed composed and, considering the heat of the moment, it was pacifying for Tommy to hear. Will knew something wasn't right with his comrade. The heat? The humidity? Fatigue? The war itself? Quite possibly it could have something to do with saving the dog.

"The dog's going with me, Will. I'm taking the dog," Tommy said, speaking to Will as calmly as Will had spoken to him.

Will and the lieutenant looked at each other as Tommy did not flinch and obviously wasn't going to back down. Peterson gave Will a nod as if to say, "I'm deferring to you. If you can get through to your friend here, then do it." Will got the message.

"OK look, Franklin," Will's voice stayed placid. "We all know the watch means a lot to you. But ask yourself this, 'What would your parents want you to do in this situation?'. I can guarantee you they wouldn't want anyone else to get hurt. Think about that."

Tommy began to remove the watch from his wrist. Will was right. With everything that had happened in the last few minutes, Tommy hadn't thought about his parents and what they would think about what he was doing. He hadn't thought about Carolyn and how she would feel about this person who had committed the unimaginable. All he thought about was a dog and saving its life. Winning a war didn't matter. Fighting the enemy didn't matter. The residents of this hamlet didn't matter. It was all about protecting the dog and keeping it safe. That was it. Cut and dried. Black and white. No backing down.

Quietly Tommy handed his watch to Will. Everything was going in slow motion and for the first time since he shot the man who just wanted his dog back, he heard the sounds of voices besides those of Ly-Tien, Lieutenant Peterson and Will. He had only been seeing actions. It was like watching a silent film. A nightmare movie. But now, he heard everything. He looked at the dog at the end of the rope and then at Lieutenant Peterson. Tommy turned around with the dog and walked away from it all. He headed in the direction his platoon had been walking just a few minutes before. Lieutenant Peterson let him go. He looked over at Will giving Ly-Tien the watch and then Ly-Tien as he handed the watch over to the man who apparently had been demanding it.

The yelling and screaming, the bickering and negotiating came to an end. The man who had received the watch showed it off to some young kids. The shouting ceased, but the villagers still cursed the American soldiers as they began to walk away. Lieutenant Peterson would let the residents of this little hamlet decide what to do with the dead man. He would also let them decide what to do with the watch. It was time to go. He told his men to pick up the pace. They were behind schedule now and all he wanted to do was get back to base. They all watched as Tommy and the dog led the way.

What Made Me Do It?

"YOU'RE IN A heap of trouble, soldier," Lieutenant Peterson said as he caught up to Tommy.

Tommy knew he would have to pay for his actions as rational thought slowly started to creep back into his brain, but he continued to justify his actions.

I had to kill the man! He would have killed me if I hadn't killed him first. If he only would have listened to me. Who knows, maybe he was a Viet Cong. An enemy soldier pretending to be an innocent resident of the village. Maybe the other villagers are glad he is dead. He could have been a tyrant. Maybe I did them all a favor. All I know is that I had to save this dog I'm walking with. I'll take him back to the States with me and he'll live a good life. I've saved the dog and I freed the villagers from an evil man. It had to be done. I had to shoot.

Tommy was hardly aware of his commanding officer's presence. Peterson was waiting for some sort of response.

"Did you hear me, Private Franklin?" the lieutenant said, still very upset and getting more and more impatient with the man that walked with the dog.

Tommy stopped, as did the lieutenant, and they looked at each other.

"I'm sorry, sir, for what happened back there. I know there will be consequences when we get back to the base. I had to save the dog, sir. I had to."

Tommy's eyes were coming back to life now. Peterson saw that and was glad that the private communicated verbally now instead of with his revolver. The apology, however, didn't make up for his actions back in the hamlet. The lieutenant was steaming.

"You're right, Private, there are going to be consequences. You could have gotten yourself or one of your buddies killed. Inexcusable, Franklin. Inexcusable. When we get back to base you'll be confined to your quarters until further notice. Understood?"

"Yes, sir, I understand. Once again, sir, I'm sorry for what happened back there. I owe everyone an apology, sir."

"That you do, soldier. I've had enough of you for now. You disobeyed a direct order and you're going to pay for that. You're in enough trouble as it is, Private. I wouldn't cause anymore."

What Made Me Do It?

Lieutenant Peterson was through talking and peeled off. As he did, Tommy apologized again for his behavior back in the village. It fell on deaf ears.

The dog, Tommy noticed, seemed to have more bounce in his step as they walked together. In fact, Tommy could swear the dog appeared to be relieved now that he was out of the village environment. Or was it Tommy trying to convince himself that nothing had happened back in the hamlet and that everything was going to be fine? The soldier knelt down beside the dog and untied the rope from around the dog's neck.

"OK, I'll let you make the decision. You're free to go back to the village or you can come with me. I might be able to get you back to the United States and show you a real life if you stay with me. Your call."

Tommy began to walk away and didn't look back. He noticed the rest of the platoon a few yards in front of him now. His comrades had all passed him by without saying anything. The guilt he was feeling pained his heart and he wondered how he could have lived with himself if one of them had been hurt or killed because of his actions? He had a lot of questions he needed to ask his inner self and he knew he'd be searching deep within for those answers. The first question he'd have to answer was, "Who was that person back there?" Two days in a row now he had crossed the line and couldn't explain why. The second question he'd ask himself was, "Who was the man I killed back there and what was his history?"

As Tommy walked a quick pace to catch up with the rest of his platoon, something off to his right attracted his attention. He turned his head. It was the dog. He would have liked to smile at the sight, but he had little energy or emotion left in him to manage that. He knelt down as the dog came walking up to him.

"So you decided to come back with me, huh? I hope you made the right decision there, boy. I'm feeling a little confused right now. But I'll be good to ya. I'll be real good to ya."

Tommy stood up and looked down at the dog. Memories of Buddy and happier times came back to him.

What would Buddy think of my actions? My goodness! What would Buddy think of what I've just done?

The soldier bent over and patted the dog on the head.

"OK then, if you're coming with me, let's go."

The dog cocked his head, stood there and watched Tommy begin walking away one more time. The private got a good fifty feet away before the dog decided to catch up with his new master.

Tommy slapped the side of his thigh as he walked. "You're a good, boy.

You got me into a heap of trouble, but you're still a good boy."

That's right! I am a good boy and I'm coming with you. I'm finding my will to live again. Give me some food and water and I'll show you exactly how much energy I have.

Will and Brian had stayed behind the others in their platoon as they continued their journey back to base. They had done it on purpose to keep an eye on their friend. Tommy caught up to them, along with the dog that was now acting like it was the center of the universe. Tommy wanted to talk, to say something, but couldn't think of the words. Will and Brian walked closely side by side, aware of Tommy's presence, but having the same problem Tommy had. What was there to say? Brian and Will would like to say, "This is a war to save humans, not dogs." They would like to say, "You could have gotten us all killed back there." There were a lot of things Will and Brian would like to say, but they remained silent and so the Oreo cookie members walked together along with their new mascot, not speaking to each other.

It was awkward for all three, but it was Tommy who was feeling the pain. He knew he would have to live with what he had done for the rest of his life. He wished somebody would say something. Will and Brian cared but were too pissed off to say anything to their friend. Really, wasn't the mission to get back home alive? Why would their friend jeopardize all that and betray them? So they walked, the three of them, the Oreo cookie, and said nothing.

Lieutenant Peterson stood at the side of the trail watching as his troops walked by. When the Oreo cookie showed up, he joined it. Finally, someone that would break the silence.

"When we get back to the base, Private Franklin, I don't want this canine friend of yours in the barracks. Find a place to tie him up and we're going to deal with all this tomorrow," the lieutenant said, walking shoulder to shoulder next to Tommy.

"Yes, sir," Tommy wisely responded respectfully, not wanting to look at his commanding officer or antagonize him any more then he had already.

Lieutenant Peterson looked at the dog as they walked and thought to himself that it did seem to be enjoying its newfound freedom. He was happy for the dog despite the trouble it had caused. He had a dog back home in the States. He liked dogs just like Private Franklin did. But this was not about dogs or even this particular dog. It was about Private Franklin disobeying orders and killing a villager he claimed came at him with a revolver. It was also very much about jeopardizing the safety of his fellow soldiers. The private wasn't thinking like the well-trained United States soldier that he was.

"You've blown it two days in a row, Franklin. That's two days. Not one, but two," the lieutenant ranted.

They had already been down this road, but Tommy understood more now just how serious this business was. He understood the lieutenant's displeasure and he would have to take the shots as they came.

"What the fuck is wrong with you, Franklin?"

Tommy looked at Will and Brian who wanted nothing to do with the conversation. He struggled to say something. He wished he were back in Brenton with Carolyn and this new friend that walked with him. Everything was wrong. What he did was wrong, he knew that. He tried to think of the future and when this would all be behind him. He wanted to think that there were happier days ahead. Right now, however, he wished he were invisible and everything would just go away.

"I don't know what's wrong with me, sir. I don't know," Tommy replied. He felt beaten. Tired. His words came slowly and deliberately. "It won't happen again, sir. I promise. It won't happen again."

"Yeah, I've heard it all before, Franklin. I've heard it all before," the lieutenant said with disdain.

Lieutenant Peterson had more than made his point and now told himself to back off a bit. As an officer you have to make your point clear and sometimes be forceful when you do it. Then after you're sure you've made your point, you have to get results. You could yell and scream all you want, but if you don't get results from your troops, then you've wasted your time and energy. The lieutenant had decided to ease up a bit on the private. He wouldn't forgive Tommy for what he'd done, not yet anyway, but now spoke in a more forgiving tone.

"You told me yesterday it would never happen again and I believed you. Why should I believe you now?" he asked the private.

"I know, sir. I know what I said, sir. I'm sorry. Trust me, Lieutenant. It won't happen again. Please believe me this time, sir." Tommy was begging for the commanding officer's trust.

The two continued to walk together in silence, both contemplating what would come next. As the head of command the lieutenant was going to have to file a report when he got back to the base and needed to think about what he was going to write in it. He looked down at the dog again and noticed the similarities between this dog and the one he had back home.

"Private Franklin ... ," he said.

"Yes, sir."

"Make sure your friend here gets food and water when we get back."

That was it. End of discussion. Lieutenant Peterson sped up and headed to the front so he could lead his platoon on the home stretch to the base

"Yes, sir!" Tommy said, loud enough to make sure the lieutenant heard him. "No problem, sir."

Tommy thought the world of his lieutenant. They had an amicable relationship since they first met and Tommy was sick and angry with himself about letting him down. Peterson had a way about him that made you feel like you would do anything for him, anytime, anywhere. Some have people skills that come naturally and the lieutenant was a prime example of that. His troops genuinely liked and respected him. Simply put, he was a great guy and he made you feel good about yourself. He made you feel important. He made you feel like you were a viable cog in the wheel. A player that "the team" couldn't do without. That's what made it even more painful for Tommy, the fact he liked the lieutenant so much and he still couldn't understand what happened that made him do what he did back in the village. But it was definitely the dog. Everything that took place these last two days, as far as the private was concerned, was because of his feelings toward the dog. All dogs. But despite that, the guilt settled in.

What have I done? What the hell have I done? I've let so many people down!

Tommy had his dog now, but there was going to be hell to pay and whatever his superiors decided to do with him, he knew he deserved it. There would be no changing the facts. Tommy continued to try to convince himself that what he did was for the love of the dog. He was sorry for everything that had happened. Killing the man, who could have been a good family man with a wife and kids, would haunt him the rest of his life.

THE OREO COOKIE had been walking together for what seemed to Tommy like a very long time without speaking. Tommy looked over at Will and Brian who stared straight ahead. Will sensed he was being looked at and stole a glance toward his friend. Will would have liked to get into Tommy's head to know what he was thinking. The dog trotted gleefully along in front of them.

I'm free! I'm free! I wonder where the humans are taking me? They seem to like me! I like them. I like these humans in uniforms.

Suddenly, to Tommy's surprise, Will broke the silence.

"I'm going to say this one time and one time only, Franklin. I consider you a friend, but you're also a fuckin' idiot. We're all trying to get home alive and you're pissing off just about everyone we run across. Are you losing it after three months, Franklin? We still have a long way to go. You've never done anything like this before, man. What the hell is wrong with you and what the fuck are you going to do with that dog? Have you lost your marbles?"

Will shook his head realizing that what he was saying probably wouldn't get a response and he didn't really care. He knew Tommy could hear him and he was not done yet.

"Don't ask me to look after him when you're in the clink, Franklin. Peterson's going to throw the book at you when we get back to the base. Shit, man! I'm glad I'm not you."

Will had said what he had wanted to say and decided to pick up the pace so he didn't have to walk with his friend any longer. As far as Tommy was concerned, Will might as well have stabbed him in the gut with a bayonet. The words hurt that much.

Tommy chose to remain silent. Brian walked past him and said nothing. Private Franklin was on his own now. He and his dog. It would be a few more hours before they got back to the base and Tommy would have time to think about a lot of things. The hike to the meeting point with his platoon, that was thoroughly disgusted with him, was punishment enough. Yet there was more to come. He asked himself over and over why he had done what he did and the only answer he could come up with was that he put his feelings for the dog over the safety of his colleagues and had showed a total disregard for another human's life by killing the villager.

Just save the dog! Kill or be killed. Why can't we all just get along?

This day, this mission, wasn't about saving a dog. It was about looking for signs of the enemy seeking refuge in these little hamlets that dot the landscape. The American soldiers were trying to establish good relations with the locals. Get them on their side. Tommy had lost sight of that and become more concerned, obsessed, with this dog now walking by his side. He wouldn't be surprised if no one in his platoon ever trusted him again. He didn't want that, but that could be the price he would pay for his recklessness. He wanted to be a good soldier and he felt he had been one. What had come over him? Will had made a good point; what was he going to do with the dog now? Could he stay at the base? If he couldn't, then what? Was he going to be able to take the dog home with him? What would happen to this dog after Tommy's tour of duty was up if he couldn't take him home? Tommy didn't like the way he was feeling. He didn't like being ignored by the members of his platoon. He watched Will and Brian a few yards in front of him, walking and talking. He wondered if they were talking about him and how crazy he was. The emotional island he was on now was a very lonely place.

Am I crazy?

What was going to become of the Oreo cookie? Their friendship, had he blown that? Tommy stopped, knelt down beside the dog and patted him behind the ear. He took solace in the animal. A bond began to form. The dog seemed to understand that Tommy had set him free and put a paw up on Tommy's knee.

"I've said this once and I'll say it again; you're a good boy. Only a few more hours to go and we'll get you some food and water. We'll fatten you up a bit too, OK guy? You're going to like the fellows at the base. We need a mascot and you'll be perfect. You're going to be just fine boy, just fine. Do you like riding in helicopters? I hope so."

Tommy turned his head and saw Will and Brian walking back toward him.

"That's Dempsey and Dodd. They're good friends of mine ... I think. You'll like them, they're good people."

Brian stopped a few feet away as Will walked up to Tommy and knelt down next to him and the dog, patting the freed animal on the head.

"Franklin, you can't be lagging behind. We know how you're feeling, but ya gotta keep up."

Will studied the dog and scratched him underneath the chin.

"He seems friendly enough, hey Franklin?" Will said, looking Tommy in the eye for the first time since they left the hamlet.

Tommy appreciated the soft tone of Will's words and the eye contact.

"Yeah Dempsey, he seems pretty friendly. He'll be fine as soon as we get some food and water into him."

Tommy and Will stood up. Private Franklin looked at Private Dempsey and somehow felt all was not lost in their friendship. Tommy exchanged glances with Brian.

"Let's get going, Franklin. I'm antsy to get back to the base," Brian shouted at Tommy, sounding friendly.

"OK, Dodd. I'm coming."

As the three joined up again, Tommy attempted to offer another apology for the way he had behaved.

"It's OK, Franklin. I'm sure we'll get over it," Will said. "But if I were you, I'd watch your ass from now on. We need you and we need you to act sane, not fuckin' crazy. It'll be OK. Don't worry, it'll be OK, just keep your shit together."

"FRANKLIN, WAKE UP! Wake up!"

Brian was almost shaking Tommy right off his bed. It was the middle of the night. It was the first night back after the incident in the village twelve hours before. Private Franklin was having a nightmare and woke up drenched in sweat. He sat up quickly, not sure where he was. He looked at Brian and didn't recognize him. He looked around the barracks. Some of his fellow soldiers glared at him while others, including Will, managed to sleep through the disturbance he had caused. Tommy had been screaming in his sleep and Brian had run over to wake him up. Tommy looked at his friend with a blank stare.

"You OK, man?" Brian asked a confused Tommy.

Tommy looked around the room again and then back at Brian.

"Fuck, man," Tommy said, slowly becoming aware of his surroundings and feeling a little embarrassed. "I was having a nightmare. Did I wake everybody up?"

"Not everybody, Franklin." Brian knew the last twenty-four hours must have been torturous for his friend and the fact he had had a nightmare didn't surprise him. "Are you going to be able to go back to sleep?"

Tommy rubbed the top of his head. If he weren't confined to his quarters he would get up and go outside to check on the dog that was tied up somewhere. But he knew he couldn't and wouldn't dare.

"Yeah, I think so, Dodd. That was one hell of a nightmare."

Brian slapped his friend on the back, said goodnight and started to walk away.

"Dodd!" Tommy said, just barely loud enough to get Brian's attention. Brian turned around and took the couple of steps back to Tommy's bed.

"What is it, Franklin?" he asked, looking around, thankful everyone had put their head back down on their pillows.

"The dog's been fed right? And he has lots of water?"

Tommy had been told this by Will before they went to sleep, but needed reassuring.

"Yeah, Franklin. It's all good. The dog's fine. Go to sleep."

"Dodd ... ," Tommy didn't want Brian to walk away, but he also didn't want to appear weak. The nightmare had been hellish.

"What is it now, Franklin?" Brian stopped and turned around again.

"Thanks ... that's all. Thanks," Tommy said, still looking a little confused from being woken up.

"You're welcome," Brian said quietly. "Go back to sleep. You need it."

Brian went back to his bed as Tommy lay with his hands behind his head and stared at the ceiling. He knew he wouldn't be able to get back to sleep. He had lied to Brian about that, but only because he didn't want his friend to worry. His mind was racing and it mostly revolved around the man he had killed the day before. It bothered him deeply. So deeply, it would haunt him to his grave. He didn't know that yet, but in time he would come to realize the effects war could have on even the most stable and brave soldiers. Tommy rehashed over and over in his mind what he would or could have done differently. But nothing was going to change that now. The deed was done. He would have to live with what he did ... or at least try.

THE MORNING AFTER the troops returned to base was a morning Tommy came to dread. He knew it was coming. He was read the riot act by Lieutenant Peterson and Captain Palmer. He was threatened with this and warned about that. He was lectured once again about what it took to be a smart soldier. He was humbled and, as he had been told already, "confined to quarters until further notice." That meant no visits with his canine buddy. However, the dog, he was informed much to his relief, could stay on the base.

Will had a change of heart and he and Brian assured Tommy they would look after the newly designated camp mascot until Tommy had his freedom again. That would come in eight days. All he knew during his confinement was that the dog was tied up away from the barracks over by the machine shop and garage where the mechanics worked on the camp vehicles. It was a shady spot under a tree and not too far from the kitchen, which of course was a good thing. Will, Brian and some others built a doghouse out of some scrap wood they found and although it wasn't exactly a work of art, it served the purpose.

Tommy got his daily reports from Will and Brian and sometimes they were quite comical. Apparently the dog was enjoying being the center of attention and adjusting to "Army life." Food was always being tossed his way as soldiers walked by with scraps from the kitchen. Eat, drink, sleep and play. It's a dog's life. The mascot was let off his rope on occasion and was thankful for that. The soldiers would let him come to the makeshift basketball court or baseball field and join them in the fun. He loved to run and chase whatever the soldiers threw for him. If the dog could talk it would say to Tommy, "Thank you for rescuing me."

But where is this guy they call Tommy? How come he's not around? Why did my new friend desert me?

The eight-day confinement seemed much longer than it actually was. Tommy couldn't wait to see how his friend was doing, although it sounded like he was doing quite well. On the morning of the eighth day Lieutenant Peterson walked into the barracks and saw Tommy sitting on the edge of his bed reading a letter. Tommy noticed his lieutenant, stood at attention and saluted.

"Good morning, sir!"

The lieutenant came up to Tommy and threw him some mail to read.

"At ease, Private. Here are some more letters for you."

"Thank you, sir."

Tommy relaxed, sat back down on his bed and went through the letters. He was pleased as he saw another one had come from Carolyn. Lieutenant Peterson sat down on the bed across from Tommy's.

"How are you this morning, Private Franklin?"

"Not bad. Could always be better."

"Yeah well, we all could," the lieutenant agreed.

Peterson clasped his hands between his legs and thought for a moment before he spoke. Tommy wondered what was coming next.

"Private Franklin ... ."

"Yes, sir."

"Private Franklin, I've said this more than once, but I'm going to say it again; I need to trust you. What I haven't done was ask you directly, can I trust you? That's why I'm here. I need to know that what happened a little over a week ago will never happen again. You're a good soldier. A good man. But for the sake of the others, I need to know if you're going to act like a responsible soldier from now on. To survive war, we need to rely on each other. A lot of us have lost faith in you. Guys think you're a loose cannon. My gut tells me differently. We've all been around each other long enough to get a feel for each other. My heart tells me you're special and that you just slipped up. Slipped up big time. But you can't do it again. Do you understand what I'm saying here, Private?"

Tommy did understand. He had been hoping all week that he would have a chance for a conversation like this with one of his superior officers and he was glad it was Lieutenant Peterson. Someone he felt comfortable with. Someone he respected immensely.

"Yes sir, Lieutenant. I fully understand."

"Then I can trust you?" the lieutenant asked looking the private in the eye.

Tommy looked him back in the eye. He wanted his lieutenant to know that this would be a vow.

"Yes, sir. You can trust me, sir."

"And your fellow soldiers can trust you?" Lieutenant Peterson continued to glare at Tommy trying to read him clearly.

"Yes, sir."

"Then I believe you, Private Franklin. And you ... you believe that we're all in this together, right?"

Tommy didn't hesitate in his response and there was clarity in his voice. "Yes, sir."

"You're one of us, Private Franklin, and we have to trust each other. I know you mean your promise and want it to be true, but under the circumstances, we are both going to have to be vigilant."

The "Yes, sirs" kept coming and Lieutenant Peterson felt in his heart the private was being honest. He thought back to the incident in the village and it was the treatment of the dog that set Tommy off. That wasn't necessarily a bad thing. Soldiers have emotions and that's a good thing. No one would ever know if killing the man in the village was the right thing to do. Maybe it was self-defense. Only Tommy really knew. But it was done. It was over. Private Franklin had set a bad example among his peers and Lieutenant Peterson was hoping these last eight days confined to the barracks had given Tommy time to reflect. He hoped time had healed the wounds and wanted this American soldier to get his confidence back. This might be the time to put it all behind them, starting now. They had inherited a dog that Tommy would have to be responsible for and only he knew why he did what he did. Or did he? Lieutenant Peterson truly liked Tommy and in these last few days even he had come to admire the dog. He was ready to move on.

"So listen. I've come here to tell you that you have your freedom back. You can leave the barracks and go say hello to your dog."

Tommy couldn't believe his ears. He was elated, but stayed restrained.

" ... and Private Franklin," the lieutenant continued.

"Yes, sir."

Peterson stood up from the bed he had been sitting on. Tommy quickly got to his feet. The lieutenant spoke in no uncertain terms.

"I can't be more sincere. You better be on your best behavior, Private. War is a serious business and we need you. We all need you to act responsibly."

There was a pause as Tommy waited to hear if that was it.

Are we finished?

They were.

"Yes, sir. Nothing like that will ever happen again, sir. I promise, sir."

"I believe you."

Lieutenant Peterson was pleased with Tommy's reaction to their conversation. The commanding officer offered a handshake that Tommy accepted. The two soldiers saluted each other and Peterson gave Tommy an understanding slap on the arm.

"You have a good day, Private Franklin. Dismissed."

What Made Me Do It?

"Thank you, sir. You have a good day as well," Tommy replied and watched the lieutenant as he walked between the rows of beds and made his exit.

Private Franklin couldn't believe his relief as Peterson walked through the exit door. He stood momentarily staring at the door and felt a little stunned by what had just gone down. He was free again. Free to go see his dog. As he picked up his mail, he heard the door reopen. Lieutenant Peterson poked his head back in.

"Private Franklin."

Tommy stood at attention one more time.

"Yes, sir."

"I meant to give you one more piece of advice. You should get a name for that dog. Nobody knows what to call it."

Tommy smiled.

"Yes, sir. I'll do that today, sir."

"... and then let me know what you've decided on, OK Franklin?"

"Yes, sir. I will. As soon as I think of one I will let you know," Tommy answered, showing his emotions for the first time in over a week.

Lieutenant Peterson closed the door as Tommy looked down at the mail in his hand. This was going to be a bittersweet ... great day. Not only had he won his freedom once again, but he had received letters from the people who meant the most to him in his life: Carolyn, his mother and father and his sister Kathy. He was alone in the barracks, but screamed with delight. He was feeling good about himself again. Good about being a soldier in the Army. Good about being a son and brother. Good about having Carolyn as his girl and good about having another dog in his life. He couldn't get to the exit door fast enough.

When he stood on the small porch he saw Lieutenant Peterson walking away. Tommy stopped and watched the lieutenant head out over the dirt. It was an honor to serve under a commanding officer that he respected so dearly. He'd never let him down again. It was too much pain to deal with and it had been a disappointment for them both.

Tommy turned his head and looked in the direction where he thought his dog was tied up. His heart pounded. Free again. He noticed the busyness of the camp and wondered where Will and Brian were. He walked hurriedly toward the machine shop. He turned the corner of the Social Club and there he was. His pal was tied up outside his doghouse, lying in the shade and chewing on a bone. The dog actually looked like it had put on some weight. Tommy stopped just a few feet shy of where the dog lay and observed. With his back toward Tommy, the dog hadn't yet noticed Tommy's presence.

"Hey, guy!" Tommy called out. The dog stood and looked at his friend that had rescued him. "Remember me?"

Sure do. How could I forget?

The dog began wagging its tail and ran up to Tommy. Tommy knelt down and hugged his new friend.

"How ya doing there, boy?"

He had been worried about the reaction he would get from the dog when they saw each other again. But now he saw that there had been no need for that. The dog was doing what dog's do when their owners disappear and then reappear, waiting. This dog had known that the human who had rescued him would return one day and now he had.

I'm pretty smart. I knew you would come back to me.

"You're a good boy, ya know. You're a good boy."

Tommy looked over at the dog's house "the boys" had put together for his canine friend. Obviously it hadn't been built from a set of blue prints.

"Gees, I like your digs there, big fella."

No, it wasn't the Ritz, but it was the thought that mattered. It wasn't air conditioned, but it had room service. Tommy got a big lick in the face.

"Hey, boy. I brought some letters. How about if I read you some letters?"

Tommy stood up, walked over to the dog house and sat down leaning his back against one side of it. The dog followed and sat down beside him.

"Come on," Tommy patted the ground. "Lay down, boy. I'll read you all the news from back home."

He opened the letter from Carolyn first as the dog lay down and put his chin on Tommy's leg. "This here is a letter from my girl back in Michigan. Maybe you'll meet her one day. Wouldn't that be cool?" The freed soldier began reading as the dog listened. There was no war going on right now. Only companionship. It was exactly what this young man from Brenton, Michigan, U.S.A. needed. It was therapeutic. It was trust and understanding. It was being best friends.

WILL AND BRIAN had been playing a pick-up game of basketball in the dirt that served as a primitive basketball court on the base. They had noticed Tommy when he came around the corner of the Social Club.

"Hey, look who's out of the joint, Dodd. Our friend, Franklin," Will said, tossing the basketball to Brian.

Brian shot the ball up toward the basket.

"I sure hope he has permission."

What Made Me Do It?

Will went after the basketball and, when he got to it, held it underneath his arm. He stood and looked at Tommy.

"Well, let's go see."

Will took one last shot at the basket, then he and Brian left the ball where it lay and headed in Tommy's direction.

"Is he reading the dog a letter?" Brian asked as they walked toward their comrade.

"He's reading it something. Maybe Franklin went off the deep end while he was doing his time," Will lightly joked.

"Personally, I think he went off the deep end a long time ago," Brian followed up.

The Oreo cookie members were still good friends in spite of everything. Even though Tommy hadn't been allowed out of the barracks the last eight days, the three of them and usually a fourth, still played cards at night and tried to make life a little more bearable for their friend. Will and Brian believed that Tommy was sincere in his apologies for what happened and the apologies continued night after night. Tommy was also sincere in his concern for the dog, always asking how he was doing. Was he being looked after? Was he getting enough food and water? Was there enough shade for him? But what was always in the back of Tommy's mind was the guilt of letting his platoon members down while he was saving the dog. It tore him up inside. Was it worth it? Tommy still didn't know. Thank goodness no soldiers got hurt and thank goodness the dog was alive and in a safe place.

"Hey, Franklin," Will called from forty feet away. "You think that dog understands what you're reading to him?"

Tommy looked up and saw his two buddies approaching. He was delighted to see them and jumped to his feet.

"Does the lieutenant know you're out here, Franklin? Cause if he doesn't I'm just gonna keep on walking," Brian said as he and Will walked up to Tommy and the dog.

"Hey guys, how ya doing?" Tommy gave Will and Brian a quick man hug each. "Yeah, he knows. He came by just a few minutes ago and cut me loose. I'm a free man again."

"Good for you, Franklin," Will said, giving Tommy a pat on the arm. "Whatta ya reading to the dog?"

Tommy looked at the letter in his hand.

"Aw, just a letter from Carolyn I got this morning. I thought he might want to hear what's going on back stateside."

Brian squatted down and petted the base mascot.

"You know we have to come up with a name for this guy sooner or later. Everybody just keeps referring to him as "the dog." We talked about this the other night, Franklin. Ya gotta give this guy a name."

"Yeah, man. Give this thing a name," Will jumped in. "How would you like it if everybody referred to you as "the human?""

"Peterson said the same thing. So let's do it then. No time better than now." Tommy said, feeling stoked about having his freedom and being with his dog and two good friends.

Will and Brian looked at each other and contemplated what name might be good for this big mutt.

"How about Lucky?" Brian asked "Yeah. I mean let's face it, he's pretty darn lucky to be here."

Tommy was not sure about Lucky and said so. Brian and Will continued to think.

"How about Dinner?" Will said and laughed. "Isn't that what he was going to be before he got rescued?"

Tommy forced out a chuckle over the thought of calling him Dinner. It brought back the memory of that day back in the hamlet and he wanted to erase those images from his mind as quickly as possible. If possible.

"Naw, I don't think so, Dempsey. I don't know if that would be real appropriate. Keep thinking."

Brian tried again.

"Hey, Franklin. That watch you gave up for this guy, what kind was it?"

"It was a Timex. My parents gave it to me," Tommy informed Brian.

Tommy didn't want to revisit the fact he had given up the watch that had been a gift from his parents when he got home from boot camp. It had meant a lot to him and what were his parents going to think when they found out he traded a watch they were so proud to give him, for a dog? That time, when it came, wouldn't be easy. They would be hurt. Maybe. But then, knowing his parents, maybe not. They were always understanding and forgiving. And besides, they were dog lovers as well. Just maybe they would understand.

"Well, there ya go then. Name him Timex," Brian snapped back.

Tommy thought about that. He kind of liked the name Timex. His parents knew how their son felt about dogs. When he told them he had traded the watch for a dog maybe they'd get a good laugh out of it and perhaps they would be flattered he named his dog after the watch they had given him. Tommy contemplated for a couple of seconds and, yes, Timex had a nice ring to it.

"Dodd, you're a genius!" Tommy appreciated everything about Brian's suggestion and his parents would, of course, understand. Tommy knew that.

"Hey," Brian said, pleased that Tommy liked his idea. "Your folks are going to find out what happened sooner or later. Maybe not the whole truth, but you have to tell them something, man. The least you can do is name this mutt after the watch they gave you."

The dog fed off the Oreo cookie's excitement and didn't know who to jump on so he tried jumping up on all three.

"Down Timex, down," Tommy wrestled with Timex and tried to calm him down.

"Dodd, you're too cool, man. OK, Timex it is. Good boy, Timex. Good boy," Tommy gleamed.

"Well, god damn it! I'm glad this guy finally has a name. Stop the presses!" Will said, kneeling down to pat Timex as the dog gave Will a big kiss in the face. "Oh, yeah! Oh, yeah. What do they say in that TV commercial? Keeps on licking even while ticking? Something like that."

It was a good day. Tommy had his freedom. His dog had a name and the Oreo cookie had a good laugh together. The war was forgotten for the moment. The war. What war?

Full Alert

WHAT WAR? THE war that raged all over Vietnam and never slept. That one. Two weeks after Tommy got his freedom his company got the news that a major battle was brewing. Everyone was told to get ready because a forthcoming Viet Cong offensive was coming and it was going to be something like this war had never seen. Camp Brotherhood was on full alert as the enemy that surrounded them bore down and dug in. They could hear the bombs and artillery fire off in the distance, day and night. The Oreo cookie had been involved in some minor skirmishes up to this point, but a big battle was now looming. Everyone had been informed that tomorrow was going to be the day the whole company headed out to meet the enemy face to face. Will, Brian and Tommy sat at a picnic table just outside the mess hall eating their dinner. Timex sat at the end of the table a few feet away, well behaved and enjoying the little tidbits of food tossed his way.

"Did you talk to Johnson about looking after Timex while we're out on our little adventure?" Will asked Tommy, referring to Cal Johnson who worked in the kitchen and would be staying behind.

"Yeah, I spoke to him. He's OK with it. No big deal. Feed 'em, make sure he has water and play with him when we can. Shouldn't be too difficult," Tommy replied between mouthfuls of dinner.

"I'm sure Johnson will be bringing him lots of goodies from the kitchen. He'll probably double in weight by the time we get back," Will said as he tossed Timex a small piece of meat.

"Did you tell Johnson no chicken bones, Franklin?" Brian voiced a mild concern.

"Yes, Dodd. I told Johnson no chicken bones and only Grade A steak for breakfast, lunch and dinner. He'll be eating better than we will."

The three continued to eat their meal and said very little. It was the same for the other troops sitting around the tables. The mood was somewhat somber during this dinner hour as most thoughts were focused on the next few days and the fighting that was to come. No one really wanted to discuss it and, as a result, conversation was kept simple and light. That is before Brian decided to broach the subject with a little bit of cynicism.

"So I guess tomorrow's the big day. I can hardly wait." Brian thought it would be healthy to talk about the unavoidable bloodshed that was going to be a big part of their lives the next few days.

"It's what we've been trained for," Tommy said, not looking up from his plate of food.

"You guys ever think about dying?" Brian continued.

"Dodd, give it a rest," Will said, not wanting to talk about dying, living or anything else at the moment. But Brian persisted.

"Hey man, we're all going to die sooner or later. Look at Duncan, he didn't make it."

Paul Duncan, their grumpy card player that no one would forget, had been killed in action a week before while out on patrol with his platoon. It was an ambush that could have happened to anyone in this group of American soldiers. In fact, it happened all the time across this country. Ambushes were part of the enemy's tactics. Sometimes when soldiers were killed in battle, all you knew was their name and it didn't feel that close to home. Even though the Oreo cookie members weren't fond of Paul, he was still one of them. Because of the card game they played, there was in fact a face with the name. It brought it all a little closer to the heart. Tommy, Will and Brian, all three thought a lot about Paul's death. Did he have family? They didn't know. If he didn't, that would have made his passing all the more sad. Did he have friends? Another mystery. Who was going to look after his burial and funeral services when his body was sent back to the States? If he was alone, the government would take care of it of course. But, who would the military notify about his passing? Did he have anyone that cared about him? At least with the Oreo cookie members they had friends and family who cared. If one of them was killed in action, everything would be looked after and there would be lots of people at the funeral. In Brian's case, he was comforted by his belief in a God who would provide for him in the afterlife. But Paul? He could have died without anyone caring except for maybe one of the many fantasy girlfriends he claimed to have had. Hopefully that would be the case. Hopefully one of his fantasy girlfriends would care. No one should die alone.

"Yeah we know, Dodd. We all know about Duncan," Will said, a little irritated. "He was doing his job, man. Just like the rest of us. God rest his soul."

Brian took that last little bit of Will's comment as a possible affirmation his friend did believe in God.

"So you do believe in God after all. Hey, Dempsey."

Will finished off the last couple of bites of his meal and put the plate on the ground for Timex to lick clean. Timex was more than pleased to do that as Will gave him a pat on the head. Will stood up and looked Brian square in the eye.

"Dodd. We live … we die. Haven't we been down this road before? We live … we die. That's about as simple as I can put it to you. You hang onto your beliefs, Dodd. They're good for you. But for me, we live, we die and that's the way it is."

Tommy continued to eat and stayed out of the conversation. He agreed with Will. This subject about the existence of God always seemed to be a sensitive one and came up more often than it should. To each their own. Tommy looked at Will, then at Brian. Was it his imagination or did everyone seem a little on edge?

"That's fine, Dempsey. You're right. We live, we die," Brian said and wanted to keep the topic going. "But some of us will keep on living after we die because we made a choice in our lives. Wouldn't you like to go on living after you leave this earth, Dempsey?"

Will stood up, stretched his arms upwards, looked at the blue sky and then back down at Brian.

"What's the catch, Dodd?"

"All you have to do … ," Brian started explaining and then was interrupted by Will.

"Yeah, I know what we have to do, Dodd. You've told us a few times. No thanks. If there's a catch, I'm not interested. I am who I am, dude. I'll see you guys back in the barracks. You two up for a card game if we have time?"

"Count me in," Tommy said, holding his empty plate down to his side to let Timex get some licks in.

Will looked at Brian.

"How about you, Dodd? Could be the last one for a while."

Brian's thoughts were elsewhere, but he told his non-believing friends it sounded like a good idea.

"OK, I'll see you guys in a bit. See ya, Timex." Will departed as Brian watched him walk away.

"I don't know why you guys don't get it, man," Brian said, directing his attention to Tommy. "God's watching over us. I'm telling ya, he's watching over us."

Brian held his plate and stared straight ahead.

Tommy looked at his plate that Timex had just made sparkling clean and was impressed. He showed it to Brian.

"Look at this, Dodd. It doesn't even have to be washed. Good job, Timex."

"Yeah good boy, Timex," Brian laughed to himself. "Maybe Johnson will put you to work in the kitchen while we're gone."

Tommy stood up, about to make his exit and follow Will back to the barracks. But Brian still had one more thing to say about the God issue.

"You know what I'm talking about, right Franklin?"

Tommy would rather play dumb on this one.

"Not really, Dodd. I kind of agree with Will. I'm not really a God kind of guy."

"You can live in all eternity in his name," Brian said, still not wanting to let it go.

"Whose name?" Tommy asked, playing the dumb part well and knowing what was coming next because he'd heard it all before.

"Jesus' name," Brian said, standing up from the picnic table.

"Oh yeah right, him."

Tommy wanted to think for a moment and phrase his statement so that it didn't show disrespect toward Brian's beliefs or hurt his feelings. How many times had he tiptoed through this subject with Brian before? He looked out over the base and around the outside of the mess hall where many soldiers were enjoying their meal. He knew that in a few days some of them wouldn't be back here eating their dinner and he might be one of them. It was pretty certain they were not all going to return. That's the nature of war isn't it? It was like Will had said so clearly, "we live, we die." Soldiers get killed in action. It's the nature of war. It was a nice thought that Brian had put forth. Wouldn't it be nice to live forever? To Tommy it didn't make sense and hadn't for a long time. What about the enemy soldiers he had killed and would kill again? Who was right and who was wrong in this war? The enemy felt the same way the American soldiers did; they were all fighting for what they considered a just cause. Whose side was God on and why would he chose sides anyway? That wouldn't be right, would it? That was part of the problem Tommy had with all this God stuff. For lack of a better explanation, he thought it was all a bunch of bull shit. But he wouldn't say that to Brian. He believed what he did and that didn't bother Tommy a bit. He didn't agree with Brian's constant preaching over the past few months, but it wasn't enough to test a friendship. Tommy had let go of his Christian beliefs long before, much to his parents' disappointment. But he was comfortable in his own shell and knew Brian had a slight problem with that. Brian thought everyone should be a believer like him.

Tommy looked down at Timex and that raised another question; were dogs entitled to this eternal life? It was all very interesting to Tommy, only not very convincing.

"Well, Dodd, I don't know. How many times do we have to have this discussion? I'm fine, you're fine, Will's fine. We're all fine and we're all good no matter what we believe. It ain't for me, man. But hey, you keep preaching. Maybe you'll get a conversion out of someone yet. But it won't be me and I seriously doubt it'll be Dempsey. I'm gonna go tie Timex up and head back to the barracks. See ya later. Let's play some cards. Come on, Timex."

Tommy walked away with his dog jumping up at his side. Just as he had watched Will walk away, Brian watched Tommy and Timex leave. He thought about how Timex had been good for Tommy. The dog seemed to have mellowed Tommy out and soothed his soul. It was obvious he had a thing for dogs and must have a history with them. He recalled Tommy mentioning more than once in a conversation something about a dog named Buddy that he had when he was growing up. He remembered the look on Tommy's face whenever he talked about that special friend. The look in people's eyes could tell you a lot and Tommy's eyes, when he talked about Buddy, led straight to his heart. It was Tommy's heart talking whenever he spoke about his boyhood friend. Now here was Timex, another special friend to give Tommy comfort.

"God, please look after those two will you? They need each other," Brian pleaded in words only audible to himself.

He tapped his fingers on the table and watched Tommy and Timex disappear around the corner of the Social Club. What would tomorrow bring for the Oreo cookie? Next month. Next year. For now a trip to hell was in store.

"Dear God, have mercy on our souls."

Brian got up from the table and started to make his way back to the barracks. It was time for one last card game.

WORDS OF COURSE, could never describe the ferocity of a battle when it was happening full bore. This was what was going on at the moment and the Oreo cookie members were in the thick of it. The North Vietnamese Army was very much on the offensive on this second day of the fight and although the daytime had been relatively quiet, all hell broke loose as dusk fell and daylight gave way to darkness. Like the day before, the heavy fighting came during the night. Until now, the Oreo cookie had only been involved in minor clashes with the enemy. Small time stuff, but small time stuff that still killed. It had been mostly "hit and run" exhibited by the enemy. But now it was different. This battle was anything but "hit and run." It was toe-to-toe fighting and neither army was going to back down. Tommy's platoon had been ambushed more than a couple of times in the past, but they hadn't suffered any causalities. They had always come out of those minor skirmishes by chasing the enemy off and killing the ones they got in their sights. Neither Tommy, Will nor Brian enjoyed the killing aspect of war. It was dreadful, but they were infantry and that's what infantry do. It isn't about the killing. It's about doing whatever you have to do to stay alive. It was thinking about your family and friends back home that gave you the will to survive at whatever cost. Survival is the only thing that war is about and in every war, it means killing the enemy. The enemy, who also had friends, sons and daughters, mothers and fathers. War isn't always understood by those on the battlefield dodging bullets and mortars. In a firefight it is not about "my ideology against your ideology," protecting my land against your aggression. It is a mentality that says what has been said so many times before: kill them before they kill you.

I'm going back to my family and friends alive and I don't really give a shit if I have to kill you to get back to them.

When the bullets go ping-ping by your head and you're firing your rifle or machine gun as fast as you can, there isn't much time to think. There's only time for killing and that's what was going on right now, lots of killing. Tommy lay on his back in a trench putting more ammo into his M16 rifle. The battle was in full force now as darkness took over. He fought beside a dozen soldiers he didn't even know. Where had Will and Brian gone? The three of them had been fighting side by side just a few moments before. He quickly looked in both directions down the trench to see if he could see either one. He couldn't and began firing again through the darkness. They were being bombarded by mortars non-stop. They fell just short of the trench or just behind him. There hadn't been any direct hits yet and there was no time to wonder why. Tommy fired back in the direction from which the bullets that zipped by his head were coming. His mind was telling him to get ready for hand to hand combat. He slid back down and noticed one of his comrades bloodied in the face and lying still just a few feet away. He crawled over to the soldier and looked to confirm what he already knew. Not that he had seen it that many time before, but Tommy knew death when he saw it now. He cursed.

Just beyond the dead soldier he heard more moaning. The light from a nearby explosion let him make out the identity of the fallen warrior. It was Lieutenant Peterson. Tommy screamed for a medic, but he could barely hear his own voice over all the explosions and the firing of rifles around him. He sprang to the top of the trench, fired off some more rounds and fell back down to where Lieutenant Peterson lay severely wounded and lay down beside him.

"Peterson, its Franklin. You're going to be OK. You're going to be OK."

Another mortar hit a few feet away spraying earth on the two soldiers.

Tommy covered up the lieutenant.
Where the hell is a medic?
More explosions. Tommy quickly examined the lieutenant to see where he had been hit and if there was anything he could do. The lieutenant's eyes were lifeless, but Tommy noticed him blink.
"Stay with me, Lieutenant. Stay with me."
Peterson's eyes closed. Tommy cursed again and as he rose to yell one more time for a medic there was a sharp undeniable pain in his abdomen. He had been hit and fell back down beside the lieutenant. He looked at his hand that he had placed over his mid-section the moment he got shot. It was bloody. He closed his eyes and once again, barely audible to even himself, he called for a medic. The war was over for Tommy Franklin and life was over for the man that lay beside him. A man that Tommy had respected more than anyone else since he came to Vietnam. A man who had a wife and two young children back home, plus a dog. As Tommy slipped into unconsciousness he thought of his own family. His parents, his sister and of course Carolyn. He began to worry about Timex and who would look after him now? The last thing he remembered before passing out was asking himself, "Why can't we all just get along?"

TOMMY LAY ON his back in a hospital bed. He opened his eyes and then closed them quickly. The lights were so bright.
Where am I? Am I alive or dead?
He kept his sensitive eyes shut and listened. He heard faint noises he didn't recognize. Tommy continued to listen and tried opening his eyes again, squinting this time. The medication had taken its toll over the last couple of days while he had been unconscious.
Am I in a hospital?
He was, but it was hard for him to determine that, with his mind clouded by the medicine. He managed to get his eyes open enough to squint at the ceiling with its bright lights. His eyes blinked rapidly in a reflex to the brightness as he continued to take in the sounds. He heard soldiers in obvious pain. He was not in the trench fighting anymore and that had been his last recollection.
What happened to me? I was in a firefight and then there was a pain in my gut ... .
Tommy moved his fingers and then his toes. That was a good sign.
What's going on? How did I get here?
His eyes began to adjust to the light of the room. Slowly turning his head

one way and then the other, he saw that he was not alone. There were many soldiers in this big, wide open room. He felt an intravenous needle in his left arm and saw the tube running up to a clear liquid being pumped into him. The confusion lingered.

I can't be alive. I can't.

He tried to lift his right arm, but it was useless. Tommy was too weak to move any of his limbs. A few beds down a nurse noticed that Tommy had regained consciousness and walked over to him. Tommy managed to turn his head slightly and look at her. His vision was blurred, but he could make out that she was Afro-American and held a clipboard. She leaned over and spoke in a soft voice.

"How are you this morning, Private Franklin?"

With a blank expression on his face he stared at her. It was comforting to hear a human voice. He wondered to himself if he would be able to speak ... now or ever. The nurse walked to the other side of the bed and informed Tommy that she was going to take his pulse, which she did. Tommy's eyes followed her and as his vision cleared he watched her. Their eyes met and she smiled. He tried to smile back as it slowly came to him that he was in fact, alive.

The nurse let go of his wrist, bent over and said that exact thing, "You're alive, Private Franklin."

Never had words felt so powerful.

Did she say I am alive? I am alive! I can't believe this! I am alive!

"You're in a surgical hospital in Pleiku."

She took his hand and held it. He didn't realize it when she was taking his pulse, but realized it now, he hadn't lost his sense of feeling. He could hear. He could see. He could feel. Tommy wanted to talk to this woman and ask her so many questions, but he was weak and his mind was not sharp. The nurse sensed his anxiety and filled him in with some basic information.

"Private Franklin ... you're recovering from a very serious wound and you're on some very strong medication. The doctors say you're going to be fine, but it will take a while for you to get back on your feet." Tommy listened intently. "Your family has been notified, but right now the doctors just want you to rest, rest and rest some more."

My family! Mom, Dad, Kathy, Carolyn. Timex. Will. Brian. Lieutenant Peterson. I am Private Tommy Franklin! I was in a firefight.

Names and places suddenly popped into his head. He hadn't lost his memory. Tommy squeezed the nurse's hand lightly and was determined to speak.

"What is your name?" he asked weakly.

"My name is Amy and you'll be seeing lots of me. It's OK to call me Amy. But for now, we won't do any talking. When you get your strength back we'll have lots of talking to do. It's nice to see your eyes open, Private Franklin. You had us worried there for a while. I'm going to go tell one of the doctors you're awake and I'll send one over."

"Wait!" Tommy's voice was barely audible and somewhat panicked.

Amy only had time to take one step before Tommy stopped her.

"What is it, Private Franklin? What can I do for you?"

Amy grabbed Tommy's hand again to console him.

"How did I get here?" the private wanted to know.

The nurse squeezed Tommy's hand.

"Some very brave soldiers brought you in."

Amy let go of Tommy's hand and walked away. By the time Tommy could get a faint "thank you" out she was too far away to hear him. He shut his eyes and began to think about family and friends. He was alive and he wondered how Lieutenant Peterson, Will and Brian were doing and if they'd been in to see him. He wished he had asked the nurse if any visitors had come by to check on him these last couple of days.

What about my mail? I wonder if I have a letter from Carolyn to read? My sister? My mom and dad?

Tommy continued to feel anxious. He wanted to get out of bed and get on with life right now. His thoughts also travelled back to Timex.

Surely someone is taking care of him. Brian or Will must be around. They'll make sure he's doing OK. Gees, I'd love to see Timex. I want to see Timex.

Tommy fell back asleep and started dreaming of the place where he grew up. In Brenton there was no war. No killing. Only good times and laughter. In his dream were all his old friends, his parents and Buddy. He was with his friends at the lake in the summer doing what they always did. Amy, the nurse who had just paid him a visit, sat at a picnic table watching the kids have their fun. She wasn't in her nurses uniform, but dressed in summer casuals and smiling at the local youth. The dream was short and the last thing that took place was Buddy running up to Amy and getting a pat and hug from her. Tommy would never forget that dream. It was a beautiful dream and one that inspired him on his road to recovery.

IT WASN'T A moment that Brian had been looking forward to and the guilt he felt for not visiting Tommy in the hospital was now more than he could bear. What was he going to say to him? He had been thinking about that ever since he found out yesterday that Tommy had regained consciousness. Now the time had come. Today would be the day. As he walked from the barracks to the hospital, his mind raced. Hopefully, Tommy would be awake and he could just get it over with. Walking up the steps to enter the hospital he hesitated. It was still morning. Maybe it would be better to do this in the afternoon. He turned around to leave, but then thought, "No, Tommy is my friend. Now is the time."

The hospital, crude as it was—wood floors, wood partitions, wood ceiling and not very many windows—still served a huge purpose for those injured in battle. The medical technology was all the latest despite the dismal surroundings. The injured soldiers were well looked after and made to feel as comfortable as possible. It wasn't one of the squeaky clean white hospitals you would find back in the States, but in a war zone, this was as good as it got. Brian walked through the fronts doors and looked around. He had been told to ask for a Dr. Morgan. He saw a receptionist dressed in a nurse's uniform sitting at a desk off to his left and thought that might be a good place to start. She was studying a file as Brian walked up.

"Excuse me, mam."

The nurse looked up at Brian and acknowledged him.

"I've come to visit a friend of mine, but I was told to see a Doctor Morgan first."

"That's him right over there," the receptionist said, pointing to a doctor sitting in a chair all by himself about thirty feet away and looking at some charts.

"Thank you very much."

Brian took his time as he strolled over to the doctor. He was still unsure if now was the time to see Tommy, but tried to pull on his strength.

"Doctor Morgan?"

The doctor stood up and offered a handshake.

"Yes, I'm Doctor Morgan." Brian shook the doctor's hand, his mind going in slow motion. There was an awkward silence before Brian spoke again. "I was told to see you before I paid a visit to my friend."

"And you are ... ?" The doctor asked.

"Private Brian Dodd. I'm here to see a Private Tommy Franklin."

"Ah, yes. Private Franklin." The doctor put an arm over Brian's shoulder. "Let's take a short walk, Private Dodd."

The doctor led Brian to a corner of the lobby where they had a discussion about Tommy's condition and what Brian should expect when he saw him.

Brian listened intently and understood why the doctor needed to have this time with him. When it was over, the doctor shook Private Dodd's hand again and walked away. Brian watched the action in the lobby and down the hallway and looked at the two double doors he was about to walk through. He had to think some more. But knew he couldn't back down now if for no other reason than that he wanted, at the very least, to see his friend. He took the first few steps and then stopped. More hesitation.

I can do this. I have to do this.

Brian knew there could be no more delay; he made his way to the doors and walked through. He looked at all the injured soldiers. There must be close to fifty. Where's Tommy? He looked at each bed. Some faces he recognized, most he didn't. He slowly walked down the aisle that separated the beds on either side of the room looking at all the faces. Some were sleeping while others were sitting up looking thoughtful. A couple of them sat on the edge of their beds and stared at the floor. He stopped halfway down the row and a nurse walked up.

"May I help you?"

"Yes, thank you. I'm looking for Private Tommy Franklin."

The nurse pointed, "Last bed on your right. He's awake."

"Thank you so much."

Brian saw his friend sitting up in bed. A good sign. This wasn't going to be easy and he knew it, but seeing his friend somewhat alert and sitting up brought a reluctant smile to his face. When Brian got a few feet away from Tommy's bed, Tommy noticed him and could hardly contain his excitement.

"Dodd!" Tommy's first impulse was to get out of bed, but he was quickly reminded of his wounds and that he was not there yet. Not even close.

"Hey, Franklin. Relax, man. Take it easy," Brian said extending his arms to signal "stay put."

The grimace on Tommy's face told Brian all he needed to know. He leaned in and gave his friend a gentle embrace. It seemed like so much longer than just a few days since they last saw each other on the battlefield.

"Good to see you, Franklin."

Brian adjusted the pillow behind Tommy's back to make it more comfortable for him to sit up.

"Thanks, Dodd. Man, it's good to see a familiar face. How the hell are you doing?"

Tommy wanted to put on that he was better than he looked, but was not very convincing.

"I'm doing ... OK. The bigger question is, Franklin, how the heck are you doing?" Brian put a hand on Tommy's shoulder.

"I'm OK. The doctors tell me I'm alive and my instincts tell me to believe them. I gotta do the rehab thing and apparently I'll be heading back stateside in a couple of weeks or something like that. Whenever they say I'm good to go. I don't know all the details. I'll just go with it. I'm feeling better today than yesterday and I guess that's how it's supposed to go."

Tommy was elated to see one third of the Oreo cookie.

Brian got the impression Tommy was in a talkative mood and knew the moment he wanted to avoid would be coming soon.

"Yeah that's right, Franklin. One day at a time. You're in good hands. They'll have you up and out of here in no time."

Eye contact became difficult for Brian and he slowly paced beside the bed.

"How's my buddy Timex doing?" Tommy asked.

"Oh, he's doing fine. Getting spoiled. Keeps asking, 'Where the heck is that Franklin guy?'"

"I can't wait to see him. Tell him to hang in there. I'll make it up to him when I get out of here." Tommy's pain almost seemed to disappear when he heard that Timex was doing well.

Brian thought talking about Timex was a good and welcomed diversion. "I'll do that. What the heck are you going to do with him when you go home, man?" Brian felt the longer he could avoid the inevitable, the better.

"I've been thinking about that, Dodd. He's going back with me. Somehow, someway, I'll work it out. I'm not leaving him here. Won't happen. He's going back to the States with me."

"Yeah well, good luck with that, Franklin. That would be cool. I hope it works out for you."

Private Dodd knew the time had come and there was only one more thing to talk about.

"Dodd," Tommy's voice changed to a more serious tone. He had wanted to ask the question, but felt he already knew the answer and it would be something he didn't want to hear. "How did the lieutenant make out?"

Brian came back to the head of the bed and looked Tommy in the eye. They both knew what was coming, but it had to be said. Brian choked up before he spoke.

"The lieutenant didn't make it, Franklin. He didn't make it."

Brian stared down at the floor as Tommy looked out the windows behind the beds across from him. There was not a lot to say. It was difficult for both. Tommy softly cursed and raised his eyes toward the ceiling as if to ask, "Why?" He thought about his lieutenant and how much he meant to not only him, but to all the soldiers who served under him. Then there was the guilt he suddenly felt, wondering if there was something more he could have done to save the lieutenant's life. His memory was fogged by his medication and the psychological impact that the battle of a few days before had on him. It was hard trying to remember and maybe, just maybe, he didn't want to. Why couldn't it have been him? Lieutenant Peterson had a wife and two kids. Tommy, for the first time, started thinking about how much he hated war and all the killing. Lieutenant Peterson was a good man and Tommy was hurting.

"There's more, Franklin," Brian said shaking his head and not looking up.

Tommy drew a blank. What more could there be? What next? He hadn't a clue and didn't know what to expect. It was bad enough that he had to hear the news about the passing of his wonderful lieutenant. What else was there? An awkward moment of silence passed and Brian would just as soon have walked away.

"There's more?" Tommy asked looking at his friend now.

Brian fought to keep his hands from shaking. He and Tommy looked at each other trying to read the other's mind.

"What is it, Dodd?"

Brian took his turn looking up at the ceiling then back down into the eyes of his friend.

"Franklin ... Dempsey's gone. He didn't make it either."

There, it was done. He said what he didn't want to say, but had to. The Oreo cookie was no more.

"That's fucking impossible, Dodd. Don't bullshit me," an upset Tommy said, not believing Brian. But it was true and his Oreo cookie friend didn't have anything to add to what he had just said. Brian had been agonizing about this moment he knew was coming and he hadn't been sleeping well because of it. The loss of Will had been tearing Brian up and now it tore Tommy up. Tommy, with what strength he could muster, grabbed Brian's uniform at chest level and fought back tears.

"Uh-uh, man. Don't fucking tell me Dempsey's dead, Dodd. Don't fuckin' tell me that."

Brian took Tommy's arm and pushed it away and then gave him a hug. They sobbed and shared each other's pain.

"Dempsey's not gone, Dodd. Where is he? Is he outside playing with Timex? Where is he, Dodd? Playing cards?" Tommy demanded another answer.

Brian couldn't speak and continued his attempt at consoling Tommy.

"I'm so sorry, Franklin. I'm so sorry. He was a good man. He is with his maker now, Franklin. Both him and Peterson. They're in good hands now."

They're in good hands now? With their maker?

That's the part Tommy didn't understand.

They're in good hands now? No! They're gone. They're dead. That's what's happened. They've been killed in a war never to walk on this earth again. I don't believe in God or heaven. Give your head a shake, Dodd. This is bull shit. Lieutenant Peterson's family, what are they thinking? "Oh good, Dad's in heaven now and we'll never see him again alive on this planet. Aren't we lucky?" And what about Dempsey's parents and siblings? Same thing, "We had an amazing big brother and now he's gone." Dempsey's parents will be devastated.

Brian held Tommy's hand.

"Would you say a prayer with me, Franklin? A little prayer for our two friends."

Tommy stared at Brian.

Man, he really does believe this shit. But if this is what he needs, then so be it. It doesn't really matter if I pray with Dodd or not. Nothing is going to change. Lieutenant Peterson and Dempsey won't be coming back no matter how much the two of us pray. It's done. It's over. In war lives are lost and it just goes on and on and on. We live. We die.

Tommy didn't respond at first to Brian's request so Brian asked again.

"Just pray with me, Franklin. It's won't hurt you, man. Let's just have a quick prayer for our two friends and for this war to end soon."

This was no time to put off his good friend and Tommy knew it. They still had each other and that meant a lot to both of them. Tommy was feeling exhausted by the news he had just received and closed his eyes as Brian began a prayer. As Brian prayed, Tommy thought about the brief time he had known Will and how much they had enjoyed each other's company. They had become good friends. He thought about Lieutenant Peterson. And Carolyn. And his parents. And his sister. And Brenton. And as Brian finished his prayer and said, "Amen," Tommy thought about how much he would just like to go home.

"Amen," Tommy said and then thought, "the hell with this war."

BRIAN QUICKLY FINISHED his breakfast in the mess hall and did what he had been doing for the last week; he headed to the hospital. He hadn't missed a visit with Tommy since he gave him the news about Will and Lieutenant Peterson and spent as much time with him as was allowed. Every day seemed to be a step forward for his buddy emotionally, and physically, and it made

Brian feel good to witness Tommy's progress. But today, today was going to be something special and he couldn't get to the hospital fast enough. Brian walked in the front doors and looked around the lobby. He knew exactly what he was looking for and saw it. A wheelchair. He walked up to the nurse at the reception desk.

"Excuse me. Is that wheelchair over there available to take a friend of mine out for some fresh air?"

The nurse concurred that it would be fine.

"Just bring it back when you're through," she said politely.

Brian got the wheelchair and pushed it through the double doors into the ward where Tommy had been for the last week and a half. He could barely contain his excitement as he saw Tommy at the far end of the room walking on crutches and doing rehab, helped by a nurse. Brian walked up without being noticed by either one.

"Excuse me. Hello there, people. Pardon me, nurse. I have permission from Doctor Morgan to take this gentleman out for some fresh air."

Brian placed the wheelchair so that all Tommy had to do was fall back into it.

"Is that right?" the nurse replied and looked at Tommy and smiled. "How do you feel about this, Private Franklin?"

Tommy looked at Brian.

"Well, I don't know. First of all I don't know who this guy is and secondly, its sounds like a kidnapping to me."

"Shut up, Franklin. Just get in the wheelchair." Brian gave his friend a gentle push and Tommy gingerly sank into the chair. Brian looked at the nurse. "Thanks," he said as he quickly headed away.

"You take it easy on Private Franklin. We don't want a setback," the nurse warned Brian, pleased that this man she had been looking after the last few days could get outside and see the sky once again.

Brian looked back at the nurse. "Don't worry. I'll have him back in just a little while, all in one piece ... hopefully ... maybe."

As Brian approached the double swinging doors that lead out into the lobby, he told Tommy to kick them open with his feet which Tommy managed to do. Out into the lobby they went and then out into the great outdoors, down the ramp and onto the dirt.

"You seem to be in a bit of a hurry, Dodd. Remember what the nurse said. I have to come back in one piece," Tommy said, suspecting he knew where they were going.

Brian pushed the wheelchair over the ground in the direction of the Social Club.

"Yeah I know, Franklin. Don't worry about it. I'll get you back in one piece. Or two. Or maybe three. Or whatever. I have a little surprise for you I want you to check out."

Brian knew there was nothing in the world Tommy would rather do right now than see his good friend Timex. Private Franklin didn't let on that he knew what was going on.

"We're going to the Social Club for a drink, Dodd? Sounds good to me."

"No, we're not going to the Social Club, partner. That can wait," Brian said pushing the wheelchair even faster now.

Tommy was enjoying the ride. They turned the far corner of the Social Club and headed toward the mess hall. One more corner to go. As Brian got to the back of the Social Club he wheeled Tommy around and there lay Timex, chewing on a bone of course. Brian stopped pushing the wheelchair so his friend could have a front row seat.

"I thought you two might want to get reacquainted."

Tommy looked at Timex and was overcome with emotion. Timex looked at Tommy and hadn't forgotten who he was. Now allowed to run free, Timex ran up to Tommy and planted his front paws on Tommy's lap. With tears in his eyes, the man who had rescued him gave his pal a hug. Somehow Brian knew this would be their reaction toward each other.

"Hey, Timex," Tommy said softly, overcome with emotion. "How ya doing ol' buddy? Good to see you. Man, is it ever good to see you."

Timex licked Tommy's face and all was well.

"I told you I would come back, Timex. I told you." Tommy continued to hold the dog in his arms and hug him.

"This guy's been asking where you have been, Franklin," Brian interrupted. "Couldn't put it off any longer. I told him today was the day and Private Brian Dodd always keeps a promise."

Tommy tilted his head back and smiled up at Brian.

"It's so good to see him, Dodd. Thank you so much. This feels good. Oh, so good."

Tommy and Timex continued to show their affection toward each other as Brian took a couple of steps away and watched. He was proud of getting these two together. Every once in a while a soldier needed something like this to help him forget about the hell they had all been through. Especially an injured soldier. Every once in a while these sorts of things had to happen in order for them to keep their sanity. Every once in a while it was nice to forget about this thing called war. And every once in a while soldiers can find something to smile about in a war zone. It was working, Brian observed.

TOMMY STOOD NERVOUSLY on the tarmac leaning on his crutches and looked around, expecting to see something. He was among other injured soldiers heading home.

Where's Brian? He said he would come and see me off. And what about Timex? Captain Palmer said he would do everything he could to send Timex back home with me.

Tommy thought about the request he had made to Captain Palmer a couple of days before to see if it would be possible to get Timex crated up and sent back to the States with him.

"It would mean so much," he had told the Captain.

Captain Palmer said it would be a tough assignment to get it all arranged on such short notice and that he had a lot of other things on his mind. But he didn't close the door on the matter and promised Tommy he would make an honest effort to send the two home together.

"I heard you fought a courageous fight a few weeks ago, Private Franklin. You're a good soldier and maybe the army owes you one," the Captain had said, complementing the private on his bravery.

Tommy was distracted as he looked for either Brian or Timex and didn't see Doctor Morgan walk up.

"Hello, Private Franklin," Doctor Morgan extended a greeting and caught Tommy off guard. Tommy attempted to salute, but the doctor informed him it wasn't necessary. "So you're heading home, hey Private Franklin?"

"Yes, sir. Thank you, sir."

It was one day shy of four weeks since Tommy had been wounded and the doctor was impressed with his progress.

"You're making a remarkable recovery, Private Franklin. You've really surprised a lot of people considering the condition you were in when they brought you in from the battlefield. Congratulations! Keep it up."

"Thank you, sir. I will. I'm feeling better each day. I'm looking forward to going home," Tommy said.

He was hoping he didn't appear rude as he tried nonchalantly to watch the activity in the distance to see if he could recognize anything.

"I've contacted everyone at the Veteran's Hospital in California and you'll be well looked after there," the doctor continued to explain. "They're expecting you and they're going to make you feel right at home until you're fully recovered. They're good people. You have a good flight back and best of luck, soldier."

Doctor Morgan shook Tommy's hand.

"Thank you again, sir. I really appreciate what you and the other's did here. Best of luck to you too," Tommy said, focused on the doctor's eyes. He owed his life to a lot of people and the doctor was certainly one of them.

"You stay well, Private Franklin."

"You too, sir."

Doctor Morgan turned to walk away so he could speak to some of the other injured soldiers leaving on the flight. Just as he did, Tommy remembered something he wanted to mention to the doctor and called out.

"Doctor Morgan!"

The doctor stopped, turned around and walked the few feet back to where Tommy stood.

"Yes, Private Franklin."

"When I first came to my senses, there was a nurse, a black nurse, Tammy, Amy, Cammie. I can't remember her name. I only saw her once. She was right there when I first opened my eyes and if by chance she remembers who I am, can you just tell her 'thank you' from me. There was something about her presence that made me feel comfortable and safe. But that was it. I never saw her again to speak to her. If you can just pass that on I would appreciate it."

"That won't be a problem, Private Franklin. I'll make sure she gets the message."

"Thank you so much, sir."

The doctor turned and walked away one more time. He didn't know why he didn't say anything to Tommy, perhaps not to confuse him or maybe because he was in a rush to speak with the other injured soldiers, but the doctor knew there were no black nurses on staff at the hospital and, considering the fact Tommy would have been heavily medicated when he first came to, he could have been delirious and hallucinated the whole thing. It didn't matter.

The conversation with Doctor Morgan put Tommy more at ease for a brief moment, but he still wondered where Brian and Timex were. Something was wrong, he felt, and he began to get anxious as he saw the first of the injured soldiers being helped onto the plane. He noticed the cargo doors still open and that instilled hope.

Good! They're not done loading yet.

Forklifts loaded crates into the cargo hold. There was still time. It would be a few minutes yet before the transport plane was ready to go. Tommy noticed something in the distance that caught his eye. Around the corner from one of the warehouses came another forklift carrying a crate that appeared to have bars across the front. Someone was sitting next to the driver of the forklift and they were headed toward the plane.

It was Brian and Captain Palmer! That had to be Timex they were bringing! Tommy took a couple of steps toward the machine that was bringing his friends. As they roared up, Tommy dropped his crutches to greet the threesome.

"Hey! It's about time! Nothing like cutting it close!" Private Franklin shouted.

Brian was driving and shut off the motor as they came to a stop a few feet in front of the waiting Tommy. A very elated Tommy. Captain Palmer jumped off the forklift as the private saluted.

"At ease, Private Franklin. We have a special delivery for you," the Captain said, returning the private's salute.

Tommy bent over and grabbed one of his crutches to balance himself and then knelt down so he could stick his arm through the metal bars to pet Timex.

"Hey, Timex. How ya doing, buddy. We're going home, Timex. We're going home!"

The three words "we're going home" choked Tommy up. He was an adult male. He was a man. He was a brave soldier. But the thought of he and his dog, both of whom had almost lost their lives, going home together on the same plane was emotionally draining. He leaned his head against the bars to get a lick from Timex. Brian and Captain Palmer watched the scene unfold. They looked at each other and congratulated themselves on a job well done.

"Had ya scared didn't we, Franklin?" Brian said, getting off the forklift and standing next to his Captain.

Tommy looked up at the pair.

"Yeah, I'd say so. I was wondering where the hell you guys were. Thank you so much for doing this, Captain Palmer." Tommy stood up and offered the Captain a handshake that Palmer accepted.

"It took some doing. There's been a little bit of paperwork and he'll have to be quarantined when you get back. But it's done. He's all yours. Take good care of him. You're lucky to have each other," the Captain said, proud that he was able to pull it off and send Tommy and Timex home together.

"Yes sir, I will. I'll take good care of him," Tommy assured Captain Palmer.

"We're going to miss you two, Franklin," Brian said, getting back onto the forklift and starting the motor. "I better get this guy over to the cargo hold. He's got water and food in the crate for now, but make sure you look after that on your layover, hey Franklin."

"Thanks, Dodd. I'll make sure I check on that when we stop in Hawaii. You're a good man, Dodd."

Brian drove off as Tommy picked up his other crutch.

"I spoke with the doctors, Private Franklin," Captain Palmer said as he watched Brian load Timex onto the plane. "and they seem to think you're going to be OK. That's good."

Tommy turned to look at Captain Palmer. "I'm feeling better all the time, sir. I'll be fine. I'm going to miss you guys. It's been one hell of a ride these last few months, Captain. One hell of a ride."

"That it has been, Private. Look, I have to go. I want to talk to some of the other men before it's too late. You have a safe journey back."

The two shook hands one last time. As Tommy watched the Captain walk away he saw, just past him, four soldiers lifting Timex into the cargo hold. Brian backed the forklift away and headed back in Tommy's direction. He pulled up to a stop and got off.

"Well, that's it, Franklin. He seems OK with it. This time tomorrow he'll be on U.S. soil. The good ol' United States of America. Sorry I can't go with you, Franklin."

Tommy looked at his wartime buddy and wasn't exactly sure what to say.

"Yeah well, Dodd. We'll have to make sure we stay in touch. I'll be thinking of you a lot. You be careful over here. You only have a few months to go."

"That's right, Franklin. Don't you worry about me. I'll be fine and I'll see you back stateside. I've gotta get this forklift back. The guys over in the warehouse made me promise I'd bring it right back when I was finished. You take care." Brian gave his friend a hug and patted him on the back. "Peace and love and all that other stuff, man," Brian said, hopping back onto the seat of the forklift and turning the key to start it. "Do me a favor Franklin and stay out of trouble."

"You do the same, Dodd." Saying good-bye to his friend was hard and Tommy struggled with it. "... and Dodd," Tommy got Brian's attention just as he was about to drive off.

"Now what, Franklin?"

Tommy just stared at Brian who sat patiently on the fork lift waiting for Tommy to speak.

"Dodd ... God bless."

That brought a huge smile to Brian's face.

"Yeah, same to you, Franklin. God bless. We'll see ya back stateside."

Brian drove off thinking that was a nice thing for Tommy to say and Tommy chuckled a little as he gave Brian the thumbs up and watched his friend head off on the fork lift. Tommy scanned the panoramic view of the base he had called home for the past six months and whispered to himself, "Yeah, it's been one hell of a ride. One fucking hell of a ride." He turned around and faced the plane that was going to take him back to the good ol' United States of America, as Brian had said.

"OK, Timex. Let's go home. Let's go home, boy. It's time."

Rehabilitation

TOMMY HAD NEVER been to Southern California before, but if this was where the Army had one of their Veterans Hospitals and if this was where they wanted to send him to rehabilitate, then so be it. The building was modern and clean and the grounds provided beautiful landscaping, trails and fresh air. The government had it right when it came to looking after their battle-scarred soldiers. It wasn't a resort, but it was close. It could have fooled a lot of people in the way it was maintained and how the staff behaved. The ambience assured any wounded soldier they were going to be well looked after. Then there was the weather. The weather was unbelievable for late February. Pleasant and warm. It wouldn't be like this in northern Michigan where it would still be snowing and the temperatures would be below freezing daily. No, this wasn't bad at all. There could be worse places to regain your health. Southern California was an OK place to be for now.

As Tommy went through his day-to-day routine of physical therapy and recovering from his wounds, there was one thing he couldn't get his mind off of; it was that place he still called home, Brenton. It didn't matter if it was freezing cold or there might be four feet of snow on the ground, all he could think about was getting on a plane and heading back to that paradise he loved. He felt it was paradise anyway and it didn't matter what anyone else thought. Winter or no winter, it was home and that's where his heart was. Southern California wasn't bad and maybe one day he would come back for a visit, but being homesick was a real emotion and all he could think about now was that small town in northern Michigan.

As Tommy sat in the lobby of this beautiful hospital reading a magazine and waiting for his visitors, he knew as soon as he saw them he would be overpowered by his homesickness and that he would have to control his emotions. He looked around the lobby and up at the clock on the wall. It was ten minutes before twelve. They said they would be here "around noon." He walked to the front doors that automatically opened as he approached and decided to continue walking to the outdoors. He was free of his crutches now, but still walking gingerly. The road back to normal health had been slow but steady, without any serious setbacks. There was light at the end of the "recovery" tunnel and the doctors and nurses keep saying how amazed they were at his day by day progress. So was he.

Tommy exited the hospital's front doors and headed for a bench strategically placed in the middle of a small flower garden. Still holding his magazine, he looked out across the parking lot to see if there were any familiar faces coming his way or if there were any cars driving in. Nothing. His thoughts turned to Timex as they did a hundred times a day. His dog would be quarantined for ninety-days and to Tommy that felt like a long time. Timex was somewhere in southern California as well, probably living the good life in some five-star luxury dog kennel. When he did get his freedom again, Tommy would make sure he was sent back to his parents place until Tommy got his release papers from the army. Then there would be one glorious reunion.

Hopefully he won't forget me. Man, I wish I could just go see him. It'll be so nice to be together again.

Tommy opened his magazine and thumbed through it looking for the article he had been reading. He heard a vehicle in the distance and looking up he saw it was a taxi cab pulling into the parking lot.

This has to be them!

He stood up and walked to the curb as the taxi made its way toward him. Through the glare of the sun he made out what looked like four passengers inside, three in the back and a man up front.

It's them!

The cab pulled up to the curb where Tommy stood and inside were his parents, his sister Kathy and Carolyn. He opened the front passenger door where his dad sat and in one fluid motion Mr. Franklin got out of the cab and hugged his son. Just as quickly the three women got out the back doors and ran up to Tommy, jumping up and down and screaming. Tears flowed. Mrs. Franklin sobbed uncontrollably as she embraced her son with all her strength. She managed to get out an "Oh, Tommy" and wouldn't let go.

"It's OK, Mom. I'm fine. I'm fine. It's so nice to see everyone. Man, this is beautiful!" Tommy put his hands on his mother's shoulders and gently pushed her back. "You going to be OK, Mom?"

He smiled as his mother nodded and wiped away tears.

"I'm OK. Sorry, Tommy. I didn't mean to fall apart like this," Mrs. Franklin said, wiping her nose with a handkerchief. She had known full well this was going to happen when she saw her son again.

"That's OK, Mom. It's OK."

Tommy's dad stood behind him and patted Tommy on the back.

"Some things never change, son. You know how emotional your mom can be."

Tommy chuckled at that and turned to his sister.

"Hey, Kathy."

"Hey, little brother."

They embraced as Kathy started up with the crying again.

"You sure had us worried there, little brother. So glad you're home."

Tommy held his sister and looked at Carolyn who stood a few feet away observing and letting the Franklin family get reacquainted. It was déjà vu from when Tommy had come home from boot camp. He gave her a wink and she put a hand up to her mouth hoping to curtail another emotional outburst.

"I'm not home yet," Tommy said to his sister still clinging to him. "But we're getting closer."

Tommy and Kathy let go of each other and he walked up to Carolyn, who had been patient. They wrapped their arms around each other. Tommy said nothing and neither did Carolyn. There was nothing much to be said. It was all in the feeling and touching to see if the moment was really real.

"I missed you so much," Tommy whispered in her ear.

Carolyn would have liked to respond verbally, but her trembling lips couldn't get the words out. She squeezed tighter. She composed herself and looked into Tommy's eyes, shaking her head. Now she was composed enough to speak.

"You scared the living 'you know what' out of us, Tommy Franklin."

She hugged him again and put her head sideways on his chest. Tommy held her head with one of his hands.

"I didn't mean to. I really didn't."

The recovering wounded soldier let go of Carolyn and grinned at his family all standing together.

"I couldn't sleep last night, you know. Not a wink. Come on, let's go. We'll take a shortcut through the lobby. There's a beautiful garden out back where we can sit."

"You lead the way, son. We're with you," Mr. Franklin said, still feeling the high from seeing his son for the first time in what seemed like a long, long time.

Tommy got between his parents, put his arms around their shoulders and the three of them walked together. Kathy and Carolyn followed behind, arms wrapped around each other and relishing the moment. None of the Franklins or Carolyn had been to Southern California before and, like Tommy, were enjoying the warmth and sunshine. They walked through the lobby joking and laughing and then headed for the beautifully landscaped gardens where they found a bench to sit on. For the next couple of hours they talked and caught up on all the latest news, especially the news from back in Michigan.

"How is school going for you, Carolyn?"

"How is so and so doing, Kathy."

"Mom, how are things going with all your church activities?"

"How is the business doing, Dad? Are you keeping busy?"

Questions and more questions. They talked and talked and talked some more. They talked about everything except the war. Tommy didn't want to broach the subject and everyone respected that. He told them all about Timex and what a wonderful dog he was. He didn't, however, tell anyone the details about how he had acquired him. How could he ever tell his family the truth? He couldn't and wouldn't.

"I found him abandoned in the jungle. It's a long story, but I couldn't believe anyone would leave a dog alone in the middle of the jungle to die. I still can't believe it!"

Tommy made up another lie about how he lost the watch his parents had given him while out on patrol one day. The same day he found Timex. "… and that, in a roundabout way, is how Timex got his name," he informed them.

Tommy told more than one lie and was in fact, living a lie. A lie that would stay with him forever. One that would never leave his memory. But he couldn't tell his family the truth because the Tommy that evolved in Vietnam was not the Tommy they knew before he went off to fight and he didn't want them to know that Tommy. He still didn't know who that person was.

Mr. and Mrs. Franklin promised they would visit Timex in the facility where he was being quarantined. "We'll do it every day we're here, Tommy." They also assured their son that Timex could come to their property when the quarantine was over and when Tommy got better and was released from the Army, they'd all be together again at home in Brenton.

It was a wonderful way to spend the afternoon, and the next few days, with his family and Carolyn visiting him, continued to be wonderful. It was just what Tommy needed. Time to forget about the war and talk about the future and the future was going to be Tommy getting out of the service and heading back to Michigan to work for his father in the home building business. It was going to be spending lots of time with Carolyn and Timex and introducing him to his friends and everyone else in Brenton. Timex would become "that dog from Vietnam" and the stories of his rescue would become legendary. More exaggerated and wilder each time they were passed on from one person to the next. But the truth would never become known. Tommy Franklin would never allow that to happen. Did the truth really matter? It was only important that he and Timex would spend the next few years together and that Tommy would give him a wonderful life. The future was going to be bright and promising and Tommy looked forward to it. Carolyn, Tommy and Timex. What a trio they were going to be. That's exactly how it would happen. It would all come to pass. It would be like a fairy tale. Camelot. Tommy could feel it inside.

TOMMY WAS AWARDED the Purple Heart and was a war hero when he returned home. It was unusual for Vietnam vets back in the late sixties to be heroes anywhere. But life was good. He spent the next year working with his dad and learned more about the business of building new homes, renovations and additions. He spent the summer with Carolyn as much as time would allow. Carolyn worked as an activities director at a summer camp just outside her hometown of Clear Lake and Tommy joined her on the weekends, helping out with the kids, playing games and going canoeing. During the school year, while Carolyn was pursuing her Marine Biology degree at university, Tommy made the two-hour drive down state to visit her and they went to sporting events or some of the other activities on campus. Holiday dinners would always be at her parents' house or Tommy's parents'.

The war was done for Tommy except for the frequent nightmares he experienced. The war was done except for a heavy heart and the guilt he carried with him that would never leave. The war was done except for the secret he kept inside and how difficult it was to live with. He wished the war would become a distant memory, but it didn't.

When Tommy came home after the war he felt like he was in high school again. Carefree. Doing the things he used to do with his friends. He had grown up, matured and done things in the war he wished he hadn't, but being home with his girl and his family and friends somehow made it feel like old times. It wasn't and never would be again, but there were flashes of the past that made him feel good and capable of living a normal life again. The Tippy's crowd was different now, but Tommy still went there with whoever would join him and usually it was just Timex. Timex instead of Buddy now. Whenever any of the old gang got together, they had their stories about work and university and travels and they also wanted to hear Tommy's war stories, but he would never talk about the war. There was no way he would talk about the war. His friends would always ask what it was like getting shot and if he ever killed anyone and on and on. But no ... the subject was taboo for Tommy.

If only I could live in the past ... before the war.

About a year and a half after leaving the Army and returning to Michigan, a feeling came over Tommy that he couldn't really explain. He liked working with his dad. He enjoyed beyond words his time with Carolyn, but he was feeling like it was time for a change … again.

He felt like doing something different, like he had when he joined the Army, and yet he wasn't sure what. He was still young and adventurous. He thought about it for a long time, often thinking about it as he lay in bed at night.

Time to do something different. Time to go somewhere. Time for a change.

IT WAS THE end of a very busy summer. Tommy and his dad had been working long hours, sometimes seven days a week. It was a Saturday and time to pack up and go home. Father and son were loading tools and material in the back of the new pickup truck that Tommy had bought in the spring. Timex looked on. Timex went everywhere with Tommy, including work and if Timex could be helpful in any way, he would be. He especially liked the handouts at lunch time. Timex and Tommy were inseparable. Just like it had been with Buddy. Carolyn kidded Tommy at times that she wished she had been born a dog.

"I'd get to spend more time with you if I were."

They laughed and joked about it. Carolyn was number one in Tommy's life and Timex ran a close second. Whenever Tommy and Carolyn went out on dates and were cruising around in Tommy's truck, Timex would always be sitting between the two, alert and proud. That's just the way it was and Carolyn came to love Timex as much as Tommy did. When the three of them were together it was a good feeling and for Carolyn, that was all that mattered.

Tommy pulled the tailgate down on his truck, hopped up and had a seat. Mr. Franklin looked at him and wondered why he had done that.

"What? You're not ready to go home yet?"

Tommy laughed.

"Yeah, I'm ready. I just need to talk to you for a minute."

Tommy's dad was flattered and jumped up onto the tailgate to have a seat next to his co-worker.

"Oh, gees. Don't tell me you want another raise!" he kidded.

"No, no, no," Tommy said, throwing a stick for Timex that he had picked up from the ground. "It ain't about money, Dad."

Mr. Franklin watched Timex chase the stick and then bring it back.

"Good boy, Timex," Mr. Franklin said as Timex lay down at their feet chewing his prize piece of wood. "You were kind of quiet today, Tommy. What's on your mind?"

Tommy watched Timex and wasn't sure where to begin discussing what he'd been thinking of or even if, in fact, he wanted to talk about it at all. His dad had always been a good listener and he felt comfortable talking about anything with his father. But this was different and it was going to be hard to get the subject at hand started. Mr. Franklin honored the silence for a brief moment to let his son think it out.

"OK, I'm ready when you are, son."

Tommy jumped down from the tailgate, grabbed the stick away from Timex and threw it again. He looked at the ground, removed his cap and scratched his head.

"Well, Dad, it's like this. This has been great, this time working with you, living at home and saving money, but ... it's beginning to feel like I want to make a change."

Mr. Franklin let what Tommy had told him sink in and then tried to offer up a mild attempt at humor.

"Was it something I said?"

Tommy chuckled at his dad's remark.

"What kind of change are you talking about?" Mr. Franklin continued talking and tried to gauge his son's body language. "What? You wanna be a plumber? An electrician?"

Tommy sat back up on the tailgate.

"No. I'm not talking about that kind of change. I've been thinking about moving somewhere. Maybe Southern California. Maybe taking a road trip out there. I don't know. I'm just feeling antsy."

Timex jumped onto the tailgate, sat between the two men and got the attention he expected.

"A road trip? Why California?" Mr. Franklin inquired.

"I have a couple of buddies from high school out there in Los Angeles. You remember Jerry Smith and Ron Conley?"

Mr. Franklin thought for a moment as he scratched Timex on the chest.

"Yeah, vaguely. Ron, more than Jerry. Didn't you date Ron's sister for a while?"

"Yeah, a very brief while. Nothing serious. She was a couple of years younger and we went out maybe half a dozen times, if that."

Mr. Franklin continued to digest the thought of Tommy moving away. He would miss his son terribly and hoped that it might be just a passing thought. His wife would be heartbroken if Tommy moved away from Michigan. Both of them enjoyed having Tommy around the house. But young lads do grow up and that's understood. He'd been a man for a long time now. They had almost lost him when he was in Vietnam and that would never be forgotten. So it had been good to see him every day and he had seemed to be quite comfortable doing what he'd been doing. But you couldn't live with your parents forever and apparently he felt the time had come to explore more of the world. Tommy hadn't really said much about it, but after spending time in Southern California in the winter when he was recovering from his wounds, he thought it was a pretty darn nice place and wouldn't mind visiting there again.

Tommy continued. "Ron's working as a carpenter out there and said he could get me a job, no problem. Sounds pretty inviting. Something I'm thinking about."

Mr. Franklin looked at the house he and Tommy were building and thought about how much he would miss working with his son. He was such a hard worker and they worked so well together. But he knew in his heart his son was right and it didn't surprise him that Tommy was feeling the way he was. This day was bound to come sooner or later. A young man needed to spread his wings and fly and Mr. Franklin wanted to be encouraging.

"Well look, son. You went through hell with that war and almost getting killed and you're certainly old enough to make your own decisions. Your Mom and I will miss having you around, but if that's what you're thinking, then I say go for it."

There, it was said. Mr. Franklin didn't want to say anything negative about what his son might be planning.

"If you can go out there and work, why not? It would be a great adventure for you. But … ," Mr. Franklin put his arm around Timex and pulled him close. "You have to leave this guy here behind. Ya can't take Timex with you. Sorry."

Father and son laughed together as Timex sensed he was being talked about.

"I don't know, Dad. I don't think I could go anywhere without this guy. We've been through a lot of shit together, whoops, I mean stuff together and I don't think there's any separating us. I'm sure he'll love Southern California as much as I do. Right, Timex?" Tommy roughed up the fur on Timex's head as his dog licked him in return. "Where I go, you go. Right, boy?"

Mr. Franklin hopped down off the tailgate.

"We should get going. Your Mother's going to have dinner ready and I told her we'd be home by six."

Tommy and Timex got down off the back of the truck and Tommy headed around to the driver's side.

"We have everything, Dad?"

Mr. Franklin looked back at the house they'd spent the last month on and thought for a couple of seconds.

"Yeah, it's all locked up. I think we've got everything. We're good. Let's go."

Mr. Franklin got in the passenger side as his son opened the driver's door and Timex jumped into the cab. "Good boy, Timex," Tommy said as he got in and started the truck up. Before putting it into gear to drive off he had more to say.

"So, Dad, let's not tell Mom what I'm thinking just yet. Nothing's definite and I haven't made a final decision. It's all still in the fantasy stages and I don't want to upset Mom if it can be avoided."

Mr. Franklin looked over at his son.

"Yeah well, that's your call. I don't like keeping secrets from your mother, but in this case … I'll do my best. Don't let it go for too long. If you decide to do this you're going to have to be the one to tell her. It won't be easy on her. I know she'll understand when it comes right down to it. She'll be glad you're going back to Southern California and not Vietnam. Don't worry about it. It'll be OK."

Tommy put the truck into gear and drove off.

"Yeah, thanks Dad. I'm sure it will be."

The house the two Franklin men had been working on was about fifteen minutes out of town and twenty or so minutes from home. It was on an acreage and isolated, and the road to get back to the highway was dirt and full of pot holes. Tommy drove slowly and maneuvered around them the best he could.

"Man, this road seems to get rougher every day."

Timex sat obediently between his two friends and stared at the scenery straight ahead. Mr. Franklin agreed with Tommy about the road being not very well maintained. The two made small talk and nothing more was said about Southern California until they reached the smooth pavement of the two-lane highway. Tommy turned left and headed for town. Mr. Franklin realized he hadn't asked Tommy exactly when he was thinking of doing this trip out west and asked the question.

"I don't know, Dad," Tommy said, being truthful. "Sometime before the winter sets in and work slows down. November. December. January. Hard to say."

"Well, it would be nice if you could stay until after the holidays. I've got enough worked lined up to last us until the end of the year. But that's up to you. I know your mom would be pleased if you could wait until after Christmas."

Tommy thought for a moment. His dad was right and it would be that much more money he could save.

"Yeah, I don't think I'll be leaving before the end of the year. It'll be nice to be here for the holidays and January would be a good month to skedaddle on out of here. I'd like to help you finish the jobs you have coming up and it'll put more cash in my pocket. So it should work out fine. You need to stop for anything in town?"

"No, not that I can think of," Mr. Franklin said, looking at his watch. "Your mom's going to be wondering where we are if we don't head straight home."

Not much more was discussed as they drove through the heart of Brenton. Tommy felt melancholy and wondered how many more times he'd be doing this drive through the center of his hometown. Mr. Franklin broke the silence with one more question he had on his mind.

"Have you talked about your plans with Carolyn?"

Tommy concentrated on his driving. He looked at all the small businesses as he drove by. He'd been in every one of them multiple times. There's something to be said about growing up in a small town. This wasn't Los Angeles and if he made the move he knew there would probably be some culture shock. The question his dad had asked ran through his mind.

"No, not yet. You're the first one I've discussed this with. She's not going to be happy when I tell her. Yeah, I don't know, Dad. I think I'll hold off telling anyone else for now. Keep it under your hat and it'll be our little secret."

"Well, that's going to be a tough one, Tommy. As I said, I don't like keeping things from your mother. She'd kill me if she found out I knew what I know now. You're asking a lot. I'll do it, but sooner or later you're going to have to say something to her. Preferably sooner."

Tommy and his dad got to the far end of town and had another few minutes to go before they were home. Tommy sped up as they made their way back onto the highway.

"Yeah, I'll do that. I'll do that. But I still have a whole lot of thinking to do. A lot of thinking." Tommy put his right arm around Timex while his other arm rested on the window ledge and controlled the steering wheel. "Boy, I'm starved. What did Mom say she was having for dinner?"

"Your and my all-time favorite, spaghetti and meatballs."

"Aw, man. Perfect. You sure did all right marrying her, Dad." Tommy also knew he'd done all right by having her as a mother.

"Yeah, I think so. She's a good woman. I'm blessed," Mr. Franklin said as he thought about the woman he had married and had two wonderful kids with.

Tommy, his dad and Timex sat quietly and enjoyed the scenery as it passed by. One thing Tommy hadn't given much thought to was how much he would miss his mother's cooking if he did move to Southern California. Mrs. Franklin loved to cook and every meal, especially dinner, was a royal treat. He started thinking about other things he would miss when he left. Certainly family and most definitely Carolyn. But there would be other things as well. Lots of things. It would be another tough decision he had to make in his young life. Right up there with his decision to join the Army.

He had had a similar feeling when he graduated from high school and didn't really know what to do with his life. He was like a lot of youth who go through a period in their lives when they don't know what direction to head in. Tommy had agonized over joining the Army. That was a huge decision to make and he had made it on his own without consulting his family or friends. Now the time had come to make another decision that would hugely impact his life. He was going to weigh out the pros and cons and come to a conclusion one way or the other. Job security and working with his father was great and if he left it didn't mean he couldn't ever come back. He knew that wouldn't be a problem. His dad would always have a job for him.

But for the first time in his life, as much as Brenton and northern Michigan were in his blood, he was getting a little bored with the small town atmosphere and wondered what it would be like living in a big city. He had briefly thought about moving down to Chicago or Detroit, but their winters were cold like Brenton's and that was another thing Tommy thought about; wouldn't it be nice to live somewhere that the winters were warm and the weather was pleasant all year round? It was very enticing. The more he thought about it, the more he leaned toward making a change in his life that would include a warm climate, even if it were just for a year or two, and he knew in his heart he could always come back home. It wasn't like he was running away from anything. He thought about a new adventure as running toward something. Timex would be with him and he'd love the nice weather as well.

Or do dogs really care about the weather?

All that Timex cared about was that he was with his best friend. That's what all dogs care about, being with the ones that love them so they could give the love back. There was, of course, another love that would make leaving Michigan difficult. His love for Carolyn. More than once he had asked himself what would happen to their relationship if he left. Deep inside he knew it would have an impact and that was troubling.

Is this something I really want to do?

Could he realistically expect her to wait for him to come back? No. Would she ever consider giving up her education to go on this adventure with him?

Absolutely not. He had always encouraged her to stay the course and get her degree. He was her biggest fan in that respect. He had left the girl he was in love with once before when he went to war, but this was different. Completely different. This was going to be his decision, his choice and it wouldn't be the U.S. government telling him where to go. It was going to hurt more than one person if he made the decision to head for California and he really didn't want to hurt anyone.

Why would I want to leave her? I don't. How do you make a decision like this? Am I being selfish? If I stayed right here in Brenton I would have a steady job, Carolyn would graduate next year and chances are we would get married and settle down right here where we have grown up. But do I want that? What's making me think that I want to go to Southern California on another adventure? But life is an adventure isn't it? Do I really want to take a chance on blowing the beautiful relationship I have with this incredible girl?

Tommy turned off the highway onto the secondary road that would take them to the Franklin driveway. He looked over at his dad who was staring out the window and seemed to be in deep thought. The younger Franklin thought about saying something to strike up another conversation, but decided instead to let it be. He himself had been thinking about a lot of things and his dad didn't interrupt him, so he felt he should return the favor. He only wished he knew what his dad was thinking. He pulled into the driveway a few minutes later. In his head he said to himself, "Home sweet home."

Mr. Franklin turned to his son. "I think I can smell that spaghetti from here."

"I hope Mom made lots. I'll have at least two helpings for sure," Tommy said, heading up the driveway.

"Well you know, one thing about your mom, she always makes enough. I wouldn't worry about it too much. There will be plenty, I'm sure," Mr. Franklin said, glad to be home.

Tommy pulled in front of the house and honked the horn. He and his father got out as Timex ran up onto the veranda and beat them to the front door. The dog knew that smell. He knew he'd be licking plates in about half an hour. He also knew the same thing Tommy and Mr. Franklin knew: it was home sweet home.

California Calls

THE AUTUMN COLORS had hit their peak about three weeks earlier, but most of the leaves were hanging on, still splendid in all their glory. It was really something to witness, this transformation from summer into a kaleidoscope of brilliant colors that dotted the landscape throughout the Midwest. People from these parts always tell their visitors, "Don't go to your grave without seeing the fall colors or the Northern lights." It was a collage of color that you could only experience if you lived in or visited this part of the world. You never got tired of witnessing it. Tommy was driving now to Carolyn's parents' house where he had been invited for some homemade cookies that Carolyn said she was going to bake. "A new recipe," she had said. Carolyn had told him to come over after dinner. Her parents were going out to a movie and when he heard about that he figured it would be a good time to do what had to be done. Tommy thought about missing all the fall colors and in the winter the spectacular Northern Lights. But then again, maybe the big city lights of Los Angeles would be just as exciting. He was hoping. Tommy had made his decision to leave for L.A. in January and, on this Thanksgiving Eve, he was going to tell Carolyn about his plans. On one hand he wanted to share his excitement about his trip. On the other, he was quite sure he knew how she would react. He kept his fingers crossed that all would go well.

It was dusk when Tommy pulled up in front of the Russell house.

"Well, Timex. Here we go," Tommy said to his faithful partner. "Ya gotta help me through this, OK my friend?"

He and Timex got out of the truck and Tommy watched the house for a minute while Timex smelled cookies and headed straight for the front door.

Spaghetti, cookies ... always head for the front door.

There were not many lights on and Tommy thought that Carolyn must be in the kitchen and didn't hear him drive up. She usually came out to greet him. He gathered up his composure and walked to where Timex sat waiting for him. Knowing her parents weren't home he thought he might just walk in, but changed his mind and decided to knock. Just as he was about to do that, Carolyn swung open the front door and jumped into his arms.

"Hey, there. Hi, there. Ho, there," Carolyn said planting a kiss on his lips. "I heard you drive up, but I couldn't stop what I was doing. Hey, Timex ol' buddy." Carolyn knelt down and gave Timex a pretend kiss on the nose. "You're looking good there, Timex. You like cookies? Too bad. Cookies are bad for dogs, but you can come in anyway." Carolyn sprang up and the trio walked into the house. She was always glad to see Mr. Timex, even more so since Molly had passed away in her freshman year of university. Molly had lived a good long life and Carolyn's parents had yet to replace her. Seeing Timex helped fill the void.

"I hope you like these cookies I'm making, Tommy. It's a new recipe, but it sure sounds good."

"Of course I'm going to like them. If they have chocolate as the main ingredient, that's all that matters."

Tommy noticed that Carolyn seemed to be in an exceptionally good mood. The mission at hand was not going to be easy. He began to have second thoughts about this whole matter of telling her the news he brought with him. He wasn't expecting her to be so giddy and upbeat, but then again, she was usually like this. Tommy remembered a few years back when he had told her he had joined the Army. It was right before a holiday and he wondered to himself why he had waited until just before another important holiday to give her news that could possibly upset her. Sometimes Tommy's timing wasn't all that good. Tommy and Timex followed Carolyn into the kitchen.

"Man, those sure smell good!" the seeker of cookies said.

Timex sniffed around as Tommy took a seat at the kitchen table.

"I'm so excited," Carolyn said, going over to the sink and washing some of the dishes she had dirtied. "Gees, I hope they turn out OK. Sorry, but you're going to have to be my guinea pig, Mr. Franklin. I just put them in the oven so it's going to be another fifteen minutes before they're ready. You'll have to be patient."

"Really?" Tommy joked. "You're asking me to be patient when there are chocolate cookies involved?" He looked at Timex who had settled down at his feet. "Timex, did you hear that? She wants us to be patient."

Tommy looked over at Carolyn doing dishes. She turned her head, looked at him and smiled, then turned back. It was her smile that made Tommy hesitate, just for a moment, about what he had come to tell her.

Do I really want to leave that smile behind? This is going to be hard.

Carolyn looked at the reflection in the window above the sink and saw Tommy and Timex behind her.

Life is a beautiful experience. I'm in love. I'm going to graduate in the spring. How could one girl be so lucky?

"Do you have any of the cookie dough left over that I can sample?" Tommy asked like a little kid.

"No. Sorry. You'll have to wait for the real thing there, guy. Gees, you're impatient."

"I'm not impatient. I'm just hungry. I didn't have much dinner," Tommy whined.

"I doubt that."

Carolyn finished washing up, walked to the kitchen table and sat down across from Tommy. For now he was going to avoid a certain subject at all costs. They talked about how things were going at university for her and how things were going for him at work. They laughed and joked about their lives in general. That was what made their relationship so special. It had been that way for years.

Do I really want to leave this behind?

They were two peas in a pod when it came to the joking. The kidding and one-liner quips went on while the cookies baked. The oven let out a ding-dong telling Carolyn the cookies were done. She got up from her chair and walked over to the stove.

"Well, let's see what we have. Here goes nothing."

She put on an oven mitt, opened the oven door and pulled out the cookie sheet.

"Can you hurry up?" Tommy asked, still sitting at the kitchen table.

"Oh, hush up. Wow, look at this, they're not burnt," Carolyn said as she put the cookies on top of the stove.

Tommy got up and walked over.

"Whoa, they look great! Can I have one?"

The cookie monster started to reach for one and Carolyn slapped his hand away.

"Forget it! They're still piping hot!"

Timex knew the smell of a good thing and came over to where Tommy and Carolyn were standing, investigating with his nose in the air.

"You have to wait until they cool down, Timex. You have to be patient like me," Tommy told his trusting friend.

"Forget it, Timex. You better not give him one, Tommy Franklin. Chocolate is bad for dogs. Do you understand?" Carolyn warned Tommy as she grabbed a spatula and started putting the cookies on a serving plate.

"Aw, man. Gees, that's not very fair. One won't kill him," Tommy said, thinking he knew better.

"Do not give Timex a cookie. I'm not going to tell you again." Carolyn slapped Tommy on the bicep with her spatula. He groaned in complaint and followed Carolyn back to the kitchen table where she put the cookies down.

"Where'd you say your parents went?" Tommy asked, saying anything that would take his mind and hopefully her mind off the cookies.

"I told you they went to the movies. It's a Thanksgiving Eve tradition with them. Timex, get your nose down."

Carolyn gave Timex a love tap at the end of his nose that was sticking up above the table. A telephone rang from another room.

"You better get that," Tommy said, thinking this might be his chance to sneak a cookie.

Carolyn headed for the living room to answer the phone. She stopped, turned and looked at Tommy and Timex who had been watching her leave.

"There are twenty-four cookies there and there better be twenty-four when I get back or there'll be hell to pay."

"You don't have to worry about us. You can trust us all right. They're still too hot to eat anyway. I'm sure," Tommy said, sounding unconvincing.

Carolyn gave Tommy a look that said she meant business.

"I mean it, Tommy. Don't you dare."

She left the room on a trot to get the phone before the person on the other end decided to hang up. Tommy and Timex stood in silence looking to where Carolyn had just made her exit. Tommy looked down at his friend.

"I don't know, Timex. This is not good! Why would she leave us alone with all these sweet smelling cookies? It's a test, Timex. It's a test."

Timex took a couple of steps back toward the table and put his snout back on it. His eyes could barely see above the table's edge, but they could see enough.

"What would you do, Timex, if you were me?" Tommy asked his canine partner in crime. "Should I try one or not? I probably should taste one to see if they're OK for people to eat. We'd be doing a community service. What's that, Timex? I should try one? OK, but remember, this was your idea not mine."

Tommy took a cookie and had a bite. He looked at his buddy.

"Whoa! These are really good!"

Tommy took another bite and gave a little piece to Timex. He walked to the far end of the kitchen to see if he could hear Carolyn talking on the phone. He could. He went back to the kitchen table where Timex encouraged his master to try another one.

"I don't know if I should take another one, Timex. We're probably in big trouble as it is," Tommy hesitated and debated inwardly. "OK, one more and then that's it. Stop licking your chops, Timex. You're going to get us busted." Tommy took another cookie and gave Timex a little bite. "Hurry, Timex. Get rid of the evidence. She'll be back any second."

Just as Tommy and Timex were through chewing their treat, Carolyn walked back in, came directly to the table and counted the cookies.

"There better be twenty-four here or you two are in big, big and I mean big trouble."

Tommy walked away a couple of steps knowing what was coming. Timex looked at his master, then looked at Carolyn and was positive she was going to give him another sample of a cookie. Carolyn looked at Tommy and gave him the look that could kill.

"What?" Tommy said, playing dumb.

Carolyn put her hands on her waist. "You know what!"

"I like your apron. Is that yours or your mom's?" Tommy asked, knowing the unavoidable was about to come.

"Don't try and change the subject there, fella. There are two missing. Obviously you had one and Timex had one. Were they good? I hope you enjoyed them because you're not getting any more." Carolyn looked down at Timex who still thought she was going to give him a treat. "You wanna tell me what happened, Timex?" Timex sat and pawed at Carolyn's apron. "No, you're not getting another one, Timex. You're busted!"

Carolyn walked over to a cupboard and grabbed a cookie tin as Tommy carefully made his way to the kitchen table and began counting the cookies.

"Don't be coy, Tommy," Carolyn said, giving it to him good. "You know you're guilty as charged. I thought I could trust you."

The wheels were turning in Tommy's head and he had to think fast.

"OK, OK. I can explain what happened."

"Oh, can you?" Carolyn asked as she began to put the cookies in the tin container. "This should be good."

Tommy began explaining and he knew it'd look bad if he tripped over his words.

"When you were on the phone I thought I would count the cookies in case you made a mistake. If there happened to be twenty five, I could have one and you wouldn't know the difference. But when I finished counting there were only twenty-two. That's when I said to Timex, "Boy, we're in trouble." So I decided to count them again hoping I had been wrong, but as I was doing that I accidentally knocked one off onto the floor and Timex wasted no time scooping it up. So I thought to myself, 'It's not fair for him to have one and not me.' So I decided to have one as well. I mean, you don't think it's fair that Timex have one and not me, do you?"

Carolyn was not buying it and stared at Tommy, letting her silence tell him everything he needed to know. She took the cookie tin and set it on the kitchen counter by the sink.

"Do you know that story made no sense at all, Tommy Franklin? Why would you lie to me and where did you learn to count?" Carolyn walked over and put her arms around Tommy. He reciprocated. She looked him in the eye. "You're so full of it!"

"Hey, I'm telling you the truth," the guilty as charged replied, "the whole truth and nothing but the truth."

Carolyn looked down and noticed some cookie crumbs on the floor. She knelt down and tapped the floor to get Timex's attention.

"Here, Timex. You missed some." Timex licked the crumbs up and looked around the floor for some more. "You didn't answer my question, Tommy. Were they good?"

Tommy sat back down at the kitchen table.

"Unbelievable. The best I've ever had. I'm serious. Where did you get the recipe?"

Carolyn sat on Tommy's lap and put an arm over his shoulder.

"From my roommate's mother. She brought us some about a month ago and I couldn't believe how good they were." Carolyn stood back up and took off her apron.

"Yeah, they're pretty good, that's for sure. When do I get another one?" Tommy was feeling greedy and sensed his girl may be vulnerable.

Carolyn got out a little brown paper bag and started putting cookies in it. Tommy was hopeful she was doing that for him. She walked over to her lover and gave him the bag.

"Here, you can take these home with you and share them with your folks. Make sure you share them!" Carolyn emphasized the "share them" part.

"Absolutely. That won't be a problem," Tommy said opening the bag and looking inside.

"I mean it," Carolyn said, threatening to break his arm if she heard differently.

Tommy left the bag on the table, got up and paced around the kitchen.

"What do you feel like doing tonight? You wanna watch TV or go out?" he asked the cookie maker.

He had almost forgotten why he came over. It was still his intention, but ... timing. How do you go from a light hearted moment like they had just shared to a serious discussion that could upset her? He didn't want to watch TV and he didn't want to go out. He wanted to have a talk and get it over with. He was thinking and wavering. Right now they were both emotionally up and in an

California Calls

exceptionally good mood and tomorrow was Thanksgiving. He didn't want to put a damper on the holiday season, but still there was something for them to discuss.

Maybe this should wait.

Carolyn and her parents were coming to the Franklin house the next day for dinner. How would the news Tommy was about to break to her going to affect the mood later, not to mention Thanksgiving?

"I don't care. What do you feel like doing?" Carolyn said, putting the ball back into Tommy's court.

He wanted to buy time and was waffling.

No, I came here to tell her what I'm going to do and I might as well get it done.

"You want to play a board game?" Carolyn asked.

Tommy thought that might be a good idea. He'd find an opening when they were playing and keep it casual.

"Sure. Whatta ya feel like?"

"Your call," Carolyn responded.

Tommy looked down at Timex.

"Timex says he'd like to play Yahtzee."

"So Timex wants to play Yahtzee does he? Sure. Sounds like fun. Good choice, Timex."

Carolyn walked by Timex and patted him on the head.

"I'll go get the game and I'll be right back."

Carolyn got a few feet away from the end of the kitchen table, stopped and turned around.

"What am I thinking?"

She went back to the kitchen counter, picked up the cookie tin and glared at Tommy and Timex.

"I don't think I'll leave these here with you two again. It didn't work out the first time did it?"

Tommy didn't say anything and put on a stunned look as Carolyn left the kitchen.

"She's good, Timex. And smart. Imagine not trusting us in a room alone with a bunch of stupid cookies. I don't like cookies anyway. Cookies are stupid, right Timex?"

Timex cocked his head and looked at Tommy.

Whatever you say, boss. If you say cookies are stupid, then I say cookies are stupid. But they sure do taste good even if they are stupid.

Carolyn came back into the kitchen with the Yathzee game and sat down at the table.

"Remember the last time we played this and I whipped your butt?" she asked, taking the dice and paper out of the box container.

"You were lucky, that's all. It was just pure luck, Miss Russell."

"Here's a pencil and score sheet for you, buster and it was skill, not luck," Carolyn retorted.

"Yeah, OK. We'll see. I'm ready. We'll show her. Right, Timex?"

Tommy couldn't get the thought out of his mind about how he was going to bring up the subject he wanted to discuss with Carolyn and if she had been paying closer attention she would have seen he was a bit distracted. He looked at the clock on the wall and thought if he wanted to have this conversation he should do it before her parents get home.

"What time are your parents going to be back?"

"They said about nine-thirty. Somewhere around there." Carolyn took a dye and rolled it. It came up a six. "There, beat that," she challenged Tommy.

Tommy knew he couldn't roll a higher number to determine who went first, but for formality sake he rolled a dye and it came up a one.

"That's not a good sign," he lamented as Carolyn laughed at his expense.

"You sure you want to play? You're taking on the queen of Yahtzee you know," Carolyn boasted.

"Come on, come on. Get the game started. You don't scare me."

And so the game began.

"Whatta ya say there, bub, best out of five?" Carolyn suggested.

"Sure. Best out of five it is." Tommy snarled at Carolyn in a make believe way and then looked around the kitchen. "What did you do with the cookies?"

"Forget the cookies. I'll make you a deal. The winner of best of five gets a half dozen to enjoy. Take it or leave it." Carolyn put the five dice in the game cup, rolled them and was thrilled with the result. "Whoa, look at that!"

"OK, I'll take it," Tommy said, feeling confidant. "That's a half a dozen, right? A half a dozen after I win. Did you hear that, Timex? We'll be eating cookies on the way home."

Carolyn looked at the man who brought her so much joy and smiled.

"Bring it on, Franklin. Bring it on."

The clock ticked, the game continued and Tommy kept waiting for the opening he had been hoping would come, but didn't. When the game ended and Carolyn had won once again, Tommy realized time was running out. He looked at the clock and it was just before nine. There might still be time. He and Carolyn had just finished counting up the scores on their score sheets and Tommy came to the realization that maybe, in fact, she was a better player.

"Damn! Shit! You cheated!" he accused his competition.

"Nothing but skill there, Tommy my man. Nothing but skill," Carolyn boasted.

The two lovers began picking up the game and putting it back into its box.

"What 'cha feel like doing now, Mr. Franklin? Any more games I can beat you at?" Carolyn asked.

"No, I've learned my lesson for tonight. Go ahead and gloat. I'll get you next time."

Carolyn did in fact gloat as she pranced away to put the game back from where she got it. Tommy sat and thought it was now or never. Her parents would be coming home soon and then it would be too late and he couldn't do it tomorrow on Thanksgiving. Carolyn had said she wanted to head back to university the day after, so it had to be now. She walked back into the kitchen prancing and humming.

"OK, OK. That's enough of that, little lady. Gees, give it a rest," Tommy complained in a fun manner.

Carolyn teased him some more and sat back down at the table.

"Would you like to go sit outside on the veranda?" Carolyn asked "It's cool out, but it's clear and there's a big full moon. Let's do that. Let's go out and sit on the porch swing."

It was the opening Tommy had been waiting for. He thought it was a wonderful idea and grabbed his jacket that was draped over one of the kitchen chairs.

"I'll go get a sweater and meet you out there," Carolyn said, jumping up and giving Tommy a peck on the lips.

"OK, see ya out there. Come on, Timex. You wanna join us?"

Timex lay on his side and lifted his head.

What? I gotta move? Oh, OK.

Timex slowly got up on all fours and stretched. He and Tommy walked out the side door and around the covered veranda to the front of the house where Tommy had a seat on the swing. Timex plopped down a few feet away hoping he didn't have to move again for a while.

Carolyn came out of the house, leaned against a post at the top of the stairs and looked up at the sky.

Tommy got up from the swing and leaned against the other post at the top of the stairs.

"I remember in some of your letters from Vietnam how you talked about the night sky and all the stars you could see. It was very poetic," Carolyn said in a reflective tone.

It was true. Tommy thought back to how clear the sky was in Vietnam at night and tonight was like one of those. But no matter how beautiful the night sky was in Vietnam, he didn't like thinking about any aspect of those days of war. He didn't want to talk about the night time sky in Vietnam or anything that had to do with that time in his life.

"That's a pretty bright moon too," Carolyn went on. "You wouldn't need a flashlight tonight, that's for sure."

Tommy looked at Carolyn still gazing at the night sky.

"Carolyn ... ," Tommy wanted to get started with the matter at hand, but got interrupted by the girl engrossed in the beauty of the darkness and all the twinkling going on.

"Tommy ... sorry, I didn't mean to interrupt."

"That's OK. Go ahead. Ladies first."

"I know we've discussed this before, but do you ever think about going back to school? It would be such fun! You could become an astronomer."

Tommy chuckled and sat down on the top step.

"Well, no. I like carpentry and one day I hope maybe I'll start up my own business somewhere. It's what I do. It's what I enjoy."

Carolyn sat down next to him and put her arm through his and her head on his shoulder. She wasn't making it easy on him. He put his arm around her and knew the time had come.

"Well, if that's what you want to do, then so be it, Tommy Franklin. Whatever makes you happy," Carolyn said, looking up into his eyes.

"Yeah, it does make me happy. There's still a lot to learn and right now I have a great teacher in my dad and I might as well take advantage of it."

"Then you do it, Tommy. You do it," Carolyn said, always having a way with that encouraging voice of hers.

Tommy began to get impatient with himself and realized he would have to take charge of the conversation. He stood up and walked down the couple of steps to the ground and looked out over the black silhouetted landscape lit up by a bright moon. The moment of silence stretched out and it was too long for Carolyn. She sensed something.

"Tommy? You're not going to get serious on me are you?" she asked, as she studied his body language.

Tommy turned around and faced Carolyn who was still sitting on the top step. He'd had serious conversations with her in the past and it was never easy. "Well ... yeah. Just for a minute if that's OK."

"Sure it's OK. Don't beat around the bush, just blurt it out ... you didn't like my cookies did you?"

Carolyn couldn't read his mind and had no idea what he wanted to discuss with her. She thought he was half kidding when he said it was something serious he wanted to talk to her about. Now that the time had actually come, Tommy wanted to frame the words as delicately as he could.

"Carolyn … ," he hesitated some more. He wanted to look at her, but instead chose to stare at the ground. Carolyn suddenly became worried that maybe this wouldn't be a pleasant conversation after all and stood up. She walked down the steps and took one of Tommy's hands into hers.

"What is it, Mr. Franklin? What's troubling you? Are you this upset about losing to me in Yahtzee and you're going to tell me you never want to play with me again?"

Tommy smiled at that comment and with his free hand pulled her head to his chest.

"No, that didn't bother me, I'll get you next time."

Do I want to leave this? She's so beautiful and makes me laugh. I do love her.

Tommy held his sweetheart close and the words began to spill out.

"Carolyn, I'm thinking of moving."

Carolyn stood back and looked at her friend. She thought it was about time he moved out of his parents place and got his own apartment or maybe even rented a house. Of course she was thinking that he was talking about somewhere in town, somewhere local. He would never leave the job he had with his dad.

"Well that's great, Tommy. You need your own space. I'll help you look for a place. We can look together. Are you thinking about moving into town?"

Tommy returned to the steps and had a seat.

"Not exactly," was all he could get out.

Still not even remotely thinking that Tommy was about to tell her he was moving across the country, Carolyn asked him a very innocent question in a very innocent way, "Where are you thinking of moving to?"

"California."

Carolyn didn't react or say anything.

Is he joking?

She flashed back to the time when he had told her he had joined the Army and just like then, wished she hadn't heard what Tommy said. She turned around and walked a few feet away from the front steps and with her arms folded gazed straight ahead. She felt that he must be joking, but the quietness of the night suggested something different. Tommy continued to sit in silence and felt uncomfortable. Carolyn began to notice the chill in the night air.

"California?" she asked in a barely audible tone, still with her back to Tommy.

"Yes California, Carolyn."

She turned around and looked at him.

"Moving out there or just visiting?"

Tommy had known this was going to be awkward, but now it had gone from awkward to painful. He sat with his hands clasped in his lap. He kept the tone of his voice soft, hoping it would smooth things over.

"Well I ... I'm thinking of moving out there. I don't know, really. You remember Jerry Smith and Ron Conley from high school? They're living out there and I've been talking to them and I'm going to go out for a visit and if things work out, I'll stay. But let's not get ahead of ourselves, Carolyn. I need a change, some sort of adventure. Here I am still living at my parents' house and it's time to move on."

Carolyn remained stunned at Tommy's words and was finding it very hard to comprehend. She felt she should start crying, but wasn't exactly sure what emotions she was feeling. Somehow, she managed to stay composed.

"Where in California?" she asked "Where are Ron and Jerry living?"

"Los Angeles. A beach community called Venice. They share a house out there and Ron said he can get me work as a carpenter. He's a carpenter and he told me he stays busy all the time. It sounds like a good opportunity and ... ."

Tommy continued to talk, but Carolyn was still mulling over his earlier words and couldn't keep up with what he was saying. She interrupted him.

"Tommy ... ."

The man sitting on the steps stopped talking and looked at her. She came over and sat by him.

"Tommy, what about Carolyn Russell? What about us?"

If the task at hand was hard before, it was suddenly becoming impossible. Tommy didn't know what to say and felt whatever he said would be the wrong thing.

"Carolyn Russell will be fine. I'm not disappearing off the face of the earth. I'm just going out to California and if I don't like it, I'll be back."

Carolyn got up and sat back down on the porch swing. Something dawned on her regarding Tommy's friend Ron Conley. She remembered Ron and Jerry vaguely and even though they all went to a small high school, they never really socialized and she didn't know them very well. She knew the answer to the question she was about to ask, but did so anyway.

"Didn't you used to date Ron's sister?"

"Yeah ... Cheryl. We had a couple of dates and that was it. It was nothing."

California Calls

Tommy decided to join his girlfriend back on the swing. The mood was solemn as both parties thought about what to say next.

"Change is good, Tommy," Carolyn said halfheartedly.

The comment caught Tommy off guard.

Does that mean she's going to support this or is she resigned to the fact it's over between us?

She continued, "Follow your heart if that's what you want to do. I'm sure it'll all work out."

Tommy wondered where this was all headed as Carolyn had even more to say.

"But for me, Tommy Franklin, this is very painful. It's hard enough not seeing each other when I'm away at school and now ... now you're going to be so far away. How is this going to work between us?"

How is it going to work between us?

The question ran through his head a dozen times and he had no answer.

"Tommy, I'm not interested in doing a long distance relationship. It would be hard on both of us. You know it as well as I do. It wouldn't work. You know that, right? I'm just trying to be realistic here."

He knew she was right. His heart ached as much as hers did.

Carolyn always had been the practical one. Always seeing the practical side of things. That's who she was, the Practical One. She disguised her pain in both her words and actions. If this was what Tommy had decided to do, she would once again show that she supported him.

Tommy pondered everything that had been said and wondered if this was all about the two of them breaking up. It didn't really cross his mind that this would happen right here, right now, but it could be and probably was.

"I guess it would be hard," Tommy said, feeling he had to say something. "I can't say I want this to be over between us, I don't. You graduate next spring, if I end up staying out there would you consider moving out there with me?"

The offer was nice, but no. As much as she loved Tommy, they were still young and, in her rational way of thinking, maybe he had to live his life and she would have to live hers. Maybe this was the way it was supposed to be. Besides, she wouldn't consider leaving her family or Michigan any time soon. She liked her life the way it was and part of the pain she felt was that Tommy wouldn't be part of it. If he was choosing to leave, it would hurt, but life had to go on. Time would tell what happened after she graduated and started looking for a job. She could end up anywhere with a degree in the field of Marine Biology. Staying in Michigan would be her first choice, but if it took her elsewhere, that would be fine. This was youth growing up and going their different ways. They had witnessed it many times with their other friends. Carolyn decided it would be best for both of them if she called the shots and not him. She knew he was having trouble handling the discussion and that he was feeling uncomfortable. "Typical of men," she thought to herself. She was strong, not weak and Tommy was not living in a rational world right now if he thought they could carry on a long distance relationship. She was the Practical One after all.

I'm going for my education that I'm committed to and nothing's going to distract me from that. I think the world of Tommy and love him so much, but obviously he needs to go find himself ... or whatever. This isn't the end of the world and it's not the end of us. It's just a break.

Carolyn took one of Tommy's hands and held it in both of hers.

"You're trembling," she said.

"I am?" Tommy asked, surprised.

"Yes, you are. It's OK, Tommy. Relax," Carolyn said calmly. "We're both going to be fine. If you do this, Tommy ... if you do this, it'll be a great adventure for you and I'm sure it will all work out. Aren't you excited?"

The tables had turned. Before he began this conversation he thought he would be dealing with a very emotional Carolyn, but it was she who was being the rock. He thought he had prepared for every reaction, but not this one. This was perhaps in part why he loved and respected her so much. She knew what she wanted out of life at a very young age and no one, not he or anyone else could stand in her way. It was obvious that more than anything, even more than having a lasting relationship with him, she wanted her education.

Carolyn loved her university life and studying about marine biology. She lived in Michigan for goodness sakes! A peninsula surrounded by water on three sides. There were the Great Lakes, thousands and thousands of inland lakes and rivers galore. She had known for a long time she was meant to be a marine biologist and she was almost there. A few more short months and she would graduate and begin her search for work in the field she had so much enthusiasm for. It was nice of Tommy to suggest that she could come out and see him if he decided to stay in California, but she would have to decline. Everything would be fine. He would be fine and she knew she'd survive.

Tommy looked at the girl he was in love with, but her words didn't register. His blank look told her that he had missed her question.

"Aren't you excited?" Carolyn repeated herself.

His mind was going a million miles an hour thinking of everything that was happening at the moment. He spaced out. Carolyn had picked up on that. She squeezed his hand to get his attention.

"Tommy, did you hear me? Aren't you excited?"

Tommy slowly nodded his head before the words could come out. "Yeah, I'm excited. I'm real excited," not sounding all that convincing.

"It'll be great spending the winters somewhere warm. Right, Timex?"

He deferred to Timex who was trying to sleep on the veranda a few feet away. Timex didn't even raise his head. Tommy's mind kept working hard trying to find a way to create a resolution to the conversation, but he was still too confused.

Is it over between us or not? It sounds like it is.

"Well, you should both be excited. When are you two dudes thinking of going on this trip?" Carolyn asked, resigned to the fact that Tommy was going to leave her. And it became obvious to her boyfriend that, as someone who was always upbeat and positive, she would never change. Tommy relaxed a bit thanks to Carolyn's demeanor and her genuine enthusiasm for him and his buddy, Timex. He didn't expect the mood to change so fast, but this was good. If Carolyn was one thing, she was mature beyond her years.

Always the rational one. Always so grounded. Always right. Always up. Always so caring.

This is the girl I'm leaving behind? What's wrong with me?

"I'm not sure," Tommy replied. "I'm thinking maybe in January. I'll stick around for the holidays. That would make my parents happy."

"Have you told them yet, Tommy, what you're doing?" Carolyn let go of Tommy's hand and shifted over to the opposite end of the swing.

Tommy felt he had to tell a little bit of a white lie. He wanted her to think she was the first to know about his plans.

"No, I haven't told them yet. I wanted you to be the first to know. I'll probably wait a couple of more weeks before I say anything. I don't want to upset Mom too much. That's going to be a tough one."

"Well, don't put it off until the last minute. That won't be good."

Carolyn stood up and looked out over the front yard once more. She thought to herself how life always had its surprises and tonight was another one.

"I'm getting cold. Let's go inside and talk about your little adventure some more."

Carolyn went in the front door as Tommy sat and thought about what had been said.

So, I guess that's it. I'm going to California and Carolyn and I are done for now. This is what I want, but don't want. Come January warm weather will look pretty inviting. It will all be good. Carolyn and I will stay in touch and then we will have to wait and see what happens. Am I doing the right thing?

Tommy got up from the swing and told Timex it was time to go back inside. As he entered the front foyer he yelled through the house, "Hey, can I have another cookie?"

In the upcoming months Carolyn and Tommy would go in different directions. Would it be for the good? No one knew just yet what would happen. But there would always be hope deep inside that one day they would pick up where they left off.

One thing they couldn't have known when Tommy broke the news to Carolyn was that this journey was going to be very long and difficult before they got back together. It would, in fact, take years.

BY THE NEXT day's Thanksgiving dinner, Carolyn had done a lot of thinking and resigned herself to the fact that Tommy would make his move and their relationship as boyfriend and girlfriend would have to be put on hold. She would miss him dearly, but in her own way was genuinely happy for him. It might be a good idea for him to get this adventure thing out of his system and one day maybe he would come back to Michigan and they could spend the rest of their lives together. If not, then she would deal with it. She knew what she wanted and wished Tommy the best.

Thanksgiving came and went and after being apart for another month until Carolyn came home for the Christmas break, it seemed like the two of them were getting along better than ever over the holidays. They had been friends for so long and both wanted to carry on their friendship … only differently now.

Carolyn bought Tommy a road atlas for Christmas and Tommy bought her a book on fresh water marine life. They went and saw a couple of movies over Christmas break and got together with some old high school friends. They were behaving very "grown up" about their romantic break up and were being very "mature" regarding their "new" friendship. It was different from the past, but remaining friends mattered to them. So on January 2, 1970, when Tommy packed up to leave the freezing cold and snow and head for warmer parts of the world, Carolyn was right there to see him off and wish him well.

"It was great spending the holidays with you, Tommy," Carolyn said, handing him Timex's dog food that Tommy put under a tarp in the back of his truck. She had just driven over to Tommy's parents' house, worried she was going to miss saying good-bye to him. She herself was headed back down state to finish her last semester of university before graduation. Tommy had told her he would be leaving at noon and she thought she had given herself enough time but, being January in Michigan, the road conditions weren't all that great. They had received another four inches of snow overnight on top of the almost two feet that was on the ground already and road crews were having a tough time keeping up.

Today, however, was a picture perfect winter day. Nothing but blue sky and lots of white and no matter what, Tommy would never have left without saying good-bye to the girl he still loved.

"Yeah, that was fun wasn't it?" He said, checking his belongings and arranging things underneath the tarp. He looked over at Carolyn standing on the other side of the truck and smiled. "I wonder where we'll be this time next year?"

"Do you want me to pull the tarp over this way a bit?" Carolyn asked.

A year from now was way too far into the future for her to think about when it came to the two of them and she didn't comment. She preferred to let it go.

"Yeah, if you can pull it a little toward the front," Tommy said.

The two of them worked together to secure everything and tie down the tarp that Tommy was hoping would protect his cargo from the elements. Timex lay in the snow a few feet away. He knew something was up, but didn't dwell on it as he was much too occupied with sticking his face in the snow. Tommy's parents had been helping him earlier, but had gone back into the house when Carolyn pulled up thinking she and Tommy might want some time alone together. Now they came back out and walked up to the truck.

Mr. Franklin examined the work being done by the two young people. "You guys making out all right?"

Tommy tightened down a rope tied to the side of the truck. "Yeah, thanks, Dad. I think we're just about ready to hit the road."

These were not the words his mom wanted to hear. She had been having a tough time accepting Tommy's inevitable departure ever since he had told her. She kept trying to convince herself to be cheerful and supportive when this moment came, but he was still her little boy and it was too hard to understand why he wanted to leave his family and the place where he grew up. But ... at least he's going to California and not Vietnam. She held a small brown paper bag and offered it to her son.

"What's this?" Tommy asked with a big grin.

He knew it had to be something good.

"Just some treats I thought you might like as you're traveling," Mrs. Franklin said, understating the truth. She knew when he opened the bag he was going to love what he saw.

"That's awesome, Mom. Thank you so much," Tommy peeked inside. "Oh, dear! Can someone tell me why I'm leaving this all behind?"

It was his mom's world famous brownies. World famous in Brenton, Michigan anyway. Mrs. Franklin stood with arms folded, thrilled at Tommy's reaction. She knew that even though Tommy had had these brownies a million times, they were still his favorite. It was the least she could do. Like many mothers, she never forgot the meals and treats that her kids liked. It didn't matter how old her children were, this loving mother wanted her kids to be happy. If baking some of Mom's "world's best" brownies for Tommy to enjoy while traveling on his trip out west was a way to remind him of home, then she would bake him brownies.

Don't ever forget about home Tommy and where you came from. Please don't ever forget about home.

Tommy took the bag and put it on the front seat of his truck.

"I don't know what's in that bag, but it must be something special," Carolyn said, walking around to the side of the truck where Tommy stood with his parents.

"Oh, it's just Mrs. Franklin's incredibly delicious double chocolate brownies. Man, oh man. If I had known I was going to get a bag of brownies for leaving town I would have left a long time ago."

Tommy kidded his mother and gave her a hug. He didn't know how she was feeling or what she was thinking, she hid it well and on the outside appeared strong ... except when she got emotional and cried. Her actions at this moment though did not let on what she was feeling inside. Sure her son had been through a war and he was old enough to make his own choices, but she was the caring mother and it was hard to let go. Mrs. Franklin was good at making people laugh with her sense of timing. She could listen to a humorous conversation and say nothing at all, but when the timing was right she would say something out of the blue that would have everyone rolling with laughter. Now was the time for that sense of timing. It would help with her pain and keep the moment light.

"Well, if I had known that all it was going to take was a bag of brownies to get you out of here I would have baked these a couple of years ago."

Everyone laughed.

"Mom, you crack me up."

Mr. Franklin walked around the truck double checking everything for the hundredth time. Like moms, dads had to do their thing as well. He checked the tires once more and the bed of the truck, making sure everything was secure.

"Looks like you've done a good job, son. Remember to check the things in the back here a couple of times a day. You don't want to lose anything."

"Oh, yeah. We'll keep a close eye on things. Thanks, Dad," Tommy said before things turned silent. Nobody wanted to be the first to say good-bye and it created an awkward moment. Tommy didn't like it and took charge.

"OK, I guess this is it. Time to roll. Are you ready, Timex?" Tommy opened the front driver's door and Timex jumped in.

I don't know where we're going; I just go where you go, Tommy.

"Ah!" Carolyn shouted, remembering something she had brought for Tommy, but left in her car. "I have something for you too. Can't leave yet." She trotted back to her car and grabbed a small box from the front seat. "Here," she said, walking back up to Tommy. "Between your mom and me you're going to be eating pretty well."

Tommy peeked inside the lid and saw it was a number of those delicious cookies Carolyn had made for him over the Thanksgiving holidays.

"You gotta be kidding me!" Tommy was delighted. "Holy smoly!" He turned to Timex sitting in the cab. "Hey, buddy. We're going to be living the high life with all these goodies. Unbelievable!"

"Tommy!" Carolyn slapped him on the arm to help her make a point. "No chocolate for Timex. We've talked about this before. It's not good for dogs."

Tommy turned to Carolyn and gave her a peck on the forehead.

"Don't you worry there, Miss Russell. These are all mine."

Tommy knew it was time to say good-bye and turned to his mom. This would be hard for both of them and he hoped they could, together, be strong. He held out his arms for a hug and walked up to her. He squeezed her tight and thanked her for all the holiday home-cooked meals. He looked her in the eye.

"We'll be in touch, Mom. I'll write you, you write me. OK? You have the address where I'll be staying. Make sure you write."

Mrs. Franklin smiled and wiped a tear from her eye. So much for being strong. Tommy noticed this and gave her another hug.

"Don't worry, Mom. You and Dad come out for a visit and you'll have a place to stay. OK?"

Mrs. Franklin regained her composure.

"Yeah, and we'll all go to Disneyland. That's something I've always wanted to do. I'll go inside and start packing my bags now."

That got a chuckle out of Tommy as he turned to his dad and shook his hand.

"OK, partner. I'll keep ya posted on work out there if you ever wanna come out to Southern California and pound some nails."

"We'll keep that in mind and you know you always have a job here if it gets too warm for you in California," Mr. Franklin said, giving Tommy a firm handshake.

"We'll see ya, Dad. Take care."

Tommy looked at Carolyn sitting sideways on the seat in the truck with the driver's door open.

"You're welcome to come with me if you want."

Carolyn jumped out of the truck.

"No thanks. I don't like warm weather this time of year. It's unnatural."

The two former lovers stared at each other for a moment, waiting for the other one to say something.

"I'm going to miss you," Tommy said, meaning every word of it.

"Yeah, I'm going to miss you too, Franklin. Follow your dream. You have to promise to write me and your mom on a steady basis. OK? Promise?"

"Yes, I will do that, Miss Russell. I promise."

Tommy and Carolyn had one last embrace that felt bittersweet. He climbed into his truck, closed the door and rolled down the window.

"Tell Kathy I'm sorry she couldn't make it and I'll be in touch."

No sooner were the words out of his mouth than he saw and heard a vehicle speeding up the driveway, slipping and sliding in the snow. He recognized it as Kathy's car and his grin went from ear to ear.

"Hey, what is she doing here? I can't believe it."

Tommy got back out of his truck as Kathy's car came to a stop a few yards away. She quickly got out of her vehicle and ran into Tommy's arms.

"Gosh, I thought I was going to miss you," Kathy sobbed from the stress of running late because of the road and deep snow. "I've been trying to call for the last hour and a half to tell you I was coming. Tommy, I'm so glad I made it."

Tommy was too. He and his sister had a loving relationship like no other brother and sister they knew. She was so important to him. She was the perfect sister.

"What are you doing here? I'm so glad you came. I was just pulling out."

They had said their good-byes the previous night because Kathy was scheduled to work at the Oakville pharmacy where she was a pharmacist. A perfect job for her. She had gone to pharmacy school, graduated the previous year and immediately found a job in Oakville about an hour's drive south of Brenton. She couldn't stand the thought of not seeing her younger brother off one more time. It was eating her heart out to the point that she finally had to ask her boss if he would mind her taking a couple of hours break to drive up to Brenton and say one last good-bye to someone that was very special in her life.

"Go for it!" was her boss's reply and so she did.

She was worried the whole drive up that she would miss saying good-bye to him.

"I called before I left. I stopped at a gas station to call. Doesn't anyone around here answer the phone?" Kathy asked, giving everyone a good ribbing. She held onto her brother by wrapping one of her arms through his.

"So you think you're going somewhere do ya?" she smiled up at her brother.

"Didn't we go through this last night, sister?"

"Yeah, but it had been driving me nuts at work this morning the more I thought about not being here to see you off. So here we are. Oh, sorry ... ." Kathy realized she hadn't even said hello to her parents and Carolyn. "Hi, Carolyn. Hello, Mom. Hello, Dad."

"I hope you didn't get any speeding tickets on the way up, Kathy," Mr. Franklin kidded his daughter.

Tommy had another long embrace with his sister.

"OK, I gotta go everyone. It gets dark early and it's after twelve now," the younger male Franklin said.

Kathy walked to the truck with Tommy and gave Timex a smooch and hug.

"You look after my brother, OK Timex? You take good care of him." Kathy stood aside as Tommy got back into his truck.

"OK, folks. This time for real," Tommy said, starting up his truck. "We love you guys. Mom, I'll give you a call tonight just to let you know how far I get, OK?"

"That would be great, Tommy. You drive carefully." Mrs. Franklin reached through the open window to touch Tommy one last time on the shoulder.

The four most important people in Tommy's life stood side by side and waved. Timex climbed over Tommy's lap, stuck his head out the driver's window and barked. It was his way of saying good-bye.

"See ya next time," Tommy said, pushing Timex back to the middle of the seat.

He put the truck into gear and drove off. Carolyn quickly made a snowball and tossed it at Tommy's truck hitting the back window. She obviously had good aim. Tommy looked at the four in his rear view mirror and couldn't help but smile. He stuck his arm out the window and gave a backward wave.

"Man, its cold out there, Timex. You're going to like where we're going, boy. Warmth and sunshine all year round." Tommy rolled up the window and gave Timex a pat on the head. He reached the end of the long driveway and turned left onto the secondary road that headed south toward Illinois where he'd catch a highway that went west.

"Next stop L.A., Timex. Are you ready for this?"

Timex sat in the middle of the seat and with tongue hanging out and tail wagging, he stared out the windshield.

I'm with you, Dad. Wherever you go I'll follow.

Tommy put his arm around his traveling friend. The man and his dog both felt like they were on cloud nine. He was feeling good and confident that everything would be fine and he was doing the right thing. This was going to be another new chapter in his life and he was excited to get on with it. But not a mile down the road his thoughts turned to Carolyn. He remembered the words she said in a recent conversation they had.

"Both our lives will carry on. You will follow your dreams and I'll follow mine. Time will pass and in the end it will all be good."

Tommy leaned forward and patted the maps on the dashboard to make sure he had them all. He looked up through the passenger window and saw nothing but blue sky.

"It's a good day for traveling, Timex. A good day for traveling."

... and in the end, of course ... in the very, very end, it will all be fine.

TIMEX IN LOS ANGELES – 1970

Road Trip

TOMMY HAD NEVER lived anywhere in his life except Brenton and Vietnam. Outside of that he had never been anywhere except Southern California when he was in the hospital and Hawaii when he was on a layover on his way to and from the war. Other than that, all the traveling he had done in his life was inside the state of Michigan, going on camping trips as a kid with his family and later on as a teenager with his friends. He had always wanted to see "the rest of the country" and there was no better way to see it than from the road. So as he traveled south through Illinois and then west across the Mississippi. He got a good dose of American pride as he talked to all sorts of people. He talked to the locals in small towns that reminded him so much of where he had grown up. Tommy took in the scenery and the more he traveled, the more he got a better idea of why the United States was such a great country: it was the people and the physical beauty that made it that way. Crossing over the flatlands of Nebraska, into Colorado and Denver and over the Rockies in the dead of winter would be quite an adventure for anyone, and Tommy enjoyed every second of it. It was a trip that Tommy would never forget and he'd tell those stories about traveling across this grand country for years to come. Stories about the people he met and the winter storms he encountered crossing the plains and up into the mountains. There were times when he thought he and Timex would have to turn back because of the weather conditions, but they persevered and finally made it. Tommy was always proud of that fact.

Once into Utah they headed south to Phoenix and then due west to L.A. on Highway Ten that would take them to the Pacific Ocean. When Tommy parked his truck in downtown Santa Monica and walked out onto the Santa Monica Pier with his buddy, Timex, he knew he had made the right decision.

"That's the Pacific Ocean, Timex," Tommy said to his friend as he leaned on the metal guard railing and looked out over the beautiful sandy beach. Timex stuck his head between the railings and saw other dogs on the beach running and playing.

This kind of looks like it might be a fun place!

"On the other side of that ocean, Timex, is where you came from."

If you could have ordered perfect weather for a January day, this would have been it. A bright blue clear sky and sixty-six degrees. Tommy couldn't believe it as he stood in a t-shirt and not a winter jacket.

"Well, I don't know, Timex. You think we'll be able to handle this kind of weather?"

Timex barked at the dogs on the beach. His master was mesmerized by the scene he was witnessing. The ex-soldier once known as Private Franklin was liking it more and more by the minute and couldn't wait to get to his friends' house. He turned around and looked at all the activity on the pier: the arcade, the merry-go round, people of all ages enjoying the day strolling in both directions, young kids eating cotton candy, bicyclists and palm readers. And here it was January, the middle of winter. Looking south he saw volleyball nets, for as far as the eye could see, a boardwalk, shops and restaurants and people loving the day. He wondered to himself how far the boardwalk went. He remembered in a phone conversation with Ron not long before, when his friend spoke of a boardwalk, that it was a great place to while away the day. He was amused by it all and couldn't wait to be part of the action. Timex sat quietly by his side.

Tommy looked down at him. "OK, pal, I guess it's time to go find this place called Venice. If I'm right it's just a little bit south of here."

The two made the five-minute walk back to the truck and began their search for the house they would be staying in for the next little while. A house that would be the starting point for this next chapter in Tommy's life and one that, like the war in Vietnam, would be an adventure that impacted him for the rest of his days.

New Highs

IT TOOK MORE time than he thought it would, but after forty-five minutes of trying to find Ron and Jerry's house he pulled his truck up in front of the address he had been given. He had managed to get lost a couple of times in the process, but was feeling elated that he finally got it all sorted out. The neighborhood was rundown and old and the two-story house that Ron and Jerry were living in was somewhat dilapidated. That bothered the visitor from Michigan slightly. Tommy looked at the piece of paper with the address on it one more time to make sure they were where they should be.

"Looks like this might be the place, Timex. Let's go knock on the door and meet your new friends."

Tommy and Timex got out of the truck and headed up the walkway. When they got to the front door, Tommy knocked. It took a few seconds before his old acquaintance from his high school days, Jerry Smith, answered the door. He was genuinely excited to see Tommy and his dog.

"Franklin! Fuck, man. Good to see you!" Jerry gave Tommy a welcoming hug. "You made it, you son of a bitch! Come on in, man."

Jerry, slender with long brown hair, short beard and a couple of inches taller than Tommy, was dressed in the typical hippie garb of the day that was so popular in the sixties and early seventies: tie dye t-shirt, bell bottom jeans and sandals. Tommy had never met a hippie before. They weren't all that common in rural northern Michigan. He had witnessed their demonstrations against the war on TV and seen them in magazines and newspapers, but Jerry here was the real deal in every sense of the word. Tommy looked down at Timex and wondered aloud if it was OK for his dog to come in.

"God damn right it's OK for your dog to come in." Jerry stopped in the foyer, bent over and gave Timex a pet on the head. "Who's this, Franklin?"

"This is my buddy from Vietnam, Timex," Tommy said proudly.

Jerry looked at Tommy a little perplexed.

"Your buddy from Vietnam?"

"Yeah, it's a long story. I'll have to tell it to you and Ron one day. But that's where he's from all right."

The three walked into the living room and the men plopped down on a couch that had seen better days. In fact, as Tommy looked around he got a feeling it was all secondhand furniture and appeared somewhat abused.

"And how the heck did he get a name like Timex?" Jerry inquired.

"Aw gees, Smitty. That's another long story. I traded my Timex watch for him is the long and short of it."

"Well, it's good to see you, man. We're glad you're here." Tommy liked hearing Jerry's enthusiastic welcome.

Even though he had been encouraged by his friends to come out to California and they had offered their house as a place to stay, he hadn't been absolutely sure what the vibes were going to be upon his arrival. Initially they were good and Tommy was thankful for that.

Timex sniffed around the living room like dogs do when they enter a new building and Tommy told him to go lie down. Timex obeyed, finding a spot on a tapestry throw rug. Jerry lit some incense and grabbed a jar from the coffee table that contained rolling papers and marijuana. He did it all quite naturally. Tommy watched this and even though he might be from "the sticks," he was no longer that naïve and knew what was about to happen.

"So how was your trip out here, man?" Jerry asked as he began to roll a joint.

"It was great. It's a beautiful country we live in. I hit some snow storms in the Rockies, but we got through it all right. As soon as we headed south from Utah things got better and south of Flagstaff it actually got quite pleasant. Didn't have any problems with the truck, so there ya have it. We're here safe and sound."

Tommy sat back in the couch and watched his host do his thing. He considered what he would do when Jerry offered him some dope. He decided to go with the flow. He was the new guy in town and when in Rome ... .

Jerry licked the Zigzag cigarette paper and finished rolling the joint. He pointed at a lighter at the opposite end of the table closer to Tommy.

"Can you hand me the lighter there, Franklin."

"Sure can."

Jerry lit the joint, took a hit and offered it to Tommy, assuming that his friend, like most everyone else in this part of the world and who lived in the hippie culture, smoked pot.

"You smoke weed, man?"

Tommy took the joint and held it, still not certain if taking a hit was the right thing to do. He looked at it and figured OK ... .

"You know, I never have, but I guess there's a first time for everything."

He took a drag and passed it back to Jerry. He wasn't sure what to expect from smoking marijuana, but he didn't feel any different after taking his first hit.

"I've never smoked much of anything to be honest with you. I like my beer is all I know."

"I can do that," Jerry said, getting up after taking a puff and handing it back to Tommy. "I'll bring us back a couple of cold ones. Sit tight." As he left and headed into the kitchen he shouted back. "I can't believe you've never smoked dope, Franklin! What the hell did you do in Vietnam?"

"I did things I wished I hadn't," he thought to himself. Tommy looked at the cigarette he was smoking and decided to take another hit. He checked out the décor around him and was amused by it. Psychedelic posters and posters of rock stars and rock groups were hanging on the walls. The place wasn't all that tidy and he wondered who did the cleaning, if anyone. There was a stereo and a big set of speakers off in one corner with at least a couple of hundred albums on multiple shelves in another. He didn't know it now, but his new place of temporary residence was a "hippie den." He took another puff as Jerry walked back into the room with a couple of beers.

"I can't believe you never smoked dope over in Nam, Franklin," Jerry said in disbelief as if there hadn't been a break in the conversation. "It's supposed to be primo stuff over there. Are ya nuts?"

Tommy laughed.

"I guess I was too busy fighting the war. You know sometimes a war can seem to get in the way of everything."

He handed the joint back to Jerry and had a swig of the beer given to him.

"Yeah, well. It might be easy for me to say, Franklin, but forget the war. I didn't go. No thank you. And I'm glad you survived. You must have a few stories to tell. But yeah, forget it, man. You're here with us now and the only thing that's happening is partying and getting high, peace and love and all that shit. Ron's got a job for ya and you're gonna be fine. It's twenty below in Michigan right now. Think about it, man."

Forget the war?

That comment caught Tommy by surprise.

Forget the war?

Anyone who's been in a war knows you don't forget about it. It was bad enough just being in Vietnam fighting an unpopular war without coming back to a country that was divided about what was going on over in that southeast Asian country. Then there are the people who make you feel like you are the enemy.

Forget all that? Not likely.

But this was not the time to go on the defensive. He needed Jerry and Ron for now and he was confident that they all would get along. He hadn't travelled this far to upset someone's apple cart or get upset about some comment coming from someone who had never been in a war. Their phone conversations back and forth, while he was still in Michigan, were upbeat, encouraging and positive. It would all work out.

He would never forget the war or the things that happened. He relived it over and over in his nightmares and guilt. The nightmares especially.

I never wanted to kill anybody, but I did. I joined the infantry because I wanted to fight and see action. I did. But the action didn't become real until I found myself fighting for my life and killing other human beings. Looking back, I never really wanted to kill. But I did. You don't forget that.

Jerry put the joint on a roach clip and handed it back to Tommy who was thinking it might be a good idea to talk about the weather as opposed to the war in Vietnam that was still going on. With all due respect to Jerry, there was no way Jerry could understand how war effected young soldiers. Tommy could. He had seen the horror of it all. He'd been shot. He had barely survived. He had close friends that were killed. The pain ran deeper than even Tommy himself knew. Forgetting about what went down in Vietnam would never happen ... so the weather was a good place to take the conversation.

"Yeah, I really can't believe how nice it is and here it is January. Holy smoke! Is it like this all year round?" Tommy asked, hoping his tactic of changing the subject worked.

Jerry got up and walked over to the sound system in one corner of the living room and started looking through the albums.

"Yeah, pretty much. When you live at the beach there's always a nice ocean breeze. It never seems to get too hot or too cold. You're going to like it here, man. What kind of music do you listen to?" Jerry asked.

Tommy had to think about that. In truth he liked everything. It didn't really matter what music his host put on.

"Whatever you've got is fine with me."

Jerry picked out an album and put it on the turntable.

"You like Santana?"

Suddenly Tommy realized he might not be as "hip" as his friend. Tommy had never smoked pot before and was vaguely familiar with a rock group called Santana.

"Yeah, I like Santana. I don't know too much about them, but I like what I've heard. I think the guys used to play them in Nam."

"Ron and I have put together quite a collection as you can see," Jerry said with pride. "Help yourself anytime, Franklin. Play whatever your heart desires. There's lots of good jazz in here too. Are you hungry, man? Have you eaten?"

"I'm good for now," Tommy replied. "I had a big breakfast and some snacks in the truck I devoured on the way in."

Tommy wondered why, after sharing the joint with Jerry, he didn't feel any different.

How were you supposed to feel after smoking this stuff?

"Did you get a buzz off that shit?" Jerry asked as he turned the volume down once the music started.

"Can't say that I feel anything," Tommy stated in all honesty.

"It usually takes a couple of times before you actually feel high, man. Hang in there. We'll get ya there," Jerry said, not wanting his friend to get discouraged.

Tommy wasn't sure he wanted to go "there" wherever "there" might be. He had gotten this far in life without engaging in illicit drugs, including avoiding them in Vietnam, and he didn't really see a need to get involved in them now as he sat with Jerry. He told himself to be polite. Smoking a little weed wasn't going to hurt him this one time, although Jerry began to roll another joint and it looked like they might be doing it all over again.

"So how are things back in Michigan, man?" the person rolling the joint asked.

"Cold and getting colder. I was working with my dad, but things started to slow down because of the weather. Always do this time of year. It's nice to feel some warmth. I keep telling Timex it's hard to believe we're in the dead of winter and here I am in a t-shirt."

"Get used to it, Franklin." Jerry lit up another joint, inhaled and passed it to Tommy. Tommy almost said, "No thanks," but relented, took it from his friend and had another hit.

"Maybe I should bring some of my stuff in," Tommy said, feeling like he needed a diversion.

"Sure, we can do that," Jerry said, leaning back onto the couch. "We're going to put you in the living room for now. This folds out into a sofa bed," Jerry said, patting the couch, "and we'll find a place to stash your stuff. Don't worry, it'll all be good. Cheryl's in the bedroom downstairs here and Ron and I have the two bedrooms upstairs."

Cheryl? Did Jerry say Cheryl? I didn't know she was here!

"Ron's sister is here?"

"You didn't know that, Franklin? Yeah, man. She's been out here for, I don't know, four or five weeks. Conley didn't tell you?"

Tommy laughed.

"No. And I think I forgot to tell you guys I had a dog. I guess communication isn't our strong point."

Jerry shared Tommy's sentiment and both chuckled.

"Yeah, well. It doesn't matter, Franklin, if you have a dog with you and Cheryl was just coming out here for a quick visit, but decided to look for a job and found one. What difference does it make? What can I say? It's nice having her around. She's a waitress at a restaurant down at the beach. She knew you were coming, man. She said you guys had a couple of dates back in high school."

"Yeah, went to the movies a couple of times," Tommy confessed.

Jerry put his feet up on the coffee table and looked very relaxed. Tommy began to think he might be feeling a little different.

Is this what getting high feels like? The music sure sounds good.

He looked at Timex sleeping on his side on the throw rug.

"Well, Cheryl's all grown up now and a good looking kid with no boyfriend, so watch out," Jerry warned a daydreaming Tommy who was still observing Timex. Jerry looked at Tommy. "You feeling stoned, Franklin."

Tommy looked back at Jerry. "Yeah ... well. I think the second one might have done it, Smitty. Couldn't tell ya if I'm stoned or just real tired. Maybe both."

"Did you hear what I said about Cheryl?" Jerry asked.

"Oh, yeah. That's cool, man. It'll be nice to see her. I've got a girl back home though. You remember Carolyn Russell?" Tommy leaned back feeling a little light headed and suddenly quite mellow. He was also lying about Carolyn.

"Yeah, I remember her," Jerry recalled. "She was one of the smart kids. I liked her. You and her have a thing going on?"

"Yeah, have been for a couple of years now. She isn't too happy about me coming out here, so I don't know what's going to happen. She's in her last year of university. It would be nice to get her out here after she graduates. We'll see."

"Well that's cool, man. I hope it works out for you two," Jerry said, taking another swig of his beer. He happened to look out the front living room window and saw Cheryl walking up the sidewalk. "Hey, speak of the devil, man. Here comes Cheryl."

Tommy got up, stood by the side of the couch and looked out the front picture window. Sure enough he saw a young lady. Timex raised his head as he heard someone enter through the front door. She was an attractive-looking hippie girl with long blond hair wearing a colorful flowing skirt and sandals.

As soon as she entered the foyer she acknowledged Tommy and ran up and gave him a hug. She was all smiles, thrilled to see him.

"So nice to see you, Tommy Franklin. Long time, no see." Cheryl was pretty and had matured since Tommy last saw her.

"Good to see you too, Cheryl. How the heck are you?" Tommy replied, mesmerized by her beauty.

"I'm fantastic. I thought that might have been your truck outside. Not too many trucks around here with Michigan plates."

Timex came up to Cheryl and got her attention with a low friendly growl.

"Hey, who's this?"

Cheryl knelt down and gave Timex a hug around the neck. Just what Timex was hoping for.

"That's my friend, Timex. He'll lick you to death if you're not careful," Tommy warned Cheryl. "Timex, be good."

"Oh that's OK, Timex. I like dogs. You're fine with me." Cheryl stood back up and looked at Tommy who was intrigued with Cheryl's physical beauty and bubbly personality. "When did you get here, Tommy?"

"I don't know. Maybe half an hour ago."

"Ready for a doobie there, Conley?" Jerry asked Cheryl, already knowing the answer as he grabbed the jar with the marijuana in it and started rolling yet another joint.

"I'm ready Dr. Smith. Man, what a day," Cheryl exclaimed, plopping down on a cushioned chair on the other side of the coffee table from the couch.

"Busy?" Jerry asked.

"Yeah, busy. Real busy. That's OK. Tips were good."

Tommy found his seat back on the couch and Timex went over to Cheryl and nudged her arm. She gave him a pat on the head, kicked off her sandals and stretched out her legs. She put her head back and closed her eyes.

"Yes, you're a good boy, Timex. A good boy," Cheryl said, gently scratching behind of one of Timex's ears.

"Timex, leave Cheryl alone. She's a tired gal." Tommy told Timex to go lie down. He went back to the spot that he had claimed on the throw rug earlier and would be his "lie down place" for the next couple of months.

"That's OK. Tommy, it's so good to see you," Cheryl said, putting the emphasis on the word "see" and squinted her eyes as she looked at Tommy.

Jerry finished rolling the joint, lit up and handed it over to Cheryl.

"Thanks, Jerry. God, I need this." Cheryl took a puff, rose up from her chair and offered it to Tommy. Once again he would have liked to say, "No," but once again, when in Rome … .

New Highs

"Can you believe this guy never smoked pot before?" Jerry said to Cheryl.

Tommy was neither embarrassed nor ashamed, but Cheryl chuckled and looked at him in good-natured disbelief.

"You've *never* smoked pot before?"

Tommy took a drag and then passed the joint back to Jerry.

"Well, sorry to let you down, Cheryl. This is it. This is the first time."

"You never smoked dope over in Vietnam?" Cheryl asked, still in a mild shock.

"Nope, never did. I saw guys doing it, but to be honest with you, it never really crossed my mind. Guess I was too busy doing other things," Tommy spoke the truth.

"Well, that's cool I guess. It won't kill ya. Marijuana won't kill you like war will. Right, Smitty? Hasn't killed us yet," Cheryl said, almost proud of the fact.

Jerry had picked up a sports magazine and was thumbing through it.

"Hasn't killed us yet and I don't think it will. You should have brought some of that shit back from Vietnam with you, man. You could have made a lot of money. I hear it's pretty good stuff over there."

Jerry salivated at the thought of the money he could make with some honest to goodness genuine Vietnam dope.

"Well, I wouldn't know. I've heard the same thing. Where is this stuff from?" Tommy asked, referring to the dope they were smoking and was really only slightly curious.

"It's called Michoacán from central Mexico. It's not bad. Are you feeling anything yet?"

"I'm not too sure how I'm supposed to feel. I feel good I know that. But, like I say, I'm also feeling good and tired. Is that how you're supposed to feel?"

Tommy wasn't sure if he was confessing or being ignorant. He did feel somewhat different, but it wasn't anything dramatic.

"You'll get the hang of it, Tommy. It takes a couple of times before you actually realize, 'Hey, I'm stoned!'" Cheryl said, speaking from experience.

"Well, I guess we'll just have to keep working at it." Tommy decided to try and take the conversation elsewhere. "So, you just got out here a few weeks ago, Cheryl?"

"Oh, yeah," she responded. "I'm thinking of becoming a California girl. I found a job right away and I kind of like it out here. You will too."

"Yeah, I guess I could easily become a California guy." Tommy sat on the arm of the couch. "Who wants a beer? I'm buying." he said, thinking he'd rather do more beer than dope.

"They're in the fridge. Bring one for the lady. I'm sure she would appreciate it," Jerry said, handing the joint back over to Cheryl.

"A beer would taste real good right about now," Cheryl said, smiling at Tommy.

"I'll be right back."

Tommy headed for the kitchen with Timex close behind to see what his master was up to. When he got into the kitchen Tommy noticed that, compared to the rest of the house, it was quite clean. He grabbed three beers, returned to the living room and passed them out.

"Thanks, Tommy," Cheryl said, accepting the beverage. "You know Ron's going to be home any minute. I can't wait for you two to talk. He's pretty sure he has a job for you."

Tommy walked over to the shelves holding the multitude of albums and began going through them.

"Well, I'm ready. That's why I'm here," he said. "I'll start tomorrow if they need me."

"Chances are they will, Franklin. Ron's been busy ever since we came out here together," Jerry chipped in.

"Well, let's do it," Tommy said. "I brought all my tools with me. The sooner the better."

He was amazed at the record collection Ron and Jerry had. Most of the albums he was somewhat familiar with, but others he had no clue at all who the artists were. Cheryl walked up to Tommy and offered him the joint that was almost down to its end. He finally found the courage to say, "No thank you," and no one was offended.

"You like music, Tommy?" Cheryl asked, turning away and heading back to her chair.

"You bet. I thought everybody did. I'm really impressed with what you guys have here. Looks like you've been collecting for a while."

"Yeah, most of them are Ron's, but I've got a few in there myself, for sure," Jerry said, putting the roach out in an ash tray.

"What kind of music do you like, Tommy," Cheryl wanted to know.

"I like all kinds. You guys know being from Michigan, it's hard to avoid the Motown sound. We listened to a lot of that over in Nam."

As soon as Tommy said the word "Nam" he knew he had made a mistake and wished he hadn't. He wasn't thinking. Whenever he said "Vietnam" or "Nam" in a conversation, it seemed to stir things up. Civilians had a curiosity about the war and about the country of Vietnam itself and that always seemed to lead to questions about a subject he didn't really care to discuss. He knew what was coming next. It was quite possible Jerry and Cheryl had never talked to someone who had been in Vietnam as a fighting soldier and he understood why, like others, they had questions.

"What was it like being over there, Franklin? Weren't you in the infantry?" Jerry leapt right in, proving Tommy was right in his thinking.

"It was no picnic, Smitty. I don't like to talk about it much." Tommy paused. "You know I got shot, right?"

Jerry had heard it from Ron, but no one had bothered to mention it to Cheryl, which perturbed her.

"I hadn't heard that, Tommy," Cheryl said. "Shit! That's awful! How come no one told me, Jerry?"

Jerry, feeling guilty and getting a nasty look from his friend's sister, claimed that he and Ron must have overlooked it and apologized.

"Sorry, Cheryl."

Tommy tried to downplay it while reading the backside of an album cover. He looked at Cheryl.

"Hey, I survived. Some of us did. Some of us didn't."

Tommy's thoughts turned to Will and Lieutenant Peterson and others. Maybe it was the marijuana, but for a couple of seconds the images playing out in his head seemed more vivid and dramatic than the reality around him. He showed Jerry the album he was holding. It was by the Rolling Stones.

"Mind if I put this one on, Smitty?"

"You go right ahead, Franklin. It's a good album … fairly new."

Tommy put the album on the turn table and took the liberty of turning the volume up slightly. Cheryl was still curious about Tommy's time spent overseas fighting a war. She took a swig of her beer.

"What do you think of that war, Tommy?" she asked.

"Hey, I signed up to go fight it." Tommy began with a little speech he had given a few times. "I did my time, paid my price and here I am. I know it's not a very popular war, but it had nothing to do with me. I just followed orders and fought to stay alive. I could honestly say that after a while of being over there I still thought I was fighting for some just cause. A lot of guys said the same thing, but then you find out real quick that the reason you fight is to stay alive. The cause may be just, but you fight only to stay alive. I did my time and don't plan on going back. And neither does Timex. Right, boy?"

Timex lay on his side at his new favorite spot, raised his head and while still lying down stretched his legs and groaned. He didn't know what everyone was talking about and didn't really care. He just knew he was with his master and that he was comfortable. The words Tommy had just spoken gave Jerry and Cheryl something to think about and there was a brief lull in the conversation. Tommy sat back down on the couch and felt a little awkward. He had joined the military as a patriot and still was, but he felt the war machine was something the human race could do without. Cheryl decided to make a statement.

"That war sucks! I don't think anybody gets it. Does it bother you with all the protests that are going on?" she asked the ex-soldier.

Tommy was OK with Cheryl being inquisitive and understood why she would seek his opinion. He'd been there in the thick of things and of course he would be the one to ask. Not all civilians got this opportunity. But they couldn't read his mind and he didn't want to sound rude by saying he didn't care to discuss it anymore. So, just like in the past when he'd been put in this situation, he remained tolerant.

"There were protests going on even before I went over there. Didn't bother me then and it doesn't bother me now. This is a free country. There've been unpopular wars in the past and there will be unpopular wars in the future. What can I say? There will always be wars and I guess somebody's got to fight them."

Jerry finally sensed his guest was ill at ease talking about the subject and decided to take the conversation in another direction. He picked up the sports magazine he had been reading. It had football players on the cover and maybe that was something they could talk about.

"Well, ya done good, Franklin. We're glad you're here." Jerry tossed the magazine over to Tommy for him to have a look at. "The Super Bowl is happening this Sunday. Should be a great game. Who do you like?"

Tommy, having been on the road for the last few days, hadn't stayed in touch with national affairs and he wasn't even sure who was playing. He looked at the magazine cover and saw that it was going to be played in New Orleans between Minnesota and Kansas City. He liked all sports and came by it honestly as he grew up playing organized sports and his parents loved watching games on TV.

"Tough call," he said, actually liking both teams. "I might lean toward Minnesota a little. They could be tough to beat." It dawned on Tommy that he hadn't noticed a TV in the house. "You guys have a TV?"

"No, we're not quite that advanced," Cheryl said mockingly.

"We'll probably go down to the bar to watch it or over to a friend's house," Jerry said, sounding a little disappointed they hadn't invested in a TV yet. Not that any of them cared much about what was on but, for special events like a big game, it would be nice to have.

"One day we'll get a TV. Probably sooner rather than later," he added.

"About the only thing I watch on it is sports," Tommy said. "Nothing else really interests me. I especially can't watch the news with all the Vietnam War coverage. Drives me nuts!" Tommy had said it again without any intention.

Vietnam War. When will I learn? Are we going to go down this road again or maybe with some luck we can keep talking football.

"I don't think we're missing anything by not having a TV," Cheryl said. "I'd rather read a book or go out to a movie. Much more entertaining."

The men agreed with Cheryl's assessment. TV was a waste of time.

"If you roll another doobie, Jerry, I might find it in my heart to go start dinner. Deal?" Cheryl said, making Jerry an offer he couldn't refuse.

"Consider it done, Conley. I love it when you cook." Jerry didn't hesitate and began to seal the deal.

"I know you do, Smitty. Who's been doing all the cooking since I got here? Huh?" Cheryl said, ribbing Jerry as she got up from the chair and smiled at Tommy. "You want to give me a hand, T.F.?"

"Sure," Tommy answered.

He didn't know why she called him T.F. and it was the first time he'd ever been called that. But if Cheryl wanted to call him by his initials, then so be it.

"Are my things OK in the back of my truck for now?" Tommy asked.

"Yeah, they'll be fine. We'll help you bring your stuff in later," Jerry said rolling one more joint.

Man, these people sure like their dope.

"Do you like spaghetti, T.F," Cheryl asked, entering the kitchen with Tommy and Timex close behind.

Dogs may not understand the complete English language, but food-related words seem to catch their attention somehow. So when Timex heard two words he was familiar with, kitchen and spaghetti, he decided to follow his master and this new female friend and see what they were up to. He knew "kitchen" was where the food was and "spaghetti" was a dish that when the humans were done eating he got to lick the plate. He did it in Michigan all the time.

"I love spaghetti, actually," Tommy confessed, "and especially homemade spaghetti. What can I do?" Tommy asked as Cheryl began pulling out pots and pans and chopping knives. She was obviously on a mission.

"You can begin by grabbing an onion out of the fridge and chopping it up. Look in the vegetable bin," Cheryl said, putting a chopping board on the counter.

Tommy found an onion and told Timex, who had his nose deep inside the open fridge door, "Get away. Go lie down, Timex. You don't know anything about making spaghetti."

Cheryl was amused at Tommy and Timex's relationship. They were obviously best friends and it showed.

"So where did you get Timex from and how did he get a name like that?" she asked as she put a pot of water on the stove and turned a flame on underneath it. Once again, Tommy didn't want to get into it, but it was no use.

How many times do I have to tell this story ... and lie?

He began chopping the onion and hoped he got the "lie" right one more time. He had caught himself in the past telling different versions on how he obtained Timex and if by chance people started putting two and two together, it wouldn't look good and someone would have reason to question the "truth." He took a deep breath and began telling the lie just as Jerry walked into the kitchen with a gift for Cheryl.

"Where are the matches?" Jerry asked her.

"Well, they're on the coffee table or ... look here, what are these?" Cheryl said, raising her eyebrows and shaking her head as she grabbed a box of matches from the back of the stove. "How long have you lived here, Smitty?" Jerry didn't say anything as Cheryl handed him the matches. "Have a seat," she ordered him as he lit another joint.

"Tommy's going to tell us the story about how he got Timex."

Jerry sat down at the kitchen table puffing away.

"OK, Franklin. Let's hear how you got the mutt."

Tommy finished chopping the onion, turned around and leaned against the kitchen counter.

"Well, it's not really that interesting or that long of a story. We were on patrol walking through a village and talking to the residents when some guy saw the watch on my arm and started mumbling something in Vietnamese."

Jerry offered the joint to Tommy who accepted reluctantly, but realized he was losing the battle. He took a puff and walked over to Cheryl. She had both hands full so he held it to her mouth so she could take a drag.

"Thanks, T.F."

Tommy walked back over to Jerry and handed the marijuana cigarette back to him.

"Our embedded interpreter came up and said the man would like to trade something for my watch." Tommy pulled out a chair and sat down at the table. "But the only thing this guy had of any interest to me was a dog. You know where this is going, right?"

Jerry smiled and handed the joint back to Tommy. "Yeah, I think so. But go ahead," he said.

Cheryl walked from the stove to the table and put her hand on Tommy's shoulder, waiting for him to finish his puff and pass it to her.

"Anyway ... ," Tommy continued, "there was a lot of negotiating and bickering going on 'cause I didn't know what I was going to do with a dog in Vietnam and I love dogs, man, don't get me wrong, I've always had one, well sort of ... ." Tommy had to stop. He felt like he was rambling and possibly not making sense.

Am I stoned?

"... so like anyway, this went on for a few minutes and my commanding officer walked up and got involved and he didn't think it was a good idea, but when I told him the dog was going to be this guy's family dinner that night he had a change of heart and let me make the deal." Tommy didn't recall the story ever taking this long to tell. Maybe it didn't, but it sure seemed like it.

Is this the long version or short version I'm telling? This is weird! I think for the first time I'm high.

"So to make a long story short or a short story long, I gave the man the watch that my parents had given me and it happened to be a Timex. Hence, the name."

Cheryl walked over to Timex lying in the sun shining through one of the kitchen windows. She knelt down and scratched his belly. He rolled on his back, his four legs reaching for the ceiling.

"Is that true, Timex?" the beautiful hippie girl asked her new dog friend. "You mean you were going to be somebody's dinner? That's not good. That's not good at all, Timex. Well, welcome to America, boy. We don't eat dogs here. You're safe here. Yes, you are."

Timex loved the attention he was getting and Tommy liked the fact that the people he would be staying with were going to enjoy having his dog around.

Tommy was feeling different now. He was feeling, in hippie lingo, "stoned." He thought back a few years to his high school days when he and Cheryl had a few dates and went out to the movies. There was never any intimacy and, except for what at the time seemed like too much of an age difference, he remembered her being good company. Now as he watched her show affection toward Timex, he realized how much they had both grown up.

"That's quite the story, Private Franklin," Jerry said. "How the hell did you get him back to the good ol' U.S. of A.?" Jerry wanted to know.

"My superior officers pulled a few strings and we had him crated up and brought back." Tommy didn't think it necessary to go into any more detail than that.

There was a brief silence as everyone seemed to be relishing the moment and thinking about the story that had just been told. Tommy got up and walked over to Timex and Cheryl. He squatted down and gave Timex a rub on the head. He knew the story he had told was not the truth and he knew Timex knew. Dogs know everything. But he'd known for a long time he could never explain the insanity that overcame him that day when he took possession of his best friend. Whatever made him behave that way would never be explained and to this day it still scared him. But Tommy came to understand, the longer he spent in Vietnam, that war can take a person out of character. Sometimes in a good way, sometimes in a bad way. It was a place and time he didn't want to go back to. He got his dog. He lost his watch. He saw his friends get killed and he did some killing of his own. The question he couldn't answer was, "Would I do it all over again to save this mutt?" Life was funny. It's an old cliché. Life can also be tragic. Life can be many things. But in the real world you can't undo what's been done. As much as he loved this dog, knowing what he knew now … .

Would I do it all over again?

Tommy pondered that question now as he had done before and the answer never changed.

I love Timex so much ... but I don't know.

He loved dogs, but he had taken a man's life and had tried to rationalize, since the day it happened, that he had done it in self-defense. Only he knew the truth, but he didn't want to believe it. It seemed like so long ago now. But in his heart, deep down inside, he knew what he did was wrong. He had decided to do something he shouldn't have been doing and he ended up killing a man to save a dog. Why?

Ever since Buddy passed away he had been thinking about him almost every day, even when he was in Vietnam, and those memories brought a smile to his face. The memories were therapeutic. Buddy had been his best friend and Tommy couldn't get him out of his mind and didn't want to. Buddy was special and so was Timex. The circumstances surrounding Timex's rescue could never be changed, and here was Timex now living the good life with his master and new friends. It felt good to Tommy. They had come a long way together and traveled across a vast country as their latest adventure and everything was feeling right. Just perfect. Better than perfect. Right or wrong nothing would ever change the past.

The big pot of water on the stove began to boil over and Cheryl heard it.

"Uh-oh. Sorry, Timex. Gotta get back to my cooking. See ya later, boy." Cheryl gave Timex one last rub on the chest, quickly made her way back to the stove and turned down the heat. "You've got more chopping to do, T.F. Come on, get with it," Cheryl dictated to Tommy in her always friendly manner.

"I'm on it," Tommy said, rising up and walking back over to the kitchen counter where Cheryl handed him some carrots.

"Chop that up and throw it into the pan with the ground beef along with the onion."

Tommy chuckled at the way Cheryl was giving him orders. She was all business. Jerry remained at the kitchen table observing.

"You guys are doing a great job. I like watching other people work," he said, knowing it was going to get Cheryl's dander up.

"Oh, shut up, Smitty. You'll be doing dishes. Don't worry about that," Cheryl promised him.

"I'll just hand it over to Timex. I'm sure he'll do a dandy job licking everything clean," Jerry said, liking his plan. Jerry assumed that, like all dogs, Timex was an excellent plate licker.

"I don't think so," Cheryl said, opening a can of tomatoes and putting them in with the other ingredients. "Why don't you make yourself useful and roll another doobie for when Ron gets home."

Cheryl liked to look after her brother who was two years older. Jerry complied by getting up and going to the living room to get the marijuana jar.

The hippie girl chef turned her attention back to Tommy. "So how are things back in Michigan, T.F.?"

Tommy finished chopping the carrots and threw them into the frying pan sizzling on the stove.

"They're fine. Cold back there. Everything else is the same too," Tommy answered.

It had been hard leaving Michigan and the ones that he loved behind, but this trip out west was about him and what he needed to do. He may be stoned, but he felt good about the company he was in.

"I'm so glad I came out here," Cheryl said, adding spices to the spaghetti sauce. "I really like it here and there really weren't any reasons for me to stay in Michigan. I can be a waitress anywhere. Might as well do it somewhere where it's warm in the winter."

"Good for you." Tommy liked her rationale and could relate to it. "That's pretty much how I feel. I spent time in the hospital here and really enjoyed the weather during the winter. It's good to be back."

Cheryl was mildly curious about his stay in the Veterans Hospital.

"So where did you get shot, Tommy?"

It was another question he'd been asked a thousand times and he had a standard answer that tried to make light of it all.

"In Vietnam," he said biting his lip.

Cheryl hit him with the cloth she was using to dry her hands off with after rinsing them in the sink.

"I didn't mean that. T.F. I mean where on your body?"

"Oh, was that what you meant?" Tommy walked over to the sink and ran his hands under the water as well. "I got shot in the gut. It hurt."

"I can very well imagine," Cheryl responded with genuine sympathy. "Are you OK now?"

"Yeah, I'm fine. Got some minor aches and pains, but no big deal. I'm alive and functional."

Jerry had been quiet as he rolled another joint for when Ron got home. He tossed it onto the kitchen table. "There ya go, Conley. Happy now?"

"You know he'll appreciate it when he gets here. Thanks, Jerry," Cheryl said, giving Jerry a wink.

Tommy still found it hard to believe how much marijuana these people smoked.

Is this normal?

Cheryl stood at the stove breaking up spaghetti noodles and putting them into the boiling water. She suddenly perked up as through an open kitchen window she heard the sound of a vehicle with no muffler pulling up in front of the house.

"Hey, it sounds like big brother is home."

She rinsed her hands once again and headed out to the front door to meet her brother. Tommy followed. It had been a few years since they last saw each other and he was very appreciative of the fact that Ron was being so kind and willing to be so helpful by opening his house to him. They had never been best friends and it meant a lot to Tommy that Ron and Jerry encouraged him to come out to Southern California and stay with them until he found a place of his own. Timex ran up behind Tommy just as he and Cheryl exited the front door. Ron drove an old beater truck and stood next to it pulling out a six pack of beer from the bed. He saw Tommy and Cheryl coming his way and was elated.

"Hey, Tommy. You made it! Good to see you."

Cheryl stopped to let Tommy have the first greeting. Ron put his beer and lunch pail down, shook Tommy's hand and followed that with a friendly hug.

"Good to see you too, man. Been a while," Tommy said, smiling.

Timex came up and sniffed Ron so he could get familiar with another new friend. Ron knelt down and gave Timex a rub on the neck.

"Who's this?"

"This is my dog, Timex. He's everybody's best friend ... or at least he thinks he is."

Ron stood up and grabbed his six pack of beer and lunch bucket. "Well, welcome to California you two. We didn't know you were bringing a dog. This is a bonus."

In all the phone conversations Tommy and Ron had before Tommy decided to come to California, he forgot to mention Timex. Tommy was pleased with Ron's reaction toward his dog. He hadn't intentionally kept it a secret, so it was comforting to know his three new roommates were so accepting. Ron finally acknowledged his younger sister who had been standing patiently by.

"Hey, Cheryl."

"Hi, Ron. How was your day?" the little sister asked the big brother.

"It was fine, just fine. Are you ready to go to work, Franklin?" Ron said, turning his attention back to Tommy.

Those were the words Tommy wanted to hear and it made his day. He related to Ron how excited he was to get started.

"Well, you can start tomorrow if you feel like it," Ron informed him.

Tommy replied that nothing would suit him better. The three made their way up the front sidewalk, along with Timex, and entered the front door. Everyone followed Ron into the kitchen where Jerry sat lighting a joint.

"You must have read my mind, Smitty," Ron said, putting the beer on the table and his lunch pail on the floor next to the fridge.

"I did," Jerry said, handing the joint to Ron.

"Who's up for a beer?" Ron inquired as he cracked the pull tab off of a can.

"We all are," Cheryl said, speaking for everyone.

Ron cracked open three more beer and passed them out. Tommy looked at the clock on the wall above the sink. It was only ten past five.

Boy, these people sure like to smoke their dope and drink their beer. When does it stop?

Ron got up and walked over to Tommy leaning against the kitchen counter in front of the sink and handed the joint to him. They toasted their beer cans and Ron again welcomed his guest to California.

"So how was your trip out, Tom," Ron asked.

Tom? He couldn't remember the last time he was called Tom. He had, for his whole life, always been called Tommy or Franklin as the boys in the Army called him. Didn't matter. Tommy, Tom, Franklin, T.F., it was all the same to him.

"It was just dandy," he said, taking a puff from the joint. "It got a little dicey coming over the Rockies and I hit a couple of snow storms, but we made it. Truck did good. No problems there."

Tommy handed the joint over to Cheryl. He was convinced he was now officially stoned. He felt distracted by almost every action and sound and was finding it hard to put thoughts together that made any sense. "It's not a bad thing," he told himself, but he was not quite sure this was how he wanted to feel. He looked at Timex lying down by the back door and wondered what his dog was thinking.

"Your truck will come in handy for work. Do you have all your tools with you?" Ron wanted to know.

"Yep, got all my tools and more. How far away is the job?" Tommy wondered.

"It's in Beverly Hills. A condominium project. Takes about twenty, twenty-five minutes to get there, depending on the traffic."

Jerry got up from the table. "I think we need some more music. Anybody have any requests?"

"Your choice, Smitty," Ron said.

"How about some blues or jazz," Cheryl suggested, still busy preparing dinner.

"You got it, Cheryl. Sounds good," Jerry said, leaving the kitchen.

"Anything else I can do here?" Tommy offered Cheryl.

"Well, you can set the table. It's still going to be a few more minutes, but if you want to do that, it'll be great."

Cheryl told Tommy where the plates, glasses and silverware were and he began his chore.

"Ron, did you know Tommy had never smoked dope before today?" Cheryl informed her brother as she handed the joint to him.

Ron looked quizzically at Tommy who was setting the table. "You never smoked dope before?"

Tommy laughed as he lay down some forks and knives. "Guilty as charged, I'm afraid."

Ron shook his head and thought about that for a moment. "Well, we won't hold it against you."

Music began to blare from the living room. Jerry had put on some John Coltrane.

"You never smoked it in Vietnam?" Ron asked the same question that the other residents of the house had already asked him.

Tommy was a little perplexed as to why everyone thought that all soldiers who went to Vietnam smoked marijuana. It was only a minority, but it seemed like civilians thought it was the opposite.

"No, Conley. Never did. Today's the first time. Maybe if I had known it was going to make me feel this good I would have taken it up."

He was lying. He wouldn't have wanted to feel like this and be in the thick of a battle or even just relaxing on the base. Tommy didn't feel quite right and he couldn't imagine being in this frame of mind and trying to fight a war. He was a tad bit confused and war demanded a clear head, not the one that currently felt clouded. He seemed to be more aware of some things, smells and sounds, but had trouble with some of his thoughts that seemed scattered and made him feel like his mind was racing. Even though the spaghetti meat sauce was smelling exceptional right now—it reminded him of his mother's cooking—and the music coming from the other room seemed to be transmitting right inside his head, he still didn't feel sharp. He couldn't explain it and didn't know why soldiers in a war would smoke dope and take the chance of not being in their natural state of mind. What did it do? Did it make them forget about the war? That would be impossible. Did it make them more brave? Not likely. So why? It was a question he couldn't answer and he knew better than to be judgmental. He also knew he was glad he hadn't indulged when he was fighting overseas. Time would tell whether or not he smoked dope ever again. For now, it was all about fitting in with the group. Peer pressure still existed even at his age. He didn't want to come across as a "flake." He was the new kid on the block. He wanted to be "cool" just like Ron, Jerry and Cheryl. So if this was being cool, then for now, that's what he would do. It didn't really bother or matter to him that he felt stoned and not in complete control of his faculties in this current environment. Alcohol did the same thing, only with different results and he certainly would never have considered drinking beer before going into battle. Same difference. He had always enjoyed his beer and he had been drunk more than a few times in his life. He'd survived that. Maybe he'd end up liking marijuana more than beer. Who knew? For now, Tommy would just live in the moment and be content and thankful he was where he was. Everyone had been so welcoming to him and Timex. That was what mattered.

"You know if you had brought some of that Vietnam shit back with you, you could have made yourself a ton of money." Jerry's business mind spoke out once again, repeating what he had said earlier.

Now Tommy got it.

"Yeah, and I can imagine that would of gotten me in a heap of trouble. I can see the headlines now, 'Wounded Soldier Busted for Smuggling Dope.' That would not have been a good thing."

The four friends chuckled over that image.

"Jerry does a little dealing, speaking on that subject," Ron interjected. "Hope you don't mind, Tommy."

Ron felt he had better get Jerry's drug dealing out in the open. Not everyone would be comfortable living in a house where drugs were being dealt, but Ron assured Tommy that Jerry was smart and kept a low profile. Supposedly there were no transactions done at home and not even Ron or Cheryl knew exactly how his "deals" went down, and they didn't really care. It was how Jerry made his living and if he kept the traffic away and did it all outside the confines of where they lived, they were fine with that. Ron and Jerry had been friends since their childhood days in Brenton and Ron trusted Jerry one hundred percent. Jerry would never do anything stupid. He was intelligent about how he conducted his business and he wouldn't betray Ron's trust or put anyone at risk by doing his dealings from their home. It actually wasn't just a little dealing he was involved in. He wasn't a small time dealer anymore. He had worked his way up the ladder and now dealt in quantity. He was on the verge of going "big time." This was his job and it was the reason that there was always dope around to smoke, whether it was marijuana, hashish or opium. There was always something to get high on. Life was good. Jerry was a cool businessman and Ron and Cheryl had free drugs at their beck and call, whenever, wherever. These were happy times for the residents of this house and from all appearances it looked like they didn't have a worry in the world.

Tommy picked up on that. These were three people enjoying life and now he was going to be part of it ... for the time being. There was laughter. That was important. There was trust. That was important. There was music and drugs. That was important to the hosts, the drugs were anyway. And if Jerry was a drug dealer and Ron and Cheryl were cool with that, what did it matter? That's the way Tommy Franklin was feeling right now. Maybe it was because he was stoned ... he hadn't figured that one out yet.

"Hey, that's fine with me, man. Sorry I don't have any connections in Nam, Jerry. Otherwise I'd help you out."

Tommy and Jerry shared a laugh.

"That's OK, Franklin. You just go pound your nails and I'll make sure we all stay high. Trust me, nothing gets done here. I don't do business here, man. In fact, I don't even live here," Jerry said and Tommy got the message.

"Yeah, he's invisible, Tommy. Pretend you can't see him. I do it all the time," Cheryl said, seeing the opportunity for a zinger as she took the pot of boiling noodles off the stove and carried it over to the sink where she emptied it into a strainer.

Tommy liked the fact that everyone was getting along and enjoyed each other's company. If he had been feeling good about being here before, he was now feeling euphoric. In being honest with himself, he hadn't been sure what to expect when he arrived. He was hoping deep down inside that he had made the right decision leaving Michigan and moving to Southern California. It had been a huge decision and a lot of thought went into it. Leaving his family, his friends, his job and his lover for the sake of a new adventure. But now, being in the presence of these three people who were acting like he'd been here all along, that was special. Very special. The whole thing of moving out here could have backfired and although he'd been here less than a couple of hours, he felt great about the reception he had received.

These were beautiful people, these hippies. Depending on your point of view maybe, like the war in Vietnam, the hippie movement wasn't a bad thing after all. That's what made America great. You could protest the war in Vietnam and still be a patriot. You could curse the hippies and their lifestyle, but you were still a patriot. Everyone had an opinion on this, that and everything else, but you were still a patriot and at the end of the day, you were still an American. The real enemies were the ones that resorted to violence. That was un-American and, despite all the wars American soldiers had fought in the past and would fight in the future, the American people at their core were non-violent. Hippies were for peace and so was the American soldier. And there was always that lingering question in the back of Tommy's mind that he knew no one could answer, *Why can't we all just get along?* Get along like the four people in this room. Was that so difficult?

Tommy directed a question to Cheryl.

"Do invisible people eat spaghetti? Cause if they don't I'll have his share," he said.

Jerry finished the last drag on the joint and put it out in an ashtray.

"Invisible people love spaghetti, Tommy," Jerry retorted in a friendly manner. "In fact, spaghetti makes us more invisible. So watch out, you might become invisible too."

"It wouldn't be good for Timex if I were invisible. Can you just imagine that? I'd be calling him and he couldn't see me! That might make him crazy."

Timex heard his name and raised his head. He had been taking in the smells even though it appeared he was sleeping. Dogs can do that. It may look like they're not paying attention, but they always seem to know what's going on even when they're pretending to be asleep. Timex put his head back down knowing his time would come when the humans were finished eating. They'd call him and he'd get to lick the plates. Why should it be any different in California than Michigan? Dogs have been licking dinner plates since the beginning of time.

"That's Jerry's job," Cheryl said, putting four glasses of water on the table, "to make all of us crazy. OK, let's eat."

Tommy joined the other two men at the table as Cheryl brought over bowls of noodles and meat sauce.

"Looks and smells good, Cheryl," Tommy complemented her on a job well done. Cheryl went to the fridge, pulled out a green salad and set it on the table.

"You're magical little sis. I don't know how you do it!" Ron wondered how this meal had come together so quickly.

"Yeah, I know. It must be magic. Amazing how it all just came together," Cheryl responded with just a slight tone of sarcasm. "Here's some garlic bread," Cheryl added one more item to the meal and sat down. The three men were polite enough to at least wait for Cheryl to join them.

"Dig in, fellas. Come on. What are we waiting for?" she said to get things rolling and took some salad as the others helped themselves. "Jerry, Mr. Invisible Man … ."

"Yes, Ms. Conley."

"Don't make yourself invisible when it comes time to do the dishes, OK?" Cheryl warned her friend.

"Ms. Conley, when have I ever ditched out on doing the dishes? I'm surprised you would even say something like that!" Jerry smiled at her as he had a bite of his dinner.

Cheryl stared at Jerry as she sipped water from a glass. She said nothing. She didn't have to. Tommy looked at Cheryl, then at Jerry. Smitty refused to make eye contact with Cheryl. He knew "the look" and didn't bother with a visual response. Tommy admired their interaction. It was apparent they liked kidding with each other.

"This is delicious, Cheryl," Tommy exclaimed, amazed at how much it tasted like his Mother's, " and Jerry, I'll do the dishes. Don't worry about it."

Jerry looked up at Cheryl with a little smirk on his face. Cheryl glared back at him.

"That's OK, Tommy," Jerry said. "You can help if you want. I know my place. Ms. Conley here will get all bent out of shape if I don't do the dishes. She tends to get that way sometimes."

Ron sat quietly eating his meal and taking it all in. He was used to the friendly bantering between his sister and his best friend. If Jerry hadn't had a girlfriend already, Ron was sure these two would be a couple. In the short time his sister had been in Southern California, they had formed a very special and friendly love/pretend-to-hate relationship and a deep respect for each other. It was all in good fun and quite entertaining. They obviously enjoyed each other's sense of humor.

"If you think this meal is amazing, Smitty, wait until you see the dessert I made last night after you went to bed. That is if you didn't find it in the back of the fridge and eat it all today," Cheryl said, grabbing a piece of garlic bread.

Jerry had missed that one. He had been in the fridge a couple of times during the day and somehow managed to overlook it.

"No, I didn't eat your dessert, Conley. I would have if I had found it, though. Good job on hiding it. You win, OK? I'll do the dishes if I can have some dessert."

Ron knew it was Cheryl's turn to respond and looked at his sister. He also knew his friend was no match for her. He had known for a very long time, since they were kids growing up, that Cheryl was a tough cookie and you better listen and obey. She didn't back down and had a knack for getting people to do things for her. She was a natural at that and Ron had always told her that she would be a good businesswoman. For now, though, she was a waitress and wasn't sure what she wanted to do with her life. Like most hippies, she lived for the moment and for getting high. She enjoyed her life right now and the future would take care of itself.

For a lot of young people in the nineteen sixties and seventies, the thought of planning ahead and thinking about life down the road wasn't important. Live for the day. Get high. Peace, love, sex, drugs and rock and roll. These were the good times. Who cared about tomorrow or next week or next year? Cheryl knew what she wanted today and didn't really think beyond that. She was intelligent, obviously quick witted and liked her dope. Getting stoned was what mattered most at this point in her life. Cheryl was happy and carefree and life couldn't be any better. Let the good times roll.

"OK, Smitty, here's the deal." Cheryl began to lay down the conditions which Jerry was going to have to honor. "When we're done eating, we'll clean up and get the dishes ready and then we'll have some dessert. I made some apple pie and bought some vanilla ice cream and after dessert you'll do the dishes. Is that gonna work for you?"

Jerry couldn't believe what he had just heard. Neither could Tommy and Ron.

"Apple pie with vanilla ice cream?"

Even Timex raised his head.

Did she say what I think she said?

Cheryl looked at the three male faces and was amused at their inability to speak.

"Finish your dinner first, boys, or there'll be no dessert," Cheryl said, threatening them in a way that only she could do.

"You know, this is probably the best spaghetti I've ever tasted," Jerry said, trying to score points for perhaps a bigger piece of pie.

"You said that last time," Cheryl fired back.

"Yeah, but I mean it this time. Honest. Did you do something different?"

Spaghetti had become a staple in the household because it was so easy to make, and they seemed to have it at least once a week since Cheryl's recent arrival. Ron would make it occasionally, but it wasn't this good. Obviously, his sister had the touch.

"Jerry, you're such a slime ball. And a liar. I make it the same way every time and I've made it what ... four times? You're worried about getting dessert aren't you?"

"Yeah, I guess," Jerry confessed. "But I'm not lying. This batch is the best you've ever made. Unbelievable!"

"Oh, shut up," Cheryl said, getting up from the table and grabbing some more salad dressing from the fridge. "The salad's good too, isn't it?"

"The best. The best salad you've ever made. This is unreal. This whole meal. God, I can't believe it!" Jerry laid it on thick and heavy.

Cheryl managed a good hearty laugh.

"Maybe you should smoke another joint there, Mr. Smith. You're so full of shit it makes me ... never mind. Not at the dinner table."

And so the conversation went among these friends. Light hearted and good natured. Tommy was impressed with the camaraderie between the three and hoped he fit in. Everyone finished eating and plates were put on the floor for Timex to lick. The three men helped Cheryl clean up and dessert was served. The evening came and the four smoked more dope, listened to more music and played a game of cards. Ron, Jerry and Cheryl continued to do little things that made Tommy and Timex feel more and more comfortable. This had been a good first day in the great metropolis of Los Angeles. When bed time finally came, Tommy unloaded his truck and got his things ready for the morning. His tools, his work clothes. He was ready to go, excited and glad he had made the trip. He pulled out the sofa bed and Cheryl helped him put the sheets on.

"Thank you once again for dinner, Cheryl. That was very tasty," Tommy was gracious as he fluffed a pillow.

"You're very welcome. See you in the morning," Cheryl said, smiling as she disappeared into her own room.

Tommy climbed into bed and stared at the ceiling. Timex jumped up and lay next to his friend. Tommy told Timex he didn't think that was a good idea, but relented and let him stay with him. Timex rested his head on Tommy's shoulder. The man from Michigan thought of his parents, his sister and his former girlfriend. He had mixed emotions as he had been missing them since the day he left, but yet was glad to be where he was. This was the beginning of something new and exhilarating. He felt if it all worked out he would be here for a very long time. He would write to Carolyn soon and start planting seeds to hopefully get her out west. She would love it, he felt. No snow. No brutal cold weather. Who could have imagined it? Even if it were artificially induced by all the pot they had smoked this day, Tommy sensed that life was beautiful. He gave thought to all the dope they smoked in such a short time and how, in fact, like his friends had told him, "It's not going to kill ya." He was feeling like he was in a good space and wondered if it was the marijuana that made him feel this way. It was no big deal. He'd probably do it again tomorrow. It wasn't a bad feeling at all. He fell asleep with Timex at his side. It was the end of day one in L.A. Who knew what tomorrow would bring? Who cared?

Why Doesn't He Call?

CAROLYN CARED. SHE cared about her future and it showed in her commitment to school and the fact that she was scheduled to graduate in April, a few short months away. She was thrilled about it and proud of her accomplishment. She also cared about her best friend Tommy and worried that it had been three weeks since he left and he hadn't called or written. She had spoken with his parents a couple of weeks before and they had talked to him on the phone and informed her that he had arrived safe and sound in Southern California. He told his parents to tell her "hello" from him, but that did little to ease the pain of his not calling or writing her. He said he would call after all, "As soon as I get there." It crossed her mind to get his phone number from his parents and call him. But no.

He'll call.

He would probably be really busy with his new job. There would be a good reason he hadn't picked up the phone and gotten in touch with her. She was sure of it. No matter how far apart they were or how much their relationship changed, she wanted Tommy in her life, even if only as a treasured friend.

We don't have to be lovers, but please, let's stay friends.

She also cared for Timex and wondered how he was enjoying the big city. She missed them and didn't like not being able to hear Tommy's voice on a regular basis. Carolyn hoped everything was OK and worried.

Why doesn't he call? Why doesn't he write?

Carolyn also cared about the future for both her and Tommy. Three weeks after he left, the reality of his being so far away started to set in. He was no longer just a two-hour road trip away. He was over two thousand miles away. That was different. Very different.

Carolyn sat at her desk in her dormitory room doing what she always did, studying. The holidays seemed like a distant memory now and school was back in full swing. She had a two-hour break between her morning classes and her afternoon schedule and had come back to the dorm to catch up on some school work. Her desk was in front of the window that looked out over the snow-covered campus. She paused to look out at the pure whiteness and blue sky.

It is so beautiful!

Why Doesn't He Call?

She began to daydream and was lost in her thoughts when someone down in the lobby yelled up the stairs and through her partially open door she heard her name being called.

"Carolyn!"

"That would be me," she muttered to herself, got up from her desk and went out into the hallway.

"Hello!" she answered back.

"You have a letter," the female voice Carolyn recognized as a resident answered back.

"I'm coming."

She hurried down the hallway and down the one flight of stairs to the lobby. Letters were always exciting no matter whom they were from, but she always held out hope that if Tommy wasn't going to call, maybe he would write a letter instead. Could today be the day? Carolyn quickly walked over to the dorm lobby desk where her friend Candice stood holding an envelope.

"Thanks, Candice."

Carolyn smiled and before she even had a chance to see where it was from, Candice informed her, "It's from California."

She looked at the return address and saw that not only was it from California it was from a Tommy Franklin.

"Oh gosh, finally." Carolyn was ecstatic. "This is a good friend of mine who moved out to California a few weeks ago," Carolyn said to Candice, opening up the letter. "I've been waiting to hear from him."

Candice, whose volunteer job was to sort the mail that came to the dorm and put it in the proper mail slots, had a suspicion that Carolyn would be waiting for this letter. She had heard Carolyn talk about this "person" before and that's why she had called up the stairs to get Carolyn's attention.

"Do you want these too?" Candice asked, handing Carolyn a couple of more envelopes.

"Oh thanks, Candice. Thanks so much."

"They're not from California," Candice teased.

Carolyn chuckled.

"That's OK. I'll still read them."

She strolled over to a couch set against one wall across from the mail slots, plunked down and began reading Tommy's letter. It was five pages long and she was pleased that he hadn't written just a couple of paragraphs. The first part of the letter tingled her skin as she read it. He talked about his drive out west and some of the snow storms he had run into. He wrote of Timex and how much Timex was enjoying himself. But it was when she got to the second part of the letter that she became concerned by his words. He talked about how he had tried marijuana and found it quite pleasing. "We'll have to smoke a joint next time we're together," he suggested. "Not likely," she thought to herself. Carolyn had no interest in drugs of any kind and why was he offering up this information? Some things were better left unsaid. She continued reading and found out that Ron's sister Cheryl was living in the same house. Carolyn barely knew Cheryl, but did recall that Cheryl and Tommy had dated a few times back in high school. She wondered once more why he felt he had to tell her this. Was there something she should be concerned about? Carolyn thought that maybe it would be a good idea to call him and hear his voice and perhaps get a better sense of where their relationship was at. Was it really over? She didn't want to admit that this might be the beginning of the end. She was hoping not, but needed to know one way or the other. In any case, she wanted to save the friendship. The love affair they had was beautiful, but it was being best friends that was the fiber of their relationship. That, in her opinion, was something she treasured and knew was worth saving.

Tommy wrote more about Venice Beach and all the hippies, the free concerts and the beautiful weather. He mentioned that he had decided to let his hair grow and that he was going to try sporting a beard. It amazed Carolyn that he'd made all these decisions in such a short time. She tried to envision him with long hair and a beard and thought about the "hippie culture" she had been hearing about for years. It certainly didn't interest her. She might be considered a "square" by some of her friends and acquaintances, but she was OK with that. She wasn't interested in drugs or being part of this hippie craze. She cared about her future. The thought of being a marine biologist thrilled her and she knew it was going to be a great career. She couldn't wait to graduate and find a job. She had already put some feelers out about employment opportunities and had gotten some very positive feedback. It had also crossed her mind that possibly one day she would be Mrs. Tommy Franklin. But that dream was beginning to fade with each word she read.

Was this what they called traveling down different roads? Going down different paths? Was Tommy maybe thinking they could carry on a long-distance relationship. Carolyn's feelings for him weren't going to change with the content of one letter, but she was a realist and smart. Was she supposed to wait for him while he did his drugs and lived so far away in this place called Venice Beach? The sensible side of her told her that it was over for now and it broke her heart. He hadn't called when he said he would and it took him over three weeks to write. His mind was on other things, not her.

Some of the little things Carolyn had noticed when Tommy returned from

Vietnam and never talked about were now starting to make sense. She had heard from his mother about the nightmares he was having. There were times when he had seemed detached and uncaring. She had never seen Tommy angry or upset, but there were times when he looked edgy and anxious. She had never questioned him about any of these new character traits and she was sure that he didn't have them before he left to go off to war. Carolyn knew in her heart he wouldn't have discussed them anyway and would have insisted that everything was "just fine." Tommy had so much talent in the field of carpentry and so much personality. Why did he run away? Was that what he did? That's exactly what Carolyn was thinking to herself. He's running away from something. Was it her? Was it more than just wanting to leave Michigan? Was he running away from life and commitment? The war? She put the letter down in her lap feeling a little perplexed. The communication from Tommy that she had been waiting for was a letdown. Disappointing. Painful. Sad. How was she going to respond and what was she supposed to say? "Glad you're growing your hair long and doing drugs?"

She picked up the letter, looked at it again and read certain parts over. It didn't help to ease the hurt she was feeling. She got up from the couch, headed back up the stairs to her room and sat back down at her desk. Carolyn decided she was going to write a letter back to him right now. She would keep it light and tell him all the news from home. She would say how much she missed him and Timex, figuring there was nothing wrong with telling the truth. She'd poke fun at him for growing his hair long and becoming a "hippie." She would not say anything about his indulging in drugs. Carolyn would write about university and ask him if he could come back for her graduation. It would mean a lot to her. She would also touch the surface of what happened next in their relationship without making it sound like she was worried. It had survived his time in Vietnam, why wouldn't it survive the duration of this new adventure he had gone on? She would write the letter once, and then write it again. Carolyn wanted the wording to be just right and hopefully the next time he wrote to her it would be soon and he'd say how he'd decided not to let his hair grow long and had given up smoking dope. He'd be the old Tommy once again and he'd say he was coming back to Michigan. This was what Carolyn was wishing. Maybe she had been jumping to conclusions and worrying when she shouldn't be.

Let's just wait and see. Things might work out.

She had known her good friend for a very long time. He'd be fine. They'd be fine. Everything would be fine. With pen in hand she began to write because she cared. Always had and always would.

The Effects of War on a Godless Dog Lover – KB Fugitt

WISHFUL THINKING WAS all it could be for now. One month after Carolyn wrote Tommy back, she still hadn't heard from him. The phone call she was hoping for never came, nor did another letter. It was going to be March soon and spring would be coming shortly after that. She couldn't believe that he hadn't replied at least to tell her if he could make it to her graduation or not. Her pain turned to anger.

How can he do this to me? Who does he think he is? Why would he want to throw everything away that we had together?

Carolyn had wanted to call him, but not anymore. She had resisted and was glad she did. If he wanted to hear her voice he could call her. Carolyn had stopped in to see Tommy's parents when she was home for the weekend three weeks earlier and they had received only one more letter from him that didn't say much. Only that he had been working and enjoying the beach. What was really peculiar was that there was no mention of Timex. Surely an oversight. In her heart she knew she and Tommy were going their separate ways. In her mind she was deeply concerned for a good friend. She didn't want to underestimate Tommy, but female intuition told her she should worry about him and in this short life she had lived, she always went with that. But no longer could she let this lack of communication with him be a distraction.

Carolyn remained focused on the mission ahead, graduation. When they saw or spoke to each other again, she was sure it would be like they had never missed a beat and would pick up right where they had left off. But for now, it was study, study and study some more. Yes, she was a "square," but when it came to the future and her career, at least she would be a happy "square." There was no reason for anyone to worry about her. Carolyn knew what she wanted and nothing would ever get in the way of that. What she wanted more than anything right now was an education and as much as she wanted to be with and hear from Tommy, that was now secondary to everything else going on in her life. She felt it was time for him to make the next move, to act. In the meantime, there was nothing she could do. She focused first and foremost on herself: her needs, her wants and her goals. For now, that was the way it had to be.

And as much as she thought about Tommy Franklin, she was also thinking about a wonderful dog named Timex. Was he being looked after? Timex and Tommy were best friends and surely that wouldn't change. Or would it? No, it couldn't possibly. Tommy loved dogs and it should be the least of her worries to think that Timex wasn't being spoiled as usual. Maybe more than spoiled. Carolyn couldn't shake the thought that Tommy was getting into drugs. That

Why Doesn't He Call?

just wasn't him. It was amazing because, after all, he hadn't been gone that long. She thought maybe she was jumping to conclusions. Was it really possible for a person to change so suddenly? She tried to understand all that. But it wouldn't go away; those images of him, growing his hair long and smoking dope, were not ones she enjoyed. If only he would call. If only he would write. Her gut told her something was going wrong—terribly wrong.

TOMMY AND TIMEX rolled up in Tommy's truck in front of the house where they had been living for the past three months. It was the end of March, a Friday and a payday. The work that Ron had promised him had been steady since the day after Tommy arrived. In fact, it had been more than steady. He was extremely busy. They had been looking for a great general contractor and he fit the bill. They would sometimes work overtime on Saturdays and had been told they could work as many hours as they wanted. Life was good and so was the money.

Tommy had been saving up as much as possible and started to look for a place to call his own. He and Cheryl had discussed going in on a place together as roommates. They wanted to stay near the beach and loved being in Venice. He didn't want to overstay his welcome at Ron and Jerry's, although they had assured him everything was "cool" and he could live there for as long as he wanted. But it had been three months and it was time to move on. Cheryl felt the same way. She loved her brother and he and Jerry had been kind but, like Tommy, she'd never had a place she could call her own and it was time to do that. It was all part of this new adventure both she and Tommy were on. Tommy thought that having a place of his own would be exciting and it would give him and Timex more independence and a place where his friends and family could come stay. He was looking forward to it.

Tommy got out of the truck with a six pack of beer and Timex jumped out behind him. They headed for the front door and entered the house to hear the phone ringing. Tommy quickly put the beer down and scrambled into the kitchen to grab the phone.

"Hello?"

"Is Tommy Franklin there?"

"Speaking."

"Tommy, its Kathy!"

It's my sister! Holy cow!

Tommy couldn't believe he was hearing his sister's voice. The first thing that popped into his head was how he was going to smooth over not being in touch these past few months. He was guilty and knew it and wouldn't be able to explain it. He was embarrassed. Tommy was always thinking about his family, but communication since he had moved to California hadn't been his strong point. For his part, it completely broke down. Tommy had been busy working so many hours and then there was the time put into smoking dope and drinking beer. His family knew where he was and what he was doing. Surely they would understand why he didn't write more often or call. Wouldn't they? They didn't. They couldn't. They wondered why? Especially his mother who had been afraid something like this might happen. He felt bad that he hadn't made more of an effort to stay in touch these past months. Time seemed to have passed by so quickly and for whatever reasons, none of which were legitimate, he just didn't find the time to sit down and write or call. Now his sister was on the other end of the line and he felt awkward and he knew he shouldn't. If only he had made more of an effort to stay in touch.

This is Kathy, my sister and best friend. Just like Carolyn is my best friend and my parents are my best friends. Why have I been so lackadaisical in communicating with them?

"Kath, I can't believe this! How the heck are you?"

"I'm fine." Kathy was elated to hear her brother's voice. "I'm so glad I caught you at home."

"I just walked in the door and heard the phone ringing. Good timing!" Tommy replied.

They talked and talked. Hearing his sister's voice was music to his ears. He couldn't believe how good it was to hear from a family member. The magic of a telephone call as he and his sister conversed made him feel wonderful. Tommy shook his head and beat himself up for being out of touch. Not only that, he had only written three letters to his parents and none to Kathy since he came to California. The answer wouldn't come to him, but he kept asking himself, "Why? Why didn't I bother to write or call? It's not like me." He couldn't change that now. He hoped his family would forgive him. They would. They did. They loved him. They cared. Kathy and Tommy talked for a good twenty minutes before she got to the reason she had called in the first place.

"Paul and I are getting married in August."

Tommy was thrilled to hear the news; in fact, he couldn't have been more pleased. Paul was a good choice for a husband and Kathy's brother approved. Kathy and Paul had met in university and had been together for five years. Paul was a school teacher and taught Junior High Math. They were a perfect match and Tommy had known that for a long time. They would be happy together.

"Paul would like you to be one of the groomsmen, Tommy. Can you make it back here? Pleeeeease Tommy, please!"

Kathy didn't have to beg or plead. That was silly.

"Are you kidding? I would be delighted. Honored. Tell Paul I'm flattered. You're getting married! I can't believe it and I'll be there!"

"... and Carolyn is going to be a bridesmaid," Kathy continued. "Isn't that cool?" The excitement in Kathy's voice pleased her brother.

"Good choice," Tommy said and thought how great it would be to see everyone again.

Just like coming back from the war, it would be a grand reunion. Brother and sister continued to talk for another hour. They talked about everything: Mom and Dad, Carolyn, Timex and California, sports, you name it. Nothing was left out. They touched all the bases. Tommy felt mildly homesick. You would have thought it had been four years since Tommy had left instead of just four months.

Cheryl came home, Ron came home, Jerry came home and Tommy hogged the phone as everyone else went about their business. It was heavenly talking to his sister and he promised her he would either write or call their parents.

"They're wondering why you don't call, Tommy. Call them. OK? Call them!"

"I will, Sis. I will."

Tommy hung up the phone and walked into the living room where his three roommates sat. Marijuana smoke was thick in the air. Timex lay on the couch with his head in Cheryl's lap getting spoiled as usual.

"Sorry to tie up the phone like that. It was my sister calling from Michigan. She's getting married in August."

Tommy sat down on the couch at Timex's bum and gave him a pat on the side.

"That's cool," Ron said. "Are you going to go back there for it?"

"Oh yeah, for sure. Her fiancé wants me to be in the wedding party. No, I wouldn't miss it for the world," Tommy said, noticing Jerry sitting across from him in a stuffed chair putting hashish in a pipe and lighting it.

"You'd look cute in a tuxedo, T.F," Cheryl said, turning away from the book she was reading and had been holding with one hand while petting Timex with the other.

"Yeah, I'm sure I would." Tommy had an image in his head of him wearing a tux. "She's pretty excited and her boyfriend Paul is a good guy."

Jerry leaned over toward Tommy and handed him the pipe that Tommy took a puff off of before passing it to Cheryl. Tommy thought about what Kathy had said about Carolyn being in the wedding as a bridesmaid. Carolyn and Kathy had become good friends over the years with Tommy being the common denominator that brought them together. He knew he wasn't being a very good long distance friend toward Carolyn and he still felt the guilt he had when he was talking to Kathy on the phone. He was ashamed of himself.

How can I be so lazy?

His problem with not being able to communicate from a distance had to be a personality quirk of his that he couldn't explain. He didn't have this problem when he was overseas. He would write all the time and would get many letters back.

Tommy took another toke from the hashish pipe and made the decision to go into the kitchen and write Carolyn a letter.

"I better go take care of some business and write a friend of mine," he said, getting up from the couch. "You boys want to play some cards later if you're around?" he asked as he made his exit?"

"Sounds good to me. Lana is coming over and I don't think we're doing anything. Count us in," Jerry said, referring to his girlfriend.

"Heather and I are going out so it'll be the four of you," Ron said, referring to his steady.

"Looks like you and I will be teaming up tonight, T.F. Think you can handle that?"

Tommy looked back at Cheryl.

"Yeah, I think I can handle it. We'll whip butt."

Jerry got a laugh out of that comment and fired back.

"I don't think you've played cards with Lana yet, have you Tommy? She's pretty good. You might regret those words."

Tommy stopped right before entering the kitchen.

"What time is Lana coming over?"

"She said around eight," Jerry replied.

"Well, if everyone can make it till then I'll order some pizza. My treat."

"That might work, T.F. Let's do it!" Cheryl was all in whenever they ordered take out of any kind and then didn't feel like she had to cook.

She had been thinking about what she was going to do for dinner and really wasn't in the mood to make anything. She'd been hoping they would order in like they usually did on Friday nights. Cheryl was the one who always organized the meals, especially dinner. The boys were usually good about pitching in, but she certainly didn't object whenever they had food delivered. She offered to go out and get some beer for later and take Timex for a walk.

"That would be great, Cheryl. I brought in a six pack, but I'll give you money for some more." Tommy was in a good mood and feeling generous.

Timex and Cheryl got off the couch as Tommy reached into his wallet and handed Cheryl some dollar bills.

"I'll be back in a bit," she said. "Do you want to go for a walk, Timex?"

Of course I want to go for a walk. That's what I live for: eat, sleep, walk, play and go to the store to get some beer.

Tommy went into the kitchen and pulled a pad of paper and pen out of one of the drawers. He sat down at the table and tried to think what he was going to say. It was more difficult then he thought.

Hi. Remember me?

He sat for a moment, then thought back to the conversation he had had with his sister on the phone. It wasn't that there was nothing to talk about, it was that he had trouble getting the words right. He decided to begin by telling Carolyn that he had just talked to Kathy and started writing a letter about the upcoming wedding and how much he was looking forward to his trip back to Michigan. Then the words started to flow easily and he couldn't stop. He virtually repeated what he had discussed with his sister. He sat and wrote for an hour and when he was finished, it felt good. He was proud of himself and vowed to do it more often. He hadn't written many letters since moving to California and this was by far the longest one. He signed it "Love, Tommy," sat back in the chair and listened to the music that was always coming from the living room. How could he have been so thoughtless toward the people that mattered so much to him? He would try to do better.

Tommy got up and walked to the window that overlooked the back yard. He noticed the lawn needed cutting. That would be a weekend project he decided he'd tackle. Then his thoughts turned back to his friends and family. He didn't recall ever feeling homesick before. Not even when he was in Vietnam. It was a weird emotion that was affecting him now. He walked over and grabbed an envelope out of the same drawer where he found the pen and pad and from his wallet pulled out the piece of paper that had Carolyn's mailing address. Tommy addressed the envelope and took it back into the living room where he laid it on one of the side tables. The room was empty and quiet. He had been so intent on writing the letter he barely remembered Ron and his girlfriend coming into the kitchen and saying, "See ya later." And he forgot what Jerry said he was doing. Maybe he went upstairs to have a shower before Lana arrived. He walked over to the stereo, looked at the albums and replaced the one that had just ended.

Where the heck is Cheryl? She and Timex have been gone a long time.

Tommy walked back to the sofa bed that he had been sleeping on for the last several months and had a seat. He put his feet on the coffee table, looked at the paraphernalia that sat on top of it and reflected how his lifestyle had changed in such a short time. He liked the drugs and this new-found freedom he had been experiencing since he came out west. He even liked his new appearance with the hair getting longer along with his beard. Things were different in California. This wasn't Brenton where things always seemed so conservative and somewhat behind the times, never changing. Things here were more progressive and people were more accepting and forward thinking. He felt comfortable in this environment. He missed home and where he grew up, but now he felt this was becoming his new home and there was nothing wrong with that. Michigan would always be in his heart, but California was running a very close second at the time and it had all happened quickly. His feeling of homesickness disappeared.

Tommy put a jazz album he hadn't heard before on the turntable and left the volume low. The music sounded nice as he enjoyed the peace and quiet of the house. Timex must be getting a nice long walk with Cheryl. They probably went down to the ocean. Both of them loved the beach and this wasn't the first time Cheryl had taken Timex for a long walk by herself. Timex liked her and she liked him.

Tommy thought of Cheryl and considered that he might be getting a little bit of a crush on her. His instincts told him the feeling could be mutual. They had talked about sharing a house together as roommates. He wondered if they were both thinking the same thing. Maybe they could be more than roommates. He had resisted making a pass at her for more than one reason. The main reason was, despite his incompetence in letter writing and making phone calls, Carolyn was still very much on his mind and his feelings for her were still strong. Secondly, Cheryl was Ron's little sister and he didn't want things to become awkward with all of them living in the same house. He and Carolyn had been sexually active for a long time and just like any young sexually active male, he missed it. He thought about it. He thought about Cheryl and wondered if she were maybe interested in having a little "fling." Would that mean being unfaithful to Carolyn? But he and Carolyn hadn't made any commitments to each other and they were a couple of thousand miles apart. So essentially he was single.

The way he was feeling, it meant that if the opportunity presented itself he would take it on. If it wasn't going to be Cheryl, it would be one of the many girls that seemed to float in and out the house. Female friends that Ron and Jerry had made and were always coming and going. They came for the free drugs mostly or to buy some if they had the money; even though Jerry always claimed he never did "business" from the house, it was obvious he did. The girls came to hang out and get high. It was a "social house" and a place where people always knew they were welcome.

Even though hippies came and went regularly, they were always respectful and never stayed late or called or came over in the middle of the night. Friends would stop over in the early evening for an hour or so just to see what was going on and then they would disappear. There were good "vibes" and a lot of laughter, and as much as Tommy enjoyed the camaraderie, it was also time to move on and get a place of his own. This had been fun, but more peace and quiet would be nice. If he and Cheryl got a place together there would certainly be less traffic and distractions. He would like that and thought Cheryl would too.

Cheryl walked in the front door with Timex. "Did you miss us?"

Tommy was slow in reacting. He had been enjoying the solitude and was caught daydreaming in a world all his own. He sat up and turned around just in time for Timex to come jumping onto his lap.

"Whoa, Timex! Hey, you're wet!" Tommy yelled good naturedly.

Tommy stood up as Timex dashed around, glad to be back home. Like a typical dog when it's wet and sandy, he ran around from room to room making sure he spread the mess.

"I'll get a towel," Cheryl said and quickly headed for the laundry room.

Tommy called Timex and calmed him down. "Obviously you had a good time down at the beach, hey Timex!" Timex reacted by licking Tommy's face. "OK, settle down, boy."

He thought it might be a better idea to dry him off in the kitchen where there was a linoleum floor and took Timex there. Cheryl walked in with a couple of towels and immediately started drying the hyper canine off. Tommy grabbed a towel and did the same.

"You guys were sure gone a long time."

"I'm sorry," Cheryl said. "We were having so much fun and we met some friends down there. I took a couple of tennis balls and you should have seen Timex crash through the waves. He actually attracted a crowd."

Tommy knew exactly what Cheryl was talking about. Timex loved the water and he lived for chasing the tennis balls. You could throw one for him as far as possible and Timex would swim beyond the crashing waves and search for the ball until he found it.

Tommy looked at Cheryl and smiled. Yes, it was "Timex the wonder dog."

"Maybe we should start charging admission next time we take balls down to the beach. Could be some extra cash," Tommy said as he stood up. Timex of course had to give one more good shake to make sure he was dry. "OK, Timex. That's enough."

Timex ran into the living room and dived head first into the shag carpet pushing himself around with his rear legs. Tommy and Cheryl followed him in and just shook their heads.

"I think he's happy," Cheryl stated the obvious. Timex stopped and faced the two humans watching him.

You guys wanna play? I'm all wound up!

Tommy told him once more to settle down and, being a dog, he responded to the tone in the human voice. Timex understood and mellowed out. One more face rub on the carpet and he went over to his favorite spot and lay down. Suddenly he realized how tired he was.

I think I may have overdone it.

"Maybe I should vacuum the carpet," Tommy suggested.

"Wait until tomorrow. It's too late. Where is everybody?" Cheryl asked, referring to Jerry and his girlfriend Lana, knowing her brother had gone out.

"I don't know," Tommy said, wondering the same thing. "Ron and Heather went to the movies and I thought Jerry might have been upstairs. I don't know. I haven't seen or heard anybody. Hopefully we still have a card game going on."

"Well, let's order some pizza. I'm starved. You're buying right? You said you would," Cheryl said, walking into the kitchen where they kept the phone book.

Tommy followed her. "You betcha. I did say that. We should get enough for four, right?"

"Yeah. I don't know where Jerry and Lana are, but they'll show up. I'm looking forward to playing cards. How about you?"

Tommy agreed with Cheryl that it'd be a good night to stay home and have some fun. It was going to be a nice relaxing evening and that would be just fine with him. He and Ron had put in a lot of hours during the week and he was feeling too tired for much of anything else.

"Did you pick up some beer?" Tommy asked. He had noticed when she came in she was empty handed.

"Oh, shit! I forgot. It's outside."

Cheryl laughed at herself and plopped her head down on the open phone book lying on the kitchen table. She raised her head back up and told Tommy it was just outside the front door. Tommy had a laugh of his own at Cheryl's expense and offered to go retrieve it. As he left the kitchen, in walked Jerry and

Lana through the front door. Jerry held the case of beer that had been left on the steps.

"Somebody lose something?"

Tommy walked over to Jerry and grabbed the beer from him.

"Hi, Lana. Yeah, our absent-minded friend," Tommy said, tilting his head toward Cheryl walking out of the kitchen, and raised his eyebrows, "lost her train of thought and left it outside. Please forgive her."

Cheryl leaned against one side of the archway that divided the kitchen from the rest of the house, her arms folded across her chest. "Sorrrrrry!"

Timex, who'd had enough rest, got up and went over to Jerry and Lana.

You guys wanna play? I'm rested now and ready to go again.

Lana, who loved dogs as much as everyone else, squatted down to give him a big hello.

"Hey, Timex. You feel wet. Have you been to the beach?"

"Yeah, we just got back," Cheryl said, walking up and taking the beer from Tommy. "I'll put these in the fridge. Everybody ready for one?"

It was affirmative for all and Tommy told Timex to get back to his spot.

"I had to go pick up Lana. Her car's not running," Jerry explained why he had disappeared.

Tommy had been so intent with his letter writing he hadn't even noticed. "We were wondering where you were. Sorry about your car, Lana."

The three entered the living room and found seats.

"It's an old clunker. There's always something going on with it. Oh, well. I'll call my mechanic on Monday. He makes a good living off of me," Lana said as she leaned back in one of the two stuffed chairs that surrounded the coffee table along with Tommy's sofa bed. Jerry brought out a little piece of aluminum foil about the size of a marble and began unwrapping it.

"I scored some good opium for this occasion. You're going to like this shit," he said.

That would be Jerry. Forever the salesman. Always providing the best drugs the market had to offer. Every time he brought in some sort of new improved marijuana, hashish or opium, it was always "the best" and he was usually right. He had his connections and it had paid off many times in the quality of his product. Tommy had no qualms with the high he got from opium. It was pretty mellow in fact. A good high. All the drugs they smoked were pretty much the same if not just slightly different. The marijuana, the hashish and opium all seemed to have their own personality and were manageable when ingested. That didn't bother him. After all, he trusted Jerry and if Jerry said that tonight they were going to be smoking some of "the best," then he was looking forward to it. Cheryl walked in with four bottles of beer, two in each hand and put them in front of the card players.

"I ordered the pizza. It'll be here in about forty-five minutes."

"Good job, Cheryl," Jerry said lighting the pipe with the opium in it and passing it on to Lana.

"I ordered a vegetarian one and a pepperoni one. That's what we all agreed on, right?" Cheryl asked her friends.

"That will be just fine," Tommy assured her.

Lana grabbed the deck of cards lying on the coffee table and took them out of their container. "Are we doing Hearts tonight?" she asked.

"Yep. We're doing Hearts," Jerry answered and then asked "You guys wanna play for money?"

Nobody saw a problem with that and they all agreed on twenty-five cents a point.

"Best of seven?" Tommy threw the question out and the players agreed on that as well.

Hearts was the game of choice in this house and got played at least two or three times during the week. Along with smoking dope and drinking beer, it was a relaxing way to pass the time. Jerry cut the cards and Cheryl ended up dealing and the Friday night card game began. The pizza was delivered, the opium was smoked along with some marijuana, the beer was drunk and life was just fine.

When the card game ended just before midnight and Jerry and Lana went to bed, Tommy asked Cheryl if she would like to go with him to take Timex out for a late night walk down to the beach. She replied that she would like that. As tired as Tommy was he had to be a good dad to his son, Timex, and his dog needed to go out one last time to do his thing. He had being lying patiently letting the humans play their silly card game and not bugging them. But just when everyone thought he wasn't paying attention he heard the word "walk" and jumped into action, making his way to the front door before anyone else.

"Hang on, Timex," Tommy told his canine son. "We'll go as soon as we're done cleaning up."

Tommy and Cheryl took away the pizza boxes and empty beer bottles and made the living room look somewhat presentable again ... for a hippie house.

"Thanks again for the pizza," Cheryl said, repeating what she had said earlier.

"That's OK. My pleasure," Tommy said as he put on a pair of runners at the front door.

"You think it's going to be cool out?" Cheryl wondered aloud.

"Nope. It's going to be nice and pleasant," Tommy said, always optimistic about the weather in Southern California.

"I hope you're right, T.F., but just to be on the safe side ... ." Cheryl opened the entry way closet and grabbed a hand knitted shawl.

Timex had his nose pressed to the front door and was more than ready to make his escape. Tommy opened the door and Timex squeezed through before it was even fully open.

"I think he's ready," Tommy said and gestured with his hand for Cheryl to make her exit as well. "After you, partner."

Tommy and Cheryl walked out into the night air that felt refreshing and warm. Pleasantly warm. Timex waited on the front sidewalk to see which way they were going to turn. One way meant to the beach and the other way was a short walk to a small local park they visited on occasion. They turned and headed in the direction of the beach and Timex went ahead and showed them the way. It was going to be a trip to the beach and all was well.

TOMMY AND CHERYL sat in the sand by the water and had a long discussion. Tommy appreciated Cheryl's ability to hold a conversation without any awkward lapses. She was gifted that way. It sometimes reminded Tommy of Carolyn, who had the same talent. Cheryl had brought a joint and some matches with her and lit up. Timex ran back and forth on the shoreline and finally found a stick that he brought to Tommy, dropping it in front of him. Tommy stood and threw the stick into the ocean hoping it would entertain Timex for a while. Timex swam around in the dark, a dog, who never gave up, on the hunt for his reward. Tommy and Cheryl laughed at the fact that Timex was going to be all wet again and agreed that when they got back they would dry him off outside before letting him into the house.

After solving most of the world's problems Tommy said, "I'm ready to head back. How about you?"

They had been at the beach for nearly an hour.

"Yeah. That sounds good to me," Cheryl said, also feeling tired and agreeing it was time.

Tommy wasn't sure yet if the feeling was mutual, but he had a sense that tonight could be the night that his relationship with Cheryl could become physical.

When they got back to the house it was all quiet. They sat next to each other on the sofa couch and chatted some more. Tommy chose his words carefully and after a few minutes of idle talk he asked Cheryl if he could sleep with her.

She responded by putting a hand on his cheek and planting a soft kiss on his lips. They embraced each other and began kissing and making out. Before things got too carried away, Cheryl suggested they retreat to her bedroom. Tommy told Timex to "stay" and he and Cheryl went to her room and spent their first night together. It was passionate and felt long overdue. When the lovemaking was over and they began to talk as they lay in bed, they discovered that each of them had been thinking of this moment for a while.

"I was hoping this would happen one day," Cheryl confessed.

"Do you still want to get a house together?" Tommy asked her, wondering if the lovemaking had changed anything.

"Yeah, I do," Cheryl said bluntly.

Tommy rose up on one elbow and rested his head on one hand, while the other hand stroked her hair. He kissed her on the forehead. "It's been great living here with your brother and Jerry. They've been so nice, but I'd really like to get a place of our own."

"Yeah, it's time and hopefully soon," Cheryl said, relishing the thought of living together. "We'll find something. I'm looking forward to it." Cheryl lifted her head and gave Tommy another kiss on the lips. "Sweet dreams, T.F. That was nice. You're a good lover."

"You weren't bad yourself, C.C." Tommy figured if she could call him by his initials he could do the same to her.

Cheryl turned over and put her back into Tommy's chest as he put an arm around her. The sex felt good and he was happy he had waited to have made love to someone that he genuinely cared for. As he closed his eyes to sleep, it was Cheryl on his mind and not the other girl from Michigan named Carolyn. For certain now, Tommy and Carolyn were on different paths and going down different roads. It had been happening for a while. The boy and girl, that had been a couple for a very long time and friends for even longer, were a couple no more. When Tommy had chosen to move to California, do drugs and now sleep with someone else besides Carolyn, he knew his life was changing and changing fast. He didn't seem to mind. He felt in his heart that all the changes were for the good and he was following his heart. He was content. As he fell asleep next to the girl he had longed for and Timex slept in the living room, everything felt just right and Tommy looked forward to tomorrow. His life was changing, again.

Nightmares

"Tommy, Tommy … ," Cheryl shook Tommy out of his nightmare.

The same nightmares had been happening since his days in Vietnam. They were brutally vivid. So real. So awful. He hadn't had one since he'd moved to California and he had started to think that perhaps they were gone forever. Now, as he woke up from the hell he was reliving in a dream and saw Cheryl on her knees above him, he realized the reoccurring nightmares were not over. He sat up in a hurry, drenched in sweat and shaking. He looked at Cheryl with a blank stare as if he didn't know where he was. Words could not come out of his mouth.

"Are you OK?" Cheryl asked him in a soft tone.

Tommy's actions before she woke him startled her. She had never witnessed anything like it. He was convulsing and screaming. He looked at the wall straight ahead still affected by what he had dreamt. The nightmares were all basically the same with only a slight variation each time and they were always about his experiences in the war. In one nightmare, he was in a firefight, there were bombs exploding all around him and death everywhere. He never saw any faces, but he knew he had to save all of the dying and wounded soldiers. Then, just like what had happened in real life, as if he were having an out of body experience in his dream, he saw himself get shot. Then another enemy soldier came along, pointed his rifle at him and pulled the trigger to finish him off. That was when he woke up screaming. He could never go back to sleep and the effects of the nightmares lasted well into the next day. Sometimes, and even more disturbing, were the nightmares he had about killing a man to save a dog.

Tommy looked at Cheryl. "Sorry," was the only word he could get out.

He pushed himself back and sat up against the headboard of the bed. Cheryl wondered if anyone else had heard Tommy's screams and listened, but didn't hear anyone shuffling around upstairs. Timex had, though, and stood outside the bedroom door that was cracked open only a few inches and whimpered. He knew when Tommy behaved like this something was wrong and he wanted to be by his master's side. Cheryl got out of bed and opened the door enough for Timex to get in. She told Tommy she was going to get a cold wash cloth to wipe the sweat that seemed to permeate from his whole upper body.

"I'll get you a cold drink of water as well," she added.

Tommy sat and stared straight ahead as Timex jumped up and put his front paws on the bed trying to get his master's attention. Tommy was too drained of energy to respond. He would give anything, do anything, to get these nightmares to end. They seemed to have become less frequent and just when he thought they were done for good, he got a reminder like this that told him they were not.

He had gone to counseling and therapy sessions before he was discharged from the Army that seemed to help some, but in the end, not enough. "Nightmares aren't uncommon to soldiers who have been in combat," he was told in his therapy sessions. But reliving the war in nightmares took its toll on a lot of soldiers and Tommy was not immune. Some soldiers could deal with it better than others. Tommy had found it difficult to say the least.

Cheryl came back in with a glass of water and set it on the bedside table. She took a wash rag and wiped her lover's forehead. It felt good and Tommy managed to comment on that. He was thankful Cheryl was here and at the same time felt bad that she had had to witness what had happened. In the past, when he had these nightmares, he was usually by himself and always felt alone, helpless. It might be a bit selfish of him, but he was glad Cheryl had been sleeping next to him when it all started. Tommy shook his head and kept saying he was sorry. It was hard putting thoughts together as he tried to make his mind blank and erase any lingering images from the hellish dream.

"It's OK. You don't have to apologize. Everything is going to be all right."

Cheryl continued to wipe Tommy and cool him down. She noticed the sheets were drenched from his sweat and planned to change them before they went back to sleep.

"I'm sorry, Cheryl. I have these nightmares every once in a while." Tommy finally managed to put more than a couple of words together.

Cheryl was relieved that he was talking and made an attempt at some humor that she hoped would relax him.

"You know, if you're going to have nightmares like this every time we make love, you're going to be in for a lot of sleepless nights."

It worked. Tommy managed a grin, grabbed her free hand with one of his and squeezed it.

"I'm so glad you're here, Cheryl."

They sat and talked a few more minutes as Tommy regained his senses. He helped her change the sheets and they lay down and tried to go back to sleep. It took a while for Cheryl as she worried about her new lover. For him it would be impossible and he knew the night was lost as far as sleep was concerned. He lay and stared at the ceiling. He was afraid if he closed his eyes the images would come back. Timex, who had been sitting a few feet away watching Cheryl care for his master, got up and walked over to Tommy's side of the bed, stood there and put his head down on the mattress where his best friend could reach over and scratch him behind his ear. Tommy tilted his head, looked at Timex and smiled. What more could a man ask for? Cheryl lying next to him on one side and Timex on the other. It was very healing to his soul. He went back to staring at the ceiling and continued to pat Timex on top of the head.

Will the nightmares ever go away?

Tommy was glad he didn't have to go to work in the morning. If he did fall back to sleep at least he wouldn't have to get up early and was thankful for that. He started planning for the next day. He'd cut the lawn and help clean house, maybe cook a big breakfast for everyone and then spend the rest of the day down at the beach with Cheryl and Timex. The thought of being with those two couldn't please him more. For everything the nightmares were, Tommy understood they were just that: nightmares. They upset him and depressed him every time they occurred and he held out hope that one day they would end. But the counseling he'd had, the few therapy sessions he'd attended and, the research he'd done, had only presented one conclusion: it was possible they would never stop. No one knew for sure. What he did know for sure was that in real life he was living a beautiful dream in California. Everything had gone well the last few months and now there was a new girl in his life that he adored and looked forward to living with. The hell with the nightmares.

The hell with them!

Tommy thought and analyzed and thought some more over the next couple of hours before his eyelids finally became heavy and he fell back asleep. When he did, he had a wonderful dream about him, Cheryl and Timex, all playing on a glorious sunny day down at the beach. For now, anyway, as he dreamt about the good things in his life, the war from years past was far, far away, hopefully never to return. For the ex-soldier though, the nightmares were only gone for the moment.

THE SEARCH FOR a house to live in took longer than Tommy and Cheryl had expected, just over a month, but they found a small, cute older two-bedroom bungalow that was exactly what they had been looking for. It was closer to the beach than Ron and Jerry's and like Ron and Jerry's, it wasn't in the nicest of neighborhoods. It didn't matter. The rent was cheap and, as small as it was, Tommy, Cheryl and Timex didn't need a lot of space. Like the house they were moving from, it had a fenced back yard which was great for "Mr. T." as Cheryl called Timex occasionally, just like she still called Tommy T.F.

Today was moving day. They had bought some of the necessities they needed and it only took three trips of hauling stuff in Tommy and Ron's trucks to get the move done. There were many thanks given to Ron and Jerry who helped on this lovely Saturday afternoon. Tommy and Cheryl didn't have much furniture and they were going to have to buy some more. For now, it was a good thing that their new digs were small. It didn't look too barren considering what little furniture they had. In due time they would accumulate things and with each of them having steady work, they could buy things when they felt like it. It wouldn't take long and the house would become a home.

Ron and Jerry entered Tommy and Cheryl's new pad with a couple of kitchen chairs that didn't match. It was the last of the furniture to be moved. The new occupants stood in their tiny living room and talked about where to put what.

"I assume you want these in the kitchen?" Ron asked his sister.

"Perfect, Ron. Thank you so much," Cheryl replied.

Jerry followed Ron and after putting the chairs in the kitchen they came back out and joined the other two. There was one couch and one small square coffee table for living room furnishings. It would have to do for now. A stereo and other chairs would have to come later and were high up on the wish list. The old interior walls were of plaster and had rounded crown moldings. The color of the walls was a medium shade of green that they could live with temporarily. They planned on painting the rest of the rooms as well and had approval from their landlord. Tommy and Cheryl were excited and it showed.

"I sure am glad we got this thing in the front door," Tommy said, referring to the bulky couch he and Cheryl had bought at a garage sale the week before. He plopped down on it.

"That was a tough one. Everything after that was pretty easy," Jerry said as he and Ron sat down on the floor next to the coffee table.

"Oh," Cheryl said, jumping up from the seat she had taken next to Tommy, "I have beer in the fridge."

"Good girl," Ron said to his little sister.

"Hurry back! I've got something to celebrate with," Jerry said as Cheryl exited.

"OK, OK. I'll be right back."

Jerry took out a small packet that looked like it contained a white powder. He had been keeping it in his top shirt pocket along with a small mirror.

Tommy observed.

What's this?

He watched as Jerry poured some out onto the mirror then took a razor blade from his wallet and began chopping the white powder.

"Jerry scored some really good coke. You're going to like this stuff," Ron said nonchalantly.

Coke as in cocaine?

"Sounds good to me," Tommy said, not wanting to spoil the party.

"It'll be a good way to celebrate your new hacienda," Jerry said, still chopping and putting some of the white powder into lines on the mirror.

Cheryl walked in with beer for everyone and saw what Jerry was doing.

"What 'cha got there, Jerry boy?"

"A special treat for a special occasion." Jerry rolled up a twenty dollar bill, snorted two of the lines then passed it to Ron. His roommate did the same and passed it to Cheryl.

"Don't say we never gave you anything, little sister," the older brother said.

Cheryl had never done cocaine.

"You have to hold one nostril with a finger and snort with the other nostril," Jerry instructed her.

Cheryl tried doing a line, but went too slowly and the drug didn't quite make it through the bill. Ron and Jerry laughed.

"No, you gotta do it fast. Really fast. You gotta snort really hard. Go ahead, try again," Ron told her.

The second time she was successful.

"Ah, I see. The faster the better," she said, wiping her nose off with a thumb and index finger.

She passed the mirror to Tommy. He had been watching and thought he had it figured out.

The faster you snort the better.

He did it like an expert. It was easy. He did two lines and passed the mirror back to Jerry.

"You did that like you've done this before," Jerry kidded Tommy, knowing his friend hadn't ever touched the white powdery drug before now.

For a few seconds Tommy wondered what all the excitement was about, then suddenly he realized he felt more alert and somewhat euphoric. It was a good feeling, he thought, and took a swig of his beer.

"That's kind of nice," Tommy understated. He looked at Cheryl sitting to his right. "You've never done cocaine before?" he asked his girlfriend.

Cheryl had a little bit of a dazed look on her face as if she were analyzing the drug and concentrating on its high. She shook her head.

"No, I haven't. I kind of like it though. Thanks, Jerry."

Ron raised his beer bottle toward the center of the coffee table.

"Cheers, guys. Here's to your new home."

Everyone clinked their beer bottles together and toasted. "Cheers!" they all said.

Ron pulled out a joint and lit it. Jerry cut up more lines of cocaine for the group to ingest.

Tommy inquired about the coke.

"How much does it cost?"

"How is it sold?"

"How long does the high usually last?"

Jerry answered all his questions with a depth of knowledge coming from experience.

"I've added coke to my drug store if you guys ever want to buy any. I guarantee you good quality."

Cheryl remarked that they better buy some of the things they needed for the house first. The drugs were great, but it would be nice to have a TV and some music for their home.

"Well, you know where to find me," Jerry said as he slid the mirror over to Ron for one more round of snorting.

Cheryl did her lines then stood up and looked around the living room. She couldn't wait to get started on making her new home feel special. Her mind was racing as she thought about paint colors and where to hang some pictures. She turned back to the three men.

"So next week we'll play cards here OK? Maybe have a little party. You guys bring Heather and Lana. You OK with that?" she asked her brother and Jerry.

"Yeah, we're cool with that. It's a date," Ron said, accepting his sister's invitation.

Timex, who had been investigating his new house, walked over to the couch and without hesitation climbed up on it and lay down next to Tommy, putting his head in Tommy's lap. Tommy looked at Cheryl and didn't know if this was going to be allowed or not.

"Are we going to let him do this?" he asked his live-in lover.

She put a finger to her lips and thought about it for a second.

"How about if we get a cover for it? We can't tell Timex, our good ol' pal not to share the furniture. He would feel bad."

Tommy appreciated Cheryl's rationale and it was one more reason why he had fallen for her. He agreed and patted Timex on the head. Timex knew what they were talking about. He also knew they would never kick him off the couch. He was family. At least Tommy had always let him get away with getting on the furniture. Why should things change now? Tommy leaned back into the couch and really got into the high he was experiencing from the cocaine. It was nothing too dramatic and yet quite pleasurable.

Nothing wrong with this stuff.

"Well, if that's it then," Ron said, standing up, "I've gotta get going. We'll see you guys later. I said this already, but I like your new place."

"Thanks so much for your help, big brother," Cheryl said, giving Ron a hug.

"You're welcome."

Ron told Jerry, "Thanks for the snort," and walked out the front door.

"Here. I'll leave you two a couple of lines. I have to be leaving too." Jerry put a couple of more lines of cocaine on the coffee table. "Enjoy," Jerry told them as he got up and said his good-byes.

Tommy, Timex and Cheryl walked him to the door and out onto the front lawn.

"We'll see you and Lana next Saturday, if not before, OK, Smitty?" Cheryl reminded Jerry.

"Sure thing, Cheryl. You guys enjoy your new shack," Jerry said as he walked toward his vehicle.

Cheryl and Tommy stood in front of their new house and waved as Jerry got in his car and drove away. They turned around with arms around each other and admired the new home they would be sharing for what they hoped would be a long time to come. The house would never win any awards for beauty and neither would the neighborhood, but for two young people starting out it was fine for now. One step at a time.

"Should we go inside and do those last lines of coke?" Tommy asked Cheryl, already knowing what she would say.

"Yeah, sure." Cheryl thought it was a wonderful idea.

"What do you think of that stuff?" she asked Tommy as they headed to the front door.

"I think it's a nice high. Real nice in fact." Tommy called Timex who was standing on the sidewalk thinking, as usual, that they were going to go for a walk. "We'll go later, Timex. Come on in, boy. Let's go."

Timex sprinted to the front door and beat the two humans in. Tommy and Cheryl went back to their spots on the couch and finished up the lines of cocaine. They discussed changes they would like to make to the house and what furniture they would need. They would clean the place up, improve it and make their landlord glad he had them as tenants. They sat back and enjoyed the high they were on while Timex, for some reason, thought his spot for now was under the coffee table. The two lovers were excited about their future together. Everything was falling into place perfectly and it was all going to be fine, wonderful, awesome … as long as the white powder didn't get in the way.

IT WAS A classically beautiful Michigan May day and a great one for an outdoor graduation ceremony. Carolyn, prideful and all smiles, stood with the other graduates in cap and gown, just beside the stage that had been put up on the football field for this very special occasion. It had seemed like such a long journey, but the moment had finally arrived for these young people, who had been so focused and committed, to attain their degrees. No one had said it was going to be easy and for some, it wasn't. But here they were now, standing and waiting for their names to be called so they could march up onto the large stage, get their diplomas and let the world know they had arrived and were ready to enter into yet another "new life" that was now beginning. It felt similar to when they graduated from high school; everyone was just a little older now. Another mission accomplished. Yes, older now and more mature, hitting the books and studying when it could have been so easy to do what a lot of their friends had done when they got out of high school—go get jobs, travel or party.

There wasn't anything wrong with that, but knowledge was power and these graduates knew it. Depending on what they were pursuing, some would continue on with their studies to become doctors and lawyers and architects or young entrepreneurs and professors. You could see in this group that this was a special day for them. You need look no further than the smiles. You need look no further than the proud parents, family members and friends that were sitting in the audience. Especially the parents of one particular girl. Mr. and Mrs. Russell couldn't be more proud of their only child. It also showed on the faces of Tommy's parents and his sister Kathy who sat on either side of the Russells. They were all happy for Carolyn and here to let her know. This was her day and Tommy Franklin barely flickered across her mind as she stood waiting to walk up the steps and march to center stage to get that valuable piece of paper.

Tommy, once again, hadn't been communicating with her and in the last letter she received he told her he wasn't going to be able to make it back for her graduation.

She was elated to have Tommy's parents and sister here along with her mom and dad. She couldn't think of five other people she would rather share this moment with. The line to walk up on the stage was moving quickly and as Carolyn got just a few feet away from the stairs and there were only half a dozen more graduates in front of her, she stood on her tip toes and craned her neck to see her parents sitting at ground level about ten rows back from the stage. Perfect seats for this. She caught her mother's eye and waved. Mrs. Russell waved back discreetly. Now her dad looked at Carolyn and the daughter blew her parents a kiss.

"Carolyn Ann Russell ... ."

That's me!

The dean said some more words into the microphone, about Carolyn Russell and her degree, that Carolyn didn't even hear. She was too full of excitement and not bashful about walking up onto the stage. She grabbed her cap as it almost slid off her head and laughed at herself. Then things started going in slow motion as she walked up and was handed her diploma. A tear of joy ran down her cheek as she turned and looked down at her parents and their guests.

This is special! Oh, so special. I am special!

She had done it. Carolyn had finished what she had started four years before. Whatever distractions there had been in her life all seemed to have disappeared now with a diploma in her hand. No one could take it away. It was magical. And the one distraction that bothered her most, the one that was about a friend by the name of Tommy Franklin, was gone as well. She walked across the stage and down the stairs into a new world. A new world she was going to love and enjoy from this day on.

Home for a Visit

FOR TOMMY TIME moved quickly. August had come at a blinding speed as he looked down at the landscape from his window seat on the jet plane that made its descent toward Traverse City Airport. It seemed like only yesterday that he had left his home state. He thought about his life these last eight months and how many changes there had been, not only in his life, but Carolyn's as well. He knew it was going to be tough seeing her for the first time since he left. Tommy also knew that if the subject came up he would have to explain why he had chosen not to write or call. He thought about that and didn't really have an explanation. He hadn't had one five months before when he last wrote and didn't have one now. Just because he wasn't communicating didn't mean relationships had to change. What difference did it make if he hadn't stayed in touch? Carolyn didn't write anymore either, but his mom and Kathy wrote or called every two or three weeks and he always assured them that he would try harder to return the favor. He didn't. Maybe this visit back for Kathy's wedding would make up for everything. He was hoping.

The plane landed and Tommy made his way to baggage claim. He got his suitcase and headed for the doors that would take him to the waiting area where he knew Kathy would be sitting and watching for him so she could run up and give him a big hug. As the automatic doors opened and Tommy began looking around for his sister he heard "Tommy." He turned to his left and saw a beaming Kathy rushing toward him. He put his suitcase down as she jumped into his arms.

"Hey, Sis," he said, squeezing her tight and relishing the moment.

Putting her down, Tommy grabbed his suitcase and they began to make their way for the exit doors with mouths flapping at two hundred miles an hour. There was so much to talk about and Kathy tried to get everything in with one big breath and in one sentence. She barely recognized him with his long hair and beard and said so. She didn't really care for that kind of appearance in a man, but if that's who he was these days, she would accept that and told him the opposite of what she thought.

"I like your long hair and beard. It looks good on you."

"Thanks," Tommy said as they walked out the exterior doors and headed for the parking lot. "I guess I'm what they call a hippie now," Tommy joked

Home for a Visit

and that got a laugh from his sister. He commented on the heat and humidity, which seemed kind of high for this part of northern Michigan.

"Hey, it's August. You know what it can be like here in August," Kathy said, trying to refresh his memory. "My goodness, you haven't been gone that long. It was hot and humid when you were in Vietnam and I'm sure it must have been worse than this."

Tommy loved his sister more than anything, but he wished she hadn't mentioned that country he had gone off to fight a war in. It seemed like such a long time ago on one hand and on the other, when he had the nightmares or someone mentioned "that country" and he was forced to think about it, it would seem like it was only yesterday when he was there. Even though his family was aware of the problems he had with the dreams that tormented him, he never made anyone aware of how much he wished he could just erase from memory the time he spent in the war overseas. He didn't make any reference to the humidity in Vietnam, deciding instead to talk about the reason he was here.

"So I guess it would be an understatement if I were to say you're a little excited about your wedding?" the hippie brother said to his straight-looking sister.

Kathy looked at him as they got to the car and grinned. "Tommy, I am sooooooo excited and sooooooo glad you made it. Hop in. We have so much to discuss on the way home."

Tommy threw his suitcase into the back and got in the passenger side of Kathy's car. They did have a lot of things to talk about and the hour's drive back to Brenton would seem like two. Tommy was anxious to see his parents. He had known it was going to be just Kathy picking him up as his parents were busy with other matters. Mr. Franklin had been working double time trying to get a work commitment done and their mom had promised to help out with a church activity she couldn't get out of. The parents were both disappointed that they couldn't go to the airport with their daughter.

It was Wednesday, but Mrs. Franklin was involved with her church—as she was seven days a week. Her life revolved around the commitments she made to her place of worship. That's where her friends were and it kept her busy. It was what she enjoyed most in her life outside of her family. There was always something going on with the church and she was the one who volunteered first to organize something and donate her time. So it was fine with Kathy when her parents asked if she were available to pick her brother up and it was fine with Tommy that his parents were busy doing other things.

Kathy pulled the car out of the parking lot and off they headed, south to their hometown. The conversation never stopped. You would have thought

Tommy had been gone for years. He told his sister how much he had always liked her fiancé Paul and how pleased he was for her. Kathy and Paul had become engaged a year and a half previously and Tommy had told his sister then how happy he was for the two of them. Kathy told Tommy about Carolyn's graduation back in May and that she was dating some guy named Jim that Kathy had met only once. "He seems very nice." This was the first time Tommy had heard about Carolyn dating another guy and he had mixed feelings about it. It was no secret that their lives were moving in different directions and he didn't expect Carolyn to hang on to their relationship from such a long distance. She had been a big part of his life for such a long time that you didn't just turn the emotional switch off and "poof" the feelings were gone. Human nature didn't work that way when you had loved someone that had been dear to you for so long. Carolyn would forever have a special place in Tommy's heart and it would be impossible to deny that. Because Carolyn meant so much to him, he felt that he should be happy for her and her new beau. He had known he was going to see her on this trip back to Michigan and he knew now he was going to meet this new guy, Jim. He'd take the high road and be happy for the two of them and it'd all be good. Carolyn and Tommy would always be friends and nothing would ever change that.

"Tell me a little bit about this girl, Cheryl, you're living with, Tommy," Kathy inquired. "She would have been more than welcome to come to the wedding," she said.

Tommy looked out the passenger window and admired the scenery that was beautiful no matter what time of year it was. The shores of Lake Michigan were as pretty as anywhere in the world and were among the planet's best-kept secrets. He told Kathy all about Cheryl and where they lived and how much he loved living in California. It even made Kathy a little envious, even though her heart was in Michigan. She had no interest in ever living anywhere else, but warm weather in the winter did sound enticing. Tommy continued and told his sister about how busy he was with work and touched, just briefly, on why he didn't write or call as much as he should. It sounded lame and a really poor excuse, but he felt like he had to say something and wanted to get it out of the way. There really were no excuses.

"Well, you're just going to have to try harder. It upsets Mom when she doesn't hear from you," Kathy mildly scolded him.

It hurt when Kathy said that, but he knew it was the truth. The last thing he wanted to do was cause his mother distress. He assured Kathy he'd change that when he returned to California. He told her how much Timex enjoyed living close to the beach and considered it his own personal playground. He talked at length about Timex because it was the easiest thing in the world for him to talk about. Kathy was happy to hear that Timex was doing well and listened intently as her brother talked about his dog.

"This is the first time I've ever left him behind since I got him out of quarantine. He's probably wondering what's going on, but he's in good hands with Cheryl. She loves him to death and spoils him rotten."

The way Tommy talked about Cheryl, it sounded as if she was good for Tommy. Kathy had always hoped her brother and Carolyn would tie the knot, but that was unlikely now that they'd both gone their separate ways. Kathy and Carolyn were good friends and they would have made great sisters-in-law.

Kathy pulled into the Franklin driveway. It was just before five in the afternoon and the ride down from the airport hadn't taken as long as Tommy and his sister thought it would. The conversation didn't lapse the whole way.

"Dad's not home yet, but Mom's here," Kathy said as their parents' house came into view.

Mrs. Franklin, in the kitchen as usual cooking and baking, was back from church and heard Kathy's car approaching the house. She quickly wiped her hands and made a mad dash for the front door, running outside to greet her son. She hadn't been able to get Tommy out of her mind all afternoon and, since she had arrived home, had been walking back and forth from the kitchen to the living room to look out a window what seemed like every thirty seconds, hoping to see Kathy's car. She knew what time his plane got in and had been expecting to see her two children any minute. Tommy saw his mom and a smile broke out from ear to ear. As soon as Kathy's car came to a halt, he jumped out and ran up to his mother, giving her a hug only a loving son could give.

"Hey, Mom."

Mrs. Franklin looked at her son and couldn't believe what she was seeing. His appearance had changed so much from when she last saw him eight months ago.

"Oh, Tommy. It's so good to see you." She put one arm around Kathy and one around Tommy as the trio headed for the front door. "Gosh, look at you," she said, rubbing his head with her hand. "Your Father is going to get a kick out of this."

Mr. Franklin would indeed get a kick out of Tommy's new look and, just like his wife, would accept it for what it was. Kids grew up. Kids changed. Kids changed their appearance. Every generation was different. There was always something new brought in by the next generation whether it was clothes, music or the way they wore their hair or the way they danced. It was always something different. The fact that Tommy had decided to let his hair and beard grow was all about being part of a generation expressing themselves. The Franklin parents weren't going to love their son any less just because he wanted to look a little different. They were quite aware of the "hippie generation" and they felt that some of the philosophy of this sub culture was good for the world. Love and Peace. Peace and Love. Wouldn't the world be a better place if everyone shared that ideology? In the way that the elder Franklins thought, wasn't this what Jesus preached? Love and peace. They heard it every Sunday in church. Love. Peace. Jesus never preached war and hate. He would have been a good hippie, excluding the drugs. The parents of this hippie, veteran, brave soldier were a perfect example of tolerance and acceptance. Did it matter what our spiritual or religious beliefs were? Were we not all one?

Another reason why Tommy had always loved his family so much was that they always tried to understand. To a certain degree they understood why he hadn't been in touch like he should have been. They understood why he had changed his appearance. They understood why he had moved to California and why he was living with some girl they had never met. That's who they were and the only thing that really mattered was that he was home for his sister's wedding. The next few days were going to be filled with fun and laughter. Tommy joked with his mom and sister that his father would probably get out the chain saw and start hacking away at his locks.

"Knowing Dad, he probably will," Kathy said, lagging behind her mom and brother as she carried his suitcase.

Mother and son walked into the house with arms around each other laughing and joking. Kathy followed, shaking her head at all the nonsense and bantering going back and forth. She put the suitcase down in the front foyer and watched the two continue into the kitchen. Kathy looked at her watch, remembering she was supposed to call Paul as soon as she got back from the airport with Tommy. She listened as her mom and brother carried on in the kitchen. It was going to be a great evening and, as she thought about her upcoming marriage to her best friend, it would be a great life and she couldn't be happier having her brother here.

Mr. Franklin arrived home just in time for dinner and was elated to see his only son home for the first time since he had moved to California. Mrs. Franklin had prepared not only Tommy's but everyone's favorite meal: roast beef and mashed potatoes with green beans and homemade apple sauce. It was a delight for all, including Paul, who arrived at the same time as Mr. Franklin.

They sat around the dining room table catching up on all the latest gossip

Home for a Visit

and news since the son and brother had left eight months before. Tommy couldn't believe how much he was enjoying himself. His mom's home cooking was still like he remembered, the best in the world. He had missed it more than anything when he was in Vietnam and was once again reminded that there were no meals like the ones Mom prepared.

"I made a chocolate meringue pie for dessert," Mrs. Franklin informed her son halfway through the meal.

"You're kidding, right, Mom?" Tommy said. He knew that his mom knew it was his favorite. "Why couldn't we have started with dessert?"

Most of the talk centered on Kathy and Paul's upcoming wedding, which was what Tommy had hoped would happen. Still everyone wanted to know about his time in California, this new girl Cheryl and how Timex was doing. Tommy complied with short answers that told them what they wanted to know. There would be plenty of time to talk about him. This was supposed to be his sister's time in the limelight and that's the way he wanted it. So with every answer he gave about his life in California, as soon as he was done he deflected the attention away from him to either Kathy or Paul to hear more details about their big day.

"The rehearsal dinner is Friday night, Tommy. You'll get to see Carolyn," Mrs. Franklin commented.

"Yeah, it'll be great to see her." Tommy meant it and hoped it wouldn't get awkward when they did in fact see each other again.

But knowing Carolyn, it would be like old times. Old times as in still good friends. He knew she would have every reason to be cool toward him, but that was not her and he knew it. He was sorry for everything: not writing, not calling, having their romantic relationship end in such a bizarre fashion.

Carolyn had found out about Cheryl through Kathy. It had hurt at first, but she was one to let bygones be bygones and her life had moved on with her graduation and her own new boyfriend, Jim. He knew that remaining friends meant a lot to her and true friends always wished each other well. Tommy was looking forward to seeing his ex-lover once again and was certain everything would be fine.

Dinner finished, Mrs. Franklin brought out dessert. No one could make a chocolate pie quite like hers. It was delicious. Absolutely scrumptious. Tommy, his dad and Paul cleared the table and got things organized in the kitchen to do the dishes. Kathy and her mom remained seated at the dining-room table and enjoyed the moment of letting the men clean up. They talked about the wedding and some last-minute preparations as the three men attacked the dirty dishes while engaging in some guy talk. Why discuss a wedding when you could talk about the upcoming football season and work and fishing and hunting?

Tommy appreciated the quality time together with his father and future brother-in-law. He was glad to be home, but couldn't get Cheryl and Timex off his mind. As Tommy wiped dry the last plate that his dad had just finished washing, he asked if he could call "home" to see how things were "back there."

"Of course you can," Mr. Franklin said, smiling at his son.

"I'll call collect."

"No you won't. Just call direct,"

"Thanks, Dad. I won't argue with ya."

"You better not."

Tommy walked over to the phone hanging on the wall by the back door where it had always hung and dialed Cheryl. He sat on the chair that was there for that purpose. He talked to his girlfriend for twenty minutes. It was nice to hear her voice and he was glad he caught her at home. She informed him that Timex was doing well "... we are having a great time together, although he does get lonely when I have to leave for work." They talked about things in general and Cheryl told Tommy about the, "really good coke that Jerry brought over tonight." Tommy thought about the cocaine he had in his suitcase and just talking about it with Cheryl put him in the mood to go do a line.

"OK, I gotta go. I'll call you again before I head back," Tommy said, sitting in the kitchen all by himself now. "Give that Timex a big hug from me and I'll see you in a week. Love you."

"I love you too," Cheryl said back. "Be sure you call again."

They said their good-byes and Tommy hung up the phone, walked to the back door and looked out the window. The sun was starting to set and the high clouds were turning different shades of pink and gray. He reflected back about how wonderful his childhood was growing up in such a special place. There was lots of room to run and play. He looked in the direction where Buddy was buried about fifty yards from the house. Without telling anyone he opened the door and headed for that spot and those memories from long ago. He wondered if there was still the small cross that designated Buddy's grave. As he got close he could see the cross was leaning a little crooked. He walked up and straightened it. The memories of his first dog come flooding back. They were fond memories that brought a smile to his face.

Buddy you were such a good dog.

That he was. Tommy smacked a mosquito that had landed on his bare arm and then looked back toward the house.

Home for a Visit

What a day it's been!

With a combination of the day's travel and his mother's incredible dinner, he was feeling fatigued. He'd go back to the house and wouldn't be surprised if someone suggested playing cards or a board game. That would be OK. As tired as he was, playing any kind of game was something he couldn't resist doing with his family. In fact, maybe he'd suggest it. He was home after all and that's what the Franklins did: have fun and enjoy each other's company. Play games.

"See ya later, Buddy. You take care," Tommy said in a soft voice to his old friend.

He walked back to the house where everybody was sitting in the living room entertaining themselves with some lively conversation.

"Where'd ya go?" Mrs. Franklin asked, putting down some pictures she had been showing her daughter.

"Oh, I just went out to say 'hello' to Buddy."

"How's he doing?" Mr. Franklin asked.

"He's doing fine. He wanted me to say 'hello' back to everyone."

Tommy found a seat next to his mother to check out the pictures.

"Oh, gees! I haven't seen these in a long time," breaking out in laughter as he viewed some family pictures from long ago.

He held up one of Kathy and showed it to Paul. She was eleven years old and standing somewhere on their property making a silly face.

"Are you sure this is the girl you want to marry, Paul?"

Paul laughed as Kathy grabbed the picture out of Tommy's hand.

"Which one is it?" Kathy asked and looked at the little girl having some fun with the person behind the camera. "Oh, gosh! Not this one!" She laughed as well, not believing the picture still existed. She handed it back to her mother. "Wasn't that on my birthday or something?"

Mrs. Franklin reflected for a moment.

"Yes, I believe it was. It was obviously nice weather and, if I remember correctly, you were cutting up for the camera just before your friends arrived for your party."

Kathy put her face down in one of her hands and shook her head.

"Sorry, Paul. I guess these things probably should come out before Saturday. Do you still love me?"

Paul laughed as he leaned back in his chair.

"Well, I don't know ... ."

Mr. Franklin jumped in with his two cents worth.

"I know how you're feeling, Paul. There were a lot of things I didn't know about Mrs. Franklin until after we got married. If I had known them before hand, well, things might have turned out a little differently."

Mrs. Franklin grabbed a throw pillow lying next to her and tossed it at her husband.

"John Franklin, you're lucky you have me."

Mr. Franklin took the pillow and put it behind his back.

"Thanks, honey. I needed that. My back was getting sore."

Mrs. Franklin turned her attention to Paul.

"Don't you worry, Paul. You're getting the cream of the crop."

Paul looked at Kathy and smiled. "I know I am, Mrs. Franklin. I know that one hundred percent."

Tommy had been looking at the pictures while the kidding was going on and ran across a few of him and Buddy. Even after all these years, looking at them still put a lump in his throat. He would never forget the years they had together, they were so special. Tommy thought again about how one's life can change in a second. Whether it was the sudden passing of a pet or rescuing another dog in a faraway land, it was something you never forgot. It impacted you for a lifetime.

He put the pictures down and asked everyone if they would be interested in a card or board game. The vote was unanimous and they all headed for the kitchen to sit around the table. It was like the days of yesteryear. Mr. Franklin said he'd pop some popcorn and Mrs. Franklin asked what everyone would like to drink. The joking and kidding with each other didn't stop for the rest of the evening.

When the games ended way after midnight and everyone had helped clean up, ready to head for bed, Paul told the Franklin family exactly how he felt.

"I want to say that not only am I lucky to be marrying your daughter, Mr. and Mrs. Franklin and your sister, Tommy, but I feel blessed to be marrying into such a nice family."

Paul scored bonus points with that comment and got hugs all around. Good nights were said as Paul left and Tommy headed for the bedroom he had slept in as a boy. It felt a little strange to be coming back to this place that had been his home for so many years, but he admitted to himself that, in fact, as the old cliché goes, "home is where the heart is." But when he got into bed and started thinking about "home," his heart told him he had a new home in a place called Venice, California. His heart was there as well. It belonged on the West Coast with a girl by the name of Cheryl and a dog named Timex. He wished they could be here with him and one day maybe they would all come back for a visit. They'd all come so Cheryl could meet his family and they could meet the girl that possibly one day he would marry. He knew he was back here in

Home for a Visit

Michigan for only a week and this was just his first night away, but already he couldn't wait to get back to the new life he had been living in California.

Tommy closed his eyes and fell asleep in a matter of a few short minutes. It had been a long day. An incredibly, fun, feel-good day. He had a beautiful dream about a time long ago when he was growing up. There were two characters in this dream and they were at a lake on the beach having fun chasing each other around. One of the characters in the dream was a dog named Buddy and the other was a girl named Carolyn. It was not a nightmare about war and killing that terrorized him, but a beautiful dream about when times were innocent, youth had the world on a string and life was no more complicated than throwing a stick for your dog to chase or taking your gal to the local drive-in for a milk shake. If it could be that simple as an adult in real life, then it would be the most beautiful dream of all.

TOMMY HAD THOUGHT about calling Carolyn on Thursday to say hello, but he had heard through Kathy that she was busy so he didn't bother. He actually spent Thursday going to work with his dad, pleased that he could help his father, if only for a day, to catch up on a job Mr. Franklin was trying to finish.

"Just like old times," his dad said on the drive back home after work.

Yes, it was just like old times and he enjoyed it so much on Thursday that Tommy decided to help his dad on Friday for half a day before they both knocked off and headed home to get ready for the wedding rehearsal dinner. The rest of the afternoon on Friday was spent in a lazy manner until five o'clock when Tommy and his parents headed for the Brenton Community Center where everyone in the wedding party plus a few friends were going to meet to have a potluck dinner. Tommy rode in the back seat of the Franklin car and in between conversing with his parents he thought about the moment when he'd see Carolyn and meet her boyfriend, Jim. He looked forward to it. It'd be nice to see her again and they would have much to talk about.

Mr. Franklin pulled his vehicle into the Community Center parking lot and the three of them got out and entered the hall. Judging by the numbers, it looked like most everyone was here. Tommy and his parents were greeted in the foyer by people that Tommy hadn't spoken to in a long while and he was held captive there for a few minutes before he could escape and make his way through the double doors that led into the large main room where all the activity was. He stood just inside the doors taking in the scene and recognized most everyone. He scanned the room for Carolyn, but didn't see her.

Maybe she's not here yet.

He shared some small talk with more people as he made his way toward the front where he saw Kathy and Paul chatting with some friends. As Tommy walked by the swinging doors that led into the kitchen, Carolyn came walking out holding a coffee urn and saw Tommy before he saw her.

"Tommy!" she screamed with excitement.

Tommy turned around and looked at the person he was hoping to see.

"Carolyn!"

Only a few feet apart, Carolyn put the coffee urn down on the floor and they fell into each other's arms. Tommy's heart was pounding with relief that this moment didn't turn out to be awkward and wondered why he had even worried about it at all.

"It's good to see you, Carolyn. How the heck are you?"

Carolyn, all smiles, couldn't believe her eyes and like everyone else had already, she commented on Tommy's long hair and beard and also, just like everyone else, whether they meant it or not, she said she liked it. She picked up the coffee urn.

"Come on, follow me. I just have to put this over on the table."

"Here, I can carry that," Tommy offered.

"It's not that heavy," Carolyn said, walking like she was late for an appointment.

Tommy did as he was told and followed. His best friend of the past reached her destination and put the coffee urn down on a table where all the drinks and food had been placed. She turned around and gave Tommy another hug.

"I'm so glad you made it! Come on, there's someone I want you to meet."

She took him by the hand and led him over to a long rectangular table where a group of half dozen people were seated and chatting. The young man sitting at the closest end of the table was the one she wanted to introduce to Tommy.

"Jim, this is Tommy Franklin, Kathy's brother from California."

Jim stood up and shook Tommy's hand.

"Nice to meet you, Jim," Tommy said.

"Nice to meet you, Tommy. Here, have a seat with us."

Jim seemed pleasant enough and gestured to a couple of empty chairs across from him. If first impressions meant anything, Tommy liked this guy already. He sat down across from Jim as Carolyn informed the two she had a couple of things in the kitchen to do before she could join them. The two men enjoyed a friendly conversation, talking about Tommy's life in California and Kathy's upcoming wedding. When Carolyn returned, Tommy wanted to know

Home for a Visit

how things had been since her graduation and how her new career in marine biology was going. It turned out that Carolyn and Jim worked together for the same company and that was something Tommy hadn't been aware of.

"It's really nice working with Jim. We're doing field work upstate on some rivers there. It's fun stuff," Carolyn informed an attentive Tommy.

Dinner was served and the three enjoyed their meal together as the conversation flowed freely between two old friends and a new one. Tommy got a sense that Carolyn was happy in all aspects of her life and he was happy for her. They had gone on separate journeys at this point in their lives yet, despite Tommy's lack of an effort to communicate, they apparently remained good pals. It made them both feel good.

"That was a great meal," Tommy said, getting up from his seat. "I'm just going to use the restroom. Hold my spot. I'll be right back."

It was easier said than done as Tommy had to stop and talk with some more people he hadn't had time to converse with earlier. When he finally reached the restroom he was alone and locked the door. From his pants pocket he pulled out a small, two-inch square packet and unfolded it. He laid it on the back of the toilet and pulled out his wallet. From that he took a razor blade and dispersed some of the white powder in the packet on the back cover of the toilet. He chopped up the small particles of cocaine, took out a bill, rolled it up and snorted the lines he had put out. He folded the packet up and put it back in his pocket. He had wanted to do some of the cocaine he had brought with him ever since his conversation with Cheryl the other night. He wiped his nose with a thumb and index finger, walked over to the sink and splashed water on his face. He liked everything about the drug. The taste, the feeling of euphoria and how it made him feel so alert.

Too bad I can't feel like this all the time.

He exited the bathroom just as his dad was about to enter.

"My turn?" Mr. Franklin asked.

Tommy knew his family would be heartbroken if they knew what he had just done. He'd have to be careful when he was here in Michigan visiting. He wouldn't want to hurt anyone, but he enjoyed the drug too much to leave it alone. As he headed back to the table where he had been sitting, he saw that Pastor Michaels from his parents' church had joined Carolyn and Jim. Tommy remembered Pastor Michaels from when he was a kid and went to church with his parents and sister. The pastor was only in his late forties, but he'd been pastor of the church for more than twenty years. Tommy had always liked him and his easy-going demeanor. He was good for the church and good for the community. Everybody in town knew him and he was well-respected. Good looking and physically fit for his age, you could tell he looked after himself and was a "practice what I preach" type of leader. He was one of the few in the hall tonight that Tommy hadn't had a chance to talk to.

Tommy walked up, shook the pastor's hand and sat across the table from him. Tommy had long ago lost his religion, but remained respectful of other people's spiritual beliefs. He knew there was no religion that could make him feel the way he was feeling now, high from the white powder he had just ingested. For him, believing in God was a thing of the past. Believing in drugs was his future. Pastor Michaels and Tommy had a brief, but informative, discussion and then the pastor started telling people it was time to get organized and on with the rehearsal. Even though the wedding ceremony itself was going to be in the church the next evening, Kathy and Paul had decided they could walk through the rehearsal here in the community center and have a potluck dinner with family and friends. Tommy looked around the room and picked up on all the laughter and people having a great time.

This is so good for Kathy.

His sister called him up to the front of the hall to participate in the rehearsal and everyone walked through their steps. There were more laughs and camaraderie. Pastor Michaels had done this many times before and quite enjoyed it. He made it fun and that in turn made it comfortable for everyone in the wedding party. Eventually, the evening wound down, but not before Tommy made another trip to the restroom to indulge in some more of his wonder drug. It would keep him up late tonight, but he figured when everyone got back to his parents' house he would be able to coax them into some sort of card or board game again. Knowing his family, that shouldn't be too hard to do. The actual games they played were secondary to all of them being together, laughing and enjoying each other's company. When they did get back to the Franklin house, Tommy's scheme worked. His parents, Kathy and Paul all joined him in a game of Monopoly.

This is what life is all about ... family, friends ... and drugs.

THE WEDDING WENT off without a hitch.

"I now pronounce you man and wife. You may kiss the bride." Pastor Michaels made it official and Tommy looked on as his newly married sister and her husband walked back down the aisle toward the church exit. Kathy was beaming and couldn't have looked happier. Tommy stared over at Carolyn who had never looked prettier.

Jim is a lucky man. Maybe they'll be next. They'll be good for each other.

Home for a Visit

Kathy and Paul walked out of the church and the rice flew as they headed for a rented limo with the traditional "Just Married" sign on the back and a long string of tins cans tied to the rear bumper. Weather wise, the day couldn't have been nicer. That was good because the reception was going to be outdoors at a local community park on Lake Michigan, which was a popular spot for receptions. Bentley Park had kitchen facilities and a covered eating area and was always booked this time of year for family reunions, parties and wedding receptions, as well as other events. There was an outdoor stage for a band to play music and you could walk on the beach forever. The community of Brenton had great foresight in building such a venue to bring people together in a beautiful setting and it was a perfect place for Kathy to have her friends and family come and celebrate her special day. Tommy loved to dance and managed at least one dance it seemed with every female, including his mother and Carolyn. Except for when he snuck away to do his lines of cocaine, a slow dance with Carolyn was the highlight of the evening for him.

Without a doubt, it was a very special day for the Franklin family and the last one they would have together in this life. No one could see disaster coming that beautiful day. Everything appeared to be just fine with Tommy except maybe for his appearance and that wasn't anything to be judgmental about. Tommy himself couldn't have imagined what the future was going to bring. He was unaware of it, but he was well on his way to a living nightmare, comparable to the nightmares he had on occasion when he slept. But for now, he was happy and carefree. He was working lots, had a beautiful girlfriend that he cared about and of course he had Timex ... and he also had the drugs.

IN THE WORLD of the drug culture back in the early seventies, there were a lot of things people couldn't see coming. What they did see was they liked their drugs and always wanted more. Sex, drugs and rock and roll. That was their anthem. The sex was good for the youth of the day because the inhibitions hadn't carried over from their parents' generation. The rock and roll was great and energizing. The hippie youth of that day couldn't get enough of it. But the drugs were sometimes deadly and misunderstood. Especially the hard drugs. A drug was a drug was a drug was a common way of thinking for "the hippies" of that era and for others that were involved in that "live for today" attitude. It didn't matter what kind of drug or what it did. "Just give me some drugs!" and life would be fine. That's all Tommy wanted was for life to be fine and in his way of thinking it became fine shortly after he moved to L.A. The drugs made everything better. Artificially better. The marijuana, the cocaine, the hashish, opium, it all worked. It didn't stop his nightmares about the war, but they helped make functioning in life's daily routine more tolerable ... or so it seemed. He could work while he was stoned, he could drive while he was stoned. He could have sex while he was stoned and eat while he was stoned. The reality of life when stoned was so much better than the reality of life not being stoned and he had a partner, a girlfriend, who felt the same way.

After his sister's wedding, Tommy couldn't wait to get back to Cheryl and the drugs. So when Tommy finished having the time of his life at Kathy's wedding and got to see Carolyn one more time, he boarded the plane that would take him back to California. No one foresaw what the next few years were going to bring for a favorite son and a favorite brother. Tommy Franklin misconstrued that he was going to be fine traveling down the road he was on. Naïve.

The world of hard drugs can be a road of no return. With drug abuse, like in war, some lived, some died. Lives were wasted. Even for those that survived, the mistakes of the past could come back and haunt them years later. So they didn't really survive, they just managed to hang on a little longer than some. It was all because the drugs were there and easy to get. The mind thought it needed to get high and the body demanded it.

"It's the high, man. It's the high."

"You gotta try this shit."

"It's the best."

"I can get you a good deal on it, man."

It was the early seventies. Sex, drugs, rock and roll and good times. But also a little bit of death, despair and sadness mixed in.

EVEN THOUGH TOMMY promised his family and Carolyn he would try harder to communicate with them when he returned to California, he didn't and it was a fault he couldn't overcome or explain. Without understanding why, he seemed to be phasing his family out of his daily thinking at that time in his life when perhaps he needed them most. It was a mystery he couldn't explain, and the chances were it had a lot to do with his lifestyle. The drugs, his girlfriend, work and other little simple distractions. It was party time, but more than anything, it was the drugs and getting high time, and family became secondary.

The next three years were not kind to Tommy for that reason. The drugs took over his life. At times it appeared Tommy was hell bent on self-destruction. Even his friends in California became worried about him and

Home for a Visit

worried about Cheryl. Timex was witness to it all and noticed how things changed slowly over time. Less attention. Fewer walks on the beach. Sometimes they forgot to feed him or left an empty water bowl.

What have I done to make my master and best friend treat me this way? Something's not right. Why are they behaving like this? Why do they forget about me? Don't they love me anymore?

Dogs don't understand the effects drugs have on humans. They have no idea.

But it seemed like every time Tommy and Cheryl were snorting the white powder, he was all but forgotten. Then they started cooking a different drug over a candle and injecting it into their arms and Timex knew when he saw that, he might as well forget about his walk or getting any attention.

Why have these humans who love me so much, changed so drastically?

Timex watched Tommy and Cheryl's behavior change over time and it became confusing and frustrating. When he had to pee he learned that he could go to the back door and whine and would sometimes have to bark to get their attention. Eventually one of them would get up and let him out. It wasn't that long ago that the three of them would go out to the beach almost every night or to one of the parks nearby. There Timex could run and play and chase the ball or fetch the stick and feel proud bringing his treasures back to his loving master or his master's loving girlfriend.

What happened? What did I do to make them not like me?

Now he was lucky to just get out into the back yard and even luckier to get back into the house. How many times did they let him out and then forget about letting him back in? He would do the same routine and stand outside the door and whine or bark until one of them came to the door to let him inside. Sometimes he was totally forgotten about and would have to sleep outside. Timex felt lonely and depressed during these times.

Timex was also sad and worried. He was sad because this house he lived in used to be full of life and energy, laughter and joy. Now it was quiet and depressing. He was worried because the humans that he loved and lived with were acting indifferent toward him and he didn't think for a moment that this was who they really were. He had seen it enough times now and it had something to do with the white powder and the sticking of the sharp pointy things into their arms. There was no routine anymore.

His human friends hardly ate meals now compared to when they used to sit down at the kitchen table, especially for dinner, and he would always get his treats. That was a thing of the past. Before this "white powder" thing came into their lives, they always used to keep their home neat, clean and tidy. He had noticed that it was no longer the way. They might do the dishes once a week or clean house once a week, but that was a maybe. Timex had reason to be sad and worried. It had been a dream life for a dog that had been rescued from a war-torn country and brought to this wonderful place called the United States of America. He spent time in somewhere called Michigan and now in this place called California and had enjoyed both places immensely. He had loved every second of it ... but now, now what was happening was something he couldn't comprehend. Like every dog that had, or had had, a loving master, he wanted to remain loyal ... but he worried.

This will pass. Humans are a very interesting species. Tommy and Cheryl are just going through some changes and one day soon we'll all be back at the beach happy and playing again.

Timex didn't know the truth of the matter. As with all dogs, he just wanted to be loved. But the happy days were over. His dad and his mom were drug addicts. They were into themselves and the drugs and the dog they had paid so much attention to had become an afterthought in their lives. It had happened quickly. At least it seemed that way to Timex. The move to California was huge for him and his master, and he had put all his trust in Tommy that whatever they did, wherever they went, all would be well. All would be fine. Why would he ever stop trusting Tommy? Now, with everything that had been going on in the last year, he was not so sure he could trust Tommy or Cheryl.

What next? Who can I trust? What is this white powder the humans seem so enthralled with?

What happened over the few years, after Tommy had discovered drugs, seemed to happen with the speed of light. Tommy and Cheryl, with their hard-core drug addiction, were too out of it to even see it coming. Tommy's parents were in complete distress over what had happened to their son, not knowing where he was or what he was doing. Was he alive or dead? It was the same emotions they felt when Tommy was in Vietnam. The "not knowing" would stress out any loving parent and no two parents could have loved their child more. They started blaming themselves and wondering where they went wrong. They wished they had done more in trying to talk Tommy out of joining the Army, but he did that on his own and he didn't tell them until it was done. Even though they wished he hadn't gone off to war, they were proud of their patriotic son for serving his country.

What Tommy's parents couldn't see were the scars of a war that had been left on their son's soul and Tommy would never share that with anybody.

Soldiers had to be strong and not appear weak. It was sometimes hard for soldiers to share their feelings about war and what happened during battle. The things they did could be completely out of character. If they were quiet about their experiences and didn't share them, maybe the nightmares and guilt would just go away.

Not a day went by that this one soldier's mom didn't get a tear in her eye whenever she thought of her lost son. The last phone call she had from him was over a year ago now. His voice had sounded funny and his words seemed scattered and disconnected. It gave her reason for concern and she tried to rationalize that he must be really tired or not feeling well. Now she wondered, "Was it something else? Drugs? His war experiences? Both?"

Where did we go wrong? Tommy had everything in life as a child and what he had most of all was a loving mother and father. How could this happen to us? To Tommy? We were such a loving family.

Kathy felt the same way her parents did. Hurt. Sad. "Why has he done this to us?" She thought back to the last time she had seen her brother when he came to her wedding. Sure, he looked like a hippie, but not all hippies took drugs and disengaged themselves from their families. She recalled Tommy on his last visit and he hadn't seemed to be acting any different from the brother she had known her whole life. Like her parents, it pained her not knowing why Tommy had seemingly disappeared off the face of the earth. She knew, but wouldn't admit it to herself, that it was probably drugs that had messed him up. Or maybe it wasn't drugs at all. Maybe it had something to do with Vietnam and what happened over there that was haunting him. Kathy wondered, just like her parents did, if it could be a combination of both. Kathy knew, whatever it was, this person who no longer communicated with his family, was not her brother. It was someone else. Tommy would never do anything to hurt his family. She knew that for certain. If only he would call again. If only he would write.

If only he knew how much we love him.

Like Kathy and Mr. and Mrs. Franklin, Carolyn also felt the pain of Tommy's decision, conscious or not, to vanish from the planet. And even though Tommy was constantly on their minds, everyone moved on with their lives. Kathy focused on her work and her remarkable marriage to Paul. Even though she felt the emptiness of not having Tommy in her life, she was concentrating on her own life now. Carolyn and Jim had moved in together and lived a one-hour drive from Brenton. They were both employed by Michigan Fish and Game doing their marine biology work and felt blessed that they had jobs in their home state that allowed them to stay in a place they loved. It was important to them that they got to stay close to their families and friends.

Carolyn's heart wouldn't let her forget about her lifelong friendship with Tommy Franklin, but over the last couple of years, she made her choices and he made his. She would never even attempt to understand what had happened to Tommy's personality that made him cut off his family and friends. She was a marine biologist, not a psychologist. She loved her life and, whatever Tommy was doing in California, she hoped that he loved his life as much as she loved hers. What she didn't know was that his life was spiraling downward and out of control. What she didn't know was that the next time she spoke with him she would be speaking to a lost soul. What she didn't know was that the next time she saw and spoke with him it would be the saddest day of her life.

Drugs Take Their Toll

CALL IT HARD luck or call it the choices Tommy made. He chose to go to California. That was fine. He chose to immerse himself in the drug culture. That would be a bad decision for anybody and it took him down the road to the point of no return. He and Cheryl alienated everyone around them except those who had the same problems or could offer them drugs. Cheryl had lost contact with her family as well and Ron, who had managed to quit all drugs, tried to help her any way he could. Ron also became upset with Tommy and blamed him for Cheryl's drug addiction, although he should have been blaming Jerry who was their main supplier. It was far reaching, the pain Tommy and Cheryl caused everyone. Ron and Jerry had parted ways and were no longer living together. Cheryl told her brother to mind his own business. Ron got pissed off and wouldn't speak to either Tommy or Cheryl for weeks on end.

Even on the job, Ron gave Tommy the cold shoulder and that went on until finally Tommy got fired for missing so much work. When Tommy got other carpentry jobs, it didn't take long for his boss or foreman to realize that he had a drug problem and he got fired again. Tommy could never figure it out. It was always somebody else's fault that he was let go. The fact that he had a drug issue never occurred to him. His work was slow and his mistakes were many and that jeopardized the safety of others. All of his talents went to waste. Everything his father had taught him was forgotten or clouded by the heroin and cocaine that he now indulged in and he couldn't understand why the world had turned on him. He had burnt bridges. No one would hire him. He and Cheryl constantly fought and eventually broke up. Cheryl moved out and Tommy eventually lost the house they had lived in when he couldn't pay the rent. Any money he had went for drugs. It's the curse of the drugs. It continued until Tommy and Timex had to live out of his truck, spending their nights in parking lots until they were booted out of them in the middle of the night by private security or the police. Timex thought to himself that he must hang on because one day things were going to get better again.

Hang on ... hang on. It's going to be all right.

Timex did hang on. Even after Tommy sold his truck, what used to be his pride and joy and then he and Timex started living on the streets, Timex still hung on. He hung on for as long as he could. In this now crazy world that

Timex was living in, even a dog could be forced into making a decision. Timex loved Tommy and Tommy, at one time, loved Timex. But Tommy loved getting a fix more than anything and Timex, like any animal with survival instincts, had to do what was best for him.

TOMMY LAY ON top of an old sleeping bag curled up in a Venice alley just off the boardwalk. The few belongings he had left were near his side along with Timex. He had managed once again to score both the cocaine and heroin and mixed a nice drug cocktail called a "speedball." It was another typically beautiful sunny day where the ocean meets the sand in Southern California. The boardwalk was busy as usual with the tourists and locals doing their thing in the warm sun. No one knew what was going on behind the scenes just a few yards away. It was where the homeless and drug addicts hid in the shadows. It was where a young man that grew up in Michigan in the good ol' U.S. of A. was slowly dying. A young man from a loving family that only wished they knew where he was and what he was doing so they could help him. A young man that had fought for his country and served so proudly in the Armed Forces. A young man that somehow lost his way and all of his possessions. His family, his girlfriend, his home, his job. A young man that had so much worth and talent ... gone. A young man that had an incredible childhood and wonderful memories from his youth. A young man that had been normal in every sense of the word ... and then he went off to fight.

If I do the drugs, it'll help me forget about the war. If I isolate myself from the rest of the world, it will help me forget the guilt.

He was good at blaming everybody but himself. He was good at denying he had any problem at all. He was good at insisting he didn't need any help.

We are not killers. We were doing what was asked of us. War? Is this how we survive as a species? Killing each other? We are not killers or murderers. We were fighting for our country. To defend freedom! I am a good human being and we ... we are all brothers and sisters!

Tommy was not alone. He was only one of thousands of war vets who came back to their country of birth and, once they became civilians, found themselves rejecting society. They were our heroes, but it seemed like the government and many civilians didn't see it that way. They couldn't possibly understand. Some war vets survived, some didn't. Some would discover the streets weren't meant for them, get help and eventually find their way back. Others just wanted to be left alone to do their drugs or alcohol. They were not killers or murderers. They were beautiful human beings that had lost their way.

Drugs Take Their Toll

That's where Tommy was now. A beautiful person, a brave ex-soldier, a kind and caring son and brother that managed to lose his way and now lay in this alley with his long dirty hair and unwashed clothes and only cared about how he was going to get his next fix. He had also lost his way as a responsible dog owner and his dog was the last thing he had left to lose. He was someone that used to care for and love his dogs. He asked nothing of Timex now and Timex asked nothing of him. The walks were done and Timex never knew when he was going to get food or a drink of water. Timex had survived the war in Vietnam, but he knew he couldn't survive Tommy's drug addiction and his master's own personal war.

Like so many ex-soldiers on the street, some dogs survived, some didn't.

Timex lay next to Tommy and realized the time had come to make a decision. He was hungry. He was thirsty. He stood up and looked around the alley.

Where do I go to get some food and water?

He made his way toward the boardwalk only a few yards away and observed the scene. There were people walking in all directions and groups sitting outside on the restaurant patios, eating and laughing. Tommy, stoned out on heroin, watched with glazed eyes as Timex walked to the end of the brick building that he and Tommy had been lying next to. The broken dog continued to look up and down the boardwalk. Tommy wondered what Timex was going to do, but had no strength to call him back. Timex turned and looked back at his lost friend. He wasn't sure what to do until his survival instincts finally took over.

I have to eat. I have to drink.

Timex turned back and again looked up and down the boardwalk.

Which way should I go?

He made his decision, turned the corner of the brick building and headed down the promenade, walking out of Tommy's life forever.

TOMMY SAT IN his drugged-out stupor and slowly realized his buddy, Timex, was out of his sight with no collar, leash or tags. He managed to put that thought together somehow. He struggled to get up and slowly, as if he were drunk, made his way to the boardwalk. By the time he got there, he couldn't even remember in which direction Timex had headed. Tommy looked one way, then the other. No Timex. He felt nauseous and leaned against the brick building, then slid back down to the ground. The homeless drug addict turned his head and looked toward the beach and the ocean and watched the pounding waves in the not so far-off distance.

What was I looking for again? Oh yeah, Timex. He probably went down to the water to play. I'll wait for him here. He'll be back. He'll come back.

No he wouldn't. Timex had gone to find food and water. He went to find someone who would give him a pat on the head and perhaps realize how hungry and thirsty he was.

Maybe I can find someone to make me feel better. Maybe I can find someone to look after me and my master. Somebody help me, please! Someone help my master!

Tommy sat on the ground leaning up against the brick building and waited. And waited. An hour passed by and no Timex. Two hours passed and still no Timex. As he came down from this last high, it became clear to him that something was wrong.

Timex would never leave me. Somebody's taken him.

He got up from his concrete seat and made his way back to his sleeping bag and a couple of garbage bags that were full of what was left of his belongings. He gathered them together and in a panic headed down the boardwalk in search of his dog, not realizing he was heading in the opposite direction that Timex had gone. It was hopeless. Tommy was hopeless. Timex was gone. Tommy's last friend had hung on for as long as he could. But a dog had to eat and drink. A dog needed love and attention and Tommy ... Tommy needed another fix.

IT WAS DUSK and Timex had drifted down the boardwalk not knowing where to go or what to do. He was starving and was becoming dehydrated. He found some shade underneath a palm tree on a little grassy area between the boardwalk and the sea. The grass was cool and felt good. He thought that perhaps this was where he'd spend the night and tomorrow, if he were still alive, he would find food and water. Timex had been watching the people on the boardwalk stroll back and forth all day. No one approached him to say hello or even give him a pat. He wondered if he should have stayed with Tommy. He was too tired to go back and look for his friend and put his head down between his front paws. The look on his face was sad. Just as he was about to close his eyes for the night a lady he had noticed sitting on a bench a few yards away with a small dog got up and walked toward him. He raised his head back up.

Is she coming to see me?

She was. The woman, thirtyish, Afro-American, came up to him and knelt down, slowly extending a hand pointed downward so that Timex could smell it.

It smelled wonderful.

"Hey, there. How you doing, Timex?" The woman's voice was soft and soothing. "You don't look too happy. Tommy's not looking after you, is he?"

How does she know about me and Tommy?

She patted Timex on top of the head and it made him feel wanted again. He managed to roll over on his back so she could pet his chest.

"My name is Amy and this is my dog, Missy. We don't live too far from here. Would you like to come home with us and I'll give you some food and water? Come on, come with us." The lady stood up, looked down at him and smiled.

Food? Water? OK. I recognize those words. I don't know who you are, but if you want me to come with you, I will.

Timex stood up and with what strength he had left in him began to follow the woman who called herself Amy. He wondered who she was, where she came from and why she had been sitting on the bench watching him for so long. All he knew for now was that he was drawn to her and understood the words food and water. Timex was walking out of Tommy's life and into another person's life. Her name was Amy, she was friendly and had offered him two essentials for living, food and water … and one other … hope.

CAROLYN SAT AT a desk in the den of the house she and Jim had rented and was doing work on a project for the company she worked for. It was just before eight in the evening and her eyes were starting to get tired. Despite the time, she felt like she was ready for bed. It had been a long day. She loved her life and everything about it, including the lover she lived with. He was kind and they had much in common, even outside of their work. She felt lucky. At work, at play, at home. She pushed her chair back from the desk and put her feet up on top of it. She stretched her arms and decided it was time to give her mind and body a break and put off thinking about tomorrow and the work at hand. Carolyn also thought about the upcoming weekend. She and Jim were planning to go upstate and do some camping. It was one more thing they loved doing together. Being outdoors as much as possible was their passion. They shared hobbies and their love for the movies, but it was the great outdoors that gave them the most enjoyment. Both were impulsive when it came to fun ideas and it was never a challenge to get the other one to join in. Doing something spontaneous was more the norm than not. It was a good life without a worry in the world. They worked hard for it and reveled in it.

Carolyn closed her eyes and thought about the wonderful times in which she and Jim were living. One thing she didn't think about much anymore was what Tommy Franklin was doing. She had finished worrying about him a long time ago. She had suffered through the pain he caused her and his family and knew he was out there somewhere, but she didn't lose any sleep over him. Not anymore. These days, she didn't give him much thought at all. He was still in her heart somewhere, but she didn't know where. Sometimes she might be somewhere and see something, or perhaps hear a song that reminded her of Tommy, but it was always fleeting. There was nothing she could do about the decisions he had made in his life these past few years. She was busy with her own life and didn't need the distraction of worrying about an ex-lover and friend. He was becoming a distant memory, all be it, a fond one, but she worried no more. That had passed and she was through with it … or so she thought.

Tommy Franklin was far from her mind when she heard the phone ringing in the living room where Jim was watching TV. She hoped it wasn't work related for either of them, only because they were both tired and wanted a quiet evening. They loved their jobs and gave them their all, but neither one felt like talking about work on this particular night. Jim would answer the call and, hopefully, whoever it was could wait for a call back until morning, unless of course, it was family. Jim got up, turned the sound down on the TV and made his way over to the phone on a small table in a front corner of the living room. He looked outside the big picture window and saw that it looked like it was going to be a pretty sunset. Like Carolyn, he didn't really want to answer it, but one never knows, it might be important.

"Hello," Jim said, speaking into the phone.

"You have a collect call from a Tommy Franklin in Los Angeles, California. Will you accept the charges," the long distance operator asked.

Jim couldn't believe what he had just heard. It had been a long while since that name had come up. What the heck could Tommy Franklin possibly want? Strange. Why was he calling collect?

"Yes, we'll accept the charges," Jim said, wondering what he was going to hear next.

Tommy's crackling voice spoke from a pay phone on the Venice boardwalk.

"Is Carolyn Russell there?"

Jim knew instantly this wasn't a casual courtesy call from an old friend just wanting to say "hello." The sound of Tommy's voice hinted to Jim that the

Drugs Take Their Toll

person on the other end of the line appeared panicked or confused, maybe both, Jim wasn't sure.

"Hi, Tommy. It's Jim here. Been a while. How are you doing?"

Either Tommy didn't want to hear what Jim had just said or it didn't register because of the state of mind he was in. With a voice that began to sob, Tommy asked once again, "Is Carolyn Russell there?"

Jim hesitated for a moment to assess the situation before responding. It was a little perplexing to hear Tommy's voice.

"Hang on, Tommy. I'll go get her."

He made his way to the den where Carolyn still sat with her feet up on the desk. She looked at him as he stared at her for a second, still trying to figure out what this old friend of hers wanted. They hadn't heard from him in a couple of years and it seemed a little odd. Carolyn assumed that Jim had come to tell her the call was for her and wondered why he wasn't spitting the words out.

"Phone for me?" she asked, not terribly enthused if it was.

"Yeah, it's Tommy Franklin. He called collect." Carolyn put her feet on the floor and swiveled her chair around.

"Tommy Franklin?"

She was as perplexed as Jim was. She stood up and began walking toward the living room, passing Jim on the way. She had a "question mark" look on her face.

Why is he calling here and why is he calling collect? How did he get my number? He must have gotten it through information. I do have a listed phone number. This is very strange. Interesting.

Carolyn hadn't given Tommy her number since she and Jim moved in together and wondered how Tommy even knew what town they lived in. It must have taken a lot of work to track her down. As Carolyn walked by Jim he informed her, "Be prepared. He doesn't sound too coherent."

"Thanks, Jim," she said and continued on her way to go pick up the phone.

"Hello. Carolyn here."

"Carolyn, its Tommy Franklin."

He was relieved to hear her voice after all this time and she picked up instantly that he did in fact seem to be sobbing.

"Hi, Tommy. It's been a long time. How are you?"

She didn't sound overly enthused, but only because she had an initial concern about what the phone call was about and why Tommy didn't sound right.

"Carolyn ... ," Tommy struggled with getting any words out between sobs.

"Tommy, are you OK?"

Carolyn immediately thought of Kathy and Tommy's parents. Why wasn't he calling them? Something was wrong and old feelings toward this friend and ex-lover were starting to resurface once again. For everything Tommy had done that so many people didn't approve of, he would always be someone that was a part of her life and he was still a brother and son and loved by his family. Carolyn sat down on the cushioned chair next to the table where the phone was. She was now genuinely worried about this person on the other end of the line.

"Carolyn ... ," Tommy still couldn't get the words out because of his crying.

"Tommy, calm down. This is Carolyn. You can talk to me. What's wrong? Tell me what's wrong, Tommy."

Jim walked into the living room and sat down on the couch. He studied Carolyn's body language and listened. She too was getting upset and looking like she could be on the verge of tears.

"Carolyn ... I've lost Timex." Now that he had gotten the words out, his crying became more intense. "I've lost Timex, Carolyn."

Knowing how much Timex meant to Tommy and how much she herself had been attached to Tommy's best friend, Carolyn wiped away a tear and didn't know what to say next.

"I can't find Timex, Carolyn. I can't find Timex," Tommy cried, sounding even more distressed, if that were possible.

"Tommy, it's OK. Listen to me. When did you lose Timex?"

She wished Tommy would calm down and she didn't think for a second she was getting through to him. He continued to bawl into the phone.

"I don't know where he is, Carolyn. Why did he leave me? I can't find him anywhere. I can't find Timex. I can't find Timex. Why did he leave?"

Tommy, standing on the boardwalk late in the afternoon in Venice, California, dropped the phone and let it dangle as he walked away and headed out into his world of personal chaos.

"Tommy?" Carolyn, two thousand miles away on the other end of the line, sensed something had happened. "Tommy? Tommy, are you still there?"

There was silence. No response. Carolyn began to cry softly as Jim got up, walked over and put an arm around her to console her.

"Tommy, please answer me. Are you still there? Please answer me, Tommy."

She knew he was not going to answer. He was messed up and she felt helpless to do anything. Jim took the phone and hung it up as Carolyn buried her head in her hands. Her live-in boyfriend got down on his knees in front of her, rubbing her arms and touching her, trying to comfort her. He was aware of the history between the two friends. He felt for her, as she would for him if it were the other way around. Her pain was his pain. She raised her head, looked at Jim and hugged him. She was so glad she had him and that he was there for her. Jim patted her on the back and calmly told her it was going to be OK. He leaned back and wiped away her tears.

"What was that all about?" he asked.

Carolyn grabbed Jim's hands and shook her head.

"I wish I knew, Jim. I wish I knew," she said through the sniffles. "He's lost his dog, Timex. But he sounds so messed up. There's something terribly wrong with him. Something's not right."

Jim tried to measure his words before talking.

"Drugs, Carolyn. Drugs. You told me a long time ago you suspected it and that's what it sounds like to me. It's more than just about losing his dog. It's more than that."

The two stared at each other for a moment.

"He needs help, Jim. He needs help. I'm worried now. I'm so worried."

Carolyn settled down a bit and Jim walked back over to the couch and had a seat. They didn't talk as they thought about what had just happened and what to do next.

"You have to call Kathy and tell her you've heard from him and then either you or Kathy has to call his parents," Jim voiced the obvious.

Carolyn knew he was right and it would have to be done tonight. She got up, walked over and sat down next to Jim, grabbing one of his hands for comfort.

"I'll call Kathy in a few minutes. I have to get my composure."

Carolyn put her head on Jim's shoulder. He let go of her hand and put his arm around her. She needed to think and relax for a few minutes. For the moment, Jim knew it was best not to say anything. Let her think. Let her do the talking. She wiped away the last of her tears. The vision she had in her head right now was a vision of the truth about Tommy. She had heard enough. She pictured him strung out on dope. He was. She pictured him homeless and living on the streets. He was. But she couldn't picture him without Timex. Yet he was. And now she had to inform his family. She felt helpless, but needed to do what had to be done. The pain of the conversation with Tommy ran deep. There were more sniffles as she realized something.

"Jim," she said, looking up at him as he held more tightly to let her know he was there and ready to listen. She sobbed. "I don't even know where he was calling from!"

Carolyn buried her head in Jim's chest as he held her even more tightly. He had been thinking that as well. The operator said the collect call was from Los Angeles and Jim informed Carolyn of that.

"Maybe we'll find out more information when we get the phone bill," Jim said, trying to strike a positive note. But then what and why would it matter? It did to Carolyn.

She already knew what she wanted to do and she also knew how the Franklin family would react when she told them how she felt about Tommy's well-being. They'd have to go looking for him and she knew they would all agree on it. There wouldn't be any second thoughts. It had been so long since any of them had heard from Tommy and now, knowing he was still alive, they would do whatever it took to find him and get him help.

Carolyn stood up and looked down at Jim. Her next move was going to be back to the phone to call Kathy.

"Jim ... ." He didn't say anything and that was the signal for her to continue. "We're going to have to go and find him wherever he is. I know that's what his family will to want to do and I'm going to be part of it."

Jim looked at her and nodded his head.

"And so am I. Count me in."

IT TOOK ALMOST two weeks from the time Carolyn let Tommy's family know she had heard from him until they all got on a plane and headed for Southern California. Mr. and Mrs. Franklin, Kathy, Paul, Carolyn and Jim all knew it was going to be like looking for a needle in a haystack and the odds were not in their favor. But to do nothing was not an option and something not one of them was willing to live with. With six of them looking and putting up posters in that area called Venice, maybe, just maybe, someone would be able to help them. They all agreed to spend a week in California. They would contact the police and do whatever it took to locate Tommy and get him the help he needed. They wanted him to know he was still loved and that he had family and friends who still cared for him. They had been hoping that after the phone call to Carolyn he would call back again, but he didn't. Who knew if he was still in the community by the ocean? It also crossed their minds that maybe they would find Timex as well. They would look in all the dog pounds and shelters and again, who knew, maybe Timex would turn up. It was a shot in the dark and Mrs. Franklin prayed every night that her God would guide them to her son.

Drugs Take Their Toll

Wouldn't it be a miracle if we found both of them? Please help me find my son. Oh, Lord! Please help us find Tommy.

Tommy's mother had never prayed harder to her Lord, asking for him to do something that would lead them to her son, a troubled soul that needed God's love and guidance. A hurting mother prayed and prayed.

It was all in God's hands now.

THE WEEK PASSED by quicker than anyone thought possible. No Tommy. No Timex. The task at hand had been an overwhelming undertaking for all of Tommy's family and friends. They scoured Venice beach and neighborhoods multiple times over. First the beach area, then the back alleys, the residential neighborhoods, time and time again. They must have talked to a couple of hundred people in all if not more. Police officers, street people, the walk-in clinics. Even the county coroner, all to no avail. They went to the homeless shelters and talked with ministers of the local churches. They put up hundreds and hundreds of posters with a picture of a long ago happy and smiling Tommy and his best friend Timex. It was a picture taken the day he left Michigan on his road trip to California almost five years ago now. On the same poster was a lone picture of Tommy with his long hair and beard taken at Kathy's wedding.

The week came to an end with no success and the flight back to Michigan seemed much longer than the one they had taken seven days before that was filled with so much hope. Deep inside, to a person on the way out to California, they felt luck would be on their side. But Tommy and Timex eluded them and that broke everyone's heart. They all took it exceptionally hard and the plane ride home was quiet and left everyone depressed. Especially Mrs. Franklin. She had put her faith in her God, that he was going to show her the way back into her son's arms. But not this time. Not now. Maybe another time. Being a true believer, she knew God wouldn't let her down in the long run and if he did, he would have a good reason.

Her God worked in mysterious ways. If something bad happened to Tommy, worse than what had already happened, God would have a reason for it. And if God decided to bring Tommy back to his family, it would be a miracle and glory and praise be unto him. Mrs. Franklin knew one way or the other, her God would look after Tommy, whether it was in this life or the next one. But, for now, she was left to cry her tears and wonder, "Why," and, "Where did it all go wrong?" She would keep praying and waiting for God to make his decision about what to do with the lost soul. Kathy also prayed and, in his own way, Mr. Franklin said a prayer or two as well. Not into prayer or religion anymore, Carolyn and Jim hung onto hope and for now kept Tommy in their thoughts. They had done what they had to do in making this trip and, as sad as the results were, they were glad they had done it. The next move might have to be Tommy's.

ONE YEAR LATER Kathy and her new-born son made their way to the mailbox on a quiet residential street in Fairlee, another town a hop, skip and a jump from Brenton where Paul taught school. Tommy was an uncle now and didn't know it. Everyone got on with their lives after the trip to California, with Tommy forever remaining in the back of their minds.

It was late summer and Gregory Thomas Franklin was three weeks old and too young to know that his middle name was in honor of his Uncle Tommy. Kathy had wanted to be a mother so badly and her wish finally came true with the birth of her son. Hopefully, this would be the start of the large family she envisioned. Paul was going to be a good father and she would make a good mother just like the one she had when she was growing up. And Tommy, she knew, if he ever turned up again, would be a good uncle.

Carolyn and Jim also had magical lives. They continued to work together and enjoyed all their outdoor adventures of camping, climbing, backpacking and cycling. Carolyn occasionally thought of Tommy, but it was always in the context of was he alive or dead? It had gotten to a point where it wouldn't have surprised her if it were the latter.

The one having the worst time dealing with what had happened to Tommy was Mrs. Franklin. She hadn't gotten over the failed trip to Los Angeles. She wanted to go back and try again, but it was too expensive and she knew, like the last time, it would probably be futile. Every time the phone rang, she hoped it would be him. Every time she went to the mailbox, she hoped there would be a letter with a return address that had the name Tommy Franklin on it. She couldn't let it go. She couldn't accept the possibility of never seeing him again. If it wasn't for her faith, her friends at church and her family, she didn't know what she would have done. Everyone prayed for her and prayed for Tommy. That gave her comfort that she so badly needed.

Mr. Franklin had also tried to move forward, but it was as difficult for him as it was for his wife. The construction business had been busy and he had hired a young man in his early twenties to help him with his heavy workload. Times were good in the building industry, but times were bad emotionally. Being busy was good for Tommy's father. It was a man's way to distract himself from the things he didn't want to think about. But, every time Mr. Franklin looked at his helper, he couldn't help but think of Tommy and of days past when they had worked together. He didn't know if it was his imagination or if it was the way the young man handled himself, but there were so many little things his young employee did that reminded him of his son.

Now, as Kathy reached her mailbox and took out a handful of letters, bills and flyers, all their lives were about to change once again. She cradled Gregory in her arms and, in a way only a mother knew how, sifted through the mail with her free hands. A couple of bills, a flyer from the local hardware store and then a letter that, when she saw the return address, buckled her knees; it was a letter from Tommy. She covered her mouth with the hand that held the letter and looked upwards to the sky. She couldn't believe Tommy had written. As she looked back down at the arm that held Gregory Thomas and the hand that held the letter, she got a better look at the return address. It was from a California State Penitentiary.

Oh, my gosh! What has he done? How did he get my address?

It didn't matter. She couldn't believe she was holding a letter from her brother and couldn't get back into the house fast enough. She put Gregory in his crib in her bedroom and began ripping open the letter. Paul was out running errands and she wished he were here to share the excitement.

We've finally heard from Tommy! I can't believe this! But my Lord! What has he done to end up in prison?

She took the letter out and saw it was a long one, perhaps a dozen pages she guessed. She began reading it with joy in her heart. It started out with apologies. That meant he still had feelings, Kathy thought to herself. That was wonderful! He admitted he had been wrong in disassociating himself from his family and that he had no explanation for that. He tried to bring her up to date, starting from the very beginning of when he first moved to California and up until now as he served time for drug trafficking. He told a sad story about getting into drugs that ended up with him living on the streets and getting caught selling drugs to support his addiction. None of this surprised Kathy. She had suspected something like this for a long time. It ripped her heart out as the image of a homeless drug addict went through her head and that it happened to be her brother. For the first time he confessed that the war had messed him up, but went on to say he didn't want to blame his problems on Vietnam. A lot of guys had gone through the same things he had and didn't end up on drugs or living on the streets. He said he still had his nightmares every now and then and they disturbed him deeply. He acknowledged he'd probably have to live with them for the rest of his time spent here on earth. He didn't go into detail, but said there were things that happened in the war that he was ashamed of and would burden him with guilt until his dying day. It wasn't just one particular incident, there were several. He didn't dwell on the atrocities of war and simply asked for forgiveness. As Kathy read that part of the letter, she sobbed and then looked at her infant son.

Will my son grow up in a world filled with war and hate? Will he become a soldier and have to go fight?

Kathy went back and forth between joy and sorrow as she read Tommy's words, but was elated that he had contacted his family once again. It saddened her to hear her brother's story in his own words. She thought how hard it must have been for him to write this letter after all this time, and she hoped it was therapeutic for him. Maybe this would be the beginning of the Franklin family becoming whole again. Maybe this would be the beginning of Tommy finding his way back to life again.

Kathy continued reading and Tommy informed her that he had gotten a two-year sentence for dealing heroin and had been in prison for five months. He said he didn't know what he wanted to do when he got out and a lot of that would have to do with how much liberty the parole board would give him. He didn't want to stay in California and mentioned moving to Alaska. Somewhere far away. "I'd like to come back to Michigan for a visit to see Mom and Dad, but I won't stay long and I don't want to live there."

Kathy wished he would at least consider moving back to the place where he grew up and in a selfish way thought it would be the best thing for him. He and his dad could work together again and that would please her father so much, and it would most certainly help mend their mother's heart. It was something she and her mother could pray for. Alaska was so far away and it would be just like when he went to California ... why?

Tommy! You belong in Michigan.

He described how he had cut his hair short and was clean-shaven now. "I look civilized again." The apologies continued throughout the letter as he appeared to be reaching out, sorry for all the worry and pain he knew he must have caused his family and friends.

"That would be an understatement," Kathy mumbled under her breath and wiped away a tear.

Then about three quarters of the way through the letter he said how, of all the things he'd had to deal with in his life, losing Timex had been the most painful.

"He was my best friend and he gave me so much hope and I let him down so badly. I am so sad when I think of him. I can never get over what happened in Vietnam and I'll never get over losing Timex. What is wrong with me?" Tommy asked in his letter.

Just come home, Tommy and we'll make it right. Just come home when you get a chance.

Between the war, drugs, living on the streets of L.A. and now prison, Kathy understood that her brother was troubled and needed help, but he had to make the decision to get help on his own and follow through with it. His family could give him love and support, but ultimately, it would have to be Tommy's decision about what he wanted to do with the rest of his life. Knowing her brother, knowing the Tommy of old, if anyone could do it, he could.

Having read the letter quickly the first time, Kathy read it again. She felt like she could have read it a thousand times. When she finished it for the second time, she walked over to the baby crib and picked up a smiling and content Gregory Thomas.

"You're going to meet your Uncle Tommy one day, Gregory. That's my brother. My wonderful, wonderful brother. You're going to like him so much and he's going to love you like a good uncle." She hugged her son as if she were hugging her brother.

Kathy headed for the living room to look out the front window, hoping to see Paul's car in the driveway or possibly pulling up.

"Where's your daddy, Gregory Thomas? I need him to get home soon. I have some exciting news for him."

Kathy went to the kitchen where the phone was and put her son in a cradle by the kitchen table. She sat down in a chair and took a minute to compose herself. She knew she had to call her parents and it couldn't wait another minute. Her mom, she suspected, would fall apart on the phone when she heard the news and that would trigger a chain reaction that would affect both of them and they would cry together. Her dad would have to be the strong one, but could he be? This was the news they'd all been waiting years to hear, never giving up hope that one day Tommy would walk back into their lives. Prayers had been answered. What had happened in the past didn't matter to anyone. Tommy was alive and that was all they could ask for.

Kathy went to the phone and began dialing, then hung up. She took one more deep breath and dialed her parent's phone number again. Mrs. Franklin picked up at the other end.

"Hello?"

"Hi, Mom. It's Kath."

"Oh, hi dear. How are you?"

"Mom ... ," Kathy paused as the words were hard to get out and she couldn't understand why. This was the happiest news she could give her mother right now, but she hesitated.

"Is everything OK, dear?" Mrs. Franklin asked, wondering why Kathy had stopped speaking.

"Mom ... I just went to the mailbox and there was a letter from Tommy."

Then it happened just like Kathy knew it was going to happen. Mrs. Franklin broke down. Kathy cried with her as she held the letter in her hand.

"Oh gosh, Kathy!"

The mother was weak and needed to sit down. Her emotions had never drained her like this before.

"Let me read the letter to you, Mom."

Kathy began reading the letter and by the time she was done, she and her mom had had a good cry and discussed everything that needed to be discussed. It was well over an hour before mother and daughter took a deep breath and stopped talking. The letter saddened Mrs. Franklin but, just like her daughter, it brought her twice as much joy.

"What a life he's lived!" the loving mother stated.

She felt sorrow when she first heard the words, "He's in prison." But again, like Kathy, she was grateful to their God that Tommy was alive.

"Oh, thank God in heaven. Oh, thank you so much, dear Lord."

The not knowing what had happened to Tommy was the worst part of the last few years. Now they knew where he was and what he was doing. Mrs. Franklin couldn't wait to tell her husband the exciting news. Mr. Franklin was working on a job only a couple of miles away.

"I have to go tell your father, dear. Oh, my gosh, I have to go tell your father."

"Don't get a speeding ticket, Mom. Drive carefully," Kathy pleaded to her mother.

"I will dear. Thank you so much for calling. When I get back from telling your father I'll call you back and we'll start making plans to go out to California to visit him. Won't that be exciting?"

"We won't be able to get out there soon enough, Mom. Do you think they're allowed phone calls in prison?" Kathy asked. "Surely they must be!"

"Look into it Kathy. It would be so nice to hear his voice. You should call Carolyn and let her know. I'm sure she would like to know as well."

"I'm going to call her as soon as I hang up, Mom. Now go. Go tell Dad."

"Love you, sweetie."

"Love you too, Mom."

Kathy hung up the phone and checked on Gregory who had fallen asleep,

Drugs Take Their Toll

but was now just waking up. He had been so good while she was talking on the phone. An angel just like her brother. She thought she'd feed him quickly before she called Carolyn. She didn't want to push her luck.

"Where is your daddy? He should have been home long ago. I need to talk to him, Gregory. I need to talk to him badly."

Paul did come home shortly after Kathy finished feeding Gregory. He was elated to hear the good news about Tommy. Kathy tried to get in touch with Carolyn, but had to leave several messages on her answering machine to, "Call me as soon as you get in," without giving a reason why. Kathy didn't want Carolyn to hear this amazing news from a machine. She needed to tell her in person over the phone. When Carolyn finally did call back, around seven in the evening, they cried together.

"If your parents don't mind, Jim and I would love to make the trip with you. But if your family wants to do this on their own, we'll certainly understand," Carolyn said. Carolyn's feelings for this old friend had always been there, lingering below the surface and now resurfacing. Like Tommy's family, she was ecstatic he was alive.

"He sure has been through a lot," Carolyn related to Kathy.

"I know. My mother said the same thing."

So the evening went and no sooner had Kathy hung up the phone from talking with Carolyn when the phone rang again and it was her father wanting Kathy to read the letter to him. He listened intently, not interrupting his daughter once. He also rode the roller coaster of emotions between being joyful one minute, then sad the next.

Maybe there is something to all this praying. God surely must have heard our prayers for this to happen. God must have spoken to Tommy and told him to contact us. God has saved my son and the world is a beautiful place again.

By the end of the night it all seemed like a dream. But it wasn't. Tommy was on his way back to the land of the living once more. By the end of the night three letters had been written to him. One from his mother, one from his sister and one from an old friend that cared for him just like family. Tomorrow would be a day of investigating, to see if he could get phone calls and planning a trip out west to see him. Everyone agreed they would do this as soon as possible.

"Within a couple of weeks," Mrs. Franklin insisted.

She also called her minister, Pastor Michaels, just before she went to bed. It brought her even more comfort to speak with him and share the glorious news.

"What a night it's been, Pastor Michaels."

"Nadine, I'll compose a letter to him right now and give it to you on Sunday at church so you can mail it to him."

"That would be so kind of you, Pastor. God bless you."

"God bless you, Nadine and Praise the Lord. Now tonight you get a good night's sleep and dream about your son. I'll talk to you tomorrow."

That was exactly what Mrs. Franklin did when she fell asleep. She dreamed about a young boy growing up in a small town in northwestern Michigan, being chased across a field by a dog that tackled him and they wrestled and played and then chased each other some more. It was the most wonderful dream she had ever dreamt.

In a prison cell in California, a certain prisoner was also having a dream, only it was in the form of a nightmare. The same nightmare he had been having since he got back stateside after the war and had been having for years. He couldn't seem to lose it. He couldn't shake it. He never would. A guard took his nightstick and clanged it along the metal bars, waking the incarcerated Tommy.

"Franklin, wake up!" the guard yelled as Tommy jumped up. "You're waking everybody up again, Franklin, and you're not going to be very popular tomorrow. What's wrong with you, man?"

Tommy was drenched in sweat and wished someone, anyone, could just understand what was going on in his head when he had these disturbing dreams. The mind was a funny thing and tonight, as in past nights, no one understood why he yelled in his sleep. Not the prison guard, who stood and told him to keep quiet, and not the inmates whom he had woken up. If ever there was a definition for being truly alone, this was it.

How did I get here and how do I escape my inner madness? Where is Timex when I need him?

Permanent Change

"THAT WAS A wonderful sermon, Pastor Michaels," Mrs. Franklin said as she shook the pastor's hand upon exiting the church on a clear and warm late August morning. "Thank you so much for mentioning Tommy in your prayers."

"Yes, thank you so much, Pastor Michaels. That was very nice of you," Mr. Franklin reiterated his wife's words as he stood next to her and also shook the Pastor's hand.

Pastor Michaels, as he did at the end of every Sunday sermon, stood outside the church's front door and shook the hands of all his parishioners. They left for their cars to enjoy their Sunday the way the Lord would want them to, with their families and friends. It was a close-knit group of worshippers and Pastor Michaels, believing he should lead by example, always had. He was compassionate, sincere, genuine, soft-spoken and admired by his congregation. They felt blessed to have him lead the flock. He was a father and loving husband. He was everything a minister should be ... pure and honest.

Now in his early fifties, and still as handsome as he was over twenty years before when he first came to Brenton to preach the word, he always felt that if he could make one person smile in the course of a day or comfort someone in need, then it would be God's will. He was just a messenger and was doing what his God had asked him to do. Pastor Michaels and his family had been the perfect match for this small church in this small community. Everyone liked him and he liked everyone without prejudice. He was joyful and positive. For a pastor, he was progressive in his thinking and his actions, very conscious of social issues and of those less fortunate. He was a man of God and it showed in everything he did.

"Well, you're very welcome," the Pastor replied as he reached to his inside suit pocket and pulled out an envelope. He handed it to Mrs. Franklin. "Here, I wrote a letter to Tommy like I said I would. You'll mail it for me?"

Mrs. Franklin took the letter and was touched, but not surprised, by the pastor's thoughtfulness.

"You know I will. You never cease to amaze me, Pastor Michaels. He'll be thrilled to hear from you."

"It's not much more than just letting Tommy know we're all thinking about him here in Brenton. I'll continue to pray for him, Nadine. God will make it right. Just keep praying."

"Oh, I will, Pastor Michaels. I most certainly will."

"Hopefully, one day we'll get him back here and back into the house of the Lord."

"Amen, Bob," Mr. Franklin said, calling the pastor by his first name.

Tommy's parents told the pastor once again how grateful they were for his support and his acts of kindness and then walked down the front steps of the church.

"I know I've said this before, John," Mrs. Franklin said as they walked down the sidewalk in front of the church, "but we've been so lucky to have Pastor Michaels all these years. He certainly is God sent and I mean that literally."

Mrs. Franklin put an arm through her husband's as they made their way to their car in the parking lot at the side of the church.

"Yes, dear. We are blessed in ways too numerous to count," John said, agreeing with his wife's assessment of their pastor. Mr. Franklin stopped in his tracks for a moment and looked at the blue sky. "Sure is going to be a beauty of a day, Mrs. Franklin. You got any plans?"

Mrs. Franklin stopped and looked up. These caring parents, so much in love with each other, began walking again with more than the blue sky on their mind.

"Well, I don't know. I'd like to spend it with you, Mr. Franklin if that's OK."

"That sounds like a good plan, my love. How about if we spend it together doing nothing?"

"It's a date, Mr. Franklin. That'll be fine by me."

Mr. Franklin opened the passenger door for his wife, walked around the car, climbed into the driver's seat and started up the motor.

"I'm not in a big hurry. Whatta ya say we take the scenic way home, darling?"

Mrs. Franklin slid over to the center of the front seat to sit closer to her husband.

"I think it's a wonderful idea," she said, putting an arm on the back of the seat and around her husband's shoulders. "I can remember Tommy as a youngster always saying, 'Dad, take the scenic way home," when we left church and you always would. We haven't gone that way in a long time. It'll be nice."

"OK, the scenic way it is."

Mr. Franklin put the gear shift into reverse, backed out and pulled forward onto Main Street. That would lead them to County Road Number Twelve, which followed the Bander River for a few short miles before it joined up with the secondary road that ran by the Franklin farm. As a family, years ago, this is what they had referred to as the scenic way home. It took about ten minutes longer to get back to their house, but it was well worth a lazy Sunday drive and that's what this late morning felt like to Tommy's parents. It was a trip down memory lane and they could reminisce about happier days when the kids were younger and Buddy was always there to greet them when they pulled up the long driveway, barking and running alongside the car as it made its way to the front of the house. As Mr. Franklin pulled onto the county highway, it all started to come back to him how those days were so innocent and carefree and expressed that to his wife.

"My, how the world has changed."

Mrs. Franklin was all smiles as she looked down to her right at the river that paralleled the winding country road. She put her head on her husband's shoulder, opened her purse and took out the letter that Pastor Michaels had written to a lost sheep. She was appreciative of the Pastor's thoughtfulness and said so.

Mr. Franklin shared his thoughts with her about missing the good old days. "Maybe I'm just getting old.".

"Well, I couldn't agree with you more." Mrs. Franklin had a hardy laugh as she didn't mean for the words to come out that way. "I don't mean you're getting old. I ... I mean I long for the good old days as well."

Mr. Franklin shared his wife's laughter.

"I heard what you said. You think I'm getting old. That's a low blow, Mrs. Franklin."

He knew what she had been trying to say. It had just come out wrong. His wife tried to cover her tracks, but dug herself a deeper hole and the laughter became contagious between the two and got in the way of their words.

"What I meant to say was that I agree with you about missing the good old days. You're not getting old. I didn't mean it that way," she said for what seemed like the tenth time.

Mrs. Franklin squeezed her husband's arm to assure him she was speaking the truth.

"No, you meant to imply that I am getting old, Mrs. Franklin. My feelings are hurt. I can't believe you would say something like that!"

"Oh stop it!" his wife said as she slid over to the passenger door and put the letter from Pastor Michaels on the dashboard. The bantering went on.

"You're as young as you ever were and getting younger," the wife said to her husband. "I wish you would share your secret with me about the fountain of youth."

Mr. Franklin looked over at the mother of his children and smiled. His lover of many years smiled back and giggled. The conversation stopped briefly as Mr. Franklin focused on the winding road and Mrs. Franklin admired the scenery. Silence seemed appropriate for the moment as thoughts of their son went through their heads.

"This has always been such a lovely drive," Mrs. Franklin interrupted the quietness.

"Yeah. It's a beautiful drive any time of year" her husband responded. "Any time of year, really."

"I can't wait to see Tommy," the mother said as she daydreamed about her son and looked out the passenger window. "I know I've said it a million times, but I can't wait. I just can't wait."

It had been quite an eventful week for the Franklin family. They heard Tommy's voice for the first time in over six years by making a phone call to the prison. He sounded good, better than they expected, if not a little distant in his manner of speaking. That they figured could be due to being embarrassed and ashamed at what he had done with his life. They only got to speak to him for fifteen minutes and it seemed like thirty seconds as both parents and Kathy all wanted to say their hellos. Tommy shed no tears, but the three on the other end of the line couldn't help themselves. The son and brother had been hardened by war, the streets and now prison. He was a changed man. So much different from that young, innocent boy that had grown up in Michigan in the fifties and early sixties.

He had repeated on the phone what he had written in the letter he wrote to Kathy, when he got out of prison he wanted to get away from it all. Go somewhere far away. He had hit rock bottom and now it was time to climb back up. He knew that many things would work against him when he was free again—his prison record, his past drug addiction—but Tommy had a lot of time to think in his prison cell and he had learned that prison and the streets weren't for him and also, no longer, were the drugs.

When I get out I'm going to make something out of myself. I've done enough damage and hurt too many people. All I need is a chance. That's all I want. One more chance to make my life right.

In that phone conversation, Tommy's parents had assured him that he could work with his dad once again and live at home if he desired.

"Just please stay in Michigan. Everyone is here including your new nephew. It's where you belong," his mother pleaded.

Rejecting the invitations, he repeated that he thought he would head for Alaska and attempt to start up a log home building business. He had taken an interest in log homes and had been reading magazine articles and books from the prison library. It was something that years ago, when he worked with his father, he thought would be a great idea and tried to talk his dad into building one. Mr. Franklin always replied that it sounded like a good idea and they should do it one day. It never happened. But Tommy did say that he would come back to Michigan for a visit and was looking forward to it. It was just that he wouldn't stay long. His family and friends would have to understand that and, of course, it all depended on whether or not his parole conditions let him.

Mrs. Franklin took the letter written by her pastor from the dashboard and held it in her hand. She wondered what was in the letter, but was certain that, with his talent for words, Pastor Michaels had said all the right things. Mrs. Franklin looked at her husband as he looked over at her. She turned her head to take in more of the scenery when she suddenly let out a scream as a deer bolted up the embankment of the river and into the path of the Franklin car. There was no time for her husband to react or even step on the brakes as he hit the large buck. It rolled over the hood and smashed against the windshield. By the time Mr. Franklin managed to step on the brakes, the car had swerved to the right and headed down the river bank, rolling over and landing upside down in the water. A son's mom lay unconscious and began to float inside the car as water poured in. A dazed and disoriented husband wanted to help, but he was bleeding profusely and struggled to breath, choking from both water and blood. In less than two minutes it was over. Their God had called them home. A white envelope containing a letter from a special person to a special person floated down the Bander River hoping to make its way to a prison cell somewhere in California.

TOMMY, IN HIS prison cell, wrote his first letter to his parents in over six years on the Sunday that his parents went to meet their maker. They had been on his mind constantly since their phone conversation and he had promised them that he would write.

He began the letter: "It was good talking to you on the phone. Be patient. I'm OK. I'll survive and get on with my life when I'm out of here. It's been a rough few years. I can't wait to see you again and I'm so sorry for the pain I have caused. I'm sorry to you, to Kathy, to Carolyn and others. Somehow I will make amends. Tell Kathy I can't believe I'm an uncle and that I will be a good one to her son ... . "

There would be a few things Tommy wouldn't believe in the near future. A lot of things had changed in the years he had been out of touch. There would be a lot of catching up to do when he saw his family.

He continued to write the letter to his parents and when he was done, he decided to write one to Carolyn. He was hardened, but the letters were therapeutic and helped him come out of his shell. It was a start. He was hopeful things would be normal again. It was a start to a new way of thinking and maturity. Maybe, in fact, his life really was starting over. It was always possible.

Yes, there would actually be a lot of things Tommy wouldn't believe in the near future and one of the things would be what had just happened on a road he used to travel on as a child whenever the Franklin family took the scenic way home from church.

CAROLYN SPED IN her car to Kathy's house, an hour's drive away. When Carolyn had received the phone call from her good friend, she had sounded distraught and broken. Carolyn's mind raced as she concentrated on the road. She wanted to get there before dark and daylight was fading fast. So many things were going through her head right now, one of which was how to tell Tommy what had happened? And why? Why did it happen?

How much pain can one family endure? How much? If there were a loving God, why would he have done this? Mr. and Mrs. Franklin were true believers who wanted to see their son so badly one more time.

Why God? Do you exist? Do you? Then tell me why? Was it better this way? I have never understood the reasons why some God would do things like this and I never will. Why would a loving and caring God take these beautiful people at this time when they were so happy about being back in touch with their son? Is it any wonder I find it impossible to believe in such nonsense? Why should I? Mr. and Mrs. Franklin were the nicest people I have ever met outside my own parents. They loved life and their family so much. All they wanted to do was visit their son they hadn't seen in such a long time. God Almighty, can you tell me ... why? You're supposed to be a loving God, but I can't make myself believe that no matter what.

Time couldn't go by fast enough as Carolyn continued to drive. She knew the pain Kathy must be feeling. Carolyn was driving too fast. Her rational thought was lost in the circumstances. She just wanted to be there with her friend. Now. They had shared a good cry on the phone and Carolyn knew she was going to have to be strong for Kathy. This was devastating news for someone who was so close to her parents and loved them with all of her heart. What news could be worse for any person? Mr. and Mrs. Franklin had been on cloud nine with the arrival of their first grandchild and then having their prayers answered that put them back in touch with Tommy. Carolyn couldn't stop asking herself "why" over and over. Through her tears the road was blurry.

The last time Carolyn had seen Kathy she had been so up and happy. "My life seems so perfect right now," Kathy had told her. Now this. How would Kathy tell her brother? How was he going to take the news? Carolyn could very well imagine he would take it just as hard as his sister and only hoped it wouldn't send him into a tailspin and back into doing drugs. One minute Carolyn was angry at life for being so unfair and the next minute she cried uncontrollably as she made her way to Fairlee.

Why is this trip taking so long? Why did Jim have to be out of town at a conference? Why did I have to be alone when I got the call from Kathy?

She had tried to get in touch with Jim at his hotel with no luck and left a message with the desk clerk for him to call her at Kathy's. Carolyn tried to think of the next few days and what had to be done to provide Kathy with all the help she could. She wouldn't leave her friend's side for a second. Her mind continued to go at a million miles an hour before she finally arrived at the home of Kathy, Paul and Gregory. She pulled up front as daylight gave way to the night darkness. All the lights in the house were on and numerous vehicles were parked in the driveway and on the street. One thing Kathy would have was support from the people in her church that she joined soon after arriving in Fairlee. Carolyn assumed the vehicles must mostly belong to them. She looked at the front door and knew she must go inside and help comfort an aching heart. Putting her hands back up on the steering wheel, she buried her head in her arms and cried like she had never cried before. When she was composed, Carolyn looked once more at the door that would lead her into Kathy's arms. She opened the driver's door, got out and stood beside her car knowing the time had come.

ON THE FIFTH day after the accident and the first day after the funeral, Kathy and Carolyn disembarked from a commercial airliner in California and made their way to a rental car agency where they would rent a car and drive to the prison that housed a brother who didn't yet know that his parents had passed on. Kathy decided he must be told in person and not on the phone and she asked Carolyn to come along to be her strength. She had also brought Gregory Thomas along to introduce him to his uncle. Things had been happening fast since her parents' death and this was the moment she had come to dread. Telling Tommy would be difficult if not impossible. There were not many words spoken between Kathy and Carolyn on the two-hour trip from the airport to the prison. Neither one was looking forward to when they would have to face Tommy with the news that would break his heart. It weighed heavy on Kathy's mind about how she was going to do this.

So the decision was made that she and Carolyn would go together along with Gregory Thomas and do what had to be done. Carolyn offered and it was agreed that she would break the news to her old friend.

"I just don't think I can do it, Carolyn. I really don't think I can," Kathy confessed.

That was understandable and if the two of them did this together, it would be easier on both. Especially Kathy. So Carolyn drove the rental car as Kathy nursed Gregory Thomas and the landscape rolled by. It wouldn't be long now. An old friend, a sister, a brother and uncle would all cry together. Just like the night when Carolyn got the news about Kathy and Tommy's parents and she drove to Kathy's house to comfort her friend, she now drove through the California countryside still asking, "Why?"

Tommy sat on the bed in his prison cell reading a magazine about how to build log homes. A prison guard walked up.

"OK, Franklin. You're up. Your visitors are here."

Tommy lay the magazine down on the bed, got up and walked out of his living space behind bars. He didn't act excited because the fact was he wasn't too sure how to act. He had taken the incentive to get back in touch with his family, but now, whether it was nerves or just the hardened person he had become, he didn't show much emotion. He was thinking how difficult and awkward it was going to be seeing his parents and his sister after all these years. The phone conversation he had with his parents less than two weeks before was uplifting for him, but the conversation didn't last long. Both his parents said how much they loved him and missed him. It made him feel good, but he had doubts that he was worthy of their love after everything he had done. He remembered how candid the conversation had been.

"Why would you still love me, Mom? I've hurt you so much."

"Tommy, you did hurt us, but we still love you and we worry about you so much. You're still our son. You'll always be our son and we'll always care for you and love you. Your parents will never change in that way."

"Dad, look, I'm not the same person. I've been through a lot. I don't know why I did the things I did, but I'm all messed up. The war, the drugs, losing Timex. Dad ... I've changed. I'm not the same."

"It's OK, son. It doesn't matter. I know you still have feelings and that you still have a heart. You reached out to us and we're reaching back and if you look way down deep inside you, you'll see that in fact you are still the same. You're still Tommy Franklin. Son. Brother. Uncle. Friend. Caring. Kind. You will always be my son and my good friend. Years have gone by, but down deep inside you'll always be a wonderful human being. Deep down inside you haven't changed."

The words his mother and father spoke in that last phone call moved him. He thought about those words. He did still have feelings. He knew that now. He still cared about his family and friends. He remembered among other things what his dad said in a quick five minutes of conversation that, "It's not too late to do something with your life." That stuck with him because Tommy was now feeling that same sentiment. He had been down the road to darkness and back. That was over. Fighting the war was not a way of life he enjoyed, he found out, even though he felt at the time he was doing the right thing and it was for a just cause. It was something as a young adult he had thought he wanted to do, but he was young, way too young and naïve.

But it had happened and unfortunately the war still lived inside him in the form of nightmares and in the conscious memories he wished he could dispel. Then there were the drugs and the living on the streets. He'd never understand that and never would be able to explain how that era in his life had evolved. It just happened because that's what was going on at the time. A simplistic excuse, but true nevertheless. He thought he was enjoying it, but now, looking back, he had to ask himself, "Why did I do that?" He didn't know it then, but he knew it now. He hadn't been truly happy and, never able to forget the incidents in the war, he needed to escape reality.

A drug addict? Living on the streets? Who was that person?

As the guard escorted him to the prison visiting area, he thought how nice it would be to see his parents and what he'd say to them. There would be much to discuss and seeing Kathy and Carolyn again would be the icing on the cake. He hoped he didn't come across the wrong way. He knew he had changed and was still recovering from his mistakes and addictions. He couldn't even remember the old Tommy Franklin from his pre-army days when he was a lover of life, carefree and full of energy. The new version of Tommy Franklin was more guarded, bordering on paranoia. He struggled to get back his self-esteem. But he knew he could do it. It would take time and today would be the first official step back in that direction. Meeting with his family would be comforting and reassuring and he knew they would all say the right things and encourage him to "hang in there." They'd also say, "We're here for you," and mean it. This was what he needed in his life right now to get him going again.

The time had come as the prison guard walked him through the door into the visiting area and Tommy began to get anxious. Outwardly, it didn't show and he couldn't force it. Inwardly he was feeling uplifted by the anticipation of seeing everyone again. He sat down in his designated chair, rested his arms on the counter and looked through the glass that would divide him from his visitors. He saw a slight reflection of himself before looking around the room and noticed he was the only one there.

I wonder why that is?

The guard stood behind him quietly. The prisoner looked through the glass partition toward a door that had a one-way mirror in the upper half of it and wondered when his parents would come walking through. It wouldn't be long now. He knew they would never be late. Tommy leaned forward and rested his chin on his two thumbs staring at the reflection that stared back at him. He wanted to smile, but couldn't. Neither could he relax. His gut feeling told him that it was just a matter of seconds before someone he recognized came walking in. Who would be first one he wondered, his mom or dad?

Kathy held Gregory Thomas as she and Carolyn looked through the one-way mirror and saw Tommy sitting and waiting. As soon as they saw him walk into the visiting room they both started tearing up and sobbing.

"There's your brother, Kathy. There's your brother," Carolyn said.

Kathy felt this was a miracle moment. She was overcome at seeing her brother. She had lost her strength both emotionally and physically and couldn't possibly do what she knew had to be done. She was so grateful that Carolyn was at her side. Kathy's body trembled. Carolyn wasn't in much better shape, but understood how her friend was feeling and would do anything for her … including what she was about to do. Carolyn also knew this would be the hardest thing she had ever had to do.

She gave Kathy and Gregory a hug and found it difficult to let go. Tommy, she feared, would suspect something was wrong as soon as he saw the state she was in. It would be obvious she had been crying. As she tried to compose herself, she expected to fall apart once again as soon as she walked through the door. She let go of her hug from Kathy.

"Kathy, I'm going in now. He's waiting for us."

Kathy nodded her head, unable to speak and clasped onto Gregory. Carolyn put her hand on the swinging door and pushed. She stepped into the visiting

Permanent Change

room, stopped and looked at Tommy as he turned his head in her direction. She covered her mouth with her hands, walked the few paces to a chair and sat opposite her friend. Tommy noticed the redness in her eyes.

Are they tears of happiness or is there something else going on? How come Carolyn is the first one in and not one of my parents? There must be a good reason for this and that's OK. It's good to see Carolyn and I'm so glad she has come. Where are the others?

Carolyn shook her head, not knowing why she was doing this. She knew, but didn't know. It was for her good friend, Kathy. Tommy leaned forward and picked up the phone connection so that he and Carolyn could converse. His visitor slowly picked up her phone receiver.

"Hello, Carolyn," Tommy said, trying to simulate a smile.

Carolyn stared back. She thought to herself that this might be impossible.

"Carolyn, is everything OK?" Tommy wondered why she didn't respond.

"Hi, Tommy."

She finally managed to get out two words knowing how much more difficult the next ones would be. She sniffled and sobbed quietly and struggled to maintain her emotions. It was useless and she knew she had to move forward. Tommy didn't think for a second that something could be so dramatically wrong. It was an emotional moment for both of them after all these years.

"It's nice to see you, Carolyn."

"It's so nice to see you, Tommy," Carolyn said, continuing to stare back at him as everything became surreal.

Tommy still didn't have a hint as to what was about to happen next.

"It's been a while," he said, feeling her awkwardness. "How have you been?"

"I'm OK, Tommy," she said as things seemed to be moving in slow motion on one hand, but didn't seem to moving fast enough on the other.

She had no idea how she could have responded with, "I'm OK," when it was the furthest thing from the truth. It just came out. She hadn't rehearsed for this and had no idea how this moment was going to play out. All she knew was that she wished it were over. Kathy watched and saw how difficult it was going by watching Tommy and Carolyn's body language. She asked her God for strength. Tommy studied Carolyn as they stared at each other and for the first time he wondered if Carolyn's tears were supposed to be telling him something more than just, "Nice to see you."

She wants to tell me something, but what? My parents couldn't make it? Kathy couldn't make it? What is it she has to tell me?

He decided to cut to the chase.

"How are my parents doing, Carolyn. Did they make it out here?"

Carolyn didn't respond and put her hand on the glass wishing she could touch Tommy. That signaled to Tommy that something was not right.

"Carolyn ... what's wrong?"

His longtime friend began to speak and told him the news she had come to deliver. He didn't believe what he was hearing. He forgave Kathy for not telling him immediately, after hearing about how his sister felt this was something that had to be done in person. It would have been different if he weren't in prison. Tommy put his hand up to the glass wishing he could feel Carolyn's skin. He could not cry because none of it was happening. All he wanted to do was look his parents in the eye and tell them how sorry he was for his actions of the past. All he wanted to do was share a smile and laugh with them. All he wanted to do was ask for their forgiveness. Now he knew that would never happen. He bowed his head trying to hide a tear that wouldn't come. He still had feelings. He knew that. But it had been so long since he felt them.

"Tommy, I'm so sorry," Carolyn said repeatedly through her tears. "Kathy is waiting to come in, Tommy. I'm going to go ask her come in now. I'm so sorry, Tommy."

Carolyn got up from her chair and looked down at the young man not wanting to make eye contact. She walked through the door from which she had entered and let Kathy and Gregory enter. Kathy sat down in the chair Carolyn had occupied and gazed at her broken brother. He finally looked up and put his hand back on the glass. Kathy managed to do the same while holding Gregory with the other. Through the sobbing and tears, Kathy managed to pick up the phone and introduced Gregory Thomas to his uncle. She lay the receiver down and took one of her son's hands and put it up to the glass where Tommy pretended he was touching it and tried to connect with his nephew. He picked his phone receiver up as did Kathy.

"I am going to be a good uncle, Kathy. One of the best uncle's that ever lived."

Home Again

"HE'S COMING, GREGORY Thomas. You're Uncle Tommy will be here any moment now. Just be patient."

Kathy held her son's hand and walked with him outside the Brenton bus station. She flashed back to a time long ago when she was waiting with her parents and Carolyn here at the depot for Tommy to get home from boot camp. It brought back fond memories, but also saddened her in a way. Gregory was not yet two and his mother wasn't sure just how much he understood, but she spoke to him as if he could grasp every word that came out of her mouth. The young toddler led his mom pretty much wherever he wanted to go. She had his hand, but he was in command.

"Uncle Tommy is going to be so excited to see you, Gregory. I bet he brought you a present."

The mother and son walked back and forth in front of the bus depot. It was late October and the fall air warned of a change in the weather. October was the border-line month that could extend an Indian summer or give you the first hint of winter. It could tilt either way in northwestern Michigan this time of year. Today it was cool and clear and thankfully not raining. The previous few days had been quite pleasant for this time of year. Today was an autumn day that would be considered a keeper in this part of the world even if it was on the cool side. Gregory Thomas had been walking now for a few months and, like most toddlers his age who have learned to walk, that's all he wanted to do. Walk and walk some more. Kathy obliged and continued the back and forth pattern in front of Paul, Carolyn and Jim, who sat on a bench. All of them waited patiently for the bus that would bring Tommy home for the first time in years. He had been released a week earlier, but wanted to spend time alone in a hotel before he came back to the state of his birth. He had been given his freedom prematurely because of his good behavior and his parole conditions allowed him to return to Michigan and report to a parole officer there. It was what he had been hoping for. He was done with California and when his parole terms were met, he would be done with Michigan. He loved them both, but he wanted to put those two states behind him and go somewhere he felt he could fit in. This ex-con, former drug addict, dealer and war veteran needed a place where he could hide and get away from it all. Alaska had that appeal and was an attraction for a lot of people with his background. He had heard that up in the far north country they accepted everyone for who they were no matter what their backgrounds were. Everyone had a history and a story up there. For now though, he would hang his hat in Michigan, which was fine with him.

His parole conditions dictated that he had to remain at least six months in Michigan and if everything went well, by next spring he could make his move. Besides, there was business to be taken care of here in his home state. Kathy still hadn't sold their parents' home and Tommy made it very clear he didn't want anything to do with it. He would stay at his parents' house over the winter, maintaining it and repairing what needed to be repaired, if anything. Considering how their father took such good care of the place, it was likely to be in fine shape. Tommy and Kathy had agreed to put the house on the market come spring. Tommy didn't want to live there permanently and his sister and her husband were too busy with their own lives to keep it up.

Tommy had told his sister, "It would be a shame to let it get run down. Mom and Dad wouldn't want that. They would want us to sell it to someone who could look after it and keep it as a family home." Kathy was in favor of that. They would do everything to sell it when winter had passed.

Kathy looked at her watch. Ten minutes before four. It had been a long afternoon with all the anticipation about Tommy's return to Brenton. She looked south down Main Street knowing that was the direction the bus would be coming from. Carolyn, Paul and Jim sat on a bench just under a window that said "Bus Depot" and chatted about the football season and whatever else came to mind. They had all come early to meet the bus. They didn't want to take any chances on not being here when it arrived. It was important for them to be here when Tommy stepped off. Kathy was making one more turn around with Gregory Thomas when she heard Carolyn shout, "Here it comes."

In one swift motion Kathy swept Gregory into her arms and looked down Main Street. The bus was coming. She was ecstatic.

"Here comes your Uncle Tommy, Gregory. I told you he was coming."

The group that was here to welcome Tommy back home ran through the front door of the bus station and out the back door where the bus would park and let its passengers disembark. It was the same routine from years before when he had come home, but this time it wouldn't be a proud American soldier in uniform. It would be a broken man who had just gotten out of prison and this time there would be no parents here to greet him.

The Greyhound bus slowly turned off onto the side street and into the wide alley that would take it behind the bus depot. It pulled up and angled its way into a parking spot, just as it always did. The motor was turned off and the

Home Again

passenger door was opened. The four adults and one toddler stood only ten feet away, waiting. Kathy was beside herself with anticipation. The first person off the bus was a young male teenager. Then another passenger stepped off, then an elderly lady with her husband right behind. Another middle-aged lady came down the steps and then right behind her was the guest of honor everyone had been waiting for, Uncle Tommy. Kathy quickly handed little Gregory to Paul and ran into her brother's arms just as he put his suitcase down. He squeezed her tight and looked over his sister's shoulder to the other three adults who were standing and smiling. As he hugged his sister he made a gesture to the others with his hand as if saying, "Hello." After their embrace Kathy took a step back.

"Oh gosh, Tommy. I can't believe you're here," Big sister said to little brother.

Tommy did something he hadn't done in a long time; he smiled.

"Well, believe it, Sis. I'm here. I'm back," Tommy said, sounding tired and downtrodden.

Grabbing his suitcase, he walked over to Paul, Jim and Carolyn. He shook Paul's hand and took notice of his nephew.

"How ya doing, Paul? Hey, Gregory. How's my little nephew doing?" He looked back at Kathy. "Gees, I can't believe how much this little guy has grown. What are you feeding him?"

Kathy laughed as she took Gregory Thomas from Paul. "Wheaties and spinach. Breakfast, lunch and dinner."

Tommy smiled again, turned to Jim and shook his hand. "Nice to see you, Jim. Nice to see all of you. Thanks so much for being here. Hello, Carolyn."

It was especially heart-wrenching for him to see his old friend again. The last time wasn't under the best of circumstances. He hadn't been expecting Carolyn to be here and would have understood if she hadn't come. Their relationship, he knew, had deteriorated a few years back, but was now slowly starting to mend. It meant a lot to him for her to show up and it said so much about the woman he had once loved. She was that amazing person who had come to see him in prison and told him the heartbreaking news about his parents and he knew she had done that for Kathy. Carolyn was a beautiful person in every sense of the word. After she had delivered the devastating news about his mom and dad, they had written back and forth on a regular basis. It was starting to feel like old times again. He was humbled by the sight of her and Jim here to welcome him back. Now, he and Carolyn had a cordial hug.

"You're looking good, Tommy. Welcome back to Brenton," Carolyn said, biting her lips to help keep her emotions intact.

"It's good to be here."

Paul took Tommy's suitcase and pointed in the direction of the cars they had all come in.

"Cars are over here, Tommy. Welcome home."

"Yeah, welcome home, Tommy," Jim said, coming up to his side and putting an arm over the parolee's shoulder. "We've all been waiting patiently for this moment. It's good to see you," Jim said and couldn't have been more sincere.

"Thanks Jim. Thanks, Paul. It's good to be back."

They had all walked a few paces toward their cars when Tommy suddenly realized something.

"Oh, hey Paul. Let me have my suitcase."

Paul handed Tommy his one piece of luggage. Tommy laid it on the ground and opened it. He ruffled through his belongings and pulled out a teddy bear. Standing up, he handed it to his nephew.

"Here, Gregory Thomas. I brought you a little present."

Gregory took the little stuffed bear and examined it.

"See, Gregory Thomas. I told you he would bring you something," Kathy said, never having a doubt in her mind. "I just knew he would. Whatta ya say?"

Gregory muttered a "thank you" and Tommy accepted that.

"You're very welcome, Gregory Thomas. You're very welcome," Uncle Tommy said, ruffling up Gregory Thomas' hair.

"Here, go to your Uncle Tommy." Kathy handed her son over to her brother and neither the uncle nor his nephew seemed to mind.

"How ya doing little buddy?"

Gregory Thomas ignored his uncle, enthralled with his new possession. After Kathy reorganized Tommy's suitcase and closed it back up, the group continued their walk to their vehicles. Once there, good-byes were said.

"We'll get together this weekend OK, Tommy?" Carolyn suggested, hoping the answer would be yes.

Tommy stood by Kathy and Paul's car admiring the nephew in his arms.

"Yeah, for sure. I would like that very much. And thank you so much for being here, guys. This means so much to me."

"We'll give you a call tomorrow, Tommy, and we'll make plans for the weekend if you're up to it," Jim said as he and Carolyn were about to get into their car.

"Let's do that. I'll talk to you tomorrow. Good to see you two." Tommy held Gregory and watched Carolyn and Jim drive away.

Tommy looked at his sister knowing where their next stop was going to be. "I'm ready," he said nodding his head. "I'm ready."

KATHY, PAUL, GREGORY Thomas and Tommy pulled up the long driveway of the childhood home of the Franklin children like they'd done a thousand times before. Paul drove as Tommy sat in the back seat alone in silence as memories from the past began to take over his train of thought. It was melancholy, it was sad. No one said anything and everyone seemed comfortable with that. There were no words to describe what was going on inside their minds. The pain of not having their parents here to greet them was unbearable for the brother and sister. All the memories of growing up here flashed through Tommy's head in a matter of a few seconds. Paul pulled up and parked in front of the Franklin home. As if in a trance, Tommy sat and looked at his parents' house. The maple tree on the north side still hung on to its leaves and was in brilliant color. The house itself was no worse for wear as Kathy and Paul, some neighbors and people from their parents' church had all tried to keep an eye on things. At first glance the barn looked good and the only thing that might need tending to was the grass that looked like it needed cutting even though it was late October. Tommy would take care of that and it would probably be the last mowing until next spring.

"Here we are, Gregory Thomas. Grandma and Grandpa's. This is where your Uncle Tommy is going to stay," Kathy said, looking back at Tommy and forcing a smile as she held onto her son and got out of the car.

"The place is still in good shape, don't ya think Tommy?" Paul asked as he exited the car.

Tommy didn't say anything initially as he got out of the back door on the passenger side and stood beside Kathy looking at their parents' house. Paul walked around the front of the car and took his son from his wife.

"Thanks, honey," Kathy acknowledged her husband's gesture as Paul put Gregory Thomas on the ground and began walking to the front porch.

Tommy realized he'd been quiet and hoped no one read anything into it.

"Yeah, Paul. Place is lookin' good, thanks to you guys putting your time in. It'll be great spending the winter here," he said with mixed emotions.

Tommy and Kathy made their way to the veranda and sat on the porch swing. It was their mom and dad's favorite place to sit just about every night except for when it was too cold. You could still feel their presence all around and people who had visited and helped out, looking after the place, said that if you looked hard enough, you could still see them sitting on the swing next to each other with Mr. Franklin's arm around his wife. There was more silence as Tommy and Kathy reminisced inwardly about days long past.

"Tomorrow we'll go up to see Mom and Dad's grave at the cemetery and take some flowers," Kathy said, breaking the silence.

Tommy looked out toward the barn and nodded slowly.

"That would be nice."

Suddenly it all sank in and came crashing down on Tommy's heart. Sitting on the porch with his sister in the swing had brought it to light. He was home. He was back on the farm, the place of his youth. He knew it all so well, but the difference was that there were no parents now. No parents and no dog to play with. He turned his head and looked out to where Buddy was buried. It was another grave he'd visit tomorrow. The last time he had visited Buddy's grave was a few years back when he was here for Kathy's wedding. His thoughts then turned to Timex and he wondered what could have happened to him. Like the pain of war that would never go away, neither would the pain of losing his parents and Timex and Buddy. The pain would always be with him. He put his arm around his sister.

"I'm glad you and Paul are going to stay with me for a few days, Kathy," Tommy spoke as his feelings came to the surface. "I really don't want to be alone right now. I've been alone enough the last little bit. I'm so sorry for all the pain I've caused. I know I keep saying that, but I'm so, so sorry. Please forgive me."

Kathy watched as Paul and Gregory moved to the front lawn and chased each other around. It warmed her heart to know she had such a wonderful husband who also happened to be a wonderful father. She turned her head and looked her brother in the eye and said a silent prayer to herself.

My Lord. He's been through so much. Could hell possibly be worse than what my brother has experienced? Oh, God please help him to see the light. Please see to it that he rediscovers who he is and that he is a kind and caring person and loved by so many people, especially you, dear Lord.

"Tommy ... ," Kathy searched for the right words as her eyes began to moisten. She thought for a second, then she began her speech. "Look, Tommy. What's done is done. The past is the past and I feel I can speak for Mom and Dad as well. We never stopped loving or caring for you. The past is behind you. You're going to be OK. You're going to be fine. Listen to me. This is your sister talking. You're going to move forward. I know you're thinking of only staying here over the winter, but everyone would love to have you stay permanently. You have a job. You would have a place to stay. You have family and friends and you have a nephew that I would love for you to watch

Home Again

grow up. Everything is here for you, Tommy. But whatever you decide about your future we will all respect that. For now, we're just so happy you're here. We're just happy you're here, Tommy"

The brother contemplated what his sister had said. He knew she had made some good points in her little address to him. Everything was here for him and it always would be. This would be a good place to start over and get his life back in order. Part of the conditions of his parole, if he came back to Michigan, was that he had to have a job lined up and that came as a blessing when the young man who had been his dad's helper and continued in the business on his own, had hired Tommy even without ever meeting him. His name was Peter Johnson and he had met Tommy's dad at church. They got along tremendously and Peter was so impressed with Tommy's credentials, he didn't give it a second thought when Kathy approached him about the idea of giving Tommy a job so he could meet his parole terms and move back to the place where he grew up.

"I've heard about all Tommy's talents from your father and I have enough work lined up that should get us through the winter," he had told Kathy. "I would love to have some help."

Tommy and Peter had only talked on the phone, but Tommy had liked what he heard and so did Peter. The local contractors that Mr. Franklin had worked with were mostly church connections and there were also the repeat customers from many years of being in the community. After conferring with Pastor Michaels, Peter was assured that his taking over Mr. Franklin's business, for a while anyway, was what Mr. Franklin would have wanted.

At the time of his death, nearly two years before, Tommy's dad had had several projects unfinished and more on the horizon. It was a bit awkward at first, but Peter managed to keep everyone happy by carrying on and looking after Mr. Franklin's business work load, even if he was only babysitting it until Tommy took over ... if he wanted to. It was going to work out one way or the other. Both parties felt, just from their phone conversations, that they would be a good team. Yes, Kathy was right in so many ways and maybe Tommy would change his mind about his dream of moving to Alaska. Maybe he would settle back in Michigan and realize this was where he belonged.

"Don't get me wrong, Kathy," Tommy began, hoping to ease Kathy's concerns. "It's good to be here. It's great actually. The parole board dictates what I do for now and where I can live. They may not let me go to Alaska. It's complicated and I have to abide by the rules. But let's take this one day at a time. A lot of ex-cons don't have the support I have and I'm aware of that. This is good. It's all good. We'll see what happens next spring." He hoped this reply would help ease his sister's mind. Tommy stood up and leaned up against one of the posts supporting the veranda roof. He looked down at his sister gently swinging back and forth and watching Paul and Gregory laughing and playing and running toward the barn.

"Seriously, Kathy. I can't put into words how nice it is to be here. I feel good. I feel healthy again. I took care of myself in prison. It was a real eye opener. I've cleaned myself up."

Tommy knew he didn't have to convince his sister of any of this, but he had to say it just the same. She believed in him and he knew that, and for the first time in years he was starting to believe in himself again. It had been a slow process, but his self-esteem was making a comeback. The price had been paid and Kathy was right; what was done was done - the past was the past.

It's all up to me now. Start living again or die. Those are my two choices.

"Is it too early to start planning on having Thanksgiving here?" Tommy asked.

Kathy had been trying to absorb his words, just like he did hers. It had been so long since they'd had a serious discussion like this. It pleased her that her brother wanted to extend such an invitation. It turned the conversation back to being light hearted; she felt that was best.

My brother's home. That's all that matters right now.

"That would be great, wouldn't it?" Kathy suggested.

"I'll even help with the cooking. How's that sound?"

Tommy's spirits were lifted by the thought of Thanksgiving dinner at his late parents' home. It would thrill them if they knew that was the plan. Maybe they did know the plan. Who knew? Anything was possible. Maybe it was actually their plan. Maybe they somehow channeled it through their son. It could have been exactly that.

Kathy giggled as she tried to picture Tommy cooking.

"That sounds too good to be true and I'll believe it when I see it."

As she headed for the front door, Kathy continued to chuckle as she kidded her brother some more about him trying to cook.

Kathy shouted to her husband, "Paul, we're going inside."

Paul waved as he and his son continued to have fun in the front yard.

Kathy looked at Tommy. "Wanna see the inside?"

Tommy grabbed his suitcase on the steps and walked to the front door that he and his sister had walked through at least a million times before.

"Sure. Let's have a look at the inside. It's been awhile."

If Tommy had any second thoughts about returning to Michigan to serve out his parole, they were quickly erased by this first day back. The day he was released from prison, he had some doubts about coming to the place where he grew up. He was nervous and didn't know what to expect. Things had been moving quickly since he got his freedom. Tommy felt more than guilty about everything he had done in the past and asked himself over and over if coming back home would be the right thing to do. It took a lot of soul searching before he decided to take a chance. He went with his instincts that perhaps being around the people who believed in him and cared for him would help him get through this transitional period. He did what his heart told him to do.

After the greeting he got at the bus station, he knew almost immediately that he had made the right decision. It would work because of his sister and people like Carolyn who cared so much for him. It would work because of the people in the community who knew him and also cared for him. It would work because he was the son of Mr. and Mrs. John Franklin and that was all that anyone who lived in and around this community needed to know. He was the Franklin boy and he was "one of us." He was family. It would work because the members of the church his parents attended were kind and loving and Pastor Michaels cared as much as anyone. So many people were interested in helping out and giving him support. Yes, he was family whether he wanted to be or not. This was Brenton and that's the way things worked around here.

TOMMY FRANKLIN SPENT the winter in Brenton and quite enjoyed it. Many people genuinely wanted to help him recover from past wounds and get him settled back down in this place he had always known as home. The holidays were heartwarming and lifted his spirits even higher. Thanksgiving was a huge success and he did, in fact, help cook the holiday meal like he said he would. Christmas was celebrated at Kathy's and he brought Christmas presents for the first time in years. He started to feel whole again. Human. It was a time for recovery and leaving the past behind. He knew there were certain things in his life that he never wanted to revisit ever again: war, drug addiction, living on the streets and prison. This was also a time for giving back whatever and whenever he could. He was lifted up even more when he gave back to the people who had been so kind and helpful in this delicate period of his life. It was all about, as Kathy said, "moving forward."

It was now early April and even with patches of snow still on the ground after a harsh winter, it felt like spring was in the air. For Tommy, time flew by and he wasn't sure he liked that. He had convinced himself in early winter that his plans to move to Alaska were still intact and come spring, certainly no later than early summer, he would make it happen. He had a job offer to work with a company building log homes that he found out about while in prison and he was going to have to make a decision soon about whether to accept it. His parole board had approved the idea of him moving up to the 50th state and he was excited about the opportunity. He knew in his heart he was going to make it happen, but when?

Many people were going to be hurt and disappointed, but remembering Kathy's words from a few months back, he knew they would accept his decision. He thought another move would be healthy and it would in fact be "moving forward" and getting on with his life." His own life. Tommy thought long and hard about it. Moving so far away from what was left of his family and friends would be disappointing for them, but he figured he would never know if he could move forward if he didn't follow his dreams.

He had a plan. He would work for a couple of years with the log home building company and then start up a business of his own doing the same. If that didn't work out, well then, so be it. He knew there would always be the option of returning to Michigan. He had enjoyed working with Peter over the winter and, except for Peter's fruitless attempts at trying to get Tommy back into religion and back into the church, they got along fabulously. He took Peter's attempts at trying to convert him with a grain of salt and they both joked about it. Maybe one day Tommy would find his way back to the church, but not likely. And maybe one day he and Peter would work together again if things didn't pan out in Alaska. But his mind was made up for now … no religion and no staying in Michigan. But was his mind really made up? Sometimes he would flip flop back and forth about his future. It was going to be difficult telling everyone when the time came that he was leaving, which now wasn't far off.

There was still something missing in his life and some business he had to attend to. It wasn't someone of the opposite sex that he had met and was having second thoughts about leaving. Tommy had been careful not to let that happen. He had a couple of dates with some nice girls that people from his parents' church fixed him up with and he had dated a friend of his sisters for a month, which was pleasant. He appreciated everyone's good intentions, but he wasn't looking for that kind of relationship or even a female companion. Whenever a little piece of his past came to light, barriers were put up and he felt that being an ex-con and former drug addict made most girls he dated feel uneasy. The company of a female was something he enjoyed and he liked the interaction, but that was as far as he wanted it to go and he was sure the parents of these girls thought their daughters could do better. It didn't bother Tommy.

He knew who he was and now, for the first time in a long time, he knew what he wanted out of life. The Tommy of the early and mid-seventies was done ... through ... finished forever. There was a new Tommy now striving to better his life and make things right, not only with his inner self, but with his family and friends. He liked the frame of mind he was in and, looking back, he was not sure who that person was from a few years before. He no longer dwelt on it or tried to psychoanalyze it to death. It was over. What happened in his past, happened. His parents were gone, but not their presence or influence. He would make them proud, he told himself. And he would.

Surely Mom and Dad are looking down and smiling and rooting for me. Surely from somewhere they must be doing that.

There was also something else on his mind. Something he couldn't block out and it felt like every second of every day he thought about it and couldn't let it go; there was a void to fill and there was only one way to do it ... take action.

A DOG NAMED BEN

More Healing

IT WAS SATURDAY and Tommy pulled his truck up to the front of the Bonford Humane Society. The thirty-minute drive down from Brenton had been as pleasant as the spring weather. He was by himself and what he was about to do was something he wanted to do alone. He had known this day would come. His heart broke when he lost Buddy and it broke again when Timex left him. But Tommy loved his past two dogs to no end and he always considered them his best friends. He had lost his parents and two loving dogs. He knew pain, and the healing process would take years. But, on this day, Tommy decided to take the healing process another step in the right direction to a full recovery. Timing was everything and now, Tommy felt, was the time for a new best friend.

"Good morning," the middle-aged female standing behind a counter said to Tommy as he walked in the front door.

"Good morning. How are you?" he replied.

"I'm fine. Thank you. May I help you with something?"

Tommy explained to the lady that he was looking to adopt a dog and he had come to see if they happened to have any looking for a good home.

"Yes, we do as a matter of fact," the lady in a Humane Society uniform said. "You've come at a good time. Follow me into the back and I'll show you what we have."

The employee put down some papers she had been going through and grabbed a set of keys.

"Right this way, sir. My name's Jen. What's yours?"

"My name's Tommy. Nice to meet you, Jen."

Tommy followed Jen through a door and into the kennel area where all the dogs in the world, or at least it seemed that way, were barking and jumping up on the gates to their cages and wagging their tails.

"Take me. Take me," they were all saying.

Above all the noise Jen began pointing out which ones were up for adoption and said only positive things about each of them.

"This one gets along with anything and anybody."

"This one really loves kids."

"This one gets along great with other dogs and even cats."

"This one is full of beans and loves to play."

"This one just needs to be loved and is very low maintenance."

Jen went on and on and Tommy hung onto every word. This was going to be a tough call for him to make and wished he could take them all home. There was one that reminded him of Buddy. Another one reminded him of Timex. It brought back memories. When they got to the end of the kennel Jen showed him a litter of puppies that had been abandoned by the mother and brought in by one of the local farmers. They were young, very young.

"They just came in yesterday and we're guessing that they're maybe eight to ten weeks old. The mother is missing, not to be found anywhere. They're kind of cute don't ya think?"

"That would be an understatement," Tommy replied. "What puppy isn't cute?"

"They look like they could have some Golden Lab in them," he commented as Jen opened the gate so she could hand Tommy one of the seven that all wanted to be held and cuddled.

"Yeah, Golden Lab and something else. They're going to grow up to be a fair size. Look at their paws," Jen pointed out.

Tommy did that as Jen held one in her arms.

"Big paws all right!" he agreed.

"Here, you hold him," Jen said, handing the little rascal over to Tommy.

"Hey guy or girl. How ya doin'?"

Tommy looked at the underside of the puppy to see what sex it was. As he cradled the puppy he flashed back to a time long ago when he had held another puppy at the Russell farm and he met, for the first time, a girl named Carolyn. That brought a subconscious smile to his face.

"Gosh, Jen. I don't know. All these guys need a home don't they? Can I just take them all home?" It was a question he had asked his father many years ago.

"Yeah, sure. Go ahead," Jen was joking of course and would be quite pleased if Tommy decided to take just one. He seemed like a nice enough fellow to her. "What are you looking for? A puppy or something full grown? A male? Female?"

"I guess I should have given that more thought before I came in. I honestly like all dogs, but I've always had big dogs and males and that's sort of what I'm thinking about now. Gosh, I don't know. I like them all. This is a tough one."

Jen had seen this all before. Yes, it was a tough one. Every person was different. A young family would come in and want a puppy. An elderly couple would come in and want an older dog. But they all had one thing in common;

they were all dog lovers. She had seen enough over the years not to try and predict what kind of person would take what kind of dog. She'd been surprised way too many times. It was all good as long as the dog found a good loving home. She had never pressured anyone and wouldn't start now.

"Take your time, Tommy. There's no rush. How about I leave you here with the puppies and you can come and get me out in the front office if you want to spend time with any of the others."

Tommy was euphoric.

Leave me alone with all these dogs! I have died and gone to heaven.

"That sounds good, Jen. I'll do that. This isn't going to be easy. I'll start with these little guys and go from there."

As Jen made her exit, Tommy walked up and down the row of kennel cages holding the puppy she had given him and looking at the other dogs one more time. He spent a lot of time trying to make a decision and slowly narrowed things down by finally deciding that he would settle on a puppy. Tommy didn't really know why he made that decision as the older full grown dogs tugged at his heart as much as the puppies did. But he concluded it would be nice to raise a dog from its early life like he did with Buddy. He had gotten Jen's permission to take each of the puppies outside one by one and spend time with them and that's exactly what he did.

They all had such neat personalities and he eventually made another decision that narrowed things down even more; he would choose a male. There were four in the litter and he spent equal time with each one of them. Finally, after an hour of playing and talking with the four male puppies, because this was serious business, he made his decision and carried the "winner" out into the main lobby where Jen sat at a desk.

"Well, I think I finally made my mind up," Tommy said, interrupting Jen from her paper work. "Man, that was hard."

Jen got up and walked over to where Tommy stood on the other side of the counter. She smiled and patted the puppy Tommy had put on display for her.

"It's never easy, Tommy, and it's not easy on me either. We'll miss this little guy."

Jen walked back to her desk and grabbed some papers.

"We just have to fill out some paperwork and he's all yours. Got a name for him yet?"

"Not yet," Tommy admitted. "Don't have a clue what I'm going to call him. I'll let you know though as soon as I come up with something."

Jen handed Tommy a writing pen as he put the puppy on the floor.

"I need you to fill out these forms and I need to see some identification to get things rolling."

Tommy obliged, reached for his wallet and pulled out his driver's license. The puppy he had chosen sniffed his way around the lobby, wagging his tail as he explored and investigated. On the form he was filling out, under "name" for the puppy he was adopting, he put Ben. He didn't know why, it just came to him.

It must have been in my subconscious somewhere.

"I think I'll call him Ben," he told Jen.

"That's a good name. It rhymes with Jen. I like that one," Jen said as she watched Tommy fill out the forms while keeping one eye on Ben. Tommy finished filling out the paperwork, walked over and picked up his new best buddy.

"I'll bring him by every now and then to say hello," he assured the Humane Society worker.

"Please do. We would love to see him grow and it would be wonderful if you did that."

Jen reminded the new dog owner that part of the agreement he had signed meant he had to do all of Ben's follow up shots.

"He's had all his initial ones so just drop by in a couple of weeks and show us proof he has gotten the rest of his shots. You don't have to bring Ben with you, but it would be OK if you did," she hinted with a smile.

Tommy smiled back and shook Jen's hand as he held a squirming Ben in his arm.

"See you in a couple of weeks then." Tommy said as he began to make his exit through the front door.

"Thank you so much, Tommy. I'm feeling good that this little guy has found himself a good home."

He stopped in the doorway and turned back to face Jen.

"He has. Trust me, he has."

IT WAS SPRING and Ben raced around the Franklin home with a stick in his mouth. Tommy gave chase. Although Tommy could catch him easily because Ben was still a clumsy puppy, he knew it was not about catching Ben; it was all about the chase and tiring Ben out. These were the moments for having some fun with the little tike and Tommy's new puppy thought he actually was escaping this big person in hot pursuit. Tommy stopped at the front of the house and realized he was the one getting tuckered out. He bent over, rested his hands on his knees and looked at Ben who had stopped a little further along

More Healing

and lay chewing on the stick, daring his master to begin the chase again.

"I could catch you if I wanted to, ya know. You're not as fast as you think you are, Ben."

Tommy tried to stare Ben down and started taking deliberate big steps in slow motion toward the puppy that couldn't destroy the stick fast enough. It seemed to Tommy that all dogs were the same when it came to play and Ben reminded him so much of Buddy when Buddy was a puppy. He got about ten feet from Ben and stopped as Ben got up on his hind legs while still crouching down on his front ones.

Go on! Make another move human person and I'll take my stick and beat it around the house again. You'll never catch me.

It became a showdown between Tommy and the good guy. Ben made a puppy growl and that forced his master to laugh. Tommy made a sudden motion in Ben's direction and the puppy high tailed it toward the back of the house once again. Tommy decided he'd trick Ben by coming around the house in the opposite direction from the one they'd been running in for the last ten minutes. It worked. When Ben saw Tommy, it surprised him so much he went head over heels, losing his stick in the process. He quickly recovered, backtracked to his stick and grabbed it just as Tommy dove and almost got Ben by the tail.

Nice try, human being. I keep telling you that you'll never catch me. I'm way too fast.

Tommy lay on the ground laughing as he watched Ben disappear back in the direction from which he had come. He rolled over on his back and told the blue sky, "One day I'll catch you, Ben and then you'll be sorry." He put his hands behind his head and checked out the wispiness of the high clouds.

So beautiful.

Tommy reflected on things from the past, but only the good things. He was slowly coming to terms with the mistakes he had made in his life and his heart, his soul and his mind told him that was all done now. From here on it was all about the future and making things right. He daydreamed about moving to Alaska and knew the time was fast approaching when he'd be loading up his truck and he and Ben would go on an adventure just like he and Timex had in another life. Only things would be different this time. He had grown up, drug free and sober. As he had discussed with his sister, the house would go up for sale next week and he'd take his share of the money he and Kathy got from that and head north. It wouldn't be easy saying good-bye, but he felt good about what he was going to do.

Deep in thought about Alaska and the near future, Tommy was suddenly licked in the face by a puppy that wondered why he wasn't being chased anymore. It was a sneak attack. Tommy grabbed Ben and held him above his head.

"Hey! Whatta, ya think you're doing sneaking up on me like that ya little mutt?"

Ben wiggled and fought to get free. Tommy put Ben down and Ben took off, absolutely positive his human friend was close behind. Tommy watched him run around to the front of the house, but didn't get up right away to chase his puppy. He stayed lying in the grass contemplating where and what he would be doing a year from now.

Is the sky in Alaska as blue as it is here?

He got up and calmly walked around to the front of the house trying to remember how this all got started in the first place. It seems, he recalled, that he had come out to do some yard work when this puppy somehow managed to distract him and he ended up chasing the little stinker. As Tommy made his way around the corner of his parents' home, he saw Ben up on the porch gulping down water from his bowl. The second Ben noticed Tommy he scampered down the front steps and bolted around the side of the house again.

"Forget it, Ben. I have work to do."

Tommy laughed to himself as he walked to the lawn mower and pulled the starter rope to cut the grass for the first time this spring. The mower didn't start with the first pull, or the second, or the third. He bent over to take the cap off to check the gas again. As he did, he heard something and looked up to see a vehicle coming toward the house.

"That looks like Carolyn's car," he told himself.

It was indeed Carolyn and she was by herself. Tommy said the heck with mowing the lawn and walked toward the dirt part of the front yard where he knew Carolyn would pull up and park. She did just that and he opened the driver's door for her.

"Well gosh, by golly. This is a pleasant surprise! How ya doing old friend?"

"Hey, I'm doing great, Tommy Franklin. How are you doing?" Carolyn responded getting out of her car.

"Not bad, not bad at all," Tommy answered. "Better now that Ben and I have company and I have a good excuse not to mow the lawn."

It didn't take Ben long as he came racing around the corner of the house to see that another playmate had arrived. No sooner was Carolyn out of the car than she was attacked by a very exuberant puppy.

"Hey, who's this?" she said, bending over and picking Ben up.

"This is Ben. Ben, meet Carolyn. Carolyn, meet Ben." Tommy did a formal introduction as Carolyn got kissed by Tommy's new friend and then kissed back. She giggled and managed a, "Nice to meet you, Ben."

"He's full of beans, so watch out," Tommy warned her.

Carolyn put Ben down and Ben immediately went looking for a stick or something, anything, to put in his mouth in case the humans might want to play chase again. Tommy and Carolyn watched Ben for a second before Tommy turned his attention back to his company.

"Nice to see you," he said, straight from the heart.

"Nice to see you too, Tommy," she replied with the same cheerfulness.

"Haven't heard from you in a while. Everything well?"

"Everything is just fine," Carolyn chuckled as she watched Ben running around with a small stick he had found. "That little guy is too cute."

"Yeah, he's a handful. He doesn't lack for energy that's for sure," Tommy understated.

Carolyn leaned against the front fender of her vehicle, enjoying the entertainment Ben was providing, thrilled that Tommy had gotten another dog.

"I'm so happy for you. I was beginning to wonder if you would ever get another dog."

Tommy leaned against the car beside Carolyn.

"It wasn't a matter of if, but when. The timing was right. He'll be a good boy and I love having the company."

Carolyn looked up at Tommy and smiled.

"Good for you. It's been hard visualizing you without a dog. Does Kathy know?"

"Yeah, I told her the day I got him. I guess you two haven't talked."

"No, I've been working out in the field for a couple of weeks. Kind of been out of touch," Carolyn confessed.

"Yeah, seemed like it," Tommy agreed. "When's the last time we talked?"

"I don't know .... It's been too long though. Seems like a month or more. Are you mad at me?" Carolyn asked, kidding her friend.

"No. Never. It's just been a while. My fault as well. You know my track record." Tommy admitted his penchant for not communicating.

Ben ran up and Tommy managed to grab him and take away his stick.

"Whoa! Got 'cha. Tricked again little buddy." Tommy looked at Carolyn and laughed. He took the stick and threw it for Ben to give chase. "How about if I get ya a cold drink?" Tommy suggested as they headed for the front porch.

"Sounds good. I'm so glad I caught you at home. I should have called first, but I took a chance."

"Well, then," Tommy beamed. "It's my lucky day."

The two friends walked up onto the veranda as Ben stopped at the bottom of the steps wondering what the heck was going on.

They're not chasing me! I don't understand. Life is all about chasing. What are the humans going to do now?

"What's your drink of choice?" Tommy asked as Carolyn sat down on the porch swing. "Seems that I remember it might be lemonade."

"That sounds good. Can I help?"

"Nope. You just sit there young lady and I'll be back in a flash. Maybe entertain the little guy while I'm gone."

"That could be fun," Carolyn said as Tommy entered the house.

Carolyn started chatting it up with Ben and threatening to take his prized stick away. Ben's eyes were fixed on her as she got up from the swing. He was delighted to have a new friend and playmate. Carolyn made slow and deliberate moves just like Tommy had done a few minutes before and walked to the top of the steps as Ben watched intently.

"You can trust me, Ben. Just put the stick down and back away slowly."

Silly human! I've already heard that a few times today.

Ben would have nothing to do with it and made a mad dash to nowhere thinking it might be safe to run circles around Carolyn's car. His new friend watched with amusement thinking his actions were quite comical. She turned back and sat down on the swing as Ben continued to run away from his invisible chaser. Tommy returned with a tray of lemonade and snacks and set them on a small table by the porch swing. He saw Ben running around Carolyn's car.

"It's nice that he can entertain himself," the host said.

Carolyn laughed.

"He sure doesn't want anyone to get that stick of his."

"No. No. Good luck with that. He thinks he's pretty important with a stick in his mouth." Tommy sat down on the swing next to Carolyn. He poured a glass of lemonade for each of them. "I know I said this already, but it's good to see you. Cheers!"

Tommy and Carolyn touched their glasses in a toast.

"Cheers to you," Carolyn said.

"How is Jim doing?" Tommy asked.

"Jim's doing fine. He's taken a job down in Florida."

Tommy was genuinely happy for Carolyn and her live-in lover and showed his enthusiasm.

"That's great! Now I'll have an excuse to come visit somewhere warm if

Alaska gets too cold in the winter. Good for him. Where in Florida?"

Carolyn had a sip of her drink.

"Fort Lauderdale. He'll be doing marine research with a federal agency down there that regulates domestic fishing laws."

"Have you ever been to Florida before?" Tommy asked.

"No, I haven't. Never even made it down there on my college spring breaks. What a pity. I was such a square in university," Carolyn confessed as she grabbed some cheese and crackers off the tray of snacks.

"Well, you never know. You might like it down there. Warm winters. That'll be nice," Tommy said, grabbing a cracker and cheese for himself.

Carolyn was hesitant before speaking again.

"Well Tommy ... I'm not going with him. I couldn't be happier for him, but we're breaking up."

Tommy didn't know what to say.

"Are you serious?" was the only thing he could think of.

He was surprised by her words and for a moment felt awkward. He gave Carolyn a funny look and Carolyn patted his hand.

"Yes, I'm serious and it's OK. This job thing had been in the works for a while and once I made it clear to Jim I was staying in Michigan that kind of put a kibosh on our relationship. Hey, it was beautiful and it ran its course. We both had a great time and we're OK with moving on with our lives. No biggie. These things happen. I've decided I'm going back for my master's degree and I want to do it here."

Tommy listened as she talked, but was still stunned by what he was hearing.

I thought they were in love!

He had those two pegged getting married and living happily ever after and yet Carolyn sounded so confident about what she wanted to do and talked matter-of-factly about the break up. He was not sure how to react. Tommy felt badly she and Jim were going their own ways and he considered Jim a friend as much as this girl he'd known for so many years.

"If you're going back to school and Jim is moving to Florida to further his career, I'm happy for both of you. It's just I thought you two would never break up. I'm sorry."

Carolyn held her glass up for Tommy to see and smiled.

"This was really good lemonade, you know."

Tommy returned the smile she flashed at him.

"Thanks. It's my own secret recipe. Don't ask me for it."

"I won't."

Carolyn took another drink and saw Ben rolling on his back on the front lawn with a stick in his mouth.

"Tommy, look. Jim and I are still good friends and I wish him nothing but the best, but we're adults and it's all going to be fine. Trust me. We both know we had a good thing going, but people change and he's moving on and I'm moving on. It wasn't meant to be forever or for the rest of our lives or anything like that and we enjoyed it for what it was. We had a great run. What can I say?"

Well, you sure fooled me.

Tommy didn't know what else she could say. She had said it all.

"Well, OK then. I guess that's just the way things go sometimes. Is that what you're trying to say?"

"Yeah, that's what I'm trying to say. And you're right. Jim is a good man. He's happy to be moving to Florida and starting a new job and I'm happy that I've decided to stay here and go after my master's. We'll both survive."

Carolyn put her glass down and walked down the steps. Ben, ever alert, noticed her and got ready for another chase. Carolyn bent over and clapped her hands as she faked a run toward Ben. The puppy headed off to nowhere once again. She turned around and faced Tommy still sitting on the swing trying to digest the conversation the two had been having.

"Wanna go for a walk around the property?" Carolyn asked, waving her hand to Tommy signaling, "Let's go."

Tommy got up from the swing, amused at what was happening and the words that had been spoken in the previous few minutes.

"Well, there goes the yard work," he said with a slight chuckle.

The yard work could wait until later or tomorrow. A lazy walk around his late parents' property sounded like a good thing to do with his longtime friend. Carolyn walked up to Tommy and put her arm through his.

"I'll help you with the yard work later. Deal?"

Tommy looked at her and said, "OK, it's a deal."

The two strolled away from the house and headed up to the fields out back with Ben leading the way. Tommy had known since he got back that when spring arrived the fields were going to need some attention. They had changed little since he was a boy, but he saw he would have to get his dad's old tractor out and do more than just a little yard work. But for now, it was going to be a walk about with his new friend Ben and his old friend Carolyn and he hadn't felt this good in a very long time.

TOMMY AND CAROLYN'S late morning—and afternoon, as it turned out—was more than a casual walk around the Franklin farm. It was a full day of relaxing and talking and playing with a puppy that had no lack of energy. They spent more than an hour walking up the creek that ran through the backside of the property and through the neighboring farms. They came back to the house and decided to go into town for some lunch. They ended up getting take out, going to Clear Lake and sitting at a picnic table while Ben ran in and out of the water, being a nuisance with another dog that was there visiting. It was a day that both friends needed and enjoyed immensely. They talked and laughed about their high school days and all the crazy things they did as teenagers. The days of innocence, when it was Buddy entertaining everyone and now here was Ben filling those shoes. They remembered the time Buddy saved Tommy's life and it reminded him how lucky he was to be still alive ... in more ways than one. He had survived almost drowning, getting shot up in a war, drug addiction, homelessness, prison and now here he was once again sitting on the shores of Clear Lake with this person who really had been his best friend, on and off, for what seemed like eternity. She was a confidant, a past lover, a rock, a supporter and an inspiration to him. He was feeling reborn and today, sitting at the picnic table with Carolyn, he felt better about himself than he had in a very long while. It was long overdue this feeling. There was something magical about this girl he sat with and talked to and laughed with. Something special. He had loved her in so many different ways in the past, as a friend and as a lover and he knew that he would always love her in one way or the other. That would never change.

TOMMY PULLED HIS truck up in front of the Franklin home and parked as Carolyn opened the passenger door to let out the puppy that had been sitting on her lap. The two humans sat for a moment and watched Ben scamper away.

"Would you like to stay for dinner?" Tommy asked, hoping the answer would be yes.

Carolyn looked at her watch. "I can't believe it's five-thirty."

She hadn't expected an invitation like this and contemplated for a second about whether she should or shouldn't accept. She looked at Tommy.

"Are you sure?"

"Of course I'm sure, silly. I'll barbeque up a couple of steaks. The company would be nice."

Carolyn didn't give it much more thought.

"OK, sounds good. You talked me into it."

Carolyn and Tommy got out of the truck and walked toward the house.

"Oh wait!"

Carolyn stopped at her car, opened up the back door and took out a bottle of wine.

Tommy laughed. "You always go around with bottles of wine in the back of your car?"

"Maybe," Carolyn said coyly and smiled.

"I wish I could join you, but my parole conditions say no alcohol."

That was fine with Carolyn and she remarked, "It'll be more for me."

Tommy looked at Ben running toward the barn for what appeared to be no particular reason and yelled to him, "Ben. Come on. Dinner time."

Ben knew those words already in his young life and made a quick U-turn.

"What can I do to help?" Carolyn asked, walking up the front steps.

Tommy held the front door open for her.

"Come on in, partner. I'll find something for you to do. That won't be a problem."

THE TWO FRIENDS sat at the kitchen table talking. They had finished eating almost an hour before and both were enjoying the other's company, relishing the moment. Ben was tuckered out and lay sleeping next to the back door, so that if anyone tried to escape they'd have to go through him.

"I can't believe he finally ran out of gas," Carolyn said, looking at Ben and emptying the last of the wine into her glass.

"It's been a big day for him that's for sure," Tommy agreed.

Carolyn held up the empty bottle.

"I bet you didn't know I was such a lush."

Tommy laughed.

"I'm glad you enjoyed it."

"It was good wine all right," Carolyn said, holding the bottle up to the light and observing it.

Tommy got up from his chair, grabbed some dishes and headed over to the kitchen sink.

"Would you mind if I spent the night?" Carolyn asked.

That question came from out of nowhere and Tommy wasn't sure of the implications. He turned around, headed back to the table and grabbed some more dishes.

"Well, considering how much you've had to drink, that might be a good idea. There's plenty of room here at the inn."

Carolyn got up with some dishes of her own and put them in the sink. She told Tommy that the reason she was in town was to visit her folks,. "I'll have to call my parents. They were expecting me home by now."

Tommy began running water to do the dishes.

"Tell them that you're in safe hands. Ben and I will protect you."

Carolyn chuckled as she headed to the phone hanging on the wall by the door where Ben lay with eyes closed.

"That's reassuring," she said, looking down at the sleeping puppy whose paws were twitching, proving he could still run and chase things even when he was in dreamland.

Carolyn made her call and had a casual chat with her mom as Tommy did the dishes. She hung up the phone and giggled to herself.

"How old am I again ... still checking in with my parents? I'm such a good daughter."

Tommy wiped his hands on a drying cloth.

"Hey, if they were expecting you home, it's good that you called. And yes, you are a good daughter. They would have worried if you didn't ring in."

"You're right, Mr. Franklin," Carolyn walked up to where Tommy stood over the kitchen sink and began drying some dishes. "I didn't bring an overnight bag or anything. I wasn't planning on spending the night here. Honest," Carolyn said, nudging Tommy.

"You should at least carry a toothbrush with you," Tommy said, nudging Carolyn back. "You should keep one in your glove box. Never leave home without a bottle of wine and a toothbrush. You never know when they might come in handy."

Carolyn laughed and it made her feel good that after everything Tommy had been through in life, his sense of humor had returned. She recalled that when he had first come back to Michigan the previous autumn, he had seemed serious and somewhat despondent. Detached. Embarrassed by the past few years. She realized after spending this day with him that the old Tommy might be slowly returning. He wasn't back all the way yet, but there was hope.

Before he went off to war, he had a great sense of humor and an uncanny ability to make people laugh. The war changed him. When he first came back to Michigan after his stay in the veterans' hospital, the whole experience over in Vietnam seemed to have had some profound effect on him. At first, nothing was funny anymore. You couldn't make Tommy laugh no matter how hard you tried. His sense of humor wasn't there like it was before he joined the service. But it wasn't the military that took away his comical quips. It was the war. Today, Tommy's actions, especially around Ben, were funny once more.

Would it be that way tomorrow? The next day? Today was an exhibition of the old Tommy, fun loving and expressing his sense of humor. How long would it take for her friend to completely shed the baggage he had carried with him these past few years? Maybe he wouldn't. Maybe a troubled mind never heals. You tuck your problems away somewhere in the subconscious and hope they stay there and don't resurface. Or maybe they come and go to remind you of where you've been and where you don't want to go back to.

"Yeah, well. So I brought some wine and forgot my toothbrush. Got a problem with that?" Carolyn asked, joking with Tommy as they finished the last of the dishes.

"No, not at all. In fact, it just might be your lucky day. I think I have an extra toothbrush that's never been used."

"Wow! And you'll let me use it?" Carolyn asked mockingly.

Tommy walked over to the stove, grabbed a tea kettle that was sitting on top and walked over to the sink, putting some water into it.

"I don't know. I have to think about it. Let me see your teeth."

Carolyn slapped Tommy on the arm.

"Forget it!" she said defiantly, then having a split second change of heart, she bared her teeth for Tommy to check out. "OK, see!"

Imitating a dentist, Tommy had a keen look at Carolyn's teeth and reached a conclusion. "Yeah, I have a toothbrush for you if you promise to brush your teeth tonight before you go to bed and then again in the morning. They look like they could use a good brushing."

Carolyn slapped Tommy's arm again.

"Oh, stop it! I was just at the dentist two weeks ago and had them cleaned. I have beautiful teeth."

Tommy put the kettle on the stove and turned on the heat.

"Yes, you do. You have beautiful teeth. Nicest teeth I've ever seen. Amazing teeth. Incredible teeth. The most ... ."

Carolyn interrupted him. "OK, OK. Forget it. Enough already!"

The two laughed together. "How about some tea and a game of cribbage?" Tommy suggested to Carolyn.

She accepted the challenge and more. "How about best of five and I whip your butt?"

Tommy walked over to a buffet and took out some cards and a cribbage board.

"Whoa! Feeling a little feisty are we?"

Carolyn had a seat at the kitchen table.

"Bring it on, Franklin. Bring it on!"

Tommy sat down on a chair next to his competition.

"Loser makes breakfast in the morning?" Tommy asked, laying down the stakes.

"I'll have Eggs Benny and orange juice, Chef Franklin."

"You're on, Russell. You're on."

It was déjà vu. They had played the card games before and she always won and he always lost. Again this time, she won, he lost. What did it matter? They were together again and for this moment that was what was important. Only now it wasn't Buddy or Timex sharing time with them, it was Ben and it couldn't get any better than this. Buddy and Timex would be proud.

"WELL, THAT DIDN'T go according to plan," a disappointed Tommy said as he watched Carolyn peg out and therefore win the best of five tourney, three games to one.

The champion gave the loser a cocky look and said nothing. She didn't have to use words to rub it in. The look she was giving Tommy said it all. It was the look she had given him years before when they had played Yahtzee together and with the same results.

"Yeah, yeah. Don't get a swelled head," Tommy warned her. "We'll do this again another time and the results will be different. I let you win this time, next time, no."

Carolyn remained silent which made Tommy fidget.

"I'm going to take Ben out for his nightly pee," he said. "Care to join me?"

They both stood.

"I can't believe how good I am," she gloated. "It's like I'm the best crib player ever!" she said, rubbing it in now. "You and Ben go have your pee. I think I'll go brush my teeth. Where's the toothbrush you were talking about?"

"I've changed my mind," Tommy fired back. "You can't use it now."

"Oh, I'm sorry. Is poor little Tommy upset because he lost to the best cribbage player in the world? That's OK. I'll just use yours," Carolyn threatened her pouting friend who must have learned it from his fun-loving father.

Tommy stood at the back door with Ben whose bladder was telling him it was time to go.

Why are you stalling, Dad? You lost at cribbage to Carolyn. So what! Get over it. She just told you she's the best player in the world. Open the stupid door before I have an accident right here and now.

Tommy tried not to smile. He would rather put on the "woe is me" charade like his dad used to do, but couldn't help himself and grinned.

"You know you really have a knack of getting under my skin."

Carolyn walked up to Tommy and gave him a soft punch in the stomach.

"And I love every second of it."

"Bite her, Ben. Bite her leg off."

Ben didn't want to bite anyone's leg off. He just wanted to go outside and relieve himself.

"Go to the upstairs bathroom and in the medicine cabinet is a red toothbrush still in its packaging. It's yours if you let me win next time."

Carolyn turned and began to head out of the kitchen.

"OK, deal. I'll let you win next time. Maybe." She stopped and looked at the pair still standing at the back door. "I think Ben needs to go out."

Tommy opened the back door for Ben and the eager puppy darted out into the night.

"Yeah, I guess he does. I'll be back in a minute and I've got some clean towels for you if you want to have a shower. I'll find something you can wear for pajama's as well. The light for the stairs is on the wall at the bottom. You can't miss it. You can sleep in Kathy's old room."

"I think I'll wait until morning to have a shower. Thanks anyway. Brushing my teeth is all I can handle right now."

Tommy laughed and shook his head. "I'll be right back."

"HELLO!" TOMMY KNOCKED on the partially open door to what was once his sister's bedroom where Carolyn sat on the bed looking at a photo album.

"Oh, hi. Come in. This was on the dresser," Carolyn said.

Tommy walked in with an armful of linen and a sweatshirt for Carolyn to use as a nightie. Ben was right behind him. Tommy sat on the bed next to Carolyn and looked down at the pictures she had been leafing through.

"Old photos are fun," he said. "My mom was always taking pictures."

It just happened that the page the album was turned to had a picture of Tommy and Buddy. It brought joy to his heart. Pictures of Buddy had always done that to him.

"Hey, remember this guy?" it was more of a statement than a question.

"Good ol' Buddy," Carolyn sighed as those fond memories came back to her as well. Ben jumped up and put his front paws on the bed. "Come on up little guy," Carolyn picked Ben up and put him on the bed where he decided the best spot was between his best friend and his new best friend.

"Here's some clean linen and the only thing I could find for pajamas was

More Healing

this sweatshirt," Tommy said, laying the things he had brought in on the bed behind Carolyn. "It's clean and it's a large so hopefully that will work for you."

"It'll be fine. Thanks so much," Carolyn said as she patted Ben on the head. "You are so cute, Ben. I can't stand it."

"He can sleep with you if you like," Tommy offered.

"Really? Oh, that would be so much fun, Ben. You and me. What a way to end the day. You don't mind?" Carolyn asked as Tommy got up and leaned against the bedroom door frame.

"I don't mind at all. You might want to leave the door cracked open a little bit in case he changes his mind. I'm just down the hall. I'll leave my door open so the little rascal can come and bug me in the middle of the night like he usually does."

Tommy watched Carolyn talk with Ben and give him the attention he was used to.

She's a natural at it. Always has been.

"OK, I'm going to bed Miss Russell. Thank you for the day. You were good company."

Carolyn got up from the bed, walked over to Tommy and gave him a peck on the cheek.

"Thank you and don't forget you're cooking breakfast in the morning. Do you remember what I like?"

"I think so. Burnt scrambled eggs. Burnt toast. Burnt bacon and burnt hash browns. Right?"

Carolyn walked back to the bed and picked up the sweatshirt.

"Eggs Bennie, Franklin and don't forget it. See ya in the morning."

"See ya in the morning. Good night, Ben," Tommy said, giving Ben a wink. Ben stood on the bed with a quizzical look on his face.

Hey! What's going on? Where ya going, Dad? You can't leave me here. Wait for me!

Tommy got about two steps out into the hallway when Ben jumped off the bed and came dashing out of the bedroom. Tommy picked him up and headed back to the doorway of the bedroom where Carolyn was waiting to get changed.

"Well, I may have lost at cribbage tonight, but I'm the real winner because it looks like Ben wants to sleep with me. Sorry about that."

Carolyn walked up to where Tommy held Ben in his arms and gave Ben a kiss.

"That's OK, Ben. My feelings are hurt, but we'll do it another time. You just remind your dad in the morning what he has to do."

Tommy raised his eyebrows. "He won't have to remind me. Don't worry."

When Tommy got half way back to his room he yelled out loud enough for Carolyn to hear behind the now closed door, "Did you remember to brush your teeth?" To which Carolyn yelled back, "Good night, Tommy Franklin."

Tommy walked into his room laughing and put Ben down. "You know, Ben, I personally don't know why you'd rather sleep with me instead of Carolyn because I'd rather sleep with her than you, good buddy. Ah, but you're probably too young to understand."

He sat down on the chair at the desk in his room and began taking his shoes off. He thought how nice it would be to sleep with his former lover, but something told him the timing wasn't right. He wondered if she would be at all interested in him again. His self-confidence with women wasn't very high right now. But if there was one woman in the world he would like to make love to, it was the one in the bedroom just down the hall. She had always had a way about her that made him feel good about himself. Maybe one day it would happen again. Maybe … one day.

CAROLYN WASN'T SURE what woke her up. It had been so quiet, like it usually was in a house in the country. She had been sound asleep and was having a nice dream. It was disappointing that it got interrupted. She turned over on her back, listened and tried to make out what she was hearing. Carolyn rubbed her forehead and couldn't quite yet get her eyes open. Lying still, she thought that maybe she hadn't heard anything at all and turned over onto her other side. There it was again. This time she opened her eyes and listened more carefully. Whatever she heard was unrecognizable in her sleepy state. She sat up now, knowing that she was definitely hearing noises. It sounded like someone yelling or screaming. Someone in agony or in pain. She wasn't sure. It became a little unnerving. She looked at the bedside clock. It was almost four. There it was again. Did Tommy hear what she was hearing she wondered? Carolyn got out of bed, walked to the bedroom door and poked her head out. It was quiet for a moment as she looked up and down the hallway. She listened for a few more seconds and nothing. No sooner had she turned to go back to bed than another cry came. It sounded like it came from Tommy's room. She remembered back a long time ago Kathy telling her about the nightmares Tommy had since his return from Vietnam.

Carolyn decided to sneak a few steps down the hallway with floorboards creaking as she did. When she got to Tommy's bedroom the door was partially open. Ben sat guarding the entry way and gave a puppy whine. He was not acting like he wanted to play; he was watching and protecting his friend who was having a nightmare. Bending her knees and stooping over, Carolyn said a quiet hello to Ben. He was glad to see her and calmed down. Ben was not too sure what was going on when his master acted this way. This was only the second incident in the few weeks he'd lived here. It was the middle of the night and he had been sound asleep on Tommy's bed when all of a sudden his best friend started tossing and turning and making those awful sounds he had heard once before.

"Hey, Ben. Everything OK?" Carolyn whispered as she picked Ben up and took a step inside Tommy's room.

He seemed to be sleeping peacefully, suddenly he screamed again. Carolyn put Ben down and quickly walked over to the bed. Her friend was obviously having an agonizing dream. Before she even had time to shake him awake she could see in the ambient light he was wet from sweat.

"Tommy. Tommy. Wake up. Wake up."

Tommy tossed and squirmed and acted panicky. With both hands on Tommy's shoulders and shouting his name, Carolyn managed to give a shake hard enough to wake him up. He sat up as if he was shot out of a cannon. He screamed a couple of swear words before he realized he was awake and the nightmare was over.

"Tommy, it's OK. It's Carolyn."

Tommy gave his friend a blank stare just like he had given Cheryl years before and others who had witnessed his nightmares. He was stunned and not quite sure where he was or what was going on. It was always this way. Always the same. Carolyn took hold of Tommy's hands and tried to calm him down. His palms were wet from sweat. Tommy continued to struggle with his whereabouts and hung his head. His body was drained of all energy. Carolyn let go of his hands and pulled his head to her shoulders.

"It's OK. It's OK. Ben and I are here with you. It's OK."

Carolyn gently rocked back and forth holding her traumatized friend. Tommy decided he wanted to sit up on the edge of the bed and put his feet on the floor. Ben watched his every move.

It's kind of strange for my human friend to be acting like this. I wonder what's wrong?

Ben sat on the floor, then suddenly decided to jump up and put his front paws on Tommy's lap. Tommy gave Ben a pet on the top of his head. He was subdued and his undershirt and boxer shorts were wet from perspiration. Tommy looked at Ben who had just licked his master's forearm.

The Effects of War on a Godless Dog Lover – KB Fugitt

"Sorry, Timex. I didn't mean to scare you," he said quietly and weakly.

Timex?

Carolyn wondered to herself if Tommy had been dreaming about Timex. She sat, saying nothing, and let Tommy gather his thoughts together as he continued to stroke Ben on the head.

"Sorry, Carolyn. Of all nights I ... ."

Carolyn stopped him right there.

"Don't be sorry. It's OK. Is everything all right?"

Feeling confused, Tommy stood up and looked around the room.

"Yeah, everything is fine. I'm sorry I woke you."

"Tommy, please don't be sorry. I'm glad I was here." She stood up in front of her friend and looked him in the face. "I'll get a towel and some dry sheets. Where do you keep your sheets?"

"Towels and sheets are in the hallway linen closet. Thanks so much."

Before Carolyn got to the bedroom door, Tommy stopped her.

"Carolyn ... ."

She stopped and saw that her friend had something to say.

"Yes."

He searched for words, but couldn't find them. Not the right ones anyway. Carolyn turned on the bedroom light and Tommy rubbed his eyes.

"Carolyn ... every once in a while I get these nightmares ... ."

"I understand, Tommy. You should get some dry clothes on. I'll be right back."

Carolyn turned and entered the hallway. Tommy went to his dresser and grabbed some dry underclothing. Ben sat and watched. Carolyn was gone for only a brief moment and came back into the bedroom. She was thinking how troubling these nightmares must be for a veteran soldier. What were they about? The war? His homeless days in L.A.? Prison? His parents passing? And was Timex in them? How did he manage when he was by himself? Whatever the content of the nightmares, they were obviously upsetting. She felt more than anything though that they were probably about his experiences overseas when he was doing things he wished he hadn't. Tommy told Carolyn he was going to change his clothes and headed for the bathroom. Ben was right on his heels. He was not going to let Tommy out of his sight for a second. Carolyn remade the bed with some clean linen and finished up just as Tommy came back in.

"Now then. Where were we?" he said, feeling somewhat normal.

"Well, I think we were sleeping," Carolyn said light heartedly, making an awkward attempt at being funny.

"Yeah, I think you're right," Tommy replied.

Ben looked at the pair standing close together.

Yeah, you're both right. We were sleeping. Remember? Do you think we can get back to that? If I'm going to be full of beans tomorrow like I am every day, I need a good night's sleep.

"Tommy," Carolyn said as she once again took his hands into hers.

"Yeah?"

"Do you mind if I stay here with you and Ben?"

Tommy related to Carolyn that he would like that very much. Ben climbed into bed between the two to prevent any hanky panky. Tommy and Carolyn lay facing each other, both petting Ben.

It's more fun with two humans in bed with me instead of just one. I like all this attention.

"You going to be OK?" Carolyn asked her friend.

Tommy looked at her and could just barely see the white in her eyes.

"Yeah. I've been through this a few times and somehow survived."

Having been through it a few times was an understatement. He took his hand and put it through Carolyn's hair to which Ben became jealous and tried to nuzzle in between Tommy's hand and his new friends head.

"It's OK, Ben. I can pet Carolyn too."

Carolyn's eyes meet Tommy's.

"Do you mind if I go back to sleep?" she asked.

"No. Not at all. Go back to sleep." Tommy stroked her hair a couple of more times.

"Carolyn."

"Yes."

"I'm glad that you were here."

She snuggled up closer to Tommy and Ben felt like he was getting squished.

"I'm glad I was here too." she said.

She closed her eyes and thought about how, in a few short hours, Tommy would be making her breakfast. She also thought about the special place she had in her heart for this good and forever friend. But, Carolyn also worried about his troubled mind and how deep his issues must go. And as she thought of him, Tommy fell back asleep thinking of her. He was thankful she was nearby and understanding about what had happened. The last thoughts on his mind right before he fell back asleep were about what he could do to make her the best breakfast she'd ever had.

TOMMY OPENED HIS eyes and saw Carolyn staring at him. Ben was sound asleep still. They had all managed to get in a few more hours of sleep since the incident that got everybody up earlier in the morning. Morning light shone through the bedroom window, signaling that another day had begun and faintly, in the background, birds were singing.

"How long have you been staring at me?" Tommy asked the girl in his bed.

"I don't know. A few minutes I guess."

Tommy was amused in a happy way.

"Are you getting impatient for breakfast?"

"I'm hungry whenever you're ready to get it going. I'm going to have a shower first if that's OK."

"That's fine. What do we do with sleepy head here?" Tommy said, referring to an "out like a light" Ben.

Carolyn came to his defense.

"Hey, he had a big day yesterday. He should be allowed to sleep in. He's a tired puppy. Poor guy."

Ben squirmed, moaned and stretched his legs in a feeble attempt to push Carolyn off the bed. She laughed at that.

"He sure is a bed hog."

"Yeah, he is." Tommy agreed. "I have to put up with this every night."

Ben opened his eyes and no sooner did he do that than he realized he had to pee and put the morning routine into full gear.

"OK, Ben. Settle down. I'll take you out." Tommy threw back the covers and climbed out of bed as Ben jumped onto the floor. Tommy looked down at Carolyn looking up at him. "It's a guy thing. When ya gotta go, ya gotta go. I'll be back and get breakfast started. Hang tight."

Carolyn stretched her arms above her head. "I'm in no hurry. Take your time."

She turned over back toward the wall and closed her eyes again, admitting to herself she wouldn't mind a few more minutes of sleep. She did get a few more minutes of solitude, but just as she was about to doze off again she heard the bedroom door open and looked back over her shoulders. Tommy came in without Ben and closed the door. He still had his boxer shorts on and an undershirt. Carolyn rubbed her eyes.

"Do you always go out in your boxers when you do your morning routine?" she asked.

Tommy laughed as he crawled back in bed with Carolyn.

"No. I just let him out and stand by the back door until he does his thing and sniffs around and then he realizes it's time for breakfast. He's chowing down right now and should be content for a while."

Tommy and Carolyn faced each other and he put an arm around her waist. She didn't mind and with one of her hands felt his morning stubble. Nothing was said, but minds were read. He took a chance and placed a kiss on her lips and then backed off and looked her in the eye. Didn't they do this many years ago on a beach? Carolyn reciprocated and kissed him back. The lovemaking began as did a new day. For both it felt like old times, only these were new times. For both it felt like maybe this was the way it should be. For both it felt like nothing had changed from when they were lovers years ago. For both it was simply a time to enjoy the moment. And that's what they did.

CAROLYN SAT AT the kitchen table and enjoyed watching Tommy cook her breakfast. She held her morning coffee cup with both hands and sipped at it.

"Is this going to take all day? It'll be lunch time before you're done!"

She thought it was kind of fun witnessing him work in the kitchen and even though Tommy was hard at it, he thought it was kind of fun as well. He hadn't felt this good in a long time and Carolyn, he came to realize, certainly hadn't forgotten how to make love. Right now, with the way he was feeling, he'd make her breakfast, lunch and dinner if that's what she wanted and if it would keep her with him for one more day.

"Just cool your jets. I'm getting there. The best breakfast you'll ever have isn't going to happen in five minutes. I'm an artist at work here. Don't distract me."

"I've already had the best breakfast I could have," Carolyn said, referring to their passionate love making earlier.

Tommy appreciated the little tease and gave her a smile. His feelings came to the surface and he blushed.

"Yeah ... OK ... well, maybe this will be the second best breakfast you've ever had. Be patient. It's coming." He cooked away at the stove as Carolyn got up and hugged him from behind. "Thanks," Tommy said, soaking up the attention he was getting. "But like I said, don't distract me."

Even though she'd had her shower, Carolyn was still wearing the long sweatshirt that Tommy had given her to sleep in.

"OK, fine. How about if I go get dressed?"

"Don't be too long. It's almost ready," he told her.

"Smells good. I'll be back in a flash."

Ben lay at the back door watching Tommy's every move. It was just a matter of time before his master wouldn't be able to help himself and would offer him a treat of human food. Right on cue, Tommy walked over and gave Ben a little slice of ham.

"Here ya go, Ben."

Tommy tried to get Ben to sit and shake a paw, but the puppy hadn't quite figured that one out yet.

Why should I sit and shake a paw when I know you're going to give it to me anyway? Gees!

Tommy turned and walked away telling Ben, "Sooner or later you're going to have to listen and obey. Sit means sit and shake means shake."

Thanks for the piece of ham, Dad. Got any more?

Ben sniffed the floor around him, thinking there must be more than what he was given.

Nope. Guess not.

Carolyn came back into the room dressed and brushing her still-damp hair. Tommy began to set the table.

"Can I help?" Carolyn volunteered her services.

"No. You just relax. It's all good to go. Have a seat," Tommy commanded her in a friendly manner.

She did as she was told. Tommy grabbed the coffee pot and refreshed her cup.

"Why thank you, sir."

"You're very welcome." The host served up breakfast, stood at the table and checked to make sure he had everything. "OK, I think that's it."

"Sure looks like it to me. Now will you please sit down and join me." Carolyn respected how hard Tommy had worked at this wonderful meal and now it was time to feast. "You'll make some lucky lady a good husband one day Tommy Franklin, if you can cook like this."

"I don't know about that. Eat up."

Tommy had a seat at the table across from Carolyn as Ben came over hoping for some more food that just might drop onto the floor. Tommy ordered his canine friend to go away by gesturing with his fork. After a couple of bites, Carolyn complimented Tommy on a job well done.

"Best Eggs Benny I've ever had."

"Hmmmm." Tommy reacted and had his doubts.

"I'm serious. This is fantastic. You should open a restaurant, Tommy."

He gave her a "you gotta be joking" stare.

"OK, well maybe not." Carolyn said. "Just trying to be complementary."

More Healing

"I think I may have gotten lucky. I don't know if I could do this twice in a row." Tommy admitted. He pondered for a moment then added, "But if you want to stay another night I just might pull out my cookbook and see what else I can come up with."

Carolyn looked at him and laughed.

"Yeah well, we'll see. Ya never know."

They took a few more bites in silence before Ben started to whine impatiently.

"Forget it, Ben. You've already had yours," said the controller of the food.

Carolyn ate and thought about her old friend and everything he'd been through in his still young life. She had thought about this often. She didn't remember prying into his feelings or having an intimate talk with him in recent years and wondered if this would be a good time to try and get him to open up. Would he be offended? Maybe some things were taboo and he wouldn't discuss them. But he did seem comfortable around her. She felt this might be a good time to reach out to him and decided to take a chance.

"Tommy."

"Yes, Carolyn."

She hesitated for a moment then carried on.

"Where do you want to be five years from now?"

As Tommy took a sip of orange juice, he studied her and wondered why she was asking that question. He put his glass down.

"I know exactly where I'm going to be five years from now." He looked down at his plate of food and cut another bite of Eggs Benedict. "You know," he said talking with a mouth full of food. "I do have to admit, these are some pretty good Eggs Bennie."

Carolyn could take a hint and didn't want to push too much. But she also felt the question was innocent enough and didn't mean any harm in asking it.

"I'm glad you're enjoying them," she said and told herself she'd try another tactic. "Would you like to know where I would like to be in five years?"

"Sure," Tommy said, giving in to Ben's persistence and handing him another little piece of ham.

Carolyn put her elbows on the table and rested her chin on her thumbs.

"Well, I'm going to go for my master's degree in marine biology and continue to pursue my career in that field .

"I thought you were already doing that?" Tommy said, wolfing down more food.

"Well, yes, I am. But you know what I mean. I'd like to take it to another level. I really like working in that field," Carolyn said, sounding like a woman

353

who knew what she wanted out of life, which in fact she did.

"Well, you've done pretty well with it so far," Tommy complemented her.

The tactic Carolyn chose seemed to be working and stirred up Tommy's curiosity. He took the conversation further and asked her where she would like to be living five years from now.

"Wherever my job might take me," she replied. "But I really, really like it here in Michigan. I'd like to stay if I could."

"Well, why not just stay with the company you're working for now?" Tommy asked.

"It's a possibility. We'll see if they'll hire me back after I've gone back to school."

Carolyn finished off her last bite of breakfast and took her plate over to the sink. Tommy was right behind her.

"Of course they will. They're not stupid."

Carolyn appreciated hearing the flattery as she rinsed off some dishes, but she wanted to turn the subject back to him and hear about his plans.

"OK, so what about you? You said you knew where you were going to be in five years. Where? Doing what? You can tell me. I'll keep it a secret. Promise."

Tommy snickered as he ran water into the sink to do the dishes.

"You'll keep it a secret will ya?"

Carolyn continued to help Tommy, just like she had after dinner the night before.

"Of course I will. Honest."

Tommy smiled and shook his head. "Well, it's no secret. I think you already know what I have my heart set on."

Carolyn did know, but didn't want to accept it.

"You're moving to Alaska. Good for you."

"Thanks," Tommy said as he put some dishes into the sink. "I'll do these later. Let's go out onto the porch and continue this conversation out there."

He dried off his hands and headed for the front door. Carolyn knelt down to pet Ben, who was still hoping for some more tidbits.

"Come on, Ben. Let's go outside with your dad."

Tommy was already sitting on the porch swing when Carolyn and Ben came out. He patted the swing.

"Come on. Have a seat. Ben, go find a stick or something."

Amazingly enough, Ben happened to already know that "stick" word and headed down the steps and into the yard to find something to play with.

"So ... ," Tommy began picking up where they left off. "Five years from now I'm going to be a log home builder in Alaska ... ."

Carolyn was impressed that he had said it so matter-of-factly and she couldn't help but believe him. She knew him well enough and wouldn't bet against him or doubt him. She knew he meant what he said. His past had made him more determined to make something of himself. She understood that. And he knew that if by chance his parents were looking down on him, they would be an inspiration as he got his life back on track in a positive way. He would make them proud of their son. Carolyn was certainly proud of her friend and wished him well. But once again, like in the past, her selfish side wanted him to stay close by and to try his luck in the state and town where he grew up.

"Why don't you try starting up a log home building business right here in Michigan?"

As soon as she asked the question she wished she hadn't. Tommy didn't hesitate to answer.

"I feel like another adventure, Carolyn. That's it. I feel like going to Alaska and checking it out just like I did when I went to California."

Yeah, and we all know what happened in California, Carolyn thought to herself. Tommy continued as they gently swayed back and forth in the swing.

"You're the first one I've told this to, but I have a job offer up there to serve as an apprentice. It's all good to go and we just have to sell the house and get on with it."

Ben ran up with a stick and Carolyn took it from him, walked to the top of the steps and threw it. She took notice that, like yesterday, today was going to be a nice day. She sat down at the top of the steps and turned to Tommy.

"I really hope things go well for you," she paused pensively. "You're going to be far away and everyone is going to miss you so much."

Tommy realized that and told her he was going to miss her and his sister and her family. He'd miss Michigan and the house he grew up in, but he didn't want to stay. The wheels were in motion and there would be no changing his mind. His parole board had once again approved his move and he was anxious to get on with another phase of his life. He had known all along that coming back to Michigan was only going to be temporary. It had started when he was in prison and read about Alaska and building log homes. The two went hand in hand. Just like California was a part of his past, Michigan was going to become that as well. The past was the past and his future, Tommy Franklin's future, was going to be in Alaska.

Carolyn watched Ben play with his trophy stick, daring her to come chase him. She knew Tommy meant what he said and she had to come to terms with that. She turned around and watched him gently swing back and forth, looking quite comfortable.

"So can I come and visit you sometime?"

Tommy got up from the swing, walked up to Carolyn and took her hands in his.

"Anytime. I would like that."

He walked down the steps onto the grass and started chasing Ben around just as if the puppy had been planning it all morning. Carolyn came down off the porch and helped her friend in the chase. Ben headed in the direction of the barn full steam ahead. Tommy and Carolyn stopped, bent over and rested their hands on their knees. Tommy looked over at his friend.

"I think he's all wired up and ready to go." He strolled over to her and took her by the hand. "Would you like to go for a little walk?"

"Are we going to Alaska?"

He laughed.

"No. No, I don't think so. Not today."

As Ben led the way, they headed past the barn and into the back fields. Carolyn picked up where the conversation had left off.

"OK, then, I'll come and visit you. I'm going to miss you so much, but I'll definitely come and visit."

"Don't bother calling. Just come. I'll be there and the door will be open."

"And you'll make me a breakfast like you did this morning?"

"If you let me beat you at a game of Cribbage."

Carolyn had to think about that for a moment and concluded that sounded fair.

"OK. Fine with me. A deal's a deal."

TOMMY STOOD STARING down at Buddy's grave with Ben sitting by his side. He had been standing for a few minutes meditating and reminiscing. With mixed emotions, he was now saying good-bye to everything that was part of his childhood. His parents' house had sold quickly and he had enough money to make a new start. Tommy had convinced himself that this was what his parents would want him to do and this new start, for reasons he couldn't explain, would begin in the North Country.

"Well, Buddy. This is it. We're leaving you, Ben and I. We'll come back and visit you if we ever get the chance. Wish us luck. Take care."

Tommy turned and started walking back to the fully-loaded truck he had bought during the winter and was ready to make his journey to Alaska. In the front yard were Carolyn, Kathy, Paul and Gregory Thomas. Gregory was being chased around the front yard by the adults and Ben, seeing that, joined in on the fun. Before anyone noticed the man who was departing, Tommy stopped and watched the joyful scene with mixed emotions. This wasn't California he was leaving for this time, but somewhere much further. This wasn't the old Tommy, this was the new Tommy, more mature, older, wiser.

The New Frontier was what some people called Alaska. It was the land of opportunity. This was why Tommy had decided to go there: opportunity and a place where someone with his past could go and blend in, make a new start. It was going to be a positive adventure and he looked forward to the new challenges that was going to bring. Maybe, in a sense, he was running away, but he would like to think he was running forward to a new life that he wanted to get on with. He was ready and anxious. Still, the scene before him warmed his heart. He wouldn't see this where he was going. At least not from these people who ran and played, chased his puppy and laughed. This departure was melancholy, but necessary. This move was to fulfill some inner, inexplicable drive. Good times were ahead. He knew it, he felt it and it was time to get started.

He walked up to the players on the front lawn and joined in. It was another moment of quality time together and hopefully not the last. When all were exhausted and Kathy had picked Gregory Thomas up, Tommy started saying his good-byes. His sister shed the tears she had known would come as she held her son and got a hug from her brother.

"We're going to miss you so much," Kathy said. "You be good, Tommy. Just promise me you'll be good."

Tommy took her by the shoulders and looked her squarely in the eye. "You don't have to worry about me, big sister. It's all going to be fine. When I get settled up there, you, Paul and Gregory Thomas are going to come up for a visit. Got that?"

Paul came up next to his wife and shook Tommy's hand.

"That would be awesome. We'll do that, Tommy. We'll come up for a visit sometime."

"I'll be looking for you, Paul. We'll do some fishin', the three of us. You, me and Gregory Thomas."

"Excuse me!" Kathy butted in indignantly. "I happen to like fishing too. What about me."

"Well yeah, yeah, sis. You can come along. Of course you can come along." Tommy laughed as he gave his sister a peck on the forehead.

"That's more like it," Kathy said, setting a squirming son back down onto the ground.

Carolyn leaned up against the rear of Tommy's truck waiting for her turn to say farewell. He turned around, walked up and gave her a long hug before either said anything.

"You'll come up for a visit as well I hope?"

Carolyn smirked. "If you're lucky and if you stay in touch, I just might."

Tommy smiled back. "Staying in touch won't be a problem. I promise. And I would like it very, very much if you came up and saw Ben and me."

"OK, then. Deal. You stay in touch and I'll come up and visit you two," Carolyn guaranteed.

Tommy took Carolyn's hand as he walked to the side of his truck and gave her one more hug. He opened the door and Ben, attempting to jump in, just barely made it onto the floor with his front paws as his back legs dangled toward the ground. Even though Ben was now a few months old and should be big enough to jump in on his own, he still hadn't mastered the art of jumping into a truck. Tommy gave his little friend a boost and Ben scrambled onto the front seat. Tommy shook his head and chuckled. He turned his attention back to Carolyn and recalled a scene, reminiscent of this, long ago when he was leaving for the west coast. He missed his parents. They were not standing here waving good-bye and wishing him good luck. He thought about that for a second as he gave Carolyn another hug and climbed into his truck.

"OK, people," Tommy said, looking out an open driver's door window. "We've got a long journey ahead. Kathy, I'll give you a call as soon as I get there. Don't worry, OK?"

"OK, little brother. You have a safe trip. Wave good-bye, Gregory Thomas."

The little boy wasn't quite sure what was going on, only that his Uncle Tommy was going to a place called Alaska. He waved to his uncle as Tommy started his truck.

"See ya, Gregory Thomas. See ya, everybody. Alaska here we come."

And with that Tommy put the truck into gear and began driving away. Looking in his side-view mirror he could see everyone waving good-bye. He honked his horn, stuck his arm out the window and waved back. He looked beyond the people standing there and got one more look at the house he had grown up in. Tommy turned his head and looked toward the passenger side-view mirror and stomped on the brakes, throwing Ben down onto the floor. He had thought for a split second he had seen his parents in the mirror waving good-bye. It startled him. Carolyn, Kathy and Paul wondered why he made the sudden stop. Did he change his mind? Did he forget something? The mixed emotions came back for Tommy, if only momentarily, as he stepped on

More Healing

the gas again. The excitement of another adventure was taking over. Ben jumped back up on the front seat and rested his head on Tommy's lap. His master gave him a pat.

"Sorry, Ben. I didn't mean to throw you for a loop. Let's try this again. You know I did this once before with a dog named Timex ... ."

Tommy stopped the truck again to think about that event. To this day it tore at his heart not knowing what had happened to that wonderful dog he had brought home from Vietnam and then deserted in those drug-filled days in Los Angeles. He knew he had let Timex down and made a vow he would never go down that road again. He still felt the pain of losing that dog and knew it would never go away. He continued to pat Ben on top of the head and stepped on the gas once more. As the truck got to the end of the driveway, it stopped yet again.

"So, Ben. The last time I did this, I turned left to head south and then west. This time though, we're going to turn right and head north. Are you ready for this?"

Ben stood up on the front seat and poked his head out the passenger window.

Yeah, I'm ready for this, Dad. I'm with you. Where you go, I go. And if you say we're going to someplace called Alaska, then that's fine with me as long as we're together. Are we there yet?

New Life in Alaska

Hope. Sometimes it's all some people need so that they can carry on with their lives. Just a little hope. Give a person some hope that things will get better one day and, if they have the fortitude to take matters into their own hands, they will see the light and move forward. But it begins with hope. Anyone can give themselves hope if they understand that, no matter what, life is worth living.

Tommy was feeling all this. Life was indeed worth living and he had made his decision to forget the past and move on. He understood this thing called hope. He had sought out help to get his life back on track because sometimes it was a team effort, with advice and compassion coming from professionals, family and friends.

Tommy hung onto this new-found hope. This adventure he was embarking on was a calling, a calling to prove to himself and to the world that whenever you chose to follow your dreams, you are choosing to believe in hope and your future.

Not long before he had no hope. No purpose and no will to live. He still struggled with the demons from his past, especially the ones from the war. The nightmares reminded him that he was not quite there yet and possibly never would be. But, there had been a turning point in his life that affected him as much as his experiences in war that still haunted him. It was when he found out his parents had been killed in a car accident and he was unable to attend their funeral because he was in prison. He had never felt as much pain as when he heard the news. It was that day when Kathy and Carolyn had come and told him what had happened that he knew instantly his life had hit a crossroads. It was live or die, both emotionally and physically. He chose to live and the choice he made that day was what gave him hope. He chose to live because that's what his parents were telling him to do. He heard their voices in his dreams. "There is always hope."

He heard his parents talking to him. "Tommy chose life. You were and still are such a good son and a good person. Please, Tommy. What happened was God's decision. We're OK, Tommy. Your parents are fine. You are such a wonderful person. Every day is a gift, Tommy. Enjoy it to the fullest."

Not a day went by that Tommy didn't hear his dad or mom's voice. In his

New Life in Alaska

mind they were always giving him advice and encouragement. His daily decisions were based on whether or not his parents would approve of what he was doing and he felt in his heart they would encourage him to leave where he grew up and start a new life somewhere else. Start over somewhere fresh, determined to succeed. He could hear his dad with his genuine enthusiasm saying, "Go chase you dreams, son. Now is the time to do it while you're still young. You go get 'em."

Tommy had also convinced himself that if his mother were here to say good-bye, she would be in tears, of course, but no less enthusiastic. Kids do grow up and sometimes they stay close to home and sometimes they move on. His mother would be understanding of that. Going to Alaska was going to be completely different from when he went to California. He would have told that to his mother if she was here and she would have believed him. She would have seen a different Tommy than the one that went out west. His mother would have seen a lot more confidence in her son now. He had been down the road to hell and back and she would know, as a mother, that it was a place he would never choose to return to. Even as a child, Tommy had the spirit of adventure in him. He always wanted to see what was around the next bend or over the next hill and he would usually have a dog in tow. His parents would be proud of him as he headed off to chase his dreams with his friend Ben. He felt it. He knew it.

Tommy sat in his truck where the driveway intersected with County Road Twenty, looked left, it was all clear, and turned right heading north. He was turning the page once again on another chapter in his life to begin a new one. Tommy looked over at Ben who had his head stuck out of the window and ears flopping in the wind. Tommy noticed Ben had one leg on the arm rest so he pull ed over to the side of the road and rolled the passenger window part way up.

"Sorry, boy. Can't have ya jumping out the window before we even get out of Michigan. At least wait till we're in Wisconsin, OK?" Tommy pulled back onto the two-lane highway. "OK. Alaska here we come. Got that, Ben? We're on a mission."

Sure. Whatever you say, Dad. Are we there yet?

TEN DAYS LATER Tommy and Ben landed in Haley's Crossroads, Alaska to start a new era in their lives. Just as he had been promised, Tommy was hired by Frank Perkins to learn the art of building log homes. They had never met, but they had a lot in common. Both were driven to succeed in something they loved doing: working with wood and logs. Frank had been in Alaska for almost twenty years, also having come north when he got out of prison. It was one of several reasons that he hired Tommy. Frank knew how hard it was for ex-cons to find work. Frank was also a military vet just like his new employee, but had managed to miss both the Korean and Vietnam wars. He had dabbled in drugs, but not to the degree Tommy had. And just like this young man from Michigan, Frank, who hailed from Montana, came north to pursue his dreams; over time with some good luck and hard work, he had fulfilled them.

First and foremost, Frank's dream was to build log homes and have his own successful business. Check and done. He had worked diligently and put in long days for years to establish his thriving business. Frank built beautiful log homes all over the state and would travel anywhere to build them. He built commercial buildings as well: restaurants, tourist info centers and remote fishing and hunting lodges. His excellent reputation was statewide and he could always use a talented hand like Tommy Franklin to further the cause.

Originally, Tommy had seen an ad Frank had put in a log home magazine and, while he was incarcerated, wrote him a letter. Frank was sympathetic and took the time to answer. He encouraged Tommy to come to Alaska and give it a go when he got out of prison. That started Tommy feeling hopeful once again and didn't hesitate to let him know that in time, he would love to take him up on his offer. They spoke a few times over the phone after Tommy's release and Frank liked what he heard from the young man.

When Tommy arrived in Haley's Crossroads and made his way to one of Frank's job sites, they met for the first time and hit it off immediately. It had been arranged for Tommy and Ben to live in Frank's guesthouse and share Frank's property with his wife and three kids. The way everything fell into place restored Tommy's faith in the human spirit. He couldn't believe how accepting and generous the Perkins family was. They even had a dog named Max that became good friends with Ben. Life was good and remained that way for the two years Tommy lived in Frank's house. He was made to feel like one of the family. He couldn't have landed in better hands.

Someone must be watching over me.

They were. Tommy never stopped learning from Frank, whether it was about business or helping others. He learned the value of public relations and caring for those less fortunate. Tommy got to know the local townspeople with just about everyone seeming to know Frank as a friend or having done business with him in the past. Frank knew everybody. It was good for business and good for the soul. Despite working hard for the company he owned and ran, Frank always found time to do favors for people and volunteer work in the community. His whole family did. He was a good role model for Tommy at this point in his life. Hanging out with Frank and his family was good for Tommy's self-esteem and confidence. He took it all in and decided that, when the time came to venture out on his own, he would do his best to model himself after Frank Perkins.

"Pay it forward," Frank once said when Tommy was thanking him for everything he had done to help turn Tommy's life around. "Pay it forward." Tommy took those words to heart.

What would possess a man like Frank Perkins to take a stranger, an ex-con and someone with Tommy's troubled past, into his home and treat him like family right from day one? That in itself was a life lesson. But being a veteran and ex-con was like belonging to a fraternity. Tommy was open and honest with Frank right from the beginning.

Frank was everything that Tommy was hoping to be and Alaska was the place to become that. Everyone seemed to have a story to tell in this new frontier. Everyone had a past. Many Alaskan residents hadn't fit in when they tried to live in the lower forty eight and so they had come north to get away, to start over. Alaska seemed like a magnet for those people. People that were considered outcasts in other places came to this North Country to join their own kind. If they were a little different, they were also kindhearted and enjoyed the company of "their own kind." The ex-cons, the ex-drug addicts, the war veterans. Male and female. They saw themselves as one big, happy family who looked out for each other. They were in Alaska to be each other's guardian angels and give each other hope. They paid it forward.

Tommy felt that. The two years Tommy spent in Haley's Crossroads with Frank Perkins and his family were two of the best years of his life. He got to know a lot of people. Even started dating again and enjoyed it. It was something he hadn't done in a while. It was a perfect world except for the fact he had a hard time getting Carolyn out of his mind. That wouldn't change. He was feeling so good about himself and doing so well, he wanted to share it with somebody like his old girlfriend that he had left behind. He thought of Kathy and her family and how they were so happy for him. But, as for Carolyn, they wrote back and forth regularly and talked on the phone every couple of months or so. Carolyn also kept that promise to herself to go back to university and pursue her master's degree. She felt the same about her life as Tommy did his. She was doing her thing and wanted to share it with someone who was far away. She was thrilled that Tommy was doing well and pursuing his dreams. But the fact that they missed each other didn't change. Carolyn always said how she would come up for a visit, but then something would happen, usually school related, that changed her plans.

"I'll be up one day. I promised I would when you left and I will someday."

Tommy in turn would say how he would come down for a visit, but it was the same with him ... always busy. There was always some excuse. He desperately wanted to see Carolyn, Kathy, Paul and Gregory Thomas and other old friends back in Brenton that meant the world to him. "I'll be back one day soon. Just kind of busy right now." So it went for the two years Tommy stayed at the Perkins' house before Tommy finally decided to go out on his own and start up his own log home building business. If he was busy before, Tommy was about to learn what it was like to start up a business and what the word "busy" really meant.

HIS GOOD FRIEND and boss couldn't have been more helpful or encouraging.

"I've got more than I can handle," Frank told him. "I'll send you the odd contract every now and then to help you along."

That was Frank, always helpful, kind, and caring. And when Tommy informed Frank of his intentions to move to a place called Eagles Junction, Frank told him that would be an excellent place to start up.

"It's a growing little community and nobody's doing that sort of thing there."

Tommy landed on his feet when he walked into Frank's world. He was in a very special place. He knew it. Now there was going to be a new test for him. Another new adventure. He was ready. For everything Tommy had been through, he had never felt better about his future. He felt ready to start up his own business and Frank told him that he was ready. He could hear his parents tell him he was ready. And he was fairly certain that he heard a guardian angel tell him over and over that he was ready. Tommy would remain eternally grateful to Frank and his family for their hospitality and forever in debt to Frank for his generosity and for the advice he gave a young man starting over. But it was time once again to move on. The dream was now within reach. So close.

"Are you ready for another adventure, Ben?"

Sure. Where to this time? Are we there yet?

BEN WAS FULL grown, four years old and enjoying life more than ever. All he cared about was that he was with his dad full time. Tommy loved being with

Ben, of course, and Ben had always thought that was pretty cool. Like with his other dogs, Tommy and Ben went to work together, slept together and had their meals together; they did everything together. Once in a while a female human would enter Tommy's life and the routine changed a little bit, but the females didn't know who they were up against and Ben always won out in the end. Tommy's female friends had always liked Ben and Ben loved the attention he got from them, but as soon as he thought the females were getting more attention than he was, he would take action. So far he had outlasted all of Tommy's romantic interests. The female friends came and went, but Ben was always there for Tommy. Things eventually would get back to normal and then it was just the two of them again. Ben would just wait things out. He knew he was number one in Tommy's life and no female friend could ever take his place. Except maybe for one.

It was that female friend named Carolyn that he and Tommy talked about a lot. Ben got to recognize her name because of all the discussions they'd had in the past about her. Carolyn this, Carolyn that. All he had was a vague recollection of this Carolyn person when he had met her as a puppy. She seemed nice enough back then. But that was a long time ago and he could barely remember what she looked like. Tommy seemed to bring her name up all the time and he'd discuss her at meals, on the job or riding in Tommy's truck.

"She'll come up here for a visit one day, Ben. It's been a while. Maybe we'll have to go down south and visit her. Who knows? You'll recognize her when you see her. I know it's been a long time since the three of us have been together, but hopefully that will all change one day and one day soon."

Whatever, Dad. Whatever makes you happy. I can barely remember her. But if she makes you happy, then that's all that matters. We could be a happy threesome. That wouldn't be a problem. She sounds very special whenever you talk about her.

TRUE LOVE CAN always stand the test of time. The road that Tommy and Carolyn's relationship had taken over the years was a bumpy one to say the least. They had needed to pursue their dreams of either getting an education or setting off on some new adventure. The "true love" thing would have never worked in the early seventies for these two because Tommy was immature and unsettled and frankly, as Carolyn would have put it, messed up. She loved Tommy on every level, but she had her own future to consider and she was serious about her education. They had drifted apart, but that was no fault of hers. As strong as her feelings were for him, she knew she had her life to live, but had hoped that one day he would be her life partner. He thought that he wanted to be part of her life, but kept being pulled away by some inner need.

Carolyn couldn't have predicted what was going to happen to Tommy when he left for California and she didn't want to even try and predict what was going to happen to him when he moved to the Last Frontier. But she knew one thing about Tommy; he had grown up. He needed to prove something to himself and she wished him nothing but the best. They both had something in common in regards to their futures. She wanted that master's degree and she went and got it. She wanted a good job and to stay in Michigan to work in her field and got both her wishes. She had her social life and dated men she enjoyed being with. Life was just how she planned it except for the Tommy factor. He was missing in her life and she was hoping, as the years passed, that he would come to realize she was missing in his.

They stayed in touch frequently the first couple of years after Tommy's move and that was the hope they both needed. She couldn't believe how well he was doing and vice versa. She sounded happy whenever they spoke on the phone and he felt the same way about what he was doing. The conversations were casual and friendly. But it had been going on four years now since they had seen each other and four years was a long time, a very long time for a relationship to stay in limbo.

Were they eventually going to go their separate ways altogether? It was beginning to appear that way. They would get married to someone they would meet one day and raise their own families and simply remain good friends their whole lives. What really though, was keeping them apart? Selfishness? Stubbornness? It was hard to say. Kathy, Paul and Gregory Thomas had managed a couple of trips up to Alaska to visit Tommy after he started up his business and they were quite impressed with how well he was doing. Why couldn't or why wouldn't Carolyn come? Or, for that matter, why couldn't Tommy come back to Michigan and pay a visit to Carolyn? Four years? That's not four weeks or four months.

They were living their lives to the fullest, but separately. They were having a great time living out their dreams, but separately. The strange part was that they seemed quite content living their lives … separately. But one thing they weren't doing was living a lie. They still had strong feelings for each other. Somewhere in their subconscious, somewhere in their heart, was a sense that this love they shared was special and they weren't meant to be apart forever.

New Life in Alaska

ONE OF THEM, the Practical One, decided that enough was enough and they weren't going to prove anything by living apart any longer. Both parties had passed the "separation" test and one decided to "take the bull by the horns" to see if their feelings were the same after so long. Hers hadn't changed and if his hadn't, then one of them had to take charge. They could live apart the rest of their lives and could possibly be quite happy, but wouldn't they be happier if they lived together? It had gotten to a point where someone was going to have to do something. The Practical One would. She would make a move and get some answers to some obvious questions.

Were we nuts for living apart for so long? Are we going to let this life pass us by without giving it one more go?

So it was that this Practical One decided she needed to get in her vehicle and take a road trip to a small town in Alaska. It was a little bit crazy she admitted, but enough of the letter writing and phone conversations. They didn't and couldn't fill the void she had felt these past few years. She didn't need to hear how his love life was going and he didn't need to hear how hers was. Who was fooling whom? The Practical One was amazed that neither one had gotten married and already started to raise a family of their own.

Why are we doing this to ourselves? Four years?

If it was meant to be, she would find out once and for all, in person, face to face. So maybe she wasn't the Practical One all the time and with that thought in mind, Carolyn Russell had also decided not to tell Tommy Franklin she was coming north for a visit. She would just show up and couldn't wait to see his reaction. That would teach him a lesson. He should have taken the initiative long ago to come and visit her, but he was lost in his world of building log homes and enjoying success. She'd surprise him and surprise him good. She even surprised herself, this Practical One. And, as she loaded up her car and prepared for her long journey north, she told herself, "Enough of being practical."

Love in the Wilderness

TOMMY AND ONE of his four employees lifted a small log and put it in place where a picture window was going to be. The boss took a couple of steps back to have a better look.

"I think that might work, Larry. Good job."

Larry sauntered over to where Tommy was standing and agreed with the boss man.

"Yep, you're right. I did a pretty good job," Larry bragged.

Tommy chuckled and slapped Larry on the back.

"Well, let's go and see if you can do two in a row."

As Ben lay on his side with one eye open watching the pair, he lifted his head as he heard a vehicle coming up the dirt road leading to the work site. Tommy noticed the car driving up, but paid it no mind. The odd car drove past every now and then all day long. Not many, but some.

Tommy took his tape measure out of his work pouch and was starting to measure another shaved log when Larry interrupted his thinking.

"Looks like we have company!"

The boss took a quick glance, saw that the driver was a female and then got back to his measuring. Must be a friend of either Don or Roger's, his two other employees working on the inside of the house doing the interior walls. Tommy bent over to view the reading on his tape measure when he heard a car door slam and a female's voice say, "Hey, you look like you could be Ben. How ya doing, buddy? Long time, no see."

Tommy stood up straight and couldn't believe his eyes.

Larry looked at his boss and said, "Must be a friend of Ben's ... ."

"Hey, Tommy!" the woman said, waving to a stunned log home builder. "Remember when you said, 'Don't bother calling?'"

" ... or a friend of yours," Larry said, noticing the look of shock on Tommy's face.

Tommy unstrapped his tool belt and let it drop to the ground. Smiling ear to ear, he looked at Larry.

"Yeah ... she's a friend of mine all right."

Tommy's heart was pounding as he quickly marched in the visitor's direction. Carolyn put a brown paper bag that she had in her hand down on the hood of the car. She roughed up Ben and got him to think they were going to have a fun game of wrestling. Tommy said nothing as he walked up to Carolyn and gave her a long hug. That was what she wanted. It was all she needed and most of the questions she had about seeing her friend again were answered in one big, long hug. It made the hard traveling of the last week and a half all worthwhile. All she needed was a hug from Tommy and all he needed was one from her. It was a simple act that made the world feel better. It had been a while since either of them had felt the way they were feeling now. She stepped back from Tommy's hug, grabbed the brown paper bag and handed it to him.

"Here. I meant to give you this when you left Brenton. It's lunch."

Tommy laughed and still couldn't believe his eyes. He gave Carolyn another hug, then opened the brown paper bag and peered inside.

"Boy. You haven't forgotten what I like in my lunches have you?"

Carolyn kept quiet and smiled at him. Ben was still in the wrestling mood and tried to get Carolyn's attention by maneuvering a rear attack through her legs.

"Hey, you," she said, almost falling over him.

"Ben, calm down. Go on!" Ben's master gave his orders and pointed in a direction far away. Larry, Don and Roger took in this curious sight and decided it was close enough to noon to take a lunch break. They sat on one of their logs and watched the action.

"I have a feeling the boss isn't going to get much more work done today," Larry stated.

"Can't say that I blame him," Roger responded.

"How the heck did you find me?" an ecstatic Tommy asked as he took Carolyn's hand and began leading her to where his employees sat.

"Just started asking around town where I might find a dog named Ben. This Eagles Junction seems to be a lot like Brenton. Everybody knows everybody and it didn't take long for a guy in a gas station to tell me right where to go."

Carolyn made Tommy laugh.

She continued. "I'm just so glad you're here with Ben. This is a bonus. I was hoping it wasn't going to be just Ben all by himself."

Tommy squeezed her hand.

"I am so glad to see you."

They reached where the guys were eating their lunch and Tommy did the introductions. He and Carolyn sat with the employees and began to share the food that was in the paper bag. The "boys" were impressed with Carolyn and happy for their boss. Ben got his usual lunchtime handouts and all was well. There was joy in Tommy's heart and joy in Carolyn's. They shared old stories, making Tommy's crew laugh as they listened. Carolyn fit right in and everyone felt comfortable being around her. They laughed at her story about driving up to Alaska and the funny things that happened on the way.

After lunch, Tommy gave her a tour of the house they were building for a client in town and confirmed Larry's hunch when he informed the crew that he'd be taking the rest of the day off. Tommy had another log home he wanted to show his friend. One that he had built for himself and had moved in to just a couple of months before. Carolyn had been aware of that through the conversations they had on the phone and the letters he wrote. Tommy, with perhaps ulterior motives, had pleaded with her to come up and see it.

"It's big enough for two and you've got a place to stay," he had assured her more than once. "It's really Ben's house, but he said it's OK for me to have friends over."

In the first few minutes of them seeing each other for the first time in four years, the past lovers picked up right where they had left off. It made Carolyn feel good to say the least. She had decided before leaving Michigan she was going to handle whatever Tommy's reaction would be when he saw her again, but she never would have made the trip if there hadn't been ... hope. Hope for the possibility that they could get back together. It didn't take long for her to realize she had made the right choice about traveling thousands of miles to get here and Tommy meant every word when he kept saying how great it was to see her again.

"I can't believe you're here. I just can't believe you're here," he kept repeating.

She couldn't believe she was here either. What happened to being practical? She had traveled all this way on a whim ... by herself. She was as thrilled as was he. Now there was only one lingering question that had to be answered; why had they stayed apart for so long? As Carolyn reached her car to follow Tommy to the other side of town and head for his new home, Tommy made a suggestion.

"How about if Ben rides with you? Just in case we lose each other, Ben knows the way."

"Sure. Sounds good. In ya go, Ben."

Ben didn't hesitate as Carolyn opened the driver's door and in he jumped. Tommy stood with Carolyn and couldn't resist giving her one more hug.

He looked at her and asked "Are you sure you're not lost?"

She was lost. Lost in love, but wouldn't say it. She'd wait and see how things played out over the next few days.

"I don't think I'm lost. I think I did a pretty good job of finding you. Don't you think?"

Tommy smiled and felt like it all must be a dream.

"Yeah, you did." He pointed to his truck. The same truck he had when he left Michigan. "Just follow that truck right there young lady. I have something I want to show you."

"OK then, let's go," Carolyn said as she got in her car and Tommy went to his truck and drove off. She looked over at the canine passenger sitting next to her. "OK, Ben. Let's follow that truck and see where it takes us and I do hope you know the way in case we lose him. You know the way right?"

Right.

The way Ben told her to go took Carolyn to one of the most beautiful log homes she had ever seen. It wasn't a mansion, but two stories and, from the outside, tastefully done with, of course, a wraparound veranda. It was at the end of a long dirt road on the north side of Eagles Junction and definitely in the bush, without another house to be found within miles. It rested right where the power lines ended. The road itself had only recently been given a name, Crescent Trail, and the sign had been put up just two weeks previously.

Carolyn sat in her car and looked at the home Tommy had built. Not only was the home beautiful, the setting was as well. Obviously, some land had been cleared to build the house that faced south and the snowcapped mountains in the near distance made it all seem like a picture postcard. As she and Ben sat in front of the log home whose yard still needed some landscaping, only one thought crossed her mind; Tommy Franklin was alive and well and had come a long way. She couldn't have been happier for him. She and Ben got out of the car and she stood and marveled at the place he had built. Tommy had tried to explain it to her on the phone when he was building it, but words somehow didn't do it justice. The owner of the house got out of his truck and saw Carolyn admiring the structure he was so proud of.

"Well, whatta ya think?"

Lost for words, she shook her head.

"Wait until you see the inside," Tommy said, taking her by the hand.

Ben was already up on the veranda. He turned around and barked. He knew that Tommy's female friends had always given him a lot of attention—Ben that is—and this one appeared no different. Suddenly, in a way only dogs can, he recalled her smell. That triggered something.

Yeah, I remember her from another place long ago and far away. I was a puppy. She was so friendly. I liked her then and I think I'm going to like her now. She has nice smells, sort of like she needs a shower.

Well then, if she smelled like she needed a shower, to a dog, that was a good thing. Ben was excited to have her here and, being the people person he was, the more the merrier.

Tommy, Carolyn and Ben entered the front door and stood in the foyer where Carolyn saw an open floor plan that showed the interior flowing from living room to kitchen. She looked at him and shook her head once again.

"You've done well for yourself, Mr. Franklin."

Tommy was full of pride and this lady next to him was bringing it all out.

"I designed it myself. I think I told you that."

"Good job," Carolyn said as she walked into the living room area and gazed up at the high, vaulted ceiling. "Good job," she repeated. "I like the high ceilings."

"Thanks. It's just the living room area and dining room where the ceilings are high. Come on. I'll give you a tour."

Ben was all for that and bounded up the stairs that led to the second level. He'd been tricked again as Tommy decided to show Carolyn the kitchen and the rest of the downstairs first. Ben decided to lie on the landing at the top of the stairs.

They'll come up here eventually. I've been through this before.

They did. Tommy gave Carolyn a complete tour and she was impressed with what he had accomplished. They ended up back in the living room where Tommy wanted to hear all about her trip to Alaska and she wanted to know more about Eagles Junction, Tommy's business and about his life in general. They sat, talked, laughed and caught up on the last four years, filling in blanks that weren't covered in letters and phone calls. It was a great way to spend the afternoon and before they realized, it was getting close to dinner time.

"How about if I make us some supper?" Tommy asked as he headed for the kitchen.

"And breakfast in the morning?" Carolyn replied with her own question as she followed him and mimicked his steps.

Tommy stopped and turned around. He took her into his arms and planted a kiss on her forehead.

"Yeah, and breakfast in the morning."

"Isn't that where we left off?"

It was where they had left off and it was right where they picked up again to carry on with what was a very special and unique relationship. Sometimes a love is just meant to be. Peaks, valleys, bumps in the road, trials, tribulations, being apart, being together, distance, more time apart, going separate ways, new adventures, pursuing dreams, traveling down different roads, different paths. True love survives all this and it was evident right here, right now in a log home in Eagles Junction, Alaska.

TOMMY STARTED OPENING drawers and cupboards and acted like he had a plan.

"Yep. This is where we left off all right," he said, answering her question. *This is where we left off and this is where we're going to start over.*

With all the discussion that had been going on that afternoon and with so many questions being asked and answered and catching up on everything else in their lives, there was one question, in all the excitement, that Tommy hadn't gotten around to asking.

"How long can you stay for, Carolyn?"

He couldn't believe he hadn't asked the question earlier in the day. He was hoping the answer would be forever as he waited for her response.

She was busy cutting a tomato.

"As long as Ben will let me stay. I took a leave of absence from work so there's no rush to get back. I don't want to impose. As far as I'm concerned, I'm on an extended vacation"

Tommy liked what he was hearing as he put a pot of water on the stove to boil so he could steam some vegetables.

"Don't even think for a second that you'll be imposing and Ben, trust me, won't care how long you stay, but I do, the longer the better. You gotta stay long enough for me to show you some of the sights around here and trust me, there's a lot to see."

"I'd like that," Carolyn said quite honestly. "But you're busy with work and … ."

"… and I don't want to hear any more about it," Tommy said, interrupting her. He wanted her to understand how much it meant to him for her to be in his house, his part of the world. "I can use a break. You'll stay as long as you want and you'll make yourself feel right at home. That's an order."

"OK, boss," Carolyn said, not meaning to ruffle his feathers.

Tommy continued his way around the kitchen beginning to prepare a meal. As he was about to open up a cabinet drawer he stopped and pondered for a moment. He looked at Ben lying between the kitchen and dining room. Tommy had something more to say and tried to think of a way to make it clear to the woman helping him in his kitchen. Carolyn looked over her shoulder and saw that Tommy was staring down at Ben. She said nothing and continued to chop more vegetables wondering what her friend might be thinking. Tommy gathered his thoughts, took a couple of steps over to Carolyn, leaned against the counter and looked her in the eyes.

"Carolyn … you can stay as long as you want. I'm … so happy you're here, truly amazed you made this trip all by yourself and I really want you to stay. My home is your home."

The tone of his voice told her she could read something into that last statement. She believed he wanted her to stay. Carolyn also couldn't believe what she had done by making the trip up here to see him. But she had had to do it. She looked out over into the dining room and into the living room area and hesitated before replying. Carolyn turned and faced Tommy square on.

"Well, we'll see. I didn't come up here to move in. I just wanted to see you so badly. You have a great life here and I don't want to interfere. Let's take it one day at a time," the Practical One said.

Tommy was thinking he had beat around the bush a little too much and wished he could just get it into her head how much he wished she would stay forever, but he didn't want to take a chance on making her feel uncomfortable by being more blunt. It had been four years after all. Maybe things had changed more than he was aware of.

"OK. One day at a time it is. Starting tomorrow, we'll do some sightseeing and I'll show you some of the log houses I've built in this neck of the woods. OK? How's that sound for starters?"

Carolyn turned her attention back to her chopping. The sightseeing part she could handle and whatever happened after that, it would be wait and see.

"That sounds absolutely wonderful. I'm looking forward to it."

Tommy went to the silverware drawer and took out some knives and forks.

"But I meant what I said when I said you can stay as long as you want and my home is your home."

He couldn't have been more sincere in those last words. They made her feel welcome and she'd known him long enough to know when he was being truthful. But, for now, one day at a time.

AS IT TURNED out, the two longtime friends and past lovers did pick up right where they had left off so long ago. The Practical One was pleased about her decision to take a road trip to Alaska. Carolyn, as a matter of fact, ended up staying for a very long time.

All the way back to the very beginning when Tommy first came to Carolyn's parents' house to get that first puppy named Buddy, there was fate. Two ten year olds sharing a moment so many years before had now reached this moment. Destiny. Now it was two adults sharing a life in the here and now. "My home is your home," were words that Carolyn had not expected to hear when she left Michigan to come north on such an innocent visit. "Stay as long as you want," was something she simply hadn't considered when she reached her destination. She had told herself she was going on a vacation, a road trip to visit an old friend. But, in this particular here and now, at this moment in time, everything felt right.

It felt so right that Carolyn decided to stay forever and did exactly what Tommy had asked her to do; she made herself feel right at home. His home became her home. She and Tommy renewed their love for each other and their love ran deeper than ever and felt like it never had before. Fate. Hope. Timing. All of the above. It naturally came together for their final act after all the years and different roads they had traveled apart. True love could and did stand the test of time. Tommy and Carolyn were proof positive of that. They were done living apart. The past was the past and their future, from the moment Carolyn arrived in the Last Frontier, was going to be shared.

Carolyn had achieved her goals in every way imaginable. She was educated, driven, successful and madly in love. Tommy had been to hell and back more than once, but had been back in the land of the living now for a long time. He too was driven, successful and madly in love. Life, they say, is full of twists and turns and no one had more twists and turns in their relationship than these two who never gave up on each other. Fate. Hope. Timing. Two lives merged into one because there were two people who couldn't live without each other's love. It was another beginning. And Ben, good ol' Ben, couldn't have been happier to be part of it.

"COULDN'T ASK FOR a more beautiful day," Tommy said as he shoved the canoe off the shore of Dustin Lake with Ben sitting in the middle and Carolyn at the far end. It was a lazy Sunday afternoon in the middle of summer and the threesome had decided to take a hike up to an old forest service cabin Tommy knew about. The forest service also provided a canoe for the public to use and Tommy and Ben had taken advantage of it many times in the past. It wasn't a big lake, but he and Ben figured it was time to show Carolyn one of their favorite spots. It was a spectacular setting surrounded by deep woods and several cascading waterfalls coming down off the snowcapped peaks and only a thirty-minute drive from home. It was the one-year anniversary of Carolyn's arrival in Alaska and Tommy thought it would be appropriate to take her somewhere special, somewhere she hadn't been before.

Things had gone well for his best friend since she arrived. Within a couple of months of landing in the Last Frontier, she got a job with the Alaska Environmental Agency and couldn't have been more pleased. It paid well and was in the field of her choosing. She was very high on her job and had had nothing but good fortune since her move north. Tommy was always busy with his business and, although Carolyn's job sometimes took her away from home for a few days, the two of them still felt exactly the way they had the day Carolyn showed up on Tommy's job site; they were still so much in love. Tommy jumped into the canoe as it started floating a few feet from shore and grabbed the paddle.

"Off we go," he said, settling down onto his seat.

"I can't believe you haven't brought me here before. It's just lovely. So peaceful," Carolyn said, always amazed at Alaska's incredible scenery.

Tommy began paddling toward the center of the small lake.

"I was waiting for a special occasion."

Carolyn sat facing her soul mate and held his .30-06 rifle that he always took with him whenever he and Ben were hiking in bear country.

"What's the special occasion?" she wondered innocently enough.

Tommy smiled and swung the paddle from one side to the other, every time having to lift it high enough so as not to hit Ben's head.

"You don't know?"

Carolyn put her index finger up to hers lips and thought about it for a moment.

"No. What is it?"

Tommy shook his head in mild amusement.

"It was one year ago today that you arrived in Alaska, silly."

Carolyn threw her shoulders back and perked up. She had totally forgotten about that.

"Oh, yeah," she looked off into the distance as the shoreline got further and further away. "Has it been a year? My goodness! That went by quickly!"

"Easy for you to say," Tommy jokingly replied, not able to help himself.

"Watch it buster or I'll tip us over. Just keep paddling. Is this as fast as you can go?"

Tommy laughed. With her quick wit, laughing was something she had him doing often. There had been a time in his life when there was no laughter at all. That had all changed. Now the laughter was back thanks to this special person sitting in the canoe with him and he was grateful that it was. Carolyn always had that aura about her that made everyone feel good about themselves and had that ability to make people laugh. It was one of many reasons people liked to be around her.

"Ben, you know if you moved back just a foot or two I wouldn't have to swing the paddle so high every time I switch sides," Tommy said to his dog.

Ben looked at his best friend Tommy and his expression echoed the words that Carolyn just said.

Just keep paddling, Dad. You're doing a good job.

When they reached the middle of the lake, Tommy put the paddle across the canoe in front of him and let the vessel drift. This was all part of Tommy's plan for the day and everything and everyone so far had been cooperating: the blue sky, the sun. His two friends in the canoe. He had been thinking for a while of having a serious talk with Carolyn and he wanted the timing and setting to be just right. Everything was going just as he had hoped.

Carolyn had been quiet for a minute, enjoying the serenity of all that surrounded her. It wasn't the first time she had been mesmerized by the scenery in this great North Country. They lived not far from the ocean and whether it was the rivers or the lakes or the ocean itself, the water was always near. She loved being around water and Tommy knew that. It was one of the reasons he chose to bring her here for what he was hoping would be a special moment.

"It sure is quiet and peaceful isn't it, dear?" Carolyn said, looking at the water streaming down off the mountains.

"Dear" was something they had taken to calling each other. That and "honey." It was fitting and had been a long time in coming. More and more in recent months they had taken to calling each other dear and honey instead of their proper names. It was becoming a habit and sounded natural.

"Yes it is, dear. Yes, it is," Tommy replied.

He had something to say, but decided to wait and joined Carolyn in relishing the solitude. She was deep in thought, almost meditating. There was not a whisper of a breeze and the lake was calm and flat. Perfect conditions for what Tommy was about to do. As time passed for another couple of minutes and both remained quiet, Carolyn spoke up and asked Tommy a question. She was looking up at the sky when the words came out.

"Do you believe in God?"

Tommy thought, "Damn! I should have spoken first!" He didn't really want to talk about theological issues. How many times over the years did he have this discussion with other people and friends and nothing was ever resolved. They always seemed to go nowhere. Everyone had an opinion and some people think you're condemned if you don't believe what they believe. Whether it was a debate or argument, Tommy never had time for it. Carolyn knew he was not religious and he knew she was not. So where did this question come from? He didn't recall ever discussing God with her in the past, but just because the question came from her, he relented with a simple, "Not really."

Carolyn looked at him and wondered to herself if that was a good enough answer. It didn't really matter to her. She was just curious what his thoughts were on the subject. She was not going to love him any differently based on what his views of God were. It was just that she didn't remember him ever saying anything about his spirituality. Where did he get it from?

He decided to put the ball back in her court.

"Do you?"

She thought for a moment.

"Good question, Tommy Franklin, but I asked you first."

She didn't have an answer to the question Tommy had tossed back at her. Like him, she had grown up in a Christian home, but those beliefs were long gone. As far as her own spirituality was concerned, she never zeroed in on anything in particular that captured her attention or gave her comfort.

"Well, I don't know," she continued. "Being a scientist, one part of me says it's possible that this all evolved and yet another part of me says that something or someone had to create it."

"Well dear, I'm with you and I think the key word there is 'possible.' Anything's possible, I guess. In fact, I go to the Church of Anything's Possible. But ... ," Tommy had to get his thoughts together for a moment before he started up again. "I don't believe in God. Doesn't work for me."

He said that for good reason. He had the same questions that a lot of people have asked over time about a so-called loving and caring God. What's with all the misery in the world if our creator is so loving and caring? Wars? Starvation? Diseases? Tommy had been to hell enough times in his life to have his doubts that such an insensitive deity could exist and in his opinion, all religions were just a fallacy. He wasn't thrilled with the timing of this "deep subject," but he'd entertain it for now, get it over with and move on to the next topic he wanted to talk about and the reason for the two of them being here in the middle of a lake surrounded by all the beauty.

Carolyn pursed her lips and looked at him questionably. "So ... you don't believe in God?"

He looked at her and smiled. His facial expression told her he would really like to lighten things up a bit.

"Naw. Don't believe in God. Don't believe in Santa Claus or the Easter Bunny. Or the Tooth Fairy. Although I did once believe in all four. Like I say, I belong to the Church of Anything's Possible. If there's a God, fine. If not, fine. You know the expression 'show me the money?'" Carolyn nodded. "Well," Tommy kept going, "someone should call God up and tell him, 'Get your butt down here and show your children that you really do exist.' Then he or she could go back to doing their business, but at least let the folks down here know there's some hope. That's all. Show us your face. Come on down and let's have a little chat. What's the problem with that, hey?"

Carolyn admired Tommy's argument and laugh lightheartedly.

"Hey, be careful what you say. I don't want to get struck by lightning sitting here in the middle of the lake. It's a long swim back to shore."

Tommy laughed, grabbed the paddle, slammed it on the water and splashed Carolyn.

"Hey," she said, putting her hands in front of her to deflect the water. "You're getting your rifle wet!"

Tommy thought it was kind of funny and began to paddle again.

"Mind if we change the subject?"

Carolyn was OK with that as she stuck her hand in the lake and flicked water in Tommy's direction.

"OK, you win. Calm down," she said.

Once again the two settled into a feeling of pensiveness. Ben thought the splashing going on looked like fun and watched the water pass by the canoe.

Carolyn broke the momentary silence.

"It's a good life isn't it, Mr. Franklin?"

He was quick to answer.

"That it is except … ."

He had been waiting for the right moment to say what he'd been wanting to say for weeks. He saw an opening. It was going to be a tough one for him and he wanted everything to be right.

"Except what?" Carolyn asked, dragging her hand in the water and not expecting any more serious subjects to be discussed for the rest of the day.

Tommy's head swayed back and forth.

"Except … ."

"Go ahead, Franklin, spit it out. Stop beating around the bush," Carolyn enticed him.

Tommy stalled and now he was not sure if the setting or timing was right. Yet … it was perfect.

"OK," Carolyn tried to keep the flow of the conversation going. "We've covered religion, what's next, politics?"

"No, no, no," Tommy said, shaking his head. "There's something I want to ask you."

She hadn't a clue where this was going and again flicked some water off the tips of her fingers in his direction.

"Well, then go ahead and ask."

She's right! I should just go ahead and ask. Stop beating around the bush like she said.

"OK, so Carolyn ... ."

"Yes, oh Godless one."

Tommy had a chuckle at the comment and relaxed slightly.

"Have you ever thought about starting a family?"

She looked at him a little perplexed, but appreciated the question. Yes, in fact, she had thought about the subject, but it was something she certainly didn't dwell on or had thought about anytime recently. She was enjoying her work, her career, and having children, she knew, would come when the timing was right and with the right man. The biological clock was ticking for her, but there was still lots of time and was Tommy the right man? Yes, he was the right man, she knew that for certain. She wondered how she was supposed to take the question. An honest answer would have to be the only answer.

"Sure, I've thought about it," Carolyn replied and she would like to take her chances of having kids with Tommy if he were interested in being a father. She was curious though, why he asked her? "I think most women my age do," she continued. "In fact most women my age already have kids." She studied his face and tried to read his mind. "Why do you ask?"

Tommy put the paddle down in front of him and let the canoe drift again. It was his turn to look out at the distant shore. He knew why he asked her, but didn't know what to say next.

"Carolyn ... ."

Stop beating around the bush. Spit it out. I can do this.

"... would you like to marry me? ... . Would you like to get married?"

She looked at him with a blank look. He was convinced now that he had blown it and the timing and setting wasn't right after all. Especially the timing. Suddenly Carolyn realized she had never felt this good in her life.

"So if I jumped up and ran over and gave you a big hug and kiss, chances are the canoe would tip over, right?"

Now there were two people who had never felt so good in their lives. Tommy's grin went from one side of the lake to the other.

"A simple 'yes' will do," he informed her.

"Well ... do I really want a Godless man fathering my children?" she kidded him.

He chuckled.

"If you say 'yes' I could find religion real quick." Tommy picked up the paddle again and put it in the water.

"You don't have to do that," she assured him. "And yes, Tommy Franklin.

I would love to marry you and have your children. Whatta ya say we get started?"

Tommy began to turn the canoe around and head back in the direction of the forest service cabin.

"OK, Carolyn Russell my dear, let's go get started."

AND START THEY did. Three months after Tommy's summer proposal they had an early fall outdoor wedding on their property. Kathy and her family were there along with Carolyn's parents and some old high school and university friends. Local friends from town along with Tommy's employees and their families all attended. It couldn't have been a more joyous occasion. Of course, Ben and some of his canine friends that were invited had a grand old time as well. It was another new beginning for two very happy people.

A baby girl was born to the Franklin's one year after the wedding that they named Sarah Rose. Carolyn decided to leave her job with the Alaska government and devote all her time to being a mother. As with everything, she was a natural at it. A year and a half after Sarah was born along came another baby girl that they named Jessica Anne. Ben loved having babies around. He thought they were cute and he became very protective of them. As the girls grew and learned to walk and run, Ben taught them how to play. At first Sarah and Jessica couldn't throw a ball or stick very far, but it didn't matter. Fun was fun and as they got bigger, both girls could throw the ball far enough that Ben would actually have to go chase it. Kids, Ben found out, were just as much fun as adults; it just took some time for them to learn all the games that he liked to play. He also went from sleeping on his parents' bed to sleeping in the girls' room. He would switch bedrooms back and forth on different nights so he could keep everyone happy.

Over the years Tommy's log home building business got bigger and bigger. No one would have seen this coming a few years back and in reality, it wasn't that long ago. A war vet, homeless and on the streets, addicted to drugs and hitting rock bottom and finally ending up in prison, who would have guessed he would be where he was today? Where he had been in the seventies was a dead end and, fortunately for Tommy, he found enough mental strength to see that it was a place he would never go back to. Now he was a successful contractor with a wonderful family.

The nightmares, the trauma of war and the things he had done long ago, still haunted him and he was resigned to the fact it would never change, no matter how long he lived. He was still trying to come to terms with that. But with a loving wife and two kids that were his world, he only looked to the future. The sixties and seventies were done. It was his family now that got him through the difficulty of living with those horrific memories that were beyond his control. The Franklins lived an idyllic life and worked hard for everything they had. Tommy and Carolyn were big on volunteering in the community and doing things as a family. Just as the Frank Perkins family had done. As the expression goes; it doesn't get any better than this.

Loss

EARLY ON A summer weekend, Tommy sat on a boulder a few yards behind his house and sang a song to Ben. Carolyn and the girls approached with Sarah and Jessica carrying fishing poles. The girls, now seven and five years old, and Ben almost twelve, were going on a day's outing with their dad to see if they could catch some fish.

"Dad, you're hurting his ears. Stop singing. He'll start howling," Sarah said as she walked up to her father and his good friend Ben.

"He likes my singing. I always sing to Ben, you know that. Besides, when dogs howl that's their way of telling you that they like your singing," Tommy explained to his oldest daughter.

"Well, you're hurting my ears, so don't sing."

Sarah wouldn't let it go and jumped up on the boulder next to her dad.

"What about you, Jessica? You've never had any complaints about my singing have you?" Tommy asked his other daughter.

"Just don't sing when we're fishing or you'll scare them all away," she warned her dad.

"Gees. Man, oh man. You'd think I had a bad voice or something. Mom likes my singing. Right, Mom?"

Carolyn sat down on the other side of Tommy.

"I've always enjoyed your father's singing. He knows so many different songs. But the girls are right, Dad. Maybe don't sing when you're trying to catch a fish. I want you guys to bring home dinner tonight."

Tommy stood up and Ben, who was sitting behind him, jumped down.

"So exactly where are you going again?" Carolyn inquired.

Tommy grabbed his rifle and a day pack off the boulder.

"Over to Johnson Creek. We're going to take the upper meadow across till it ends and then through the woods and down to the creek. I've taken you there before," Tommy informed Carolyn.

It was one of the little discoveries she and Tommy had made on one of the exploratory hikes they often did. It was a pretty spot, but it seemed a little too far for the girls and Ben, and Carolyn expressed her concern.

"It's only about an hour's walk," Tommy explained, knowing full well his wife knew how long it took to get there. "... and we'll stop and have some lunch and take it slow for ol' Ben here. We'll be fine."

Carolyn knew her husband always used good judgment and the girls were excited to be going on their little adventure.

"Just make sure you bring back some fish," Mom said as the four headed out.

"You'll probably be looking at some nice rainbow trout in the skillet come dinner time, Mom," Tommy said confidently. "See ya when we get back. Give your mother a hug, girls."

Sarah and Jessica hugged their mom and said good-bye. Ben, not as young as he used to be, but still feeling chipper, took the lead and was the first one down the trail that led away from the Franklin home. Carolyn stood with her hands on her waist and watched and waved as her family walked out of the clearing and into the woods. She knew they'd have a great time. Dad would make sure of that. It pleased her when Tommy took the girls out and when it was just them and their dad. He loved being with his kids and they loved being with him. She couldn't have asked for a more loving father for her children. In fact, there was nothing more she could ask for out of life. It was a fairy tale. Divine ... and she'd have the whole day to herself.

How sweet it is!

"HOW'S THIS SPOT look, girls?" Tommy asked his daughters as they walked down a slight incline to Johnson Creek.

"This will be fine, Dad, as long as there's fish here," Sarah said, making her way to the water's edge.

"All you have to do is catch 'em." Dad assured his daughters that it shouldn't be a problem.

The place they had chosen was on a long, flat straightaway where they could see for quite a distance up and down the stream. Tommy wanted it that way. It was bear country and he wanted to be able to see a fair distance in both directions. There was a gravel beach the girls could stand on where the water was deep enough to fish in and the creek, at this spot, wasn't moving very fast. A perfect place for fish and a perfect fishing hole for two young girls to cast their rods.

Tommy got the girls' fishing poles ready as Ben, always willing to help even at his ripe old age, kept his nose right in the middle of things. The poles were "kids" poles and not so big that the girls couldn't handle them. Dad refreshed his daughters' memories on the art of casting and reeling in the "big one."

"OK. You two have at it. I'm going to go sit up on the rock right here," Tommy said as he walked a few feet over to a huge boulder about twenty feet away.

"Any prizes for who catches the first fish, Dad?" Jessica asked as she made her first cast.

"Five hundred million dollars," her father answered as he reached the top of the big rock jutting out into the creek giving him a good view in all directions as well as allowing him to keep an eye on his daughters. He had a seat and was feeling blessed.

"Wow! That's a lot of money!" Sarah yelled back, still playing with her rod.

"Yeah, well, better hurry up and get that line in the water there, Sarah. Time's a wasting," Tommy told his oldest daughter.

Sarah made a cast as her proud father looked on. He knew in his heart if they caught any fish it would be a bonus. This day was about spending time with his daughters. He never got tired of it. Ben leaned against his dad and enjoyed the view from their lookout. Tommy put his arm around Ben and patted his chest.

"We're pretty darn lucky aren't we, Ben?"

Before his dad could defend himself, Ben gave him a lick in the face. Just like in the good old days when he was a puppy, he still had the fastest tongue in the north.

Yes, Dad. We're pretty lucky!

Twelve years the two had been together. Longer than either of Tommy's two previous dogs. They had put on a lot of miles as a duo and done a lot of things as an inseparable pair. Where Tommy went, Ben went. When the family did things together, Ben was always included. Even on trips over the years when they went back to Michigan to visit Kathy and her family and Carolyn's parents, Ben came along. He had his crate that went on a plane and the next thing Ben knew he was running on one of Lake Michigan's beautiful beaches that his dad used to run on as a child and teenager. The thought of leaving Ben behind was something the Franklins would never consider. He was their canine child and Tommy and Carolyn wouldn't leave any of their children behind when they went away. Why would they leave Ben? There were five of them in the family and they were all one. It made Ben feel special and that's because he was.

The sun felt good as Tommy read a book he had brought with him in his day pack. Ben lay by his side, half asleep, thinking the same thing, that the sun sure felt good. The two girls had been walking up the creek for as far as their dad would let them, hoping to hook the five hundred million dollar fish. Everything about the day was perfect, especially for Tommy. It was being lazy and being with his daughters that made it all good. After about forty-five minutes of the dad reading a good book and his daughters fishing away, a voice shouted out.

"Dad! I think I caught something!"

It was Sarah.

Tommy jumped up and looked down, as did Ben. From his vantage point and through the clear water of the creek, he saw that, sure enough, Sarah had a fish on.

"Hold on to it, Sarah. I'm coming. Hold on to it!"

Tommy hurried to the back of the giant rock where he had climbed up and scrambled back down. He ran over to Sarah and, without taking the pole from her, helped her reel in her big money fish.

"Whoa! That's a beauty, Sarah. Can you see that, Jessica," Tommy asked his younger daughter as they continued to bring the fish in.

"You have to share the money with me, Sarah," Jessica declared.

Dad helped his daughter hold her pole high enough to lift the fish out of the water, then Tommy grabbed it and took the hook out.

"That's got to be about fourteen inches. Good catch, Sarah."

Ben got his sniffs in.

"You have to share the money with me," Jessica reminded her older sister once again.

"Do I, Dad?" Sarah asked her father.

"Yes, of course you do. Jess, keep your line in the water. There has to be more where this one came from."

Jessica made another cast, but kept her attention focused on her dad and older sister. Tommy hit the fish over the head with his fillet knife that he had strapped to his side, killing it, and then began to clean it on the bank.

"OK, girls. Fifteen more minutes and then we have to go. See if you can catch another one," Tommy said, laying the cleaned fish on a damp rock by the water's edge.

"Dad. We just got here," Jessica protested.

"We didn't just get here, Jessica," Dad explained. "We have to get the fish back to mom before it goes bad. Keep fishin'."

No sooner did Jessica mumble another complaint than she let out a yelp.

"Dad!"

Tommy, still standing on the gravel beach looked at the bend in his youngest daughter's pole and it told him that she had caught a fish as well. He hurried over to Jessica and helped her bring the fish in.

"Whoa, man! They sure grow them big here," Dad said, noticing that the trout Jessica had caught was about the same size as Sarah's. Tommy repeated the actions he had just done with Sarah's fish and cleaned Jessica's.

"It's going to be good eating tonight, girls," he said, looking forward to dinner already.

"Can we keep fishing for a few more minutes, Dad. Please," Sarah tried to reason with her father that there might be more fish to catch.

"Yeah, go ahead. We'll give it a few more minutes and then we have to go"

"Yippee!" the girls shouted in unison.

"I'm going back up on the rock, girls. Come on, Ben."

Tommy and his sidekick climbed back up on the boulder where Tommy had a seat and looked around. He saw something upstream that caught his attention. He had a good view of it, roughly two hundred yards away; it was a bear in the creek acting like it was searching for a meal. Tommy grabbed a pair of binoculars out of his day pack and had a better look. He kept quiet, not wanting to alarm the girls. There was still some distance between the bear and them. It looked, however, like the bear was headed in their direction and it was a huge Brown Bear. He took the binoculars down from his eyes and looked down at his daughters fishing away. He knew they were going to have to make a move if the bear kept coming their way. For reassurance, he picked up his rifle and made sure the safety was off and that it was good to go, ready to fire. When he looked through the binoculars for the second time, things suddenly got more complex. Out of the woods at the edge of the water just behind the adult bear, two cubs had arrived on the scene.

"Shit," Tommy said to himself.

He observed the mother and her cubs for a few more seconds as they continued to head downstream toward Tommy and his daughters. Tommy hurriedly gathered up everything and began throwing it all in his pack. He grabbed his rifle and softly called to Ben, who had been watching the girls. Dad quickly climbed back down the rock and ran to his daughters.

"Girls, put your poles down. Hurry. We got a momma bear coming our way with her cubs. Just leave your poles here. Let's go."

The girls without saying anything put their poles down. Sarah grabbed her dad's hand and Jessica grabbed Sarah's. They knew about bears and the danger they presented. They had grown up in bear country. Even at their young age they knew how dangerous a mother bear could be with cubs that she was trying to raise. The threesome, along with Ben, headed into the woods and found the trail that they had come in on. Tommy looked for a tree he could boost the girls up into. He found one and told the girls to climb up as high as they could go. Because of their youth things weren't moving quite as quickly as the father would have liked.

"Hurry, girls. Be careful," Tommy said and remained calm, not wanting to risk getting his daughters more excited than they already were.

Sarah and Jessica looked down at their dad who was not climbing up behind them. They were becoming fearful and started to whimper.

"What are you going to do, Dad?" Sarah said in a worried tone.

"I'll be right back," Tommy answered.

"Daddy, don't leave us!" Jessica cried out.

Tommy turned and held his index finger up to his lips to hush the girls.

"Keep quiet. I'll be right back."

The girls held on tight to the branches and tried to be quiet and not cry. With Ben right behind him, Tommy headed back to his lookout rock a few yards and seconds away. When he got there he had another look through his binoculars. The mother bear and her cubs were only about a hundred yards away now and still coming in their direction. There was still time to make a dash for it. Tommy scrambled down from his view point and ran toward the tree his daughters had climbed. No sooner were he and Ben back on the ground from the rock when Ben decided to cut off in the direction of the mother bear and her cubs. He had gotten a whiff of them and that was all it took. He had a family to protect. Tommy screamed and wished he hadn't.

"Ben!"

The dog and his old bones ran along the creek bank. Tommy knew he couldn't yell again fearing it would get the adult bear's attention if it hadn't already. He dashed to the tree to retrieve Jessica and Sarah.

"Come on, girls. We're going to make a run for it!"

"Dad, no," Sarah shouted down, now crying.

"Quick. Hurry." The two sisters came down the tree as fast as they could, scared to death. Tommy strapped his rifle over his shoulder, grabbed one daughter with each hand and the three of them made a bee-line down the trail.

"Ben, Daddy. What about Ben?" Sarah asked through her tears.

Tommy was feeling helpless and knew there was nothing he could do about his longtime friend. In his heart he knew what Ben had decided and he wouldn't stand a chance.

"He'll catch up," Tommy said, hoping his words were true.

The father and his daughters ran as fast as the little girl's legs could carry them down the trail that would take them home. What seemed like an eternity, but in actuality was only three or four minutes into their rushed escape, they stopped to catch their breath. They looked back and saw nothing but woods. It was quiet. All breathed heavily and were tired.

"Where's Ben, Daddy?" Jessica asked, barely getting the words out through her huffing and puffing.

"He'll come. Don't worry."

But Tommy was worried. As the person of strength, the one in control, the one his daughters were counting on to get them home safe and sound, he couldn't show it. But it was a good question; Ben, where was he?

"OK, we're not going to run anymore for now. We're just going to walk real fast. How ya doing? Are you two going to be OK?" Dad inquired.

No they weren't. They knew their dad would protect them from any sort of danger, but they wanted to be home with their mother. They were only seven and five and a lot had been asked of them in the last few terrifying minutes.

"Let's go, Dad. Let's go." Sarah pulled on her dad's hand.

"OK, let's go," Tommy said.

They continued their journey toward home at a brisk pace and it seemed to take longer getting back. It was about fifteen more minutes of fast walking before they all started to feel safe. It could be that the mother bear never even knew they were around. But what about Ben? Still no Ben. Another half an hour on the trail and they found a dead fall to sit on and decided to wait five minutes for Ben to catch up, if that's what he was trying to do.

"What if he doesn't show up by the time we get home, Daddy?" Jessica asked.

"Then I'll go back and see if I can find him," Tommy replied, thinking the worst.

Tommy wasn't feeling good about Ben's disappearance. He was so worried he felt sick to his stomach, but dared not let it show. So the three sat and waited. They waited ten minutes instead of five and with every passing second, they hoped Ben would appear on the trail behind them. Tommy made a father's decision that it was time to go.

"You'll go back and get him, right Dad?" Jessica asked.

"Yep. Let's get you girls home safe to Mom and if he hasn't caught up to us by then I'll go back and see if I can find him."

TOMMY, SARAH AND Jessica come out of the woods and saw the most welcoming sight they have ever seen. Home sweet home. The edge of the woods was about fifty yards from the Franklin house and as soon as the girls were in the clearing they let go of their Dad's hands and made a bee line for the rear of the house. Tommy continued to walk a normal pace and was glad for the girls that in a matter of seconds they would run into their mother's arms.

"Mom! Mom! Mom!" Sarah and Jessica screamed as they ran.

Carolyn, relaxed and reading a magazine on the front veranda, recognized those voices coming from the rear of the house and ran through the front door and then out through the back door just in time for her two daughters to fly into her arms. She looked at Tommy and waved, having no clue as to the story she was about to hear. Something was said about a bear. Her daughters were talking a mile a minute.

"OK, girls. Slow down. Slow down. What's this about a bear?"

Carolyn again looked at her husband as he approached. Out of all the excitement she put together a story about them seeing a mother bear with cubs and that they had to run for it. The girls wouldn't take turns telling their story and it became muddled in all the chatter. Bear? Cubs? Run away? Ben? Something clicked in Carolyn's head; where was Ben? Carolyn and her daughters had a group hug as the girls sobbed and their father walked up. Mother had a worrisome look on her face and asked Tommy if everything was OK.

"Not really. We're fine, but I don't know where Ben disappeared to," her husband replied.

"What happened?" Carolyn asked as she guided her children over to the back steps to have a seat.

Tommy sat down on the steps and sandwiched himself between the girls and their Mom. He began to tell Carolyn what had happened. The more Mom heard the more she was thankful everyone was home safe and sound. A Brown Bear with cubs was no match for anything or anyone. In this part of the world in which they lived with the bears, wolves and moose, their threat and presence was always a possibility. They'd seen all the wildlife before, but this was the first time they had been so close to a mother bear and her cubs. Tommy would have shot the mother bear in a second if she had gotten too close and become aggressive. He was thankful that he didn't have to do that. It was a mother bear … with cubs. Her children.

Tommy finished his story and Carolyn suggested they all go inside and have a treat. The girls remained upset and Mom thought a little treat and some milk would help them relax. As they entered the kitchen, Tommy said he was going to go back to try and find Ben. Carolyn understood, but she knew it would cause her more worry and upset.

"I'll get you a snack to take with you and some water."

Tommy said he was going out to the shed to get some more ammo for his rifle. By the time he got back into the house, Carolyn had restocked his daypack. He gave his daughters each a peck on the top of the head as they sat at the kitchen table and said he'd be back in time for dinner. Carolyn looked at the clock on the wall and saw that it was almost three o'clock already.

"Please be careful, Dad. OK?" Carolyn said, giving her husband a kiss on the cheek and a hug.

"I'll try not to be too long," Dad assured the three females in his life. "Ben's probably half way home by now. I'll be all right."

"Be careful, Daddy," Sarah said to her father.

Tommy stopped at the back door.

"Oh, Mom. Gosh, in all the excitement I forgot to mention the girls caught some fish," he said proudly.

Carolyn stood next to the kitchen table.

"You did! You caught some fish? Way to go girls. I knew you would."

Mother pulled out a chair and sat down across from Sarah and Jessica. The two young girls made their mom laugh as they described in detail their fish story and how dad promised them five hundred million dollars for catching one.

"Boy! You girls are rich. Where's Dad gonna get all that money?"

Tommy and his wife looked at each other.

"I'll be back in a little while," Father said.

"Love you, Dad," Carolyn said as her husband made his exit.

"Love you, Dad," his daughters echoed Carolyn's words as he headed down the steps and back toward the trail where he hoped he would meet up with Ben.

"Love you, girls," he yelled, loud enough for his family to hear him behind a closed back door. "I'll be back."

Jessica ran out the back door and shouted at her departing father, "Don't forget to bring our fishing poles back."

Tommy stopped and turned around. "OK, Jessica. If I get that far. Depends where I meet up with Ben. We can always buy you new ones or go back tomorrow to get them. Don't you worry."

"Thanks, Dad," Jessica said as she ran back into the house.

Tommy turned around and began his journey back up the trail.

"Love you, girls," he yelled one more time. "Love you."

TOMMY MADE GOOD time getting back to the spot where all the action had taken place earlier and was disappointed he hadn't run into Ben on the trail trying to make his way back home. He was feeling pessimistic and knew it was a possibility that something bad could have happened to his good friend. Fearing that, his heart ached. Ever on the alert with his rifle at the ready, he made his way down to where his daughters had left their fishing poles. He picked them up, took them higher up onto the bank and lay them down. He looked down at the rock where he had laid the cleaned fish and noticed the fish were gone. The bears must have had a nice little treat. Tommy then walked out onto the rock where he had first spotted the bear. Taking his binoculars out of his pack, he looked upstream. Nothing. Just beautiful scenery. He looked downstream and saw more of the same. Tommy yelled Ben's name for the hundredth time as he had been doing while he was walking the trail back. There had been no response or sighting of Ben and Tommy was feeling more and more grim about finding the family dog alive. He didn't want to admit it to himself, but in his heart he had a feeling that Ben may have taken the mother bear on, thinking he was going to protect his dad and human sisters.

Tommy climbed back down the huge boulder and decided to walk up the creek and do some more exploring. About fifty yards up the creek he noticed on some rocks at the shoreline something that appeared to be blood. He knelt down to have a closer look and his fears were confirmed; it was most definitely blood. Tommy stood up and followed droplets of blood leading away from the creek toward a small meadow. His steps were slow. His instincts told him he was close to finding something he didn't want to find. About forty feet into the long grass he stumbled upon his old friend lying still, mangled and bloodied, eyes closed, hardly recognizable.

"Shit," Tommy whispered to himself as he lay his rifle and day pack down. He got on his knees and began stroking a lifeless Ben.

"Look at you, ol' buddy. What happened?"

Ben apparently had done what Tommy suspected. He put his own life on the line hoping to protect his family.

"Why, Ben? Why? You didn't have to do that."

Tommy's emotions took over and a tear ran down his cheek. Suddenly, as he stroked Ben's side, the dog's head moved ever so slightly. Then with his hand on Ben's body, Tommy felt his friend's side heave as if he were taking a breath, maybe his last breath. Ben was alive, if only barely. Tommy leaned down to put his head closer to Ben's.

"Hey, guy. Are you still with us?" He patted the top of Ben's bloodied head. The bear had obviously done a thorough job in protecting her cubs. Tommy spoke in a soothing tone. "It's OK, Ben. I'm here. You're a good boy, Ben. I'm here, boy. Just relax, everything is going to be fine."

Loss

It's so nice to hear your voice, Dad. I was waiting for you to come back so I could say good-bye. Sorry I messed up. I was trying to protect you and the girls. Don't worry about me. Please don't worry about me.

Tommy knew his friend was suffering and couldn't stand the thought of that. He also knew what had to be done as he grabbed his rifle. Ben was dying and in great pain. There wouldn't be a chance in hell of getting him back home alive and Tommy didn't want his long time sidekick suffering any longer. Ben opened his eyes one last time.

It was a great life Dad. We had lots of good times together. I'm going to miss you and the girls and Mom. But it was a great life. The best. Thank you so much.

Tommy stood over Ben, readied his rifle and took aim.

In the woods not too far away a Steller's Jay cackled as it sat on a low branch of a Douglas fir. A rifle shot went off and the bird flapped its wings and flew to a higher branch, still cackling away. It had never heard a sound like that before. Scared, it flew off toward another tree deeper into the woods. Ben was at peace now and the Steller's Jay hoped it never heard that sound again.

Tommy collapsed by Ben's side and couldn't believe what he had done. He remembered being down this road a long time ago with Buddy. Then there was the pain of losing Timex and never finding out what had happened to him. *Why do these dogs have to get into your blood so?* No longer was Ben suffering and no longer would the two of them share good times together. *Why did it have to end like this?* Tommy sobbed as he put a hand on Ben's side and lay his head on top of it. It had been a long time since this hardened man, a teddy bear to his family, had cried. He raised his head and stroked Ben's mangled coat.

"You were such a good boy, Ben. You were such a good boy."

Tommy stood up and began looking around for something to dig a shallow grave with. The soil was loose and sandy in the immediate area. He walked into the woods and found a dead branch that he would use as a shovel. It would do. He managed to dig a hole deep enough to be a grave right next to where Ben lay. When Ben was buried and covered up, Tommy walked over to the creek and started gathering rocks of all shapes and sizes and carried them over to Ben's grave. It was a lot of work, but worth the pain and effort. He stacked them up until the monument reached three feet high. When he was done he sat down by the manmade headstone and swayed back and forth as he recalled all the wonderful times he and Ben had had together over the past twelve years. There were so many. The memories comforted him and made him smile through his tears. He talked to himself at first, then decided to have one last conversation with his late friend.

IT WAS GETTING to be early evening and Tommy was losing track of time. He took out a snack from his pack that Carolyn had prepared for him and ate it. It had been a long day and he was tired. Tommy didn't want to move. He refused to leave Ben's side. They'd been bound together for so long. This was not the time to leave Ben alone. Time passed and Tommy, in a trance-like state, continued to console his dog.

I am a dog person and dog lovers all over the world would understand why I can't leave my friend. I won't leave you, Ben. You don't have to worry about that.

This time of year in late summer, this far north, complete darkness never came. It would start to get dusk and would act like it was going to get dark, but it never quite reached the total blackness of a winter's night. That's what was happening now. It was getting dusk and Tommy had no idea what time it was and didn't care. But darkness was once again beginning to take over Tommy's life. He started to experience another trip into hell. He had thought those days were behind him. He wished that those days were behind him, but he was not going to leave his friend. He could never do that. He grabbed his daypack to use as a pillow and lay down next to Ben's grave. Once again, Tommy repeated what he had said so many times the last few hours.

"We sure had some good times together, Ben. We sure had some good times." Tommy closed his eyes and began to fall asleep as he put one arm over Ben's grave. The day had been enjoyable, stressful—especially stressful—happy, sad, rewarding, scary and emotional—very emotional. It was time to rest before another trip to hell.

CAROLYN DIDN'T UNDERSTAND why Tommy was so late and tried to hide her concern for her husband, keeping it inside so that she didn't alarm her children. Where was he though? Where was Ben? She had spent the rest of the day after Tommy left entertaining Sarah and Jessica. After all the trauma that had gone on earlier in the day, Carolyn tried to keep things light and upbeat. But she and the girls had eaten their dinner and cleaned up the kitchen and still, no Dad. She was worried and rightfully so. The three of them played a child's board game in the living room and Carolyn looked at the clock on top of the bookcase. It was almost bedtime for the girls. Surely Dad would be home to tuck his daughters into bed.

When the game ended and she asked Sarah and Jessica to run upstairs and get ready for bed, Carolyn stepped out onto the back porch hoping to see a sign of her husband. There was nothing. She went back into the house and headed up the stairs to her daughters' bedroom.

"OK, you two," Mom said. "Brush your teeth and I'll read you a story or if you like you can tell me more about your exciting day."

As the two young females headed down the hallway, Sarah had to ask one more time, "Where's Dad?"

"Well, I'm sure he's still looking for Ben. I'll send him in when he gets home, which I expect to be any moment. Now go brush your teeth."

Carolyn peered through the window that looked out over the back of the house. Still no Tommy. The light was fading and though it was not quite dark in the clearing, she knew it would be a lot darker out in the woods amongst the trees and that worried her even more. She panicked for a moment as she couldn't remember if Tommy had taken a flashlight. She didn't recall if he had one in his pack or not. She paced as she waited for the girls to return. She knew that her husband was familiar with the bush, but something was wrong. Dreadfully wrong. He would always return home before sunset. Carolyn was used to that whenever he and Ben went out exploring. They always came back before the sun went down. The girls returned and hopped into their single beds.

"So what do you want? A story or do you want to talk about your day?" Mom asked.

"What time do you think Dad will be home? He's late." Jessica still wouldn't let it go and neither would Sarah.

"Yeah, Mom. He should be home by now," Sarah said, agreeing with her sister

"Dad would be very upset if he knew you two were worrying about him. So how about if I read you girls a story?"

Carolyn walked over to the girls' bookcase and picked out a children's book to read. She sat at the bottom of Jessica's bed and began reading. Sarah and Jessica were tired and it showed. Mom knew she wouldn't have to read for long before they would fall asleep. The questions continued about Dad's whereabouts as she tried to get through the book. She kept reassuring the girls everything was going to be OK. Sarah was the first one to head into dreamland and then Jessica followed shortly after. Carolyn closed the book, gave each girl a goodnight kiss and turned out the light. In the ambience of the nightlight she could see two angels sleeping. She wished their father was here to witness it. Carolyn went back downstairs not quite sure what to do. She picked up the phone and called her friend Bonnie who lived in town. She explained to her friend what was going on and asked if she could come over.

"My gosh, Carolyn. Absolutely. I'll be there in less than an hour."

Bonnie arrived in about forty-five minutes and tried to comfort her troubled friend. It was just after nine p.m. and still relatively light out. Carolyn's continued to hope as she expected Tommy and Ben to come walking in the back door any second, but she'd been feeling that way since late afternoon. She was glad that her friend was here as they talked and bounced ideas off each other. Carolyn wanted to go out on the trail and look for her husband, but he had the only rifle they owned and she knew you couldn't head out into the Alaskan bush without a weapon. Bonnie was adamant that it wouldn't be a good idea to go out alone and tried to be positive about Tommy and Ben's return.

"Just sit tight, Carolyn. He'll show up. You know how men are."

Carolyn considered calling more friends over and forming a search party, but worried that might take too long and felt it could be an overreaction.

"He'll probably show up just about the time everyone starts arriving to go look for him," she admitted to her friend.

She also considered calling the state troopers, but once again, it would take a while for them to get to their house and then what? There was a lot of indecisiveness and that bothered her more than anything. So she and Bonnie sat and talked and paced and constantly looked out the windows in the direction Tommy and Ben should be coming from. By half past eleven there was still no sign of them.

"I can't take this much longer, Bonnie," Carolyn confessed.

"He knows the bush, Carolyn. He'll find his way home and he'll have a good reason for being so late and causing you so much worry," Bonnie said, remaining optimistic.

More time passed. It was now after midnight. Carolyn was extremely tired and having a tough time keeping her eyes open. She and Bonnie had been sitting outside on the back veranda talking and Bonnie was the distraction that Carolyn needed at this time of uncertainty. Bonnie informed her worried friend that she would spend the night or at least stay until Tommy got home.

"Where are you going to sleep, my dear friend?" she asked a dozy Carolyn.

Tommy's stressed wife got up from her patio chair. "I think I'll go grab a blanket and sleep right here," she said as she walked to the door. "Thank you so much for offering to spend the night, Bonnie. I can't thank you enough. Where do you want to sleep? You have a choice between a couple of bedrooms."

Bonnie got up from her chair and followed Carolyn inside. "Maybe I'll just sleep on the living room couch if you don't mind."

Carolyn objected, but Bonnie explained she wanted to be able to hear the girls upstairs if they got up and also so she could hear Tommy when he came in.

"OK. Have it your way. I just want you to be comfortable," Carolyn said as she got her companion a sheet, blanket and pillow and made up the couch for Bonnie to sleep on.

"Don't get eaten by the bugs out there." Bonnie reminded her friend that it was still bug season. "You come in if it gets too bad."

Bonnie wished her troubled friend would sleep in her own bed, but it wouldn't serve any purpose to say something to that effect.

"I'll be fine," Carolyn said as she headed back out onto the veranda.

The worried wife made herself as cozy as she possibly could on her patio chair and knew sleep would not come easily, if at all. Her body was tired, her mind was tired, but the adrenalin was flowing. She closed her eyes and it seemed to take forever for her to drift off. Every time there was the slightest noise her ears perked up and her eyes opened. It could be Tommy and Ben coming home. She wasn't able to do anything more than just get in some cat naps throughout the night. Carolyn had come to the realization that her husband wasn't likely to come home any time soon and it pained her. For some reason, and she had no idea why, Tommy was spending the night out in the bush. She told herself that if he wasn't home at first light she would take the initiative and go looking for him, rifle or no rifle, and she would go find him wherever he might be. Where was he? What was he doing? Why didn't he come home? Was he OK? What happened to him? What about Ben?

"AAAAAAGH!" TOMMY WOKE up screaming from another dreadful nightmare about the war he fought long ago. Only this time something was different. He was in the bush, but didn't know where in the bush. In the near darkness it looked like Vietnam. His mind was playing tricks on him. Something in the brain had short circuited. He was having hallucinations and had lost his sense of reality as he grabbed his rifle and thought he was back in the war. Tommy looked over at the moon-lit creek and on the opposite side coming out of the woods he could see enemy soldiers approaching. He fired off a round and then another. The imagined enemy soldiers fired back. He was way out numbered and knew it. There was no point in firing his rifle again. It was over. They had come back for their retribution and they kept coming and firing their rifles and machine guns. They meant business and it had taken them almost thirty years to find him. They blasted away, but Tommy was not dying and he didn't understand why. They obviously saw him. They were almost on top of him now. With all the rounds being fired, surly he must be getting hit. He didn't get it. He wished if he could only get hit and die then he could join Ben, Buddy and Timex somewhere in a land of peace and tranquility. He looked at his rifle, thinking he'd save the enemy soldiers the trouble of killing him and he'd just do it himself. The unthinkable. But as the enemy soldiers got just a few feet away, their figures started to melt into the shapes of little girls in their pajama's running toward him. It was six or seven pairs of little girls with the same two faces. He recognized the faces and was reminded of what his real life was about and all the reasons why he had to choose life over death. He couldn't remember the little girls' names, but he knew he had to live. Tommy stood up, took the barrel of his rifle, twirled around and, with every ounce of energy he had, tossed it away from him as far as he could throw it.

He turned back in the direction in which the enemy soldiers and little girls had come from. Everyone was gone. Tommy dropped to his knees and held his hands above his head as if he was surrendering and shouted out, "I'm not fighting anymore. The war is over. I'm not fighting anymore." The hallucinations stopped. No more enemy soldiers. No more little girls. He began to cry.

Where did they all go?

The proud veteran was confused and delirious. He fell back over onto Ben's grave and slowly his senses began to come back to him as he started to think more rationally. He worried about where he was and what he'd done.

Here I am thirty years after the war and still haunted by the past. Why won't it leave me alone? Why can't all this madness stop? Why must we continue to fight these wars? What's wrong with us humans?

"Where am I, Ben? What's going on?"

Tommy gave in to his fatigue and to the events that had just happened. In bits and pieces he began to remember who he was and what he was. He looked up at the sky and wondered what sky it was. Was it the one in a Southeast Asian country? Was it the sky in Michigan? What sky was it? Was it the same sky everywhere?

"Where am I, Buddy? What's going on?"

He put his head back down on his daypack, exhausted and wanting to go back to sleep. His thoughts remained sporadically irrational as he tried to get a grasp on what was real and what was not. Those little girls he saw? They meant something to him. He knew their faces. Who were they? Tommy closed his eyes and tried to clear his mind and wondered where his next feeling of comfort would come from.

"Where am I Timex? What's going on?"

Over the next few minutes his mind gave him more sense of real time and place. He opened his eyes and looked at the sky once more.

"What have I done?"

For years he had asked himself how the post traumatic effects of war could cause a person to suffer for so long, but he knew he was not alone. Long ago, after he had come back stateside, he had attended meetings and had counseling and spoke with other soldiers who suffered the same depression, nightmares and confusion that he endured. The suffering was real and for Tommy, no one could ever answer his question regarding the nightmares and images in his mind. Would they stop in this lifetime for this brave soldier? Or for that matter, for all the brave soldiers that fought the wars? Or would it follow them to their graves?

His thoughts turned once again to future wars and soldiers not even born yet. He felt for them. No one had told him all those years before, when he enlisted in the military service, that the images of war never go away and the effects of war could stay with you for a lifetime. Tommy had somehow managed to live his life around these things that he had no control over. Time, prescription drugs, therapy, nothing changed and nothing could prevent the nightmares and internal pain he felt. He had recovered from those days in the seventies when he did drugs and lived on the streets. He had made something of himself. He was a good father and husband. It was a perfect world except for the reminders of his past war experiences. The disturbing memories in his subconscious wouldn't let him forget.

Tommy raised his head and suddenly realized where he was ... lost. Alone. He began to recall having a wife and two daughters at home that must be worried sick about him, but he had no energy to pick himself up and head back down the trail. He looked at his watch. It said half past three. It would start to get light again in less than an hour. Tommy decided he must rest and if possible close his eyes one more time and try to get some sleep. As they always did, the after effects of the nightmares had left him drained of energy.

"I'm so sorry, Carolyn. I'm so sorry, Sarah and Jessica. I'm so sorry," Tommy told the night sky as he closed his eyes. "I'm so sorry Buddy. I'm so sorry Timex. I'm so sorry Ben. I'm so sorry for being Tommy Franklin."

A CHIRPING BIRD woke Carolyn up just after she had fallen asleep. That was the way the whole night had gone. She would fall asleep for a few minutes, then some noise would wake her up and she would have to get up to see if it were Tommy and Ben happily arriving home. Every time there was no Tommy or Ben. Now, cuddled underneath her blanket on a patio chair, she saw a faint sliver of light in the sky. Looking at her watch with sleepy eyes, she saw that it was five past four. Carolyn jumped up and knew it was time to take action. She ran into the house and gave Bonnie, who was sound asleep on the couch, a gentle shake. Speaking in a low voice so as to not wake the sleeping angels upstairs, she whispered, "Bonnie. Tommy hasn't come home. It's starting to get light out. I'm going to go out and see if I can find him."

Bonnie rose, put her feet on the floor and looked out one of the windows. She saw that it was really not that bright outside. Bonnie thought to herself that perhaps Carolyn should wait until there was more light, but knew it would be pointless to say anything. A little droggy, she stood up.

"I'll watch the girls, Carolyn. Let me help you get ready."

The two friends went into the kitchen and Carolyn grabbed another day pack from a closet.

"I've got some bear spray to throw in there. At least I'll have something," Carolyn said on the verge of tears. She kept telling Bonnie how worried she was about Tommy. "He's never done anything like this before. Why would he do this?"

"I'm sure there will be a good reason he spent the night in the bush, Carolyn. He's probably heading home right now as we speak," Bonnie said as she helped her friend get some things together.

The two got the day pack ready with a couple of granola bars, some water, the bear spray and a small flashlight and before she knew it, Carolyn was ready to go. As they walked outside into the back yard, Bonnie grabbed Carolyn's arm.

"Remember, you have two daughters to think about. Be safe and don't do anything foolish and please bring Tommy and Ben home."

Carolyn knew that Bonnie was right about Sarah and Jessica. Whatever happened on the trail on her way to find Tommy, she had to consider the girls as well.

"Thanks, Bonnie. Do me a favor and call the state troopers. If I can't find him, the best thing to do will be to start organizing a search party. I'm so worried."

Bonnie said she would not only call the state troopers, but also their friends and it didn't matter how early it was. The two hugged and Carolyn began a fast pace away from the house as Bonnie watched her disappear into the woods.

MORE CHIRPING BIRDS and another pair of eyes opened. Tommy saw ambient light in the sky and jumped up. He looked down at Ben's grave. In a panic, he had come back to his senses and knew it was time to head home. Now. Right now. What a night it had been. Putting Ben down had been too much for him to handle and when the nightmare followed, it was more than his mind could take. The events of the last twenty-four hours were fuzzy and right now he didn't have a whole lot of time to think about them. He knew he was Tommy Franklin and had to get home to his wife and kids. Tommy started to head back down the creek toward the trail that would lead him to his family. He stopped.

My rifle!

Tommy went back to the vicinity of Ben's grave and looked around for his firearm. He couldn't find it and didn't recall throwing it into the bush. More panic set in.

What the hell did I do with my rifle?

He was anxious to get going and thought for a second that it didn't really matter. It was the people at home that mattered. He walked in circles spreading outward from Ben's grave and just as he was about to give up, he stumbled upon it. Now he could go and go he did as quickly as his feet would carry him.

WITH EVERY STEP it seemed like the morning light was getting brighter. Carolyn was thankful for that. She was hoping beyond hope she would bump into Tommy and Ben any second now on the trail, but thirty minutes into her mission there was no sign of them. The heart was optimistic, the mind was pessimistic. Her mind fought her heart and neither one was winning. Her heart would never give up hope as her mind told her something terrible had happened. Her heart drove her faster down the trail and as it did, she saw something she wished she hadn't.

In a clearing beyond the woods, to her left, not thirty yards away, a pack of wolves were prancing across a meadow out for their morning hunt. She couldn't believe her eyes or her luck and stepped off the trail, hiding behind a tree to observe the predators. They were going in the opposite direction to her, parallel to the woods and hadn't let on that they were aware of her presence. It looked like they would pass by when one of the wolves suddenly stopped and looked in her direction. She began to tremble. The wolf stood and looked her way, put its nose on the ground and then into the air. It smelled something. Perhaps her sweat. Maybe her fear. It stood gazing into the woods for a few more seconds then decided to investigate what was drawing its attention.

Carolyn thought for a second about pulling out her bear spray, but that wouldn't do anything if the whole pack of six or seven decided to follow the one that now walked toward her. She had to find a tree and looked for one that had low enough branches to climb up.

She finally spotted one about twenty feet away and made a dash for it. She reached it safely, but dropped her pack as she began to head upward. The branches were brittle and broke as she climbed. The lone wolf had spotted her and at a slow trot came over to the tree as Carolyn managed to get up just high enough to be out of his reach. She realized immediately she had not chosen the best tree to climb as the mostly dead branches broke easily. She hung onto the trunk of the tree but it was too wide for her to get a firm grip and wrap her arms around tightly. Her feet had broken the branches underneath her as she scrambled up and her footing was braced on a couple of stubs that stuck out and didn't allow any relief for her arms that must hold her weight or else she would fall. Carolyn held on with every ounce of strength she had and began to sob. The wolf below her began to tear up the dropped backpack and munch on the treats that were in it.

As if things weren't bad enough, the rest of the wolf pack, one by one, started to show up. The one that ripped apart the backpack was obviously the Alpha male as the other wolves dared not approach him and gave him his space. She took a peek over her shoulder and counted seven wolves altogether. Carolyn was starting to realize it was just a matter of time before her strength gave out. The wolves' mannerisms were casual as they sensed it wouldn't be long before their prey hit the ground. If they were humans, they would be sitting around reading the newspaper or doing their nails. Time was on their side and they knew it. Carolyn also knew it as she hung on with what little strength she had left in her. Her head leaned on the tree realizing what was about to come. Having her life end this way was one thing, but not knowing what had happened to her husband was another. She thought of Sarah and Jessica and her heart ached more than it ever had in her life. Would her daughters be left without a mother and a father? She panicked at this thought and feared the worst. She didn't know if Tommy was alive or dead. Carolyn had another peek at the wolves as they sat and lay around acting as if there wasn't an aggressive bone in their bodies. She was crying profusely now, but somewhere deep inside she found the energy to scream out Tommy's name.

"TOMMY! TOMMY FRANKLIN! TOMMMMMMMY!"

Tommy stopped dead in his tracks.

What was that?

He was sure he heard screaming in the distance. He was quiet and listened.

He heard it again. Someone was yelling his name. It was a female and he couldn't tell for sure who it was, but it sounded like Carolyn. The fast pace he had been walking now turned into a run, full speed ahead.

The Alpha male wolf had jumped up on its hind legs and put its front paws on the tree trunk only three feet below where Carolyn's hiking boots continued to struggle in an attempt to find something, anything, to brace herself. The other wolves had gotten up and now circled the tree, pacing around the perimeter. They sensed their prey was getting weak; the time was getting near. Another wolf had jumped up with its front paws on the tree and the Alpha male didn't seem to mind. The wolves, for the first time, were showing excitement about what was going to happen in just a few seconds. Their prey was giving in to the inevitable. Carolyn was bound and determined to hang on for dear life. She didn't have enough energy left to call out her husband's name again. Instead she sobbed and with her head against the tree she softly spoke his name and the names of her two daughters.

"Tommy. Tommy Franklin. Where are you, my love? Sarah … Jessica, Mommy loves you so much."

THE TWO RIFLE shots in rapid succession startled Carolyn and got the adrenalin flowing once again. She instantly hugged the tree more tightly just when she thought there was no strength left in her to do such a thing. A third shot was fired a second after the first two, louder and closer. Carolyn looked out over her left shoulder and saw the wolf pack scrambling away. She turned her head, looked out over her right shoulder and saw Tommy not forty feet away kneeling down and firing off two more rounds at the scattering wolves. The adrenalin rush didn't last long. She lost her grip on the tree trunk and crashed to the ground. She only fell a few feet, but it was enough to knock the wind out of her. Lying on her back with her eyes closed trying to determine what hurt and what didn't, she heard one word and a familiar voice.

"Carolyn!"

Opening her eyes she saw Tommy kneeling over her. They had found each other again. Her Tommy would be coming home after all.

"Are you OK?" he asked, having witnessed her drop to the ground, concerned she may have injured herself.

Any pain she was feeling was washed away by the euphoria that overcame her.

She managed to sit up and support herself with an arm. Sobbing, she couldn't believe her eyes.

"I'm just fine, Mr. Franklin. Just fine."

Tommy put an arm underneath her, pulled her close and hugged her.

"I'm so sorry, Carolyn. I'm so sorry."

She had never felt a hug so tight from him and he had never needed her more.

"Can you stand up?" Tommy asked.

With her husband's help, Carolyn got up on her knees and he lifted her the rest of the way. Her legs felt weak as she grabbed onto Tommy and hugged him as if she would never let go. Her head was buried in his chest. She looked up at him and between the tears asked him where he'd been.

"You had us so worried."

Words could not express how sorry Tommy was. He said it over and over like he had done so many times in his life. "I'm so sorry. I'm so sorry ... ."

Carolyn squeezed her husband like she had been squeezing the tree trunk. They held each other and enjoyed a glorious reunion. They were back in each other's arms where they'd always known they belonged. When they had caught their breath and their bodies began to relax, Carolyn felt she had to ask the obvious question.

"Where's Ben?"

Tommy didn't want to talk about it or think about it as he walked over to the tree that Carolyn had just fallen out of and leaned his back against it. He closed his eyes and tilted his head back.

"He didn't make it."

Carolyn's instincts had already told her that was going to be the answer and she went to her husband and grabbed his hand. There were more emotions to be shared, more tears. Like a thirty-second movie going through her head, Carolyn recalled all the good times Tommy had with his dog named Ben. His really, really good friend. His pal. She watched the movie play out in her mind and saw Ben with the children and what a wonderful family dog he had been. He had had a good life.

"Tommy ... let's go home," she said.

Tommy opened his eyes, looked at his wife and said solemnly, "I think that might be a good idea."

He picked up his rifle, held it in one hand and took Carolyn's hand in the other. Husband and wife, friends and lovers, mother and father, together again they started walking down the trail toward home.

FORTY-FIVE MINUTES LATER Tommy and Carolyn walked out of the woods behind their house. What they saw astounded them. Friends and state troopers were at the back of their home talking and discussing a strategy to go search for the two missing people. No one was really taking notice as they approached the house. No one until Sarah, still in her nightie, saw her parents and started screaming and running toward them.

"Mommy, Daddy! Mommy, Daddy!"

Jessica, also still in her nightie and standing on the back porch, followed her older sister to her parents where they had a group hug and more tears.

"Where were you, Daddy? Where were you?" Jessica wanted to know.

"It's OK, girls. Your Mommy and Daddy are fine. Mommy's here, I'm here. It's OK," Tommy told his daughters.

Bonnie was the next one to run up and gave Tommy a long hug.

"Don't ever do that again. OK?" she said through her own emotions that were running rampant. She turned to Carolyn and gave her a long, hardy hug.

"I'm so glad to see you. Welcome home."

It had been a long twenty-four hours, but ended up right where it began. Right where it should. At home and in the arms of loved ones.

Tommy took Bonnie by the shoulders and looked her in the eye.

"Don't worry ... it won't ever happen again. Ever."

The group headed to the house to greet their other friends and explain to the state troopers what had happened since Tommy left yesterday to go search for the family dog. When it was all sorted out, everybody went their own way leaving the Franklin family alone with Bonnie. Inside the house Tommy told his daughters and Bonnie the story he had told Carolyn as they walked on the trail back home. He told them everything except about his nightmare. The story was sad for everyone. The girls couldn't stop crying. They cried tears of joy because their mother and father were home safe and they cried tears of sadness because they'd lost their canine brother, Ben. They had grown up with him and now he was gone. He had been so much a part of the family. Tommy explained to the girls that Ben was only trying to protect them and paid the ultimate price. It was something every good soldier would do to protect the ones they love and Ben ... Ben was a good soldier. He also told his daughters how he had dug a grave for Ben and buried him.

"I'll take you girls and Mom one day soon and we'll go visit his grave. I'll show you where it is so that you know."

Tommy and Carolyn also told Bonnie and the girls about the wolves. Mom said how fortunate she was to have another good soldier come along and save her life. It had been an unbelievable twenty-four hours that neither husband nor wife wanted to live through again.

"OK, you guys, I'm heading out," Bonnie said to her four good friends as she gathered up her stuff and headed to the front of the house where her truck was parked.

Tommy and Carolyn followed her out onto the veranda. Carolyn gave Bonnie a warm hug.

"I can't thank you enough, Bonnie. You are an amazing friend."

Bonnie downplayed what she had done and knew that what she did was something friends do for each other and that Carolyn would have done the same for her. As Bonnie got to the driver's side of her truck, she warned Tommy once more not to do what he had done ever again.

"I told you," a tired Tommy replied, "never again."

It was one of the most incredible stories Bonnie had ever heard up here in the North Country and she had grown up in Alaska. First the Brown Bear and her cubs and then the wolves in the morning. Only in the Last Frontier could things like that happen.

Tommy and Carolyn walked back into the kitchen and saw Sarah coloring in a coloring book and Jessica had her head on an out-stretched arm on the table. Both girls were as tired as their parents.

"How about some breakfast?" Tommy suggested.

"Wouldn't that be nice," his wife said in agreement.

Breakfast was cooked and served. Tommy and Carolyn talked to their daughters more about what happened yesterday when Daddy went back to look for Ben and also about the morning when Mom went out to look for him.

"We don't have to be afraid of the bears and we don't have to be afraid of the wolves," Tommy summarized the story that he and his wife had been telling. "But we have to respect their space. You girls know they can be dangerous if they're protecting their young or happen to be hungry. You just have to be careful when you're out in the bush."

Father was right. In all the years he had been living in Alaska he had watched and observed many bears and wolves. But he never had an encounter like he had in the last twenty-four hours. If it never happened again that would be fine with him.

After breakfast Jessica and Sarah headed into the living room to lounge around and read. Tommy and Carolyn cleaned up the kitchen and continued to discuss yesterday and last night. He didn't tell the girls, but now he told Carolyn about the nightmare he had and how he woke up and didn't know where he was. He didn't remember much about his hallucination and everything in that time frame was rather vague. He did, however, recall feeling terribly alone. His wife knew how he suffered whenever the nightmares occurred and last night's must have been more horrible with no one else around. As much as her husband wished they would stop, so did she. Tommy had known for a long time that it was possible they never would. Carolyn looked at him with compassion.

Why can't the memories of a war so long ago just let him be? He's suffered enough. If only these nightmares would stop so my husband could live in peace.

After the dishes were done and the kitchen was cleaned up, Tommy put his dishrag down and sat at the kitchen table. Carolyn joined him. Tommy stretched his legs out. He was sitting and thinking. Silence. Carolyn, with her elbow resting on the table and her chin in her hand, looked at her husband and wondered why he was being so quiet. He seemed lost in some deep thoughts.

"Everything OK?" she asked.

Tommy brought his legs up and put his feet flat on the floor. He cupped his hands on top of the table.

"Just thinking about Ben"

That didn't surprise Carolyn. Of course he would be. She put a hand on his forearm.

"Tommy … there's nothing you could have done. Ben was just being protective of you and the girls. It was an awful way for him to go, but you and I both know he would have been no match for a mother bear with cubs."

"Yeah, I know," Tommy said sadly and barely audibly to his wife. "It just happened so fast." There was a pause and silence. Tommy buried his head in his hands. "Man, he was a good dog."

Carolyn got up and hugged her husband from behind.

"Yes, he was. A very good dog. We all know that."

The previous night, when Tommy was wondering where his next comfort would come from, he should have known it would be from his wife who now hugged him and rested her head on his. The comfort in his life had always come from Carolyn and his girls. They gave him peace of mind in so many different ways in which words could not express. He was a lucky man to have such a kind-hearted wife and two loving daughters. Tommy lifted a hand from the table and took one of hers.

"Carolyn."

"Yes, my love."

Tommy had something to say and it was going to be hard and painful, but it was the way he was feeling.

"What is it, honey?" she asked him, not knowing what to expect after all the stress from yesterday and this morning.

He pulled her hand close to his lips and softly kissed her.

"I'm ... I'm done with dogs."

Carolyn let go of her husband's hand, sat back down in her chair and studied him.

He's not done with dogs. He will never be done with dogs. His best friends have always been dogs.

She understood the pain he was feeling and sensed this was something he was saying in haste without realizing exactly what those words meant. He said it again, shaking his head.

"I'm done with dogs."

Tommy turned solemn and his thoughts seemed far off. Carolyn knew her husband, and dogs had been, and always would be, a big part of his life. She was sure of it.

"What about the girls?" she asked "What if they want to get another dog at some point? What about me? A dog has always been part of our family."

Tommy said nothing and Carolyn felt she had to be careful where she tread. She waited for a response, but it didn't come.

"Tommy?"

He was aching and feeling overly tired. Physically his body was starting to crash and he wanted to just lie down and go to sleep. Carolyn as well was feeling the strain from lack of sleep and from all the events that had occurred just a short time before.

Maybe we should have this conversation another time.

Tommy threw his head back and, looking at the ceiling, rubbed his eyes and decided to speak up.

"Honey, you know I would never object if you or the girls wanted to get another dog," he looked at his wife. "And you're right, dogs have always played a big part in my life. But it's hard. It's hard when you get so attached to them and the heartbreak that comes when they die. Or get killed. Or disappear. I don't know if I can take that again. It's too painful."

Carolyn took Tommy's hand one more time.

"I know how you feel, Tommy. Why don't you go lie down and have a nap?"

They both stood up from the table and hugged.

"Go upstairs and lie down and I'll come join you after I sit with the girls for a while," Carolyn said to her husband.

As Tommy walked away to tell his daughters he was going to lie down, his wife had one more thing to say.

"Tommy ... ."

He stopped and turned around. Carolyn was going to say something positive about having a dog in the family and that one day they'd get another one, but she changed her mind. She decided to keep it simple.

"I love you."

As tired as he was those three words from the gal who meant everything to him managed to bring a smile to his face.

"I love you too."

And you're not done with dogs, Tommy Franklin. You'll never be done with dogs.

A DOG NAMED DAISY

Goodbyes and Gratitude

IT TOOK A year, a very long year, for Tommy to get over the pain of losing Ben and to start thinking about getting another dog. Then one day ... .

"You girls 'bout ready to go?" the father shouted up the stairs at his two daughters. Dad had decided it was time for the Franklin family to pay a visit to the Humane Society in Palmer, about an hour's drive from Eagles Junction. Tommy and Carolyn stood at the front door of their home waiting for the girls to come running down the stairs for a long anticipated visit to see what they could find out about adopting another puppy. The parents smiled at each other and waited for the sound of footsteps bounding down the stairs.

"Whoa! Here they come," Carolyn said and walked toward the living room to greet them. She took one little girl's hand in each of hers and the three skipped to where Tommy was waiting.

"Took you long enough to get ready, girls. Are you as excited as Mom and Dad?" the loving father said to his children.

Both Sarah and Jessica confirmed with unabated excitement that they couldn't wait to get to the Humane Society. The four headed out, got into the family vehicle and made their way north to Palmer. They had been discussing amongst themselves this past couple of weeks the subject of getting another puppy, right after Tommy broke the news to them that now might be the perfect time to get one, "No good, lowdown, conniving, canelopy, scheming looney tooney, dog." The girls had been begging for one and Carolyn was always dropping subtle hints, but they respected the fact that everyone had to be "all in" if it were going to happen. They were just waiting for Dad to come around. He had. Tommy didn't get Timex to erase the memory of Buddy because Buddy was irreplaceable. And he didn't get Ben to ease the long-time pain of losing Timex. Timex was also irreplaceable. And there would never be another dog to take the place of Ben. That would be impossible. This dog, this next dog, would be like the previous three, special in its own way. It would have its own personality just like the others did. But this one would be different in one specific way; it would be the first female dog Tommy had ever had. They talked about it as a family and voted on it democratically. Of course, the decision was unanimous. Girls have to stick together. When Tommy saw the three females in his family raise their hands on voting day and said that they all wanted a girl dog, Tommy raised his and it was a done deal.

"Well then, that's it. It's settled. We'll get a girl dog."

It didn't really matter to him. He was just excited about getting another dog into his life. Into his family's life. They had all agreed it had to be a mixed breed dog and a big one. It turned out to be a dog they named Daisy. Another Heinz 57 variety just like Tommy's past dogs and she was going to be big just like the others in his life had been. Daisy was a mixed breed by every definition of the word with a little bit of this and a little bit of that in her. A little bit of Lab and a little bit of St. Bernard and the Humane Society thought possibly even a little bit of Great Dane and, "Oh, yeah. Possibly some German Shorthair as well." Daisy looked the part. Especially the potentially big part. She had the big paws, the big ears and a long tail. She was going to be big alright and that was fine with the Franklin's. Like all puppies, she became instant family and was glad to have a home. And if you were a dog, it was the Franklin home you would have wanted to land in.

Daisy and Tommy hit it off right from day one and were inseparable, like he and Ben and Timex and Buddy had been. He took her to work like he had with Ben and she would be the first one out to Tommy's truck every morning. She knew the routine just like his previous dogs. If they weren't going to one of Tommy's job sites, they would be going to the store or the post office or wherever. It was all good as long as she and Tommy were together.

Daisy grew up to weigh almost a hundred pounds. She was a huge dog that didn't know exactly how big she really was, especially in the middle of the night when she crawled up onto the bed and squeezed between Tommy and Carolyn. If you would let her, she would get up on the couch with you and if you just happened to be trying to read something, a magazine or a book, she would put her head in your lap … along with most of the rest of her body. Daisy enjoyed being a nuisance when the girls were trying to do their homework. She was loved, lovable and loving. There was only one thing in her canine life that she wanted: to be with her family. She got that wish every second of every day.

If she wasn't with Tommy she would be with one or both of the girls and if she wasn't with any one of those three she would be under Carolyn's feet trying to help her in some way. Daisy was Daisy and quite a character. The Franklin's couldn't get enough of her and the feeling was mutual. For the Franklin family, every day was an adventure with Daisy around. She made them all laugh and was great entertainment. There wasn't an aggressive bone in her body and she was the epitome of what a family dog should be. Daisy … was Daisy.

Goodbyes and Gratitude

DAISY WAS TEN years old when Tommy first started getting abdominal and back pains. At the same time he began feeling those pains, other things were happening with his body that he noticed didn't seem right. At first he didn't give it much thought. He figured the changes were all about getting old. But deep inside he knew something was wrong and besides, mid-fifties wasn't exactly what you would call old. What he didn't know was that the past was coming back to haunt him. The lifestyle he had lived back in the seventies was now catching up to him. It was a long time before he even mentioned anything to his wife and even longer still until she finally convinced him, as hard as she had tried so many times before, to go to a doctor. A year passed from the time when Tommy started not feeling right until he finally made his first doctor's appointment. All the while, his health was deteriorating and he could feel it every day. He would still go to work and enjoyed being with his crew, but the energy level wasn't there like it used to be and his employees could see the changes.

After all the doctor's appointments and blood tests, x-rays and everything else, it was confirmed that Tommy had Hepatitis C that had degenerated into cirrhosis of the liver. The Hepatitis C virus could lay dormant for years until one day it would decide to show its ugly head. After he was diagnosed and he did his research, he came to the conclusion that he got the virus from sharing needles to shoot up drugs over thirty years ago. It didn't surprise him. He also knew he was one of the lucky ones to have lived for as long as he had. The drug and alcohol abuse didn't kill him back in his twenties, but it most certainly had killed some of his friends. Drug friends. Party friends. It was the seventies after all. The sins of so long ago had waited for thirty years before deciding to come back and kill him now.

The prognosis was that he had roughly a year to live, give or take. Tommy Franklin's life was coming to an end. A premature end. Carolyn tried to be strong and for the most part was, but in that last year she couldn't stop the tears from flowing. Every time there was an occasion when she realized it was going to be Tommy's "last" something, she would find a place to hide in private and break down. Tommy's "last" Thanksgiving. Tommy's "last" Christmas. The "last" time he would celebrate the girls' birthdays. Her birthday. His. Tommy also had some last tough decisions to make. He shut down his business and took Daisy to work for the "last" time. There were too many "lasts" in his final year. Too many to bear. But you couldn't have seen that in his face. His exuberance for life never changed.

Physically, of course, you could see the changes, but emotionally he never wavered from his creed that "every day is a gift." He knew he was a lucky man to have had the people in his life that he did. Having the life he had with his wife and daughters was more than any man could have wanted. He could have been killed in Vietnam, but he wasn't. A guardian angel must have been watching over him. He could have been killed on the streets of L.A. and overdosed. But he wasn't and didn't.

His life was coming to an end now and, as with every day in the recent past, he enjoyed every second. For what it was worth, he knew he was lucky to have lived as long as he did. His life had been about giving love and getting love in return. He didn't feel cheated. He had shared more love and laughter than many people his age had. But it was time to go. Time to check out. Time to say farewell.

IT WAS A WARM spring day and Tommy decided he would like to go for a walk by the ocean. As his health failed, he had certain things he felt he still needed to do. So many more things to do, so little time. A simple walk on the beach with Daisy was what the day called for.

"I'll be back in a couple of hours," Tommy said to Carolyn, who was doing some front yard gardening as he walked to his truck. Daisy waited by the driver's door to jump in.

"Are you sure you don't want me to come?" She had asked the same question an hour before. Tommy had declined earlier because he wanted the time alone with Daisy. But now, as he was about in climb into his truck, he had a change of heart and thought that, yeah, it would be nice to have the love of his life come along.

What was I thinking? She would like that. I would like that. She's always been there for me. Why should that change now? She's been my best friend longer than anybody.

Tommy nodded his head toward the passenger door.

"Let's go!"

She was thrilled that he had changed his mind and put her gardening tools down.

"OK, Mr. Franklin. Give me a couple of minutes. I'd love to go with you. I'll go inside and tell the girls."

Tommy smiled and opened the driver's door for Daisy to jump in.

"I'll be waiting," he said as his wife entered the front door.

Everything was quiet. He looked at the sky and was amazed at what a deep blue it was. He gazed at his home and recalled all the great memories that went on inside and outside. He looked at Daisy as she hung her head out the window and reminisced about the other dogs in his life. He gave Daisy a pat on the head.

"Every day is a gift, Daisy. Every day's a gift. Don't you ever forget that."

"I'm ready to go," Carolyn said as she came out the front door with Sarah and Jessica right behind her. Their two daughters, now nineteen and seventeen and beautiful young women in their father's eyes, had grown up to be caring and giving. They looked and acted like their mother.

"We'll be back in a couple of hours, OK girls?" Tommy told Sarah and Jessica.

"That's fine, Dad. Don't worry. You and Mom have fun. We'll see you when you get back," Sarah said maturely like the young adult she was.

"Yeah, you guys go have some fun. I'll keep an eye on Sarah for you," Jessica joked as she gave her father a hug.

"OK, Jessica. You keep an eye on Sarah and we'll be back in a little while," the proud father said, hopping into his truck.

As Tommy, Carolyn and Daisy started to drive off, Tommy stopped the truck. Carolyn looked over at him.

"What's wrong?"

"What am I thinking?" her husband replied and put the truck into reverse.

Tommy backed up to where his daughters were still standing.

"You girls aren't doing anything real important right now, are ya'?" Dad asked.

Sarah and Jessica looked at each other.

"Not really," Sarah answered.

"Well then, how about hopping in your car and following us out to Lantern Beach? We'd love for you to come along if you don't mind joining us!"

Tommy's two daughters were all smiles.

"We're on it!" Jessica almost screamed the words out.

" ... and we'll stop somewhere along the way and have some lunch." Tommy yelled as the girls ran back into the house to get ready.

The husband turned and looked at his wife who smiled and patted Daisy.

What was I thinking?

LANTERN BEACH WAS a forty-five minute drive from the Franklin home. They'd been there a hundred times over the years as a family with Ben, Daisy and the kids and it was one of Tommy's favorite spots. It was made up of big rocks you could climb on that overlooked a sandy beach that ran into the ocean and the ocean in turn ran into the horizon. A great place where one could meditate or walk forever if that's what you chose to do. Today it would be both. Walking, meditating, quality time for Tommy with his wife, kids and dog. Plus, he had a little bit of business he wanted to take care of.

Tommy and Daisy sat on a piece of driftwood that had at one time been a fair-sized tree, but now was well worn and had been made silky smooth by the elements. It was tucked inside a little cove that was barely big enough to fit the weathered log. From where he sat, Tommy could see down the beach to where his wife and daughters were walking and scouring the sand for sea shells. The sound of the surf pounding the shoreline was hypnotic and he never tired of hearing it. Tommy had an arm around Daisy and pulled it away to take out a piece of paper from his shirt pocket that he unfolded and showed to his canine friend. After Daisy sniffed the piece of paper, Tommy laid it down on his lap. He had rehearsed the speech he was about to make many times before and didn't really need to look at the paper to know what he wanted to say.

"OK, Daisy, here's the deal," Tommy began what would be a long conversation with his pal Daisy.

Tommy took one more look down the beach toward the three most important people in his life before continuing. It was going to be difficult for him to say what he was about to discuss with his dog and he only hoped she understood.

"Daisy ... there's something I haven't told you and it's only because I didn't want to upset you."

Tommy stopped and reflected some more. He had thought he was going to be OK with what he was about to do, but now realized it was going to be harder than he had anticipated.

"I think the time has come to have this little talk, Daisy, so I want you to listen up."

Tommy straightened up and eventually got his composure back. He began with the matter at hand.

"When we got you, I told myself you were going to be my last dog. Why? Because I was planning on living longer than you and at some point, when I retired, Mom and I were going to do some traveling and other stuff that might not accommodate owning a dog. So you were going it be it, Daisy. The last dog in my life ... and in a way that's true. But things changed a few months back and now it looks like you're going to outlive me."

Tommy stopped again and looked Daisy in the eye to see her reaction and if she understood what he was saying. She did and he continued with his talk.

"... and that's fine, Daisy. Just fine. It's all good. I'm OK with that. But I want to talk to you about your future ... and mine. First of all, I'm going to pass on and leave this beautiful place and I want you to rest assured that I'm leaving you behind with some very special people."

Tommy looked down the beach again and watched his family for a few seconds. Carolyn was bending over and had apparently found shells of some interest and showed them to her daughters.

"You see those lovely people walking on the beach down there? I know you already know this, but they're dog lovers. Big time dog lovers. That's one of the reasons I married Carolyn. She had always been kind and loving toward my dogs. She's kind and loving toward everybody and everything and I do mean everything. That's who she is. She has been the love of my life for a very long time and you and I have been so lucky to have had her in our lives. Damn lucky! She's an amazing woman and she'll take good care of you after I'm gone. And the girls, well, you know the girls. They love dogs as much as their mom and dad. So ... not to worry. You're going to be in good hands when I'm gone. Now that's the first part of what I wanted to talk to you about. OK? I just want you to know you're going to be well looked after. Between Mom and Sarah and Jessica, nothing is going to change. You'll still get lots of walks and lots of attention. Your routine will stay exactly the way it has always been. Except of course we won't be going to work together anymore, but we haven't done that for a while anyway. The bottom line here is that you're going to be OK. You don't have to be concerned about that at all."

I'm not concerned, Dad. I know I'll be looked after. I'm going to miss you though.

Tommy held up the document he'd been holding in his hand and had another look at it.

"Now here's the second part of what I want to talk to you about. I've been doing some thinking. Serious thinking ... deep thinking ... some soul searching and I've decided I don't want to go to people heaven. It's a place that, honestly Daisy, just doesn't appeal to me. Not that whoever runs that place would want me around anyway, but I don't think it's where I want to go from here. And, if whoever *or* whatever is in charge of a so-called heaven made any stipulations about getting in, I wouldn't be interested. No thanks. That wouldn't be Tommy Franklin. In my mind there's got to be somewhere else to go when you die. Don't you think?"

Tommy showed Daisy the piece of paper again.

"So Daisy, this here is a contract that I want you and Miss Carolyn to sign. She'll sign it here and you'll be the witness. You'll put your paw print right here ... see?"

Daisy looked at where she was supposed to put her paw print.

"Here's the thing, Daisy. We humans, as a species, haven't done a lot of good things on this planet to make me think it'll be any different in some sort of people heaven, so I think I'll just pass on that one. Now, individually, people do a lot of good things. There are some incredibly kind and caring people here on this planet we live. But overall, dag gum it, for the life of me, I can't figure out why we can't all just get along. Nope, can't figure that one out."

Tommy talked and looked out over the ocean and back and forth at his wife and kids who continued to stroll down the beach. Daisy did the same, looking out at the ocean and back and forth at her friend Tommy as he kept talking.

"I'm an optimist, Daisy, not a pessimist. I think one day we'll get it all figured out, but until then ... I don't want to roll the dice on us humans righting the ship. Too many problems. Does that make me sound like a pessimist, Daisy? I'm not. Really, I'm not. But having said all that, if there is an afterlife, and I don't necessarily believe in that either, I think I'd like to go where dogs go. That might be a safer bet than ending up somewhere where ya gotta believe this or ya gotta believe that for eternal life. Forget it, Daisy! We are who we are, we is who we is. Right, girl?"

Tommy was on a roll with his speech and had a captive audience. It was the same with Buddy, Timex and Ben. Dogs listen. They're all ears if you have something to say. Daisy sat attentively and didn't really care how long Tommy's speech was. This was quality time with her dad and there wouldn't be many more of these in the future.

How long do you want to sit here and talk, Dad? Forever? That would be OK. What else is on your mind?

Tommy had a lot on his mind and he couldn't be more grateful to have this moment with a friend who understood what he was talking about. He paused to listen to the waves and study the scenery around him. He rocked back and forth on the driftwood, looked up to the sky and wondered what was up there beyond.

Anything is possible.

He gave Daisy a hug and put his head on hers.

"Anything is possible, right Daisy?"

Daisy's dad looked down the beach and if he were a painter he would have painted the scene of his wife and daughters standing at the edge of the surf looking for shells. He wondered if they were thinking of him. Right on cue all three looked his way and waved and the loving husband and father waved back.

Goodbyes and Gratitude

They must have been thinking about me! They must have been.

Tommy had a feeling his family knew he needed this time alone with his dog. They knew him all too well and had known him all too well for a very long time now. That's what had made them so special. Especially his lifelong friend Carolyn. She knew all his emotions and the way he thought. She knew his ups and downs, his peaks and valleys, the highs and lows. His wife knew many years ago, when she handed him a puppy that he named Buddy, it was the one meant for him. She was magical in that way then, and still was to this day. Tommy knew for the most part it had been a beautiful life and so much of it was because of her. For a moment Tommy lost his train of thought. He snapped back and started up again.

"So this is what I'm thinking, girl. I might want to use you for a reference if that's OK. I would like to go where dogs go when they die. Honestly, Daisy. I can see it as the only place for me. I'm not a religious man, so I'm obviously not going to go someplace religious people go. No, no wait! Let me rephrase that. I'm actually very religious. See those three down the beach? That's my religion. That's where I find my spirituality. When I'm with you and the girls and Carolyn, for me there's no greater religious experience than that. When I'm with you guys ... that's all the religion I need."

Tommy stopped and thought about what he had said and had a question for Daisy. He looked at her quite seriously.

"I've never asked, but are you religious, Daisy?"

Tommy laughed heartily as he grabbed Daisy in a headlock and with his free hand rubbed his knuckles on top of her head in joy and delight, thinking the question he had just asked Daisy was pretty funny.

Whoever heard of a religious dog?

He let her go and laughed some more.

"I didn't think so."

Daisy, figuring it must be play time, jumped down off the driftwood and looked for something to put in her mouth. She found a stick.

"Wait, Daisy. I'm not done yet," Tommy said, trying to get his dog to settle down.

Daisy jumped back up on the log and sat next to Tommy. "This is serious stuff so I want you to listen closely."

OK, Dad. Then can we play?

"Where was I?" Tommy asked himself. "Oh, yeah. So I want you to witness this contract in front of Mom and hopefully I'll get to see you in the next world. I think it would be a good idea to have a dog's paw print on here and maybe I'll end up somewhere where there are lots of dogs and beautiful people."

Tommy reflected for another moment to think if he'd covered everything he wanted to discuss with Daisy.

"OK, Daisy. Thanks for listening. Go get your stick."

Daisy knew those words just like all of Tommy's previous dogs had known them. She jumped down onto the sand and got the stick she had had in her mouth a few moments before. Her master started chasing her down the beach toward Carolyn. He felt good about the conversation he had had with Daisy and was confidant she understood every word. She would be a perfect witness to the contract he had drawn up and hoped it would be honored. When he reached his wife, he playfully grabbed her and threw her down onto the sand to Daisy's joy and excitement. Tommy's daughters sat on him, joining in on the fun. And Daisy ... Daisy jumped back and forth over the four humans. It was all good. It had always been good for a dog living with this family.

It's playtime! That's why I love my family so much. They're always willing to play, anytime, anywhere.

TOMMY LAY IN his bed at home knowing his time was drawing near. He had had enough strength right up until the last couple of days to take Daisy on her walks and have his talks with her that comforted him. The pain and energy loss from his disease had taken their toll and now, for the last forty-eight hours, he hadn't been able to get out of bed. It seemed to be happening fast. He had fought a long battle with his cirrhosis, but it was winning and soon it would win the war. He was a fighter that couldn't fight anymore. He had been a brave soldier that every American could be proud of. He had made mistakes, like soldiers do sometimes, but he fought gallantly for his country. He was a loving husband that lived for his family. He had raised children that at one point in his life he thought he would never have. It was a dream life that happened to come true. He and his family had been relentless volunteers in the community always thinking about those less fortunate than themselves. He had never forgotten the values his parents taught him as a child and he wanted to exemplify that to those who had helped him when he was down and out. "Pay it forward," as Frank Perkins had said, because that's what makes it all work. If everyone got along in peace and harmony, then everyone could help others that were in need. And, in the end, Tommy's dying wish was for the human race to save themselves.

Save ourselves, save the planet. Stop killing each other. It's not rocket science.

Tommy's doctor had called the family together and Carolyn, Sarah and Jessica sat in chairs by his side. After a while, Mother asked her teenage daughters if they would mind waiting in the living room as Tommy's breathing became laborious and she sensed the end was near. Daisy lay on the bed with her head on Tommy's mid-section. With what little energy he had left, he stroked the top of Daisy's head. Carolyn moved from her chair to the bed and stroked Daisy's side, and as she did she heard Tommy's last words.

"You're a good girl, Daisy. You're a good girl."

That was it. That's how Tommy Franklin signed off. That's the only way he could have signed off. It was appropriate and Daisy knew she was a good girl because Tommy had told her that every day of her life.

"You're a good girl, Daisy. You're a good girl."

Carolyn took her husband's lifeless hand that rested on Daisy's neck and put it on his chest. She stood up and walked back over to the chair she had been sitting on. Softly she said, "And you were a good husband, Tommy Franklin. A good friend. A good father. And a very brave American soldier."

From the bedside table, she picked up a sealed envelope that Tommy had asked her to open when he had passed away. She walked to the bedroom door and quietly called Daisy.

"Come on, girl. Let's go see Sarah and Jessica."

Daisy stood up on the bed and looked down at her friend who lay peaceful and still. She turned and stepped down off the bed, knowing full well what had happened, and slowly walked toward Carolyn who stood at the door. The grieving wife had opened the envelope and taken out the contents. There were two pieces of paper that she unfolded. One was the contract that she was familiar with and was signed by her with Daisy as a witness. The other piece of paper had five handwritten words that simply said, "Every day is a gift." Tommy's favorite saying. Carolyn covered her mouth with one of her hands. With moist eyes she looked down at the dog that looked back up at her.

"Daisy ... how about if we grab Sarah and Jessica and go for a walk?"

A Special Place

TOMMY STOOD AND looked around. He wasn't sure where he was. It looked like a big park and it felt like a perfect summer day. In the distance up on a knoll he watched two dogs chasing each other. He turned around to check out the rest of the world that surrounded him and a few feet away he saw a middle-aged black woman sitting on a park bench with a small white dog. She was wearing a white dress and was barefoot.

"Hello, Tommy," she said.

"Hello," he replied and walked toward her. "How did you know my name?"

"Oh, I know everybody's name here," the lady informed him.

Tommy sat down next to the lady and patted her dog.

"Where is here?" he asked.

The hostess smiled at him and replied, "It's where you want to be, Tommy. The people here call it Earth and so we just go with that."

"Earth?" Tommy asked, somewhat confused.

"Yes, Tommy. As in planet Earth," the lady informed him again. "You once said, "Anything is possible and you were right. Anything is possible. Welcome to Earth."

"Hmmm," Tommy said, nodding his head and continuing to pat the dog in the lady's lap. "OK, well then, that sounds good to me." Tommy looked around and noticed more and more dogs. "Are you sure this isn't dog heaven?" he asked quite seriously.

The lady with bare feet laughed.

"No, not exactly. We love our dogs here, but no, we just call it Planet Earth. You're in the dog section, but we have all sorts of wonderful animals and beautiful people here. You'll see. You'll meet them."

"Is this people heaven?" Tommy asked, wanting to get that clarified.

The lady laughed again.

"No, it's not that either. Just go with the flow, Tommy. It's a place called Earth."

The new arrival had to think about that for a moment.

"What's your name?" Tommy inquires.

"My name is Amy and this is my dog, Missy."

"Hello, Missy. Hello, Amy," Tommy said, observing the dog that seemed quite content and calm.

"We're so glad to see you, Tommy. We heard you might be coming around this way."

Tommy noticed the greenery and how well manicured the park was. Off to his left he saw flower gardens and a big fountain that sprayed water at least thirty feet into the air.

"This is a lovely place. Have you and Missy been here long?" he asked Amy.

"Well yeah, you might say that. We're kind of like the welcoming committee," Amy said with pride.

Tommy nodded his head in approval.

"Well, you're doing a good job."

"Thank you."

The more Tommy looked around the more beautiful the place he had come upon seemed to be getting.

"I noticed some dogs on the hill over there. Are there other people here besides you?"

"A few. We just let the people in that we feel don't have to be kept on a leash," Amy joked.

Tommy joined her in a laugh.

"So you have a leash law here for people?"

He was amused by her admission.

"You're not listening, Tommy. The only people that get by me are the ones we feel don't have to be kept on a leash. The other ones we send off somewhere else."

Tommy got it and scratched the underside of Missy's chin. Missy liked the attention.

"OK, I get it. Well Amy, I want you to know that I'm really glad to be here and you won't have to worry about me being off a leash. I'm cool."

"We're not worried about you and we're glad you're here," Amy assured him.

Tommy stood up and examined the scene in all directions before looking back at Amy and Missy.

"Would it be OK if I took a walk around? I promise to behave."

"Please do. You can walk anywhere you like, Tommy. You might want to take that walkway right there." Amy pointed to a path that Tommy was just about standing on. "You may find something that will interest you. You can trust me on that one, Private Franklin."

The "Private Franklin" remark caught him by surprise, but he didn't question it.

"Yeah, I know I can. Thanks so much, Amy. Will I see you again?"

Amy smiled. "We're always here. We look after the dogs and check in the people when they show up. Yes, Tommy. We'll see each other again."

As he began to walk away he stopped and turned back to look at Amy one more time. He studied her.

"This may sound crazy, but you look familiar. Have we met before?"

Amy tilted her head and had a good look at Tommy.

"Possibly, but I don't think so. I wouldn't know where or when. Who knows?"

"Yeah, who knows?" Tommy said as he waved and began his new adventure.

For the next few minutes he walked along the trail, stopping occasionally to admire the foliage or to watch dogs playing with each other. He felt euphoric. He hadn't met any people yet and wondered if, in fact, he and Amy were the only ones here. As he came out of a small woodsy area into a clearing he saw a dog lying in the grass a few yards away. It was close enough that he decided to say "hello" to the dog that looked at him and did not move. Taking a couple of paces toward the dog Tommy stopped dead in his tracks as if he couldn't believe his eyes. It was Timex. Tommy choked up.

"Timex?"

The dog stood up and looked at the man he didn't recognize. Tommy extended a hand and took a couple of steps toward his old friend. The dog wasn't sure who this person was and became leery of him.

"It's me, Timex. Tommy. Remember me, boy? It's Tommy!"

The last time Timex had seen his master, Tommy had had a long beard and hair and was a shell of the person that he saw before him now and a lot younger. If memory served Timex correctly, he had left his friend because he was tired, hungry and thirsty. It was shortly after he left Tommy that he met Amy on the Venice boardwalk and she brought him here. Now Timex was uncertain and took a couple of steps backwards. The voice sounded vaguely familiar, but he didn't recognize this clean-shaven man who was now a lot older than the last time they were together. Tommy knelt down trying to reassure the suspicious Timex that everything was OK. The dog continued to stare down the stranger and took a couple of more steps backward.

"It's OK, Timex. You remember me don't ya? Please remember me. It's Tommy."

Tommy was overcome with emotion as he couldn't believe he was so close

A Special Place

to being reunited with a dog he had thought he would never see again. A dog whose heart he knew he had broken. A dog he had let down and never got over the guilt of losing. He was so close, but the dog turned and began walking away.

Tommy cried out to him.

"Timex, wait! Please."

A few yards away Timex stopped, turned and looked back at the man pleading with him not to leave. He thought for a moment.

That voice sounds familiar. I do remember a Tommy, but he didn't look like this.

Tommy began singing a song from the late sixties that he used to sing to Timex all the time. He had sung it all the way from Michigan to Los Angeles on their trip west so many years before. As soon as he started singing that familiar tune, Timex knew it could only be Tommy Franklin. He took a couple of steps toward the man that sang. Tommy softened his tone and pleaded with Timex to come to him. It all began to click in Timex's head. Memories started to flood back. The song had done it.

This man is Tommy Franklin. He used to be my best friend!

Timex ran into Tommy's waiting arms and was held tight in a joyous and tearful reunion.

"Timex, Timex. I can't believe it's you. I'm so sorry, Timex. I'm so sorry. I never meant to treat you like I did. I had so many problems back then. It was the war, Timex. The war and the drugs. I'm sorry, Timex. I'm so sorry."

It's OK, Dad. I forgave you a long time ago. It's so nice to be back together. Just hold me for now. You're going to like this place. Amy is so caring and looks after us. You'll be well looked after too.

Tommy hugged and patted Timex as he continued to say how sorry he was.

As Tommy and Timex got reacquainted, a man's voice came from behind Tommy and said, "He's a beautiful dog."

Tommy turned his head, stood up and looked at the man who was Asian and was about the same age as him.

The man stood a few feet away with his wife who was holding a small dog.

"Thank you," Tommy said, acknowledging the couple. "I didn't think I would ever see this guy again. This is Timex."

"Yes, I know," the man said, walking up to Timex and giving him a pat on the head. "How are you doing today, Timex?"

The man looked at Tommy. "We have met Timex many times before. He didn't have a name when we had him years ago."

Tommy was perplexed at that last statement.

What did he mean, "When we had him?"

The man started up again before Tommy could comment.

"He was just as beautiful in Vietnam, but I'm so glad the two of you went to America and lived a good life."

Tommy thought he knew who this man and woman were. The man, more than the woman. He never knew the man's name, but suddenly recalled his face and the horror of so many years before came back to him in another flash. The man knelt, patted Timex some more and spoke again.

"My name is Vu-Bao and this is my wife Qua and our little dog Beatrice. We met many years ago when you were a young soldier in my country. You came to my village … ." Vu-Bao stood up and Tommy took him by the shoulders. Tears streamed down Tommy's cheek as he stared at Vu-Bao. The former soldier was stunned and speechless.

"Vu-Bao … Vu-Bao … ."

Vu-Bao gave Tommy a hug and the veteran American soldier held on tight not wanting to let go.

"It's OK, Private Franklin. It's OK," Vu-Bao said, attempting to console the crying veteran. "That was a long time ago. All is forgiven and we are so glad you and Timex are back together. There will be no more wars, Tommy. Emotional or otherwise. All we do here is look after our dogs and each other. That's all we do."

Tommy took a step back and wiped away his tears.

"I'm so sorry, Vu-Bao. I'm so sorry."

Tommy felt ashamed to the core of his being and couldn't find the words to express how much he was hurting, his guilt, his pain. He turned to Qua and kept saying over and over how sorry he was for his actions when he was a soldier in such a faraway land. Qua walked up to Tommy and let him pat Beatrice.

"Like Vu-Bao said, Private Franklin. That was a long time ago and we forgave the American soldiers many, many years back. Things like that don't happen here. We are all one. The dogs here keep us at peace. We live in peace, Tommy. No wars, only peace."

Tommy slowly regained his composure as he looked at Timex rolling on his back in the grass. "Vu-Bao, Timex was your dog before he was mine. I want you to have him back." Those words broke Tommy's heart, but he knew it was the honorable thing to do.

"That is not how it works here, Tommy," Qua said in a soft and gentle voice. "Here, Timex is everybody's dog, but especially yours. He will always be your dog. It makes us very happy that the two of you are together again. It's going to make everyone happy to see the two of you as a team again."

Everyone?

"We have to be going now, Private Franklin," Vu-Bao said as he went over to Timex, who was still rolling on his back, and gave him a scratch on the chest.

"We'll be seeing you two at the picnic later."

Picnic?

Tommy couldn't fathom what was going on in this place he had come to, but for now he would embrace the moment and enjoy his reunion with Timex. He gave Vu-Bao and Qua one more hug and watched as they walked away. They looked back at him and waved. Tommy did the same.

"OK, then. We'll see you at the picnic later," the American veteran of war said, still unclear as to what was going on.

Timex came over to Tommy and jumped up on his long-lost friend. Tommy grabbed Timex's front paws. Pure joy came over the human as he playfully pushed Timex away and began chasing him. Wherever he had come to, he was glad to be here. A few minutes of running around with Timex and Tommy fell to the ground with the dog all over him. This was the way it was supposed to be in the afterlife, the here and now. This place called Earth. This was the way it was supposed to have been when they were together the first time. It would be a happy ending this time. They had to catch up on their running and playing. Tommy was giddy and couldn't stop laughing as Timex refused to let up.

"OK, Timex. OK. I give up. You win. You win. Take it easy on me. I'm not as young as I used to be."

Tommy sat up and leaned on Timex who got the pats he remembered from way back when. They felt as good as they had the first time they were together. They still felt compassionate and genuine. Tommy was lost in the moment when he heard another voice.

"Hello, Tommy."

He looked to his side and saw an elderly couple. It was people he would recognize no matter how old they were and he recognized them immediately. Tommy jumped up and stood in shock as Timex ran up to greet the two strollers.

"Dad? Mom?"

"We thought we would find you here," Tommy's father said.

Mrs. Franklin stood with her hands cupped over her mouth and nose. Like Tommy, she couldn't believe her eyes and began to sob. If Tommy thought the reunion with Timex was full of emotion, this was more than he could bear. With weak knees he walked over to his parents and the three had a hug that had been a long time coming. Timex, of course, tried to squeeze into the middle of them. The trio was too emotional at the moment to say anything to each other and simply had a good cry. Tommy stepped back from hugging his parents and looked at them both.

"I can't believe this. I can't believe any of this is happening."

"Believe it, Tommy. Believe it. We know now that anything is possible and that all prayers are answered." Mrs. Franklin said, managing to get out her words between sobs.

Tommy was lost for words. He thought back to the last time he had seen his parents when he was at Kathy's wedding. He knew he had broken their hearts when he got into drugs and didn't communicate with them. That ache had stayed with him his whole life. He was searching for something to say and it was impossible. He finally began by telling his mother and father how sorry he was to have caused them so much pain.

"The pain is gone, Tommy. The joy is back. The joy is back," Mrs. Franklin said, grabbing her son's hand.

Tommy gave his mom another hug. Mrs. Franklin stood back to have another look at her son. She laughed.

"Looks like we're all a little older, wouldn't you say, Tommy?"

The son smiled at the mother.

"Yeah, a little older, a little wiser."

"Tommy," Mr. Franklin said, somewhat excited as he put one hand on his son's shoulder and pointed with the other, "look who we brought with us."

Tommy turned to look where his dad had pointed. Running down a small hill, coming in his direction over the grass about fifty yards away, was another dog. He didn't know what to make of it at first, but as the dog got closer he saw that it was Buddy. Things were happening so fast Tommy could barely comprehend any of it.

"Buddy!" Tommy screamed out and started running toward the first dog he had ever owned. Timex, a little faster and just as excited to see Buddy as Tommy was, ran up to Buddy and the two started a game of chase before Tommy could get to where they were.

Hey, Buddy! Tommy's here. Tommy's here."

"Buddy! Buddy!" Tommy stopped and laughed, observing his two past dogs having so much fun.

Buddy escaped the mischievous Timex and ran up to his old friend. Tommy knelt down, but was bowled over by an over rambunctious Buddy. The two wrestled like they had done so many times in Tommy's youth. Timex joined in on the fracas and Mr. and Mrs. Franklin watched in pure delight. Tommy was not acting his age. He was acting like a teenager again. He managed to break loose from the highly energetic pair and trot back over to where his parents stood.

"This is all pretty amusing, don't you think, son?" the elder Franklin said.

"Yeah, it's pretty amusing all right. These two are obviously very happy dogs. They must serve the dogs here a lot of energy food." Tommy joked as his mother put her arm through her son's and wanted to never let go.

"They do, Tommy. A lot of positive and happy energy food. Isn't this a wonderful sight?" Mrs. Franklin asked her son as the three watched the two dogs chasing each other again.

"It is a wonderful sight. It's more than a wonderful sight," her son replied, shaking his head in agreement. "It's something I can't put into words."

"Well come on, Mrs. Franklin. Come on, Tommy. Let's keep walking," Mr. Franklin said, slapping Tommy on the back. "We're all headed to the picnic and you're the guest of honor."

The three began walking on the trail Tommy had been on.

"I heard about this get together. Sounds good to me," Tommy said in an understatement. He was also curious about who was in charge of this picnic and asked the question.

"Those two guys right there." Mr. Franklin pointing to two gentlemen about Tommy's age walking toward them. Tommy had been preoccupied watching Buddy and Timex playing. When he looked at the two figures walking in their direction, he stopped.

"Oh, my goodness!"

Yes, they were all a little older, but Tommy would have recognized the pair anywhere, at any age. It was Will and Lieutenant Peterson, dressed in casual street clothes, walking quickly toward him. Private Franklin trotted in the direction of his old service buddies. When they reached each other, there were more hugs and tears.

"Stop your crying, man. How the heck are you doing, Franklin?" Will said and had a good look at a very emotional Tommy.

"I'm fine, Will. I'm fine. How the heck are you guys? I can't believe what's been going on here. It's a bit much."

"You'll get used to it, Private Franklin. We have a lot of fun here and nothing but time. Lots of time," Lieutenant Peterson said as Tommy's parents walked up.

"Guys, I want you to meet my parents. Mom, Dad ... ."

Will smacked Tommy in the chest.

"We've already met a few times, Franklin. Hello, Mr. and Mrs. Franklin.

Your son here has a lot to learn about this place."

Tommy's parents smiled. Mr. Franklin put a hand on Tommy's shoulder.

"Just enjoy yourself, son. You'll get used to it. Come on, this guy has put a lot of work into this meal you're about to have," a father told his son.

"Yeah, Franklin. Your old man's right and you're going to like today's special. Let's keep it moving, guys," Will ordered the small group. "People are starting to get hungry."

They walked and talked and tears turned into smiles and laughter. Timex and Buddy tagged along, having heard the words food and picnic. Yes, there was a lot of catching up to do for someone named Tommy Franklin.

Tommy didn't bother to ask any more questions about this place he had come to. He figured he'd find out in time and with the way things had been going, as far as he was concerned, it really didn't matter. They kept walking for another five minutes as they told stories and shared laughter. They got to a place where the trail began to head down into a valley and Tommy saw a few dozen more people along with picnic tables and chairs. It looked to him like it was going to be quite an occasion.

As they got closer, he noticed the group was incredibly diversified and saw more people walking down the slope on the other side of the valley. Everyone seemed to have the same destination in mind. Timex and Buddy smelled food, made a dash toward all the activity and joined in with the other dogs that were playing. About halfway down into the valley, Tommy looked off to his right and saw another dog lying in the grass. It looked like he was chewing on a stick. Tommy stopped as the others continued on their way. Something drew him toward the dog and he slowly made his way in that direction. The dog looked familiar and when Tommy realized who it was he dropped to his knees.

Barely audible even to himself, he whispered, "Ben?"

It was Ben. Tommy stood up and continued walking toward the third dog he had ever owned. Ben looked up from chewing his stick and recognized Tommy. He jumped up and ran to someone he couldn't be happier to see. Tommy barely had time to kneel down when Ben jumped into his arms.

"Ben ... Ben ... Ben." Emotions ran deep once again.

"Ben ol' pal. I've missed you so much."

Tommy didn't think it was possible to have more tears in him, but he did and they flowed. He looked down to the bottom of the valley and saw everyone having a good time. He noticed Frank Perkins and couldn't wait to speak with him and all the other familiar faces. Tommy didn't know where he was and he thought back to what Amy had said when he arrived.

"You're right where you want to be, Tommy. You're right where you want to be."

He was and he knew it. Tommy stood up.

"Hey, Ben. Do you know those people down there? You probably do. Whatta ya say we join them?"

Sure Dad, let's do that.

Carolyn Meets Amy

Carolyn finished reading the paper to Daisy and put it down in her lap. Sitting on the veranda she contemplated her next move. Looking down the driveway, she saw the truck driven by the black woman that they had seen a little while before down on the road. She was obviously coming up to the house for a visit. Carolyn noticed a small dog with its front paws on the dashboard. Daisy saw this as well and bolted down off the veranda. Being the official greeter, she knew she had to take action. Carolyn got up from her rocking chair and followed Daisy as part of the welcoming committee. The truck pulled up to a stop a few feet from Carolyn and the lady got out of her vehicle.

"Hello," the visitor said, leaving her dog in the truck.

"Hello there. Hi, I'm Carolyn Franklin. I think I saw you down on the road earlier."

Carolyn walked up to the woman and extended a hand which the visitor grabbed and shook.

"Hi. I'm Amy."

"Well, nice to meet you Amy. You can let your dog out of the truck. Daisy here is friendly." Carolyn assured her guest.

Daisy had been running around the truck wondering where the heck the dog with its paws on the dashboard went.

I could have sworn I saw another dog.

Amy opened the driver's door and out jumped her small white dog. Daisy greeted the other dog and after sniffing and smelling each other, Daisy decided it was all OK and got her new friend to start playing.

"Your dog is very friendly. That's Missy," Amy informed Carolyn as the two women watched the dogs play for a moment before Amy started talking again. "I was looking at some property for sale just up the way and thought I would come by and introduce myself."

"I heard there might be some ten-acre parcels going on the market," Carolyn said, pleased that the rumor she had heard a month before was now being confirmed. "Come on up to the house and I'll make us some tea."

"I don't want to intrude." Amy hesitated to follow Carolyn's lead. "I just thought if I could ask you some questions about the area … ."

"You can ask all the questions you want and you're not intruding. I'll put some tea on. Come on."

Amy appreciated the hospitality and gave in. The two walked up to the house and into the kitchen where Amy sat at the table and Carolyn began to boil water and prepare some treats. Daisy and Missy decided to stay outside and chase each other. The hostess enjoyed having company and meeting new people. She was pleased Amy had come by and if there was any chance of becoming future neighbors, she wanted to get to know this woman.

She and Tommy had never had neighbors here in Alaska and they had discussed the subject at times saying it would have been nice to have people living nearby. They valued their isolation and the peacefulness that came with it, but they certainly weren't anti-social and having a neighbor around would have been positive in more ways than one. Especially if they had kids that their daughters could have played with when they were growing up. The isolation where they lived was something her husband had worried about before he passed on. It concerned him that Carolyn would be living too far out of town, out in the bush with no one else around. For now though, Carolyn didn't mind that. The girls were still at home and when the time came to move into town, she would do so. Sarah and Jessica had already voiced their opinions on the matter and both of her daughters felt that their mom should move closer to town as soon as possible ... but for now, no. This was her and Tommy's home, their family home and Daisy's as well. She'd stay put and would know when the time came to move on.

"Where are you moving from?" Carolyn asked Amy.

"Right now I'm living in Anchorage," Amy replied to her host. "I've always lived in big cities and now I'm thinking I would like to live out in the country somewhere, so I've been looking around. I used to come down to Eagles Junction for vacations. I know a little bit about the area and I've always liked it around here."

Carolyn found it interesting that this woman, who was the same age as she was, wanted to move out of the city and into the bush. Good for her if that's how she was feeling.

"It's a great spot," Carolyn said, proud of the fact. "I've been here more than twenty years. My husband passed away just a few months ago and for now I just want to stay put."

Amy expressed her condolences to Carolyn regarding her husband as Carolyn opened the oven door and pulled out cinnamon rolls she had quickly heated up. She brought them over to where Amy sat.

"Oh, my goodness. Thank you so very much. They look delicious."

"I just made them this morning," Carolyn said. "The tea will be ready in a minute. It's herbal tea and decaffeinated if that's OK."

"That will be just fine, Carolyn. I've already had a couple of cups of coffee. I don't think I need any more caffeine, thank you."

Amy began to cut into her cinnamon roll with a knife and fork.

"My goodness, Carolyn! What time did you get up to have rolls like this already made?" Amy asked good naturedly.

"Early," Carolyn replied as she sat down across the table from her guest.

"Do you live in this big house alone, Carolyn?" Amy inquired.

"Well, it's not that big and heavens no. I have one daughter that lives here full time and our oldest daughter stays here whenever she comes home from university. Sarah and Jessica just zipped into town to run a couple of errands. They should be back pretty soon, I would think. It would be nice if you could meet them."

"I would like that."

Amy and Carolyn sat and chatted, enjoying each other's company. Carolyn liked this potential new neighbor. It was as if they'd known each other for a long time and they acted like old friends. They talked about life in Alaska and the more they talked the more Carolyn admired this stranger that had driven up onto her property. The subject of the weather came up and how nice it was outside.

"Every day is a gift, I always say," Amy said, entertaining that thought for a moment as if in a day dream.

Carolyn couldn't believe what she had just heard. She laughed.

"Would you believe that was my husband's favorite saying?"

"You're kidding. I say it at least once a day!" Amy stated.

"Tommy did the same thing. At least once a day we would hear him say, 'Every day is a gift.'"

The two had a good chuckle at the similarities in their lives. The more they talked the more uncanny it appeared, how much they had in common. When Tommy was a soldier in Vietnam, Amy had served as a nurse there. Amy had also lived in Los Angeles when Tommy was living there. She moved to Alaska the same month as Carolyn's husband did. It didn't stop there. It went on and on and both were in near hysterics as they compared their life stories and had much fun with it.

"This is unbelievable," Carolyn said as she found herself in one of her most joyful moods of late.

"I know. I know," Amy said, agreeing and laughing with her host.

Carolyn tried to encourage Amy to purchase one of the parcels nearby.

Carolyn Meets Amy

"It will be good times. You would love it here at the end of the road."

"Well Carolyn, I'm seriously contemplating it. We'll see what happens."

Amy said she must be going and, just then, hearing the dogs bark, Carolyn walked to the front room and looked out the window. It was Sarah and Jessica pulling up in their vehicle with Jessica's dog, Sam, sitting in the middle. Amy came walking out of the kitchen.

"The girls are home," Carolyn said, excited. "I'm so glad you're going to meet them."

"It'll be my pleasure," Amy said as she and Carolyn walked to the front door to greet the girls.

Sam jumped out of the car that Sarah drove and did the standard dog salutations and rituals by sniffing Missy and being sniffed in return. Sam, a medium-sized mix, decided, like Daisy had already done, that Missy, even though she was a bit small, was OK and started running in circles hoping to get chased. Daisy and Missy obliged.

The two daughters had a good laugh at the three dogs chasing each other. They walked toward their mom and the visitor standing at the top of the front steps.

"Hi, Mom," each girl said, acknowledging their mother.

"Hello," The two sisters said to the woman they had never met before.

Amy smiled and said, "Hello."

"Girls, this is Amy. Amy is thinking about buying a ten-acre parcel just down the road."

Sarah and Jessica shook Amy's hand and welcomed her to the Franklin home.

"Let's go into the house and Amy please, please stay for another cup of tea," Carolyn pleaded.

"I can't. I really should be going. I have to get back to Anchorage today."

"One more cup, Amy. We can talk some more about this piece of property you're thinking of buying."

Amy looked at Sarah and Jessica who smiled back at her and the visitor gave in.

"OK. One more quick one. If I could use your washroom first that might help matters," Amy said, chuckling.

The four walked into the house with Jessica telling Amy where the bathroom was. Carolyn, with her two biggest fans, entered the kitchen and began to reheat the water for more tea that both girls said they would also have. When Amy was finished, she came back into the kitchen and sat at the table with Sarah and Jessica. Just as she had been with Carolyn, Amy was a hit with the girls. The conversation between the three was lively as Carolyn prepared more tea and heated up more rolls. She was proud of her daughters and they reminded her so much of their father. Mother interrupted the three to tell the girls about Amy's favorite saying.

"That's awesome!" Sarah shouted out in disbelief.

"Isn't that something, girls?" Carolyn said, holding the tea kettle and beginning to pour tea into the cups.

She looked outside through the window above the sink and for a split second her eyes played a trick on her. She could have sworn she saw Buddy, Timex and Ben playing in the front of the house instead of the three that were out there. She blinked her eyes in disbelief and then realized that, in fact, it was Daisy, Missy and Sam running about.

She continued to poor the tea and, as she did, Carolyn thought more about what Amy had said earlier about her favorite expression.

Every day is a gift.

That amazed Carolyn along with all the other coincidences that she and Amy had talked about. It brought a smile to her face. She put the kettle down and gazed at the full cups of tea as if in a daydream. She shook her head and couldn't get those words out of her head.

Every day is a gift!

She turned sideways and gazed at the three people conversing at the kitchen table. Under her breath she whispered just loud enough so that only she and her best friend Tommy could hear.

"Isn't that something?"

Yes, it is dear. It's really something! It's so true. And listen to this, my love, about what I have discovered. Tell the children, all the children ... Earth is our Heaven.

Dear reader. Thank you for showing an interest in my book. Here is a poem I have written from me to you.

I asked, "Why is it, in this place we rest, all that is new, blends in so well with all that exists?"

This is what I was told.
It's the music.
A concerto in the woods.
Look. Listen.
There's no mistaking the sound of life as it awakens to caress the morning dew.
Everything you see and hear is true.
True to this earth.
That's why.

What a duet, the Alder and the wind.
I can't believe we're here again, right where it all began.
The leaves. The breeze. The waterfalls.
The mountain peaks through the clearing.
The daylight colors reappearing.
Is there a more perfect time and place to acknowledge every new birth in the wild?
Our love for this planet?
That fawn? These flowers?
This child, that child and all the others?
If ever there was a moment to cherish, a memory that life will once again live and look at life, this is it.

We can learn so much as we sit and watch the children play.
We can learn everything we need to know by listening to what they have to say.
"Hold on forever, don't let go.
Look to the future and its promising glow.
Within this forest you are not alone.
Look around you, welcome home."

The Effects of War on a Godless Dog Lover – KB Fugitt

What is it with this thing called time?
Is it time to cry tears of joy?
In a blink everything is grown and all that is young and not yet sown
    quickly becomes part of this world.
If not for hope, dreams would turn to stone.
Together we must share our hopes and dreams.
We must live together in peace.
Together we must love all of this that lies before us and wishes for
    nothing more than compassion.
Of all things, together we must carry on.

People.
Nature sees things in us that we cannot see.
Its efflorescence abounds everywhere in this harmonious kingdom.
Its wisdom surrounds you and me on the verdurous side of paradise
    and reflects off these children that will show us the way, what will
    be.

Close your eyes and open them again.
Stop.
Think of all the places you've been.
Oh, the beauty that has circled your footsteps.
Will these children follow or will they say good-bye?
Will they return to see the tear flowing out of your eye?
Something inside you says, "Yes."
They will take the time to see what has brought them here.
They will pet the fawn, soon to be a deer.
They will paint the flowers, now in full color.
They will play with the others who are now all singing.
"Smile and laugh your way through life, around the world
and to the moon.
Smile and laugh your way through life.
It's not too late and it's not too soon."

The clarity of the music is touching your heart.
You listen more closely and agree with what we all should be feeling.
And like the music, the answer becomes more clear:

For what it's worth, be true to this earth.
To all that is old, to all that is young,
To life that has lived and only just begun.

I was free to write this book and you were free to read it.
There is a reason for that.

This book is dedicated, in loving memory, to Dollar Bill and Lion, who no longer fight the war or live on the streets. They've taken their dogs and gone home.

Made in the USA
Charleston, SC
22 December 2013